EARLY CIVILIZATION

Jane Chisholm

Anne Millard

Illustrated by **Ian Jackson**

Designed by **Iain Ashman, Radhi Parekh** and **Robert Walster**

History consultant: **George Hart,**
British Museum Education Service

Map illustrations by **Robert Walster**

Additional illustrations by **Peter Dennis, Richard Draper, Louise Nixon** and **Gerald Wood**

With thanks to **Lynn Bresler** and **Anthony Marks**

Contents

How to use this section of the book

Dates

Nearly all the dates mentioned in this section are from the period before the birth of Christ. These dates are shown with the letters BC, which stand for 'Before Christ'. Dates in the period after the birth of Christ are indicated by the letters AD, which stand for *Anno Domini* ("Year of our Lord"). To avoid confusion, BC and AD have been used throughout the section. Dates in the BC period are counted backwards from the birth of Christ. For example the period from 0-99BC is called the first century BC. Periods of a thousand years are counted in millennia. The period from 0 to 1000BC is called the first millennium BC.

Many events in ancient history cannot be dated exactly, and so an approximate date is given. Approximate dates are preceded by the letter 'c.', which stands for *circa*, the Latin for 'about'.

Much of the evidence for the dates in this section comes from lists of kings compiled by the Egyptians. These tell us how long a king reigned, who came before and after him, and during which year of the reign an event took place. Experts can then convert these into dates BC.

However some of the lists are incomplete and some experts disagree about how to interpret the available evidence. This means that the dating systems used may vary slightly in some books. This applies particularly to Mesopotamian dates, for which the evidence is especially thin.

About early civilization

The term civilization is usually applied to a people whose culture has reached a certain stage of development. This stage is characterized by the invention of writing, the use of a calendar, and the development of large social units such as towns and cities, with organized government, law codes and monumental architecture.

This section of the book concentrates on the world's first civilizations which grew up in Egypt and the Middle East in about 3000BC. It also takes a brief look at the earliest cultures of India and China, which developed soon afterwards.

How we know about early civilization

Although early civilization began over 5000 years ago, we have plenty of information about how people lived. Much of it comes from the sources listed below.

Hot, dry climates help to preserve things and a number of stone buildings, such as temples and pyramids, have survived almost intact. These tell us about building technology and styles of architecture. Since the 18th century, archaeologists have excavated a large number of sites, including ancient cities and tombs.

Egyptian tombs in particular provide a wealth of information about daily life and religious beliefs. The interiors were richly decorated with wall-paintings, showing scenes from the person's life and from the lives of the gods. Many of the colours, although faded, are still quite distinct.

In most ancient cultures, people's possessions were buried with them. Furniture, chariots, household items, glass, jewellery and even fragments of clothes and food have all been found preserved in tombs. Also found in tombs are models of people doing things, such as baking bread or herding cattle.

Ancient scripts, such as *hieroglyphics* and *cuneiform* (see pages 10-11), have been found inscribed on buildings and clay tablets, and on scrolls made from a reed called papyrus. For centuries the meaning of these scripts remained a mystery, but since the 19th century scholars have been able to read them. Ancient texts have provided details about a number of things – methods of government, legal systems, the reigns of various rulers, scientific knowledge, religious customs and stories about the gods.

Periods of Egyptian history

For convenience, experts divide Egyptian history into a number of different approximate periods. These are shown in the chart below.

The Predynastic Period c.5000-3100BC

The Archaic Period c.3100-2649BC

The Old Kingdom c.2649-2150BC

The First Intermediate Period c.2150-2040BC

The Middle Kingdom c.2040-1640BC

The Second Intermediate Period c.1640-1552BC

The New Kingdom c.1552-1069BC

The Third Intermediate Period c.1069-664BC

The Late Period c.664-332BC

The Ptolemies c.332-30BC

Unfamilar words

Italic type is used for Egyptian, Greek and Latin words, and for unfamiliar words derived from them. Words followed by a dagger symbol, such as nomad†, are explained in the glossary on page 87. If a person's name is followed by this symbol, you can read more about them in the 'Who's Who' on pages 84-86.

Reference

At the back of this section there is an appendix. This includes a detailed map of Egypt, a list of Egyptian kings, a detailed date chart which outlines the most important events of the period, biographies of rulers and other important people, myths and legends and a glossary.

The beginnings of civilization

The earliest people were nomads† who travelled from place to place, hunting animals and collecting wild plants to eat. Then slowly a more settled way of life developed, based on farming. This transition occurred in different places at different times. It seems to have happened first in about 10,000BC in a part of the Middle East that historians call the Fertile Crescent. This is the area now occupied by Turkey, Syria, Iran and Iraq. Knowledge of farming probably spread as people gradually moved into new areas.

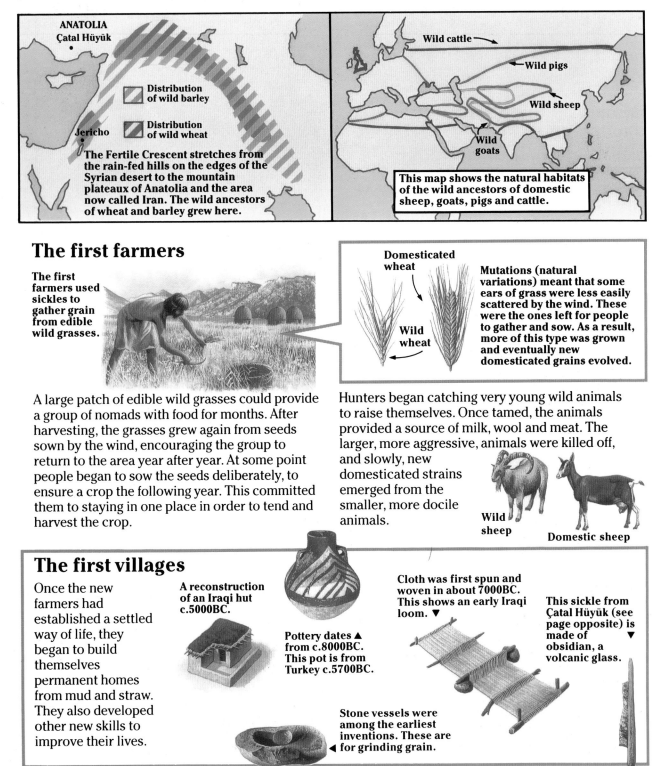

ANATOLIA
Çatal Hüyük

Jericho

Distribution of wild barley

Distribution of wild wheat

The Fertile Crescent stretches from the rain-fed hills on the edges of the Syrian desert to the mountain plateaux of Anatolia and the area now called Iran. The wild ancestors of wheat and barley grew here.

Wild cattle

Wild pigs

Wild sheep

Wild goats

This map shows the natural habitats of the wild ancestors of domestic sheep, goats, pigs and cattle.

The first farmers

The first farmers used sickles to gather grain from edible wild grasses.

Domesticated wheat

Wild wheat

Mutations (natural variations) meant that some ears of grass were less easily scattered by the wind. These were the ones left for people to gather and sow. As a result, more of this type was grown and eventually new domesticated grains evolved.

A large patch of edible wild grasses could provide a group of nomads with food for months. After harvesting, the grasses grew again from seeds sown by the wind, encouraging the group to return to the area year after year. At some point people began to sow the seeds deliberately, to ensure a crop the following year. This committed them to staying in one place in order to tend and harvest the crop.

Hunters began catching very young wild animals to raise themselves. Once tamed, the animals provided a source of milk, wool and meat. The larger, more aggressive, animals were killed off, and slowly, new domesticated strains emerged from the smaller, more docile animals.

Wild sheep

Domestic sheep

The first villages

Once the new farmers had established a settled way of life, they began to build themselves permanent homes from mud and straw. They also developed other new skills to improve their lives.

A reconstruction of an Iraqi hut c.5000BC.

Pottery dates ▲ from c.8000BC. This pot is from Turkey c.5700BC.

Cloth was first spun and woven in about 7000BC. This shows an early Iraqi loom. ▼

This sickle from Çatal Hüyük (see page opposite) is made of ▼ obsidian, a volcanic glass.

Stone vessels were among the earliest inventions. These are ◄ for grinding grain.

The first towns

Nomadic women could only carry one small child each at a time, and so they had to limit the number of children they had, if necessary even by killing unwanted babies. However, once people had settled in villages, they could try to rear all their children and the population began to increase. Some small communities prospered and grew into towns, though little is known about how this way of life developed, as very few towns have been excavated.

Jericho

One of the earliest towns to have been discovered by archaeologists is Jericho, which dates from about 8000BC. Situated near a water source, it appears to have been on an important trade route. Salt and bitumen (tar) from the Dead Sea were probably traded for turquoise, cowrie shells and obsidian (a volcanic glass used for making tools). The people of Jericho grew rich and built walls to protect themselves from envious neighbours.

A stone tower, over 9m (29ft) high, has been excavated. There were probably other towers too.

The town was surrounded by a wall over 5m (16ft) high and 1.5m (5ft) wide and a ditch over 8m (27ft) wide and 2m (6ft) deep.

At one time at least 2000 people lived in Jericho in small, round houses made of sunbaked mud-bricks.

Jericho's defences suggest that the town must have had leaders and experts to plan and organize the building work and to provide enough food to feed the workers.

Çatal Hüyük

Another early town has been excavated at Çatal Hüyük in Anatolia. The people there were successful farmers, although trade may have been the source of their wealth. They probably traded cloth and obsidian for shells and useful stones, such as flint. By 6500BC Çatal Hüyük was a flourishing centre. This is a reconstruction of part of the town.

Çatal Hüyük had an unusual defensive system. The town consisted of one-roomed rectangular houses joined to one another, with no doors.

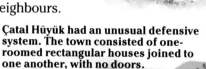

In the event of an attack, the ladders were drawn up and the enemy was then faced with solid, blank walls.

People entered their houses through holes in the roofs, which they reached by wooden ladders.

Clay stamps have been found which may have been used to pattern the cloth.

Early religious beliefs

Archaeologists have some idea of the religious beliefs of the people of this period from the number of small carved figures that have been found at ancient sites. Many people seem to have worshipped some form of mother goddess, and sometimes a young god associated with her.

Here is a selection of mother goddesses dating from before 5000BC.

Mother goddess from Tell es-Sawwan, Iraq

This is one of several shrines † found in Çatal Hüyük.

Mother goddess from Tepe Sarab, Iran

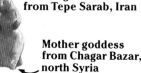

Mother goddess from Çatal Hüyük

Mother goddess from Chagar Bazar, north Syria

Sumer

The earliest civilizations all grew up in fertile areas bordering great rivers. One of the first of these was in Mesopotamia (meaning 'between the rivers'), the name given by the Ancient Greeks to the land between the Rivers Tigris and Euphrates. The most dramatic developments took place in the southern part, Sumer, situated in what is now Iraq.

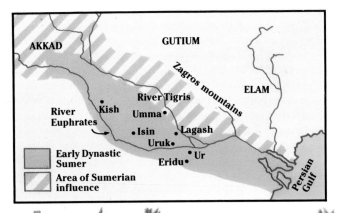

Early Sumer

The Sumerians grew wheat, barley, vegetables and dates and reared sheep and cattle.

Fishing, hunting and catching wildfowl provided additional food.

The settlements were clustered on the river banks. The houses were built of sun-dried mud-bricks and there were stables made of matting for the animals.

The farmers built dykes to protect their crops from the flood waters.

A new more efficient plough was introduced in the Uruk period. It was drawn by oxen instead of men, and later had a metal blade. This enabled much larger areas to be ploughed, which increased the crop yield.

Hut for cattle

Potters at work

The potter's wheel was invented in about 3400BC, and later adapted for transport. A donkey pulling a wheeled cart could carry up to three times as much as it could on its back.

The earliest Sumerian culture is called Ubaid, after the site where it was first discovered. By about 5000BC, farmers were established on the river banks and around the marshes. The land was flat and fertile but had little rain, and although the Euphrates flooded its banks each spring, in summer the soil baked hard. Gradually the farmers learned how to build irrigation canals in order to store the water and transfer it to the fields. This allowed more land to be cultivated and the population increased. Surplus food was produced, which allowed some people to become full-time craftsmen, traders or priests, rather than farmers. A few of the larger settlements, such as Eridu, Ur and Uruk, grew into cities and eventually into independent city states†.

In about 4000BC a new phase began, named after Uruk. During this period there was a series of new advances, the most important of which was the invention of writing in about 3000BC (see page 10). The Sumerians also devised an elaborate legal system and became skilled mathematicians and astronomers (see page 64). The reconstruction shown here is of an early Sumerian village.

Crafts and trade

The early Sumerians made objects by hammering lumps of copper. In about 4000BC they learned how to produce pure copper from copper ore by heating it at high temperatures. They also discovered how to cast molten (melted) copper, gold and silver in moulds.

In about 3500BC the Sumerians learned how to make bronze, a harder metal, by combining copper and tin. The period from 3000 to 1000BC is often called the Bronze Age, as bronze became so widely used.

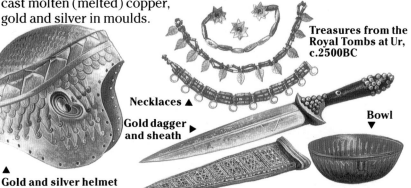

Sumerian pots ▲

◄ Clay figure

Treasures from the Royal Tombs at Ur, c.2500BC

Necklaces ▲

Gold dagger and sheath ▶

Bowl ▼

▲ Gold and silver helmet

The Sumerians traded agricultural produce, cloth and manufactured goods for timber, stone and metals. Their merchants travelled as far as Anatolia, Armenia, the Mediterranean coast and the Persian Gulf and exchanged goods with Indian traders, at a trading depot such as Dilmun (modern Bahrain).

Early Sumerian government

At first each city was probably run by a council of elders, although in wartime a leader, or *lugal*, was chosen to direct the campaigns. Wars became increasingly common. There were raids by foreigners and disputes arose between cities whose rulers competed with each other for supremacy. Massive fortifications were built and people came to live in cities for protection.

Battle chariots drawn by wild donkeys, called onagers.

The Early Dynastic Period

As wars became more frequent, *lugals* kept control for longer periods and eventually for life. From about 2900BC *lugals* became kings and founded dynasties† in the most important cities. Later Sumerian lists give details of some of these early kings. They appear to have ruled one after another, although in fact some of them ruled at the same time in different cities.

This decorated relief† (known as the Battle Standard of Ur) shows Sumerian soldiers and chariots in battle.

Dynasty III of Ur

Between about 2400BC and 2100BC Sumer was overrun first by Akkadians (see page 24), then by Gutians, a tribe from the Zagros mountains. In about 2100BC Sumerian supremacy was restored by Ur-Nammu. He founded Dynasty III of Ur and united Sumer under his rule. Later internal rivalries broke out and in about 2000BC Ur was destroyed by Elamites. However Sumerian culture lived on, as it was revived by later rulers of Mesopotamia (see page 24).

Excavations of Dynasty III buildings at Ur show that some wealthy people in towns lived in quite sophisticated houses. The reconstruction below is based on the remains of one of them.

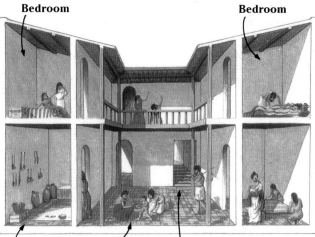

Bedroom

Bedroom

Kitchen

Doors and windows opened on to a central courtyard.

A wooden staircase and balcony gave access to rooms on the first floor.

Sumerian religion

The Sumerians worshipped hundreds of gods and goddesses. They believed that it was important to obey them and make offerings to them. If the gods were angry, they might send punishments such as floods or war. Each city had its own patron deity to look after its interests. There were gods associated with every aspect of life and death. Here are some of the most important ones.

Enki was god of 'sweet waters' and patron of crafts, learning and magic.

Ninhursag was the great mother goddess. She was married to Enlil, god of the air. He took a leading role among the gods and in the affairs of Sumer.

Enlil's son **Nanna** (later renamed **Sin**) was the moon god.

Nanna's son **Utu** (later **Shamash**) was the sun god.

Inanna (later **Ishtar**) was goddess of love and a warrior goddess. She was married to **Dumuzi** (later called **Tammuz**).

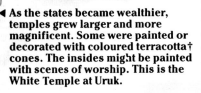

Early temples, like this ▶ Ubaid shrine at Eridu, were rectangular mud-brick buildings on low platforms.

◀ As the states became wealthier, temples grew larger and more magnificent. Some were painted or decorated with coloured terracotta† cones. The insides might be painted with scenes of worship. This is the White Temple at Uruk.

Temples

At the centre of each city was a temple to the patron deity. The Sumerians believed the gods owned the city states† and some of the land was worked directly for them by peasants and slaves. The government allotted the rest to temple staff or to farmers who paid part of their crops as rent. Few people owned land outright. Rents, offerings and farm produce were all used to run the temples and to help the poorest citizens. As well as priests and priestesses, each temple employed a large number of officials, scribes†, craftsmen, cooks and cleaners.

◀ New temples were erected on the rubble of the old ones. This raised the platform higher and higher until the ziggurat (temple platform), shown here, became the established style. This reconstruction shows the Dynasty III ziggurat of the moon god of Ur.

Priests and priestesses conducted the rituals.

Musicians and dancers performed at the ceremonies.

Key dates

c.5000BC Ubaid culture: farmers are established in Sumer (southern Mesopotamia).

c.4000BC Uruk culture: the wheel, the ox-drawn plough and writing are invented. The Sumerians discover how to smelt metal.

c.3500 The Sumerians discover how to make bronze.

c.3100-2900BC Jemdet Nasr or proto-literate period: writing is in widespread use.

c.2900-2400BC Early Dynastic Period (Dynasties I and II of Ur): kings are established in leading cities.

c.2400-2100BC Sumer is conquered by Akkadians, and then by Gutians.

c.2100BC Dynasty III: Sumerian power is restored by Ur-Nammu.

Dates for early Mesopotamian history are very approximate, as experts cannot agree on how to interpret the available evidence.

Early Egypt

While city states were developing in Mesopotamia, cultural and economic conditions in Egypt led to the establishment of the world's first great nation. In ancient times Egypt occupied almost the same area as it does today.

The Predynastic Period

The period between about 5000BC and 3100BC is known as the Predynastic Period in Egypt. In the Nile Valley three cultures can be identified that evolved one after the other. They are known as Badarian, Amratian (or Nagada I) and Gerzean (or Nagada II), after the sites where they were first discovered. The people of these cultures made tools, weapons and utensils and were skilled potters and weavers.

Badarian artefacts

Amratian artefacts

Gerzean artefacts

The early Egyptians knew how to control the Nile's annual flood with an elaborate irrigation system (see page 14). They also learned how to work metals, and the use of copper (and later bronze) tools and weapons slowly increased. At first houses were made of mud and reeds, but by Gerzean times these had been replaced by sun-dried mud-brick.

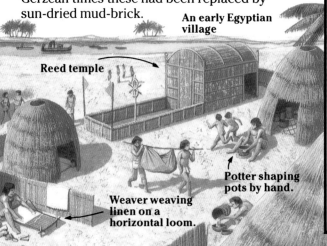

An early Egyptian village

Reed temple

Potter shaping pots by hand.

Weaver weaving linen on a horizontal loom.

Upper and Lower Egypt

By about 3300BC important changes were taking place in southern Egypt which suggest that the population and wealth of the area was growing. Towns were built, defended by high mud-brick walls, and large monuments were constructed as burial places for kings. The art of writing was also discovered at this time (see page 10).

By about 3100BC the communities of the Nile Valley had united into a single kingdom, known as Upper Egypt. The kingdom was ruled from Hierakonpolis by a line of kings who wore white crowns. The kings were buried at a sacred site near Abydos. The Upper Egyptians developed elaborate burial customs, placing personal possessions and offerings in their tombs.

Model animals found in tombs suggest that some creatures had already become linked with certain deities (see page 63).

Very little excavation has taken place in the region of the Nile Delta. However according to Egyptian tradition this area, known as Lower Egypt, had also become one kingdom by this time. Its kings wore red crowns and ruled from Buto. Evidence suggests they had close trading connections with their neighbours in the East.

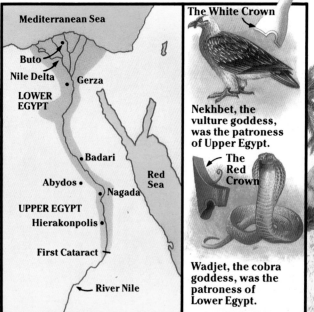

Mediterranean Sea

Buto

Nile Delta

Gerza

LOWER EGYPT

Badari

Abydos

Nagada

Red Sea

UPPER EGYPT

Hierakonpolis

First Cataract

River Nile

The White Crown

Nekhbet, the vulture goddess, was the patroness of Upper Egypt.

The Red Crown

Wadjet, the cobra goddess, was the patroness of Lower Egypt.

Writing

The invention of writing is one of the most important landmarks of civilization. It is often said to mark the end of prehistoric times and the beginning of history. This is because writing enabled people to record information accurately, and so helped them to develop a sense of their past.

The first steps towards the development of writing probably took place in Sumer between 4000BC and 3000BC. The new cities were rapidly growing and needed a way of keeping records. Pictograms (simple pictures) were used to indicate objects and quantities, such as the amount of grain or cattle owned by a temple. Later the pictures became more stylized and began to look like symbols.

Cuneiform writing

The first pictograms were drawn in vertical columns with a pen made from a sharpened reed. Then two developments made the process quicker and easier. People began to write in horizontal rows, which avoided smudging. A new type of pen was used which was pushed into the clay, producing 'wedge-shaped' signs that are known as *cuneiform* writing.

Cuneiform writing

Picture writing

Pictograms and *cuneiform* were written on clay tablets, and then baked hard in a kiln.

Egyptian hieroglyphs

In Egypt the first examples of writing appeared between about 3300BC and 3100BC. Some scholars suggest that the Egyptians may have been inspired by seeing the Sumerian script. The Egyptian script is known as *hieroglyphic*, after the Greek for 'holy writing', although the Egyptians themselves called it the 'words of the gods'. To them it had an important religious and magical significance. They believed that the knowledge of writing had been given to them by Thoth, the god of wisdom.

How hieroglyphs work

The Egyptian writing consisted of over 700 signs, or *hieroglyphs*, most of which are recognizable as pictures of things. They probably began by representing objects, and later came to stand for sounds too.

Each hieroglyph corresponded to the sound of one or more letters. For example:

=t =sw =nh.

At the same time, a sign could also represent an object. For example ⬯ meant mouth, but it also represented the sound 'r' and could be used as part of the word *nfr*, meaning 'beautiful'.

n ___ f
___ r

Hieroglyphs normally represented consonants only, though they had a few semi-vowels, such as 'y'. In order to pronounce the language, vowels have to be added and experts sometimes disagree about the correct spellings. For example, the *hieroglyphs* for the name 'imnhtp', can be written as Amenhotep, Amunhotep or Amenhotpe. ►

Sometimes a picture representing an object or movement was placed at the end of a word, to clarify its meaning. This is called a determinative.

Determinative for cat

= mjw, meaning 'cat'

Determinative for movement

=tkn, meaning 'to approach'

Hieroglyphs can be written from left to right, right to left, or downwards. If the animals or people are facing left, you read from left to right. If they are facing right, you read from right to left.

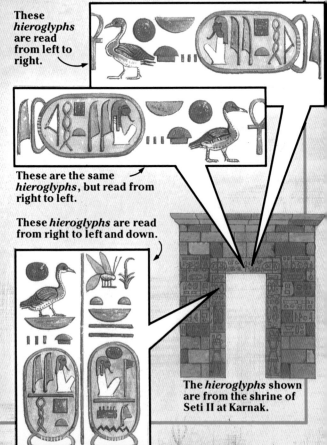

These *hieroglyphs* are read from left to right.

These are the same *hieroglyphs*, but read from right to left.

These *hieroglyphs* are read from right to left and down.

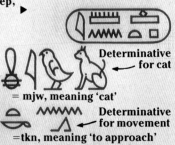

The *hieroglyphs* shown are from the shrine of Seti II at Karnak.

The Egyptian "i" is not like an English "i". It is almost silent, like an intake of breath.

10

How cuneiform writing developed

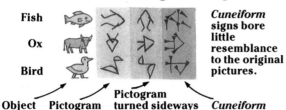

	Object	Pictogram	Pictogram turned sideways	Cuneiform
Fish				
Ox				
Bird				

Cuneiform signs bore little resemblance to the original pictures.

At first signs were only used to represent objects. Later they began to represent sounds. This meant that abstract concepts could be expressed.

For example, if you used a system of picture writing in English you could write the word 'belief' like this.

Bee   Leaf

Understanding cuneiform

Cuneiform was adapted by the Akkadians, Babylonians and Assyrians to write their own languages and was used in Mesopotamia for about 3000 years.

Knowledge of it was then lost until AD1835, when Henry Rawlinson, an English army officer, found some inscriptions on a cliff at Behistun in Persia. They consisted of identical texts in three languages (Old Persian, Babylonian and Elamite), carved in the reign of King Darius† of Persia (522-486BC). After translating the Persian, Rawlinson began to decipher the others. By 1851 he could read 200 Babylonian signs.

Writing materials

The Egyptians wrote with ink and brushes on papyrus, a paper made from papyrus reeds. They also made notes on pieces of broken pottery or flakes of limestone, known as *ostraca*.

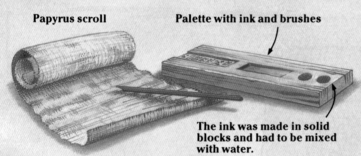

Papyrus scroll

Palette with ink and brushes

The ink was made in solid blocks and had to be mixed with water.

Scribes

Early scripts were extremely complicated and years of study were required to learn them properly. People specially trained to read and write were known as scribes. These skills brought them power and status. Scribes could get good jobs in temples or in government and were often exempt from paying taxes.

A statue of an Egyptian scribe

Shorthand scripts

The Egyptians developed two shorthand scripts for daily use. *Hieroglyphs* were kept for religious and state inscriptions.

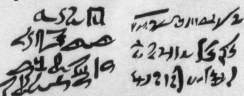

The first shorthand script is known as *hieratic* and was in use during the Old Kingdom.

During the Late Period (c.700BC), an even more flowing script evolved, which is known as *demotic*.

Deciphering hieroglyphs

The last known example of *hieroglyphs* dates back to AD394. For centuries after that no-one knew how to read them, until 1799 when French soldiers of Napoleon's army unearthed a clue at Rosetta in Egypt. It was a stone slab covered in different kinds of writing – identical texts in *hieroglyphic*, *demotic* and Greek.

The puzzle was finally solved by a French linguist, Jean François Champollion, who published the results of his research in 1822. Champollion deduced that *hieroglyphs* might stand for sounds and letters, rather than objects alone. He built on previous studies which suggested that words inside oval shapes, called cartouches, were the names of rulers.

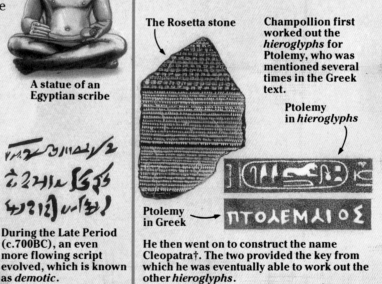

The Rosetta stone

Champollion first worked out the *hieroglyphs* for Ptolemy, who was mentioned several times in the Greek text.

Ptolemy in *hieroglyphs*

Ptolemy in Greek

He then went on to construct the name Cleopatra†. The two provided the key from which he was eventually able to work out the other *hieroglyphs*.

The Archaic Period and the Old Kingdom

In about 3100BC, a king of Upper Egypt, traditionally known as Menes†, conquered Lower Egypt. He united the two kingdoms under Dynasty I and founded a new capital on the border, at Memphis. Evidence suggests that he married a northern princess, giving their son, Hor-aha, a hereditary claim to the whole of Egypt. The Egyptians never forgot that their country had originally been two lands. The official title of the ruler was 'King of Upper and Lower Egypt'.

This slate carving shows Narmer, an Upper Egyptian king, triumphing over a Lower Egyptian prince. Many believe he and Menes were the same person.

The Archaic Period

The period of the kings of Dynasties I and II is known as the Archaic Period. The kings may have been buried at Sakkara, near Memphis, as their names appear on seals and other objects found there in brick *mastaba* tombs (see page 16). However the same kings' names also appear in tombs in the desert necropolis† at Abydos, where the predynastic kings of Upper Egypt were buried.

This disc was found at Sakkara and dates from about 2950BC.

The Old Kingdom

This wall-painting of geese is from a tomb at Meidum, c.2575BC.

The Archaic Period was followed by the Old Kingdom, one of the greatest eras of Egyptian history and culture. It was the age of the pyramids (see page 16). Egypt was united under a strong central government. Trade flourished and Egyptian traders travelled as far afield as Lebanon and Punt (see page 47). The army defended the frontiers and trade routes from Nubians, Libyans and bedouin (desert nomads†). Craftsmen produced fine works of art and scholars standardized writing and the calendar, and studied astronomy, mathematics and medicine.

Imhotep

Imhotep was one of the highest officials of King Zoser† of Dynasty III. He was the architect of the first pyramid, the Step Pyramid of Sakkara (see page 16). He was also a high priest and a doctor and may have had something to do with introducing the calendar. Imhotep's reputation for wisdom was so great that later generations worshipped him as a god. The Ancient Greeks identified him with their god of medicine, Asclepius.

Imhotep

Dynasty IV

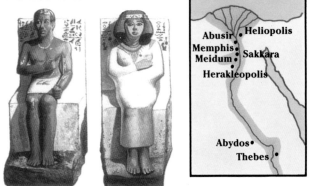

These statues show Prince Rahotep and his wife Nofret c.2700BC.

Egypt in the Old Kingdom

Abusir • Heliopolis
Memphis •
Meidum • Sakkara
Herakleopolis

Abydos •
Thebes •

Dynasty IV seems to have been torn by family feuds. Problems arose because King Khufu† had three queens. Kawab and Hetepheres II, the children of his chief queen, Meritetes, would have been the next king and queen, but Kawab died before his father. Rivalry then broke out between the sons of the two other queens. First one son ruled, then the other. The feud finally ended when the heir of one line married the heiress of the other, beginning Dynasty V.

Family tree of Dynasty IV

Sneferu = Hetepheres I

Meritetes = Khufu = Name unknown   Henutsen

Kawab = Hetepheres II = Radjedef = O

Meresankh   Khafra

△ Male
O Female
= Married
| Children

△   O Menkawre = O

Userkaf (1st king of Dynasty V) = O   Shepseskaf (last king of Dynasty IV)

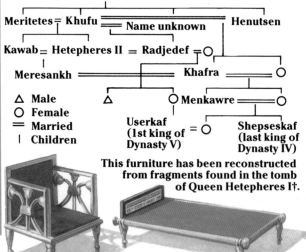

This furniture has been reconstructed from fragments found in the tomb of Queen Hetepheres I†.

The sphinx of Gizah

Workmen building King Khufu's pyramid at Gizah were left with a large outcrop of rock. They carved it with his features and made it into the head of an enormous sphinx, a statue with a king's head and a lion's body which was a form of the sun god. The sphinx was supposed to guard the pyramids.

The cult of the sun god

The Egyptians worshipped many different gods (see page 20), but during the Old Kingdom religion was dominated by the cult of the sun god, Re, whose cult temple was at Heliopolis. The Egyptians believed that Re sailed across the sky every day in a boat. In early times people thought that when a king died he joined the northern stars. However by the time of Dynasty IV it was thought that he sailed with the sun god in his boat. 'Son of Re' became one of his most important titles.

According to a popular story, the first three kings of Dynasty V were actually the sons of Re.

Temples to Re, like this one, were built near the pyramids at Abusir.

The Pyramid Texts

When a ruler died prayers and spells were said to enable him to join the gods in the Next World†. By the end of Dynasty V, these prayers were carved on the walls of the burial chambers of pyramids and so became known as Pyramid Texts. They were later modified and put on the sides of coffins and called Coffin Texts. By the New Kingdom, they were written on papyrus instead and placed inside the tombs. These texts are known collectively as the *Book of the Dead*.

An illustration from the *Book of the Dead*

The longest reigning king

The autobiography of Uni, a favourite courtier of Pepi I of Dynasty VI, relates how the king appointed him as a judge to try his sister-wife, Queen Imtes. After the trial, Pepi I married the two sisters of a powerful noble called Djau. Pepi's youngest son, Pepi II†, became king at a very young age and reigned for 94 years – the longest recorded reign in history.

This alabaster statue shows Pepi II with his mother, Meryre-ankhnes.

The rise of the nomarchs

In the Old Kingdom Egypt was divided into 42 *nomes* (administrative districts), each governed by an official. At first these officials did short spells of duty, and then returned to the capital of Memphis. However by Dynasty V they began to settle permanently in their *nomes* and took the title *nomarch*. They kept their positions for life and passed them on to their sons. This gradually undermined royal authority.

A *nomarch*

The First Intermediate Period

During Pepi II's reign the system was weakened by the growth of powerful officials, troubles abroad and a struggling economy. By the time he died, most of his children were already dead and so a dispute broke out over the succession. Egypt collapsed into civil conflict and confusion, and there were invasions by Libyans and bedouin† from the East. The irrigation system broke down and there was famine.

A new line of kings, Dynasties IX and X, took control in northern Egypt, ruling from Herakleopolis. However, they were unpopular in southern Egypt, especially after the Herakleopolitans sacked the holy city of Abydos. The *nomarchs* of Thebes led a revolt against them and eventually united Egypt under the Middle Kingdom (see page 26).

Key dates

c.3100BC	Egypt is united by Menes.
c.3100-2649BC	The Archaic Period
c.2649-2134BC	The Old Kingdom
c.2246-2152BC	Reign of Pepi II
c.2150-2040BC	The First Intermediate Period

Farming

The civilization of Ancient Egypt grew up along the banks of the River Nile. Egypt's wealth was based on agriculture and the river not only provided water, but also created fertile land in an area that would otherwise have been desert.

The Nile floods

Every spring, rain and melting snow in the Highlands of Ethiopia sent a huge quantity of water down the Nile. This reached Egypt in about July. The river overflowed and flooded its banks, depositing silt (a rich, fertile mud) on the fields. This was known as the inundation. The Egyptians developed a sophisticated irrigation system to make use of the flood. However, the amount of water varied each year. Too little could result in a poor harvest and famine. Too much could damage the system and sweep away animals and entire villages.

River Nile

Nile Delta

EGYPT

Ethiopian Highlands

Villages were built on high ground to avoid the floods.

Fields on higher ground, near the desert edge, were less productive as the flood did not reach them every year.

Gauges known as nilometers were built on the banks so that officials could check the water levels and plan for the year ahead.

The land was divided into small rectangular plots by a series of ditches and irrigation canals. The canals were used to store the flood water and supply it to the fields when needed. Each canal and ditch could be opened and closed.

The fields nearest to the Nile were the most fertile as the silt and water always reached them.

Farmers marked the limits of their fields with boundary stones, designed to stay in place during the floods. It was a serious crime to move the stones, or to block a neighbour's water supply.

Surveyors could be called in to redraw any boundaries damaged by the flood.

Water could be raised from a lower level to a higher one using a device called a *shaduf*. This technique is still sometimes used.

Beam

Leather bucket to carry water

Weight

What the Egyptians ate

The fertility of the land and the abundance of sources of food meant that most Egyptians had a varied diet.

Wheat and barley were used to make bread and beer, the staple elements of the Egyptian diet.

Many different vegetables were grown, including onions, leeks, garlic, beans, peas, lettuces and cucumbers.

Fruit included melons, pomegranates, grapes, dates and figs.

The farming year

The inundation season (mid-July to mid-November)

In July, when the fields were covered with flood water, work came to a halt. Some farmers could afford to relax for a while, while others were called up to work on royal building projects or mining expeditions.

The growing season (mid-November to mid-March)

As the flood subsided the farmers ploughed the land. They scattered the seeds by hand and drove animals across the fields to tread in the seeds. In the following weeks, the farmers weeded and watered the crops.

Wooden plough with bronze blade

Summer (mid-March to mid-July)

After the harvest, before the summer heat made the soil too hard to dig, the irrigation channels had to be repaired and new ones dug, ready for the next flood. This was done as part of the labour tax everybody paid to the king.

The harvest (March to April)

The harvest was in March and April. Before it was gathered taxmen came to assess how much grain each field would yield. From that they calculated how much each farmer should give to the king in taxes.

Men cut off the ears of grain, using sickles with flint blades. The stalks were later gathered and used for animal food.

Flint sickle

The grain was stored in granaries.

Some farmers had flute players to provide music while people worked.

Women and children picked up any ears of grain which the men had missed.

Cattle were driven over the ears to separate the grain from the stalk. This is known as threshing.

Women separated the grain from the husk by winnowing (tossing it in the air so that the light husks blew away).

Threshing-floor

The ears of grain were taken to the threshing-floor.

Drinking water was kept under a tree or in a shelter to keep it cool.

Honey from bees kept in pottery hives (shown above) was used as a sweetener. Oil for cooking was made from linseed, saffron and sesame.

Several breeds of cattle and pigs were kept.

Sheep and goats provided dairy produce and hides.

Egyptians kept geese, ducks and pigeons and caught many varieties of wildfowl.

Fish were caught in traps, by hook and line, and in nets hung between two boats. Large fish were speared.

Pyramids and tombs

In an attempt to preserve their bodies forever, the Egyptian kings had massive tombs built for themselves and their families. Pyramid-shaped tombs were introduced during the Old Kingdom.

However pyramids were frequently robbed, so the New Kingdom kings chose to be buried in tombs cut deep into the sides of cliffs. For more about how pyramids were built, see page 52

Mastabas

The first kings were buried under mud-brick buildings called *mastabas*. This is a reconstruction of one built at Sakkara in about 3100BC.

Step pyramids

At the beginning of Dynasty III, King Zoser's† architect, Imhotep†, designed a new style of tomb. He built a stone *mastaba*, enlarged it, then added other layers on top, each smaller than the last. This resulted in the first step pyramid. Experts believe that the steps were intended as a symbolic staircase up which the king climbed to reach the stars. Step pyamids were planned by all the later kings of Dynasty III, but only Zoser's and Huni's (see opposite) were completed.

The pyramid was surrounded by a vast enclosure, 547m (1790ft) by 278m (912ft).

Inside the enclosure were buildings with finely decorated exteriors. Most of them were only facades, filled with solid rubble.

Four steps

Six steps

This is a cross-section of the step pyramid. It began with four steps, but it was later enlarged to make six.

Burial chamber

Private tombs

Ordinary Egyptians were simply buried in a hole in the sand and covered with a layer of sand and stones. Those who could afford it had a deep shaft cut, with one or more chambers at the bottom.

The tombs of the wealthiest people were decorated inside with scenes of daily life. The Egyptians believed this ensured that these activities carried on after death.

Old Kingdom nobles tended to be buried in *mastabas*, like these, situated near the pyramids of their kings. They were made of stone, or of rubble or brick covered with stone.

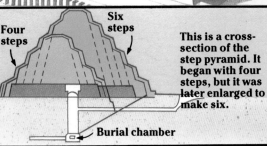

This painting is from a noble's tomb in the cliffs at Beni Hasan. Cliff-cut tombs were in use from the end of the Old Kingdom.

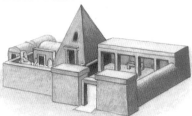

These tombs were built by the royal tomb builders at Deir el Medinah (see page 66) for themselves.

Straight-sided pyramids

The introduction of the worship of the sun god, Re (see page 13), at the end of Dynasty III affected the design of pyramids. The steps were replaced by straight sides. These represented a solid form of the sun's rays, up which the king could climb to reach his 'father' Re.

All the early pyramids were made of stone, but most kings in Dynasty XII used mud-brick, which did not wear as well. There was an outer casing of limestone, but this was often stolen, leaving the bricks exposed.

This reconstruction is based on the pyramid of King Sahure at Abusir.

Enclosure wall

Smaller pyramid for the queen

Daily offerings were made to the spirit of the king in the mortuary temple.

A covered causeway linked the valley and mortuary temples.

The king's body may have been prepared for burial on the roof of the valley temple, which was on the edge of the Nile.

Huni's pyramid at Meidum

Straight sides

Step pyramid inside

This cross-section of Huni's pyramid shows the transition between the styles. It began as a step pyramid, but Huni's son, Sneferu†, added straight sides.

The Great Pyramid

Great Pyramid

St Peter's, Rome

The Great Pyramid at Gizah was built for King Cheops (or Khufu†) of Dynasty IV. It was known as one of the Seven Wonders of the Ancient World because of its size – 146m (480ft) high. This shows its height compared with St Peter's in Rome, the biggest cathedral in the world.

Mentuhotep's temple

King Mentuhotep II† of Dynasty XI built himself a unique monument on the West Bank of the Nile at Thebes, combining a funerary temple and tomb. His successors planned similar monuments, but never completed them.

Some experts believe there may have been a small pyramid on top.

The Valley of the Kings

The New Kingdom kings and their families were buried in tombs cut into cliffs, situated in two remote valleys (the Valley of the Kings and the Valley of the Queens) on the West Bank of the Nile opposite Thebes. Although the tombs were inconspicuous from the outside, the insides were lavishly decorated.

Death and burial

The Egyptians saw death as a transitional stage in the progress to a better life in the Next World†. They believed they could only reach their full potential after death. Each person was thought to have three souls – the *ka*, the *ba* and the *akh*. For these to function properly, it was considered essential for the body to survive intact. The Egyptians tried various methods to achieve this. In predynastic Upper Egypt, bodies were buried in shallow graves. They dried out quickly in the hot sand and so were largely preserved from decay.

A preserved body from an early grave, c.3200BC.

Embalming

During the Archaic Period, kings and nobles were buried deep under the ground in stone-lined burial chambers. Away from contact with the hot sand, the bodies decayed. So the Egyptians tried to find artificial ways to preserve them instead. By the New Kingdom an elaborate process of embalming had evolved, which was used by kings, nobles and those who could afford it.

When the person died, priests recited prayers and a final attempt was made to revive the corpse. It was then washed and purified in a special shelter called an *ibu*.

The body was then taken to the *wabet*, the embalmers' workshop. First a cut was made in the left side. The organs were removed and stored in containers known as canopic jars.

Canopic jars

A salt called natron was packed around the body to dry it out. After a few days, the insides were filled with linen or sawdust, resin and natron. The body was wrapped in bandages, with jewellery and amulets† (shown here) between the layers.

A *djed-pillar*†

An *ankh* – the symbol of life

Heart scarab

A portrait mask was placed over the head by the chief embalmer, who wore a jackal mask to represent Anubis*, the patron god of embalmers. The wrapped body, or mummy, was put in a coffin.

Coffins

Early coffins were wooden and rectangular. In the Old Kingdom they were plain or decorated with a band of *hieroglyphs*. Middle Kingdom coffins, like this one, were more ornate.

Coffins were often elaborately decorated with spells.

These eyes, called *udjat* † eyes, were meant to protect the mummy.

Anthropoid (human-shaped) coffins came into use during the Middle Kingdom and remained in fashion for over 2000 years. By the New Kingdom, mummies were placed inside a nest of two or three coffins.

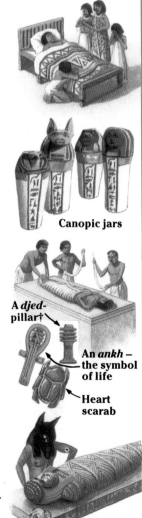

The arms were carved in relief and often shown crossed over the chest, holding amulets.

Some coffins were decorated with gold and inlaid with semi-precious stones.

*For more about Anubis and other Egyptian gods and goddesses, see pages 20-21.

The funeral

The body was taken to the tomb in a procession of family and friends. The funeral of a nobleman or woman also included professional mourners, priests, animals for sacrifice and porters carrying the dead person's belongings.

At the tomb door the priest performed the 'Opening of the Mouth' ceremony. This was supposed to revive the dead person's bodily functions and powers. Final prayers were said.

The wooden coffin was placed inside a *sarcophagus* (stone coffin), and the lid was closed. The burial chamber was sealed, although the upper chambers of the tomb were left open so that regular offerings of food could be left.

The Next World

The Egyptians believed in a life after death, which they referred to as the Next World. Although they had several different versions of what it would be like, it was thought to be a happy land somewhere in the far west. (It was often called the Kingdom of the West.) Entry depended on leading a virtuous life on Earth. When a person died he or she first had to go through a series of tests and ordeals.

First the dead man had to persuade an old ferryman to take him across the River of Death.

Then he had to pass through the Twelve Gates, guarded by serpents. The dead man had amulets and a *Book of the Dead*, containing spells, a map and information to help him by-pass the many dangers.

After passing by the Lake of Fire, he had to confront the 42 Assessors who read out a list of sins. The dead man had to swear that he had never committed any of them.

If he passed this test, he entered the Judgement Hall of Osiris, where his heart was weighed against the Feather of Truth. If he had led a sinful life his heart would be heavy. The scales would tip against him and he would be fed to a monster. If he had led a virtuous life his heart would balance with the Feather of Truth. The man could then join his ancestors in the Kingdom of the West. This papyrus showing the 'Weighing of the Heart' is from the *Book of the Dead* (see page 13).

Egyptian gods and goddesses

The Egyptians had as many as 2000 gods and goddesses. Some, such as Amun, were worshipped throughout the whole country, while others had only a local following. The most important gods had a home town where their main temple, known as a cult temple, was situated. They were also worshipped at other shrines and temples across the country. A few deities, such as Bes and Tawaret, had no temples, but were worshipped in people's homes. Some gods and goddesses represented forces of nature, such as water or air. Others were associated with aspects of daily life, such as weaving or farming. From predynastic times, many deities were identified with particular animals or birds (and sometimes with plants too). To make them easier to recognize, they were often shown in paintings and carvings with the head of that creature. Many of the gods and goddesses were linked in families. Here are some of the most important ones.

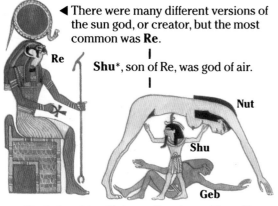

◄ There were many different versions of the sun god, or creator, but the most common was **Re**.

Re

Shu*, son of Re, was god of air.

Nut

Shu

Geb

Shu's daughter, **Nut**, was the sky goddess. She was married to her brother, **Geb**, god of the Earth.

◄ **Amun**, was King of the Gods in the New Kingdom. He was associated with Re and became known as **Amun-Re**. Temple: Karnak. Animals: goose and ram.

Amun

Mut

Mut, wife of Amun, was a mother goddess. Temple: Karnak. Animal: lioness.

Khonsu

Khonsu, son of Amun and Mut, was the moon god. ► Temple: Karnak.

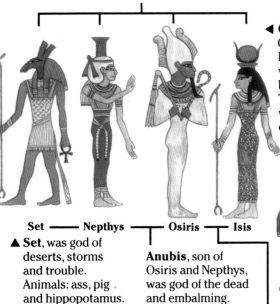

◄ **Osiris**, the son and heir of Geb and Nut was King of Egypt and introduced vines and grain. He became Ruler of the Dead. Temple: Abydos. His sister-wife, **Isis**, introduced crafts. Temple: Philae.

Horus

Hathor

Ptah was patron of Memphis. Animal: Apis bull†. ▼

Sekhmet, wife of Ptah, represented motherhood and the destructive power of the sun. Animal: lioness. ▼

Set ── **Nepthys**   **Osiris** ┬ **Isis**

Ptah ┬ **Sekhmet**

▲ **Set**, was god of deserts, storms and trouble. Animals: ass, pig and hippopotamus. He was married to his sister **Nepthys**.

Anubis, son of Osiris and Nepthys, was god of the dead and embalming. Animal: jackal. ▼

Nefertem, son of Ptah and Sekhmet, was god of oils ► and perfumes. Flower: sacred blue lotus.

Nefertem

Anubis

Neith

◄ **Min**, god of fertility. Temple: Coptos. Animal: bull. Plant: lettuce.

Horus, inherited the throne of Egypt. Temple: Edfu. Animal: falcon.
Ihy, son of Horus and Hathor, was the musician god.

┬ **Hathor**, wife of Horus, was goddess of love, beauty and joy. A mother and death goddess. Temple: Denderah. Animal: cow.

◄ **Neith** was mother of the sun, goddess of hunting, war and weaving, and guardian of the Red Crown of Lower Egypt. Temple: Sais. Symbol: shield and arrows.

Min

*Shu, as god of air, is often shown holding up Nut, the sky goddess.

Sobek

◄ **Sobek** was god of water. He was married to Renenutet. Temples: Fayum and Kom Ombo. Animal: Crocodile.

Thoth

— **Renenutet**, was the harvest goddess. Temple: Medinet el Fayum. Animal: Snake.

Bast was a mother goddess who represented the healing power of ◄ the sun. Temple: Bubastis. Animal: cat. Her son was **Mithos**, the lion-headed god.

Bast

Renenutet

▼

Thoth was god of wisdom and vizier and scribe of the gods. Temple: Hermopolis. Animal: baboon. Bird: ibis. ▲

Ma'at was goddess of ► justice and truth. She represented the harmony and balance of the Universe. Symbol: feather.

Ma'at

Satis

Khnum

Anukis

Bes the dwarf ► was the jester of the gods. He protected people's homes and children.

Bes

Taweret, a ► female hippopotamus, looked after pregnant women and babies.

Taweret

Khnum was a ► potter who created people on his potter's wheel. He was thought to control the source of the Nile. Temple: Elephantine. Animal: ram.

Khnum's wife, **Satis**, was patroness of hunters.

Their daughter, **Anukis**, was ▲ goddess of the First Cataract† of the River Nile.

The creation

The Egyptians had many tales about how the world began. According to one legend, it started with an ocean in darkness. Then a mound of dry land rose up and the sun god Re appeared. He created light and all things. Here are four other different versions of the story.

The sun god flew to an island as a falcon.

He emerged from a sacred blue lotus that grew out of the mud.

He was hatched from an egg laid by a goose called the Great Cackler.

He appeared as a scarab beetle on the eastern horizon.

The story of Osiris and Set

The Egyptians believed that Osiris and Isis had once ruled Egypt. They were good and much-loved rulers, but their brother Set was jealous. He invited Osiris to a party where he produced a beautiful casket, and announced he would give it to the person who fitted most exactly inside. The casket had secretly been made for Osiris, and once he was inside, Set had it tossed into the Nile. The current carried it into the Mediterranean, and on to Byblos. There it was cast ashore and a huge tree grew around it.

After many adventures, Isis found the body and returned with it to Egypt. Despite her attempts to hide it, Set discovered the body and cut it into pieces. However Isis and her stepson Anubis reassembled them and succeeded in bringing Osiris back to life. In revenge Set tried to harm Horus, the son and heir of Osiris and Isis. He took Horus to court, claiming he had no right to rule, and a series of battles followed. Horus finally won. He became King of Egypt, while Osiris ruled the Kingdom of the Dead.

Early civilization in India

Little is known about the emergence of early civilization in India, but it seems to have developed from small communities which were established in the Indus Valley by about 3000BC. The people made their living chiefly from farming, and later from trade. The produce and artefacts of farmers and craftsmen paid for imports from abroad, including precious metals and cloth.

The remains of over a hundred towns have been found. The most impressive ruins are those of the cities of Mohenjo Daro and Harappa, which seem to have controlled the entire area. Information from excavations there has been used in this reconstruction of Mohenjo Daro.

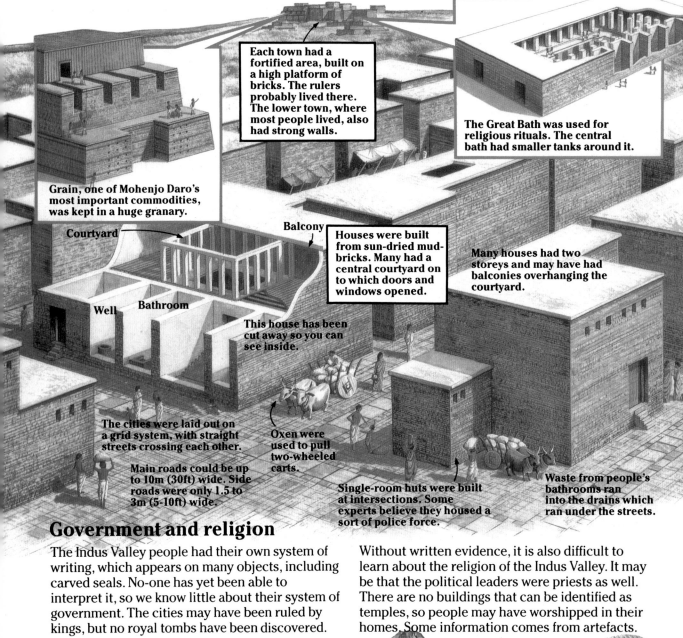

Each town had a fortified area, built on a high platform of bricks. The rulers probably lived there. The lower town, where most people lived, also had strong walls.

The Great Bath was used for religious rituals. The central bath had smaller tanks around it.

Grain, one of Mohenjo Daro's most important commodities, was kept in a huge granary.

Courtyard

Balcony

Houses were built from sun-dried mud-bricks. Many had a central courtyard on to which doors and windows opened.

Many houses had two storeys and may have had balconies overhanging the courtyard.

Well   Bathroom

This house has been cut away so you can see inside.

The cities were laid out on a grid system, with straight streets crossing each other.

Main roads could be up to 10m (30ft) wide. Side roads were only 1.5 to 3m (5-10ft) wide.

Oxen were used to pull two-wheeled carts.

Single-room huts were built at intersections. Some experts believe they housed a sort of police force.

Waste from people's bathrooms ran into the drains which ran under the streets.

Government and religion

The Indus Valley people had their own system of writing, which appears on many objects, including carved seals. No-one has yet been able to interpret it, so we know little about their system of government. The cities may have been ruled by kings, but no royal tombs have been discovered.

Without written evidence, it is also difficult to learn about the religion of the Indus Valley. It may be that the political leaders were priests as well. There are no buildings that can be identified as temples, so people may have worshipped in their homes. Some information comes from artefacts.

◄ This seated male figure, surrounded by animals, may be a very early version of the Hindu god Siva.

◄ Baked clay figures like this one suggest that goddesses played a leading role.

This statue may ► be of an Indus Valley ruler or priest.

◄ Carved seals

The civilization declines

Gradually, from about 1800BC, the Indus Valley civilization declined. The reasons for this are unclear, but there seems to have been frequent flooding, and the inhabitants overgrazed the land and cut down the trees. Excavations show a decline in trade and in the quality of the buildings. Finally war may have destroyed at least some centres, including Mohenjo Daro.

The date of the final collapse is uncertain, but it may have been connected with the arrival in about 1500BC of groups of Indo-Europeans† who called themselves Aryas (known in the West as Aryans). They occupied the Indus Valley and then drifted eastwards into the Ganges Valley.

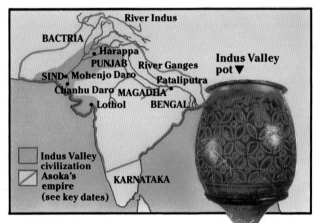

River Indus
BACTRIA
Harappa
PUNJAB — River Ganges
SIND· Mohenjo Daro — Pataliputra
Chanhu Daro — MAGADHA
Lothol — BENGAL
KARNATAKA

Indus Valley pot ▼

☐ Indus Valley civilization
▨ Asoka's empire (see key dates)

The Aryans

Much of our information about the Aryans comes from an ancient series of religious poems composed by priests. The poems were passed on by word of mouth, and by 900BC they were gathered together to form a collection called the *Rig Veda*. (Later three other *vedas* were composed.) The *Rig Veda* describes the events of the period. The Aryans set up several kingdoms, each with its own *rajah* (ruler). Most people were farmers and wealth was counted in terms of the number of cattle a man owned. In their leisure hours they enjoyed music, dancing and gambling.

Priest

Warrior

Farmer

Dravidians

During this period, class divisions started to assume an important role. There was a class for priests, another for warriors, and one for farmers and traders. At the bottom came the Dravidians (the original inhabitants), and the children of mixed Aryan-Dravidian marriages. This formed the basis for the caste† system, which has lasted into the 20th century.

By the 6th century BC some important changes had taken place. The centre of Aryan power had moved to the Ganges Basin, where four rulers struggled to gain control of the whole area. The Aryans had adopted an irrigation system and were growing new crops and using domesticated elephants. Skilled craftsmen had emerged, and specialist traders, such as merchants, moneylenders and entertainers. Money and a new writing system were both in use.

Religion

The Aryans worshipped several deities, particularly those connected with the sky. These included Indra (god of war and weather), Varuna (who governed the order of the Universe) and Mitra (protector of oaths and contracts). Sacrifices† played an important part in their worship and, as rituals grew more complex, the training and status of priests increased.

The Aryans believed that after death a person's soul passed into a new body and that behaviour in one life affected the quality of the next. Holy men gave up their possessions and wandered around preaching, trying to achieve an inner joy through poverty and meditation. These ideas, and others, provided the basis for a new religion, Buddhism, founded by Gautama, an Indian prince. He became the Buddha, 'the Enlightened One', and his teachings spread rapidly across the Far East.

Head of the Buddha from Gandhara

Key dates

c.3000BC   Farming communities are established in northwest India.

c.2500BC   The Indus Valley civilization reaches its peak.

c.1800BC   Signs of decline appear in some Indus Valley sites

c.1500BC   Arrival of the Aryans

c.560-483BC   Life of the Buddha

512BC   King Darius† of Persia conquers the provinces of Gandhara and Sind.

327-325BC   Alexander the Great† of Macedonia campaigns in India.

c.321BC   Chandragupta founds the Maurya Dynasty (c.321-185BC).

305BC   An invasion by Seleucus Nicator, ruler of the Seleucid† empire, is defeated by Chandragupta.

c.272-231BC   Asoka, grandson of Chandragupta, unites most of India under his rule (see map) and is converted to Buddhism. His empire is divided after his death and the Mauryas decline in power.

c.185BC   The Sunga Dynasty replaces the Mauryas. Greeks from Bactria (formerly part of the Seleucid empire) invade and set up small kingdoms in the Punjab.

After Sumer

By about 2500BC the area which stretched from the northern borders of Sumer (see pages 6-8) to the eastern borders of Egypt was inhabited by people known as Semites. The Semites spoke closely related dialects which form part of the language group known by modern scholars as Semitic. Sumerian culture had a strong influence on the region and many of the neighbouring Semitic tribes wanted to share in its wealth.

Akkad

The Akkadians, a Semitic people from a land just north of Sumer, adopted Sumerian culture, religion and writing from the earliest times. In 2371BC*, an Akkadian called Sargon seized the throne of the Sumerian city of Kish. He was a gifted soldier and administrator and created the first great Mesopotamian empire.

Sargon conquered the whole of Akkad and Sumer, uniting them under his rule, and so the city states† lost their independence. He also took control of Elam, a land east of the Tigris, and set up a vassal† as governor. He marched as far as the Mediterranean, conquering cities such as Mari and Ebla (see opposite) on the way. Sargon's empire fell apart after his death, but it was reconquered by his grandson, Naram-Sin† (2291-2255BC).

Sargon of Akkad

Trouble broke out again in about 2230BC, and the kingdom finally collapsed after local rebellions and invasions by tribes of Gutians from the Zagros mountains.

Northern Mesopotamia

In northern Mesopotamia there were independent cities strongly influenced by Sumerian culture. The greatest of these was Mari, which was an important trading post, both for river traffic and for overland caravans (expeditions crossing the desert).

Statue of Itur-Shamagan, King of Mari

The nomads

To the south and east of the Fertile Crescent lived groups of nomadic† Semitic tribes who wandered the edges of the deserts seeking pasture for their sheep, goats and donkeys. They came to towns and villages to trade animals, wool and artefacts for grain, dates and metal goods. Some worked as mercenaries† or labourers and a few managed to acquire land and become farmers. Others took to raiding villages and caravans. The nomads were usually easily absorbed into village life, but their numbers sometimes increased to such an extent that they threatened the stability of the city states.

Semitic nomads from a painting at Beni Hasan, Egypt

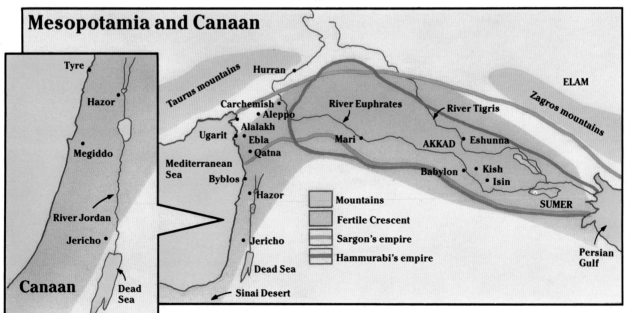

Mesopotamia and Canaan

Tyre
Hazor
Megiddo
River Jordan
Jericho
Canaan
Dead Sea

Taurus mountains
Hurran
Carchemish
Aleppo
Alalakh
Ugarit
Ebla
Qatna
Mediterranean Sea
Byblos
Hazor
Jericho
Dead Sea
Sinai Desert

River Euphrates
Mari
River Tigris
AKKAD
Eshunna
Babylon
Kish
Isin
SUMER

ELAM
Zagros mountains
Persian Gulf

Mountains
Fertile Crescent
Sargon's empire
Hammurabi's empire

Canaan

The area known as Canaan stretched from the borders of the Sinai Desert north into what is now southern Syria. By the Early Bronze Age (c.3000-2000BC), it was divided into independent city states, each with massive fortifications, palaces and temples. In the farmland around the cities, animals were raised and barley, wheat, grapes, olives and vegetables were grown. The northern cities on the east-west trade route were among the largest. One of the most impressive was Ebla, which is reconstructed here.

The upper city contained the palace and government buildings.

The walls were heavily fortified.

Most people lived in the lower city.

The ports of Canaan, such as Byblos, and the north Syrian port of Ugarit, were great trading centres. They exported cedarwood, metals, ivory and textiles (including a rare purple-dyed cloth) throughout the eastern Mediterranean. Egyptian influence was strong, especially in Byblos, but merchants also came from Cyprus, Mesopotamia and Anatolia. In about 2350BC southern Canaan went into decline. Some cities were abandoned, others were destroyed. It is uncertain what caused this as there were no written records, but it may have been due to local political upheavals.

Enamelled pendant from Byblos, showing Egyptian influence

At the beginning of the Middle Bronze Age (c.2000-1500BC), a new period of prosperity began. The Canaanites invented their own form of writing, a simple alphabetic script of 27 picture signs. It was used for short inscriptions only. All dealings between foreigners were conducted in Akkadian, which was written in *cuneiform* (see page 10). The Canaanite city states were well-situated for trade. In the Late Bronze Age (c.1550-1150BC) the Egyptians, Mitannians* and Hittites* fought over them and divided them between themselves.

Canaanite religion

The Canaanites had many gods and goddesses, who they worshipped in temples and in 'high places' – hill-top enclosures containing large upright stone structures.

Baal was god of rain, storms, fertility and war. His cult† animal was a bull.

The Amorites

One group of nomadic Semites, the Amorites, threatened both Mesopotamia and Canaan in about 2000BC. They conquered Sumer, Akkad and Assyria and set up dynasties in the city states of Canaan. These dynasties fought each other for supremacy, but were soon overshadowed by the rise of the Assyrians (see pages 74-75).

In 1792BC a young man called Hammurabi† inherited the throne of Babylon, a small Amorite kingdom in central Mesopotamia. The kingdom had been founded about a hundred years earlier, but Hammurabi extended its frontiers to include all of Sumer and Akkad. He also defeated the Gutians and took over territory from the Elamites and the Assyrians. Hammurabi was a clever administrator and diplomat, and was concerned with law, order and the welfare of his people.

Hammurabi established a unified system of laws and penalties within his expanding kingdom. This stone *stela*† records his code of laws.

Hammurabi's empire slowly declined after his death and in about 1595BC the ruler of Babylon was overthrown by Hittites who plundered the city. This left the way open for new rulers – the Kassites*.

Key dates

c.3000-2000BC Independent city states flourish in Sumer, Akkad and Canaan.

c.2371-2316BC Reign of Sargon of Akkad

c.2300BC Southern Canaan is in decline.

c.2291-2255BC Reign of Naram-Sin of Akkad

c.2230BC Akkad collapses after invasions by Gutians.

c.2000BC Increasing numbers of Amorites move into Canaan and Mesopotamia.

c.2000-1550BC New period of prosperity in Canaan

c.1894BC Amorites establish a dynasty in the city of Babylon.

c.1792-1750BC Reign of Hammurabi of Babylon

c.1595BC Hittites plunder Babylon and depose the ruler.

c.1550-1150BC Canaanite city states are divided between Egyptians, Mitannians and Hittites.

The Middle Kingdom (c.2040-1640BC)

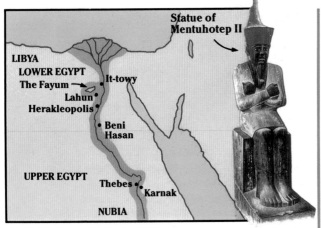

LIBYA
LOWER EGYPT
The Fayum
Lahun
Herakleopolis
It-towy
Beni Hasan
UPPER EGYPT
Thebes
Karnak
NUBIA

Statue of Mentuhotep II

In about 2040BC, the ruler of Thebes, Mentuhotep II†, defeated the Herakleopolitan king (see page 13) and reunited Egypt under Dynasty XI. This began the period known as the Middle Kingdom. Mentuhotep drove invaders from the Delta and crushed all opposition to his rule, appointing loyal Thebans to key posts in the government. From his capital at Thebes, he resumed foreign trading contacts and embarked on an energetic programme to restore Egyptian prosperity.

The soldiers' tomb

Archaeologists have excavated a tomb next to Mentuhotep's funeral monument (see page 17), which contains the bodies of about 60 soldiers, many of whom were archers. No-one knows why they were buried near a place normally reserved for the royal family. Their bodies had many wounds, so they may have been the Thebans who died in the battle that brought Mentuhotep to power.

Tomb models

In the First Intermediate Period it had become the custom to put wooden models in graves, showing scenes from everyday life, such as making bread and beer. Meket-re†, Mentuhotep III's chancellor, had a huge model collection in his tomb. It included models of a house and garden, and several boats.

Tomb models showing men catching fish

Noblemen's barges

Dynasty XII

A rebellion during the reign of Mentuhotep IV led to the emergence of a new dynasty in about 1991BC. The new king, who had been an important official in Dynasty XI, called himself Amenemhat I†, meaning 'Amun is foremost'. Amun* became the patron god of the royal family and grew in importance. A festival was introduced in his honour, called the Feast of the Valley.

During the Feast of the Valley, Amun's statue was taken in its sacred boat from the temple at Karnak across the Nile to the necropolis† on the West Bank.

Amenemhat's dynasty became one of the most successful to rule Egypt, presiding over a period of power, wealth and artistic achievement. However Amenemhat was conscious of the weakness of his claim to the throne and of the need to secure the succession. In the twentieth year of his reign, he had his son Senusret I crowned as a co-king. Amenemhat was murdered ten years later, but Senusret succeeded in holding on to power.

Very few Middle Kingdom buildings have survived. This chapel built by Senusret I was later dismantled but has been reconstructed by archaeologists.

Throughout Dynasty XII Egypt's frontiers were secure. Libyans who had settled in the rich farmland of the Western Delta during the First Intermediate Period were driven out. The Libyans were one of the most important of the 'Nine Bows', Egypt's traditional enemies. On the eastern frontier, a string of great forts was built. The garrisons there kept a check on the bedouin†, although they allowed them in temporarily to trade and pasture their flocks in the Delta. The Egyptians occupied Nubia (see page 28) and fortresses were built to guard the new frontier there.

A Libyan soldier

*For more about Amun and other Egyptian gods and goddesses, see pages 20-21.

A new capital

In order to keep better control of the 'Two Lands', Amenemhat moved the capital north to It-towy, near the Fayum (a huge dip in the desert to the west of the Nile Valley). The Fayum had once contained a vast lake that was filled from the Nile, but silt had built up round the entrance, forming a fertile tongue of land.

Senusret II began to reclaim more land by reducing the amount of water flowing into the lake. New land became available for farming and many building projects were undertaken. A royal palace was built at Kahun, as well as a town for the priests and officials who looked after Senusret's pyramid at nearby Lahun.

Art and culture

Egyptian art and culture flourished under Dynasty XII. In particular many fine statues were produced.

◀ Most earlier Egyptian scupltures were idealized portraits, like this one of a noblewoman called Sennui.

Some Middle Kingdom artists produced more individual portraits, like this face of Senusret III. ▼

From Dynasty XII, some statues were cube-shaped and showed the person squatting. ▲

The cult of Osiris

The cult of Osiris, ruler of the dead, grew in popularity during the Middle Kingdom. Evidence of this is shown by inscriptions and objects found in tombs. In earlier times Egyptians had expected the king to look after their interests after death. But in the chaos of the First Intermediate Period (see page 13), many people lost their faith in kings and turned instead to Osiris. He promised a happy life after death as a reward for a good and virtuous life on earth.

The nomarchs

At the beginning of the Middle Kingdom, the provincial governors, or *nomarchs*, still played a part in local government, ruling from their palaces in the provincial capitals. However, under Senusret III† a reorganization of government took place and the role of the *nomarchs* declined. The Vizier, the king's chief minister, was given control of the government departments and Egypt was divided into three administrative areas, each called a *waret*.

The paintings in the tombs of the *nomarchs* provide a detailed picture of the daily life of the period. This painting, of men and baboons picking figs, is from Beni Hasan.

Dynasties XIII and XIV

When the direct male line died out, a princess called Sobek-neferu† became the last 'king' of Dynasty XII. The whole system of centralized government based on a king and a strong succession broke down. The kings of Dynasty XIII were often unrelated to one another and ruled for very short periods. For the next hundred years real power was in the hands of important families of officials. Government became less and less efficient. Eventually some princes from the Western Delta broke away and formed Dynasty XIV, ruling at the same time as Dynasty XIII.

The forts were no longer properly maintained and the Egyptians lost control of Nubia. People from the Middle East who had settled in Egypt began to take over towns in the Eastern Delta. In 1674BC, the Delta was overrun by a group known as Hyksos†, who later became the rulers of Dynasties XV and XVI. This marked the beginning of a period of decline, known as the Second Intermediate Period (see page 45).

The king began wearing a blue crown called the *khepresh*.

Key dates

c.2040BC Mentuhotep II reunites Egypt under Dynasty XI. The Middle Kingdom begins.

c.1991-1783BC Dynasty XII

c.1783-1640BC Dynasty XIII

c.1674BC The Eastern Delta is overrun with people from the Middle East.

c.1640-1552BC The Second Intermediate Period

Nubia

Nubia was the land that lay immediately south of Egypt. It was hotter and less fertile than Egypt, but there was enough vegetation in the Nile Valley and at oases to support herds of cattle. These played an important part in the Nubian way of life.

The earliest cultures of Egypt and Nubia were very similar, but from about 3300BC Egypt began developing much more quickly. From Dynasty I, Egyptian kings sent expeditions to Nubia in search of valuable raw materials, such as gold, copper, cattle, slaves and semi-precious stones. Beyond Nubia they found exotic animals, such as giraffes and monkeys, and such rare items as ivory, incense, panther skins, ostrich eggs and plumes, and ebony (a hard black wood).

This painting shows Nubians offering gifts.

Nubia during the Old Kingdom

The aim of Egyptian foreign policy was to keep the country's frontiers secure and to protect trading interests. In Dynasty IV, King Sneferu† launched a devastating attack on Nubia. Egyptian records claim that 70,000 prisoners were taken. Excavations confirm that there was a sharp drop in Nubia's population and wealth.

The Egyptians built a heavily fortified town at Buhen as a base from which to trade with Nubia and the African interior. At first trade was under the direct control of the king, but later some of his powers were delegated to *nomarchs* (see page 13). The *nomarch* of Aswan was given the title 'Keeper of the Gate of the South'.

The Nubian recovery

By the time of Egyptian Dynasty VI, the Nubians were showing signs of recovery. They became involved in clashes with desert nomads†, making trade routes dangerous for the Egyptians. During the First Intermediate Period the Egyptians lost their position of power and Nubia came under the control of native Nubian princes. Archaeologists describe the Nubians of this time as 'C-group'.

Nubia during the Middle Kingdom

Trading contacts between Egypt and Nubia were resumed during the Middle Kingdom. The Egyptians soon felt threatened by the presence of prosperous, independent Nubians in the Nile Valley and so they invaded Nubia again. By the end of the reign of Senusret I, Nubia had been conquered up to the Second Cataract†.

Also seen as a threat was the Kingdom of Kush, situated in the area around the Third Cataract. In order to protect their new frontier, the Egyptians built a string of nine fortresses around the Second Cataract. These fortresses were masterpieces of military engineering and design, as well as centres of trade and government. The reconstruction shown here is based on ruins at Buhen.

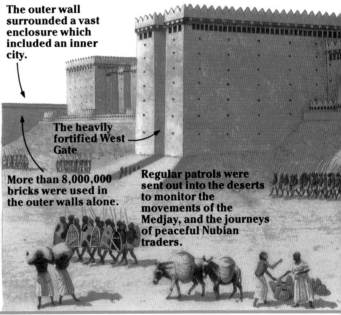

The outer wall surrounded a vast enclosure which included an inner city.

The heavily fortified West Gate

More than 8,000,000 bricks were used in the outer walls alone.

Regular patrols were sent out into the deserts to monitor the movements of the Medjay, and the journeys of peaceful Nubian traders.

The Second Intermediate Period in Nubia

After Dynasty XIII, the Egyptians lost control of Nubia. Traces of a terrible fire at Buhen and evidence of Kushite pottery there suggest that the Kushites took over. Egyptian sources describe independent kings in Nubia who formed alliances with the Hyksos†. Some of the Medjay† were hostile to the Kushites and joined the armies of the Egyptian kings who ruled from Thebes (see page 45).

Kushite pottery

The Buhen horse

The first known example of a horse in Egypt was found in an excavation of a Middle Kingdom site at Buhen. Horses had only just been introduced in the Middle East at this time, and did not become common in Egypt until much later. An official might have brought it back from the East and taken it with him to Nubia.

There was a secret tunnel to the Nile, so water and supplies could be brought in during a siege. Stone quays on the river enabled ships to dock.

The upper walls were 11m (36ft) high and 4.5m (14ft) thick. Objects could be dropped on the heads of attackers from an overhang at the top.

Carefully positioned arrow slits enabled defending archers to cover the walls with their cross fire.

The fortress had an outer and an inner ring of fortifications. The inner wall (shown here) protected the city. This contained the governor's palace, houses for army officers and officials, storehouses, a shrine and a parade ground.

Battlements protected people from enemy fire.

There were round towers on the lower walls and square towers on the upper ones.

The enclosure contained barracks where the soldiers lived, houses for their families and stables for donkeys. Some caravans† may have had as many as 1000 donkeys.

Large numbers of soldiers were needed to guard the fort. At first they returned home after a spell of duty. Later some settled in Nubia and were joined by local troops.

Nubia in the New Kingdom

The temple of Abu Simbel was one of seven temples built in Nubia by Ramesses II.

The Egyptians invaded Nubia again during the New Kingdom and extended their frontier to the Fourth Cataract. A viceroy† known as the 'King's Son of Kush' was appointed to rule Nubia. Nubians adopted Egyptian culture and religion and became loyal subjects.

Nubia

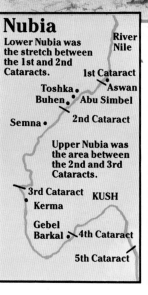

Lower Nubia was the stretch between the 1st and 2nd Cataracts.

River Nile

1st Cataract
Aswan
Toshka
Buhen
Abu Simbel
Semna
2nd Cataract

Upper Nubia was the area between the 2nd and 3rd Cataracts.

3rd Cataract
Kerma
KUSH
Gebel Barkal
4th Cataract
5th Cataract

Key dates

c.2900BC Nubians of this period are known as 'A-group'. Egyptian kings begin campaigning in Nubia.

c.2570BC King Sneferu of Egypt attacks Nubia.

c.2300BC Nubians recovery; Nubians at this time are known as 'C-group'.

c.2200BC Egypt loses control of Nubia.

By 1926BC Egypt reconquers Nubia up to the 2nd Cataract and builds fortresses.

c.1600BC Egypt loses control of Nubia again and Kushites take over.

c.1550-1300BC Egypt reconquers Nubia up to the 4th Cataract.

Travel and transport

Most people in Ancient Egypt lived close to the River Nile, so boats provided the quickest and most efficient means of transport.

The Nile flows from south to north, but the wind usually blows from the north. This means that boats can drift down the river with the current, and if they raise their sails the wind will carry them back upstream.

The *hieroglyph†* for 'going upstream' and 'south' showed a ship in sail.

▲ The *hieroglyph* for 'going downstream' and 'north' showed the sail rolled down.

The Nile and the gods

The Nile played such an important part in the lives of the Egyptians that it affected their way of looking at things. For example, they believed that the sun god Re (shown here) travelled by boat across the sky each day. At night he sailed through the Underworld†.

Reed boats

The earliest Egyptian boats were made of reeds bound together. People continued to build this type of boat throughout ancient times, but it was used for short trips only, such as going fishing.

Early reed boat

Wooden boats

By the Old Kingdom, wood (both local and imported) was used for larger boats and for sea-going vessels. Experts have been able to reconstruct a variety of different types from paintings, reliefs† and models left in tombs, and from a few boats that have actually survived. There were different boats for fishing, trading and carrying cargo, as well as barques for funerals and pleasure boats for the rich.

Old Kingdom ▲ fishing boat

Old Kingdom Nile ▲ cargo boat

Old Kingdom sea-going ship

Egyptian ships were constructed so that they could be dismantled easily. This meant they could be carried around the Nile cataracts†, and then reassembled afterwards.

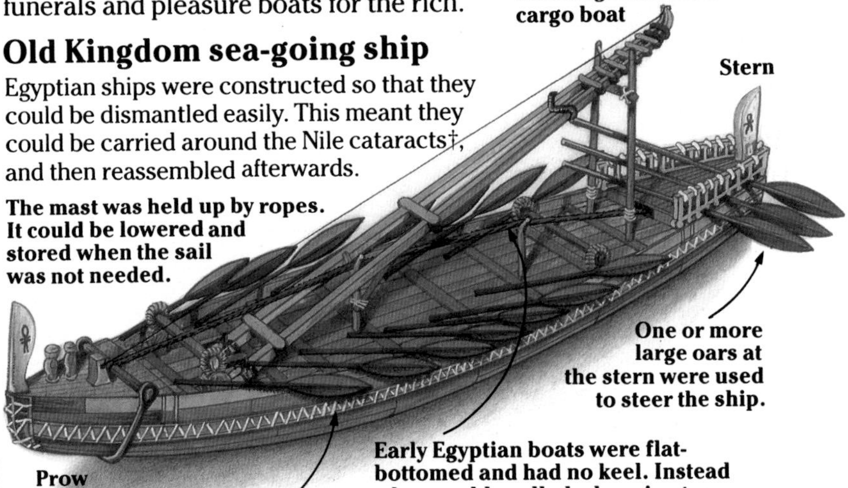

The mast was held up by ropes. It could be lowered and stored when the sail was not needed.

Stern

One or more large oars at the stern were used to steer the ship.

Prow

Many ships had oars as well as sails. This enabled them to travel against the wind if necessary.

Early Egyptian boats were flat-bottomed and had no keel. Instead a huge cable called a hogging truss ran from the prow to the stern. This held the ends up and kept the ship firm.

New Kingdom trading ship

This kind of ship was built in the New Kingdom for trade in the eastern Mediterranean. Most of the space was used for cargo. ▼

Hogging trusses were no longer necessary, as keels began to be used.

The expedition to Punt

This reconstruction is based on a relief of one of the ships that sailed in Queen Hatshepsut's expedition to Punt (see page 47). Punt was a land accessible from the Red Sea, probably in East Africa. The ships were built for speed, as they had to sail quickly past long stretches of desert.

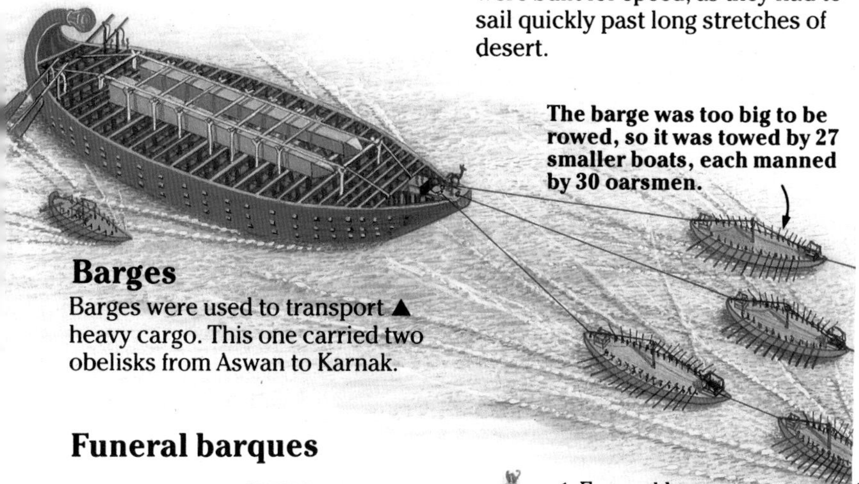

The barge was too big to be rowed, so it was towed by 27 smaller boats, each manned by 30 oarsmen.

Barges

Barges were used to transport ▲ heavy cargo. This one carried two obelisks from Aswan to Karnak.

Funeral barques

◀ Funeral barques were used to transport the bodies of the royal family or wealthy people to their tombs.

New Kingdom travelling boat

Nobles often had their own private boats for travelling around. The one shown here is based on a model from the tomb of King Tutankhamun†. Many of the basic features have changed since the Old Kingdom (see page opposite).

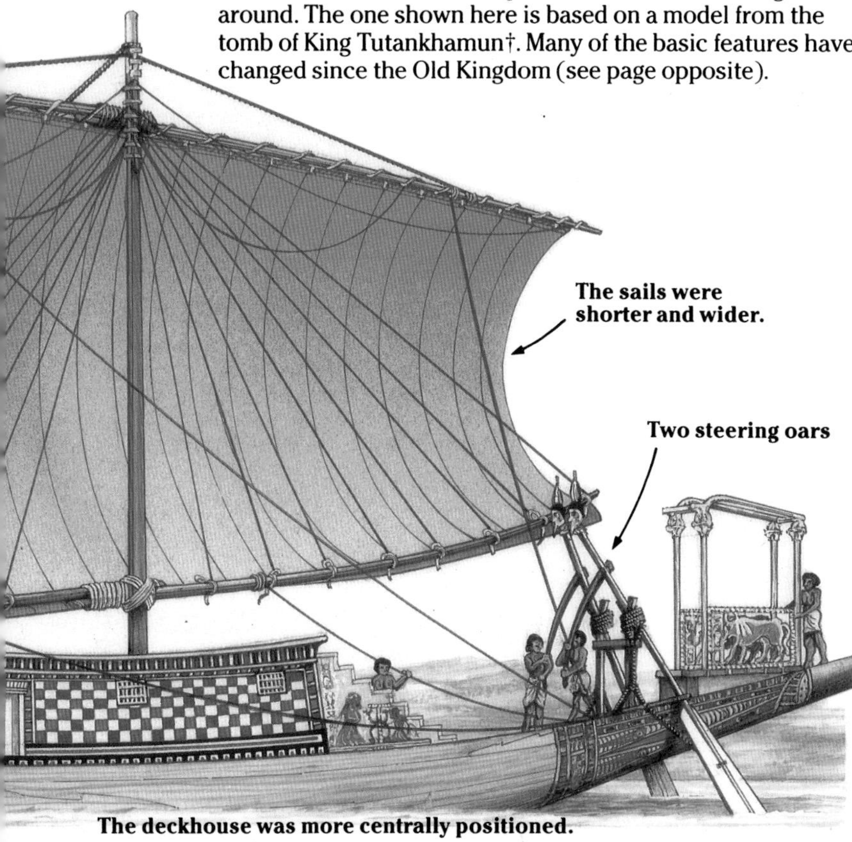

The sails were shorter and wider.

Two steering oars

The deckhouse was more centrally positioned.

The royal ship of Cheops

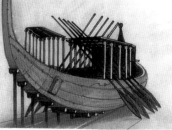

This ship was reconstructed from fragments found buried next to the pyramid of Cheops†, the Great Pyramid of Gizah.

Mesopotamian boats

In Mesopotamia boats were also the most important form of transport. The earliest were rafts, reed boats (like the Egyptian one opposite) or coracles (small round rowing boats). ▶

The frame of a coracle was made from reeds and animal hides.

The outside was coated with tar to make it watertight.

Travel on land

Although the Egyptians used the Nile whenever possible, it was sometimes necessary to travel overland. There were no roads as farming land was too precious to waste, and roads would have been washed away annually by the Nile floods (see page 14).

On long desert journeys small loads were carried by donkeys.

Nobles travelled in carrying chairs slung between donkeys, or carried by slaves.

New Kingdom nobles sometimes drove in horse-drawn chariots.

Mining and trade

The Ancient Egyptians were well supplied with a variety of stones and minerals. There were quarries in the deserts within reach of the Nile, and others in Nubia and Sinai. Mining and quarrying expeditions were authorized by the king and financed from taxes. The workforce included expert stonemasons, miners and engineers, but the majority was made up of unskilled men who worked as part of the labour tax which everyone paid to the king. On larger projects criminals and prisoners of war were sometimes used as well. In Sinai local men were often hired.

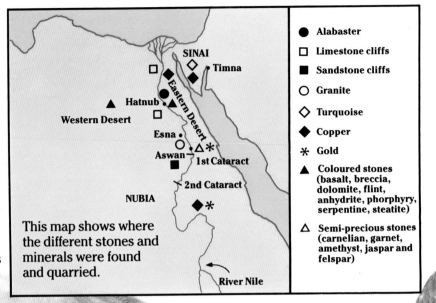

This map shows where the different stones and minerals were found and quarried.

- ● Alabaster
- □ Limestone cliffs
- ■ Sandstone cliffs
- ○ Granite
- ◇ Turquoise
- ◆ Copper
- ✳ Gold
- ▲ Coloured stones (basalt, breccia, dolomite, flint, anhydrite, phorphyry, serpentine, steatite)
- △ Semi-precious stones (carnelian, garnet, amethyst, jaspar and felspar)

A mining camp

There is evidence of Egyptian gold mines in the Eastern Desert and of copper and turquoise mines in Sinai dating back to the Old Kingdom. This reconstruction shows a copper mining camp at Timna in Sinai. Egyptian mining engineers appear to have been highly skilled. Vertical shafts up to 70m (230ft) deep led into long tunnels cut deep into the cliffs. The shafts acted as air vents and connected the tunnels to each other.

Stone barracks for the men

Storehouses

The miners dug the copper ore from the cliff sides.

Cattle stores

The copper was beaten into pieces shaped like oxhides.

The copper ore was carried away in panniers on donkeys.

Soldiers were usually sent to the camps to protect the workmen and the metal from bandits and hostile bedouin†.

Egyptian maps described the route an expedition should follow, and included details such as distances, the positions of wells, and areas frequented by nomads†. This is a New Kingdom map of gold mines at Wadi Hammamat.

The ore was crushed and then smelted (heated in a fire to extract the copper). To raise the temperature of the fire, blowpipes were used to blow air into it.

Egyptian trade

Egypt was well-placed for trade with both Africa and Asia. Crossing frontiers in search of metals and other goods often involved the Egyptians in clashes with the local inhabitants, so trade became linked with foreign policy. One of the main aims of Egyptian policy was to protect trade routes and supplies, and this led to the conquest and occupation of places such as Nubia and Sinai, especially in the New Kingdom. Foreign trade was normally under the control of the king, although temples and merchants were sometimes allowed to trade abroad too.

Syrian trading ship being unloaded

Important officials were put in charge of despatching and receiving trading missions.

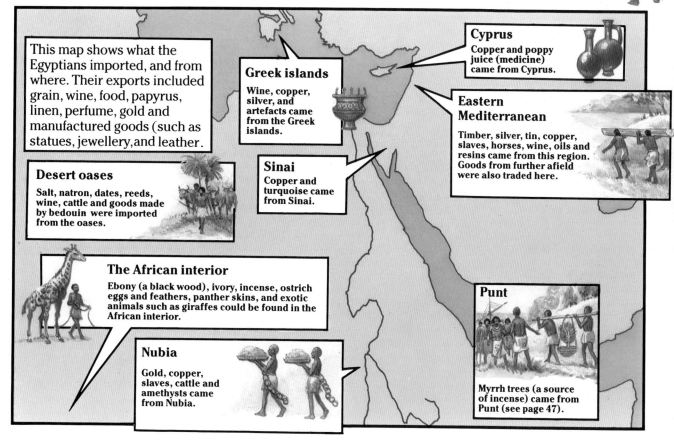

This map shows what the Egyptians imported, and from where. Their exports included grain, wine, food, papyrus, linen, perfume, gold and manufactured goods (such as statues, jewellery, and leather.

Greek islands

Wine, copper, silver, and artefacts came from the Greek islands.

Cyprus

Copper and poppy juice (medicine) came from Cyprus.

Eastern Mediterranean

Timber, silver, tin, copper, slaves, horses, wine, oils and resins came from this region. Goods from further afield were also traded here.

Sinai

Copper and turquoise came from Sinai.

Desert oases

Salt, natron, dates, reeds, wine, cattle and goods made by bedouin were imported from the oases.

The African interior

Ebony (a black wood), ivory, incense, ostrich eggs and feathers, panther skins, and exotic animals such as giraffes could be found in the African interior.

Nubia

Gold, copper, slaves, cattle and amethysts came from Nubia.

Punt

Myrrh trees (a source of incense) came from Punt (see page 47).

Buying and selling

Although a few surviving tomb scenes show small market stalls, little is known about shopping in Egypt. Craftsmen probably sold their goods from the front rooms of their houses or at royal or temple workshops. The Egyptians did not use money. They exchanged goods which were agreed to be of approximately equal value. For example, two copper vases might be considered to be worth five linen tunics. A system was later developed by which the value was assessed in copper weights called *deben*. Goods of an equal value were exchanged. Sometimes, people actually gave the *deben* instead. However a proper coinage system was not developed until the 7th century BC in Lydia (Asia Minor).

The Egyptians used scales and standard weights. This painting shows gold rings being weighed with a weight shaped like a bull's head.

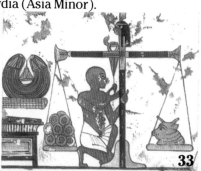

The government of Egypt

The Egyptians believed that the position of king of Egypt had been introduced by the gods at the time of the creation of the world. The kings were thought to be descended from the sun god Re*, who had been the first king of Egypt. Ordinary people believed they could communicate with the gods through the king. The king was thought to be so holy that it was considered impolite to refer to him directly. People therefore referred to him indirectly as 'Great House' (or palace). The Egyptian words were *per-o*, from which we get the word 'pharaoh'. The king had five official titles, the first and oldest of which was 'The Horus'*.

The Egyptians believed that when the king was on his throne, wearing his royal regalia, the spirit of Horus entered him. During Dynasty XVIII, the queen became closely associated with Horus's wife, the goddess Hathor.

The king's crowns

The king's crown, the Double Crown, combined the White Crown of Upper Egypt and the Red Crown of Lower Egypt. The king was often described as 'The Lord of the Two Lands'.

Double Crown

Red Crown **White Crown**

This jewelled headband, known as the royal diadem, shows the vulture and cobra goddesses (see page 9) who were thought to protect the king. The goddesses are referred to in another of the king's titles 'He of the Two Ladies'. ▶

The king's role

The king had absolute power. He also had a number of duties. It was his responsibility to rule justly and to maintain *ma'at* (the order, harmony and balance of the Universe). The king played a part in every aspect of life.

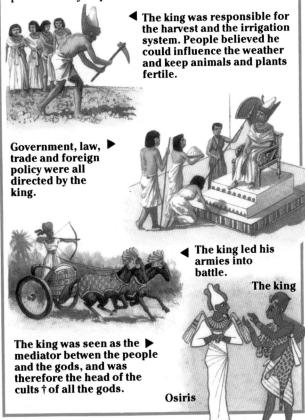

◀ The king was responsible for the harvest and the irrigation system. People believed he could influence the weather and keep animals and plants fertile.

Government, law, ▶ trade and foreign policy were all directed by the king.

◀ The king led his armies into battle.

The king

The king was seen as the ▶ mediator betwen the people and the gods, and was therefore the head of the cults † of all the gods.

Osiris

The royal succession

Marriage between close relatives, including brother and sister, was usual within the Egyptian royal family (although not for ordinary people). It was seen as a way of maintaining the purity of royal blood. The king had many wives, but usually only one queen. She was the eldest daughter of the former king and queen, and was known as the Royal Heiress. The king could nominate any of his sons as his successor (although the queen's sons were the most eligible). However in order to confirm his claim the boy would marry the next Royal Heiress (the queen's eldest daughter), who would be his sister or half-sister.

Ceremonies

There were a number of ceremonies which were designed to keep the king in power and protect him from enemies. One important one was *Heb Sed*, which was supposed to renew the king's strength and powers. It was often held after he had reigned for 30 years, although the king could choose to hold it at any time to indicate that he was making a new start to his rule.

This relief† shows the king running. This was one of the rituals of the *Heb Sed* festival.

For more about Re, Horus and other Egyptian gods and goddesses, see pages 20-21.

The organization of the government

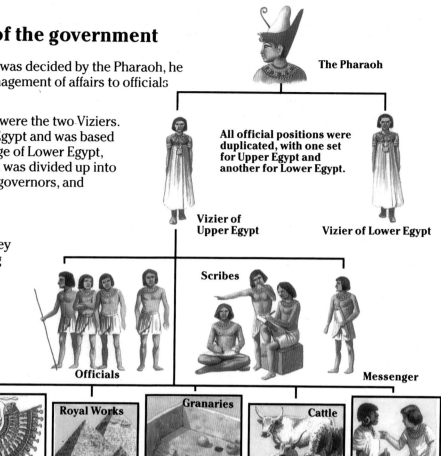

Although government policy was decided by the Pharaoh, he delegated the day to day management of affairs to officials and departments of state.

The most important officials were the two Viziers. One was in charge of Upper Egypt and was based in Thebes. The other, in charge of Lower Egypt, was based in Memphis. Egypt was divided up into rural districts, controlled by governors, and towns, controlled by mayors.

Each Vizier, governor and mayor had a staff of officials, messengers and scribes†. They were responsible for carrying out the orders of central government and collecting taxes. The scribes kept the records, which helped the system run efficiently.

There was an official in charge of each state department – the Treasury, the Granaries, Royal Works, Cattle and Foreign Affairs.

The Pharaoh

All official positions were duplicated, with one set for Upper Egypt and another for Lower Egypt.

Vizier of Upper Egypt

Vizier of Lower Egypt

Scribes

Officials

Messenger

Treasury

Royal Works

Granaries

Cattle

Foreign Affairs

Taxation

The Egyptian government imposed a number of different taxes on its people. As there was no money, taxes were paid 'in kind' (with produce or work). The Vizier controlled the taxation system through the departments of state. The departments had to report daily on the amount of stock available, and how much was expected in the future.

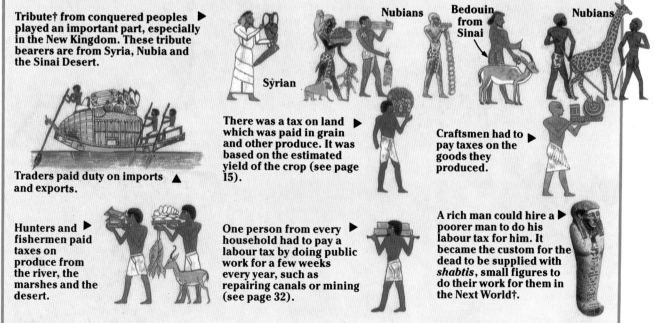

Tribute† from conquered peoples ▶ played an important part, especially in the New Kingdom. These tribute bearers are from Syria, Nubia and the Sinai Desert.

Syrian

Nubians

Bedouin from Sinai

Nubians

Traders paid duty on imports ▲ and exports.

There was a tax on land ▶ which was paid in grain and other produce. It was based on the estimated yield of the crop (see page 15).

Craftsmen had to ▶ pay taxes on the goods they produced.

Hunters and ▶ fishermen paid taxes on produce from the river, the marshes and the desert.

One person from every ▶ household had to pay a labour tax by doing public work for a few weeks every year, such as repairing canals or mining (see page 32).

A rich man could hire a ▶ poorer man to do his labour tax for him. It became the custom for the dead to be supplied with shabtis, small figures to do their work for them in the Next World†.

Costume, jewellery and cosmetics

Egyptian fashions changed very little throughout ancient times. Most clothes were made of linen, which varied from a coarse weave to a fine semi-transparent material. In winter, the Egyptians may have worn wool too, but it was regarded as impure and so has not been mentioned in texts or found in tombs. The clothes shown in tomb paintings were usually white, but this may have been simply because white was considered to be pure or because it was used for special occasions. There is evidence that the Egyptians wore coloured fabrics too.

Many people kept their hair short, because of the climate. Nobles tended to have longer hair or wear wigs (straight, plaited or curled). There were a variety of preparations for the hair – henna (a vegetable dye) to colour it, and mixtures to prevent baldness, dandruff and grey hair.

The Old and Middle Kingdoms

The basic costume for a ▶ man was a kilt, made from a piece of linen wrapped around the body and tied at the waist.

Noblemen wore pleated kilts in a variety of styles. Older men, particularly important officials, sometimes wore longer kilts. ▼

Wraps and cloaks were worn in winter. These are very rarely shown in tomb paintings, presumably because good weather was expected in the Next World†. ▲

For a woman the basic costume was a straight dress held up by two straps. ▲

When doing heavy, hot, dirty jobs, men wore a kilt or a loincloth and women a short skirt.

◀ Children usually ran around naked during the summer. They sometimes had their heads shaved, except for a long plait, called the 'lock of youth'.

Padded hairstyle

Noblewomen also wore beaded dresses. The beads may have been sewn on, or strung together and worn over the dress. In the Middle Kingdom it was fashionable to pad out the hair or decorate it with ornaments.

Some clothes were decorated with stripes, squares or diamond shapes, or made up of overlapping pieces of material. This servant girl is wearing a patterned dress. ◀

The New Kingdom

By the time of the New Kingdom, styles became much more elaborate, particularly for special occasions. Clothes were looser and more flowing and arranged with numbers of pleats.

New Kingdom hairstyles were often long, with lots of plaits and curls. ▼

Some queens are ▶ shown wearing a ceremonial costume apparently decorated with feathers, like the garment on this bronze statue of Queen Karomama. Kings also appear to have worn feathered cloaks.

A nobleman ▶ sometimes wore a long robe over his kilt. Loose, thin cloaks were also fashionable.

Belt

◀ Noblewomen wore flowing pleated dresses and shawls. The shawl was made from a single piece of cloth folded round the body and knotted under the breasts.

Masses of small sequins were found in the tomb of ▶ Tutankhamun†. Each one was pierced with two holes, which suggests that they may have been sewn on to clothes as decoration.

Shoes and gloves

People often went barefoot, although they had sandals made of reeds or leather for formal occasions. Nobles had highly decorated sandals, like the ones on the right which belonged to Tutankhamun. The gloves shown here were also found in his tomb, although gloves were never shown in paintings.

Wigs

Wigs were worn by both sexes at parties and official functions. Special boxes with a stand inside were used to store the wigs while they were not in use.

Wig with hair ornaments ▲

Toiletries and cosmetics

Cleanliness was important to the Egyptians. Most people washed themselves in the river or with a jug and basin at home. Rich people had rooms where they took showers by getting a servant to pour water over them. The water drained away through a pipe into the garden. A cleansing cream made from oil, lime and perfume was used instead of soap. People rubbed themselves daily with oil, to prevent the hot sun from drying and cracking their skin. Razors and tweezers were used to remove body hair and there were preparations to cure spots and eliminate body odours. Both sexes wore perfume and eye make-up.

Cosmetic chest

Malachite (copper ore) or galena (lead ore) was ground in a palette and mixed with oil to make eyepaint called kohl. This was kept in jars and put on with a small stick.

Make-up box →

Henna was used to paint the nails, and possibly the palms of the hands and the soles of the feet too.

Perfume jar →

Cosmetic jars →

Sticks

Mirrors were made of highly polished copper or silver, not glass.

Red ochre (a type of clay) was ground and mixed with water, and applied to the cheeks and the lips.

Jewellery

It appears that everyone in Egypt wore jewellery. For the rich there were beautiful pieces made of gold, silver or electrum (gold mixed with silver), inlaid with semi-precious stones and coloured glass. Poorer people wore copper or faience (made by heating powdered quartz).

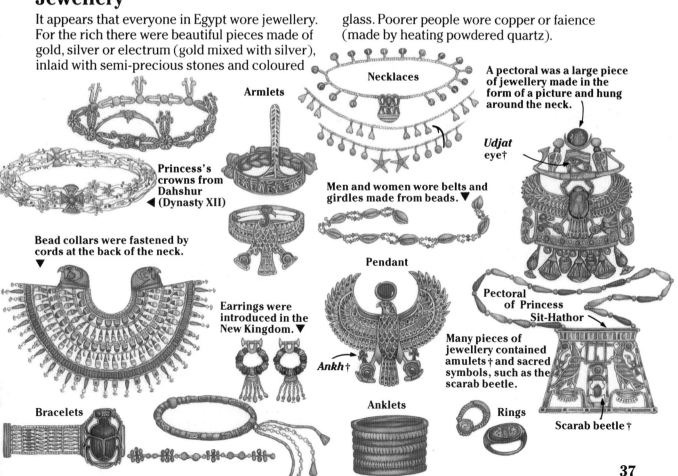

Armlets

Necklaces

A pectoral was a large piece of jewellery made in the form of a picture and hung around the neck.

Princess's crowns from Dahshur ◀ (Dynasty XII)

Men and women wore belts and girdles made from beads. ▼

Udjat eye†

Bead collars were fastened by cords at the back of the neck. ▼

Pendant

Earrings were introduced in the New Kingdom. ▼

Ankh †

Pectoral of Princess Sit-Hathor

Many pieces of jewellery contained amulets† and sacred symbols, such as the scarab beetle.

Bracelets

Anklets

Rings

Scarab beetle †

37

Entertainment

Evidence of how the Egyptians spent their spare time comes from paintings and objects left in tombs. There were no theatres, but dramatized performances held at temples told tales of the lives of the gods. Religious festivals and royal processions also provided colourful spectacles. However, one of the most important sources of sport and relaxation was the river.

The river

Many tomb paintings show noblemen catching fish, waterfowl and river animals in the marshes. They used harpoons to catch the fish, whereas peasants who fished for a living used large nets.

Wealthy families often went on outings on the river in small papyrus† boats.

A favourite game among peasant boatmen seems to have been a contest between two teams armed with long poles. Each team tried to knock the other into the river.

Swimming in the Nile was the natural way to cool off in the heat, although people had to choose their bathing places very carefully to avoid crocodiles.

Cats were sometimes taken on hunting expeditions. They may have been used to flush out the birds.

Hunting crocodiles and hippopotamuses was a very dangerous pastime. A team of hunters and boatmen was needed to harpoon the animals and bring them ashore with ropes and nets.

Hunting in the desert

Hunting desert animals was a favourite pastime for noblemen. At first they hunted on foot, but from the New Kingdom onwards they also used horses and chariots. The Egyptians usually hunted antelope, hare, fox and hyena, although paintings and reliefs show kings tackling bulls and lions too. By Dynasty XVIII, the empire had expanded and new animals, such as rhinoceros and elephant, became available. This golden fan shows Tutankhamun† hunting ostriches.

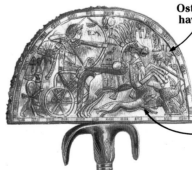

Ostrich feathers would have been used for the plumes of the fan.

The Egyptians had hounds that were specially bred for hunting. They had long legs, pointed muzzles and curling tails.

Parties, music and dancing

Wealthy Egyptians often entertained lavishly, giving large parties with plenty of food and drink. Groups of professional singers, musicians, dancers, jugglers and acrobats were hired to entertain the guests. Paintings and reliefs demonstrate many different styles of dance, some of which are shown here.

This painting shows servants offering the guests flowers and cones of perfumed fat to put on their heads. These had a cooling and refreshing effect as the fat melted.

The Egyptians loved music and singing. This wall-painting shows some of the instruments they played, which included lutes, lyres, harps and several types of flute and pipes.

Harp   Lute   Double flute made of two reed stalks   Lyre

Games

Egyptians from all backgrounds appear to have played games with counters on boards, although the rules have not survived. Gaming boards made of ebony, ivory and gold have been found in royal tombs. Most ordinary boards would have been made of mud or local wood.

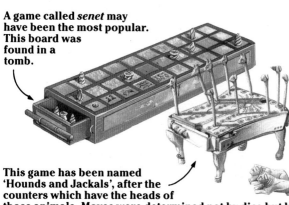

A game called *senet* may have been the most popular. This board was found in a tomb.

This game has been named 'Hounds and Jackals', after the counters which have the heads of those animals. Moves were determined not by dice but by throwing marked sticks.

Pets and zoos

The Egyptians kept a variety of pets, including dogs, cats, monkeys and geese. Small, short-legged breeds of dogs often appear in tomb scenes, and their collars were sometimes buried with their owners. References to pet cats date from the Middle Kingdom. Cats are sometimes shown at parties, sitting beneath their owners' chairs. Some pharaohs of Dynasty XVIII seem to have collected exotic animals and even set up their own private zoos.

Toys

A number of toys, like the ones shown here, have been found in children's graves. Some of them were quite elaborate, with moving parts.

Ivory dog with moving jaws ▼

Painted doll ▶

Wooden ▶ animal

Balls ▶

Dancing figures ▲ made of ivory

Wooden horse on wheels ▶

Some tomb paintings show children playing what look like team games.

Mesopotamian pastimes

Archaeological evidence suggests that Mesopotamian sports and pastimes were similar to those of the Egyptians.

◀ A silver lyre found at Ur

A board game from the royal tombs at Ur (see page 7) ▶

The law

Most of the surviving information about the Egyptian legal system dates from the New Kingdom onwards. Egyptian laws covered every aspect of life. Records were kept of each law that had been passed and any judgements that had been made in previous cases. The Egyptians' system appears to have been highly regarded by their contemporaries in the ancient world. King Darius† of Persia asked for translations of Egyptian laws to be made for him.

◀ Ma'at (shown here) was the goddess of truth and justice. She is sometimes shown in paintings standing behind the king, who was the head of the legal system on Earth. Judges often became her priests.

The Medjay used hunters and dogs to help them track down criminals. Suspects may have been rounded up before a trial and locked in an unused storeroom of a temple. There do not appear to have been any prisons.

The Medjay

The Medjay was originally a Nubian tribe that came to Egypt as mercenary soldiers. It gradually evolved into a peace-keeping force, which was joined by native Egyptians. By the New Kingdom, there were groups of Medjay stationed in all major Egyptian towns. Their job was to keep law and order, catch criminals, and to guard the frontiers and cemeteries. The Medjay had an intimate knowledge of local matters, which helped in dealing with crimes.

The law courts

The day to day running of law and order was under the control of the law courts. Justice was supposed to be available for all, not just the rich, and Egyptians regularly took each other to court. There do not seem to have been any barristers, so people had to speak for themselves. Each town had its own court, called a *kenbet*. The judges,

who were chosen from important local men, also travelled to country areas. Then came the higher courts (called the Court of Listeners), under the supervision of the district governor. Above them were two Great Courts (one each for Upper and Lower Egypt), presided over by the Vizier. This is a reconstruction of a court scene.

Scribes† kept the court records. They also drew up contracts such as wills, marriage settlements and business deals.

The judges

Bribes were forbidden, although one text claims that to win a case you needed 'silver and gold for the scribes of the court, cloth for the attendants'.

All witnesses had to take an oath. Anyone thought to be lying or concealing information was liable to be beaten.

Witnesses were cross-examined and written statements were produced in evidence.

Verdicts and punishments

Consulting the oracle

The accused was considered innocent until proved guilty. If the judges had difficulty in reaching a decision, they sometimes consulted an oracle†. People could appeal against a verdict to a higher court, to the Vizier and, in special cases, to the king himself. Punishments included fines, flogging, hard labour, mutilation, exile or death. There do not appear to have been any prisons.

Medicine

Egyptian doctors were highly regarded throughout the Middle East and some travelled abroad at the request of foreign princes. A New Kingdom tomb painting shows a foreign prince bringing his whole family to Egypt to consult a doctor.

Doctors may have been trained by other doctors in their families, although there were probably medical schools too. There is evidence of at least one school for midwives. Most doctors worked in the community as general practitioners. Others worked in temples, or as army surgeons or specialist consultants. The best doctors were appointed as court physicians.

This Egyptian doctor is treating a Syrian princess.

Egyptian doctors understood quite a lot about how the body worked. They also had some knowledge of the nervous system and the effects of injury on the spine. They knew that an injury to the right side of the head affected the left side of the body, and vice versa. Although they may not have fully understood the circulation system, they knew that the heart pumped blood through the body. They described the pulse as 'speaking the messages of the heart'.

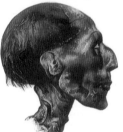

This is the mummified head of Ramesses II†. Modern medical examination of other mummies† has revealed information about ancient diseases.

Diseases and remedies

The Egyptians had specialist medical textbooks on diagnosis, treatment and medicines, as well as specialist books on anatomy, women's diseases, dentistry, surgery and veterinary science. Copies of parts of these books have survived, and Egyptian doctors consulted them when treating diseases and preparing remedies. Experts cannot be sure how effective all Egyptian medicines were, but some of the ingredients that can be identified would certainly have worked.

Egyptian surgical instruments

Papyrus scroll

Egyptian doctors were taught first to observe the symptoms, then to ask questions, inspect, smell, feel and probe. They were instructed to make detailed notes of their observations, treatments and results, for use in future cases. Evidence suggests that doctors were prepared to admit when they did not know, or were not sure, how to cure something. Operations were occasionally performed. Surgeons cleaned their blades in fire before use and kept the patient and the surroundings as clean as possible.

Some patients undergoing surgery were given a pain-killer which may have been opium. It was imported from Cyprus in jugs like these.

The gods of medicine

Religion played a part in the treatment of illness, especially when dealing with psychological problems. Prayers were always said during a treatment, and were probably seen as more important when the illness was very serious. Several Egyptian deities were particularly associated with medicine and healing: Thoth, Sekhmet, Isis and Imhotep*.

This *stela*† was meant to protect against bites and stings.

People often went to the temples of these deities to be cured. Attached to the temples were doctors, who were usually priests too. In some cases the patient was allowed to spend the night in a room near the sanctuary. People believed that the patient might be cured by a miracle†. If not, he or she might have a dream on which the doctor would base the treatment.

*See page 12 for more about Imhotep, and pages 20-21 for more about the other Egyptian gods and goddesses.

Early civilization in China

China is isolated geographically, cut off from the rest of the world by sea, mountains, and the vast freezing plains of the Steppes in central Asia. As far as we know, China had no direct contact with the West before the 2nd century BC. It therefore developed very differently from other ancient cultures. Remains of early people have been found dating back to 30,000BC.

There is evidence of farming communities by the Huang Ho River from about 5000BC. This is known as the Yangshao culture. Farmers grew millet (a kind of cereal), fruit, nuts and vegetables and kept pigs and dogs. Farming also developed along the Yangtze River, where rice was cultivated from about 4000BC. In the Longshan period (c.2500BC), settlements were better organized. Farmers kept chickens, cattle, sheep and goats, and buffalo for ploughing and transport.

Yangshao settlement

The first dynasties

After the farming cultures, China was ruled by a series of dynasties†. The first of these, the Hsia (Xia)* Dynasty, is traditionally said to have begun in about 2205BC, but little evidence of it has been found. In about 1766BC the Shang Dynasty began in what is now Henan province. The Shang eventually controlled land as far south as the Yangtze River. They moved their capital several times, lastly to a place called Anyang.

The Bronze Age in China began with the Shang Dynasty. Elaborate vessels like this were used for religious ceremonies.

Writing

Shang rulers employed men who predicted the future by scorching bones and tortoise shells until they cracked. They then interpreted the 'messages' revealed by the cracks. Oracle bones contain the first known examples of Chinese writing. The script was difficult to learn, as it had several thousand characters, each representing a word. Variants of many of these symbols remain in use in Chinese script today.

Oracle bone

The traditional spelling is shown with the modern spelling in brackets.

China

Area controlled by Shang
Area controlled by Chou (Zhou)
Area controlled by Ch'in

Great Wall of China
Anyang
Loyang
Huang Ho River

Yangshao pottery

The Chou Dynasty

At the end of the 11th century BC the Shang were conquered by a people called the Chou (Zhou)*, who extended the territory further. It was divided into smaller areas, some ruled by the king, others by appointed leaders. During this period there were many wars and political changes.

Chariots were used in battle. These chariot ornaments were found in a grave near Loyang, the Chou capital.

Trade

The Chou period was one of economic growth and increased trade. The Chinese had goods that were unavailable elsewhere, such as silk, which was made from the thread produced by the larvae of certain moths. By the 1st century BC silk was exported as far as the Roman empire. Other Chinese exports included semi-precious stones (especially jade), porcelain and spices.

Silk funeral banner

Life in a Chou city

Excavations at ancient Chinese sites reveal large walled cities with areas set aside for rulers, temples and cemeteries. Additional evidence, such as models placed in graves, tells us what a Chinese city might have looked like.

Ordinary house

Farm
City wall

The rise of the Ch'in Dynasty

During the 8th century BC Chou authority declined. The smaller states fought each other for supremacy and in the 5th century BC seven major kingdoms emerged. For the next 250 years they were constantly at war. (This is known as the Warring States Period.) Finally one kingdom, the Ch'in, dominated the others. The first Ch'in emperor, Shi-huang-ti, succeeded in uniting his territory and improving law and administration. Ch'in is the origin of the word 'China'.

Shi-huang-ti standardized coinage so that everyone used the same money all over the empire. Coins had holes in the middle so that they could be threaded on cords.

Religion and burial

The Chinese had many gods. They also believed very firmly in life after death and in the power of their ancestors. They buried food and personal belongings with the dead, often in magnificent tombs. In the Shang period slaves and animals were killed and placed in royal tombs with their masters. This custom later died out and models of attendants were used instead.

A 2nd century BC prince and his wife were buried in jade suits. Jade was thought to preserve the body.

Shi-huang-ti was buried with thousands of life-size model warriors made of terracotta†.

Philosophers and prophets

The Chinese believed that their rulers were descended from a god called Shang ti, who granted dynasties the right to rule, and could withdraw it at any time. This idea helped them to account for changes of dynasty.

In the 6th century BC other beliefs grew up. The prophet Kong zi (shown here), known in the West as Confucius, lived in a period of warfare. He believed that peace would only be restored if people obeyed a strict code of behaviour. Confucianism later became the basis of Chinese social and political conduct.

The prophet Lao-zi founded Taoism. He taught that if people were in tune with the natural world they would behave correctly.

Warriors and weapons

Many Shang and Chou warriors fought in chariots, but during the Warring States Period there were increasing numbers of footsoldiers, and armies contained up to one million men. Iron working was introduced in the 6th century BC and was used to make tools and armour. After the invention of the crossbow in about 450BC, soldiers were issued with iron armour to protect them.

Under the Chou, many nobles had built walls to defend their territory. In 214BC, Shi-huang-ti had them joined and extended to keep out the hostile Hsung nu tribe (known as Huns). The result was an immense frontier about 3000km (1865 miles) long, known as the Great Wall of China.

The Great Wall is still the largest man-made structure in the world.

Chinese soldiers

Hsung nu

Key dates

Migrations in the Middle East

In about 2000BC, groups of people known by modern scholars as Indo-Europeans drifted into the Middle East. Some settled there; some moved on. They probably came from the great plains that stretch from central Europe eastwards into south Russia. Although their cultures often differed, their languages were all related, having apparently evolved from a single common tongue. Most modern European languages are descended from that original Indo-European language, as are Iranian, Armenian and Sanskrit (the ancient literary language of India).

The Hittites

The Hittites were Indo-Europeans who settled in Anatolia (part of modern Turkey) in about 2000BC and were probably united under one kingdom in about 1740BC. The Hittites expanded into north Syria and conquered Babylon (see page 76) in about 1595BC. During the Hittite New Kingdom (c.1450-1200BC), they were one of Egypt's most dangerous enemies. They built up a huge empire, but it collapsed with the coming of the Sea Peoples (see page 71).

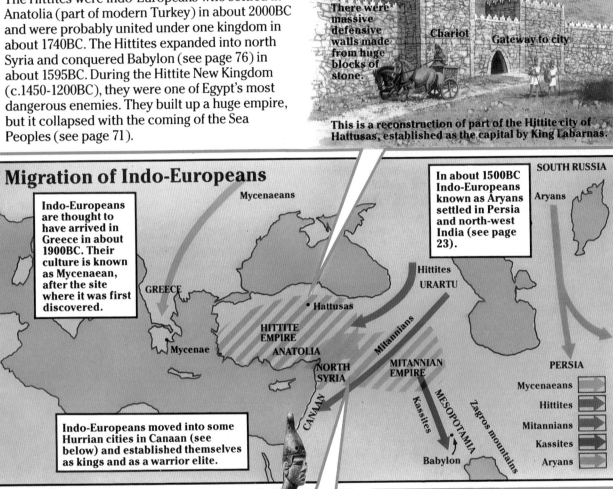

There were massive defensive walls made from huge blocks of stone.

Chariot

Gateway to city

This is a reconstruction of part of the Hittite city of Hattusas, established as the capital by King Labarnas.

Migration of Indo-Europeans

Indo-Europeans are thought to have arrived in Greece in about 1900BC. Their culture is known as Mycenaean, after the site where it was first discovered.

In about 1500BC Indo-Europeans known as Aryans settled in Persia and north-west India (see page 23).

SOUTH RUSSIA

Aryans

Mycenaeans

GREECE

Mycenae

Hattusas

HITTITE EMPIRE

ANATOLIA

NORTH SYRIA

CANAAN

Hittites

URARTU

Mitannians

MITANNIAN EMPIRE

Kassites

MESOPOTAMIA

Zagros mountains

Babylon

PERSIA

Indo-Europeans moved into some Hurrian cities in Canaan (see below) and established themselves as kings and as a warrior elite.

Mycenaeans	→
Hittites	→
Mitannians	→
Kassites	→
Aryans	→

The Mitannians

The Mitannians were Indo-Europeans who settled in northern Mesopotamia. In about 1500BC they united the Hurrian kingdoms under their rule. Between about 1450BC and 1390BC they built up an empire from the Zagros mountains to the Mediterranean. The Mitannians were keen horsemen and wrote books on horse management. Although originally rivals of the Egyptians, they made peace in about 1440BC. The kingdom broke up in about 1370BC after an attack by Hittites.

A Mitannian king

The Hurrians

The Hurrians first appeared in Mesopotamia in the 3rd millennium BC. Little is known about their origins, although they may have come from Urartu (modern Armenia), and they were neither Sumerian nor Semitic. They established kingdoms in northern Mesopotamia and later united with the Mitannians. During the 2nd millennium BC they formed an aristocratic caste† in many cities in Canaan, ruling the Amorites and native Canaanites.

Horses

Horses were native to the plains of Europe and south Russia and were probably first domesticated in about 4000BC, for use as work animals. They first appeared in the Middle East just before 2000BC, but were kept as expensive pets. Later the Indo-Europeans introduced the idea of using horses to pull war chariots. This had an effect on warfare, as it meant new military skills were needed.

Horses were used to pull chariots, like this Egyptian war chariot. They were rarely ridden.

The Kassites

The Kassites were neither Semitic nor Indo-European. They are thought to have come from the Zagros mountains, east of Babylon. Some settled in Babylon; others founded a state on the frontier. After the Hittites attacked Babylon (see opposite), the Kassites took over and set up a dynasty†

Kassite decorated brickwork

Key dates

c.2000BC Indo-Europeans drift into Middle East. Hittites settle in Anatolia.

c.1900BC Mycenaeans settle in Greece.

c.1680-1650BC Rule of King Labarnas; he is regarded by the Hittites as the founder of their kingdom.

c.1640-1552BC Second Intermediate Period in Egypt.

c.1595BC Hittites conquer Babylon and destroy the Amorite kingdom (see page 25).

c.1570-1158BC Kassite dynasty rules in Babylon.

c.1500BC Aryans settle in Persia.

c.1500BC Mitannians move into northern Mesopotamia and unite Hurrian kingdoms under their rule.

c.1450-1390BC Mitannians conquer a huge empire.

c.1450-1200BC Hittite New Kingdom

c.1440BC Mitannians make peace treaty with the Egyptians.

c.1380BC Accession of King Shuppiluliuma†, one of the greatest Hittite kings. He overthrows the Mitannian empire and captures northern provinces of the Egyptian empire in Syria.

c.1285BC Hittite coalition clashes with Ramesses II† at Kadesh.

c.1275BC Ramesses II makes a peace treaty with Hittite king, Hattusilis III, and marries his daughter.

c.1196BC Destruction of the Hittite empire by the Sea Peoples.

Egypt in the Second Intermediate Period

The collapse of the Middle Kingdom (see page 27) was caused by the invasion of a Semitic people, called Hyksos, from across the eastern frontier. After a period of fighting and destruction, the Hyksos adopted the Egyptian language and culture. They ruled Lower Egypt and northern Upper Egypt, as Dynasties XV and XVI, from their capital, Avaris.

Meanwhile, the southern part of Upper Egypt was ruled from Thebes by the Egyptian kings of Dynasty XVII. Although nominally independent, they were dominated by the Hyksos and had to pay tribute to them. The Egyptian kingdom was

The Hyksos introduced horses and chariots into Egypt.

poor, both culturally and economically, and cut off from foreign trade. However, in about 1600BC came the first signs of revival. The kings started restoring damaged monuments at Abydos and Coptos and encouraged the copying of old manuscripts. Amun*, the patron god of Dynasty XII, became the symbol of an Egyptian resistance movement against the Hyksos.

Tao and the hippos

The Egyptians had a sacred rite which involved harpooning a male hippopotamus, the symbol of Set*, the god of trouble. The Hyksos worshipped Set as the 'benefactor of mankind', so they took the ritual as a deliberate insult and a declaration of hostility. On one occasion, Apophis†, king of the Hyksos, complained to the Theban king, Tao II†, that he was being kept awake in Avaris by the hippos in Tao's pool in Thebes, over 850km (500 miles) away.

Egyptian hippo made of faience†

War with the Hyksos

War followed between the Thebans and the Hyksos, during which Tao was killed. His elder son, Kamose†, became king and extended the Egyptian frontiers as far as the Fayum. Kamose died young and was succeeded by his young brother, Ahmose†, who drove out the Hyksos and became the first king of Dynasty XVIII. This began the New Kingdom (see pages 46-47).

Battle axe belonging to Ahmose

The early New Kingdom

The New Kingdom (1552-1069BC) was the great age of warrior pharaohs and of the Egyptian empire. The occupation of the Hyksos (see page 45) had left the Egyptians with a new aggressive spirit. This drove them to conquer territory beyond their traditional frontiers and to build up the greatest empire of the day (see map, page 81). This brought them into direct conflict with other imperial powers, such as the Mitannians and the Hittites (see page 44).

Some kings put on special displays to demonstrate their military skill. Amenhotep II used to shoot arrows through copper targets while he galloped past them in his chariot.

The New Kingdom kings took on a more active military role than most earlier kings had done. They were personally responsible for planning campaign strategy and individual battle tactics, and they fought in battle alongside their soldiers. Military skills now formed an important part of the education of young princes. Friendships developed between kings and some officers. In peacetime these men were given top jobs in the government.

The age of queens

During the New Kingdom a number of queens appear to have had political influence. Teti-sheri†, the mother of Tao II† and grandmother of Kamose† and Ahmose I†, seems to have had an important role during the wars of independence.

Her daughter, Ahhotep I†, was regent† during the minority† rule of her son, Ahmose. There is

evidence that she led her troops herself during a rebellion. A necklace of 'golden flies', an award for gallantry on the battlefield, was found in her tomb.

Ahmes Nefertari†, sister-wife of Ahmose, acted as regent for her son, Amenhotep I. When he died without heirs, she helped her daughter's husband, Tuthmosis I, to become king.

Ahmes Nefertari was later worshipped as a goddess. This painting shows her with a black face, which symbolized fertility.

Hatshepsut (1490-1468BC)

The most remarkable of all the queens was Hatshepsut. As the only surviving child of Queen Ahmose, Hatshepsut became Royal Heiress† and married her half-brother, Tuthmosis II. He died young, leaving two daughters by Hatshepsut, and a son, Tuthmosis III, by his concubine† Isis. Although still only a child, the boy became king and married his elder half-sister, Neferure. Hatshepsut was made regent, presumably because Isis was regarded as unsuitable.

Hatshepsut's family tree

```
Tao I  =  Teti-sheri

Tao II  =  Ahhotep

Kamose        Ahmose  =  Ahmes Nefertari

Ahmose  =  Tuthmosis I  =  Mut-nofret
                                    Amenhotep I

Hatshepsut  =  Tuthmosis II  =  Isis

Neferure      Meryetre  =  Tuthmosis III
```

About 18 months later, Hatshepsut and her friends staged a coup during a temple ceremony at Karnak. As the statue of Amun* was carried past her it became so heavy that the priests sank to their knees. The oracle† declared this to be a sign that Amun wanted her to rule. The majority of courtiers appear to have supported this, despite the fact that there had been child kings before. As the ruler was believed to be the god Horus incarnate on earth, he was by definition male. So Hatshepsut was crowned 'king', rather than queen. Official statues show her in men's clothes and inscriptions usually refer to her as 'His Majesty'.

According to the propaganda, she was actually the daughter of Amun. He had fallen in love with Ahmose and, disguised as Tuthmosis I, become Hatshepsut's father.

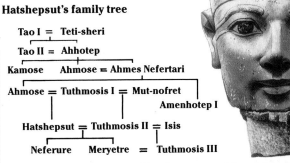

Hatshepsut's parents, Tuthmosis I and Ahmose ▶

Hatshepsut ruled successfully for about 20 years, though evidence of her reign is scarce as her official inscriptions were later wiped out. She appears to have restored many buildings destroyed by the Hyksos and extended the temple of Amun at Karnak. It was once thought that, as a woman, she could not fight and so pursued a policy of peace. However evidence from the inscriptions of her courtiers suggests that she may have fought in person in Nubia and in the East.

*For more about Amun and other Egyptian deities, see pages 20-21.

The expedition to Punt

One of Hatshepsut's achievements was to send a successful expedition to Punt, to bring back myrrh trees, which were highly valued by the Egyptians. The land of Punt was probably situated somewhere on the east coast of Africa, and the route had not been explored for over 200 years. Punt was known as 'the land of the gods', because myrrh was used as incense in religious ceremonies.

A fleet of vessels was built especially for the trip. No other Egyptian expedition had been planned on such a scale before.

This painted relief† shows gifts being presented to the chief of Punt and his wife.

Senmut

A man called Senmut was at Hatshepsut's side throughout her reign. The son of an ordinary official, he became Royal Architect and guardian of the Princess Neferure, as well as holding many other posts. He may also have been Hatshepsut's lover. This might account for a second tomb he had built for himself, resembling a royal one, and the fact that he is shown in carvings on the walls of the funerary temple he built for the queen at Deir el Bahari (reconstructed here).

Hatshepsut's temple at Deir el Bahari was built to a unique design, and much of it has survived.

The temple consisted of a series of huge terraces.

An avenue of sphinxes led up to the first terrace, which was planted with myrrh trees.

The inside walls were decorated with paintings describing events in Hatshepsut's life, including the expedition to Punt.

Tuthmosis III (1490-1436BC)

Tuthmosis III began his military career in the last years of Hatshepsut's life, and married her second daughter, Meryetre. After Hatshepsut's death, he appears to have ordered the destruction of all her statues and inscriptions. Despite having been kept from power for so long, Tuthmosis was probably the greatest of all the warrior pharaohs. He fought 17 campaigns and enlarged the Egyptian empire to its widest limits.

Tuthmosis III

Key dates

1552-1069BC	New Kingdom	1402-1364BC	Amenhotep III *
1552-1305BC	Dynasty XVIII		
1552-1527BC	Ahmose		
1527-1506BC	Amenhotep I		
1506-1494BC	Tuthmosis I		
1494-1490BC	Tuthmosis II		
1490-1468BC	Hatshepsut		
1490-1436BC	Tuthmosis III		
1438-1412BC	Amenhotep II		
1414-1402BC	Tuthmosis IV		

Amenhotep III hunting

*For the remaining kings of Dynasty XVIII, see pages 50-51.

The Egyptian army

During the Old and Middle Kingdoms, the Egyptian army consisted of the king's bodyguard and a small army of professional soldiers. Ordinary men could be called up in emergencies, but most lacked military training and so were of limited use. As the *nomarchs*† grew in power they set up armies, which the king sometimes used during a campaign.

This tomb model shows Egyptian soldiers carrying spears and large shields made of wood and leather.

Bows and arrows were the main weapons of Nubian mercenaries, employed from Dynasty VI .

The army in the New Kingdom

The need to drive out the Hyksos (see page 45) and the desire to conquer an empire had brought about a radical reorganization of the army by the New Kingdom. Horses and chariots were introduced and the army increased in size. The king was Commander-in-Chief and often led campaigns himself, while generals and officers of various ranks commanded the units. One out of every 100 able-bodied young men was liable for call-up, but there were usually plenty of volunteers. The army offered adventure and a good career, although not all soldiers went abroad on campaign. Some stayed at home to guard frontiers, suppress civil disturbances or supervise mining and building operations.

The army was made up of several divisions of 5000 men each (4000 foot-soldiers and 1000 charioteers). Charioteers were the elite troops, because of the cost of the equipment and the skill and training involved.

The organization of the army

The battle formation

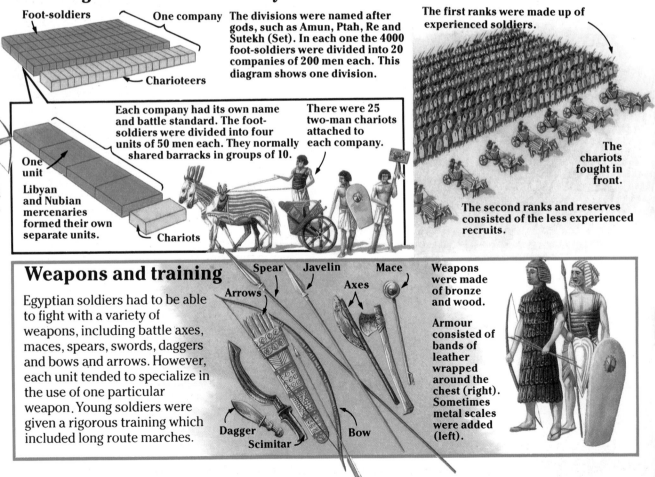

Foot-soldiers

One company

Charioteers

The divisions were named after gods, such as Amun, Ptah, Re and Sutekh (Set). In each one the 4000 foot-soldiers were divided into 20 companies of 200 men each. This diagram shows one division.

Each company had its own name and battle standard. The foot-soldiers were divided into four units of 50 men each. They normally shared barracks in groups of 10.

There were 25 two-man chariots attached to each company.

One unit

Libyan and Nubian mercenaries formed their own separate units.

Chariots

The first ranks were made up of experienced soldiers.

The chariots fought in front.

The second ranks and reserves consisted of the less experienced recruits.

Weapons and training

Egyptian soldiers had to be able to fight with a variety of weapons, including battle axes, maces, spears, swords, daggers and bows and arrows. However, each unit tended to specialize in the use of one particular weapon. Young soldiers were given a rigorous training which included long route marches.

Spear   Javelin   Mace

Arrows   Axes

Dagger

Scimitar   Bow

Weapons were made of bronze and wood.

Armour consisted of bands of leather wrapped around the chest (right). Sometimes metal scales were added (left).

On campaign

Camps were set up when the army was on campaign. The soldiers were accompanied by donkeys carrying baggage and a number of support staff. These included messengers, doctors, priests, armourers and cooks, scouts to spy out the land ahead and grooms to look after the animals. Scribes organized supplies and pay, and kept a daily journal of the campaign.

A defensive mound was dug around the camp.

Shields were placed around the top for added protection.

The tents were laid out in rows. In the centre of the camp were the king's tent and a shrine to Amun.

These golden flies, known as the 'Gold of Valour', were awarded for bravery. Other rewards for a life in the army included the opportunity to take slaves and loot (goods from the enemy), and the prospect of a piece of land on retirement.

Some officers' tents were large enough to have two or more rooms. Pictures show tents equipped with comfortable furniture and provisions. This folding bed belonged to Tutankhamun†.

Sentries

Messenger leaving the camp

Running the empire

The kings of Dynasty XVIII conquered the greatest empire of their day. At its height, it stretched from the Fourth Cataract† of the Nile to northern Syria. The Egyptians acquired great wealth by trading with their subjects and claiming tribute† from them. This is reflected in the amount of treasure buried in tombs during this period.

HITTITES
MITANNIANS
EASTERN EMPIRE
LIBYA
NUBIA
Under Egyptian control
KUSH
Area of Egyptian influence

Nubia

Although the Egyptians met considerable initial opposition in their conquest of Nubia, they managed to maintain peaceful control relatively easily. The Nubians readily adopted many aspects of Egyptian culture, religion, language, writing and architecture.

A Nubian from an Egyptian painting

The Nubian government was run on Egyptian lines, headed by a Viceroy called the 'King's Son of Kush'. He had two deputies; one was responsible for Wawat (northern Nubia), and the other for Kush (southern Nubia). The country was divided into administrative areas, each run by an official who was usually a local chief.

The eastern empire

By contrast, in the eastern part of the empire* the Egyptians encountered cultures almost as old as their own. The area was divided into small princedoms which had well-established traditions of government, law and religion. The Egyptians kept as many native princes as possible in office. Overseers were sent to important cities, but their task was only to guard Egyptian interests. It was the local princes who ruled, through their own officials and according to local laws and customs.

Egyptians storming a Syrian fortress

Trumpet calls were used to sound orders on the battlefield.

As rival empire-builders, the Hittites and the Mitannians were always ready to encourage discontented Egyptian subjects to rebel. To ensure the princes' loyalty and to discourage attacks, Egyptian troops were garrisoned in fortresses and important provincial towns. Rebellions were dealt with severely. However, there were excellent rewards for loyal princes, including opportunities for profitable trade with Egypt. In order to ensure good behaviour, the princes' children were sometimes sent to Egypt as hostages. They were educated at court and treated well. This encouraged them to remain loyal to Egypt when they eventually went home to rule. The pharaohs often reinforced family ties by taking foreign princesses as secondary wives.

This is the area known as Canaan (see page 25), now occupied by Syria, Lebanon, Israel and Jordan.

The reign of Akhenaten

The reign of Amenhotep IV (1364-1347BC), also known as Akhenaten, still causes great controversies among scholars. Amenhotep is the first person in history who is known to have worshipped only one god. He revived the ancient cult† of the sun god (see page 13), in the form of the Aten (the disc of the sun). Amehotep believed that the Aten revealed himself only to his 'son', the king. He changed his name to Akhenaten ('living spirit of the Aten') in honour of his god.

Akhenaten worshipping the Aten

Akhenaten also gave his wife Nefertiti† (shown here) a second official name incorporating that of the Aten–Neferneferuaten. Normally only kings took a second name.

A painted stone bust of Nefertiti found at Tell el Amarna (see below)

At the start of his reign Akhenaten ordered a complex of shrines to be built for the Aten, beside the temple of Amun-Re at Karnak. However, before it was completed, he decided that the Aten should have a home town of his own. The king sailed north and was inspired by his god to stop at a bay in the cliffs on the east side of the river. There, he ordered a new capital city to be built.

The city of Akhetaten

The king named the new city Akhetaten, meaning 'the Horizon of Aten'. (Its modern name is Tell el Amarna.) The court moved there in the 6th year* of his reign. Excavations have given us a good idea of what the city centre looked like. It had several temples and palaces, as well as luxurious villas for the nobles.

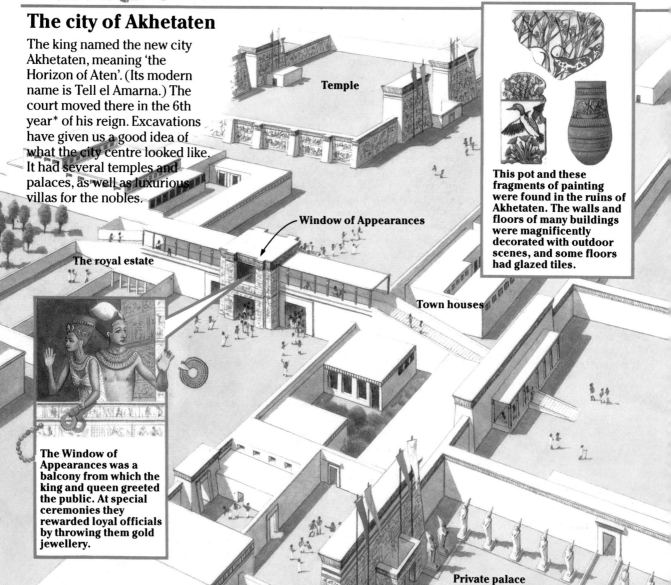

Temple

This pot and these fragments of painting were found in the ruins of Akhetaten. The walls and floors of many buildings were magnificently decorated with outdoor scenes, and some floors had glazed tiles.

Window of Appearances

The royal estate

Town houses

The Window of Appearances was a balcony from which the king and queen greeted the public. At special ceremonies they rewarded loyal officials by throwing them gold jewellery.

Private palace

Akhenaten's religious revolution

Akhenaten introduced a series of changes which amounted to a religious revolution and shocked many conservative Egyptians. Not only did he introduce the worship of the Aten, but at the same time he also banned the worship of all the old Egyptian gods and goddesses. He even had their names cut out of inscriptions.

Experts disagree about Akhenaten's reasons. His actions may have been prompted by devotion to his god, or they may have been the result of a power struggle between the king and the powerful priesthood of Amun-Re.

Offering tables

The Great Temple at Akhetaten was unlike most other New Kingdom temples. It consisted of open courtyards, where the sun's rays could reach the worshippers, with hundreds of tables for offerings.

Portraits of Akhenaten

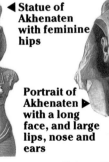

A carved relief† of Akhenaten and his family. The Aten was usually included in portraits.

Akhenaten had himself portrayed in statues and reliefs kissing his wife and playing with his children. The Egyptians were used to more formal traditional portraits and many people must have found these poses rather undignified for a king.

◀ Statue of Akhenaten with feminine hips

Portrait of Akhenaten ▶ with a long face, and large lips, nose and ears

Some of his ▲ portraits show a more normal looking face.

Kings were traditionally made to look strong, masculine and handsome. However most of Akhenaten's portraits show an almost feminine body, with a long face and large lips, nose and ears. Experts disagree on the reasons for this. If his strange shape was the result of an illness*, it is unlikely that he would have been able to have children. Yet he and Nefertiti had six daughters. So it is possible that portraits were deliberately distorted for some other reason.

The mystery of Smenkhkare

In about year 14 of his reign, Akhenaten took a co-ruler called Smenkhkare, and gave him Nefertiti's special name – Neferneferuaten. Some experts believe he was a young nobleman; others think that he was Akhenaten's brother. However a recent theory suggests that it was Nefertiti herself. According to the theory, Akhenaten believed she would never give birth to a son, so he married their eldest daughter, Meritaten, compensating Nefertiti by making her a 'king'. About the time that Akhenaten died, Smenkhkare also disappeared.

After Akhenaten

Tutankhamun† (1347-1337BC), was probably Akhenaten's son by a minor wife. He became king when he was only about nine and married Ankhesenamun†, the daughter of Akhenaten and Nefertiti. A general called Horemheb† and a courtier called Ay became regents†. They abandoned Akhetaten and restored the worship of the old gods.

Tutankhamun died very young. He was succeeded by Ay and then by Horemheb. It appears from texts written at this period that problems had developed under Akhenaten, including the loss of the northern empire (Syria) to the Hittites†. Horemheb set about reorganizing the government and restoring order. He began a campaign to dishonour Ahkenaten, tearing down many of his monuments. Akhenaten himself was branded as a heretic†.

*The illness referred to is known as Frölich's syndrome.

Egyptian building methods

From the beginning of the Old Kingdom, the Egyptians built enormous stone monuments, such as pyramids and temples. These buildings were constructed without the aid of cranes or other machinery. Instead the work was carried out by large numbers (often thousands) of men, using ropes, ramps and sledges. At first much of the building was done by peasants as a labour tax due to the king. However during the New Kingdom prisoners of war were used as well. All these men had to be housed, fed and looked after. The organization involved was a major feat in itself.

Constructing a temple

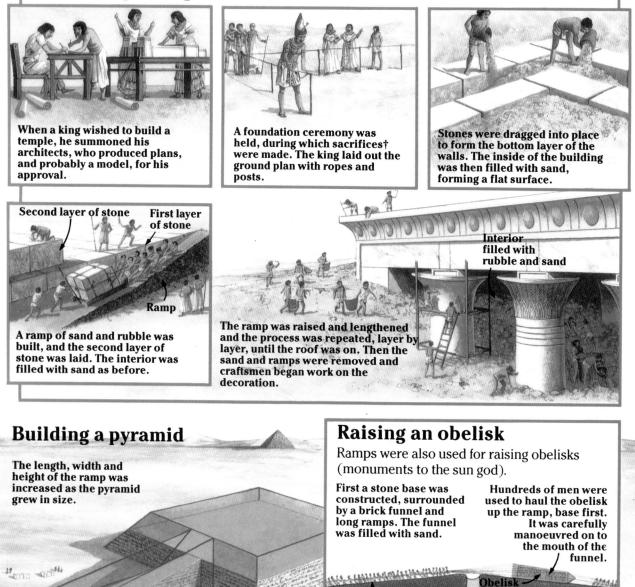

When a king wished to build a temple, he summoned his architects, who produced plans, and probably a model, for his approval.

A foundation ceremony was held, during which sacrifices† were made. The king laid out the ground plan with ropes and posts.

Stones were dragged into place to form the bottom layer of the walls. The inside of the building was then filled with sand, forming a flat surface.

Second layer of stone   First layer of stone

Ramp

A ramp of sand and rubble was built, and the second layer of stone was laid. The interior was filled with sand as before.

Interior filled with rubble and sand

The ramp was raised and lengthened and the process was repeated, layer by layer, until the roof was on. Then the sand and ramps were removed and craftsmen began work on the decoration.

Building a pyramid

The length, width and height of the ramp was increased as the pyramid grew in size.

Pyramids were also built with ramps, although there are different theories as to how they were arranged. Some experts believe that only one ramp was used. Others suggest that ramps were built on each side of the pyramid.

Raising an obelisk

Ramps were also used for raising obelisks (monuments to the sun god).

First a stone base was constructed, surrounded by a brick funnel and long ramps. The funnel was filled with sand.

Hundreds of men were used to haul the obelisk up the ramp, base first. It was carefully manoeuvred on to the mouth of the funnel.

Ramp   Funnel   Obelisk   Base

A hole was made here to remove the sand.

As the sand level sank, the men guided the obelisk so that it tilted up, slid down and rested on its base. The ramps and funnel were then dismantled.

52

Architectural details

Egyptian craftsmen reproduced in stone many of the features of the earlier reed buildings (see page 9).

Stone pillars were carved to look like bunches of reeds and flowers.

The tops of walls were often decorated with a *kheker* frieze, which represented reeds bound together.

Statues

Statues were shaped with stone pounders. Copper and bronze tools and abrasive powders were used to cut and polish the stone, and to carve details such as plaits in wigs. Some statues were colossal.

Paintings

Tombs and temples were brightly decorated, inside and out, by skilled artists. The paintings had an important religious and magical purpose. The Egyptians believed that the gods, or the dead person, could actually take part in the activities shown in the picture. For example, a painting of a banquet would ensure that the dead person ate well in the Next World†.

Carving reliefs

A raised relief (a sculpture carved on a background) was made by cutting away the background and modelling details on to the figures.

Raised relief

Sunken relief

A sunken relief was made by cutting away the stone from inside the outline of the figure and carving the details out of the body.

Before painting a wall, the artist made sure the surface was flat, usually by applying a layer of plaster. A grid was then printed on the wall, using string soaked in red paint.

The artist drew in the outlines in red. These were corrected in black by a supervisor. Then the background colour was filled in, followed by the figures, and finally details such as eyes.

Face in profile

Eye looks straight ahead

Shoulders from the front

Breast in profile

Navel in ¾ twist

Legs in profile

Egyptian painting was governed by strict rules of proportion. The figures were painted as if seen from different angles at once. Some parts were shown from the front, while others were in profile.

The paints were made from chalks, ochres (earth) and minerals such as copper and cobalt. These were ground into powder and mixed with water. The brushes were made of reeds.

Egyptian houses

The Egyptians lacked good timber but had plenty of mud and reeds, so the earliest houses were made from reeds, woven and bound together. By the Gerzean Period (see page 9), most houses were built from bricks made of sun-dried mud, and reeds were only used for temporary shelters. The reconstruction below shows a rich nobleman's house from the New Kingdom. By this time most houses, from farmhouses to luxurious villas, were divided into three main areas. There was a reception at the front where business was done, a hall in the centre where friends were entertained, and private quarters at the back where the family lived.

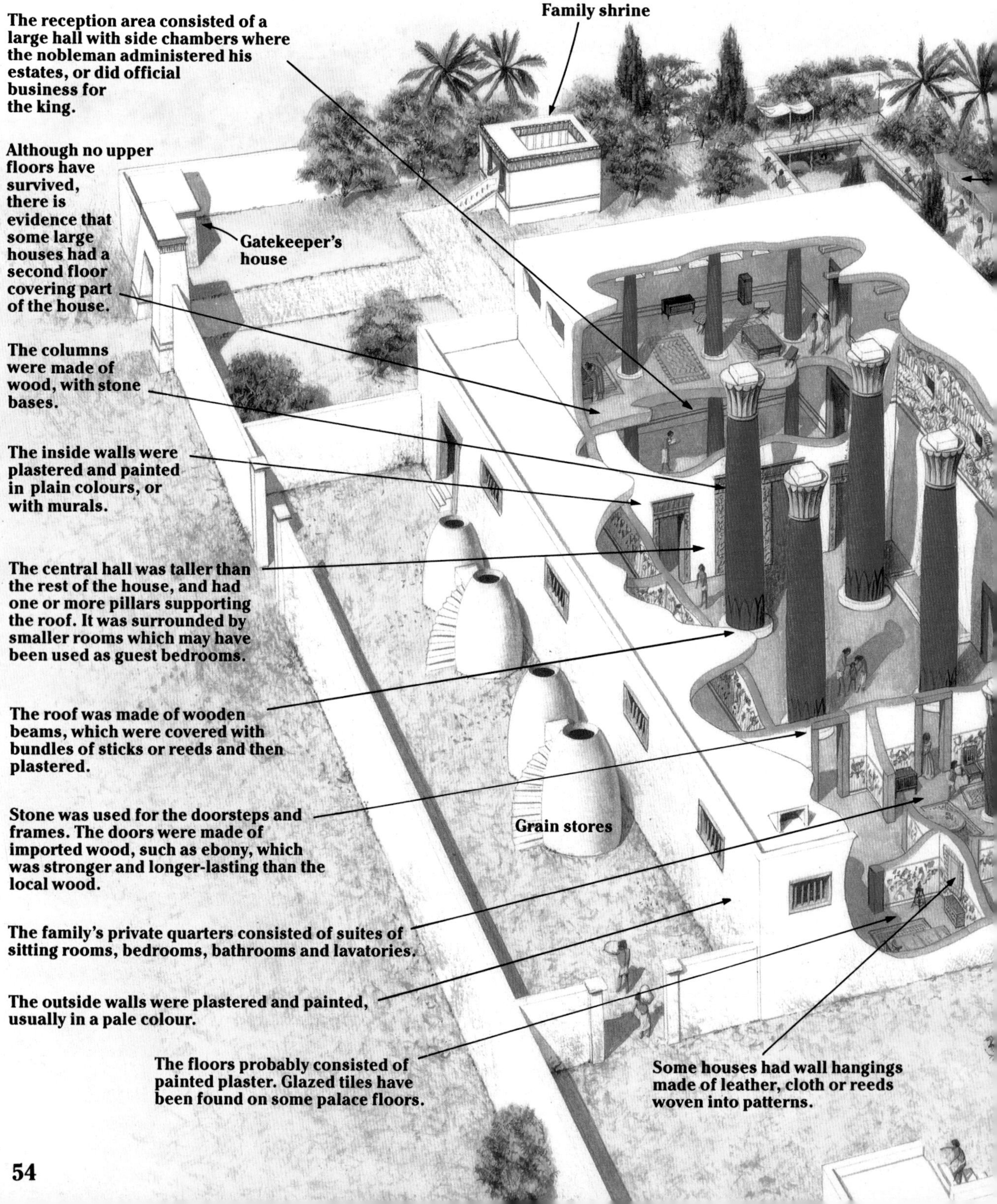

The reception area consisted of a large hall with side chambers where the nobleman administered his estates, or did official business for the king.

Although no upper floors have survived, there is evidence that some large houses had a second floor covering part of the house.

The columns were made of wood, with stone bases.

The inside walls were plastered and painted in plain colours, or with murals.

The central hall was taller than the rest of the house, and had one or more pillars supporting the roof. It was surrounded by smaller rooms which may have been used as guest bedrooms.

The roof was made of wooden beams, which were covered with bundles of sticks or reeds and then plastered.

Stone was used for the doorsteps and frames. The doors were made of imported wood, such as ebony, which was stronger and longer-lasting than the local wood.

The family's private quarters consisted of suites of sitting rooms, bedrooms, bathrooms and lavatories.

The outside walls were plastered and painted, usually in a pale colour.

The floors probably consisted of painted plaster. Glazed tiles have been found on some palace floors.

Family shrine

Gatekeeper's house

Grain stores

Some houses had wall hangings made of leather, cloth or reeds woven into patterns.

How we know what houses looked like

During the First Intermediate Period and the Middle Kingdom, pottery models of houses were placed in tombs. The model below has been used to reconstruct the Middle Kingdom farmhouse shown on the right.

A Middle Kingdom farmhouse

Mud-plastered reed columns

In the summer the family slept under a shelter on the roof.

Cooking area

Stamped earth floors

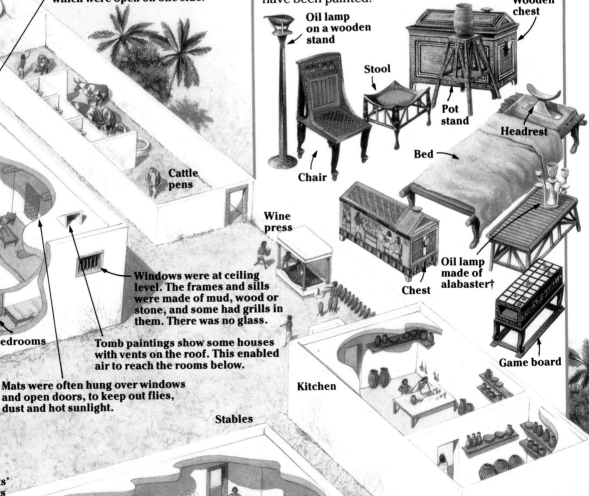

The Egyptians loved gardens and pools, but very few people would have been able to afford a garden like this one.

Plastered mud-brick stairs led to the roof and the upper floors.

In summer people may have slept on the roof. Some houses even had rooms on the roof, which were open on one side.

Well

Cattle pens

Windows were at ceiling level. The frames and sills were made of mud, wood or stone, and some had grills in them. There was no glass.

Bedrooms

Tomb paintings show some houses with vents on the roof. This enabled air to reach the rooms below.

Mats were often hung over windows and open doors, to keep out flies, dust and hot sunlight.

Stables

Servants' quarters

Furniture

The furniture of kings and nobles has been preserved in tombs. It was made of imported woods, such as ebony and cedar, inlaid with ivory, precious metals, semi-precious stones and faience†. Most furniture was probably made of cheap local wood, leather or reeds, and might have been painted.

Oil lamp on a wooden stand

Wooden chest

Stool

Pot stand

Headrest

Chair

Bed

Wine press

Chest

Oil lamp made of alabaster†

Game board

Kitchen

Town houses

Very few Egyptian towns have been excavated, as people have continued living in them over the centuries, and modern towns have been built on top of the ancient sites. However, models and paintings suggest that some houses were up to four storeys high. Towns were hot, noisy, dusty places, with narrow, busy streets. Water was supplied from private and public wells, but there does not appear to have been a public refuse or sewage system. Each household had to dispose of its own waste – in pits, in the river, or in the streets.

The family quarters were on the upper floors.

Shops and businesses were probably on the ground floor.

People spent a lot of time on the roof because it was cooler. In the summer they probably slept there too.

Cooking and eating

The Egyptians cooked in the open air whenever possible, to avoid the danger of fire. However, evidence from Tell el Amarna (see page 50) shows that some people risked cooking on the roof. Egyptian food was baked, boiled, stewed, fried, grilled or roasted.

Cooking was done on tripods (shown here), braziers or pottery stoves.

Wood was used as fuel. It was set alight with a firedrill, which created heat by means of friction.

Tripod

Paintings like this one, as well as offerings and models left in tombs, give us an idea of what the Egyptians ate and how it was prepared. Although no recipes have been found, there are references in texts to soups and sauces.

Pots and pans

Kitchen equipment found in tombs, includes pots, pans, storage jars, ladles, sieves and whisks.

Whisk

Storage jars

Sieve

Bowl

Drinking cup

Beer jar with straw

Dish

Most dishes were made of earthenware, although rich people also used faience†, bronze, silver and gold.

Bread, beer and wine

Bread and beer were the staple elements of the Egyptian diet. To make bread, the wheat was first ground into flour. Evidence is recorded of requests for pure wheat flour, sieved and free from added barley, so some people must have cheated by mixing barley with the wheat. The flour was then mixed with water to form a dough. Bread was baked in moulds inside the oven, or shaped into flat, round loaves, which were placed on the outside of it. As the flour was ground outdoors, grit often got into the bread, causing heavy wear on people's teeth.

Women ground the wheat into flour. If very fine flour was needed, it was then pounded by men.

Flavourings were sometimes added to the dough, such as honey, fruit, butter, seeds or herbs.

Bread moulds

Oven

The loaves dropped off the oven when they were cooked.

Making wine

Although the Egyptians made several types of wine, it was usually only drunk by the rich. Wine was made from dates, pomegranates and palm sap, as well as from grapes. The best vineyards were said to be in the Nile Delta.

Trellises for growing grapes

To extract the juice, men ▶ trod on the grapes in a large vat. This produced the best quality wine.

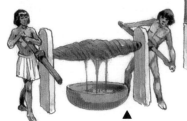

Then the fruit pulp, pips and stalks were all crushed together in a sack, twisted between two poles. This produced more juice, but it made a poorer quality wine.

◀ The juice was put in jars to ferment. The mouths of the jars were closed with a wad of leaves plastered over with mud.

Small holes were left in the stoppers, to allow further fermentation to take place without the jars exploding.

Finally the jars were completely sealed. They were labelled with details of the year, the vineyard and the quality of the wine.

Making beer

To make beer, barley was moistened with water and left to stand. Lightly baked barley loaves were then broken up and mixed with the grain in a large jar of water. The mixture then fermented (turned into alcohol).

The mixture was thick and lumpy.

Breaking bread into the mixture

Beer was strained through a sieve before being served.

Beer was served in a drinking cup. It was sometimes drunk through a straw, made from wood or metal.

Women and family life

In many ways, women in Egypt were in a more privileged position than elsewhere in the Ancient World. Although they did not hold jobs in government, they had a great deal of personal freedom and had the same legal rights and obligations as men. They were able to do business deals, enter into contracts and act as witnesses in court, and they were expected to conduct their own court cases. Women took the same oaths as men and faced the same penalties.

Children

The Egyptians regarded children as a great blessing. If a couple had no children, they prayed to gods and goddesses for help, or placed letters in the tombs of dead relatives, asking them to use their influence with the gods. Some people also tried fertility charms and magic. If all this failed, children could be adopted.

From an early age boys were taught their fathers' trades and girls worked with their mothers at home. People who could afford it sent their sons to school from the age of about seven (see page 64). Although there is no evidence of any schools for girls, some learned to read and write at home, and a few even became doctors.

Wills and inheritance

Children were expected to look after their elderly parents, and to organize funerals. At one time the person who paid for the funeral also inherited the property.

Fathers tended to leave land to their sons, and other property, such as the house, furniture and jewellery, to the daughters. However there was nothing to prevent girls from inheriting estates, especially if they had no brothers. There is evidence of Middle Kingdom heiresses who inherited whole *nomes†*.

New Kingdom land-owner supervising her estate

Jobs and careers

Although women usually married young and were expected to play a major part in bringing up their children, there were a few jobs and careers open to them.

Courts and temples employed women as singers, dancers, musicians and acrobats. Noblewomen could become courtiers or priestesses.

Professional mourner

Priestess

Acrobat

Statuette of servant girl

◄ Some women worked as servants in wealthy households. A noblewoman's maid or nanny could have great influence. The sons of some royal nannies held important positions at court.

Women also worked as perfume-makers (shown below), gardeners, weavers and professional mourners.

There is evidence of women running farms and businesses on behalf of absent husbands and sons. This scene shows a woman supervising farm workers.

Marriage

Peasant girls sometimes married as early as 12 years old; those from richer families were a few years older. The boys were usually a few years older than the girls. Parents were expected to choose their children's husbands and wives for them, although surviving love poetry suggests that some young people chose their own.

Statue of a New Kingdom couple

Details of the marriage ceremony are not known, but it probably began with a procession, followed by an exchange of vows by the bride and groom, a banquet and the giving of presents. Most couples moved into a house of their own, usually provided by the husband. Egyptian texts warn about the many problems that arise from living with parents and in-laws.

The marriage contract contained detailed financial arrangements. The wife was entitled to a maintenance allowance from her husband. She brought goods with her, such as clothes and furniture, as a kind of dowry†. But, unlike a dowry, the goods remained hers. They, or others of equivalent value, had to be returned to her if the marriage ended for any reason.

Both husband and wife could own property of their own, separate from their partners. For practical reasons, it was usual for a wife to let her husband administer her property along with his, but it was still regarded as hers.

The marriage fund

From the Middle Kingdom onwards, a joint marriage fund was set up and a written record was kept. The husband contributed two-thirds and the wife one-third; these proportions remained the same, even if the value of the fund increased over the years. The fund acted as a guaranteed inheritance for the children. When a husband or wife died, his or her share went straight to the children. If the surviving partner remarried, the children received the rest of the inheritance before a new fund was set up for the second marriage. If a couple divorced, they would each keep their own share of the fund, although the wife forfeited hers if she had been unfaithful to her husband. Some unscrupulous men accused their wives falsely, in order to confiscate their share, but the woman was allowed to keep it if she took an oath that she was innocent.

Divorce

A wife was known as the *nebet per* (lady of house). She was in charge of running the house and bringing up the children, and expected to be treated with respect. If a wife was treated badly, she usually went to her relatives for help. They might try to persuade the husband to improve his behaviour, making him swear to do so in front of them. Divorce appears to have been an easy matter, amounting to a simple statement before witnesses. A divorced woman usually had custody of her children and was free to remarry.

Concubines

Royal harem

Although kings always had several wives, an ordinary Egyptian man normally only had one. However, it was considered legal and respectable for a man to keep an official lover (known as a concubine), if he could afford one. Although the man's wife and children came first, he was also expected to look after the concubine and her children.

The king's wives and concubines all lived together in a special part of the palace. Unlike some later harems†, which were cut off from the world, this was a lively, open place, where officials and other visitors could be received.

Egyptian temples

For the Egyptians a temple was the home on earth of the god or goddess to whom it was dedicated. It housed a cult statue, a statue of the deity through which the spirit of the god or goddess was said to communicate. A temple was not like a church, mosque or synagogue, where people gather together to worship. It was a private place. Normally only priests and priestesses went inside. Most ordinary people only went as far as the entrance to make offerings and pray. At some festivals, the cult statue was carried out of the temple in a boat, called a sacred barque.

This is a New Kingdom temple. It was built inside an enclosure which contained several outbuildings, and was entered through a gateway called a *pylon*. The temple itself was divided into three areas – the courtyards (one or more), the hypostyle hall, and the sanctuary.

Priests and priestesses

Each temple had a number of priests and priestesses. The priests were divided into four groups, called *phyles*. Each *phyle* went on duty three times a year, for a month at a time. The temple also provided work for other people, including scribes, singers, musicians, craftsmen, builders and farmers.

At one time if a person wanted the god's help he or she placed a small *stela*† of a pair of ears against the temple wall. This was to remind the god to listen to the person's prayers.

Temple workshops produced goods such as furniture, statues, linen and sacred vessels.

Flagpoles

Obelisks (sacred monuments to the sun god)

Pylon

Sphinxes were carved figures with a lion's body and a ram's head. They represented the sun god.

Avenue of sphinxes†

Some people prayed before statues of the king. The Egyptians believed he was descended from the gods and could intercede with them on behalf of his subjects.

Scribes† sat at the temple gates. If someone wanted to ask the god a question, they asked the scribe to write it down. The question was then given to the priests in the temple.

The outer walls of the temple were decorated with inscriptions and scenes of the king's conquests.

Processions took place in the hypostyle hall. The walls were decorated with scenes showing processions and offering ceremonies.

The walls of the sanctuary were decorated with scenes of offerings being made to the god.

The sanctuary contained the 'Holy of Holies', a shrine where the cult statue was kept.

Sacred vessels were kept here.

Shrine for the sacred barque

Every day at dawn, noon and sunset the priests made offerings to the god. The cult statue was dressed and given food, as if it were a living person. The priests knew that the god did not really need food, but it was a way of saying 'Thank you'.

Sanctuary

The priests prayed over the offerings. The priestesses sang and recited prayers, accompanied by musicians, singers and dancers.

Hypostyle hall

The priests on duty lived in a house in the grounds.

Courtyard

On special occasions (after the birth of a child, for example), people were sometimes allowed into the courtyard to say prayers or give offerings.

Incense

Priests dressed as gods

Before going on duty, a priest's body was washed and shaved. He chewed natron (a kind of salt) and inhaled incense to purify his mouth and mind.

Water for purification was taken from a pool known as the sacred lake.

Scribes copied out religious texts.

Library

Some of the walls and columns have been cut away so you can see inside. In reality, not all of the activities shown here would have been happening at the same time.

Administrative offices

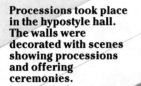

Dreams and oracles

Like many other ancient peoples, the Egyptians tried various methods to interpret the will of the gods and to predict the future. One of these was through dreams. It was usual for a pharaoh to claim that a god had appeared to him in a dream, to order him to pursue a particular policy, reassure him of support or warn him of danger.

People who were puzzled by dreams could consult priests. They were trained to interpret dreams and had books to help them. Here are two examples adapted from Egyptian texts.

If a person dreamed about looking at a large cat, it meant that there would be a large harvest.

If a man dreamed about looking at his face in a mirror, it meant he would have another wife.

Signs in the sky

People also looked for meanings in the sky. When Tuthmosis III† saw a falling star, he believed it was sent to reassure him of victory in battle.

Consulting the oracle

The most popular method of finding out the will of the gods was to consult the oracle. This was usually a cult statue†, through which the god was supposed to speak. Kings sometimes used the oracle to gain approval for royal policy, and ordinary people sought solutions to personal problems and fears.

The oracle was normally consulted on a feast day. The cult statue was carried out of the temple on its sacred barque†. Anyone could approach and ask a question. The answer (yes or no) depended on how the boat moved – forwards or backwards, or pressing down. Obviously the result of an oracle could be fixed, but most priests probably believed that the gods inspired their responses.

Mesopotamia

The people of Mesopotamia had a variety of ways of predicting the future and finding out the will of the gods. They looked carefully at the behaviour of animals. They also sought information from arrows thrown in the ground, shapes made by smoke or oil poured on water, and from the entrails of sacrificed animals. The Babylonians specialized in reading omens (signs of some future event) from animal livers.

Hiring a scribe

Between festivals, anyone who wanted to ask a question urgently could go to the temple gate. As most people could not read or write, they hired a scribe† to write their questions down. The questions were then given to a priest, who consulted the god on the people's behalf.

Sacred animals

Many Egyptian gods and goddesses were associated with a particular species of animal or bird (see pages 20-21). It became the custom for a creature of that species to be selected and kept in the deity's main temple. The animal was treated with great honour, and people believed that when certain prayers and spells had been said, the spirit of the deity passed into it. The animal could then give oracles, indicating a yes or no answer by its movements.

These are examples of sacred animals that were kept at temples. The deity's name is in brackets.

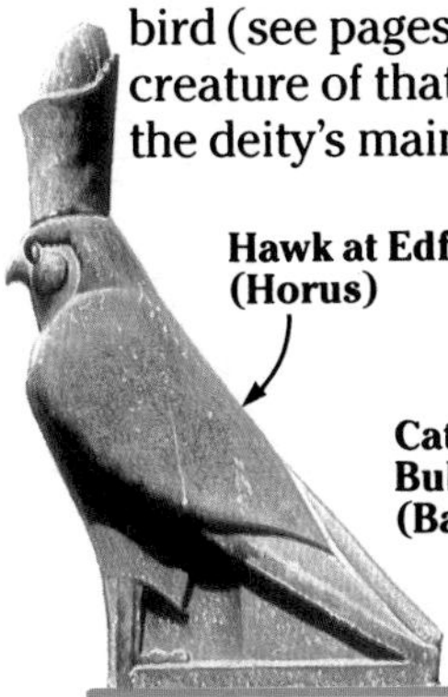

Hawk at Edfu (Horus)

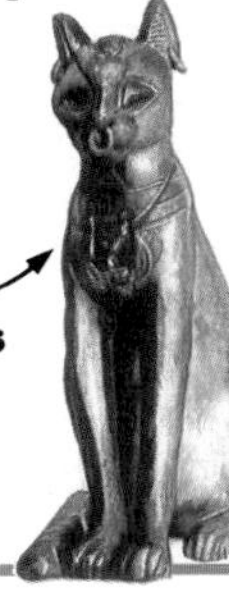

Cat at Bubastis (Bast)

Ram at Elephantine (Khnum) and at Karnak (Amun).

Crocodile at Medinet el Fayum and Kom-ombo (Sobek)

The Apis bull

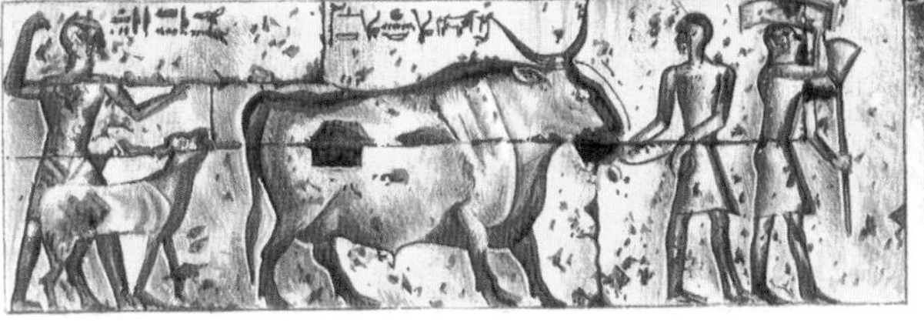

Relief† showing Apis bull ▶

The animal we know most about was the Apis bull. He was associated with the god Ptah, whose cult temple† was at Memphis. Whenever an Apis bull died, a search was made all over Egypt for his successor. The new bull had to be black and white with certain special features – a white triangular patch on his forehead, a patch resembling a flying vulture on his back, a scarab-shaped lump on his tongue, and double hairs in his tail.

Once the Apis had been identified, he and his mother were taken to Memphis, where they lived in comfort for the rest of their lives. Their dung and milk were used for magic and medicinal purposes.

Funeral procession of Apis bull

At great religious festivals, the spirit of Ptah was believed to enter the bull and he was paraded before the people so that they could worship the god through him. When the bull died, he became known as the Osiris-Apis. He was embalmed and taken in a great procession to the Serapeum (the tomb of the bulls) at Sakkara. There he was buried in a huge *sarcophagus* (a stone coffin).

Animal mummies

Mummified cat

By the Late Period, some entire species of animals were regarded as almost sacred. It then became the custom to give these animals proper burials. People believed that by doing this they would please the gods. Many animal cemeteries have been found. The largest seems to have been at Sakkara, where there are enormous underground passages. Millions of birds (such as ibises and hawks), cats, dogs, baboons and other animals have been found there.

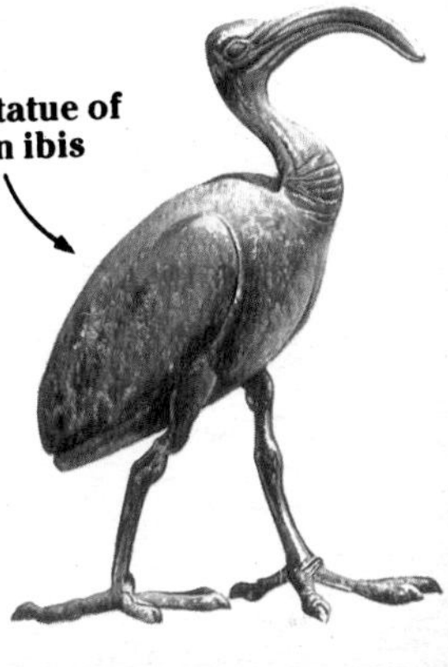

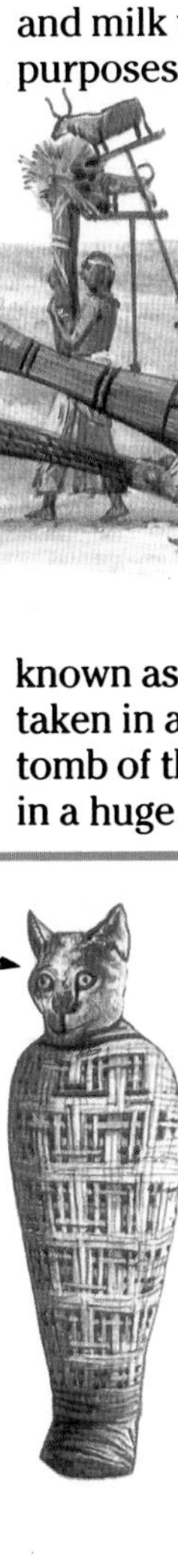

Statue of an ibis

Mummified ibis

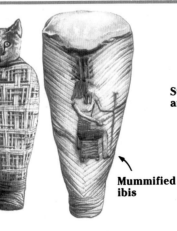

Education

During the Old Kingdom the sons of noblemen were educated at home. When they became young men, they were instructed in intellectual, social and spiritual arts by older men with a reputation for being wise.

The first evidence of schools in Egypt dates from the Middle Kingdom, although they may have developed earlier. Many schools were attached to temples; the best ones were probably at large temples, like Memphis and Thebes. There were village schools too, where a few peasant boys were taught by a local priest or scribe who wanted to supplement his income. However, most Egyptian children did not go to school. Instead most boys learned their fathers' trade, while girls helped their mothers at home.

A temple school

Temple schools were probably connected to the 'House of Life', a complex of buildings where religious texts were copied and stored.

Egyptian schools were for boys only. The boys began when they were about seven years old. They learned to read and write the three forms of Egyptian script (see page 11). Most of their time was spent copying texts.

The boys wrote on pieces of broken pottery or stone, known as *ostraca* (sing: *ostracon*), or on wooden tablets covered with plaster, which could be washed and re-used.

This is an *ostracon* with part of the *Story of Sinuhe*, a popular Egyptian tale

Higher education

At the age of nine or ten, a boy could go on to higher education. At this stage he learned how to compose letters and legal documents, and studied a range of subjects, including history, literature, geography, religion, languages, surveying, engineering, account-keeping, astronomy, maths and medicine. Evidence

Papyrus with mathematical text

suggests that examinations were held, but we do not know at what stage they were taken.

Those who could afford it went on to specialize in one or two subjects. A poor boy's family might try to persuade a rich man to be his patron†, in order to pay for his studies. Most well-educated boys eventually became scribes†. This was the most highly regarded profession in Egypt, as most people could not read and write and the whole system of government was based on keeping records. Some scribes entered government service and became important officials.

Sumerian education and learning

The Sumerians were expert mathematicians, astronomers and surveyors. They also developed elaborate law codes. Their calendar, based on the Moon, had months of 28 days. The Sumerians used two counting systems. One was a decimal system like ours, based on a unit of ten. The other, based on units of sixty, is still used for measuring circles and time. The Sumerians were the first to divide an hour into 60 minutes and a circle into 360°.

Sumerian tablet with mathematical text

A Sumerian school

Wealthy Sumerians sent their sons to schools, where they learned reading, writing and arithmetic. The boys practised writing on soft clay tablets, which could be squashed, reshaped and used again. The school day was long and discipline was strict. Boys were beaten for not learning their lessons properly.

Stars, calendars and measuring systems

The Egyptians were very interested in astronomy. They understood that there were differences between planets and stars and were able to identify Mercury, Mars, Venus, Jupiter and Saturn. They used their knowledge of the stars to work out several calendars.

Egyptian calendars

This Egyptian astronomical drawing shows the constellations (groups of stars) as gods.

The first Egyptian calendar was based on the stars. The most important star was Sirius, which the Egyptians called Sopdet (or Sothis, its Greek name). The Egyptians noticed that Sopdet disappeared below the horizon at the same time each year, and reappeared just before sunrise 70 days later. This happened just when the level of the Nile began to rise for the annual floods. It became the date of their New Year, which was called *wepet renpet*.

Their second calendar was based on the cycle of the Moon. As a lunar month consists of 29½ days, the calendar was in constant need of adjustment. However, it continued to be used to calculate the dates of some religious festivals.

The first calendar to divide the year into 365 days was introduced very early in the Old Kingdom, possibly by Imhotep†. Since there are actually 365¼ days in a year, this calendar slipped very gradually out of step with the New Year as calculated by Sopdet. When Julius Caesar† visited Egypt, he was so impressed by the calendar that he took it back to Rome and adapted it. His version, known as the Julian calendar, was used until the Gregorian calendar (the one we use today) was introduced in the 16th century.

The Egyptian year

10 DAYS = ONE WEEK

3 WEEKS = ONE MONTH (30 days)

4 MONTHS = ONE SEASON (120 days)

3 SEASONS = 360 DAYS

+ 5 HOLY DAYS

= ONE YEAR (365 days)

Holy days

The five holy days were the birthdays of Osiris, Isis, Set, Nephthys and Horus, which all came at the end of the year. These, and other important festivals, were public holidays. Every tenth day was also a holiday, rather like a weekend.

Osiris   Isis

Days

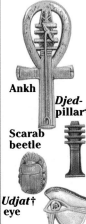

Ankh

Djed-pillar†

Scarab beetle

Udjat† eye

The Egyptians were the first to introduce the 24 hour day, which they divided into 12 hours of day and 12 of night. They believed that some days were good, while others were very unlucky. (This related to events in the lives of the gods.) On a bad day, it was considered advisable to take extra care and wear plenty of amulets (magic charms, shown here). On the worst days it was best to stay at home and pray, and wait for the danger to pass.

Dates

The Egyptians counted their years from the accession of the reigning king. So when a new king came to the throne, they began again at year 1. Since scholars know who reigned, in what order, and for how long, they can add up the reign dates and convert them into dates BC.

Telling the time

The Egyptians told the time by means of a water clock, a conical vessel with hours marked off on the inside. Water dripped out of a spout at the bottom at a carefully measured rate. As the water level fell, the number of marks that were exposed indicated the time.

Spout

An Egyptian water clock

Egyptian measurements

Egyptian measurements were based on the human body. The main measurement was called a *cubit* and was equal to the distance from the elbow to the fingertip. Seven hands, each four fingers wide, also equalled one *cubit*. A *cubit* was then divided into digits (finger-widths), and then sub-divided into fractions of a digit.

An Egyptian measuring rod

Crafts and trades

The craftsmen and women of Egypt were well-paid and respected members of the community. The most highly skilled were employed in temple and palace workshops or on the estates of nobles. There were also village craftsmen who produced goods for the local market and probably did a little farming to supplement their income.

A boy usually followed his family's trade, although he could be trained in another craft if he showed a special talent for it. After training as an apprentice, he was promoted to 'junior', and then craftsman. If he was very skilled, he became a master craftsman. There were a few trades open to women, including weaving, gardening and making perfume.

Experts have been able to learn a lot about the techniques of Egyptian craftsmen from paintings and models left in tombs, as well as from the objects they made. This painting shows goldsmiths at work.

The royal tomb-builders

Excavations at Deir el Medinah on the West Bank near Thebes have uncovered a village designed specially for the men who built the royal tombs of the New Kingdom. The village was abandoned at the end of this period, when the kings were no longer buried at Thebes.

Excavations have revealed the layout of the village. Surviving texts on *ostraca†* provide information about the lives of skilled workmen in Egypt, although as royal tomb-builders these men were probably unusually privileged. There were 60 qualified workmen, as well as juniors and apprentices. They were divided into two teams, each under the direction of a foreman and his deputy. The week was ten days long and included two days' holiday. There were also holidays for religious festivals. The working day was in two shifts, each four hours long, with a rest at midday. This reconstruction shows what the village might have looked like.

The village was surrounded by a wall. The main street was straight and narrow, and lined with small houses, mostly identical in design.

During the week the men lived in barracks in the Valley of the Kings, returning to the village for weekends and holidays.

Wages were paid in goods – food, drink, linen, oil, fuel and salt, with bonuses of silver on special occasions. The foremen were paid twice as much as ordinary workmen.

A doctor and two scribes† were attached to the village. The scribes kept records of work, tools and wages, and wrote down the villagers' questions to the oracle†.

The king provided 15 female slaves to grind grain for the villagers. Male servants carried water, cut firewood and washed clothes.

Tools and techniques

Here is a selection of different Egyptian crafts, showing some of the tools and techniques that were used.

Most cutting tools were made from flint and obsidian.

A bow-drill was used to drill holes in beads and inside stone vases.

Stone vase

Carpentry

This carpenter's workshop has been reconstructed from a painting.

Polishing wood with sandstone

Sawing

Cutting wood with a saw

Making a hollow with a mallet and chisel

Some carpenters' tools have survived in tombs. They were made of copper and bronze, and had wooden handles.

Metalworking

Egyptian metalsmiths worked in copper, bronze, silver, gold and electrum. This scene shows copper being smelted (extracted from the ore). Using bellows to keep the fire blazing fiercely, the ore was heated until it melted. The molten metal was then poured into a mould to shape it.

Bellows

Molten copper

Mould

Lost-wax casting

A technique called lost-wax casting was used to shape finer objects such as ornaments. This process is still in use.

The statue was modelled in wax around a clay core, then covered in clay to form the mould. Pegs kept the clay in place.

The clay was then heated and the wax melted.

The wax was poured away and the empty space was filled with molten metal. When it cooled, the clay was broken, exposing the statue.

Pottery

Pots were shaped on a potter's wheel. The pots were then fired (baked) in a wood-burning kiln. The fire had to be tended carefully to stop the temperature from dropping.

Kiln

Wheel

Paper-making

The Egyptians wrote on a paper called papyrus made from papyrus reeds. Strips of pith from inside the reed were laid flat. Another layer was laid across them, at right angles. This was pounded and pressed under heavy weights, until the paper was welded together.

Papyrus

Strips of pith

Boat-building

Lightweight ▶ papyrus boats were made by tying bundles of reeds together.

To build a wooden boat, planks were lashed and pegged together with ▼ dowels.

Glass-making

Glass containers were made by dipping a sandy clay core into a dish of molten glass. Patterns were made by winding glass threads around the core, and then heating and flattening them.

Egyptian glass vase

Weaving

The first Egyptian looms were laid out horizontally on the ground, and held in place with pegs. ▼

From about 1500BC vertical looms were in use. These were more practical to use indoors as they took up less space.

Leather working

Leatherworkers made a range of things, including sandals, shields, armour, arrow quivers and furniture.

The Amarna letters

In 1887 an Egyptian peasant woman, digging for mud-bricks in the ruins of the city of Amarna (see page 50), discovered several hundred baked clay tablets. They turned out to be government records from Akhenaten's† reign, consisting of letters written to the pharaoh by a number of foreign kings and princes. Although many of the tablets were damaged or destroyed before they reached the experts, the ones that survived have given historians a vivid picture of the Egyptian world in about 1350BC. The tablets (which are known as the Amarna letters) provide interesting information about the politics and diplomacy of the time.

At the start of Akhenaten's reign there were four great empires – those of Egypt, Mitanni, Babylon and the Hittites. Other major powers included Assyria, Cyprus and Mycenae.

Great importance was attached to the way rulers addressed one another. 'Brother' was only used by equals, 'father' by an independent ruler to a friendly but more powerful one, and 'lord' by a subject prince to his conqueror. We know that the King of Babylon was furious when he discovered that his former subject, the King of Assyria, had addressed the pharaoh as 'brother'.

The pharaoh

Assyrian messenger reading a letter

Ambassadors, equipped with letters of introduction and requests for safe conduct, travelled far afield to negotiate on behalf of their rulers. Messengers maintained a courier service, carrying royal correspondence in sealed pouches around their necks.

Mitanni bride

Marriages were a useful way of cementing alliances. Tuthmosis IV married a Mitannian princess as part of a peace settlement. His son and grandson also married Mitannian princesses. Egyptian princesses, on the other hand, never married foreigners, presumably to prevent a foreigner from having a claim to the Egyptian throne. When a Babylonian king asked for an Egyptian bride, he was firmly refused.

There were regular exchanges of gifts between kings, sometimes as a result of specific requests. In one letter, a Hittite king asked his 'brother' in Babylon to send him young stallions (because old ones would not survive the winters). A Mitanni king asked for gold, claiming that 'in my brother's land [Egypt] gold is as the dust'. There were complaints if a messenger arrived without a gift or if the quality of a gift was inferior.

These Babylonians are presenting horses to the Hittite king.

Diplomatic etiquette was important. It was considered necessary to exchange letters of congratulation or condolence where appropriate. On one occasion, the King of Babylon complained bitterly when he received no letters or presents from Queen Meritaten of Egypt during an illness.

However all this politeness concealed grim struggles for power. It appears that many Egyptian subject princes wrote to the pharaoh accusing rival princes of disloyalty, in the hope of taking over their land. One of them, the ambitious Prince of Amurru, attacked the cities of fellow Egyptian vassals†, claiming that they were disloyal to Egypt. One of his victims, Prince Rib-addi of Byblos, begged for Akhenaten's help, but his pleas were ignored. This attitude cost Akhenaten the northern provinces of his empire. The Prince of Amurru, having conquered several cities, defected to the Hittites, joined by other princes who believed that the pharaoh would be as indifferent to them as he had been to Rib-addi.

Ramesses the Great and Dynasty XIX

Horemheb†, the last king of Dynasty XVIII (see page 51), died without a son. The throne passed to his Vizier, a former army officer called Ramesses. He became Ramesses I and founded a new dynasty, Dynasty XIX. The new king was already an old man, and was soon succeeded by his son Seti (named after the god Set, one of the patron gods of his family).

Seti I

Seti I had the task of preserving the remains of Egypt's eastern empire from the expansion of the Hittites†. He fought several long and successful campaigns, but each time he returned home the Hittites took the opportunity to reoccupy and seize some Egyptian territory.

Seti restored some of the monuments damaged during Akhenaten's reign (see pages 50-51) and built new temples to the old gods.

Seti I ▲
(1303-1289BC)

In order to strengthen the new dynasty, Seti had his son Ramesses crowned during his own lifetime. He also provided him with a harem†, with the result that when Seti died, Ramesses II succeeded peacefully to the throne, having already fathered several children.

Ramesses II

Ramesses II reigned for 67 years and lived to be over 90. He was a great warrior (see page 70) and a prolific builder, commissioning temples throughout Egypt and Nubia. He was also an excellent self-publicist. Amongst other things, he claimed that the god Amun was his real father.

Ramesses II (1289-1224BC) ▲

This is a reconstruction of the hypostyle hall of the Temple of Amun at Karnak, built by Ramesses II.

▲ The most spectacular of Ramesses' temples were the two that were cut into the rock face at Abu Simbel in Nubia, one of which is reconstructed here.

Ramesses' other buildings included fortresses to protect the western frontier from the Libyans, and a city and palace, known as the House of Ramesses, which was built near the site of the old Hyksos† capital at Avaris. He also had his name engraved on some of the buildings and statues of previous kings, making it look as if he had built them as well.

Later generations of Egyptians saw him as one of the most successful kings in their history, although this judgement owes a certain amount to the power of propaganda.

◄ This painted relief† shows Ramesses II overpowering his enemies. The three prisoners shown are a Libyan, a Syrian and a Nubian.

Ramesses had many wives and concubines† who between them had about 200 children. He built the second temple at Abu Simbel for his chief queen, Nefertari†, as well as a tomb in the Valley of the Queens near Thebes. When Nefertari died, Ramesses married their daughter Meryet-Amun, and another wife, Isi-nofret, became chief queen. His other wives included his daughter Bint-Anath†, one of his sisters, and a Hittite princess.

This wall- ▶ painting from Nefertari's tomb shows the Queen playing a board game.

The struggle with the Hittites

In the first half of his reign Ramesses was engaged in a bitter struggle with the expanding empire of the Hittites†. After some successful campaigning, he set out in year 5* to capture the city of Kadesh, an ally of the Hittites.

Ramesses was tricked by two bedouin† who were secretly working for the Hittites. He approached Kadesh, accompanied only by his bodyguard and the division of Amun**. The bedouin had claimed that the Hittite army was about 200km (120 miles) away, but it was actually concealed behind the city, having already smashed the division of Re. The Hittites appeared just as Ramesses was setting up camp. Although the Egyptians were greatly outnumbered, Ramesses led his troops courageously and held out until reinforcements arrived. The reconstruction below shows what the battle might have looked like.

Finally the Hittites and their allies were defeated, but the Egyptian army had suffered serious losses and had to return to Egypt in ruins. Nevertheless the account that Ramesses carved on the walls of many Egyptian temples describes an overwhelming victory, won single-handed.

Eventually fear of the Assyrians (see pages 74-75) brought the conflict to an end. In year 21, Ramesses signed a peace treaty with the Hittites.

The Battle of Kadesh

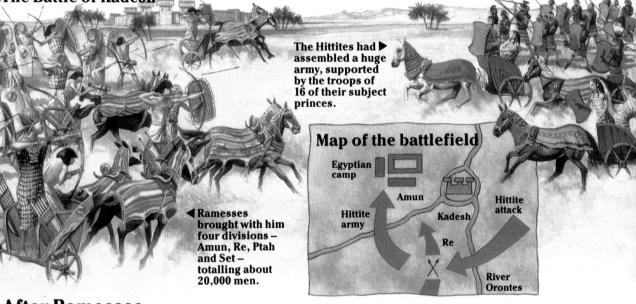

The Hittites had ▶ assembled a huge army, supported by the troops of 16 of their subject princes.

◀ Ramesses brought with him four divisions – Amun, Re, Ptah and Set – totalling about 20,000 men.

Map of the battlefield

Egyptian camp

Amun

Hittite army

Kadesh

Hittite attack

Re

River Orontes

After Ramesses

Ramesses reigned for so long that his 12 eldest sons died before him. He was succeeded by the 13th, Merenptah. Merenptah fought an invasion by Libyans and another by Sea Peoples (see opposite page). An inscription from his reign also mentions that the Egyptians had conquered the people of Israel. Merenptah maintained the spirit of his father's treaty with the Hittites, sending them grain during a severe famine. This is the first known record of international aid.

After Merenptah's death there was a period of confusion, as the descendants of Ramesses II competed with each other for the throne. Usurpers† seized power during the reign of Merenptah's son Seti II, who died without heirs. A Syrian may have taken control for a time, and for a brief period Tawosret†, sister-wife of Seti II, reigned alone as a 'king'. Dynasty XIX ended in turmoil.

Key dates: Dynasty XIX

1305-1186BC	Dynasty XIX
1305-1303BC	Reign of Ramesses I
1303-1289BC	Reign of Seti I
1289-1224BC	Reign of Ramesses II
1284BC	Battle of Kadesh

1270BC Ramesses II makes a peace treaty with the Hittites. They agree to support each other in the event of attack by a third party.

1224-1204BC	Reign of Merenptah
1204-1200BC	Reign of Amenmesse
1200-1194BC	Reign of Seti II
1194-1188BC	Reign of Sitptah
1194-1186BC	Reign of Tawosret

These gold earrings were found in the tomb of the daughter of Seti II and Queen Tawosret.

Ramesses III and the Sea Peoples

From the warring descendants of Dynasty XIX emerged Set-nakht, who became the founder of Dynasty XX. Although he may not have had the best claim to the throne, he was the strongest candidate. After a short reign, he was succeeded by his son Ramesses III. Ramesses was conscious of the weakness of his claim and attempted to

imitate the great Ramesses II, even naming his children after Ramesses' children.

The temple at Medinet Habu, built by Ramesses III

The Sea Peoples

In years 5 and 11*, poor harvests drove the Libyans to invade Egypt in search of new land. They were aided by people known as the Sea Peoples. This was the name the Egyptians gave to a loosely connected group of raiders and settlers from Greece, the Mediterranean islands and the west coast of Turkey. The Sea Peoples were first mentioned in texts in the reign of Amenhotep III. Driven by troubles in their homelands, they began by raiding around the Mediterranean. Later they brought their families with them and settled in areas that were already well-populated.

Sea Peoples travelling in carts

In year 8 a battle fleet of Sea Peoples cruised the eastern Mediterranean, capturing Cyprus and mainland coastal towns. Meanwhile an army was making its way south overland, accompanied by women and children riding in carts. After demolishing the Hittite empire, the Sea Peoples carried on towards Egypt, leaving a trail of ruined cities behind them.

As the army and fleet of Sea Peoples converged on Egypt, Ramesses gathered together all his resources to face the expected attack. Every man of military age was called up to fight; there were no reserves. Ramesses led his forces in two great battles, at sea and on land, and the Sea Peoples were finally defeated. This saved Egyptian civilization and changed the course of history in the Mediterranean (see pages 72-73).

Ramesses recorded his victories on the walls of the temple at Medinet Habu. The sea battle was the first in history about which any details have survived.

Problems at home

However, despite Ramesses' military successes, Egypt was in trouble. The eastern empire was now gone, and trade in the Mediterranean had been disrupted for years, depriving the country of much wealth. Prices rose rapidly, and signs of strain on the economy began to show. Several government officials were dismissed for dishonesty and incompetence. The wages of the royal tomb-builders were unpaid and the men went on the first recorded strike in history.

The harem conspiracy

Several of Ramesses' sons by his two chief queens died young, and there was a plot to kill him and put one of his sons by a minor wife on the throne. The conspirators, who included leading courtiers and soldiers, as well as members of the harem†, were caught and tried. The ring-leaders were condemned to death. Among the royal mummies of this period, archaeologists have found the body of a young man who had not been mummified. He had been bound, and put into his coffin alive. It is possible that this was the prince who had been involved in the plot.

Ramesses III was the last great warrior pharaoh. Eight more kings called Ramesses succeeded him, but their reigns were undistinguished and often short, and royal power declined (see page 73).

The royal tomb robberies

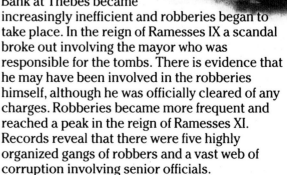

After Ramesses III's death, the guarding of the tombs on the West Bank at Thebes became increasingly inefficient and robberies began to take place. In the reign of Ramesses IX a scandal broke out involving the mayor who was responsible for the tombs. There is evidence that he may have been involved in the robberies himself, although he was officially cleared of any charges. Robberies became more frequent and reached a peak in the reign of Ramesses XI. Records reveal that there were five highly organized gangs of robbers and a vast web of corruption involving senior officials.

The world after the Sea Peoples

The attacks of the Sea Peoples (see page 71) brought about dramatic changes in the Mediterranean world. The destruction of the Hittites† left the way open for the rise of a new empire, that of the Assyrians (see pages 74-75), as well as a number of small independent states. Some Hittites headed south and formed new (Neo-Hittite) states, such as Carchemish, in the former southern provinces of the empire.

A group of nomads† called Aramaeans left the desert fringes and settled in fertile areas. They spread into Assyria and Babylonia and the area now called Syria, establishing independent cities such as Damascus. By 750BC Aramaic had become the language of international diplomacy.

In Greece, the civilization of Mycenae (see pages 106-107) soon collapsed and the Phoenicians became the leading traders.

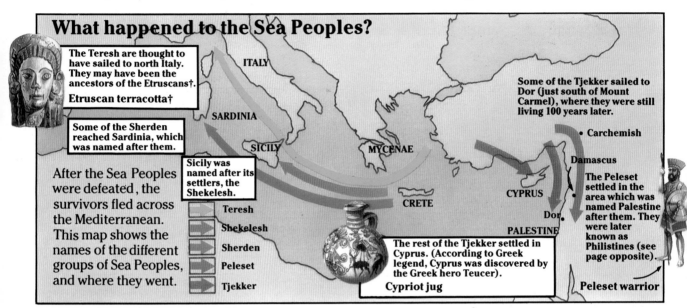

What happened to the Sea Peoples?

The Teresh are thought to have sailed to north Italy. They may have been the ancestors of the Etruscans†.

Etruscan terracotta†

Some of the Sherden reached Sardinia, which was named after them.

After the Sea Peoples were defeated, the survivors fled across the Mediterranean. This map shows the names of the different groups of Sea Peoples, and where they went.

Sicily was named after its settlers, the Shekelesh.

Teresh
Shekelesh
Sherden
Peleset
Tjekker

Some of the Tjekker sailed to Dor (just south of Mount Carmel), where they were still living 100 years later.

• Carchemish

Damascus

The Peleset settled in the area which was named Palestine after them. They were later known as Philistines (see page opposite).

The rest of the Tjekker settled in Cyprus. (According to Greek legend, Cyprus was discovered by the Greek hero Teucer).

Cypriot jug

Peleset warrior

ITALY

SARDINIA

SICILY

MYCENAE

CRETE

CYPRUS

Dor

PALESTINE

The Phoenicians

The Sea Peoples destroyed some of the great cities of Canaan, like Ugarit (see page 25), but in coastal cities such as Byblos, Beirut, Sidon and Tyre, energetic merchants took over from the Mycenaeans as the leading traders of the Mediterranean. The inhabitants of these cities from about 1100BC are known as Phoenicians. The name is derived from *phoinix*, the Greek word for a purple dye, which was their most valuable export. The Phoenicians also exported cedarwood, glass and carved ivory, and carried cargo for other nations. They developed a simple alphabetic script which was later adapted by the Greeks and became the basis of our alphabet.

The purple dye came from the Murex shellfish and could produce a range of colours from rose to violet.

Map of Phoenician colonies

SPAIN
CORSICA
SARDINIA
Gades
Carthage
SICILY
Byblos
Beirut
Sidon
Tyre

NORTH AFRICA
▨ Phoenician colonies

The Phoenicians were skilled sailors and explorers. They led an Egyptian expedition around Africa and set up trading colonies as far west as Gades (now Cadiz) in Spain, possibly as early as 1000BC. Their most famous colony was at Carthage in North Africa. The Carthaginians built a great harbour and fleet of ships. They later came into conflict with the Romans† over territorial rights in the Mediterranean.

The Philistines

The Philistines (formerly Peleset) were warriors and merchants who occupied the area known as Palestine. They dominated their neighbours, including the Israelites (see below), for nearly 200 years. The Philistines appear to have had some control over the local trade in iron, and some served as mercenaries in Egyptian frontier forts. They were led by the *Seren*, local princes who ruled from the five cities of Gaza, Ashkalon, Ashdad, Ekron and Gath.

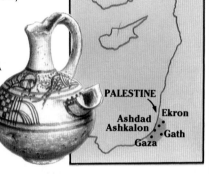

Philistine decorated pottery was considered the finest in the region. Many of the designs reveal Mycenaean influence.

The tribes of Israel

The Israelites were a Semitic people who were divided into 12 tribes, led by men known as Judges. Experts believe that they were the first people to worship one God*. In about 1030BC, the Israelites went to Samuel, one of the Judges and the most important priest, asking him to appoint a king to lead them against the Philistines. Saul (c.1030-1010BC) was appointed king, and he was succeeded by David (c.1010BC-970BC).

David fought many wars, united his people, and turned Israel into a major power in the area. Jerusalem, which he captured in about 1005BC, became the capital city. Israelite power reached its height under Solomon (c.970-930BC). After his death, the kingdom split into two: Israel, with its capital at Shechem, and Judah, with its capital at Jerusalem.

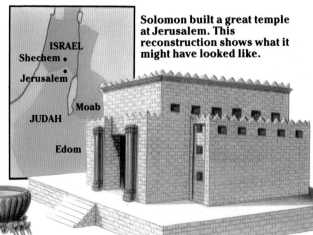

Solomon built a great temple at Jerusalem. This reconstruction shows what it might have looked like.

The Third Intermediate Period

Royal power in Egypt declined after the reign of Ramesses III. High-ranking officials ruled the country and there was widespread corruption and incompetence. Libyans invaded and settled, Nubia broke away, and Egypt lost control of the eastern empire. By the end of the reign of Ramesses XI, real power rested with Heri-hor†, a general who became Vizier and High Priest of Amun. Heri-hor controlled Upper Egypt, and the Delta was governed by his son Smendes, who married Ramesses' daughter Princess Henttawy. Their descendants ruled from the Delta city of Tanis, as kings of Dynasty XXI, while the High Priests of Amun controlled Upper Egypt. The great days of the New Kingdom now gave way to the Third Intermediate Period (1069-664BC).

Coffin of Princess Maakare (c.1065-1045), daughter of a High Priest ▶ of Amun.

These gold vessels are from the ▲ royal burials of Dynasty XXI at Tanis.

Without an empire to control, the kings of Dynasty XXI concentrated on trade, but they were still capable of some military activity. To protect his trading interests, Pharaoh Si-Amun captured the Philistine city of Gaza and gave it as a dowry† to his daughter, who married King Solomon† of Israel.

Libyan influence increased. Shoshenq, a Libyan chief, married his son Osorkon to the Egyptian Princess Ma'at-ka-Re. In 945BC Shoshenq became king and founded Dynasty XXII. Family feuds led to civil wars and rival dynasties were set up. By 730BC there were five kings in Egypt.

In 728BC Egypt was conquered by a Nubian king called Piankhi† (or Piye), who united the country under Dynasty XXV. Having been ruled by Egypt for so long, the Nubians regarded themselves as the real heirs of Egyptian civilization and encouraged a revival of Egyptian culture. However, some Egyptian princes refused to accept them and supported an invasion by Assyrians.

This finally led to the Nubian retreat in 664BC. Prince Necho† of Sais, who was executed by the Nubians for his alliance with the Assyrians, was regarded by Egyptians as the first king of the next dynasty, Dynasty XXVI (see page 78), although he never ruled Egypt.

Piankhi's son, King Taharka (690-664BC)

*Although Akhenaten† introduced the worship of one god in Egypt, this was abandoned after his reign.

The Assyrians

The original homeland of the Assyrians was a small area on the upper part of the River Tigris, around the cities of Ashur, Nineveh and Arbela. The area was culturally under the influence of its richer neighbours in Sumer and Akkad (see pages 6-8 and 24), and often under their political control as well.

However, some time before 2000BC, Assyria was invaded by large numbers of Semitic Amorites (see page 25), who established a line of kings. Under their leadership, the Assyrians built up a huge empire, which was at its greatest in the period known as the New Assyrian Empire (c.1000-612BC). They were an aggressive, militaristic people and made many enemies, among their neighbours as well as among their subjects. The empire was overthrown in 612BC by Medes and Babylonians (see pages 76-77).

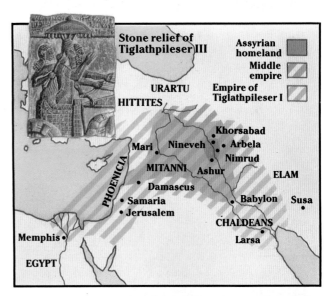

Stone relief of Tiglathpileser III

Assyrian homeland
Middle empire
Empire of Tiglathpileser I

URARTU
HITTITES
Mari
Nineveh
Khorsabad
Arbela
Nimrud
MITANNI
Ashur
ELAM
Damascus
Samaria
Jerusalem
Babylon
Susa
CHALDEANS
Larsa
Memphis
EGYPT
PHOENICIA

Assyrian cities

To reflect their power and success, the kings of the imperial age built themselves magnificent palaces and cities, such as Khorsabad and Nimrud. The walls of the palaces were decorated with painted stone reliefs†, which provide information about the lives of the Assyrians.

This is a reconstruction of the throneroom of Ashurnasirpal II at the palace at Nimrud.

Like the Sumerians, the Assyrians built ziggurats† for their gods.

Aqueducts† of mud-brick were built to provide a water supply for the palaces. The water was carried in a pipe with a waterproof lining of bitumen (tar) and stone. Arches carried the pipes across valleys.

Winged bulls with human heads feature in statues and reliefs found at Nimrud and Khorsabad.

Hunting

Hunting appears to have been a great passion of the Assyrian kings. Lion hunts in particular seem to have had an almost religious significance.

Relief† showing a lion hunt

Religion

The name Assyria comes from the chief god, Ashur, who gave his name to the main city. Many of the other important deities had Mesopotamian origins.

Ashur

Warfare and empire-building

The Assyrians were tough warriors. From the earliest days they had to defend themselves against the Mesopotamians and hostile mountain tribes. From about 800BC, they introduced a series of military reforms and developed a formidable permanent army. Campaigns were now better organized and troops were well-equipped. Their weapons included bows, slings, swords, daggers, spears, battle axes and maces. Assyrian soldiers wore leather or chainmail armour and carried shields. Most soldiers fought on foot, but there were also chariot divisions.

The Assyrians were particularly good at besieging cities.

Scaling ladders were used for climbing walls.

For demolishing walls, they used cleverly shielded battering rams that protected the men operating them.

Camels

Some Assyrian reliefs show camels carrying goods or Arab† warriors into battle. Camels were probably first domesticated in about the 2nd millennium BC. They are better adapted than donkeys for desert journeys; they can carry twice as much, they do not need to feed and drink as frequently, and they can travel faster. This enabled people to cross long stretches of desert. This was especially useful for transporting goods from Arabia.

Stone relief showing camels

The Assyrians built good roads to ensure that the army could move quickly. The kings demanded annual tribute† from their subjects, and often collected it in person. If a city refused to pay, or if a conquered people rebelled, they were dealt with ruthlessly. The city and its surroundings were destroyed, and captives were tortured to death or made into slaves. Entire populations were sometimes deported to other parts of the empire. This deprived the rebels of resources and support, and was therefore an effective way of smashing their resistance. The Assyrians relied mainly on fear of punishment to keep the different provinces of their empire under control.

Key dates

c.2000-1450BC The Old Assyrian Empire; during this period there is a very profitable trading relationship with Anatolia. This comes to an end with the expansion of the Hittites† in about 1500BC.

Assyrian merchants ▶ carried their goods on the backs of donkeys.

1813-1781BC Reign of Shamshi-Adad, a great warrior who conquers an empire from Mari to Babylon. His son Ishme-Dagan is defeated by Rimsin of Larsa, and later becomes a vassal† of Hammurabi of Babylon (see page 25).

c.1450BC Assyria passes under the control of the Mitannians (see page 44).

1363-1000BC The Middle Assyrian Empire; Ashur-uballit I (1363-1328BC) restores Assyrian independence.

1273-1244BC Reign of Shalmaneser I, who acquires the former eastern province of the Mitanni kingdom.

1114-1076BC Reign of Tiglathpileser I, who makes great conquests. He marches west to the Mediterranean, campaigns against Aramaeans (see page 72) and Phrygians†, and encroaches on Babylonian territory.

c.1000-612BC
The New Assyrian Empire; the greatest period of conquest and expansion.

Gold jewellery from Nimrud from the New Assyrian Empire

745-727BC Reign of Tiglathpileser III, who conquers Damascus and Phoenicia.

726-722BC Reign of Shalmaneser V, who conquers the kingdom of Israel (see page 73) and destroys the capital (which is now called Samaria). Many Israelites are deported to Mesopotamia and new people are brought in. They marry the few remaining Israelites, and their descendants are later known as Samaritans.

721-705BC Reign of Sargon II†; he conquers the state of Urartu (between the Black and Caspian Seas) and builds a magnificent palace at Khorsabad.

704-681BC Reign of Sennacherib†; he invades Egypt, but withdraws, and sacks Babylon in 689BC.

680-669BC Reign of Esarhaddon†, who captures Memphis in Egypt.

668-627BC Reign of Ashurbanipal II; he sacks Thebes (665BC), Babylon (648BC) and Susa (639BC).

614-612BC Ashur and Nineveh fall to the Medes and Babylonians. By 608BC Assyria ceases to exist.

The Babylonians

The Kassite rulers of Babylon (see page 25) were thrown out in about 1158BC after a series of clashes with their neighbours, the Assyrians (see pages 74-75) and the Elamites†. After an unsettled period Babylonian rule was eventually restored and several short dynasties were established.

In the 7th century BC the Assyrians claimed control of Babylon and twice sacked the city for rebelling against their rule. In 627BC the Babylonians succeeded in overthrowing them,

with the help of the Medes (see opposite) and the Chaldeans, a group of Semitic† tribes who had settled on the coast of the Persian Gulf.

The New Babylonian (or Chaldean) Empire (626-539BC) was one of the greatest periods of Babylonian history. The Babylonians conquered a huge empire, which was at its height under Nebuchadnezzar II† (605-562BC). It was finally invaded by Persians in 539BC and absorbed into the Persian empire (see map opposite).

Babylon under Nebuchadnezzar II

This is a reconstruction of Babylon as rebuilt by Nebuchadnezzar II. The city became the richest in the world.

There were many ziggurats† in the city. The greatest was built by Nebuchadnezzar II for the god Marduk. It consisted of seven platforms with a small shrine on top.

One of Nebuchadnezzar's wives was a princess from Medea. According to legend, she missed the mountains of her homeland so much that he built her an artificial mountain, terraced like a ziggurat, and planted with trees and bushes. It was known as the Hanging Gardens of Babylon.

On New Year's Day the Babylonians celebrated the marriage of the god Marduk to the mother goddess Sarpanitum with a great procession. The marriage was supposed to ensure the fertility and prosperity of the land for the coming year.

The gate at the north entrance to the city was called the Ishtar Gate, after the city's chief goddess, Ishtar, the goddess of love and war. The bricks were glazed in blue and decorated with bulls and dragons.

Key dates

1158-1027BC Dynasty of Isin; the most notable king is Nebuchadnezzar I **(1126-1105BC)** who restores national pride after the sack of Babylon by the Kassites.

1026-1006 Dynasty of Sealand

1005-986BC Dynasty of Bazi

985-980BC Elamite Dynasty

979-732 Period known by historians as Dynasty "E"; the Babylonian Chronicles, a record of historical events and astronomical observations, is begun.

731-626BC Ninth Dynasty; the Chaldeans and the Assyrians struggle for control of Babylon. The Chaldean leader Merodach-Baladin II† twice becomes king **(721-710BC** and **703BC).** The Assyrians claim sovereignty and sack the city as a punishment for rebelling.

626-539BC The Chaldean Dynasty or Neo (New) Babylonian Empire; Nabopolassar wins back Babylon, overthrows the Assyrians and takes over most of their land.

605-562BC Reign of Nebuchadnezzar II

597BC Nebuchadnezzar II occupies Jerusalem, capital of Judah (see page 73), and carries off many of its leading citizens to Babylon. After a revolt in **587-586BC** many Jews† are deported to Babylon and their descendants kept there until after the Persian conquest (see below). This is known as the Babylonian Captivity.

561-560BC Reign of Evil-Merodach

559-556BC Reign of Neriglissar

556-539BC Reign of Nabonidus†

539BC Babylon is taken over by the Persians (see opposite). They rule until **331BC,** followed by the Macedonians† **(330-307BC),** and the Seleucids† **(311-125BC).**

The Persians

In about 1500BC Aryan† tribes began settling in the area which is now named after them – Iran. Eventually one of these tribes, the Medes, emerged as the dominant group. By 670BC they had united under one kingdom, Medea, with a capital at Ecbatana. During the reign of Cyaxares, the Medes allied with the Babylonians (see opposite) and overthrew the Assyrian empire (see pages 74-75).

Another tribe, the Persians, established a rival kingdom under a ruling family called the Achaemenids in about 700BC. At first the Persians played a subordinate role to the Medes, but in 550BC Cyrus II† of Persia defeated his grandfather, King Astyages of Medea, and took over his lands. Cyrus went on to conquer the Kingdom of Lydia in 547-546BC and the Babylonian empire in 539BC. In 525BC Cyrus's son Cambyses II† conquered Egypt.

The Persian empire c.485BC

LYDIA
IONIA
ASSYRIA
MEDEA
Ecbatana
Susa
Babylon
PERSIA
Persepolis
EGYPT

Gold armlet

Babylonian empire

Persian empire

Darius I

The empire reached its greatest extent under Darius I†. He was an able and successful ruler and established a fair and efficient code of laws. He divided the empire into provinces, known as 'satrapies', each run by a *satrap* (governor). A system of roads was built to link Persia to its far-flung provinces, and to enable soldiers and messengers to travel quickly and easily. Officials known as the 'King's Ears' went on regular tours of inspection, reporting directly back to the king. Subject peoples had to pay tribute† and to provide soldiers and ships for the army and navy.

Although the capital was at Susa, Darius I began building a huge palace complex at Persepolis.

Religion

The early Persians worshipped many deities. Their priests were famous for their skills as sorcerers; they were called *magi* (the origin of the word magic). One *magus* called Zarathustra (or Zoroaster) worshipped a single god, Ahura Mazda, who created all things. Evil was represented by the god's enemy, Angra Mainyu (or Ahriman).

The wars with Greece

Between 500BC and 494BC Greek colonists in Ionia (western Turkey) rebelled against their Persian rulers. They were helped by the city states of the Greek mainland. This provoked a series of wars between Greece and Persia which lasted from 490 to 449BC (see page 136-137).

The Persian army had an elite regiment of 10,000 men known as the Immortals. Two of them are shown in this relief†.

The decline of the empire

From about 465BC the Persian empire was in decline. Its size made it difficult to govern and frequent revolts by subject peoples put a great strain on the government. Power struggles at court also undermined royal power. In Egypt there were a number of major revolts against the Persians, and the Egyptians eventually succeeded in winning independence from 404BC to 343BC.

The Persians were such unpopular rulers that in 336BC Alexander the Great† of Macedonia was able to lead his army into Egypt without resistance (see page 170). By 330BC the whole of the Persian empire had come under his control.

Key dates

c.1500BC   Aryan tribes begin settling in Persia.

c.700-600BC   Kingdoms established in Medea and Persia.

550BC   Cyrus II of Persia unites Persia and Medea under his rule. He conquers the empires of Lydia and Babylon.

525BC   Cambyses II conquers Egypt.

522-485BC   Reign of Darius I; the empire reaches its greatest extent.

500-494BC   Greek colonists in Ionia rebel against Persia.

490BC   Persians invade Greece and are defeated at the Battle of Marathon.

480-479BC   Persians invade Greece; they win at Thermopylae and sack Athens, but are defeated at sea (Artemision, Salamis and Mykale), and on land (Plataea).

330BC   Alexander the Great conquers the Persian empire.

The Late Period (Dynasties XXVI-XXX)

In 664BC, the Nubian kings (see page 73), were replaced by a native Egyptian dynasty (Dynasty XXVI). The new kings ruled from Sais and are sometimes called the Saite kings. The Assyrian invasions (see page 75) and discontent with Nubian rule had left Egypt poor, weak and divided, and it took the new pharaoh, Psamtek I, about nine

years to assert his control over the whole land. He restored Egypt's independence from the Assyrians (who were still officially his overlords†), by stopping tribute† payments.

◀ **Psamtek I and the goddess Hathor**

Under the Saite kings, Egypt entered a new era of power, peace and prosperity, known as the Late Period. Industry and agriculture recovered and trade increased. In order to promote trade, foreigners were encouraged to settle in Egypt. Greek merchants set up colonies in Naucratis and Daphnae, and there was a flourishing Jewish colony in Elephantine. After the fall of Jerusalem in 587BC, many Jews† settled in the Delta.

Bronze men from the sea

Greek mercenaries† were hired by many Late Period kings. According to tradition, the goddess Wadjet promised the throne to Psamtek if he employed 'bronze men from the sea'. One day he saw some Greek soldiers who were shipwrecked off the Egyptian coast. Their bronze armour convinced him that these were the men described by the goddess. He employed them as mercenaries and went on to become king.

A Greek soldier

The God's Wife

During the Third Intermediate Period a princess was chosen to take the title 'God's Wife'. She never married, but instead devoted her life to the god Amun. The God's Wife was rich and powerful. She headed the priesthood of Amun and governed Upper Egypt on behalf of the king. Each God's Wife adopted a girl to succeed her, who was usually a daughter of the reigning king. At the start of Dynasty XXVI, the reigning God's Wife was a Nubian princess, Amenirdis II† (shown here).

Late Period art and culture

As the Egyptian economy improved, its art and culture rapidly recovered. In an attempt to regain their former greatness, the Egyptians tried to recreate the past. They studied old documents, repaired temples, revived ancient cults and copied the artistic styles of earlier periods.

During the Late Period wealthy people were buried in deep tomb-shafts in massive stone coffins called *sarcophagi*. The *sarcophagi* were decorated with pictures and texts, and usually had a portrait of the dead person on the lid. Inside the coffins archaeologists have sometimes found the mummy† covered with an elaborate beaded shroud†, like the one shown here.

Late Period mummy covering.

Meroë

Throughout this period Nubia was ruled by the descendants of the Nubian kings who had governed Egypt under Dynasty XXV. In the 6th century BC they abandoned their old capital, Napata, and moved south to Meroë. The Greeks called them *aithiops* (meaning 'dark-skinned'). This is the origin of the name Ethiopia, although modern Ethiopia lies south-east of Meroë. Meroitic culture was strongly influenced by Egypt, but it was also open to Greek and Indian influences. In the 3rd century BC the people of Meroë invented their own alphabetic script.

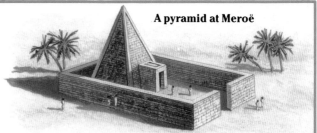

A pyramid at Meroë

The country around Meroë was greener, more fertile, and better irrigated than the Napata region. There were also large, valuable deposits of iron ore. The Meroitic people traded with Egypt, the Mediterranean, and with Arabia, East Africa and India, via the Red Sea.

Relations with Nubia

Although the Saite kings tried to maintain peace with Nubia, relations between the two countries were strained. The Egyptians resented their former conquerers, and cut out the names of the kings of Dynasty XXV from their monuments. After rumours of a Nubian attack, Psamtek II (595-589BC) invaded Nubia, marching as far south as Abu Simbel. Names carved on the walls by his Greek mercenaries can still be seen today.

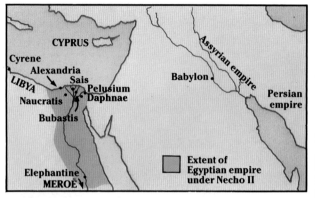

Empire and exploration

There was a brief revival of Egypt's imperial role during the reign of Necho II (610-595BC). The Assyrian empire was under attack by Medes and Babylonians, and finally collapsed in 608BC. For a short period before the rise of Nebuchadnezzar II (see page 76), Necho was left in control of a large part of Egypt's former eastern empire.

Necho sent an expedition, led by Phoenician sailors, to explore the African coast. It became the first to sail around the entire continent of Africa.

Necho's expedition sailed down the Red Sea and round the Cape, returning to Egypt via the Straits of Gibraltar (then known as the Pillars of Herakles).

Bast

The popularity of the mother goddess Bast* (shown here) grew during the Late Period. The Greek historian Herodotus† described a festival at the goddess's city of Bubastis. He reported that people arrived by boat from all over Egypt and spent days and nights dancing, singing and feasting in her honour.

A revolt against the Greeks

Ordinary Egyptians resented the presence of large numbers of Greek merchants and soldiers in Egypt. This discontent erupted into a full-scale rebellion when King Apries thoughtlessly appeared in public in Greek armour, just after his army had been defeated by Greeks. Apries was deposed and executed, and the leader of the revolt, General Amasis, became king. However, although he reduced Greek trading privileges, he continued using Greek mercenaries and maintained friendly relations with Greece.

The Persian period

In 525BC, Amasis's son Psamtek III was defeated at the Battle of Pelusium by a new empire-builder, Cambyses† of Persia (see page 77). From 525BC to 404BC the Persians ruled Egypt as Dynasty XVII. They were unpopular rulers, and some showed no respect for Egyptian culture and religion. Rebellions broke out in the reign of Cambyses' grandson, Xerxes†. The Greeks (who were also enemies of the Persians) sent a fleet to help the rebels, and it took Xerxes six years to restore order.

In 404BC the Egyptians succeeded in gaining their independence under Dynasties XXVIII-XXX. The greatest kings of this period were Nectanebo I and Nectanebo II. They kept Egypt peaceful and prosperous and embarked on an ambitious building programme. In 343BC the country was reconquered by the Persians, who punished the Egyptians by plundering the land.

Alexander the Great

According to Egyptian legend, Alexander the Great (shown here) was the son of Nectanebo II, the last native Egyptian king. Nectanebo was said to have great magic powers, which he used one night to fly to Macedonia.

Between 334BC and 331BC the entire Persian empire was conquered by Alexander the Great†. He arrived in Egypt in 332BC, and was hailed as a liberator and accepted as pharaoh. He took care to respect Egyptian religion and culture and founded a new city, named Alexandria, on the Mediterranean coast. On his death in 323BC, his generals divided the empire between them. Egypt came under the control of General Ptolemy† who went on to found a new dynasty (see page 80).

For more about Bast and other Egyptian deities, see page 21.

The Ptolemies

At the death of Alexander the Great† in 323BC, Ptolemy† took over Egypt as *satrap* (governor). He ruled on behalf of Alexander's son, Alexander, and retarded brother, Philip Arrhideus. They were both murdered and in 305BC Ptolemy became pharaoh, founding a new dynasty. The Ptolemies became involved in struggles between Alexander's generals to divide up his empire, known as the Wars of the Diadochi (323-281BC). Later there were also quarrels with the Seleucids† over possession of Palestine, Phoenicia and southern Syria. Five bitter wars were fought (274-272BC, 260-253BC, 246-241BC, 221-217BC and 202-198BC) which ended with defeat for the Ptolemies.

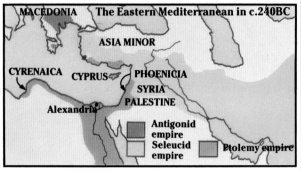

The Eastern Mediterranean in c.240BC

MACEDONIA

ASIA MINOR

CYRENAICA CYPRUS PHOENICIA
SYRIA
Alexandria PALESTINE

Antigonid empire
Seleucid empire
Ptolemy empire

Alexandria

Alexandria, the new capital of Egypt founded by Alexander in 331BC, was designed like a Greek city, set out on a grid pattern. Alexander had intended it to be a great commercial and trading centre. Two magnificent harbours were built, which were capable of sheltering the largest ships of the day. Deep channels were dug linking the harbours to the River Nile.

The lighthouse on the island of Pharos was about 180ft (70m) tall. Its fire was reflected by mirrors and was visible 50km (30 miles) away.

A causeway 1.3km (almost a mile) long joined the lighthouse to the mainland.

Alexandria became a great centre of learning, and a number of important scientific inventions and discoveries were made there. The first two Ptolemies established the Museion (or Museum), a sort of research institute where some of the greatest scholars of the Greek world came to study. It contained a huge library, with about 500,000 papyrus scrolls. Ptolemy II commissioned a history of Egypt to be written, and the translations of Hebrew† scriptures into Greek.

Life under the Ptolemies

The economy flourished under the early Ptolemies. Large areas of marshland in the Fayum (see page 27) were drained and reclaimed for cultivation, trade was promoted and exports increased. However this new wealth only benefited the monarchs and their officials, who were mainly Greeks. In general, ordinary Egyptians were taxed heavily and exploited.

This relief† shows Ptolemy VII with two goddesses, Wadjet and Nekhbet.

The Ptolemies showed respect for Egyptian culture and religion. They built temples to the Egyptian gods, and had themselves shown on monuments in traditional Egyptian style. Greek gods soon became identified with Egyptian ones.

The decline of the dynasty

In the 2nd century BC, royal power began to decline. Feuds and murders became common within the royal family, and tensions between the Egyptians and the Greek immigrants erupted into violence. Upper Egypt broke away, and between 205BC and 185BC it was ruled by native pharaohs. During the reign of Ptolemy V, Macedonians and Seleucids invaded and almost succeeded in taking control. The period that followed was one of unrest, high inflation, heavy taxation and corrupt and inefficient government.

Cleopatra and the Romans

Despite the threat of the expanding Roman empire (see pages 200-201) the Ptolemies did not give up hope of regaining the provinces they had lost to the Seleucids. Cleopatra VII† attempted to use her influence over the Roman dictator Julius Caesar†, who became her lover. After Caesar was murdered in 44BC, she married his friend Mark Antony†. In 31BC Antony and Cleopatra were defeated by Caesar's heir, Octavian, at the Battle of Actium. They committed suicide, and in 30BC Egypt became part of the Roman empire.

A Greek marble head of Cleopatra VII

Map of Ancient Egypt

- Çatal Hüyük
- River Tigris
- Hurran
- ASIA MINOR
- ANATOLIA
- GREECE
- TAURUS MOUNTAINS
- Carchemish
- Aleppo
- Alalakh
- MESOPOTAMIA
- CRETE
- CYPRUS
- Ugarit
- SYRIA
- Qatna
- Byblos
- Beiruit
- Mari
- River Euphrates
- MEDITERRANEAN SEA
- Sidon
- Tyre
- Damascus
- Hazor
- Megiddo
- River Jordan
- Nile Delta
- Ekron
- Ashdad
- Ashkalon
- Jerusalem
- Alexandria
- Sais
- Buto
- Gaza
- Gath
- Naucratis
- Tanis
- Pelusium
- DEAD SEA
- Avaris
- Daphnae
- Bubastis
- LOWER EGYPT
- Gizah
- Heliopolis
- Sakkara
- Memphis
- It-towy
- Meidum
- SINAI
- THE FAYUM
- Gerza
- Herakleopolis
- Egyptian empire at its greatest extent during the New Kingdom
- River Nile
- EASTERN DESERT
- Beni Hasan
- Tell el Amarna (Akhetaten)
- WESTERN DESERT
- Badari
- Abydos
- Coptos
- Thebes
- Nagada
- Karnak
- UPPER EGYPT
- Hierakonpolis
- First Cataract
- Aswan
- Elephantine
- RED SEA
- Toshka
- WAWAT
- Abu Simbel
- Buhen
- Semna
- Second Cataract
- NUBIA
- KUSH
- Kerma
- Third Cataract
- Napata
- Fourth Cataract
- Fifth Cataract
- Meroë
- ETHIOPIAN HIGHLANDS

This map shows Ancient Egypt and the surrounding area. Most of the cities and regions mentioned in this section of the book can be found here. The shaded area indicates the extent of the Egyptian empire at its height during the New Kingdom.

The Egyptian kings

The list on these pages contains the names and approximate dates of most of the Egyptian kings up to the Roman conquest in 30BC. In some cases, particularly during the intermediate periods, several kings ruled simultaneously. Some kings are often known by the names the Greeks gave them. These are shown in brackets.

The Archaic Period (c.3100-2649BC)

DYNASTY I
Seven or eight kings starting with **Menes c.3100**

DYNASTY II
Eight or nine kings including **Hetepsekhemwy**, **Re'neb**, **Peribsen** and **Kha'sekhemui**

The Old Kingdom (c.2649-2150BC)

DYNASTY III

Sanakht	**c.2649-2630BC**
Zoser	**c.2630-2611BC**
Sekhemkhet	**c.2611-2603BC**
Kha'ba	**c.2603-2599BC**
Huni	**c.2599-2575BC**

DYNASTY IV

Sneferu	**c.2575-2551BC**
Khufu (Cheops)	**c.2551-2528BC**
Ra'djedef	**c.2528-2520BC**
Khafre (Khephren)	**c.2520-2494BC**
Menkaure (Mycerinus)	**c.2490-2472BC**
Shepseskaf	**c.2472-2467BC**

DYNASTY V

Userkaf	**c.2465-2323BC**
Sahure	**c.2458-2446BC**
Neferirkare	**c.2446-2426BC**
Shepseskare	**c.2426-2419BC**
Ra'neferef	**c.2419-2416BC**
Neuserre	**c.2416-2392BC**
Menkauhor	**c.2396-2388BC**
Djedkare	**c.2388-2356BC**
Unas	**c.2356-2323BC**

DYNASTY VI

Teti	**c.2323-2291BC**
Pepi I	**c.2289-2255BC**
Merenre	**c.2255-2246BC**
Pepi II	**c.2246-2152BC**
Nitocris**	**c.2152-2150BC**

First Intermediate Period (c.2150-2040BC)

DYNASTIES VII and VIII (c.2150-2134BC)
Many kings who reigned only for short periods

DYNASTIES IX and X (c.2134-2040BC)
The Herakleopolitan kings

The Middle Kingdom (c.2040-1640BC)

A line of kings reigned independently at Thebes, at the same time as the kings of Herakleopolis. This family later became Dynasty XI, ruling all Egypt under the Middle Kingdom.

DYNASTY XI

Mentuhotep II	**c.2040-2010BC**
Mentuhotep III	**c.2010-1998BC**
Mentuhotep IV	**c.1998-1991BC**

DYNASTY XII

Amenemhat I	**c.1991-1962BC**
Senusret I*	**c.1971-1926BC**
Amenemhat II*	**c.1929-1892BC**
Senusret II*	**c.1897-1878BC**
Senusret III*	**c.1878-1841BC**
Amenemhat III*	**c.1844-1797BC**
Amenemhat IV*	**c.1799-1787BC**
Sobek-neferu**	**c.1787-1783BC**

DYNASTY XIII (c.1783-1640BC)
About 70 kings most of whom had very short reigns

DYNASTY XIV
Princes from the Western Delta who broke away, ruling at the same time as Dynasty XIII

Second Intermediate Period (c.1640-1552BC)

DYNASTY XV
Hyksos kings including **Apophis (c.1585-1542BC)**

DYNASTY XVI
Minor Hyksos kings who ruled at the same time as Dynasty XV

DYNASTY XVII (c.1640-1552BC)
Fifteen Theban kings including **Tao I**, **Tao II** and **Kamose (c.1555-1552BC)**

The New Kingdom (1552-1069BC)

DYNASTY XVIII

Ahmose	**1552-1527BC**
Amenhotep I	**1527-1506BC**
Tuthmosis I	**1506-1494BC**
Tuthmosis II	**1494-1490BC**
Hatshepsut**	**1490-1468BC**
Tuthmosis III	**1490-1436BC**
Amenhotep II	**1438-1412BC**
Tuthmosis IV	**1412-1402BC**
Amenhotep III	**1402-1364BC**
Akhenaten (Amenhotep IV)	**1364-1347BC**
Smenkhare*	**1351-1348BC**
Tutankhamun	**1347-1337BC**
Ay	**1337-1333BC**
Horemheb	**1333-1305BC**

These kings were crowned during the lifetime of the previous king.
**These are queens reigning as kings.*

DYNASTY XIX

Ramesses I	**1305-1303BC**
Seti I	**1303-1289BC**
Ramesses II	**1289-1224BC**
Merenptah	**1224-1204BC**
Amenmesse	**1204-1200BC**
Seti II	**1200-1194BC**
Siptah	**1194-1188BC**
Tawosret**	**1194-1186BC**

DYNASTY XX

Set-nakht	**1186-1184BC**
Ramesses III	**1184-1153BC**
Ramesses IV	**1153-1146BC**
Ramesses V	**1146-1142BC**
Ramesses VI	**1142-1135BC**
Ramesses VII	**1135-1129BC**
Ramesses VIII	**1129-1127BC**
Ramesses IX	**1127-1109BC**
Ramesses X	**1109-1099BC**
Ramesses XI	**1099-1069BC**

Third Intermediate Period (1069-664BC)

DYNASTY XXI

Smendes I	**1069-1043BC**
Amenemnisu	**1043-1039BC**
Psusennes I	**1039-991BC**
Amenemope	**993-984BC**
Osochor	**984-978BC**
Si-Amun	**978-959BC**
Psusennes II	**959-945BC**

DYNASTY XXII

Shoshenq I	**945-924BC**
Osorkon I	**924-889BC**
Shoshenq II	**c.890BC**
Takeloth I	**889-874BC**
Osorkon II	**874-850BC**
Takeloth II	**850-825BC**
Shoshenq III	**825-773BC**
Pimay	**773-767BC**
Shoshenq V	**767-730BC**
Osorkon IV	**730-715BC**

DYNASTY XXIII
A separate line of kings ruling at the same time as the later kings of Dynasty XXII

DYNASTY XXIV
Ruling at the same time as Dynasties XXII and XXIII

Tefnakhte I	**727-720BC**
Bakenranef	**720-715BC**

DYNASTY XXV
The Nubian kings

Piankhi	**728-716BC**
Shabako	**716-702BC**
Shebitku	**702-690BC**
Taharka	**690-664BC**
Tanut-Amun	**664-663BC**

The Late Period (664-332BC)

DYNASTY XXVI
The Saite kings

Psamtek I	**664-610BC**
Necho II	**610-595BC**
Psamtek II	**595-589BC**
Apries	**589-570BC**
Amasis	**570-526BC**
Psamtek III	**526-525BC**

DYNASTY XXVII (525-404BC)
The Persian kings including
Cambyses (525-521BC), Darius I (521-485BC)
and **Xerxes (485-464BC)**

DYNASTY XXVIII

Amyrtaeus	**404-c.399BC**

DYNASTY XXIX

Nepherites I	**c.399-393BC**
Achoris	**c.393-380BC**
Psammuthis	**c.380-379BC**
Nepherites II	**c.379**

DYNASTY XXX

Nectanebo I	**c.379-361BC**
Tachos	**c.361-359BC**
Nectanebo II	**c.359-342BC**

DYNASTY XXXI (341-323BC)
The second period of Persian kings

The Macedonian kings (332-305BC)

Alexander the Great	**332-323BC**
Philip Arrhidaeus	**323-316BC**
Alexander IV	**316-305BC**

The Ptolemies (305-30BC)

Ptolemy I	**305-284BC**
Ptolemy II	**284-246BC**
Ptolemy III	**246-221BC**
Ptolemy IV	**221-205BC**
Ptolemy V	**205-180BC**
Ptolemy VI	**160-164BC**
	and 163-145BC
Ptolemy VII	**145BC**
Ptolemy VIII	**170-163BC**
	and 145-116BC
Queen Cleopatra III and Ptolemy IX	**116-107BC**
Queen Cleopatra III and Ptolemy X	**107-88BC**
Ptolemy IX	**88-81BC**
Queen Cleopatra Berenice	**81-80BC**
Ptolemy XI	**80BC**
Ptolemy XII	**80-58BC**
Queen Berenice IV	**58-55BC**
Ptolemy XII	**55-51BC**
Queen Cleopatra VII	**51-30BC**

with Ptolemy XIII (51-47BC), with Ptolemy XIV (47-44BC) and with Ptolemy XV (44-30BC)

Who was who in Egypt and the Middle East

Below is a list of important people from Egypt, Mesopotamia and other early civilizations in the Middle East. If a person's name appears in bold in the text of an entry, that person also has his or her own entry in this list. Dates of reigns, where known, are shown in brackets.

Ahhotep I. Queen of Egypt (Dynasty XVII). Daughter of Tao I and **Teti-sheri**, and sister-wife of **Tao II**. She acted as regent† during the reign of her son **Ahmose**.

Ahmes Nefertari. Queen of Egypt (Dynasty XVIII). Daughter of **Tao II** and **Ahhotep I**, and sister-wife of **Ahmose**. She held the offices of God's Wife† and of Second Prophet of Amun in the temple at Karnak and acted as regent† for her fourth son, Amenhotep I. Together they founded the community of royal tomb-builders, who eventually settled in the village at Deir el Medinah (see page 66).

Ahmose (1552-1527BC). King of Egypt. The first king of Dynasty XVIII and the New Kingdom. Son of **Tao II** and **Ahhotep I**, he came to the throne while still a child, with his mother as regent†. Ahmose continued the war begun by his father and brother and succeeded in liberating Egypt from the Hyksos†. After suppressing rebellions at home, he began the reconquest of Nubia.

Ahmose of El Kab (Dynasty XVII/XVIII). Egyptian soldier in the army of King **Ahmose**. He fought on campaigns to drive the Hyksos† from Egypt and won the 'Gold of Valour', the highest award for bravery. The biography on the walls of his tomb is an important source of information about the wars against the Hyksos.

Akhenaten/Amenhotep IV (1364-1347BC). King of Egypt (Dynasty XVIII). One of the most controversial figures in ancient history. He abandoned the traditional Egyptian deities and introduced the worship of one god, the disc of the sun, known as the Aten. He changed his name to Akhenaten and built a new capital, Akhetaten. After his death all these changes were reversed and the capital was abandoned. Akhenaten's monuments were destroyed and he himself was branded as a heretic†.

Alexander the Great (356-323BC). King of Macedonia, military leader and empire-builder. After taking control of Greece, he marched into Asia Minor and conquered the entire Persian empire (including Egypt). He founded many new cities, the most famous of which was the port of Alexandria in Egypt, which became the new capital. Alexander married a Persian princess called Roxane and died in Babylon at the age of 32. His heirs were eventually murdered and the empire was divided up between his generals, one of whom, **Ptolemy**, became King of Egypt and founded the Ptolemaic Dynasty.

Amenemhat I (c.1991-1962BC). First king of Dynasty XI. In order to secure the succession, he had his son Senusret I crowned in his own lifetime. Amenemhat was eventually murdered, but Senusret remained in control.

Amenhotep IV, see **Akhenaten**.

Amenhotep, son of Hapu (Reign of Amenhotep III). Egyptian royal scribe. He held some of the highest offices in the land and statues of him were erected in the temples of Amun and Mut at Karnak. He was worshipped as a god in the Late Period in Thebes.

Amenirdis II. Nubian princess and God's Wife. Daughter of King **Taharka** (Dynasty XXV). She was obliged to adopt as her heir **Nitocris**, the daughter of Psamtek I, the first king of Dynasty XXVI.

Ankhesenamun. Queen of Egypt (Dynasty XVIII). Sister-wife of **Tutankhamun**. After his death she was married to Ay, an elderly courtier who became king.

Antony, Mark (82-30BC). Roman soldier and politician. Lover of **Cleopatra VII**, he ruled Egypt with her after the death of **Caesar**. After a quarrel with Caesar's heir Octavian, war broke out; Antony and Cleopatra were defeated at the Battle of Actium and committed suicide.

Apophis. One of the greatest of the Hyksos† kings of Egypt (Dynasty XVI). During his reign war broke out with **Tao II**, the King of Thebes. This led to the expulsion of the Hyksos and the start of the New Kingdom.

Bay. An adventurer of Syrian origin who became influential in Egypt at the end of Dynasty XIX. He tried to sieze the throne after the death of Queen **Tawosret**.

Bint-Anath. Queen of Egypt (Dynasty XIX). Daughter and wife of **Ramesses II**. She has a tomb in the Valley of the Queens on the West Bank at Thebes.

Caesar, Julius (c.100-44BC). Roman politician, writer and general who was made dictator for life. He intervened in a quarrel between his lover **Cleopatra VII** and her brother and secured the Egyptian throne for her. He was murdered on 15 March 44BC.

Cambyses (530-522BC). King of Persia. Son of Cyrus II. He conquered Egypt in 525BC. He appears to have been a cruel man, and the Greek historian **Herodotus** claimed that he was mad. According to one story, he broke into the tomb of a pharaoh and burned the corpse. He is said to have offended the Egyptians by desecrating temples and wounding the Apis bull†. Cambyses died on his return to Persia in 522BC, and was succeeded by his cousin **Darius**.

Cleopatra VII (51-30BC). Queen of Egypt (Ptolemaic Period). Sister-wife of both Ptolemy XIII and Ptolemy XIV and lover of the Roman dictator **Julius Caesar**. She later married his friend **Mark Antony**. Antony and Cleopatra were defeated at the Battle of Actium (31BC) by Caesar's heir Octavian. In 30BC Cleopatra committed suicide and Egypt was absorbed into the Roman empire.

Cyrus II (559-529BC). King of Persia and founder of the Achaemenid Dynasty. In 550BC Cyrus defeated his grandfather Astyages of Medea and united the two kingdoms under his rule. He defeated King Croesus of Lydia in 547-546BC and annexed his empire, and in 539BC he conquered the Babylonian empire.

Darius the Great (522-485BC). King of Persia. Under him the Persian empire reached its greatest extent. An able and successful ruler, he established a fair and efficient code of laws and divided the empire into provinces, each run by a *satrap* (or governor).

Elissa or **Dido**. Queen of Carthage. Princess of the Phoenician city of Tyre, and niece of Queen Jezebel, wife of King Ahab of the Israelites†. She fled with her brother to north Africa and built the city of Carthage. According to Roman tradition, the Greek hero Aeneas landed there after the destruction of Troy. Dido fell in love with him and committed suicide when he left.

Esarhaddon (680-667BC). King of Assyria. He gained the support of the Babylonians by rebuilding the city of Babylon, which had been destroyed by his father **Sennacherib**. However elsewhere he faced great problems. The empire was huge and the cruelty of the Assyrians made them unpopular with their subjects. In 671BC Esarhaddon invaded the Nile Delta and Assyrian governors were installed in Egypt.

Hammurabi (c.1792-1750BC). King of Babylon. He extended the frontiers of the kingdom and built up an empire which included all of Sumer and Akkad. A gifted administrator, he was concerned with law and order and established a unified system of laws and penalties.

Hatshepsut (1490-1468BC). Queen of Egypt (Dynasty XVIII). Daughter of Tuthmosis I and Queen Ahmose and sister-wife of Tuthmosis II. Although appointed regent† for her son **Tuthmosis III**, she took power and reigned as "king" for over 20 years. Evidence of her reign is scarce, as Tuthmosis destroyed her official inscriptions.

Hekanakhte. Egyptian priest (Dynasty XI). Letters and documents found in his tomb provide important information on the running of a large household and estate, as well as an insight into tensions and intrigues in a wealthy family.

Heri-hor. Egyptian soldier (Dynasty XX). A member of a family of officials which became influential as the power of the pharaohs declined. During the reign of Ramesses XI, Heri-hor took control of Upper Egypt. Lower Egypt was governed by his son Smendes, who married a daughter of Ramesses XI. When Ramesses died, Smendes became the first king of Dynasty XXI.

Herodotus (c.460-420BC). Greek historian, often called "the Father of History". He wrote a history of the Greeks which centred around the Persian Wars. He was one of the first writers to compare historical facts and to see them as a sequence of linked events.

Hetepheres I. Queen of Egypt (Dynasty III). Daughter of Huni, sister-wife of **Sneferu** and mother of **Khufu**. Shortly after her burial, the tomb was robbed and her body destroyed. Khufu had the remains of her burial moved to Gizah, where it was discovered this century. Although the wooden furniture had crumbled, archaeologists were able to reconstruct it from the surviving gold foil that covered it.

Hiram. King of the Phoenician city of Tyre. Contemporary with King David and King Solomon of the Israelites†. He supplied cedar and fir trees for Solomon's temple at Jerusalem and sent craftsmen to work in bronze.

Horemheb. King of Egypt (Dynasty XVIII). General and regent† during the reign of **Tutankhamun**. He appears to have had no claim to the throne except as husband of Ay's daughter **Mutnodjmet**.

Imhotep. Egyptian official (Dynasty III). Architect of the first pyramid, the step pyramid of King **Zoser** at Sakkara. He was also a doctor and a high priest and may have been involved in introducing the calendar. Later generations worshipped him as a god, and the Greeks identified him with their god of medicine, Asclepius.

Kamose (c.1555-1550). King of Egypt (Dynasty XVII: the Theban kings). Son of **Tao II** and **Ahhotep I**. He fought with the Hyksos† and extended his frontier as far as north the Fayum. He died in battle and was succeeded by his brother **Ahmose**.

Khufu or **Cheops** (c.2551-2528BC). King of Egypt (Dynasty IV). Son of **Sneferu** and **Hetepheres I**. His pyramid, the Great Pyramid at Gizah, is the largest ever built and was the oldest of the seven wonders of the ancient world. The diorite quarries at Toshka in Nubia were first mined during his reign and a fortified town was built as a trade centre at Buhen.

Meket-re. High-ranking Egyptian official in the reign of Mentuhotep III. His tomb on the West Bank at Thebes contained a magnificent set of tomb models, including models of his villa with its garden and pool, kitchens, workshops, cattle, granaries and boats.

Menes (c.3100BC). King of Upper Egypt. He conquered Lower Egypt and united the two kingdoms, so becoming the first king of Dynasty I. He may have married a princess from Lower Egypt, giving their son Hor-aha a hereditary claim to the whole of Egypt.

Mentuhotep II (c.2061-2010BC). King of Thebes in Upper Egypt (Dynasty XI). In about 2040BC he defeated the King of Lower Egypt (Dynasty X) and reunited the country. This began the Middle Kingdom.

Merodach-Baladin (or **Marduk-apal-iddina**). Chaldean prince from Sumer and champion of Babylonian independence, he challenged the powerful **Sargon II** of Assyria. He became King of Babylon between 721BC and 711BC, but was driven out by Sargon and forced to flee to Elam. After Sargon's death in 705BC, he returned to Babylon, but was expelled the following year. He fled to the marshes and waged guerilla war on the Assyrians. He died in exile in Elam.

Montu-em-het. An Egyptian official from an influential Theban family (Dynasty XXV). He married the granddaughter of one of the Nubian kings and became the most important official in Thebes. When the Assyrians invaded Egypt in 665BC, he fled to Nubia with King Tanut-Amun. He returned to Egypt when a new Egyptian dynasty (Dynasty XXVI) was established.

Mutnodjmet. Queen of Egypt (Dynasty XVIII). Daughter of Ay, a courtier who became pharaoh. She married a general called **Horemheb**, who became the next king.

Nabonidus (556-539BC). King of Babylon. An official of royal descent, he came to the throne during a period of turmoil after the death of **Nebuchadnezzar II**. He commissioned a lot of rebuilding in Sumer and studied in archives to discover how earlier buildings had been constructed. After leaving his son Belshazzar in control in Babylon, he withdrew to Arabia for several years, possibly in an attempt to secure control of the lucrative trading route from southern Arabia. When the Persians attacked Babylon he returned home, but he and his son were killed and the Babylonian empire came to an end.

Naram-Sin (c.2291-2255BC). King of Akkad. Grandson of **Sargon**. He attempted to rebuild Sargon's empire and succeeded in extending the frontiers west as far as Lebanon. The empire disintegrated after his death.

Nebuchadnezzar II (605-562BC). King of Babylon. Under him Babylon was rebuilt and the New Babylonian Empire reached its height. He captured the provinces of Syria and Palestine and dealt severely with his new vassals† when they failed to pay tribute†. In 597BC he conquered Jerusalem and carried off 3000 of its leading inhabitants. The King of Judah revolted in 587BC. After an 18 month siege the walls and temple of Jerusalem were destroyed and the people carried off to Babylon.

Necho I (672-664BC). Prince of Sais (Lower Egypt). Necho's family had never accepted the Nubian kings of Dynasty XXV. When the Assyrians invaded Egypt in 664BC Necho sided with them. He was appointed governor by the Assyrians, but was captured and executed by the Nubians. His son Psamtek escaped and returned to restore Egypt's independence as the founder of Dynasty XXVI. However the Egyptians regarded Necho as the first king of their new dynasty and for this reason he is known as Necho I.

Nefertari. Chief queen of **Ramesses II** (Dynasty XIX). One of the temples at Abu Simbel was built for her, as well as a tomb in the Valley of the Queens.

Nefertiti. Queen of Egypt (Dynasty XVIII). Wife of **Akhenaten** and mother of **Ankhesenamun**.

Nitocris (or **Net-ikerty**). God's Wife†. Daughter of Psamtek I, first king of Dynasty XXVI. She helped reconcile Upper Egypt to the new dynasty.

Nitocris. Queen of Egypt (Dynasty VI). Daughter of Pepi II. The direct male line appears to have died out soon after her father's death and Nitocris ruled on her own for about two years (c.2152-2150BC).

Pepi II (c.2246-2252BC). King of Egypt (Dynasty VI). He reigned for 94 years; the longest recorded reign in history. After his death disputes broke out over the succession. Egypt collapsed into civil conflict and confusion and the Old Kingdom came to an end.

Piankhi (747-716BC). King of Nubia and Egypt. He saw himself as the guardian of Egyptian culture and religion during a period of decadence and political division in Egypt. He conquered Egypt in 728BC, and became the first king of Dynasty XXV. He died in Nubia and is buried under a pyramid at el Kurru.

Ptolemy I (305-284BC). King of Egypt. A general in the army of **Alexander the Great**, he was appointed governor of Egypt after Alexander's death, ruling on behalf of Alexander's son and retarded brother. When they were both murdered Ptolemy became king and founder of the Ptolemaic dynasty.

Ramesses II (1289-1224BC). King of Egypt (Dynasty XIX). One of the best known kings in Egyptian history. Ramesses built a large number of fortresses, temples and monuments, including two temples cut into the rock face at Abu Simbel. During the early part of his reign he was engaged in a struggle with the Hittites. Eventually fear of the Assyrians brought an end to the conflict and peace was made between the two sides.

Ramose. Vizier of Upper Egypt during the reigns of **Amenhotep III** and **Akhenaten**. A member of the successful family of **Amenhotep, son of Hapu**.

Rekhmire. Vizier of Upper Egypt (reign of **Tuthmosis III**). His tomb at Thebes contains valuable scenes of daily life, as well as a text which describes the instructions given by the king to the Vizier on his appointment to office.

Sargon of Akkad (c.2371-2316BC). A gifted soldier and administrator, he united Akkad and Sumer under his rule and built up the first great empire in Mesopotamia. The empire fell apart after his death, but was reconquered by his grandson **Naram-Sin**.

Sargon II (721-705BC). King of Assyria. A brilliant and ruthless soldier, he conquered the state of Urartu and built a magnificent palace at Khorsabad.

Sennacherib (704-681BC). King of Assyria. The favourite son of **Sargon II**. During his reign there were constant revolts in Babylon, led by **Merodach-Baladin**. These ended when the Assyrians sacked Babylon in 689BC. The kings of Sidon, Ashkalon, Judah and Ekron also rebelled, encouraged by the King of Egypt. After defeating the rebels, Sennacherib invaded Egypt, but the Egyptians were saved by the sudden withdrawal of the Assyrian army after an outbreak of plague. Sennacherib was murdered by one of his sons who crushed him with a statue of a god.

Senusret III (c.1878-1841BC). King of Egypt (Dynasty XII). He led several campaigns against the Kushites who were threatening the frontiers of Egypt's Nubian province (established at the Second Cataract†). He also began a massive rebuilding programme to strengthen the fortresses there, and dug a channel through the rocks of the First Cataract, so that ships could sail directly upstream. Senusret claimed to have established his frontier further south than any previous king had done.

Sheba, Queen of. Sheba, or Saba, was a rich, fertile land on the south coast of Arabia. The Shebans were situated on a good trading route from Africa and the East and traded agricultural produce and incense. According to the Bible, the Queen of Sheba travelled north to visit **Solomon**, King of the Israelites†. According to Ethiopian tradition, she had a son by him, from whom the Ethiopian royal family are descended. Muslim sources give her name as Bilqis.

Shuppiluliuma (c.1380-1340BC). King of the Hittites. The greatest king of the Hittite New Kingdom; a wily and able ruler and diplomat and a successful soldier. Under him the Hittite empire reached its greatest extent. In about 1370BC he conquered the Mitannian empire and then encouraged discontented Egyptian vassals† to rebel. When **Tutankhamun** died, his young widow **Ankhesenamun** wrote to him, offering to marry one of his sons and make him King of Egypt. Shuppiluliuma eventually sent one of his sons to Egypt, but the plot was discovered and the Hittite prince was murdered. To avenge his son, he attacked the northern provinces of the Egyptian empire in Syria.

Sinuhe. Egyptian army officer (Dynasty XII). On a campaign against the Libyans, he heard that King **Amenemhat I** had been murdered, and that there was a plot to deprive his son Senusret of the throne. For some unknown reason, Sinuhe fled in panic to Syria, where he stayed for many years. After numerous adventures he returned home. His story is inscribed on the walls of his tomb and was copied and turned into a book.

Sneferu (c.2575-2551BC). King of Egypt (Dynasty III). Son of Huni and a secondary wife, he became king after the premature death of the heir. In order to strengthen his claim, he married his half-sister, **Hetepheres I**. Sneferu appears to have been tough, efficient and ruthless. He sent an expedition to Nubia and many Nubians were killed and others taken prisoner. Sneferu built himself two pyramids – the 'Bent' Pyramid and the Northern Pyramid (the first to be designed and completed as a straight-sided pyramid).

Sobek-neferu (c.1787-1783BC). Queen of Egypt (Dynasty XII). With the death of her brother Amenemhat IV the direct male line of Dynasty XII died out and she ruled alone for four years.

Solomon (c.970-930BC). King of the Israelites†. Son of David. He built a great temple at the capital, Jerusalem, and Israelite power reached its height. After Solomon's death the kingdom split into two: Israel and Judah.

Taharka (690-664BC). King of Egypt (Dynasty XXV: the Nubian kings). Son of **Piankhi**. The Assyrians attacked Egypt three times during Taharka's reign. The second invasion reached Memphis, but he escaped to Nubia and later returned. In the third invasion the Assyrians were supported by Egyptian princes such as **Necho of Sais**. Taharka again fled to Nubia, and a new native Egyptian dynasty was established.

Tao II. King of Thebes (Dynasty XVII). Son of Tao I and **Teti-sheri**. During his reign the Thebans began plotting to drive out the Hyksos† who were ruling Egypt from Avaris as Dynasty XV. War broke out between them and Tao succeeded in pushing his frontier north to Assiut.

Tawosret (c.1194-1186BC). Queen of Egypt (Dynasty XIX). Daughter of Merenptah and sister-wife of Seti II. After Merenptah's death, Amenmesse (a member of the royal family) seized the throne briefly before Seti took control. When Seti died Amenmesse's son Siptah was made ruler. Tawosret married him and when he died she reigned as a "king" until her death three years later.

Teti-sheri. Queen of Thebes (Dynasty XVII). Wife of Tao I. She appears to have been a woman of great influence who may have encouraged the men of her family into rebellion against the Hyksos†. The Hyksos were finally driven out by her grandson **Ahmose**, and he provided her with estates recaptured from them, a burial at Thebes and a monument at Abydos.

Tia. Egyptian princess (Dynasty XIX). Eldest daughter of Seti I and sister of **Ramesses II**. She married a high-ranking official and is buried with him at Sakkara. The marriage probably took place before her grandfather, Ramesses I, founded Dynasty XIX. Otherwise she would probably have married her brother Ramesses II.

Tiy. Queen of Egypt (Dynasty XVIII). Daughter of two influential courtiers called Tuyu and Yuya. Wife of Amenhotep III (who may also have been her cousin) and mother of **Akhenaten**.

Tutankhamun (1347-1337BC). King of Egypt (Dynasty XVIII). Son of **Akhenaten**. He came to the throne aged only about nine and married his half-sister **Ankhesenamun**. A general called **Horemheb** and a courtier called Ay became regents†. Although Tutankhamun died young, he is famous because of the treasures found in the 1920s in his tomb in the Valley of the Kings. Many of the tombs of the Dynasty XVIII kings had been repeatedly robbed over the centuries, but Tutankhamun's tomb had escaped attention.

Tuthmosis III (1490-1436BC). King of Egypt (Dynasty XVIII). Son of Tuthmosis II and nephew of **Hatshepsut**, who was regent† and kept him from power for the first twenty years of his reign. Tuthmosis was probably the greatest of the warrior pharaohs of the New Kingdom. He enlarged the Egyptian empire to its widest limits.

Xerxes (485-465BC). King of Persia. Son of **Darius**. He put down a revolt in Egypt and spent much of his reign fighting the Greeks. He invaded Greece in 480BC, won a battle at Thermopylae and sacked Athens. His forces were later defeated at Salamis and Plataea.

Zoser (c.2630-2611BC). King of Egypt (Dynasty III). The first pyramid, the step pyramid at Sakkara, was designed as a tomb for him by his architect **Imhotep**.

Glossary

Many foreign or unfamiliar words in this section are listed and explained in the glossary below. The names of peoples are also included. Other words related to the term appear in bold within the text of the entry. When a word in the text of an entry is followed by a dagger, that word has its own entry in this list. When the sign follows a name, see the 'Who's who' that begins on page 84.

Alabaster. A translucent, white stone veined rather like marble. It was used for decorative features, such as floors in temples, and for items such as vases and lamps in wealthy Egyptian households.

Amulet. A small figure of a god or goddess or a sacred object. Amulets were worn as charms for luck and protection by the living and the dead. Examples include the *ankh*†, the *djed*-pillar†, and the scarab beetle.

Ankh. An Egyptian amulet†; the symbol of life.

Aryan. A term used to refer to the language or people of the Iranian and Indian branches of the Indo-European† group.

Aqueduct. A man-made channel for tranporting water.

Arab. A member of a group of Semitic† people living in Arabia and neighbouring territory.

Bedouin. Nomads† inhabiting the deserts of North Africa and Arabia.

Caravan. A group of people, usually merchants, travelling together for safety across a desert.

Caste system. A hereditary system of rigidly defined social classes in India. Now a social system, but originally based on professions.

Cataract. A place where large rocks block the path of the River Nile. Cataracts often formed important boundaries in ancient times.

Concubine. A term applied in a historical context to a woman who lived with a man without being married. In Egypt it was an officially recognized relationship and a concubine had special rights.

City state. A self-governing city with its surrounding territory, forming the basis for an independent state.

Cult. The worship of a particular god or goddess, or the practice of a particular system of religious rites. Most Egyptian gods and goddesses had a home town where their main temple, known as a **cult temple**, was situated. The temple was the home of the **cult statue**, which was thought to be the means by which the deity could communicate with the outside world.

Djed-pillar. An Egyptian amulet† representing stability and continuity of power.

Dowry. Money or property brought by a woman to her husband at the time of marriage.

Dynasty. A succession of hereditary rulers. Dynasties are often referred to by a family name. Egyptian dynasties are numbered I to XXXI.

Elamites. A people from Elam, a land east of the River Tigris. The Elamites destroyed the Sumerian city of Ur in about 2000BC. Elam itself was absorbed into the empire of Sargon† of Akkad.

Faience. A type of glazed earthenware, made by heating powdered quartz.

First Cataract. See **Cataract**.

Fourth Cataract. See **Cataract**.

God's Wife. Head of the priestesses at the temple of Amun at Karnak. By the Third Intermediate Period this was a very powerful position held by a princess.

Harem. The name given to the part of an Oriental (usually Muslim) house reserved strictly for women (wives and concubines†). It is used to describe the part of an Egyptian palace where the royal women lived.

Hebrew. An ancient Semitic† language and people. The people are also known as Israelites† and Jews†.

Heretic. A person who maintains a set of beliefs contrary to and condemned by the established religion. The beliefs held by a heretic are described as **heretical** and the person is said to be guilty of **heresy**.

Hieroglyphics. The Egyptian system of writing in which pictures or signs are used to represent objects, ideas or sounds. The pictures themselves are known as **hieroglyphs**.

Hittites. An Indo-European† people from Anatolia, who built up a great empire in Asia Minor and northern Syria in the second millenium BC.

Hyksos. A group of Semitic† peoples, probably mostly nomads†, who invaded and conquered Egypt during the Second Intermediate Period.

Indo-European. A group of languages which includes Iranian, Armenian and Sanskrit (the ancient literary language of India), as well as most modern European languages. The name is also given to those groups of people speaking early Indo-European languages who drifted into the Middle East in about 2000BC. They may have originated in the area that stretches from southern Russia to central Europe.

Israelites. The Hebrew† inhabitants of the Kingdom of **Israel**.

Jews. Another name for the Semitic† people also known as Israelites† and Hebrews†; people who practice the religion **Judaism**.

Medjay. The name of a Nubian tribe some of whose members came to Egypt as mercenary† soldiers. The role of the Medjay later evolved into that of a peace-keeping force, and the term was also applied to native Egyptians who joined it.

Mercenary . A man who fights for pay in a foreign army.

Miracle. A wonderful event which cannot be explained by natural causes and is attributed to divine intervention.

Mummy. An embalmed body ready for burial.

Necropolis. A cemetery.

Next World. The place where the Egyptians thought people lived after death.

Nomads. People who do not live permanently in any one area, but move from place to place. People who live in this way are described as **nomadic**.

Nome. The Greek name for an Egyptian administrative district. Each *nome* was governed by an official called a **nomarch**.

Oracle. A message from a god or goddess. In Egypt it was usually communicated through a cult statue or a sacred animal, in response to questions posed by priests on behalf of worshippers. People consulted the oracle in order to find solutions to personal problems and fears. Kings also used it in an attempt to acquire divine approval for their policies.

Ostraca (Singular: **ostracon**). Pieces of broken pottery or stone, used for drawing or writing on.

Overlord. A supreme lord or ruler, who has power over other, lesser rulers.

Papyrus. A reed used to make a form of writing material (also known as papyrus). It was cut into strips which were pressed and dried to make a smooth writing surface.

Patron. Someone who sponsors or helps another person, usually by providing money or a job.

Phrygians. An Indo-European† people from Phrygia, an ancient kingdom in Asia Minor.

Regent. Someone who rules in the place of the actual ruler who is either absent, incapable or, more commonly, still too young to take power.

Relief. A sculpture carved on a flat background. Raised reliefs were made by cutting away the background and modelling details on to the figures. Sunken reliefs were made by cutting away stone from inside the outlines of the figures and carving the details out of the body.

Romans. A people from the city of Rome in central Italy, founded in the 8th century BC, which became the centre of a great civilization. The Romans built up a huge empire in Europe and around the Mediterranean, conquering Egypt in 30BC. Their empire reached its greatest extent in the 1st century AD and declined in the 4th century AD, but its cultural influence continues to the present day.

Sacrifice. A gift or offering made to a deity by people of early civilizations. This sometimes consisted of fruit, vegetables or flowers, but it could also involve the ritual killing of animals and humans.

Scribe. A person specifically employed to write and copy texts and keep records. This was a highly regarded profession in the ancient times, when relatively few people could read and write. Scribes were eligible for well-paid and prestigious jobs in government.

Second Cataract. See **Cataract**. The frontier between Egypt and Nubia in the Middle Kingdom. The site of the great Middle Kingdom fortresses.

Seleucid. A dynasty and kingdom founded by Seleucus Nicator, a Macedonian general under Alexander the Great†. In 304BC the Seleucids seized a large part of Alexander's empire, but it proved impossible to hold together. Large areas began to break away. In 64BC Seleucid lands were conquered by the Romans† and incorporated into the Roman empire.

Semites. Groups of peoples who, in about 2500BC, occupied an area which stretched from northern Mesopotamia to the eastern borders of Egypt. The Semites spoke closely related dialects which form part of the language group known by modern scholars as **Semitic**. Early Semites include the Akkadians and the Babylonians. Jews† and Arabs† are modern Semites.

Shrine. This is both a temple where a deity is worshipped and a container of wood, stone or precious metal in which the figure of a god or goddess is kept.

Shroud. A reactangular piece of cloth used to enclose a dead body.

Sphinx. In Egypt, statue representing the sun god. A sphinx usually had the body of an animal with the head of a lion, ram or pharaoh.

Stela (plural: **stelae**). An upright reactangular stone slab (sometimes curved at the top), carved with inscriptions. *Stelae* were used to commemorate special events and were also put in tombs to record the names and titles of the dead person and his or her family.

Terracotta. A mixture of clay and sand, used to make tiles and small statues. The statues themselves are sometimes called terracottas.

Tribute. A payment in money or kind made by a ruler or state to another, as an acknowledgement of submission. A vassal† pays tribute to an overlord†.

Underworld. Another name for the Next World†, the kindom of the god Osiris, ruler of the dead. The Egyptians sometimes referred to it as the Kingdom of the West, because it was thought to be somewhere in the far west.

Date chart

This chart lists the most important dates in the history of the early civilizations discussed in this section of the book. It also includes some dates relating to the civilizations of Greece and Rome, which developed within the same period.

From c.10,000BC   Farming develops in the Fertile Crescent.

c.8000BC   Early town is established at Jericho.

Before c.6000BC   Early town is established at Çatal Hüyük.

c.5000BC   Ubaid culture in Sumer.

c.5000BC   Yangshao culture in China; farming settlements are established by the Huang Ho River.

c.5000-3100BC   Predynastic Period in Egypt.

c.4000BC   Uruk culture in Sumer.

c.3500BC   Writing develops in Sumer. Sumerians also invent the wheel and learn how to make bronze.

c.3300-3100BC   Hieroglyphic writing develops in Egypt.

c.3100BC   Egypt is united by Menes.

c.3100-2649BC   Archaic Period in Egypt.

c.3000-2000BC   Independent city states flourish in Sumer, Akkad and Canaan. Early Bronze Age in Canaan.

c.3000-1500BC   Indus Valley Civilization in India.

c.3000-1100BC   Bronze Age in Greece.

c.2900-2400BC   Early dynasties develop in Sumer.

c.2649-2150BC   The Old Kingdom in Egypt; the pyramids are built.

c.2590BC   Pyramid of Cheops (the Great Pyramid of Gizah) is built.

c.2500BC   Longshan culture in China.

c.2500-1500BC   Stonehenge is built in Britain.

c.2371BC   Sargon of Akkad seizes the throne of the city of Kish and builds up an empire in Mesopotamia.

c.2205-1766BC   Traditional dates for legendary Hsia (Xia) Dynasty in China.

c.2150-2040BC   First Intermediate Period in Egypt.

c.2100-2000BC   Dynasty III of Ur.

c.2040-1640BC   The Middle Kingdom in Egypt.

c.2000BC   Amorites conquer Mesopotamia and Assyria and set up independent city states in Canaan. Indo-Europeans drift into the Middle East.

By c.2000BC   There is a flourishing civilization on Crete.

c.2000-1500BC   Middle Bronze Age in Canaan.

c.2000-1450BC   The Old Assyrian Empire.

c.2000-1000BC   Hurrians form an aristocratic caste in many cities in Canaan, ruling the Amorites and native Canaanites.

c.1900BC   Palaces are built on Crete.

c.1813-1781BC   Reign of Shamshi-Adad of Assyria. He builds up an empire from Mari to Babylon.

c.1792-1750BC   Reign of Hammurabi of Babylon.

1766-1027BC   Shang Dynasty in China.

c.1740BC   Hittites are united under one kingdom.

c.1700BC   Cretan palaces are destroyed by earthquakes and then rebuilt.

c.1674BC   Nile Delta is overrun with Hyksos, a people from the Middle East.

c.1640-1552BC   The Second Intermediate Period in Egypt.

c.1600BC   Rise of the Mycenaean culture in Greece.

1552-1069BC   The New Kingdom in Egypt; the greatest period of the Egyptian empire. Royal tombs are built in the Valley of the Kings.

c.1500BC   Groups of Indo-Europeans known as Aryans arrive in India.

c.1500BC   Mitannians unite the Hurrian kingdoms under their rule.

c.1595BC   Hittites plunder Babylon and destroy the Amorite kingdom.

c.1570-1158BC   Kassite dynasty rules in Babylon.

c.1550-1150BC   Late Bronze Age in Canaan.

c.1500BC   Aryans settle in Persia.

c.1500BC   Writing develops in China.

c.1500BC   Decline of the Indus Valley Civilization in India.

c.1500-600BC   The Vedic Period in India; the Hindu religion is gradually established.

1490-1436BC   Reign of Tuthmosis III in Egypt; the greatest of the warrior pharaohs.

c.1450BC   Minoan civilization comes to an end. Palaces are destroyed and Crete is taken over by Mycenaeans.

c.1450-1390BC   Mitannians conquer Assyria and build an empire from the Zagros mountains to the Mediterranean.

c.1450-1200BC   Hittite New Kingdom.

1440BC   Mitannians make a peace treaty with the Egyptians.

1380BC   Accession of Shuppiluliuma, one of the greatest Hittite kings. He overthrows the Mitannian empire and captures northern provinces of the Egyptian empire (Syria).

1364-1347BC   Reign of Akhenaten (Amenhotep IV) in Egypt.

1363-1000BC   The Middle Assyrian Empire.

1289-1224BC   Reign of Ramesses II in Egypt; a great warrior and a prolific builder.

c.1200BC   The advance of the Sea Peoples, raiders and settlers from Greece and the Mediterranean islands.

c.1200BC   Decline of Mycenaean culture in Greece.

1196BC Sea Peoples destroy the Hittite empire. Some Hittite survivors establish small Neo-Hittite states.

1184-1153BC Reign of Ramesses III; the last great warrior pharaoh. He defeats the Sea Peoples.

c.1158BC Kassite rulers are thrown out of Babylon. After an unsettled period Babylonian rule is restored.

c.1100BC Phoenicians are established in coastal cities of Canaan. They found colonies around the southern and western shores of the Mediterranean, with leading cities at Byblos, Sidon, Beirut and Tyre.

1069-664BC Third Intermediate Period in Egypt.

c.1030-1010BC Reign of Saul, first King of the Israelites.

1027-221BC Chou (Zhou) Dynasty in China.

c.1000-612BC The New Assyrian Empire; the greatest period of conquest and expansion.

c.970-930BC Reign of King Solomon of the Israelites. Israelite power reaches its height.

c.900BC The *Rig Veda* is composed in India.

c.814BC Phoenicians found the city of Carthage on the North African coast.

c.800-500BC The Archaic Period in Greece; a Greek alphabet is introduced, the first Olympic Games is held and the poet Homer composes the *Iliad* and the *Odyssey* (tales of the Trojan wars).

c.753BC Traditional date for the founding of Rome.

728BC Egypt is conquered by Piankhi, a Nubian king.

726-722BC Reign of Shalmaneser V of Assyria who conquers the Kingdom of Israel.

c.722-481BC Spring and Autumn Period in China; small states fight each other for supremacy.

721-705BC Reign of Sargon II of Assyria.

c.700BC Achaemenid Dynasty established in Persia.

c.670BC Kingdom of Medea established.

664-525BC The Late Period in Egypt begins with the Saite Dynasty; Egyptian independence is restored.

668-627BC Reign of Ashurbanipal II of Assyria; he sacks Thebes (Egypt), Babylon and Susa (Persia).

c.650BC The first coins are introduced in Lydia.

626-539BC The New Babylonian Empire.

612BC Ashur and Nineveh fall to the Medes and Babylonians.

605-562BC Reign of Nebuchadnezzar II of Babylon.

c.600-500BC Nubians abandon their capital at Napata and move south to Meroë

c.600BC Introduction of Taoism in China by the prophet Lao-zi.

597BC The Babylonian Captivity; Nebuchadnezzar II occupies Jerusalem and carries off many of its leading citizens to Babylon. After a further revolt in 587-586BC he sacks Jerusalem and again deports many of the people to Babylon.

c.560-483BC The life of the Buddha.

551-479BC Life of Kong zi (also known as Confucius), Chinese philosopher and prophet.

c.550BC Medea and Persia are united by Cyrus II. He conquers Lydia and the Babylonian empire.

525BC Cambyses II of Persia conquers Egypt.

c.510BC Rome becomes a republic.

c.500-336BC The Classical Period in Greece; the great age of Greek civilization.

490-449BC Wars between Greece and Persia.

c.481-221BC Warring States Period in China; seven major states destroy each other in struggles for power.

c.465BC Persian empire is in decline.

404-343BC Egyptians overthrow their Persian rulers and set up native dynasties.

343-332BC Persians retake Egypt.

334-331BC Alexander the Great of Macedonia conquers the Persian empire. He is accepted by the Egyptians as pharaoh.

331BC Alexandria becomes the new capital of Egypt.

323BC Alexander the Great dies and Egypt comes under the control of General Ptolemy.

323-281BC Wars of the Diadochi.

305-30BC Ptolemaic Dynasty in Egypt.

301-64BC The Seleucid Dynasty rules an empire in Asia Minor.

c.300-200BC Alphabetic script is developed in Meroë.

280-268BC The Antigonid Dynasty rules in Macedonia.

c.272-231BC Asoka of the Maurya Dynasty unites most of India under his rule.

264BC Rome now dominates the whole of Italy.

264-241BC First Punic War between the Romans and the Carthaginians.

221BC Unification of China by the first Ch'in emperor, Shi-huang-ti.

218-202BC Second Punic War.

214BC The Great Wall of China is built to keep out hostile tribes, the Hsiung-Nu (also known as Huns).

206BC-AD222 Han Dynasty rules China.

149-146BC Third Punic War ends with the destruction of Carthage.

133-31BC The Romans expand throughout the Mediterranean and build up a huge empire.

c.100BC Paper is invented in China.

51-30BC Reign of Queen Cleopatra VII of Egypt.

31BC Anthony and Cleopatra are defeated by the Romans at the Battle of Actium.

30BC Egypt becomes a province of the Roman empire.

The myths of Egypt and Mesopotamia

The people of Ancient Egypt and Mesopotamia told stories about their gods and goddesses and kings and queens, and about how the world began, to help explain the world about them. We call these stories myths and legends. Below are some of the most important ones. The names of the main characters are picked out in bold type to make them easier to identify.

The gods and goddesses of these early civilizations were capable of human failings. Some behaved badly and were punished, some were tricked, and others even died. You can read more about the Egyptian deities on pages 20-21.

Part one: Mesopotamia

In the beginning

The Sumerians had a number of different stories to explain how the world was created. According to one version, it was the work of **An** (known to the Akkadians as **Anu**). In another, four gods were responsible, and in yet another, all the gods were said to have played a part. The most popular account claimed that the world began with **Nammu**, goddess of the salty ocean. She gave birth to a son (the Sky) and a daughter (the Earth). They had a son called **Enlil** (the air). Enlil separated the sky from the Earth and then, with the Earth, created all living creatures.

All the different version agree on what the newly created world looked like. It was a flat disc with mountains all around the outside edge, floating in an ocean of sweet (not salty) water. Over the Earth, the sky stretched in a great half-circle, across which the stars and planets moved. Below the Earth was the Underworld, the realm of the dead, also covered with a half-circle of sky. This was ruled by the goddess **Ereshkigal**, with her husband **Nergal**, god of war and sickness. The Earth and the Underworld were both encircled by atmosphere and floated like a bubble in the salty ocean.

The Babylonians and the Assyrians had their own versions of the story, with their own chief gods in the leading roles. In the Babylonian version, the world began with **Apsu** (sweet waters), **Tiamat** (salt water) and **Mummu** (clouds). Apsu and Tiamat gave birth to several deities, some of whom caused so much trouble that their parents planned to kill them. The younger gods foiled the plot by killing Apsu and casting a spell on Mummu. In revenge, Tiamat declared war and created terrifying dragons and snakes which caused the gods to tremble with fear. Then **Marduk** came forward and offered to destroy the monsters, provided the gods made him their king. Armed with lightning and the winds, he set out in his chariot and killed the monsters and Tiamat too. He slit Tiamat's body in two, using half to form the sky and half to form the earth. Marduk became king of the gods.

The crime of Enlil

After the creation, **Enlil** laid down the laws by which everything and everyone, gods and men included, were to be governed. Foolishly Enlil broke his own laws. One day he saw a beautiful young goddess called **Ninlil** bathing in a river. Despite her pleas, he dragged her struggling from the water and raped her. She gave birth to **Nannu**, the moon god (known to the Akkadians as **Sin**). For this crime, Enlil was banished from the Earth.

How Enki was tricked

With **Enlil** banished, the god **Enki** (known to the Babylonians as **Ea**) took over the task of organizing the Universe. He provided pure water, rain, fish, land animals and plants. He then appointed a different deity to watch over each of his creations. He kept the magical power, which he used to control all things, in the city of Eridu where he lived.

Enki's daughter **Inanna** (later known as **Ishtar**), goddess of love, wanted her city of Erech to be the most powerful one. She held a banquet for her father and encouraged him to drink far too much. When he was hopelessly drunk, she persuaded him to hand over the magic power. She carried it back to Erech, which then became the most powerful city in Sumer. When Enki recovered and realized that he had been tricked, he flew into a terrible rage. He sent an enormous sea monster to try to get the power back, but Inanna was able to use the power to protect her city. Enki had failed.

Trouble in Paradise

Dilmun was a beautiful land, where no-one was ever ill or died. It was full of plants and trees bearing delicious fruits that the inhabitants could pluck and eat. In the centre, there were eight special trees which had been planted by the mother goddess **Ninhursag**. It was forbidden to eat any of the fruit from these trees. However **Enki** wanted to taste them and sent a servant to pick them for him. Ninhursag was furious when she found out what had happened and put a curse on him. Enki collapsed and was near death, but the other gods begged the mother goddess to relent and cure him. Eventually she agreed and Enki's life was spared.

The fate of Dumuzi

Inanna was Queen of Heaven, but she wanted to be Queen of the Underworld too. The Underworld was ruled by **Ereshkigal** from the Palace of the Seven Gates. Inanna went to the palace, but Ereshkigal was unwilling to give up her power. She had Inanna tied up and imprisoned in the gloomy world of the dead.

Despite the trick Inanna had played on him, **Enki**

intervened and asked Ereshkigal to release his daughter. Ereshkigal finally agreed, but on condition that Inanna found someone to replace her in the Underworld. If she failed in this task, she would have to return there forever.

Inanna went back to Earth, accompanied by *galla* (demon guards) to make sure she did not try to escape. She tried unsuccessfully to find a volunteer to take her place. When she reached her home city of Erech, she found her husband **Dumuzi** on the throne. He had grown tired of his wife being in charge and had taken advantage of her absence to take control. Enraged by this betrayal, Inanna told the *galla* that they could have Dumuzi in her place. The demons leapt at him and dragged him screaming to his fate.

Mankind and the chance of immortality

According to one Babylonian story, the gods **Marduk** and **Ea** created human beings from clay mixed with the blood of the slain monster **Kingu**. The blood contained evil, which is why mankind is prone to wickedness.

In another version, the first human being was **Adapa**, a man created by Ea. One day when Adapa was fishing, he cursed the South Wind which had nearly caused him to drown in a gale. As a result the wind stopped. The winter winds did not blow to Mesopotamia that year and the date crop was affected. The god **An** was furious and sent for Adapa.

Ea advised Adapa to be very humble, to admit that he ought not to have cursed the wind, and to apologize for it. He told him to expect offerings of clothes and oil, and then bread and water. Ea urged Adapa to accept the first two gifts, but to decline politely any offer of food and drink because they were the bread and water of death.

Adapa did exactly as Ea had suggested, and An sent him on his way without punishment. What Adapa didn't know, however, was that An had been so impressed by his humility and reverence that the bread and water he had offered was the food of life. If Adapa had tasted it, he and everyone after him would have lived forever. He had turned down the chance of immortality for all mankind.

The flood

Mankind had been created to serve the gods, who appointed kings to enforce the divine laws. Despite this, people became lazy, disobedient, and wicked. During the rule of King **Ubar-Tutu** of the city of Shuruppak, the population became so unruly that the gods decided to kill everyone in a flood. However, **Ea** had noticed that the king's son **Ut-napishtim** was a good man who respected the gods' laws and was humble and obedient. Ea warned Ut-napishtim of what was to happen and instructed him to build a boat. He told him to take his family, his servants, and animals of every species on board. No sooner had he done this than it began to rain.

A great storm raged for seven days, drowning everything and everyone, until even the gods were scared of the destruction they had unleashed and regretted their actions.

Meanwhile, Ut-napishtim's boat rode out the storm and eventually ran aground on the submerged peak of Mount Nisir. No land was visible in any direction. Ut-napishtim released a dove but, finding no land to perch on, it came back. Later he released a swallow, but it also returned. Finally he sent a raven. As the raven did not come back, Ut-napishtim knew that it must have found land and that the water level must be dropping. He gave thanks to the gods for saving all those on the boat, and offered sacrifices.

At first **Enlil** was furious to find that some people had survived the flood, but he calmed down when he realized that Ut-napishtim was a good man and that the other gods were pleased. He told Ut-napishtim and his wife the secret of eternal life, and the couple went to live in the beautiful land of Dilmun (see page 92).

The quest of Gilgamesh

Gilgamesh, King of Uruk, was the son of the goddess **Ninsun** and a High Priest of Uruk. Gilgamesh was handsome, strong and brave, but he was also arrogant and ruthless. His subjects appealed to the god **Anu** for help. In response, Anu created **Enkidu**, a wild hairy man of brutish strength, to teach him a lesson. The two men quarrelled and fought, but they grew to respect each other's strength and became firm friends.

Gilgamesh and Enkidu had a series of adventures together, which included the slaying of a giant who lived in the Cedar Forest. Then the goddess **Ishtar** fell in love with Gilgamesh and offered to marry him. He turned her down, reminding her that she had treated some of her other lovers very badly. Bitterly offended, Ishtar went to Anu and persuaded him to send the Bull of Heaven to ravage Uruk. But her plan failed. Gilgamesh and Enkidu were strong enough to kill the Bull. They tore the animal apart and threw a piece of it at Ishtar. The gods decided that someone would have to pay for such bad behaviour, and Enkidu was struck down with an illness that killed him.

Devastated at the loss of his friend, Gilgamesh now feared his own death and decided that he wanted to live forever. He knew that **Ut-napishtim** and his wife knew the secret of everlasting life, and so he set off to Dilmun in search of them. After many adventures, Gilgamesh finally found them. They told him of a thorny plant that grew at the bottom of the ocean, and said that anyone who ate this plant would become immortal. Gilgamesh dived deep into the ocean, plucked the only plant and brought it triumphantly to the surface. He set off for home but, exhausted by his adventures, settled down to sleep with the plant in his fist. While he slept, he lost his grip on the plant. It fell to the ground and was eaten by a snake. Gilgamesh lost his chance of eternal life, but somewhere, according to the Babylonians, there is a snake that will live forever.

The baby in a basket

Long ago, in the city of Azupiranu, a young woman gave birth to a baby boy in secret. According to the rules of the society of the day, she should not have had a child. It may have been because she was a priestess who was not allowed to marry. The woman managed to hide the fact that she was pregnant and, after the boy was born, she decided that he had to find him a new home.

She made a basket from the rushes that grew by the water's edge, and made it water-tight by coating it in tar. She then put her baby in the basket and cast it adrift in the River Euphrates. As his mother had hoped, the baby was found. A man called **Akki** was drawing water from the river when he spotted the basket and looked inside. He took the child home and raised him as his son.

As the boy grew, he showed great intelligence and courage. He entered the service of King **Ur-Zababa** of Kish. The king was impressed with him and made him his cup-bearer. This was an unfortunate move for the king. The young man's name was **Sharru-kin**, better known as **Sargon†**. He overthrew his master, seized the throne and founded the kingdom of Akkad. He brought all of Sumer under his control and went on to build the world's first great empire.

Part two: Egypt

The eye of Re

The Egyptians had many different myths to explain how the Universe was created. In most of them the sun god **Re** was the creator, but there are a number of different versions about how he came to Earth. You can read about some of them on page 21.

Re had two children: **Shu**, god of air, and **Tefnut**, goddess of moisture. Soon after their birth, they wandered off and got lost. When they did not return, Re became worried and sent one of his eyes to look for them. The eye was gone a long time, hunting high and low for the missing children. Unsure if it would ever come back, Re made himself a new one to replace it.

When the eye did return, it was furious to find its place had been taken. It cried with rage, and from its tears sprang human beings. It then became so furious that it burst into flames. Re picked up the flaming eye and turned it into a snake. He then placed the eye on his forehead, where it sits, spitting fire at his enemies if they approach.

The secret name of Re

Every god and goddess in Egypt had a secret name which gave them their power. Anyone who found out the secret name would have power over them. The goddess **Isis** had greater magic powers than any other deity except **Re**, but she wanted to be the most

powerful of all. Many times she tried to trick the sun god into telling her his secret name, but without success. Isis knew that her magic alone would never beat Re.

However, one day, she saw a drop of saliva fall from his mouth. When his back was turned, she dug up the piece of soil where it had fallen. She mixed the saliva and soil unto a clay, chanting spells as she worked. From the clay she made a magic snake and placed it on a path where Re often walked.

The next time Re walked along the path, the snake came to life and bit him. As the snake was made from his own saliva, as well as Isis's magic, it had the power to harm him. Re was in agony. Many of the gods and goddesses tried to cure him, but all failed. Finally Isis offered to relieve the pain, but only if he told her his secret name. She used magic to make the pain even worse. In the end it became unbearable and Re gave in. He whispered the secret name so that none of the other deities would hear. Re was cured and Isis became the greatest magician of all.

Hathor and the destruction of mankind

People began to look at **Re** and think that he must be growing old and frail. As they became less frightened of his power, many people became disobedient, and some even plotted against him. When Re realized this, he became enraged. He ordered **Hathor**, goddess of love and beauty, to go down to Earth to destroy his enemies.

Hathor turned herself into the fierce lioness **Sekhmet** and set about her task, killing Re's enemies and drinking their blood. However, the more people she killed, the more she enjoyed it. Re became alarmed that the human race might eventually be wiped out and decided that he must stop her.

When she was asleep, he flooded Egypt with a beer that had been coloured red by a soil called ochre. When the lioness awoke, she thought that the red beer was the blood of her victims and began to lap it up. The more she drank, the happier she became, and she forgot what she had been sent to do. She turned back into the gentle goddess Hathor and mankind was saved.

Horus and Set

The story of how the god **Osiris** was murdered by his wicked brother **Set** and brought back to life by his sister-wife **Isis** is told on page 21.

Osiris and Isis were the parents of the boy **Horus**. When Horus had grown up, he claimed the throne of Egypt as his rightful inheritance from his father who had ruled before him. Set immediately objected. He had persecuted Isis and Osiris and now wanted to rule Egypt in place of their son. The case was taken to the tribunal of the gods. Most of the gods supported Horus, but **Re** was angry because he had not been consulted, and so he favoured Set's claim. The two rivals then embarked on a struggle that was to last 80 years.

They fought each other physically, sometimes in the form of humans, sometimes as animals, and both sustained terrible wounds. At one point Horus lost his eye, but was healed by his wife, the goddess **Hathor**. During one fight, they each turned into a hippopotamus and fought in the river. Isis stood on the river bank, but angered her son by failing to harpoon her brother Set when she had the chance.

Horus and Set also tried to settle the dispute with contests, one often trying to outwit the other with tricks. Once, for example, they agreed to race in stone boats. Set built a boat of stone and of course it sank. Horus, however, built his from wood covered with a rough plaster that looked like stone. He won that race, but the fight for the throne continued.

Isis achieved the greatest success when she disguised herself as a beautiful woman. She appealed to Set for help, claiming that her son had been denied his rightful inheritance. Set, dazzled by her beauty, agreed that a son ought to be allowed to inherit his father's property. The gods heard him condemning his case from his own mouth.

Unable to reach a decision, the tribunal of the gods eventually appealed to the goddess **Neith**, the ancestress of them all, to make a decision. She ordered them to uphold Horus's claim. If they refused, she threatened to allow the sky to crash to Earth. Re obeyed Neith's command, though with some reluctance. (In some versions of the story Neith was Re's mother.) Horus became King of Egypt and, in compensation, Set was given two foreign goddesses, **Astarte** and **Anath**, as extra wives. Horus's father Osiris became ruler of the dead in the Kingdom of the West.

Seven lean years

In the reign of King **Zoser**† of Dynasty III, famine struck the land of Egypt. For seven years the River Nile had failed to flood and cover the valley with rich, fertile mud. Without the mud, the crops would not grow, and so the granaries stayed empty and the people went hungry. No-one seemed to know which of the gods controlled the river, so Zoser asked a priest to advise him. The priest travelled to Hermopolis to consult sacred books in the temple of **Thoth**, god of wisdom. From these books, he learned that the god **Khnum**, Lord of the First Cataract†, controlled the Nile from the city of Elephantine. On hearing the news, Zoser hastily ordered offerings to be made to Khnum.

That night Khnum appeared to him in a dream. He complained that, despite all he had done to help Egypt, his temples were falling into ruin and no new shrines were being built in his honour. The next day Zoser gave orders that Khnum's temples should be repaired and new ones built. He gave areas of land to Khnum, and decreed that all those who worked on the land – farmers, hunters and fishers – should always give part of their produce or catch to the god in thanks. Khnum was satisfied and the Nile rose properly that year and for many years after. The famine had come to an end.

The magician and the missing amulet

Once, when he was holding a great banquet, King **Khufu**† called on his sons to tell him stories. Each prince told a story. This is the one told by Baufre.

One day King **Sneferu**†, Khufu's father, was feeling bored and depressed. To cheer him up, one of his priests suggested that 20 of the most beautiful women in the king's harem should row him in a pleasure boat around the lake. The king agreed and the outing was arranged.

Sneferu was enjoying his tour around the lake until one of the women stopped rowing and disturbed the rest of the party. When he asked her what the matter was, she explained that her new turquoise amulet† had fallen from her hair into the lake. He felt sorry for her and promised a new one, but she was still upset and insisted that she find the missing amulet. Fortunately, the priest who had suggested the outing was also a magician. He stretched out his staff over the lake and the waters parted to reveal the turquoise amulet lying on the sandy bottom. The woman climbed out of the boat and put the amulet into her hair. She went back to her seat and the lake returned to normal. The women began to row once more and Sneferu was happy.

Khonsu and the Princess of Bakhtan

One summer the great pharaoh **Ramesses II**† was on a tour of his empire, collecting tribute† from the princes of the conquered lands. One of the princes who came to him was the ruler of the state of Bakhtan. In addition to many fine gifts, he gave Ramesses his eldest daughter. She was so clever, talented and beautiful that Ramesses fell in love with her and married her. He gave her the Egyptian name of **Neferure** and made her a queen.

They had been living happily in Egypt for a while when an urgent message arrived from Neferure's father. His youngest daughter, Princess **Bentresh**, was very ill, and he begged Ramesses to send an Egyptian doctor to try to cure her. The doctor was despatched and reported that Bentresh was possessed by an evil spirit. It would need the intervention of a god to save her.

Ramesses sent the Prince of Bakhtan a miracle-working statue of the moon god **Khonsu**. The statue was taken to the princess's bedchamber and the god battled with the evil spirit. He drove it from her and left her fully recovered. All Bakhtan rejoiced, but the prince was so impressed by the power of the statue that he did not want to return it. He built a shrine for the statue and made one excuse after another to postpone its departure from Bakhtan.

One night the prince dreamed that the god had left the shrine and had flown back to Egypt in the form of a golden falcon. When he awoke, the prince was afraid. He realized that the god wanted his statue to go home, and that trouble might befall him if he did not return it. So he ordered the return of the statue and the Egyptians rejoiced to have Khonsu safely home again.

The legacy of Egypt and Mesopotamia

The roots of civilization itself can be traced back to Egypt and Mesopotamia. However, the influence of the early civilizations there is often less obvious than that of the Greeks and the Romans, who adapted and recorded many of their ideas and discoveries. Some of the most important ones are listed below.

The wheel

The wheel, which originated in Sumer in about 3400BC, was first used by potters and only later adapted for carts and chariots. It opened up the possibility of transport and travel, and so radically altered people's lives.

Writing

One of the most crucial steps in the development of civilization is the invention of writing. The earliest known writing systems were developed in Sumer and Egypt between 3500BC and 3000BC (see pages 10-11). The alphabet we use today is based on that of the Ancient Greeks, which in turn was adapted from an alphabet devised by the Phoenicians (see page 72). However, some experts believe it may be possible to identify a connection with Egyptian hieroglyphs. In the Sinai Desert, a number of inscriptions have been found which date from the Middle Kingdom, a period when Semites† were working there for the Egyptians. The inscriptions must be alphabetic, as they contain only 27 signs. As the Phoenician alphabet may have been influenced or directly descended from this script, there may be a link between this alphabet and our own.

Law

The earliest examples of written codes of law have been found in Mesopotamia. The most famous example is the law code of King Hammurabi of Babylon (see page 25).

Astronomy

The Babylonians were the first to observe the seasonal equinoxes and the phases of the Moon. They also named some of the constellations of the stars. A few of the signs of the Zodiac have Babylonian names.

The Egyptians understood that there were differences between planets and stars and were able to identify a number of planets. They used their knowledge of the stars to work out several calendars (see opposite).

Mathematics and measurement

The Babylonians used the number 60 as a unit of measurement. They were the first people to divide a circle into 360 degrees, and an hour into 60 minutes.

The Egyptians divided the day into 24 hours and the year into 365 days. This idea was adapted by the Roman dictator Julius Caesar† and became known as the Julian Calendar. This is the basis for the calendar we use today, though it has been amended slightly to include leap years. The Egyptians also invented a water clock, which is one of the earliest successful attempts to measure the passage of time.

The Egyptians' skill in mathematics is best demonstrated by their achievements in architecture, the most oustanding example of which is the design of the pyramid. As an architectural form, the pyramid is still being used today, most notably in glass at the entrance to the Palace of the Louvre in Paris.

Medicine

Greek writers often openly acknowledged the amount they had learned from Egyptian doctors. The Egyptians had a detailed knowledge of human anatomy, acquired from centuries of embalming their dead (see pages 18-19). They also had some knowledge of the nervous system, the pulse, the effects of various injuries, and the circulation of the blood. Egyptian doctors had excellent diagnostic techniques and a knowledge of the medicinal properties of many plants and herbs.

Religion

Versions of several Mesopotamian and Egyptian religious stories have reappeared in the Old Testament of the Bible. Mesopotamian myths contain versions of stories which predate the Bible about eating forbidden fruit and a universal flood. There are also striking similarities between several Hebrew psalms and Egyptian hymns, and between the sayings of Egyptian wise men and the Book of Proverbs.

The Egyptians also had an important influence on the development of Christianity. Several of the great writers and thinkers of the early Christian Church were either Egyptian or lived and worked there. Monasticism began in Egypt in the 3rd century, when some Christians began withdrawing into the desert to live as hermits. In the 4th century the first monasteries were established there by Basil of Caesarea.

THE
GREEKS

Susan Peach
Anne Millard
BA, Dip. Ed., Dip. Arch., Ph.D.

History consultant: **Graham Tingay** MA

Edited by **Jane Chisholm**

Designed by **Robert Walster, Radhi Parekh**
and **Iain Ashman**

Illustrated by **Ian Jackson**

Additional illustrations by
**Richard Draper, Robert Walster, Gerry Wood,
Peter Dennis, Nigel Wright** and **Gillian Hurry**

With thanks to **Anthony Marks**

Contents

How to use this section of the book

Dates

Most of the dates in this section are from the period before the birth of Christ. These dates are shown by the letters BC, which stand for "Before Christ". Dates in the period after the birth of Christ are indicated by the letters AD, which stand for *Anno Domini,* meaning "Year of our Lord".

Dates in the BC period are counted backwards from the birth of Christ. The main centuries are .

1-99BC	= first century BC
100-199BC	= second century BC
200-299BC	= third century BC
300-399BC	= fourth century BC
400-499BC	= fifth century BC
500-599BC	= sixth century BC
600-699BC	= seventh century BC

Experts have not been able to discover the exact dates for many events in Greek history, and most archaeological finds can only be dated imprecisely. In this section, where a date is only approximate, it is preceded by the abbreviation "c". This stands for *circa,* the Latin for "about".

Periods of Ancient Greek history

Experts divide Ancient Greek history into several approximate periods, which are shown on the chart below. These periods have been used throughout this section of the book.

c.2900-1000BC	= The Bronze Age
c.1100-800BC	= The Dark Ages
c.800-500BC	= The Archaic Period
c.500-336BC	= The Classical Period
c.336-30BC	= The Hellenistic Period

How we know about the Greeks

Although the Ancient Greeks lived about three thousand years ago, we know a lot about how they lived. Our information comes from a variety of sources, which are shown here.

Archaeologists have dug up many Ancient Greek objects and buildings. Important sites have been excavated in Greece and in the places that the Greeks colonized. Marine archaeologists have found the wrecks of several Ancient Greek ships, some with their cargoes preserved. Greek objects have also been found in countries where they were taken by traders. For example, Minoan pots made on Crete have been dug up in Egyptian tombs (see page 101).

Archaeologists at work on a site.

Pots are some of the most useful archaeological discoveries. The Greeks decorated many of their pots with pictures of everyday life. These scenes have given experts much information about what the Greeks looked like, what they wore, what their homes and furniture were like, and the kind of lives they lived. Many scenes in this book are based on pictures found on vases.

This vase shows potters at work.

When the Romans occupied Greece in the second century BC, they were fascinated by the buildings, statues and paintings that they discovered there. They were so impressed by Greek art that they made copies of many statues and paintings. A large number of these Roman copies have survived, although the originals have been lost.

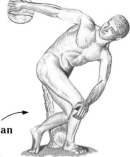

This discus thrower is a Roman copy of a Greek statue. The Greek original has been lost.

The Greeks wrote on scrolls made out of a plant called papyrus. This rots easily, so very few original manuscripts have been found. However Greek writings have survived because people from Roman times onwards made copies of them. The copies include works by many Greek writers about history, philosophy and politics, as well as plays and poems. Coins, clay tablets and inscriptions on monuments and buildings provide other written evidence.

Part of an inscription from the wall of a Greek temple.

Silver coin from Athens.

Fragment of Greek papyrus found in Egypt.

Key dates

On some pages of this section there are charts which summarize the events of the particular period or place. A chart on pages 186-187 lists all the events in this section.

Unfamiliar words

Greek words, such as *tholos*, are written in italic type. Words that are followed by a dagger symbol, such as democracy†, are explained in the glossary on pages 188-189. If a person's name is followed by this symbol, it means that you can read more about them in the "Who's Who" on pages 183-185.

Places

There are small maps on many pages, to show where events took place. Towns or cities are marked with dots, and battles are shown with crosses.

Many places now have different names from their Ancient Greek names. In most cases the ancient names have been used, and the area is made clear by the map. The area now called Turkey is referred to throughout this section as Asia Minor, which was its name in ancient times.

Reference

At the back of this section of the book there is an appendix. This contains a detailed map of Greece, summaries of important Greek myths and legends, a section that explains who was who in Ancient Greece, a chart of the important dates in Ancient Greek history, and a glossary of Greek and other unfamiliar words.

The first Greeks

The area now called Greece consists of a land-mass on the north-eastern edge of the Mediterranean Sea and the surrounding islands.

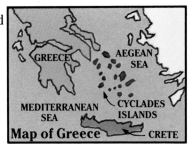
Map of Greece

The first inhabitants arrived in Greece about 40,000 years ago. They lived in caves and hunted and gathered food. Some time before 6000BC, farming was introduced by new groups of people from the east who settled in eastern Greece.

The first farmers grew vegetables and cereal crops and kept sheep.

Around 3000BC, people in Greece discovered how to mix copper and tin to make bronze. They used it to make tools and weapons. These were harder and sharper than previous ones, which had been made of bone or flint. The improved equipment made farming and building easier. The period from 3000-1100BC is known as the Bronze Age†.

These objects were all made during the Bronze Age.

Marble figure

Gold earrings

Clay jar

As farming became more efficient, many farmers had a surplus of produce which could be exchanged for goods. Some people made a living as craftsmen by selling their goods instead of growing food. Trade made people more prosperous, the population increased and some villages grew into towns.

Farm produce could be exchanged for goods such as tools, jewellery or pottery.

From 2600-2000BC the people of the Cyclades were particularly prosperous. Craftsmen produced fine goods and there was much trade between the islands. However, the Cyclades were too small to develop further and it was on the island of Crete that the first great European civilization began.

Crete

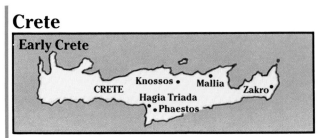
Early Crete

The first inhabitants of Crete seem to have been farmers who settled there in about 6000BC. By about 2000BC there was a flourishing civilization on the island, with a highly organized economy and system of trade, based around a number of large palaces. There were skilled craftsmen and artists, and some people could read and write.

These objects were made by early Cretan craftsmen.

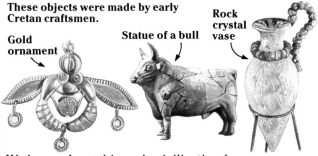

Gold ornament

Statue of a bull

Rock crystal vase

We know about this early civilization from archaeological evidence found on Crete. The first and most important discoveries were made by an Englishman called Sir Arthur Evans. In AD1894 he began excavating a palace at Knossos (see map above). Evans named the civilization Minoan†, after a legendary Cretan king called Minos.

The legend of Minos

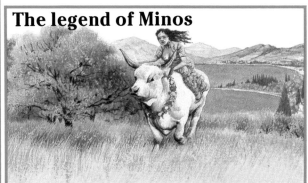

According to Greek legend, the god Zeus (see page 160) fell in love with a beautiful princess called Europa. He assumed the shape of a bull and swam to Crete with her on his back. She had three sons, Minos, Sarpedon and Rhadamanthys. Minos became the king of Crete, and his palace was at Knossos.

Although the legend says that Minos was the name of one king, experts now think that Minos may actually have been a title, like the Egyptian word Pharaoh. All Cretan kings may therefore have been known as Minos.

Life in Minoan Crete

An extra piece of cloth could be worn like an apron.

Short kilt

Flounced skirt

A belt of twisted cloth was tied around the waist.

We know what the Minoans wore because their clothes were shown on many wall paintings. Men usually wore a loincloth and a short kilt made of wool or linen.

Women wore elaborate, brightly coloured dresses with tight bodices which left their breasts bare. The skirts were generally flounced.

Most people made their living from farming. They kept animals and grew crops such as wheat, barley, olives and grapes. Fishing and hunting provided extra food. This Minoan wall painting shows a young fisherman.

Map of Minoan trade

The Minoans travelled widely, both on Crete and abroad. They used carts drawn by oxen or donkeys, but as there were few roads, people often travelled by sea.

The Greek historian Thucydides says that King Minos had a large fleet of ships, which controlled the seas. This wall painting shows a variety of Minoan ships.

The Minoans traded with many foreign countries. Their pots and other goods have been found in Greece and the Cyclades and all round the eastern Mediterranean (see map).

Writing

When the Minoans started to store and export goods, they developed a system of writing to help them keep accurate records. Their first script, which was used from c.2000BC, was a form of hieroglyphic (picture) writing. In about 1900BC they introduced a second script, which we call Linear A†. As yet no-one has been able to decipher either of these scripts.

Part of a Linear A tablet

This disc, from Phaestos, is inscribed with a third Minoan script, which has not yet been deciphered.

Pottery

Minoan pots

Before the discovery of Knossos, Minoan pots had been found in Egypt. These pots had already been approximately dated, as experts had been able to establish dates for Egyptian sites. When archaeologists found a particular style of pot on Crete, they could date it by comparing it with the dated pots found in Egypt. This also meant that they could give a rough date to the Cretan site at which the pot had been discovered.

101

The Minoan palaces

The Minoans† often built their towns by the coast, in places where it was easy to reach the sea and the fertile farmlands. Each of the larger towns was based around a palace. The first palaces were built shortly after 2000BC and were destroyed by earthquakes about 300 years later. Little remains of these early buildings because the Minoans quickly built new, even grander palaces over the old ones. Four of these later palaces have been found, at Knossos, Zakro, Phaestos and Mallia. There is also a large villa at Hagia Triada and a few smaller sites, mostly to the east of the island.

The palace at Knossos

The largest palace was at a place called Knossos. It was built and rebuilt several times between about 1900BC and 1450BC. This picture shows how it probably looked at its height, when it covered around 20,000 square metres (215,000 square feet). Experts think that over 30,000 people lived in the palace and surrounding area.

> The palace was decorated with images of a bull's horns.

> The roofs, ceilings and doors were made of wood.

The queen's bathroom

Knossos had an excellent water supply and drainage system. To prevent floods the heavy spring and autumn rains were channelled into gutters. The water was stored in tanks, then passed into the palace along clay pipes. The system served several toilets and bathrooms. This reconstruction shows the queen's bathroom.

The royal apartments

Each palace had private apartments set aside for the royal family. The royal apartments had large, airy rooms, decorated with colourful wall paintings known as frescoes. These were made by applying paint to wet plaster. The frescoes at Knossos have given archaeologists much valuable information about Minoan dress and customs. Most of the frescoes which can now be seen in the palace are modern reconstructions, based on fragments of the original pictures.

This fresco shows a young man wearing an elaborate headdress which suggests that he was a prince or a king.

Many paintings depict the beauty of nature. This is part of a fresco from the queen's apartment, which shows a school of dolphins.

Lighting

Light was let into the building through open shafts which ran from the roof to the ground floor. These are known as light wells. Staircases and corridors led from the light wells to the rooms on each level.

The throne room

The king at Knossos may have had some power over the rulers of the other Minoan palaces, and he played an important part in the religious life of the island. As well as his private apartments, the king had a number of state rooms. One of these was a throne room where he conducted state business or religious ceremonies.

When Evans excavated Knossos he found the throne room almost intact. This is what it looks like today.

The floors were supported by wooden columns, which were painted red.

Some parts of the building had three or four storeys.

The buildings were arranged round a large courtyard which was used for religious ceremonies (see page 8).

The palace was built mainly of stone.

Storerooms

Minoan trade was highly organized. Grain, wine and oil were produced on farms. Part of the crop was kept in storerooms at the palaces and was used to feed the court and to pay officials and craftsmen. The remainder was exported around the Mediterranean. The Minoans used the profits to pay for imports such as precious metals, jewels, ivory, ostrich plumes and amber. These were stored at the palaces and then used by the craftsmen.

Food, oil and wine were stored in huge earthenware jars called *pithoi*†. Some of these were taller than a fully grown man.

Pithoi used for storing liquids had a hole at the bottom with a stopper, so that their contents could be run off when required.

Ordinary houses

Not everyone lived in the palaces. Many people lived in smaller houses outside the palace grounds. These varied in size, but usually the storage, cooking and work areas were downstairs, with the living and sleeping quarters above. Some houses also had a room on the roof. This model, made of faience† (glazed earthenware), was found at Knossos. It shows what the outside of a Minoan town house looked like.

Minoan religion

Special rooms were set aside for religious ceremonies in Minoan palaces. Outdoor shrines were also used. Archaeological remains have revealed how the Minoans worshipped and the roles of some of their gods. It seems that goddesses were probably more important than gods, as they are much more prominent in statues and paintings. Some of them are shown here.

◀ The goddess on this seal is known as the Mistress of the Animals. She is shown on a mountain top, surrounded by animals. A young male god is worshipping her.

The Minoans ▶ worshipped a goddess who protected the household. She is often depicted with snakes, which were a sacred symbol.

This seal shows another important ▲ goddess who looked after crops. She is often depicted by a sacred tree and is sometimes accompanied by a young god.

Sacred symbols

The Minoans had two sacred symbols which they used to decorate palaces, tombs and pots. The bull was thought to be sacred and images of its horns were found throughout Knossos. Another common symbol was the double-headed axe, or *labrys*†.

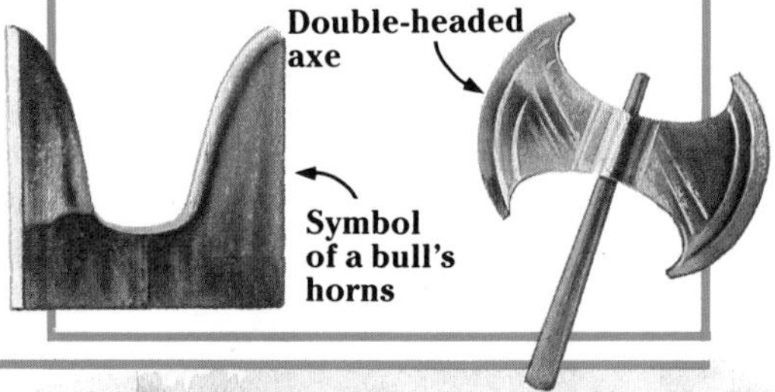

Double-headed axe

Symbol of a bull's horns

Religious ceremonies

This reconstruction shows what might have happened at a religious ceremony. Special priests and priestesses would have led the ceremony. Archaeological remains show that the Minoans made offerings of food, statues and axes to their gods.

Musicians

During the ceremony, a libation† (an offering of milk, wine or blood) was poured on to an altar

Sacred symbols and statues of gods

Altar

Offerings

Bull-leaping

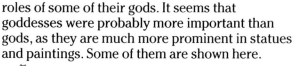

This fresco† shows part of the bull-leaping ritual. The figure on the right was there to catch the leaper.

One of the strangest Minoan practices was bull-leaping. It seems that teams of young men and women approached a charging bull. One after the other they grasped its horns, leaped on to its back, and then to the ground. Many experts believe that this was a religious ritual, as the bull was a sacred animal. The ceremony may have taken place in the palace courtyard.

Death and the afterlife

The Minoans believed in some form of life after death. They buried dead people with food and personal possessions which they thought would be of use in the afterlife. Early tombs, dating from about 2800BC, were round stone structures which were used for many burials. Later the Minoans used individual coffins.

This coffin, found at the villa of Hagia Triada, was made in about 1400BC. It is decorated with a funeral scene showing people making offerings.

The end of the Minoans

In about 1450BC all the palaces on Crete were destroyed. Many experts have linked this event to a volcanic eruption on the island of Thera, about 110km (70 miles) north of Crete. The explosions were so violent that most of Thera was blasted away, leaving only the small crescent-shaped island now called Santorini. On Crete, this may have caused tidal waves, earth tremors, flooding and destruction of crops. Recent geological evidence suggests that the eruption may have taken place about 200 years earlier, so Minoan dates may have to be revised.

Map of Thera and Crete

Area affected by the explosion

THERA

Thera before the eruption

Thera after the eruption

CRETE • Knossos

The arrival of the Mycenaeans

Natural disasters may not have been the only cause of the Minoans' downfall. According to legend, King Minos travelled to Sicily, where he was murdered by a local king and his fleet was destroyed. This may be partly true. Perhaps there was an unsuccessful expedition to Sicily, which left Crete without a fleet. We know that by about 1450BC Crete had been invaded by a people from mainland Greece, known as the Mycenaeans.

The Mycenaeans repaired and rebuilt the palace at Knossos and became the new rulers of the island.

Around 1400BC the palace at Knossos burned down and was abandoned.

About 50 years later Knossos was destroyed again. We do not know why this happened. Perhaps the Mycenaeans fought among themselves, or new conquerors arrived from Greece. Another theory is that the Minoans rebelled against the Mycenaeans. Between 1400BC and 1100BC a joint Minoan-Mycenaean culture flourished, but Crete became a second-class power. By 1100BC Minoan culture had collapsed.

The Minotaur

According to a later Greek legend, an Athenian prince called Theseus went to Crete, where he fought and killed a terrible monster called the Minotaur. It was half man, half bull and was kept in a maze called the *Labyrinth.* *

Perhaps there was some truth in this story. The palace at Knossos might well have seemed like a maze because it had so many rooms and corridors. It could have been known as the *Labyrinth*, or house of the *labrys†*, because it was decorated with so many pictures of the double axe.

The Minotaur could also have been based on fact. One scholar has suggested that the king wore the mask of a bull's head during religious rituals. It is possible that the story may have become confused. People may have forgotten about the king and begun to believe in a monster.

Key dates

c.6000BC The first farmers arrive on Crete and the Greek mainland.

c.3000BC People in Greece discover how to make bronze. Start of the Bronze Age†.

c.2000BC The first palaces are built on Crete.

c.1900BC The Minoans start to use the Linear A† script.

c.1700BC The first palaces are destroyed by earthquake. New palaces are built.

c.1600BC The first Mycenaeans arrive on Crete.

c.1450BC Traditional date for the destruction of Thera. Recent evidence suggests that this date may have to be revised (see above).

c.1400BC Final destruction of the palace at Knossos.

c.1100BC End of Minoan culture.

*You can read the full story of Theseus and the Minotaur on page 178.

The Mycenaeans

From about 1600-1100BC, mainland Greece was dominated by a people we call the Mycenaeans, who lived in small kingdoms. Their name comes from the city of Mycenae, where remains of the culture were first discovered. Some experts believe that the Mycenaeans invaded Greece from central Europe between 2000-1900BC. Others think that they had already been in Greece for some time, and only gradually became the dominant people. Although they were never politically united, the Mycenaeans were linked by their culture. They all spoke an early form of the Greek language and they shared a common way of life and religious beliefs.

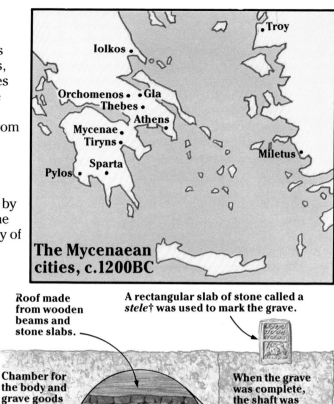

The Mycenaean cities, c.1200BC

(Map labels: Troy, Iolkos, Orchomenos, Gla, Thebes, Mycenae, Athens, Tiryns, Sparta, Pylos, Miletus)

The royal graves

Some of the first and most important archaeological evidence about the Mycenaeans comes from the royal graves at Mycenae, which date from 1600BC. There were two main styles of grave: shaft graves and *tholos* tombs.

Shaft graves

The earliest tombs were shaft graves, like the one shown on this cutaway reconstruction. A shaft grave could be over 12 metres (40ft) deep and usually contained several bodies, perhaps from the same family.

Roof made from wooden beams and stone slabs.

A rectangular slab of stone called a *stele*† was used to mark the grave.

Chamber for the body and grave goods

When the grave was complete, the shaft was filled with earth.

Low stone walls

Pebble base

Tholos tombs

By about 1500BC, shaft graves had been replaced by the *tholos*, or beehive-shaped, tomb. This reconstruction shows one from Mycenae, which dates from c.1250BC. The Roman historian, Pausanias, thought these tombs were treasuries because of the rich grave goods they contained. This *tholos* is still called the Treasury of Atreus, after a legendary Mycenaean king.*

The beehive-shaped burial chamber was over 13 metres (43ft) high.

The inside of the dome was originally covered with bronze ornaments.

Side chamber

A long corridor called a *dromos* led to the entrance.

This picture shows the main entrance to the tomb, which was decorated with carved green and red stones.

Tomb treasure

Members of the royal families were buried with many precious objects. Shaft graves were difficult for tomb robbers to break into, and so have often survived with their goods intact. The objects shown here were all found in the graves at Mycenae.

◀ A piece of jewellery showing a goddess.

Gold drinking cup ▼

Ceremonial vessel made of rock crystal. ▼

▲ The faces of some of the kings were covered with masks made of beaten gold. The masks were probably portraits of the kings.

▲
Sword and dagger blades were bronze, but the hilts were often made of gold.

Religion

There are no written records of the Mycenaeans' religious beliefs. Our only evidence comes from frescoes†, statues and shrines. From these it appears that the Mycenaeans had a very similar system of beliefs to the Minoans (see page 104).

◀ The Mycenaeans did not build temples, but there seem to have been rooms set aside for worship in houses and palaces. Shrines like the one shown on this gold ornament were erected in the countryside.

Mycenaean records mention several gods, such as ▶ Zeus, Poseidon and Dionysus, who were to be important in later Greek history. This fresco shows a figure holding ears of corn. She may be an early version of the goddess Demeter (see page 161).

Their elaborate tombs show that they believed in a life after death. They thought that goods from this world would be of use in the afterlife and would help wealthy people to preserve the privileges they had on Earth.

This terracotta† figurine represents a ▶ Mycenaean goddess. As in Crete, goddesses seem to have been the most powerful deities. A young male god is sometimes shown, but he seems to have been a less important figure.

Clothes

Statuettes and frescoes give us an idea of what fashions and hairstyles were like in Mycenaean days. They seem to have closely resembled the fashions on Crete. This fresco shows a court lady from Mycenae.

▼

▲
Young men, like the ones shown out hunting on this dagger blade, seem to have been clean shaven. Many of the gold masks from shaft graves show bearded men, but this may have been an older man's style.

Key dates

c.2000BC First evidence of the Mycenaeans in Greece.

c.1650-1550BC Grave circle A (see page 108) is used at Mycenae.

c.1600BC The height of Mycenaean power, economy and culture.

c.1450BC The Mycenaeans occupy Knossos on Crete and become the rulers of the island (see page 105).

c.1250BC Defensive walls are built around many of the Mycenaean cities. Traditional date of the fall of Troy (see page 110).

c.1200BC Start of the period of Mycenaean decline. Their cities are gradually abandoned.

c.1100BC Start of the Dark Ages.

Mycenaean cities

The Mycenaeans lived in small kingdoms, each with its own city. Their cities were usually built on areas of high ground and were surrounded by walls to make them easy to defend. This type of fortified city is called an *acropolis†*, which means "high city" in Greek.

The acropolis at Mycenae

The earliest Mycenaean cities were often destroyed when new ones were built on the same sites. The buildings shown in this view of the ruins at Mycenae were built at the end of the Mycenaean period.

An *acropolis* contained a royal palace along with houses for courtiers, soldiers and craftsmen. The palace was not just a royal residence. It was also a military headquarters, the administrative centre from which the government was run, and a workplace for many skilled craftsmen.

City walls

The lion gate

Grave circle A

Houses

The Lion Gate

The main gateway was decorated with sculptures of two lions. These may have been the symbols of the Mycenaean royal family. In about 1250BC enormous stone walls were built to enclose the *acropolis*. In some parts they were seven metres (23ft) thick.

Grave circle A

A burial ground for members of the Mycenaean royal family, now known as grave circle A, was situated inside the city walls. It consisted of a number of shaft graves† (see page 106) enclosed by a low stone wall.

Writing

Clay tablets covered with writing have been found in some Mycenaean cities. The Mycenaeans learned the art of writing from the Minoans. They combined some signs from Linear A† (see page 101) with new signs to produce a script known as Linear B. Although experts are now able to read Linear B, the results have been disappointing as the tablets only give lists of goods and inhabitants in the palaces.

Mycenaean scribes at work

An example of Linear B script

Trade

The Mycenaeans were trading as early as the 16th century BC. At first, they had to compete with the Minoans, but they found more trading opportunities as Cretan power declined.

The Mycenaeans traded extensively in the eastern Mediterranean and kept trading posts in important cities along the coasts of Asia Minor and Lebanon. They also purchased items from more distant lands, such as Africa or Scandinavia, through other traders.

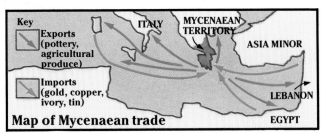

Key

Exports (pottery, agricultural produce)

Imports (gold, copper, ivory, tin)

ITALY

MYCENAEAN TERRITORY

ASIA MINOR

LEBANON

EGYPT

Map of Mycenaean trade

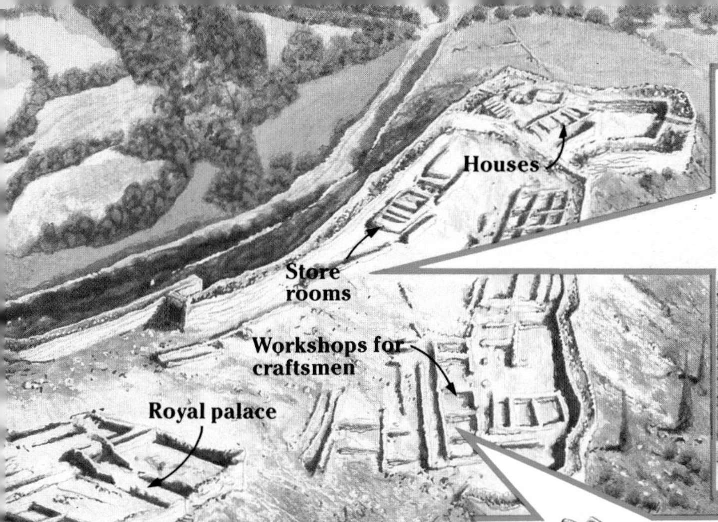

Houses

Store rooms

Workshops for craftsmen

Royal palace

Storerooms

As in Crete, the palace was the centre of economic life. Agricultural produce from the surrounding countryside was kept in storerooms on the *acropolis* to be used or exported. Objects produced by craftsmen and imported goods were also stored here.

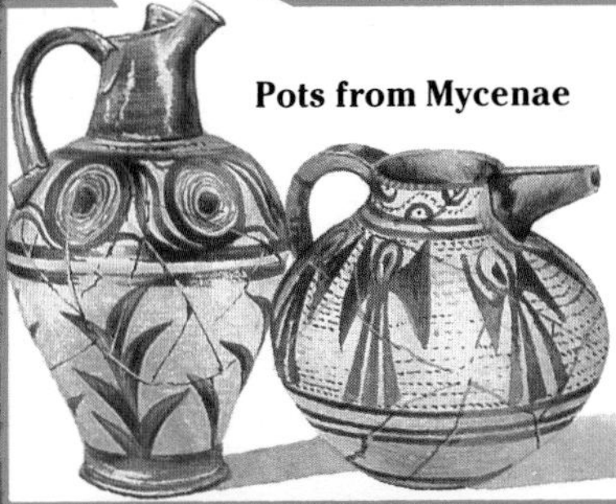

Craftsmen's workshops

Pots from Mycenae

Many artists and craftsmen worked for the king. They had workshops on the *acropolis*, where they produced goods such as pots, statuettes, jewellery, cloth and weapons. These objects were used by the household, given to craftsmen and soldiers as payment for work, or exported for profit.

The royal palace

A Mycenaean palace consisted of a number of buildings, often more than one storey high, grouped around a central courtyard. It was brightly painted, both inside and out. In each palace there was a large hall called a *megaron*, where the king held court and conducted state business. Little remains of the *megaron* at Mycenae. This reconstruction is based on the remains from other palaces, which would have been similar.

The room contained four pillars and a hearth.

The walls were covered with frescoes†.

Warriors

The Mycenaeans seem to have been a very warlike people. We know from the weapons and armour found in graves that their kings and nobles were warriors. A ruler was expected to look after his soldiers, supplying them with food, housing, land and slaves. This was organized through the palace, where many warriors seem to have lived.

Tower shield

Round shield

The Mycenaeans used three styles of shield: the rectangular tower shape, the figure of eight shape and the round shape. They were made of oxhide stretched over a wooden frame.

Figure of eight shield

◄ Mycenaean soldiers used body armour, helmets and shields. This bronze armour was found in a grave. It must have belonged to a nobleman, as it would have been very expensive. Various types of helmet are shown on vases and frescoes. Most helmets had cheek flaps and were fastened under the chin. The one shown here was made of leather, covered with the tusks of wild boars.

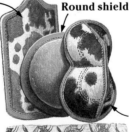

◄ Poorer soldiers, such as the foot soldiers shown on this vase, did not have bronze armour. They wore leather tunics to protect themselves.

We know very little about how a ► Mycenaean army was organized. It seems that rulers and nobles fought from chariots drawn by two horses. Each chariot contained a driver and a warrior.

109

The Trojan War

The story of the Trojan War is told in the works of the Greek poet, Homer†. He describes how a city called Troy was destroyed by the Mycenaean Greeks after a ten year siege. For many years historians thought that the Trojan War was just a story. However, at the end of the 19th century AD the remains of Troy were discovered in modern Turkey and many experts now think that there is some truth in Homer's tale. Although we still cannot prove that Homer's Trojan War happened, some experts now believe that a war on which his story was based may have taken place around 1250BC.

This reconstruction shows the city of Troy under siege from the Greeks.

The legend of the Trojan War

The cause of the war between Greece and Troy was Helen of Sparta. She was so beautiful that all the Greek kings wanted to marry her. Helen eventually married Menelaus, brother of King Agamemnon of Mycenae. Her father made all her suitors swear an oath to support Menelaus and to help if anyone tried to kidnap Helen.

Unfortunately, Aphrodite, the goddess of love and beauty, promised Helen to Paris, a prince of Troy. She made Helen fall in love with him, and the pair eloped to live in Troy. Agamemnon was angered by his brother's humiliation. He reminded the other Greek kings of their oath, and organized a great military expedition to Troy to get Helen back.

Troy was a heavily fortified city and could not be easily defeated. For ten years the Greeks laid siege to the city and the battle raged. Heroes on both sides displayed great bravery. Then Odysseus, the King of Ithaca, thought of a trick to help them seize Troy.

They built a huge wooden horse, left it outside the city and then sailed away. When they had gone, the Trojans brought the horse into the city,

thinking that it would bring them luck.

That night Greek soldiers, who were concealed inside the hollow horse, crept out and opened the city gates. The Greek army, which had sneaked back under cover of darkness, charged in and destroyed the city. They killed the men and made the women and children slaves. Only one Trojan prince, Aeneas, escaped alive with his family. He fled to Italy, where his descendants are said to have founded the city of Rome.

The search for Troy

At the end of the 19th century AD, a German called Heinrich Schliemann set out to discover the city of Troy. He had complete faith in the accuracy of Homer's account, and he used the descriptions in Homer's poem, the *Iliad*, to locate the site of the city.

A picture of the wooden horse, taken from a Greek vase.

In AD 1870 Schliemann started to dig at a site called Hisarlik, in modern Turkey. He uncovered the ruins of a city, which he believed to be Troy. Several archaeological expeditions have since excavated the site. We now know that the city was built c.3600BC, but it was rebuilt at least eight times. Experts disagree about which of the layers is the city described in the *Iliad*.

Several of the cities uncovered at Hisarlik were destroyed violently, but we do not know whether this was by earthquake or war. People from the Greek mainland may well have raided Troy and destroyed the city, but there is not yet any archaeological evidence to prove that the Trojan War took place in the way Homer described.

The end of the age

By about 1200BC the Mycenaean world was breaking up. Egyptian records show that in the second half of the 13th century BC there was a long run of poor harvests, food shortages and then famine. In Mycenaean Greece, bad harvests would also have affected trade, as agricultural produce was exported and used to pay craftsmen. Without it, the whole economic system and way of life was threatened (see diagram).

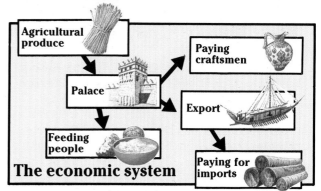
The economic system

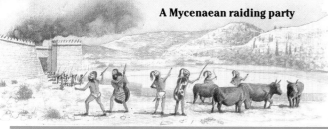
A Mycenaean raiding party

In times of shortage, the Mycenaeans traditionally attacked their neighbours to steal their cattle and crops. Enormous stone walls were built around many cities at this time and may well have been intended as protection against marauding neighbours. Some groups of Mycenaeans may also have gone on raids overseas. This may have been the real cause of the war against Troy.

The Sea Peoples

The famine may have driven some Mycenaeans to emigrate. Egyptian texts show that in about 1190BC a group of emigrants were reported in the eastern Mediterranean (see page 71). Some were travelling overland with their families, while others were at sea in a large battle fleet. The Egyptians called them the Sea Peoples. Some of the Sea Peoples seem to have been Mycenaean refugees.

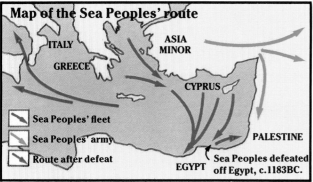
Map of the Sea Peoples' route

ITALY
GREECE
ASIA MINOR
CYPRUS
PALESTINE
EGYPT

- Sea Peoples' fleet
- Sea Peoples' army
- Route after defeat

Sea Peoples defeated off Egypt, c.1183BC.

A reconstruction of a battle between the Egyptians and the Sea Peoples, based on an Egyptian relief†.

The Sea Peoples' fleet seized Cyprus, while their army destroyed several cities and defeated a people called the Hittites in Asia Minor. The fleet and army were eventually defeated by the Egyptian Pharaoh, Ramesses III. After this the Sea Peoples dispersed around the Mediterranean (see pages 72-73). Some may have been the ancestors of the Etruscans in Italy and of the Philistines in Palestine.

The Dorians

One by one, the Mycenaean cities were abandoned. Some may have been ruined by earthquakes, while others were destroyed by enemies. As the Mycenaean world disintegrated, Greece entered the Dark Ages (see page 112) and a people called the Dorians came to prominence.

It was once thought that the Dorians invaded from outside Greece. However, many experts now think that they had been in Greece for some time, but took advantage of the troubled times to exert their influence. In the places where they settled, the Dorian dialect of Greek was later spoken. Different dialects developed in other areas (see map).

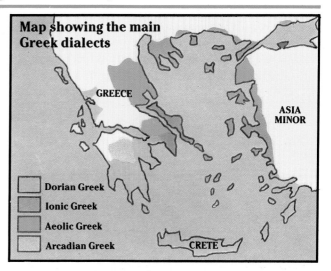
Map showing the main Greek dialects

GREECE
ASIA MINOR
CRETE

- Dorian Greek
- Ionic Greek
- Aeolic Greek
- Arcadian Greek

The Dark Ages: c.1100-800BC

This period is known as the Dark Ages because we know very little of what was happening in Greece. The art of writing was lost after the end of the Mycenaean civilization, so there are no written records. There is also little mention of the Greeks in foreign records, as they had very few contacts with other countries. By the beginning of the Dark Ages the population had decreased dramatically. There was a general decline in the standard of pottery, jewellery and architecture. Skills such as fresco† painting and cutting gems were forgotten.

Many farming communities were destroyed during the disturbances at the end of the Mycenaean period.

Architecture

In the Dark Ages the main building materials were mud brick (mud mixed with straw and left in the sun to dry) and wood. These materials do not last as well as stone, so very few buildings have survived. Most people probably lived in small huts like the one shown in the reconstruction below.

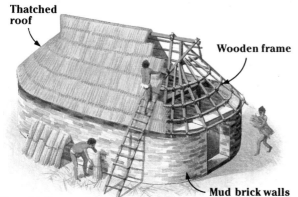

Thatched roof

Wooden frame

Mud brick walls

Clothes

Many dress pins from the Dark Ages have been discovered. They suggest that fashions were very different from the tightly laced and tied Mycenaean clothes. People started to wear simple, loose tunics, made from rectangular pieces of cloth, fastened at the shoulders with pins. This style is known as the Doric *chiton*.

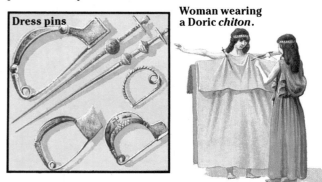

Dress pins

Woman wearing a Doric *chiton*.

Burial customs

Archaeological evidence from a cemetery in Athens has shown that cremation was introduced in the Dark Ages. The body was burned and the ashes were put in a clay jar in the grave. By about 800BC burial was once more in favour.

The Dark Age Greeks continued the Mycenaean custom of burying objects with the dead. However, people could not usually afford to bury luxury goods and most graves contained just a pottery jug or cup.

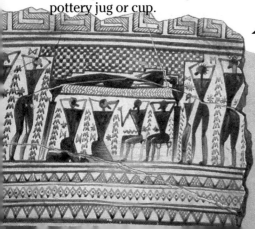

A vase painting of a funeral. It shows the dead person on a bed, surrounded by mourners who are tearing their hair in grief.

Euboea

On the island of Euboea, excavations have revealed a flourishing Dark Age culture. It was rich enough for people to put gold ornaments in their graves. As early as 900BC, the Euboeans were re-establishing trading contacts with foreign countries. However, wars between the two main cities on Euboea ended this period of progress.

These objects were all discovered in tombs on Euboea.

Terracotta† figure of a centaur

Pot decorated with human figures

Gold rings and earrings

Euboea

Athens

The Archaic Period: c.800-500BC

The Archaic Period was a time of progress and expansion. The population grew and there was a rise in the general standard of living. The standard of art improved and the Greeks had more contact with the outside world. The first Olympic Games were held in this period (see page 154).

The rediscovery of writing

About 800BC the Greeks started to use writing again. They had trading links with a people called the Phoenicians, who used an alphabet which contained only consonants. The Greeks adapted this by introducing extra signs for vowels. This system of writing was very successful, as it was much easier to learn than previous scripts.
It is the predecessor of the alphabet we use today.

Greek letter, name of letter and English sound

α	β	γ	δ	ε	ζ	η	θ
alpha	beta	gamma	delta	epsilon	zeta	eta	theta
a	b	g	d	e	z	e	th
ι	κ	λ	μ	ν	ξ	ο	π
iota	kappa	lambda	mu	nu	xi	omicron	pi
i	k	l	m	n	x/ks	o	p
ρ	σ, ς	τ	υ	φ	χ	ψ	ω
rho	sigma	tau	upsilon	phi	chi	psi	omega
r	s	t	u	f/ph	ch	ps	o

Bards

A bard reciting his poem.

Although no written records were kept during the Dark Ages, the people had a very strong oral tradition. Professional poets, known as bards, travelled widely, passing on the stories of the gods and the Mycenaean heroes.

The most famous bard is Homer†, whose poems are the earliest surviving example of Greek literature. We know very little about Homer's life. He may have come from the island of Chios, and tradition maintains that he was blind. Some time between 850-750BC, Homer retold the traditional stories about the Trojan War (see page 110). He composed two epic poems: the *Iliad* (the story of part of the siege of Troy) and the *Odyssey* (the account of the hero Odysseus' journey home to Ithaca).*

Roman bust of Homer, based on a Greek original.

Emigration

As the population started to grow, some areas of Greece became overcrowded and sometimes there were famines. Political struggles between the various Greek states also created exiles and refugees who were forced to flee abroad. From about 1000BC onwards, groups of people left Greece seeking land or employment overseas. The first emigrants travelled to the coastal area of Asia Minor, which was called Ionia. Later groups settled all round the Mediterranean, from France to the Black Sea. They settled in places with natural harbours and good farming land, where they faced little opposition from the local inhabitants. Once a colony was established, it rapidly became independent from the mother city.

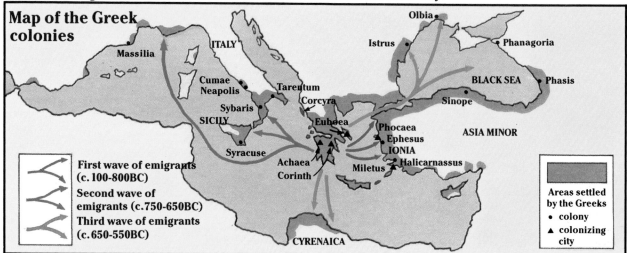

Map of the Greek colonies

Olbia
Istrus
Phanagoria
ITALY
Massilia
BLACK SEA
Phasis
Cumae
Neapolis
Tarentum
Corcyra
Sinope
Sybaris
SICILY
Euboea
Phocaea
Ephesus
ASIA MINOR
IONIA
Syracuse
Achaea
Corinth
Miletus
Halicarnassus
CYRENAICA

First wave of emigrants (c.100-800BC)
Second wave of emigrants (c.750-650BC)
Third wave of emigrants (c.650-550BC)

Areas settled by the Greeks
• colony
▲ colonizing city

*You can read more about the Iliad and the Odyssey on page 180.

113

The Greeks and their neighbours

During the Dark Ages, the Greeks had few contacts with the outside world. However, from the Archaic Period onwards, when they started to set up colonies and to trade, they came into contact with many peoples around the Mediterranean. Some of them are described below.

The Assyrians

During the Dark Ages a people called the Assyrians (see page 74-75) conquered a vast area of the Middle East. They came from the area that is now Iraq and their most important cities were Ashur (the capital) and Nineveh.

This stone carving shows the Assyrian king Ashurbanipal out hunting.

Map of the Assyrian Empire, c.646BC

ASSYRIA · Nineveh · Ashur
MEDITERRANEAN SEA
EGYPT
Assyrian territory

The Assyrians were a warlike people, famed for their cruelty. Archaeologists have discovered lists of Assyrian kings going back to 2500BC. However, it was not until around 1814BC that they started to expand their territory. Their empire reached its height in about 646BC under King Ashurbanipal.

The Egyptians

There were many trading links between Egypt and the Greeks. The Greeks purchased papyrus for scrolls, fine linen, perfumes and wine from the Egyptians. They also kept trading posts in the Egyptian cities of Naucratis and Daphnae.

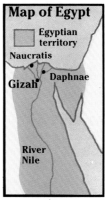

The pyramids at Gizah were built in the 26th century BC and were tombs for Egyptian Kings.

For more about Egypt, see pages 1-96. By the time of the Dark Ages in Greece, Egyptian civilization was over 2000 years old. However, after the reign of Ramesses III (see page 70) Egypt began to decline. It was later conquered by the Persians (see page 79) and by Alexander the Great† (see pages 170-171). In 30BC Egypt became part of the Roman empire.

Map of Egypt

Egyptian territory
Naucratis
Gizah · Daphnae
River Nile

The Etruscans

In about 750BC, the Greeks started to set up colonies in southern Italy. There they came into conflict with a people called the Etruscans, who were expanding their territory southward from north-western Italy. Some scholars believe that the Etruscans were native inhabitants of Italy. Others think that they were Sea Peoples who had to find a new home after they were defeated by the Egyptians. They may even have come from Asia Minor.

The Etruscans were expert sailors, who traded extensively around the Mediterranean. They were also skilled metalworkers. Their engineers knew how to build sewage systems for their towns and drain marshy areas.

Terracotta head of an Etruscan warrior

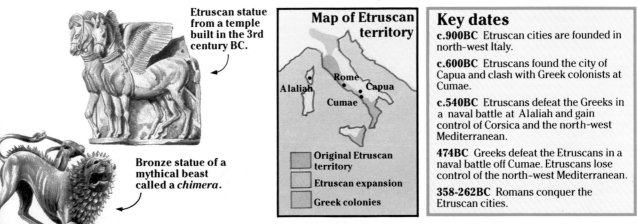

Etruscan statue from a temple built in the 3rd century BC.

Bronze statue of a mythical beast called a *chimera*.

Map of Etruscan territory

Alaliah
Rome · Capua
Cumae

Original Etruscan territory
Etruscan expansion
Greek colonies

Key dates

c.900BC Etruscan cities are founded in north-west Italy.

c.600BC Etruscans found the city of Capua and clash with Greek colonists at Cumae.

c.540BC Etruscans defeat the Greeks in a naval battle at Alaliah and gain control of Corsica and the north-west Mediterranean.

474BC Greeks defeat the Etruscans in a naval battle off Cumae. Etruscans lose control of the north-west Mediterranean.

358-262BC Romans conquer the Etruscan cities.

The Phoenicians

During the Greek Dark Ages, the most successful traders in the Mediterranean were a people called the Phoenicians. They lived on the coast in what is now the Lebanon. The Greeks called them *Phoinikes*, or purple men, after a purple dye which they produced. Their most important exports were purple cloth, timber, glass and goods made of metal and wood, including fine furniture inlaid with ivory.

The Phoenicians lived in independent city states, each of which had its own king. Their most

A Phoenician trading ship leaving port.

important cities were Byblos, Sidon and Tyre. They were daring sailors and explorers and established colonies round the south and west shores of the Mediterranean (see map).

In about 1000BC the Phoenicians invented a form of writing. Their alphabet was later adopted by the Greeks (see page 113).

Phoenician pots made from coloured glass.

Map of the Phoenician colonies

ITALY

GREECE

PHOENICIA
Sidon
Byblos

Carthage

Tyre

EGYPT

■ Areas colonized by the Phoenicians

Key dates

c.1200-1000BC Phoenicians rise to power.

c.814BC Princess Elissa of Tyre founds the colony of Carthage on the North African coast.

c.600BC Phoenician sailors circumnavigate Africa.

539BC Phoenicia is conquered by the Persians (see page 137).

332BC Phoenicia is conquered by Alexander the Great (see pages 170-171).

The Lydians

Lydian coin

Lydia was a small but wealthy state in Asia Minor. Its capital was Sardis. The Lydians were close neighbours of the Ionian Greek colonies, with whom they traded.

Key dates

c.680-652BC Reign of King Gyges. He starts a policy of attacking the Ionian Greek colonies, while trying to maintain friendly relations with mainland Greece.

7th century BC The Lydians are the first people to use coins.

560-546BC Reign of King Croesus. In alliance with a people called the Medes, he conquers the Ionian colonies.

546BC Croesus is defeated by the Persians. The Persians seize the Ionian colonies (see page 136).

Lydian and Scythian territory

■ Greek colonies

■ Scythian territory

■ Lydian territory

BLACK SEA

ASIA MINOR

GREECE

The Scythians

The Scythians were a tribe of nomadic horsemen from Central Asia who kept herds of horses, cattle and sheep. In about 1000BC, they moved into the area around the Black Sea.

The Scythians were a barbaric and warlike people. Greek colonists who settled around the Black Sea often had to defend their territory against them. However, a lot of trade was done between the two peoples. The Greeks bought wheat, salt, hides and slaves from the Scythians,

A Scythian chief, noblewoman and horse in their ceremonial costumes

and in return supplied them with jewellery, metalwork, oils and wines. The Scythians were a very wealthy people. Their graves were filled with rich goods, along with human and horse sacrifices.

Greek craftsmen made many pieces of gold jewellery for the Scythians.

Key dates

674BC The Scythians make an alliance with the Assyrians.

c.650BC The Scythians and Assyrians plunder various areas of the Middle East.

c.630BC The Scythians defeat a people called the Cimmerians from central Asia.

514BC The Scythians repel the Persians.

Earring

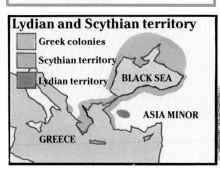

Necklace

Ornament for clothes

Social structure and government

In the Archaic Period, Greece was made up of many independent states. The Greeks called each of these a *polis*, or city state. A *polis* consisted of the city and its surrounding countryside. The largest *polis* was Athens, which had about 2,500 square kilometres (1,000 squares miles) of territory. However, most states were much smaller, many with less than 250 square kilometres (100 square miles).

The Greeks liked to keep each city state small. Even the largest city states had no more than a few thousand citizens (see below). This reconstruction shows what a typical *polis* would have looked like in the Archaic Period.

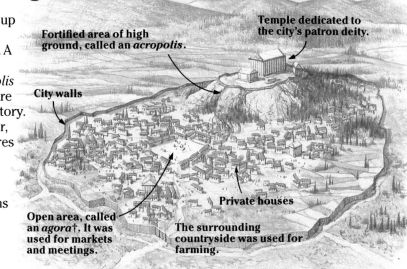

Temple dedicated to the city's patron deity.

Fortified area of high ground, called an *acropolis*.

City walls

Private houses

Open area, called an *agora*†. It was used for markets and meetings.

The surrounding countryside was used for farming.

Social structure

In Greek society there were always two main groups of people: free people and slaves. Slaves were workers who were owned by free people. They were used as servants and labourers and had no legal rights. Some slaves were prisoners of war from other Greek states. Others were foreigners purchased from slave traders. Many slaves worked closely with their owners and lived as members of the family. A few slaves were skilled craftsmen and were paid for their work.

Female slaves doing basic housework.

Male slaves at work on a farm.

In Athens, as society developed, free men (but not women) became divided into two groups: citizens and *metics*. A citizen was a free man, born to Athenian parents. Citizens were the most powerful and privileged group. They were the only people who could take part in the government of the *polis*. They had to serve in the army, and were also expected to be government officials and to volunteer for jury service (see page 156-157).

A *metic* was a man born outside Athens who had come to live there, usually to trade or to practise a craft. Many of them were very prosperous. *Metics* had to pay tax and to serve in the army if required, but they could never become citizens. They had no say in the government, could not own houses or land and could not speak in a law court.

Metics often worked as jewellers, potters or smiths.

A man born into one of these social groups could rarely move into another one. This rigid social system was enforced by a law passed in Athens in 451BC, which defined who could be a citizen. The only people who could sometimes improve their social status were slaves.

Occasionally, a master would pay to set a skilled slave up in business. He would receive a share of the profits in return. Some of these wage-earning slaves were able to save up and buy their freedom. However, freed slaves could never become citizens or *metics*.

A slave receiving his freedom.

All these social divisions applied only to men. Women took their social and legal status from their husband or male relations. They were not permitted to take part in public life.

Changing forms of government

Rule by the aristocrats: c.800-650BC

By the Archaic Period, most Greek states were governed by groups of rich landowners, called aristocrats. The word comes from the Greek *aristoi*, meaning "best people". This system of government is known as an *oligarchy*, which means "rule by the few" in Greek. As trade increased, a middle class of merchants, craftsmen and bankers began to prosper. However, they could not take part in government, and soon began to demand a say in the decision making.

In the early days aristocrats were the only people who could afford to buy armour and horses. They became leaders in war and at home.

The age of tyrants: c.650-500BC

Resentment of aristocratic power often led to riots. To re-establish peace, people were sometimes prepared to allow one man to take absolute power. This sort of leader was called a tyrant, which meant "ruler". Tyrants first appeared in about 650BC. They often tried to curb the power of the aristocrats, as this helped to protect their own positions. Some tyrants stayed in power for many years, but most only ruled for a short time.

Many tyrants were deposed by men who envied their power and wanted to be tyrants themselves.

Government in Athens: c.750-621BC

During the Archaic Period, real power in Athens lay with the *areopagus*, or council, whose policies were carried out by three magistrates called *archons†*. All the *archons* and the members of the council were aristocrats.

Many people were dissatisfied with this system and with the city's laws. In about 630BC, an aristocrat called Cylon tried to make himself tyrant, but failed. Instead the Athenians looked for someone to reform their laws, and in 621BC they appointed a man called Draco†. He drew up a new set of laws which were very severe.

Draco's laws were so harsh that even minor crimes such as stealing food were punished by death. A harsh law is still referred to as "draconian".

Solon's reforms

People were unhappy with Draco's laws. In 594BC an aristocrat called Solon† was made *archon* and given power to introduce reforms. Many of Solon's measures were popular. For example, he prevented merchants selling grain abroad, which meant there was more food for the Athenian poor. He cancelled many debts and stopped debtors being sold into slavery. Solon also reformed the system of government, so that men from the middle classes could hold administrative positions. Even poor citizens were given a say in the city's affairs through an Assembly (see page 156).

Solon arranged for debtors to be freed. Some were brought home from abroad.

The tyrant of Athens

Despite these reforms, few people were satisfied. Solon left Athens and disorder broke out again between the aristocratic families and the various social groups. About 546BC, an aristocrat called Peisistratus† seized power and became the tyrant of Athens. His rule was largely a success, and he appears to have been popular. Under his rule, Athens enjoyed a period of peace and prosperity.

Peisistratus tried to take power several times. Once he arrived in Athens with a woman dressed as Athene. He hoped to persuade people that the goddess had appointed him leader.

The introduction of democracy

When Peisistratus died in 527BC, his son Hippias became tyrant. He ruled until 510BC, when he was overthrown. Two years of civil war followed. An aristocrat called Cleisthenes†, from a family called the Alcmaeonids, eventually triumphed. In 508BC he introduced a new system of government called *democracy* (see pages 156-157).

Hippias was deposed by members of the Alcmaeonid family, helped by Spartan troops.

Sparta

In the 10th century BC, people called Dorians moved into Laconia, a province of southern Greece. They defeated the native inhabitants and founded the state of Sparta. Between c.740-720BC, the Spartans conquered the neighbouring state of Messenia. This made Sparta one of the largest Greek states and gave it enough fertile land to make it self-sufficient in food.

By the beginning of the Archaic Period, the Spartans were trading with other Greek states and importing luxury goods from abroad. Their craftsmen produced fine metalware and they also had skilled vase painters. In the intellectual field, the Spartans are said to have played a leading role in the invention of Greek music, and they had a famous poet called Alcman.

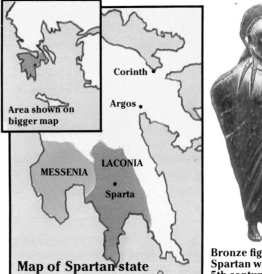

Map of Spartan state

Bronze figure of a Spartan warrior, 5th century BC.

This scene is taken from the neck of a huge bronze pot known as the Vix krater (see page 144). It was made in Sparta in the 6th century BC and shows Spartan soldiers marching to war.

In 668BC the Spartans were defeated in a war against Argos. Then, in about 630BC, the Messenians started a revolt against the Spartans, which lasted for 17 years. These events convinced the Spartans that they must make drastic changes in order to keep the rebellious population under control and to defend themselves against any possible foreign invasion.

They set up a system dedicated to producing warriors. Every male Spartan had to become a full-time soldier and spent his life training and fighting. Spartans lived in very hard and uncomfortable conditions, without any luxuries. They distrusted any form of change and had as little contact with the outside world as possible.

By the Classical Period, Sparta had become the strongest military power in Greece, and its soldiers were famous for their bravery. However, this was achieved at the expense of its cultural development. There were now no philosophers or artists in Sparta.

This Spartan plate was made in c.560BC.

Social structure

Only men of Spartan birth were regarded as citizens†. They were an exclusive group who never admitted any outsiders, and there were probably never more than 9000 of them. All citizens served in the army and could vote in the assembly.

Men who were not full citizens were known as *perioikoi*, which meant "neighbours". Although they were under Spartan rule, they were free men who were allowed to trade and to serve in the army. They lived in separate small villages.

Descendants of Sparta's original inhabitants were known as *helots*. They farmed the land and had to give part of their crops to their Spartan masters. The *helots* outnumbered the Spartans heavily. The Spartans kept them oppressed, to prevent rebellions.

Life in Sparta

Physical fitness was very important to the Spartans, as only strong and healthy men could become soldiers. Each new baby had to be examined by state officials. If it showed signs of weakness it was left outside to die.

A boy was educated by the state until he was 20 (see pages 148-149). Then he had to join the army and be elected to one of the military clubs. He lived in the club's barracks, where conditions were very harsh.

Each soldier was allocated land and *helots* to work it by the state. This left him free to pursue his military career. He supported his family and helped to supply his barracks from the produce of his land.

Spartan men did not usually marry until they were 30. Even then they spent most of their time at the barracks, and just visited their wives and families. Only old men were allowed to live in their own homes.

Spartan women had to keep fit so that they would give birth to strong babies. They trained and competed against each other in athletic events, wearing short tunics. Other Greeks were often shocked by this behaviour.

Foreigners were not allowed into Sparta. Only the *perioikoi*, who looked after trade, had any dealings with outsiders. The Spartans did not use coins and usually bartered for goods.

Government in Sparta

The Spartan system of government included a monarchy, a council of elders and a popular assembly. Their various functions are shown on this diagram. According to legend, a leader called Lycurgus set up the government institutions and laws. Experts now disagree about whether or not he was a real historical character.

Sparta had two royal families and two kings, who always ruled together. Their main responsibility was to lead the army in war. At home, their powers were strictly limited to religious duties.

More actual power lay with the five *ephors*, or overseers, who were elected annually by the Assembly (see below). They looked after the day-to-day running of the state.

The *gerousia*, or Council, was made up of the two kings and 28 councillors. Councillors were men over 60 who had been elected for life by the Assembly. The councillors decided which policies Sparta should adopt. They also created the laws and acted as judges.

The Council's proposals had to be passed by the *apella*, or Assembly, which consisted of all citizens aged over 30. The Assembly could not debate or amend a measure, it could only vote for or against it. Spartans voted by shouting "yes" or "no": the loudest group would win.

The Peloponnesian League

The Spartans realized that they did not have enough soldiers to fight an enemy abroad and suppress a *helot* uprising at the same time. In the 6th century BC, they therefore made a series of alliances with their neighbours in the Peloponnese (the southern part of mainland Greece). This is known as the Peloponnesian League. Sparta's allies remained independent, but they had to give Sparta military assistance when required.

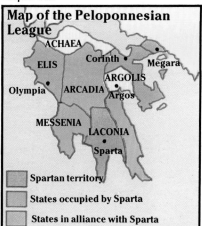

Map of the Peloponnesian League

ACHAEA
Corinth
ELIS
Megara
ARGOLIS
Olympia
ARCADIA
Argos
MESSENIA
LACONIA
Sparta

Spartan territory
States occupied by Sparta
States in alliance with Sparta

Farming and food

Most people in Ancient Greece made their living from farming. Even the citizens of towns often had a farm in the country which provided their income. However, the landscape and climate of Greece made farming difficult. About three-quarters of the land area was mountainous and therefore of little use for agriculture. Land could be farmed on the coastal plain and in some inland areas, and in places the soil was very fertile. Only a few areas, such as Thessaly, had good pasture land. Very little rain fell between March and October, so crops were grown during the winter.

A Greek farm

This scene shows a typical Greek farm. They were usually quite small, and only produced enough food to support a single family. They were worked by the owner, his family and a few hired hands or slaves. If the owner lived mostly in the town, he paid a servant called a bailiff to run the farm.

Areas of high ground or poor soil, which were useless for other crops, could be used to grow olive trees.

Grapes were grown in vineyards on the lower hill slopes.

Farm buildings

Grain was grown on the fertile plains. It was the most important crop, as bread was the main element in the Greek diet.

Farmers grew fruit and vegetables to feed their families.

Many farmers kept animals (see below). They grazed on the hillsides and were looked after by one of the farm workers.

Farm animals

Many horses were reared in Thessaly, where there was lots of pasture land. Elsewhere they were expensive to keep and were only used by the rich.

In fertile areas cows were kept for their milk.

Fish were plentiful and many varieties were found in the seas around Greece.

Most milk came from sheep and goats. They were also eaten, and their hides were used for leather.

Oxen were used to draw the plough and mules were kept as beasts of burden.

Farmers often kept pigs and poultry for their meat.

Grapes

Grapes were picked in September. Some were kept for eating, but most were made into wine. They were trodden underfoot in big vats. This first squeezing of the grapes made the best quality wine. The last drops of juice were extracted in a press. The juice was then left in jars to ferment.

Olives

An olive press

The picture on this vase shows the olive harvest.

Olives were either picked by hand or knocked out of the trees with sticks. Some olives were eaten, but most were crushed in a press to produce oil. Olive oil was an essential product. It was used for cooking, lighting and in many beauty products. In the state of Athens it was a criminal offence to uproot an olive tree.

The grain harvest

1. Grain was sown in October, so that it could grow during the wettest months of the year. One man steered a wooden plough, pulled by oxen. Another man walked behind him, sowing the seeds.

2. In April or May, the crops were harvested with curved knives called sickles. Afterwards the field was left fallow (unplanted) for a while so that the soil could regain its goodness.

3. The grain was threshed (separated from the stalks), by driving mules over it on a paved threshing floor. Some floors were positioned so that the wind would blow away the chaff (the outer cover of the grain).

4. The grain could also be separated from the chaff by throwing it into the air, so that the chaff would blow away. This is known as winnowing. The husks were then removed by pounding the grain in a pestle and mortar.

What people ate

Most people in Greece lived mainly on porridge and bread. This was usually barley bread, as wheat was more expensive than barley. Other common foods were cheese, fish, vegetables, eggs and fruit. Wild animals such as hares, deer and boars were hunted to supplement the food supply. A typical day's food is shown in the picture on the right.

Coriander and sesame were popular seasonings. Bees were kept in terracotta† hives to provide honey, which was the only form of sweetening.

Rich people had a more varied diet. They ate more fish and meat and could afford bread made from wheat.

Breakfast usually consisted of a lump of bread soaked in wine.

The main meal of the day was dinner. This was often barley porridge or bread with some vegetables.

Lunch might be bread with a piece of cheese or some olives and figs.

A Greek house

Very few Greek houses have survived, so we cannot be sure exactly what a typical house looked like. We do know that Greek houses were usually built around a central courtyard from which doors opened into the various ground floor rooms. Any windows on the outside walls of the house tended to be small and could be closed with shutters. This made the house very private and secure. Stairs led from the courtyard to an upper storey, where the bedrooms and servants' quarters were situated. Men and women lived separate lives and had separate rooms within the house.

This reconstruction is based on the remains of a house found in the city of Olynthos. Some walls have been cut away to show the layout of the rooms. Not all the activities shown in this picture would have happened at the same time.

The roof was made of pottery tiles.

The women's quarters were called the *gynaeceum*. Women spent most of their time in these rooms, organizing the household, spinning, weaving and entertaining their friends.

The exterior

The outside walls were built from mud bricks, sometimes reinforced with timber. These bricks were cheap and easy to use, but they were not very strong. Burglars sometimes broke into houses by tunnelling through the walls. Doors and shutters were made of wood with bronze hinges. Wood was a valuable material, as it was very scarce.

A statue of the god Hermes, called a *herm*, often stood by the main entrance to the house to ward off evil. Wealthy people often employed a doorman to receive visitors.

Herm

The men ate and entertained their friends in a room called the *andron*. They reclined on couches and were served by slaves.

Mosaic floors were used in some rooms from the 5th century BC. They were made from coloured pebbles.

Heating was provided by burning charcoal in portable metal braziers.

Furniture

Furniture was usually made of wood. Rich people had more highly decorated furniture, which was often finely carved with inlays of ivory, gold and silver. Some items were made of bronze.

Chairs

A *thronos* was a seat of honour used by the master of the house. It was a large chair with arms.

The ladies used chairs with backs. This style was called a *klismos*.

Most people sat on stools. The legs could be fixed or folding.

Tables

Tables could be round, oval or rectangular and were usually low, so that they could be pushed under couches when not in use. They either had three legs or a single central support.

Slaves' room

Walls were usually painted in a plain colour. They were often hung with richly coloured and patterned tapestries, which were made by the women of the household.

The kitchen contained an open fire used for cooking. There could be a chimney shaft to allow smoke to escape.

Bedroom

Altar

The courtyard usually contained an altar where prayers were said. Some households also had a well there to supply water.

There was often a room set aside where the family could gather together round a hearth. This room was dedicated to the goddess Hestia.

The bathroom contained a terracotta† bath with a drain which led outside. A basin on a stand was used for washing.

Couches and beds

Beds and couches were similar in design. They had a wooden frame, strung with leather thongs or cords. On top of this was a mattress, pillows and a cover.

Storage

Small personal items, such as jewellery and make up, were kept in small boxes and baskets. Larger items, such as clothes or bedlinen, were stored in chests.

Lighting

Rooms were lit by small oil-burning lamps made of pottery, bronze or silver. The oil was put in the round body of the lamp, with a wick in the spout. There were special bronze stands on which lamps could be stood.

Clothes and jewellery

Greek clothes were very simple. Both men and women wore pieces of material draped around their bodies to form either a tunic or a cloak.

Clothes were usually made of wool or linen. However, in the 5th century BC the Greeks also started to use cotton, which came from India. By the 4th century BC silk was being produced on the island of Kos. Other luxury cloths were imported from Egypt, Persia and Phoenicia. Only the rich could afford any of these exotic materials. The poor wore clothes of poorer quality materials, such as undyed or unbleached wool and linen.

Women's clothes

The basic female dress was called a *chiton*. It was made from a single rectangular piece of cloth.

There were two main styles of *chiton*, the Doric and the Ionic.

The *chiton* was fastened with buttons or brooches.

A girdle could be tied around the waist.

The *chiton* was fastened on the shoulders with long pins or brooches.

A girdle was often tied around the waist.

A *himation* could be a light, gauzy scarf.

This travelling cloak was also a *himation*.

The Doric *chiton* originated on mainland Greece The top quarter of the material was folded over and it was then wrapped around the body, leaving one side open.

The Ionic style of *chiton* was said to have been invented in the Greek colonies in Ionia. It was fastened at intervals across the shoulders.

A woman's other basic item of clothing was a rectangular-shaped wrap called a *himation*. It varied considerably in size and thickness.

Changing fashions

Paintings on vases show that in the Archaic Period highly patterned, brightly coloured fabrics were fashionable and women's dresses tended to fit closely to the body.

In later years there was a reaction against too much display. Dresses were made of material of one colour, but sometimes had a band of colour or a small pattern at the edge. The garments fitted more loosely.

In the 4th century BC this trend was reversed. Patterned materials, including ones with gold ornaments sewn on to them, were in favour again. The materials were fine and clung more revealingly to the figure.

Men's clothes

Young men wore thigh-length tunics.

Slave wearing a loincloth.

Old men and the rich usually wore ankle-length tunics.

Greek men wore a simple kilt or a tunic sewn up at the side and fastened on one or both shoulders. Craftsmen and slaves often wore a loincloth.

Men also wore a *himation*. It was ▶ usually rectangular in shape but varied considerably in size and texture. Sometimes it was worn over a tunic.

The *himation* was wrapped around the body with the end thrown over one shoulder.

The *chlamys* was fastened with a pin or brooch.

◀ There was also a shorter cloak called a *chlamys*, which was usually worn by younger men, particularly for hunting or riding, or by soldiers.

Footwear

Leather sandal. The straps could be tied in many different styles.

Leather boots were often lined with felt or fur for warmth.

Leather shoe

Hats

Many people went barefoot most of the time, especially indoors. The most common footwear was leather sandals, although shoes were sometimes worn. Horsemen and travellers wore calf-length boots.

Both men and women wore hats with brims when they were outdoors to protect themselves from the sun.

Jewellery

Many pieces of Greek jewellery have survived in tombs, as it was the custom to bury a dead person's jewellery with them. Paintings, sculptures and lists from temples give us other details. Rich people had jewellery made of gold, silver, electrum† and ivory. Less wealthy people had jewellery made of bronze, lead, iron, bone and glass.

Greek jewellers worked gold into many different shapes and textures and sometimes added touches of enamel for colour. It was not until the Hellenistic Period that coloured stones were used to decorate jewellery.

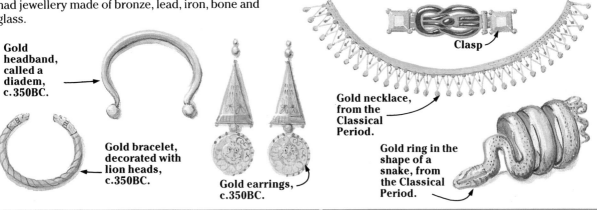

Gold headband, called a diadem, c.350BC.

Gold bracelet, decorated with lion heads, c.350BC.

Gold earrings, c.350BC.

Clasp

Gold necklace, from the Classical Period.

Gold ring in the shape of a snake, from the Classical Period.

Hairstyles

In the Archaic Period, Greek men wore their hair long with a head band and they had full beards.

Hair styles became shorter during the Classical Period. Beards were also worn shorter.

In the Hellenistic Period it became fashionable for men to be clean-shaven.

Women always wore their hair long. In the Archaic Period it was held in place by a head band.

In the Classical Period hair was usually worn up, held in place by ribbons, diadems, nets or scarves.

In the Hellenistic Period, waves and curls were fashionable, although the hair was still usually worn up.

Pottery

Greek pottery was intended for everyday use. But as well as being functional, it was often beautifully decorated with paintings. The pictures on many pots show scenes from everyday life which have given us vital information about how the Greeks lived.

Styles of decoration

The Geometric Period: c.1000-700BC

During the Dark Ages the marine and plant decorations of the Bronze Age were abandoned in favour of geometric patterns. Early designs consisted of simple shapes such as zigzags and triangles. ▼

In the 9th and 8th centuries BC bands of decoration featuring animals and humans were added. The figures were shown as silhouettes against a light background and the scenes often depicted funerals. ▼

▲ In about 900BC very elaborate geometric patterns like this became common.

The Orientalizing and Archaic Periods: c.720-550BC

◄ As the Greeks started to have more contact with foreigners, oriental motifs such as lotuses, palms, lions and monsters became common on pottery.

In the Archaic Period, scenes from ► Greek mythology and from everyday life started to appear on pots. The figures were more detailed and realistic than those of the Geometric Period.

Athenian pottery: c.550-300BC

Athenian pottery dominated the market for over 200 years. The pictures on Athenian pots showed episodes from the lives of gods and heroes, as well as scenes from daily life.

At first, the ► Athenians made pottery known as black figure ware, which consisted of red pots decorated with black figures. This style was fashionable from about 550-480BC.

The Athenians also produced white pots with painted decorations. ►

▲ In about 530BC the Athenians developed red figure ware: black pots decorated with red figures. This style became very popular and eventually replaced the black figure style.

The Hellenistic Period: c.300BC onwards

In the Hellenistic Period, black and red figure ware were virtually abandoned in favour of plain coloured pots. These often had raised patterns on ◄ the pot.

Identifying shapes

Pots were made in many different shapes and sizes according to their use. Some of the most common styles of pot are shown here.

An *amphora* was a two-handled ▲ storage jar with a wide body and narrower neck. *Amphorae* were used to store wine, oil and many other commodities, and varied greatly in size and shape.

A *krater* was a large vase in which wine was mixed with water before it was served. Two different styles of *krater* are shown here. ▼

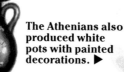

Volute krater

Calyx krater

The mixture of ▲ water and wine was transferred from the *krater* into a jug called an *oinochoe*, ready to be poured into wine cups.

How pots were made

Greek potters were skilled craftsmen who made a variety of things, including large storage jars, fine black and red figure ware, cooking pots, lamps and perhaps even roof tiles. The more decorative pots were usually made by two people (the potter and the artist who painted them), although sometimes one man did both jobs. Pots were often signed on the bottom by both the potter and the artist.

In Athens the potters had their own quarter, which was known as the *Kerameikos*. Potters' workshops were usually small and employed only five or six men. This reconstruction shows the inside of a typical workshop.

Large pots were made in separate sections and joined together. Handles were made by hand and joined on last.

The finished pot was decorated by a painter.

Pots were fired (baked) in a kiln like this one, which has been cut away to show how it worked.

Air vent

There was usually a hole in the loading door, so that the potter could see what was happening inside the kiln.

The finished pot, was turned upside down and smoothed to produce a fine surface.

Some Greek pots were moulded by hand, but most were made on a wheel. An apprentice often turned the wheel for the potter.

Wood or charcoal was burned here to heat the kiln.

Making black and red figure ware

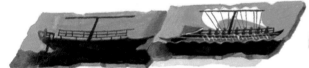

This type of pottery was made from a clay that turned red when fired. The areas of the pot that were to be black were painted with black slip, a paint, made from clay, water and wood ash.

On black figure ware, details could be carved into the black surface so that they would show through in red. Touches of white and dark red paint were used to provide extra details.

At a certain point in the firing, all the vents and openings in the kiln were shut. This cut off the oxygen supply and caused a chemical reaction which turned the whole pot black.

The temperature was then allowed to drop and the vents were re-opened. The areas painted with the black slip stayed black, but the rest of the pot turned a clear red colour.

Skyphos

Water was fetched from the fountain in a jar called a *hydria*. It had three handles: two were used to lift it and the third to pour. ▼

Alabastron

◀ An *aryballos* and an *alabastron* were flasks used for perfume, perfumed oil and ointments.

Aryballos

Kylix

A *loutrophoros* ▶ was a large vase used to bring water for a bride's ceremonial bath (see page 146).

A special type of ▶ *amphora*, filled with oil, was given as a prize at the Panathenaic Games. It was decorated with a picture of the event for which the prize was awarded.

Kantharos

▲ A *kantharos*, a *kylix* and a *skyphos* were all drinking cups. They had big handles so that people lying on couches could hold them easily.

Hydria

▲ Toilet box called a *pyxis*.

Markets, money and trade

In early times there was no money. People either exchanged goods for other goods of a similar value, or for an agreed amount of metal. Coins were probably invented at the end of the 7th century BC in Lydia, a kingdom in Asia Minor (see page 115). The first coins were made of electrum, a natural mixture of gold and silver.

From Lydia, coins spread to the Ionian Greek colonies and then to the Greek mainland. People soon came to prefer solid gold or silver coins. The Greeks used silver for most of their coins and a round, flat shape soon became standard. It became a sign of a city's independence to issue its own coins. The one exception to this was Sparta, where they continued to use iron rods instead of coins until the 4th century BC.

Greek coins

Early electrum coin from Ionia, marked with parallel lines, c.650-600BC.

Electrum *stater*, a coin from Lydia, showing a lion and a bull, c.561-545BC.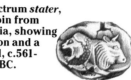

Athenian coin showing an owl (Athene's sacred bird), 5th century BC.

Silver *stater* from Corinth showing Pegasus the winged horse, c.520BC.

The first coins were small lumps of electrum, stamped with official marks to show that their weight and purity were guaranteed by the state.

From 600-480BC animals were the most popular image on coins. They were usually the symbol of the city that issued the coin.

Coin from Katane in Sicily showing Apollo, c.405BC.

Herakles fighting a lion. Silver coin from Herakleia, early 4th century BC.

Gold *stater* from Macedonia depicting Philip II, 359-336BC.

Silver coin from Macedonia, showing Alexander the Great, 336-323BC.

By 480BC, coin-making techniques had greatly improved and the human face and body were shown. Coins usually depicted a god or hero.

In the Hellenistic Period, the quality of the designs on coins declined. One new development was to show portraits of rulers.

Trade

Most trade was done by private merchants who sailed from port to port, buying and selling goods. The states did not normally interfere, except to charge custom duties. There was a great deal of trade between the various states within Greece and with the colonies. The colonies also acted as staging posts for Greek trade with the rest of the world. In the Classical Period, Athens was the leading trading centre, with Corinth a close rival. Each region exported surplus goods or produce. Areas became associated with particular products: for example, Thessaly and Macedonia exported horses, while Athens exported honey and silver. The main Greek exports were oil, wine, pots, statues, metalwork, cloth and books. The main imports are shown on this map.

Map showing major Greek imports

Olbia
Tyras
Phanagoria
ITALY Timber, grain, meat, pottery
Istrus
Tomi
BLACK SEA
Phasis
Messembria
Grain
Apollonia
Taras: Wool, linen
Sardis: Wool
Miletus: Wool, beds, carpets
Silk from CHINA
SICILY Grain, cheese, hide, pigs
Athens
Carthage: Wool, rugs, cushions
Syracuse: Dyed wool
CYPRUS Grain, oil, timber, copper
PHOENICIA Dates, flour, ointment, purple dye
CRETE Cypress wood
Gems, ebony, spices, elephants from INDIA
Cyrene: Wool, oil, ivory, lotuses
EGYPT Grain, gems, linen, ivory, papyrus

The grain trade

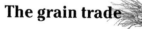

Grain was the most vital import, as many of the city states could not grow enough of it to feed all their citizens. Athens, for example, had to import two-thirds of the grain it needed. Grain was so important that its trade was controlled by the state, and at one time it was a capital offence to export it. Much of the imported grain came from the Greek colonies around the Black Sea.

Markets

At the heart of every Greek city was the *agora*, or market place. It was the centre of the city's commercial activity, and it was also a social centre where people met their friends. This picture shows what a typical *agora* would have looked like.

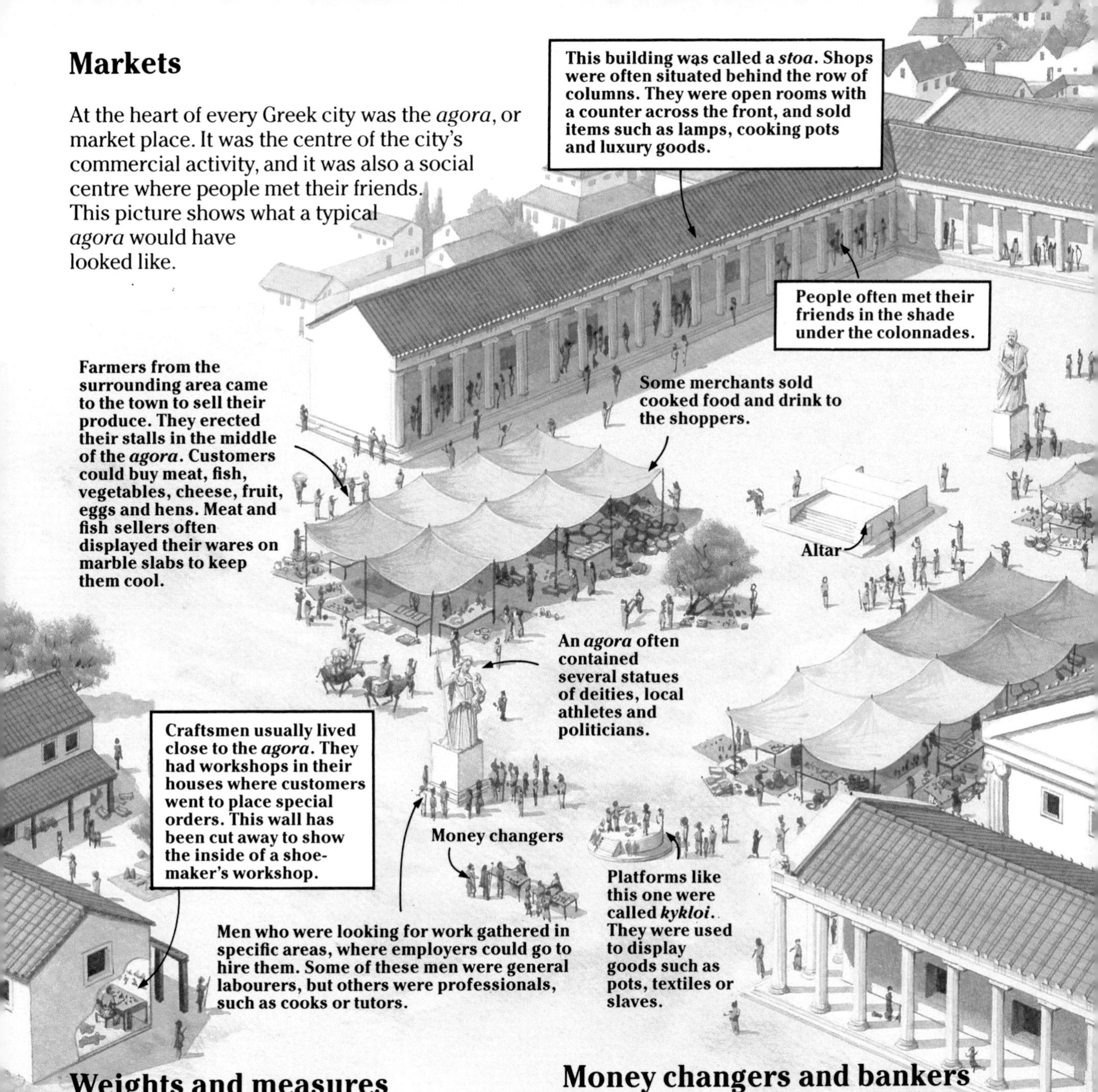

This building was called a *stoa*. Shops were often situated behind the row of columns. They were open rooms with a counter across the front, and sold items such as lamps, cooking pots and luxury goods.

People often met their friends in the shade under the colonnades.

Farmers from the surrounding area came to the town to sell their produce. They erected their stalls in the middle of the *agora*. Customers could buy meat, fish, vegetables, cheese, fruit, eggs and hens. Meat and fish sellers often displayed their wares on marble slabs to keep them cool.

Some merchants sold cooked food and drink to the shoppers.

Altar

An *agora* often contained several statues of deities, local athletes and politicians.

Craftsmen usually lived close to the *agora*. They had workshops in their houses where customers went to place special orders. This wall has been cut away to show the inside of a shoe-maker's workshop.

Money changers

Platforms like this one were called *kykloi*. They were used to display goods such as pots, textiles or slaves.

Men who were looking for work gathered in specific areas, where employers could go to hire them. Some of these men were general labourers, but others were professionals, such as cooks or tutors.

Weights and measures

Traders in and around the *agora* were controlled by various officials. In Athens, ten *metronomoi* were chosen annually to check weights and measures. Other officials called *agoranomoi* checked the quality of goods, while *sitophylakes* controlled the grain trade.

This is an official set of weights, against which the seller's weights were checked.

Money changers were known as *trapezitai*, or "table men", because they worked at tables in the agora.

Money changers and bankers

Every city state issued its own coins, so people who wanted to trade with another city had to go to a money changer. They charged a fee for their services and often made so much profit that they were able to lend money. This was the start of banking. A borrower had to pay back his loan by a set date and pay some interest. If he failed to pay he would lose whatever he had pledged to guarantee the loan. This could be his house or his land. People with spare money could also use a banker. He would find a suitable venture to invest it in and would pay the depositor interest from the profits.

Travel by land and sea

As Greece is a very mountainous country, land travel was extremely difficult in ancient times. One of the easiest and quickest ways to travel was by boat. There were many safe harbours and people could pay to travel on one of the merchant ships which sailed around the coast.

Sea travel had its risks too, as dishonest sailors sometimes robbed their passengers once they had put to sea. Ships could also be becalmed or driven off course by the wind. To ensure a safe voyage, a sensible captain always made a sacrifice to the sea god Poseidon before sailing. Ships were also at risk from pirates. It was only in the 5th century BC, when Athenian naval power was at its height, that the Aegean could be successfully policed and the number of pirates was reduced.

Merchant ships

Merchant ships did not normally sail in stormy weather, but even so some were caught and wrecked. Several wrecks have now been located and are being excavated by underwater archaeologists. This reconstruction of a trading ship from about 300BC is based on a wreck discovered off Cyprus.

The ship had a large, square sail made of linen.

The mast was made of spruce and the hull of pine. This timber had to be imported from Thrace and Macedonia.

Ropes were made of flax or hemp.

Cargo was stored below the deck. Liquids such as wine or oil were transported in large jars called *amphorae*.

The ship was steered with two rudder oars at the back.

Anchors

Early anchors were made from stones. They had a hole through the top for a rope. The modern shape of anchor was invented by a Greek called Anacharsis.

Navigating techniques

Merchant ships often travelled long distances across open sea, which required great sailing and navigating skills. A Greek called Thales of Miletus studied the Egyptian methods of astronomy and land surveying. He used these to devise a method by which a captain could calculate his distance from land, and a system of navigating by the stars. Anaximander, who lived in the 6th century BC, is said to have been the first person to draw a map of the world. Unfortunately it has not survived.

The kerkouroi

Merchant ships normally relied on sail-power, but writers speak of a ship called a *kerkouroi*, which had both a sail and oars. It had a ram at the front which could be used to fight pirate ships. This picture from a vase painting probably shows a *kerkouroi*.

Greek explorers

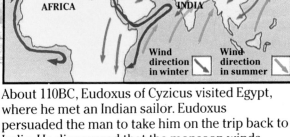

In about 325-300BC, a Greek called Pytheas from Massilia (modern Marseilles) set out to explore northern Europe. He landed in Cornwall and then tried to sail round Britain. After sailing north for six days, he reached another island. Modern scholars are not sure where this was. When he returned home, Pytheas wrote an account of his voyage, but most Greeks did not believe his tales.

About 110BC, Eudoxus of Cyzicus visited Egypt, where he met an Indian sailor. Eudoxus persuaded the man to take him on the trip back to India. He discovered that the monsoon winds carried ships to India from May to September. Then, from November to March, they blew in the other direction and took ships back to Africa. Eudoxus also sailed around the west coast of Africa.

Land travel

Travelling on land was not easy as the country was mountainous and there were few roads. The only good roads led to religious centres such as Eleusis (see page 165). Elsewhere, the roads were often in poor condition and there were hardly any bridges over rivers. Wars between the Greek states meant that people were often forced to make long detours in order to travel in safety.

When most ordinary Greeks went on a journey they had to walk.

Carts were used to transport both people and goods. They could only be used where there was a road, or at least a reasonable surface, to run on.

Rich people often travelled on horseback.

Merchants carrying goods on uneven tracks or over hilly ground used mules and donkeys as pack animals.

Many roads were plagued by bandits who attacked travellers.

Accommodation

Travellers often arranged to stay with relatives or friends along their route. There were inns on the main roads, but many did not provide food, so people had to take supplies with them. In towns, travellers could sleep under the porches of public buildings, but in remote areas they had to sleep in the open.

In some important centres, there were hotels, known as *katagogia*. However, these were often reserved for important visitors. This is a reconstruction of a hotel which has been found at Epidaurus. It had 160 rooms arranged around four courtyards and was two storeys high.

The army

At the beginning of the Archaic Period, the most important part of a Greek army was the cavalry. Warriors had to provide their own equipment, so rich aristocrats† came to dominate the army, as they were the only people who could afford a horse and armour. Foot soldiers usually came from the poorer classes, so their weapons and armour were of lower quality.

This statue shows a mounted warrior from the Archaic Period.

Later in the Archaic Period, trade increased, there was more demand for goods, and the middle classes started to prosper. They could now afford good armour and weapons and became heavily armed foot soldiers, known as *hoplites*. By the 7th century BC, foot soldiers were the most important part of the army.

A group of hoplite soldiers

A hoplite's equipment

All hoplites used similar armour and weapons. Most armies did not have a uniform, although in later years some standard elements were adopted to make soldiers recognizable in battle. Spartan hoplites always wore scarlet and the Athenians had shields decorated with the letter "A", for example.

Shields were normally round, and were large enough to protect the body from neck to thigh. They were made of bronze and leather. A hoplite could choose the decoration on his shield and often used a symbol of his family or city. The white legs on this shield were the emblem of the Alcmaeonid family of Athens.

Helmets were made of bronze and often had horsehair crests on top. The shape of helmets changed over the years. Some common styles are shown here.

A hoplite wore a joined breast and back plate, known as a *cuirass*. Early cuirasses were made from two bronze plates, secured with straps at the side. Later, hoplites used a more flexible cuirass, made of leather and bronze.

Bronze cuirass

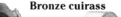

Illyrian helmet

Attic helmet

Corinthian helmet

Thracian helmet

Leather cuirass

A hoplite normally carried two weapons: a long spear and a short, iron sword.

A hoplite wore bronze leg guards, known as greaves, to protect the lower part of his legs.

How the army was organized

Each state had its own procedures for raising and leading its army. In Athens, a man went on to the active service list at 20 and could be called up when there was a war. Men of 50-60 went into the reserve and were used for garrison duties. In an emergency, both young men and veterans might have to fight.

The Athenian forces were led by ten commanders, called *strategoi*, one from each of the Athenian tribes. They were elected by the Assembly. Only one or two *strategoi* were sent out with each military expedition. Each of the ten tribes had to provide enough soldiers for one *phyle*, or regiment, of the army.

In Athens, young men of 18 had to do two years' military training. They were known as *ephebes*.

132

Battle tactics

As hoplite soldiers began to dominate the Greek armies, new battle tactics were needed and methods of fighting changed completely. In the Bronze Age, warriors had fought individually. Hoplite soldiers, however, fought in organized formations which required good discipline and precise training.

Hoplites fought in a unit known as a phalanx, which was a long block of soldiers, usually eight ranks deep. When a soldier in the front line was killed or injured, his place was taken by the man behind him.

Exposed side

Each hoplite was protected partly by his own shield and partly by his neighbour's. The man on the right-hand end of a line had no neighbour to protect him and was half exposed.

When attacking, a phalanx charged forwards so that the full weight of men and armour smashed into the enemy. If the enemy line did not give way, the two phalanxes had to push until one line broke.

Weak right wing

Enemy phalanx

The right wing of the phalanx was the most vulnerable to attack because the soldiers at this end were partly unprotected. In battle, a general would often try to attack the enemy phalanx on this side.

For the phalanx to be effective, it was important for the men to stay in lines and move as a unit. They used flute music to help them keep in step. This vase painting shows a hoplite phalanx being piped into battle.

Thracian soldiers

In the 5th century BC, the Greeks came into contact with Thracian soldiers, known as *peltasts*. Their tactics were to dash out from cover, hurl javelins into a phalanx and then retreat. When the phalanx formation was broken, the *peltasts* would pick off individual hoplites. To fight them, the Greeks used soldiers known as *ekdromoi*, or "runners out". They were fit, young hoplites, who would run out of the phalanx to chase off the *peltasts*.

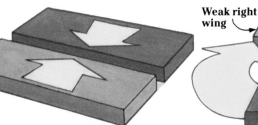

A *peltast* carried a small, crescent-shaped wooden shield called a *pelta*.

An *ekdromos* did not use a cuirass or greaves, as these would have weighed him down.

Auxiliary soldiers

Poor men who could not afford the full armour and weapons of a hoplite usually served in lightly armed auxiliary units. These units included archers, stone slingers and soldiers known as *psiloi*, who were armed with clubs and stones.

A *psilos* wore no armour. He used an animal pelt wrapped around his arm to defend himself.

The cavalry

Once hoplites came to dominate the army, the cavalry was much reduced in numbers. By the time of the Persian Wars, the Athenians had only 300 cavalry soldiers. However, horsemen proved to be very useful, both as scouts and to break up an enemy phalanx. The Athenians therefore started to build up their cavalry. By the middle of the 5th century BC they had 1000 cavalrymen.

Each of the ten Athenian tribes was responsible for supplying one squadron of cavalry soldiers. The cavalry was led by two commanders called *hipparchs*, who each controlled five squadrons.

Cavalrymen wore a metal helmet, a cuirass and boots. They were armed with spears, javelins and swords.

Siege warfare

When one Greek state fought another, a common tactic was to lay siege to the enemy city. The army would surround the city and then destroy the enemy's crops, which were usually grown on the plains outside the city. The enemy city would eventually be starved into submission, but this could take a long time.

The besieging army might also try to take the city by force. They used a variety of weapons to attack the city walls and kill the defending soldiers. Some of these devices are shown below.

A city under siege

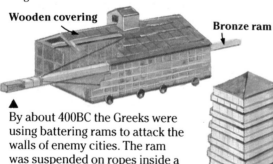

Javelin

◀ The Greeks invented the catapult in the 4th century BC. Early versions were based on the crossbow and fired arrows or javelins, but later catapults could throw large rocks.

Cauldron containing burning coals, sulphur and pitch.

Bellows

Hollow tree trunk

A flame-thower was sometimes used to destroy wooden walls. Huge bellows pumped air down a hollow tree trunk. This sprayed fire from a cauldron on to the target.

Wooden covering

Bronze ram

▲
By about 400BC the Greeks were using battering rams to attack the walls of enemy cities. The ram was suspended on ropes inside a wooden covering, and was moved backwards and forwards by a team of men.

Siege towers were used to enable ▶ soldiers to climb on to enemy walls. They were sometimes divided into storeys, each of which housed archers or a catapult.

The navy

Whereas Greek merchant ships relied on sails to propel them, their fighting ships had both oars and sails. They could be used simultaneously in open sea, but only the oars were used in a battle.

The more oarsmen a warship had, the faster it could go. At first, oarsmen sat in two rows, one on each side of the ship. Then the Phoenicians invented a ship called a *bireme*, in which the oarsmen on each side of the ship sat in two rows, on two different levels. This doubled the number of oarsmen. In the 6th century BC, the Greeks invented the *trireme*, a ship with three levels of oarsmen on each side.

The trireme

Triremes were fast and easy to manoeuvre. They probably carried crews of up to 200 men, of whom about 170 were rowers. Archaeological evidence from the Athenian dockyard at Piraeus shows that triremes were about 41 metres (135ft) long and 6 metres (20ft) wide. Experts think that in good sea conditions they could reach speeds of around 16 kilometres per hour (10mph).

Triremes had some disadvantages. They were unsafe in stormy sea conditions. There was also no room on board for the crew to cook or sleep, so the ship had to stay close to the coast and land each night. However, they were for many years the most successful warships in the Mediterranean and continued to be used into Roman times.

The captain of the ship was called a *trierarch*. In Athens, he was a rich man, chosen by the state to pay for the running of the ship for one year. The *trierarch* would often appoint a professional sailor to run the ship for him.

The ship was steered from these two oars at the stern.

Each oar was over 4 metres (14ft) long.

These leather covers were normally rolled up and tied to the rails. They could be lowered to protect the oarsmen during a battle or to stop water entering through the oar holes.

Early ships

In the Archaic Period, the standard Greek warship was a *penteconter*. It had 50 oarsmen. Some experts believe that the oars were in a straight line, others think that the oarsmen sat on two levels.

By the 8th century BC, the Phoenicians were using a warship called a *bireme*. It had two rows of oars on each side of the ship and a raised deck which carried archers and warriors.

The oarsmen

Greek oarsmen were free men and professional sailors, who were usually recruited from the poorer classes. We do not know exactly how the three rows of oarsmen were arranged on a trireme. Three possible seating plans are shown here. Experts now think that the first arrangement was most likely.

Battle tactics

At the time of the Persian Wars, trireme tactics were to row hard and ram the enemy ship. This would sink or at least incapacitate it. The Greek troops then fired arrows at the enemy crew. If necessary, they boarded the enemy ship and defeated any remaining crew in hand-to-hand fighting.

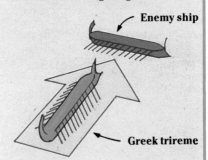

As triremes became swifter and lighter, tactics changed. A trireme would row towards an enemy ship, but swerve away at the last moment. The rowers pulled their oars on board and the trireme glided past the enemy ship, breaking its oars. The disabled ship could then be rammed and boarded easily.

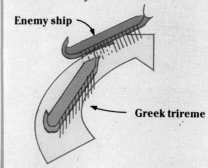

The mast was usually made of a wood called spruce. The wood was specially imported from Thrace and Macedonia. The mast was lowered on to the deck before a battle.

The sail was probably made of linen. It was used when the trireme was in open sea, but was lowered before a battle. The ship was more stable and easier to manoeuvre when the sail and mast were lowered.

A trireme carried a number of archers and soldiers, who travelled on the upper deck. In a battle they fired at the enemy crew and tried to board their ship.

The prow of the ship was equipped with a bronze ram, which was used to sink enemy ships. The whole prow area was heavily reinforced, sometimes with metal. The front of the ship was often decorated with a painted eye to scare the enemy.

The Persian Wars

In the 6th century BC, the Greeks were threatened by a people called the Persians, who came from the area that is now Iran (see page opposite). As the Persians expanded their empire westwards, they tried to seize Greek territory. In 546BC, they conquered the Ionian states on the west coast of Asia Minor. In 500-499BC the Ionians became discontented with Persian rule and rebelled, helped by a naval force from Athens and Eretria. The Ionians were successful at first, but the Persians eventually crushed the revolt. This was the start of a series of wars between the Greeks and the Persians, which lasted from 490-449BC.

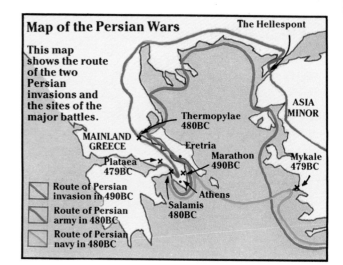

Map of the Persian Wars

This map shows the route of the two Persian invasions and the sites of the major battles.

The Hellespont

ASIA MINOR

MAINLAND GREECE

Thermopylae 480BC

Eretria

Marathon 490BC

Mykale 479BC

Plataea 479BC

Athens

Salamis 480BC

Route of Persian invasion in 490BC
Route of Persian army in 480BC
Route of Persian navy in 480BC

The Battle of Marathon

The Persians did not forgive Athens and Eretria for helping the Ionians. In 490BC, led by King Darius, they crushed Eretria. Then they landed at Marathon, a place on the coast north east of Athens. The Athenians and their allies raised an army of 10,000 troops, led by a general called Miltiades†. Although the Greeks were heavily outnumbered by the Persians, they won the battle. This was due to Miltiades' superior military tactics and the strength of the hoplite† phalanx (see page 133).

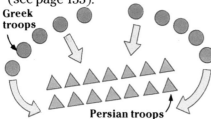

Greek troops

Persian troops

The Greeks concentrated their troops on the wings. They were able to attack the Persians at the sides and then from behind.

The second Persian invasion

Many Greeks thought that the Persians would invade again. A politician called Themistocles† persuaded the Athenians to improve their city's defences by building up its navy. In 480BC the Persians did invade, led by King Xerxes. Many of the Greek states joined forces to fight the Persians. The Athenians consulted the Oracle† at Delphi (see page 164) and were told that Athens would be saved by a wooden wall. Some Athenians believed the Oracle was describing the wooden city walls, but Themistocles convinced them that the message in fact referred to the wooden ships in the city's navy. He therefore prepared for a naval battle.

In 480BC the Persians crossed the Hellespont (see map) on a bridge made of boats. Their huge army was said to have taken seven days to march across.

The Battle of Thermopylae

The first battle between the Greeks and Xerxes' army took place in 480BC in a narrow mountain pass called Thermopylae. A small army of Spartans and Boeotians, led by King Leonidas, were able to prevent the Persians getting through. However, a Greek traitor showed some of the Persians another route around the pass. Leonidas knew he would be surrounded and sent most of his soldiers away to safety. He fought on with just a few troops. They were hopelessly outnumbered and were all killed.

The destruction of Athens

After Thermopylae, the Persians marched south to attack Athens. The Athenian leader, Themistocles, was still determined to fight the Persians at sea, so he withdrew most of his troops and allowed the Persians to seize the city. They murdered the few defending Athenians, burned the temples on the Acropolis† and plundered the city.

The Battles of Salamis and Plataea

The Persians also sent a naval force to attack the Greeks. There was a decisive sea battle in 480BC around the island of Salamis, off the coast of Athens. Themistocles lured the Persian fleet into the channel of water between Salamis and the mainland. There the Greek navy took them by surprise. The Persian ships were unable to manoeuvre in the narrow waters and after a fierce battle they were defeated.

The Battle of Salamis

In 479BC the Greeks assembled an enormous army, led by the Spartan general, Pausanias, and defeated the Persian army at a place called Plataea. At the same time the Greek navy attacked and burned the Persian fleet, while it was beached at Mykale on the coast of Asia Minor. This marked the end of the Persian invasion.

The Delian League

Many Greeks believed that it was only a matter of time before the Persians tried to avenge their defeat. In order to be ready for this, many of the Greek states formed a league, led by Athens.

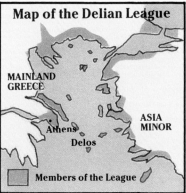

Map of the Delian League

MAINLAND GREECE

Athens

Delos

ASIA MINOR

Members of the League

Members of the league contributed ships and money to provide a navy to defend them. It is known as the Delian League, as it first met in 478BC on the island of Delos, where the common treasury was kept.

The end of the Persian Wars

Although the Greeks had succeeded in stopping the Persian invasion of mainland Greece, the wars did not come to an abrupt end. The Greeks and Persians continued to fight over various territories around the Mediterranean, such as Egypt, Cyprus and Ionia. In 449BC the Delian League signed a peace treaty with Persia, but most Greeks continued to dislike and fear the Persians.

The Persians

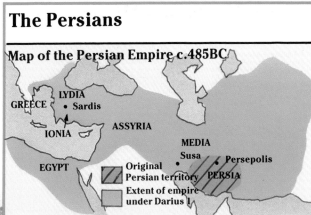

Map of the Persian Empire c.485BC

GREECE

LYDIA
• Sardis

IONIA

ASSYRIA

EGYPT

MEDIA
Susa •
• Persepolis

PERSIA

Original Persian territory

Extent of empire under Darius I

The Persians came from the area now called Iran. In 550BC they conquered the neighbouring kingdom of Media and started to expand their territory, eventually acquiring an enormous empire. Their empire was divided into 20 provinces, each governed by an official called a *satrap*. A system of roads made communication between the king and the provinces easy.

The Persians owed their success to an extremely efficient army. Most of their troops were Persian, and there was an elite force of 10,000 warriors, known as the Immortals.

Picture of two Immortals from the palace at Susa ▶

Part of the staircase from Darius' palace at Persepolis ▼

Key dates

550BC King Cyrus II of Persia defeats the Medes and founds the Achaemenid dynasty.

522-485BC Reign of the Persian King, Darius I. The Persian Empire reaches its largest extent (see map above).

500-499BC The Greek colonies in Ionia revolt against the Persians, but are defeated.

490BC First Persian invasion of Greece. The Persians are defeated at the Battle of Marathon.

480BC Second Persian invasion of Greece; Battle of Thermopylae; destruction of Athens; naval Battle of Salamis.

479BC Battle of Plataea; the Greeks defeat the Persian invasion.

465-330BC Persian Empire declines and is eventually conquered by Alexander the Great† (see pages 170-171).

The city of Athens

Athens is dominated by a rocky hill called the *Acropolis*, which means "high city" in Greek. People settled there from the earliest times because it had a spring of water and was easy to defend. In Mycenaean times there was a small city on the Acropolis, surrounded by stone walls.

By the end of the Dark Ages, the Acropolis had become a sacred place used only for temples and shrines. Other public buildings and people's houses were built around the base of the hill.

In 480BC Athens was sacked by the Persians (see page 136) and the temples on the Acropolis were destroyed. A few years later, a massive rebuilding programme was launched by the politician, Pericles†. The temples which still stand on the Acropolis were built at this time.

By the Classical Period, there were probably over 250,000 people living in Athens and the surrounding countryside. The city had its own port on the coast at Piraeus, about six kilometres (four miles) away. This reconstruction shows what the city of Athens probably looked like at the end of the Classical Period.

The Acropolis

This temple, called the *Erechtheum*, was built in 421-406BC. It was constructed on the site of the contest between Poseidon and Athene (see right) and a sacred olive tree grew in its courtyard. The temple was named after Erechtheus, who was the legendary ancestor of the city's Mycenaean kings. It contained a wooden statue of Athene, which the Greeks believed had fallen to earth in ancient times.

This huge, bronze statue of *Athene Promachos* (Athene the Champion) was made by the sculptor Pheidias†. On clear days, it could be seen by sailors returning to the port at Piraeus.

This gateway leading to the sacred enclosure was called the *Propylaea*. It was built in 437-432BC by the architect Mnesicles.

The temple of *Athene Nike* (Athene the Victorious) was built in 426BC by the architect Callicrates.

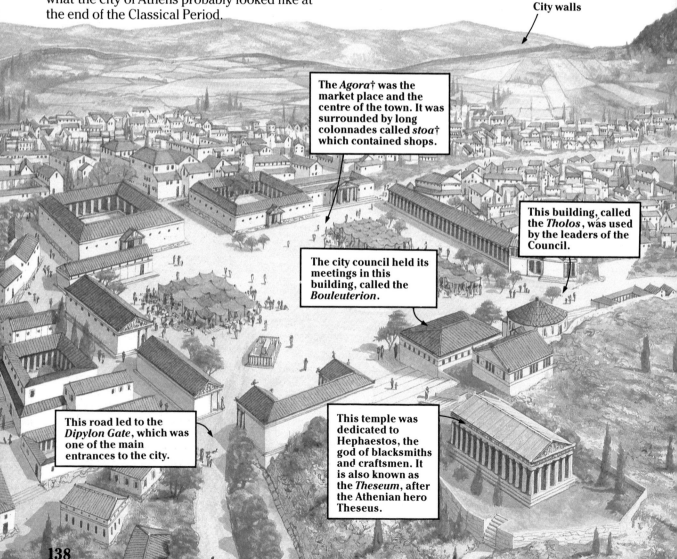

City walls

The *Agora*† was the market place and the centre of the town. It was surrounded by long colonnades called *stoa*† which contained shops.

This building, called the *Tholos*, was used by the leaders of the Council.

The city council held its meetings in this building, called the *Bouleuterion*.

This road led to the *Dipylon Gate*, which was one of the main entrances to the city.

This temple was dedicated to Hephaestos, the god of blacksmiths and craftsmen. It is also known as the *Theseum*, after the Athenian hero Theseus.

The *Parthenon* was built between 447-438BC by the architect Ictinus. It was a temple to the goddess Athene, who was the patron goddess of the city. Athens was named after her.

Altar

This concert hall, called the *Odeon*, was used for contests of music and poetry.

A drama festival was held in this theatre each year in honour of the god Dionysus.

Acropolis

The *Panathenaic Way* was the main road to the Acropolis. It was the route used by a special procession, which took place every four years in honour of Athene.

The Court of Justice was situated on this hill, called the *Areopagus*. It was named after the god Ares who, according to legend, once stood trial here for murder.

The Assembly of Athenian citizens met on this hill, called the *Pnyx*, to take decisions on the government of the city.

Houses near the agora were often occupied by craftsmen. Many blacksmiths' forges were situated close to the temple of Hephaestos.

The naming of Athens

According to legend, the gods Athene and Poseidon quarrelled over the naming of the greatest town in Greece. Poseidon thrust his trident into a rock on the Acropolis. Sea water gushed out, and Poseidon promised the people riches through sea trade if they named the city after him.

Athene planted an olive tree as her gift to the people. It was decided that she had given the more valuable gift and the city was called Athens in her honour. Athene's sacred olive tree was burnt when the city was sacked by the Persians, but when it later threw out green shoots it brought new hope to the Athenians.

The return of Theseus

Theseus was a legendary king (see page 178), said to have ruled Athens in the Mycenaean Age. At the Battle of Marathon in 490BC, the spirit of Theseus was said to have charged towards the Persian ranks, inspiring the Athenians to victory.

After this the Oracle of Delphi (see page 164) ordered that Theseus' bones should be brought back to Athens from the island of Skyros, where he had died. On the island, the Athenians saw an eagle tearing at the ground. They dug in this spot and discovered a coffin containing bones and bronze armour. They knew this must be Theseus, and reburied him in Athens.

Architecture

The Greeks attached little importance to the building of private houses, which were usually simple structures made of mud and brick. Instead, they devoted their money and skills to public buildings. The most important of these were temples, which provided a focus for both civic pride and religious feelings. In the Classical Period, the city state was therefore the most important patron for architects, sculptors and painters.

Building materials and techniques

From the 7th century BC, temples and other large, public buildings were made of stone. Limestone or marble were the normal materials, but in the western colonies sandstone was also used. Parts of the building, such as the roof frame and ceilings, were built from wood. Roof tiles were usually made of terracotta†, although some great temples had stone tiles. This scene shows how a temple was constructed.

Blocks of stone were brought from the quarry on wagons.

Each block was joined to the ones beside it with pieces of metal called cramps, and joined to the ones above and below with rods called dowels.

Cramp

Blocks were shaped on the ground. Masons used hammers, mallets and various kinds of chisel to shape the stone.

Ropes and pulleys were used to lift the blocks of stone. They were then manoeuvred into place with levers.

When they were in place, the stones were polished with a hard stone and a lubricant.

Columns were made from a number of cylindrical pieces of stone, called drums, held together with metal pegs.

The grooves on the pillars, known as fluting, were started when the drums were on the ground and completed when the columns had been erected.

Public buildings

▲
A *tholos* was a round building with a conical roof, surrounded by columns. The *tholos* in Athens was used as a meeting place for members of the city's council. This reconstruction shows the *tholos* in Delphi, which was probably used for religious purposes.

A *stoa* was a building with a row of columns at the front. It was used to provide shelter from the sun and rain. *Stoas* were often built round an agora and often contained shops or offices behind the colonnade.

▼

Treasuries were built at religious centres to house the offerings made by a *polis*† and its citizens. They resembled small temples, and consisted of a single room with a porch in front. This is the Athenian treasury at Delphi.

▼

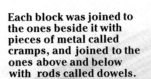

▲
Altars were erected in the open air, often in front of a temple entrance. They were usually just a slab of stone, but some could be very large and ornate. This reconstruction shows the altar of Zeus and Athene at Pergamum, which was built in the Hellenistic Period by King Eumenes II.

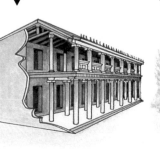

Architectural styles

The design of most Greek buildings was based on a series of vertical pillars with horizontal lintels. This style probably came from earlier buildings in which tree trunks were used to support the roof. The proportions, such as the number and height of the pillars and the distance between them, were carefully calculated to achieve a balanced effect. In the architecture of temples, two main styles, or orders, emerged. They are known as the Doric and the Ionic Orders.

The Doric Order

This style was popular in mainland Greece. It was a simple style with sturdy columns whose tops, or capitals, were undecorated.

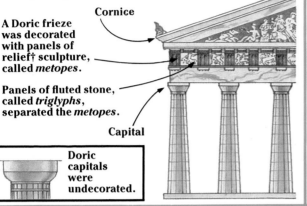

A Doric frieze was decorated with panels of relief† sculpture, called *metopes*.

Cornice

Panels of fluted stone, called *triglyphs*, separated the *metopes*.

Capital

Doric capitals were undecorated.

The Ionic Order

The Ionic style was popular in the eastern colonies and on the islands. It was a more elegant style than the Doric, and had thinner columns with decorated capitals.

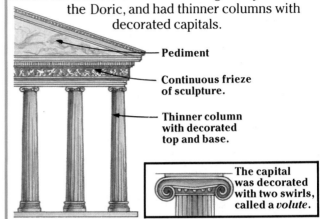

Pediment

Continuous frieze of sculpture.

Thinner column with decorated top and base.

The capital was decorated with two swirls, called a *volute*.

Other column styles

An early form of the Ionic column has been found at Smyrna and on Lesbos. This style is known as Aeolic. It is thought to date from the 6th century BC.

The Corinthian column was a later variation of the Ionic. It had an elaborate capital, decorated with acanthus leaves. The Greeks did not often use Corinthian columns, but they became very popular in Roman times.

Sometimes a statue of a girl, called a *caryatid*, was used as a column. The most famous *caryatids* are in the *Erechtheum* on the Acropolis in Athens.

A votive monument was one erected in honour of a hero, or of a great victory in an athletic competition, a festival or a war. This lion was built as a memorial to the Theban soldiers who fought in the Battle of Chaeronea in 338BC. ▼

▲
A *propylaea* was an elaborate gateway, which formed the entrance to the sacred enclosure at a religious sanctuary. The most famous *propylaea* is the one on the Acropolis in Athens which was built in 437-432BC.

Decoration of buildings

The statues, friezes and sometimes also the walls of public buildings were painted. Fragments from early mural paintings show that a flat, two-dimensional style was used. In the Classical Period a more realistic style was introduced, and the Greeks became the first people to make use of perspective in their pictures. In the Hellenistic Period, wealthy people often had their houses decorated with murals.

Very few Greek murals have survived. However, this painting from Pompeii in Italy was probably painted by a Greek artist.

Sculpture

The Greeks made large numbers of statues, as they used them for a wide variety of purposes. Sculptures were used to decorate temples and people's homes, to commemorate famous people and to mark graves. Although some Greek statues have been lost, others have been preserved, sometimes in rather unusual ways. For example, the remains of may broken statues have been discovered on the Acropolis† in Athens, where they were buried after the city had been sacked by the Persians in 480BC (see page 136). Other statues, which were lost in shipwrecks, have recently been recovered from the sea. Many Roman copies of famous Greek statues have also survived although the originals have been lost.

Stone statues

Sculptors used a chisel and mallet to carve the stone.

Clothes were painted in bright colours, such as red or blue.

Hair was painted yellow.

Stone statues were made from limestone or marble. As large blocks of stone were difficult to transport, they were usually cut in the quarry to the rough shape of the statue. The more detailed carving was done later in a workshop, like the one shown here.

Finished statues were originally painted, but most of the paint has now worn away. Sometimes inlaid glass, coloured stone or ivory was used for the eyes. Details such as weapons, crowns, jewellery or horses' tackle were made of bronze fitted on to the stone.

Terracotta

Terracotta is a mixture of clay and sand which was used to make small statues and plaques for temples. Small figures illustrating scenes from daily life were also made of terracotta. This one from the 6th century BC shows a barber at work.

Wood

◄ In early times, statues were probably made of wood, but as it decays quickly few of them have survived. This rare wooden statue showing Zeus and Hera was made in c.625-600BC.

Bronze

The Greeks also made many bronze statues, but only a few of them have survived. Some of these are shown on page 144.

Styles of sculpture

The Archaic Period: c.800-480BC

At first statues were only made in a ► limited number of poses, which were copied from Egyptian art. Normally the figure was standing in a very stiff, formal position, with its left leg forward and arms at its side. Its facial expression was always a half-smile.

The Classical Period: c.480-323BC

In this period, it ► was fashionable for sculptors to portray deities or god-like men and women, with detached and serene facial expressions. This is a Roman copy of a statue by Praxiteles†, c.350-330BC.

Sculptors liked to show figures in the middle of an action. This discus thrower is a Roman copy of a statue made by the sculptor Myron† in c.460-450BC.

The Hellenistic Period: c.323-100BC

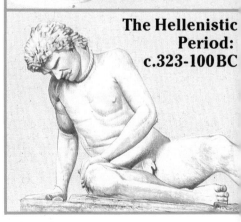

Egyptian statue

Greek statue of a young man, called a *kouros* (youth).

Greek statue of a *kore* (maiden).

Greek artists soon became dissatisfied with this formal approach and began experimenting with relaxed and supple figures and more adventurous poses. This statue of an archer was made in c.500-480BC. ▼

Sculptors also started to show the folds of material in clothes. At first these were just rigid lines, but they became more realistic, as shown on this figure of a goddess made in c.480BC. ►

As sculptors became more skilled at showing facial expressions, they began to produce portraits of the famous. This is the Athenian leader Pericles (see page 158). ►

In this period, sculptors also made reliefs – figures carved on flat slabs of stone. They were often used to decorate temple walls. This scene from the Parthenon shows riders in the *Panathenaic* procession (see page 163). ▼

Athens was a famous centre for carving gravestones. This gravestone for a woman called Hegeso was made in c.400BC. ▼

◄ There was also a growing interest in portraying the female body. The first known female nude is this statue of Aphrodite by Praxiteles, made c.350-330BC.

◄ Sculptors also produced special reliefs which people left in temples to thank the gods for favours. This one was dedicated to Asclepius, the god of medicine.

In the 4th century BC sculptors ► became more interested in human qualities. Facial expressions on statues were often gentle and tender. This Roman copy shows the mythical characters, Eirene and Ploutos, by the sculptor Kephisodotos.

In the Hellenistic Period, sculptors started to portray a wider range of characters. Old age, childhood, pain and even death were now acceptable subjects. This is a Roman copy of a ◄ statue showing a dying man.

Physical deformities were also shown. This boxer with battered ◄ features is a typical example of the new subject matter in the Hellenistic Period.

Hellenistic sculptures ► could be highly dramatic. This Roman copy shows a man killing himself and his wife.

Metalworkers and miners

During the Mycenaean period the principal metal used for weapons and tools was bronze. Iron was introduced during the Dark Ages, but it was only used for a limited range of objects and many things continued to be produced in bronze. Gold and silver were always used for luxury items.

In Athens, the metalworkers had their own quarter near the temple of Hephaestos, who was their patron deity. Most smiths worked in small workshops in their homes.

Bronze

Bronze is an alloy which is made by adding a small amount of tin to copper. The Greeks imported copper from Cyprus and the eastern Mediterranean and tin from Spain, Brittany and even Cornwall. They used bronze to make a wide variety of objects, some of which are shown below. As bronze was a valuable metal, it was often melted down and re-used, so few large items have survived.

Bronze was a favourite material for statues. Some of the statues we have were originally lost at sea in shipwrecks and have only recently been found by underwater archaeologists.

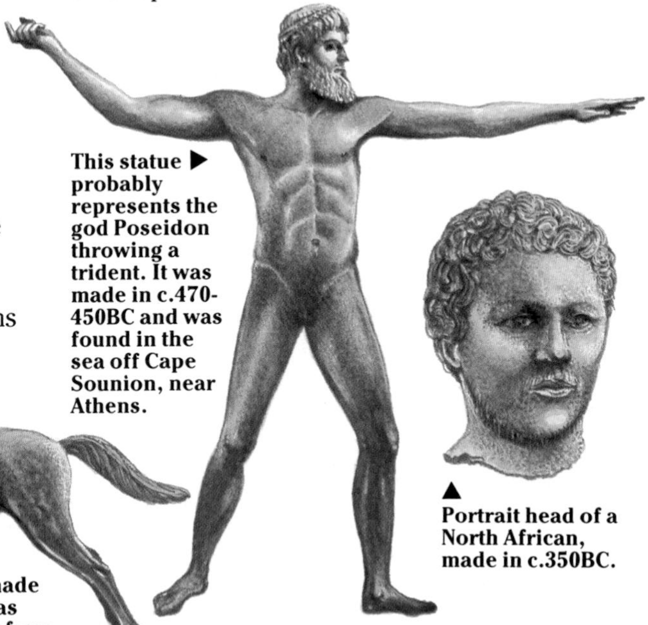

This statue ▶ probably represents the god Poseidon throwing a trident. It was made in c.470-450BC and was found in the sea off Cape Sounion, near Athens.

▲ Portrait head of a North African, made in c.350BC.

▲ A boy jockey and his horse, made in c.330-310BC. This statue was probably a victory monument from the Olympic Games.

◀ Armour was usually made of bronze (see page 132). This vase painting shows an armourer at work on a helmet.

Bronze was used to make household articles, such as vases, mirrors and kitchen utensils. This bronze mirror from Athens was ◀ made in c.500BC.

◀ This enormous bronze *krater* was discovered at Vix in France. It is 1.64 metres (5.4ft) high, weighs 208 kilos (458lb) and holds about 1200 litres (317 gallons).

Methods of working bronze

Hammering
The earliest bronze statues were made from sheets of bronze hammered and riveted over a wooden core.

Casting
Later, small statues were made of solid metal, cast in moulds.

The lost wax method
Not all statues were solid metal. Some were made by the lost wax method, shown below. Large statues were made in sections and joined together.

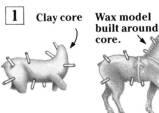

1 Clay core   Wax model built around core.

First a clay core was made and pins were stuck in it. The statue was modelled in wax around the core.

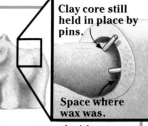

Clay core still held in place by pins.

Space where wax was.

2

The model was covered with more clay and heated. The wax melted and then ran out, leaving a space.

Finished statue

3

Molten bronze could then be poured into the gap. When the bronze had set, the clay mould was removed.

Iron

Iron was first used in Greece in about 1050BC and steadily increased in importance. Iron was used principally for tools and weapons, as it could be made sharper and harder than bronze.

The use of iron required the invention of new technology. In bronze-making, the furnace only needed to be heated to around 1090°C (1994°F), but to work iron a much higher temperature was required.

This reconstruction of an iron furnace is based on one shown on a vase painting. When the furnace was heated, the molten iron gathered at the bottom and could be removed with tongs.

The furnace was built of brick and lined with clay to retain the heat.

Layers of charcoal and iron ore were placed in here.

One man pumped these goatskin bellows to increase the temperature in the furnace.

Iron from the furnace had to be hammered while it was still red hot to remove impurities.

Special tongs were used to move the hot metal.

This golden casket was found in the royal Macedonian tombs in Vergina, and is thought to have held the ashes of King Philip II (see page 169).

A silver jug from the Macedonian tombs.

A gold bowl from Olympia, c.620BC.

Gold and silver

Precious metals were used to make coins, jewellery and luxury goods. We also know of several large statues made of gold and ivory, such as the statue of Athene in the Parthenon (see page 162). Few gold and silver items from Ancient Greece have survived, as they were often melted down so that the metal could be re-used. In addition, they were often stolen by tomb robbers or conquerors. When the Romans occupied Greece in the 2nd century BC (see page 201), they stole huge numbers of gold and silver objects.

Silver mining

Most of the Greeks' silver came from the mines at Laurion near Athens. These mines were worked from at least the 8th century BC.

The mines were owned by the Athenian state, but they were leased out to private contractors. The mining itself was done by slaves, who were hired by the contractors from their owners. By the 5th century BC there were as many as 20,000 slaves working at Laurion. Conditions were grim, with miners working shifts of up to ten hours. This reconstruction of a mine shows how the ore was extracted.

Narrow galleries fanned out into the seams of silver ore. In some places miners had to crawl along them and then lie on their backs to work.

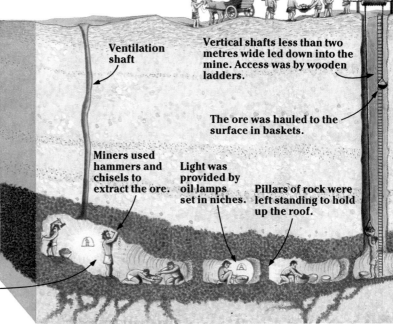

Ventilation shaft

Vertical shafts less than two metres wide led down into the mine. Access was by wooden ladders.

The ore was hauled to the surface in baskets.

Miners used hammers and chisels to extract the ore.

Light was provided by oil lamps set in niches.

Pillars of rock were left standing to hold up the roof.

The role of women

Women in most states in ancient Greece led very sheltered lives and were not permitted to play an active role in society. They could not take part in the running of the city. They were not allowed to inherit or own property, or to conduct any legal transaction. They could not even buy anything that cost over a certain amount of money. Throughout their lives they were always under the control of a male relative: first their father, then their husband, brother or son.

Marriage

A girl was only about 15 when she was married, but the bridegroom was likely to be much older. Plato said that 30-35 was the best age for a man to marry. A girl's father chose her husband and provided her with money and goods, called a dowry. This was administered by her husband, but would return to her father if she were divorced or left a widow without children.

Loutrophorus

Servants dressing the bride

On the day before her wedding a bride sacrificed her toys to the goddess Artemis, as a sign that her childhood was ending. She bathed in water from a sacred spring, brought in a vase called a *loutrophorus*.

On the wedding day, the bride wore white. Both families made sacrifices and feasted. In the evening, the bridegroom went to the bride's house. This was often the first time that the bride and groom met.

The bride and groom then rode to his house, in a chariot if they were rich, or a cart if they were not. They were accompanied by a procession, led by torch bearers and musicians.

They were met at the door by the groom's mother. The bride was carried over the threshold and then led to the family hearth to join the religious life of her new family.

The bride and groom shared some food before the hearth as a symbol of their union. Then they were showered with nuts, fruits and sweets to bring them luck and prosperity.

Finally the bride was led to the bedroom, amidst much laughing and joking. On the following day both families met at the husband's house for a party and presents were given.

A wife's duties

In a wealthy household, a bride had many duties. Each day she inspected the stores, and ensured that the house was clean and tidy and that meals were ready on time. She looked after the children and any sick members of the household, and managed the family finances.

The women of the household produced all the cloth needed for clothes and furnishings. Spinning and weaving therefore occupied a large amount of a wife's time. This reconstruction, based on a 6th century vase painting, shows a wife supervising the various stages involved in making cloth.

The mistress of the household would have been seated. Here she is preparing some wool for spinning and supervising the work.

This woman is spinning the wool. She holds the wool on a distaff and uses a spindle to stretch out the thread.

These women are weighing bales of wool on a pair of scales.

The thread is woven into cloth on a loom.

These women are folding the finished piece of cloth.

Social life

The slave carried a parasol to protect the lady from the sun.

In Athens, married women from good families did not often leave the house. They normally went out only for religious festivals and family celebrations, or to do small bits of personal shopping. Whenever they went out, they were accompanied by a slave.

Sometimes they were allowed to visit their women friends. This terracotta† shows two ladies chatting. Women also gave dinner parties for their female friends, but we know little about them. Men and women only mixed at strictly family parties.

Generally, the richer the family, the less freedom the wife was likely to have. In poor families, the women had to do the housework themselves. This involved going shopping and fetching water from the fountain, which were good opportunities to meet friends.

Divorce

A woman had to be virtuous and absolutely faithful to her husband. She would be divorced and lose her dowry if he suspected that she were not.

If a man wanted to divorce his wife, he just made a formal statement of divorce in front of witnesses. It was much more difficult for a woman to end an unhappy marriage, because she could not take legal action herself. She had to go to an official called an *archon* (see page 157) and persuade him to act on her behalf.

In a divorce, the husband kept the children and sent his wife back to her nearest male relative.

Hetairai

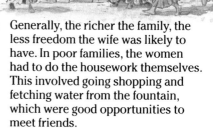

Hetairai were invited to men's dinner parties. They were trained to join in the conversation.

Not every girl was brought up to be a virtuous wife. Some girls, usually from the lower classes or foreigners, would become *hetairai*, or companions. They had to be pretty and clever, and were carefully trained to be skilled musicians and witty, interesting speakers. They took wealthy lovers who could support them in comfort.

Beauty

Oil bottles in the shape of feet.

Greek ladies spent a lot of time, effort and money on making themselves beautiful. It became the custom to have a bath every day. After the bath, perfumed oil was rubbed into the skin to prevent the drying effect of the sun.

This vase painting shows a woman washing her hair. Oil was also used on the hair to make it shine. Some women dyed their hair or used wigs. Others used padding to improve their figure, or wore thick-soled sandals to make themselves taller.

Many women wore make-up. They used rouge to make their cheeks pink and darkened their eyebrows. It was fashionable for the skin to be pale and make-up was used to make the skin white. This vase painting shows a woman admiring herself in a mirror.

Childhood and education

Greek citizens were taught that it was their patriotic duty to get married and father sons. In Sparta, for example, penalties were imposed on men who stayed single for too long. The State encouraged people to have sons to provide future citizens and soldiers.

Parents also benefited from having a son, as it ensured that there would be someone to support them in their old age. Daughters could not do this because they were not permitted to inherit property or money. If a man did not have a son, he could adopt a boy who would inherit from him.

Babies

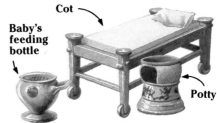

Cot

Baby's feeding bottle

Potty

When a baby was born, the mother presented it to her husband. If he did not believe that it was his child, or if the baby was handicapped, he could reject it. The baby would then be abandoned and left to die. Baby girls were most often rejected.

People who did not want another child, or who could not afford to raise one, might also abandon their babies. In some states unwanted babies were left in a specific place. People could go there, adopt a child and bring it up to be their slave.

A family who could afford it would hire a poor neighbour or a slave as a nurse for the baby. Wealthy families would also have special furniture made for their children, some of which has been found on the sites of excavated houses.

Seven days after the birth of a baby, the front door of the house was decorated with olive garlands for a boy or woollen ones for a girl. The family would make a sacrifice to the gods and a party was held for all the relatives, who brought gifts.

During the celebrations, a ceremony called the *amphidromia* took place. The women of the house carried the baby round the hearth to bring it into the religious life of the family. The baby was named at this ceremony or on the tenth day of its life.

At the age of three, a child's infancy was considered to be over. In Athens this was marked at the *Anthesteria* festival (see page 163). On the second day of the festival, children aged three were presented with small jugs like the one shown above.

Education in Sparta

Spartan schooling emphasized physical fitness. The most important subjects were athletics, dancing and weapon training. Pupils were also taught music and patriotic songs, Spartan law and some poetry. However, these more academic subjects were not considered important, as the aim of the Spartan system was to produce tough, healthy adults who would become warriors and mothers of warriors.

At seven, a boy was sent to live in a barracks, supervised by a teacher called a *paidonome*.

Each boy was allotted to a group, and several groups made up a class. The boys elected leaders, who helped to organize the work.

Boys had to make their own beds from rushes and they were not allowed to have covers.

Each boy was given one tunic to wear throughout the year. From the age of 12 boys also went bare-headed and bare-footed.

148

School

Greek education aimed to produce good citizens who could participate fully in the running of their state. Physical fitness was considered to be as important as learning. A boy's education usually began at the age of seven, and could go on until he started his military training at 18 (see page 132). As education had to be paid for, it is unlikely that the children of the poorer citizens received more than a very basic schooling. Girls did not go to school and were usually taught by their mothers at home. A rich family often hired a slave called a *paidagogos* to supervise their son's schooling. He escorted the boy to school and stayed during the classes to keep an eye on the boy's behaviour.

Wax covered tablet

Grammatistes *Paidagogos*

A boy attended three schools. The first was run by a teacher called a *grammatistes*, who taught reading, writing and arithmetic. Each pupil wrote with a stylus on wooden tablets covered in wax. They used pebbles or an abacus to do sums.

Poems were written on scrolls of papyrus.

A boy was taught music and poetry by a teacher called a *kitharistes*. He was taught to play the lyre and the pipes. He also had to learn extracts of poetry by heart, as an educated man was expected to quote the great poets in his conversation.

The third type of school was run by a *paidotribes*, who taught dancing and athletics. He probably took his pupils to the *gymnasium*† (a training ground) or a *palaistra* (a wrestling school) to practise. His pupils could take part in competitive games (see page 154).

Higher education

There was no formal higher education, but from the 5th century BC teachers called *sophists* travelled from place to place instructing young men in the art of public speaking. Philosophers like Socrates† often taught informally at a *gymnasium* and attracted groups of devoted young followers. In the 4th century BC, Plato†, Aristotle† and others set up permanent schools at *gymnasia* in Athens. By the Hellenistic Period, it was common for *gymnasia* to provide lecture rooms and libraries as part of their facilities.

Philosophers taught their pupils under the colonnades or in the dressing rooms at a *gymnasium*. They discussed subjects such as mathematics, science, politics and history.

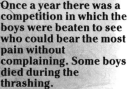

The food was inadequate and the boys were encouraged to steal extra food from local farms.

Once a year there was a competition in which the boys were beaten to see who could bear the most pain without complaining. Some boys died during the thrashing.

Boys bathed in the river.

Boys were allowed to attend the men's meals in the barracks. They listened and took part in the discussions, but absolute respect and obedience to their elders was expected.

Spartan girls were also educated in order to produce physically fit and disciplined women. They were trained in gymnastics, music, singing and dancing, and took part in athletic competitions. This picture shows a Spartan dancing class.

Music and poetry

Music was very important in the daily lives of the Greeks. There were songs and music for most social events: songs to celebrate a birth or lament a death, drinking songs and love songs. There were work-songs for farmers, and warriors and athletes trained to the sound of pipe music. Music was also used to accompany poetry, and as part of religious festivals and theatrical performances (see page 152).

The sons and daughters of citizens were usually taught music. This vase painting shows a child being taught to play the *auloi* (see below).

Musical instruments

We do not know what Greek music sounded like because it was not normally written down. Only some small fragments of pieces of music have been found and it is difficult to interpret what the symbols mean. However, we do know what Greek musical instruments looked like because they were often depicted on vases and in paintings. Some common instruments are shown here.

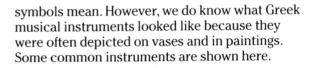

Cymbals

The *syrinx* or pan pipes.

The *kithara*. This was a more elaborate version of the lyre. It was played with a plectrum and tended to be used in musical contests and by professional musicians.

The lyre. According to legend, the lyre was invented by the god Hermes. He made it from the shell of a tortoise and the hide and horns of an ox he had stolen.

The harp

The *timpanon*

The *auloi*, or double pipes. They were made of two separate pipes with a reed mouthpiece. The musician played the two pipes simultaneously.

Poetry

In Greece, music and poetry were closely linked. Poetry was usually performed in public, rather than read privately. The words were sung or chanted, often with a musical accompaniment.

Men called *rhapsodes* made their living by reciting poetry at religious festivals or at private parties. They knew long epic poems such as Homer's *Odyssey* and *Iliad* (see page 113) by heart.

This vase painting shows a *rhapsode* reciting from a podium.

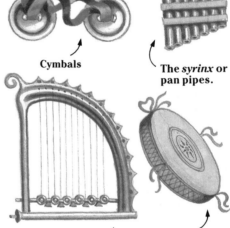

Apollo and the Muses

Apollo was the god of music and poetry and is often shown with a lyre or a *kithara*. According to legend, the lyre was invented by Apollo's half-brother, Hermes, who gave the instrument to Apollo in exchange for some cattle which he had stolen from him.

Apollo is closely associated with nine goddesses called the Muses, who were believed to inspire and guide people's creative and intellectual activities. Each of them was responsible for a particular art, such as poetry, music or dance.

Parties and games

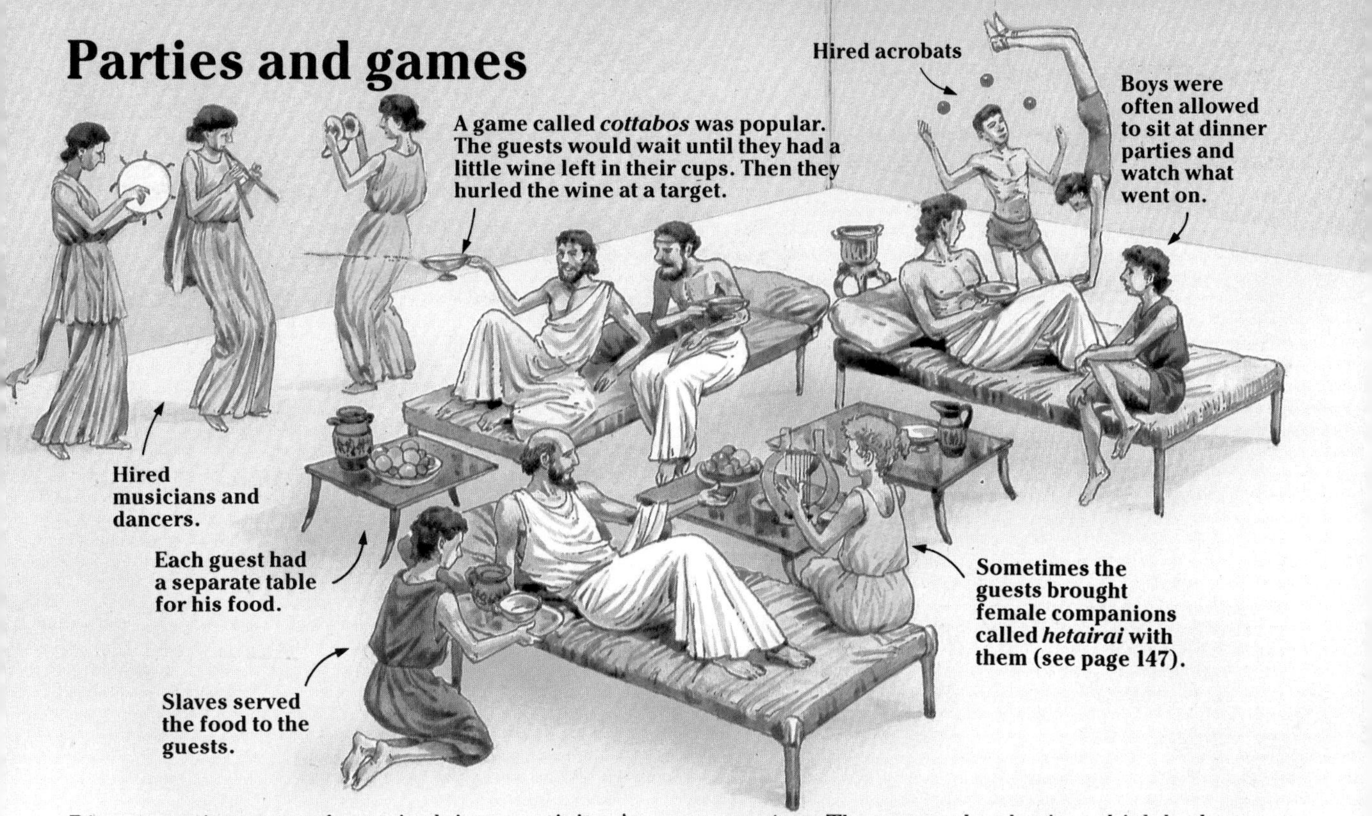

Hired acrobats

A game called *cottabos* was popular. The guests would wait until they had a little wine left in their cups. Then they hurled the wine at a target.

Boys were often allowed to sit at dinner parties and watch what went on.

Hired musicians and dancers.

Each guest had a separate table for his food.

Slaves served the food to the guests.

Sometimes the guests brought female companions called *hetairai* with them (see page 147).

Dinner parties were a favourite leisure activity. A man would invite several male friends to his house for a meal. The guests were met at the door by slaves who washed their hands and feet. Then they lay on couches in a room called the *andron*, where food was served by slaves. There was a choice of several dishes for each course.

Once the food was cleared away, the drinking and talking began. This was known as a *symposium*. The guests drank wine which had been mixed with water in a big vase called a *krater*. The conversation might be a serious discussion about some aspect of life, such as morals or politics. But often parties were more relaxed, with guests playing the lyre, reciting poetry, telling jokes or posing riddles. Additional entertainment might be provided by a troupe of hired musicians, dancers or acrobats.

Toys and games

Animal fighting was considered a sport. Cocks, quails, or a cat and dog would fight each other to the death.

This vase painting shows two warriors playing a board game similar to draughts or chess.

The Greeks also enjoyed sport. This carving shows a game which seems to resemble modern hockey.

Adults often played dice, either at home or in special gaming houses. Another favourite was a game called knuckle bones, in which small animal bones were thrown like dice.

Whipping top

Baby's rattle   Doll

Wealthy families gave their children many games and toys to amuse them

Hoop and stick

Yoyo

in their leisure hours. Some of them are shown here.

The theatre

The origins of theatre in the western world can be traced back to Ancient Greece. It developed from a countryside festival, held in honour of the god Dionysus. In Athens this developed into a more formal annual event, known as the *City Dionysia*. Songs were specially composed each year for the festival and were performed together with dances by a group of men known as a *chorus*. Prizes were awarded for the best entry.

At first, the *chorus* performed in the market place, but later a huge open-air theatre was built on the slopes of the Acropolis near the temple of Dionysus. Later, theatres were built all over the Greek world. Most of them could hold at least 18,000 spectators.

One of the best preserved Greek theatres is at Epidaurus. It was built on a hillside and could seat around 14,000 spectators.

The theatre building

The scene on the right is a reconstruction of a typical Greek theatre. It shows how it would have looked when a play was in progress.

Important people, such as leading citizens, distinguished foreign visitors or competition judges, sat at the front of the theatre. Special stone seats like this one were reserved for them.

The people from each district of a city had their own block of seats. Tokens like these were used as tickets. The letters on them show which block of benches the ticket-holder could sit in. Seats cost two obols. From the time of Pericles† the State paid for poor people's tickets.

The Athens theatre festival

In Athens the *Dionysia* was one of the city's most important religious celebrations. The festival, which lasted for five days, was a public holiday so that everyone could attend. The first day was devoted to processions and sacrifices. The remaining four days were taken up with drama competitions.

The *Dionysia* was organized by an official called an *archon* (see page 157). He picked a number of wealthy citizens, known as the *choregoi*, who had to pay for the production of the plays. Greek plays soon developed into two distinct types: tragedies and comedies. There were therefore two sections to the Athenian competition. Each year three tragic writers and five comedy writers were entered.

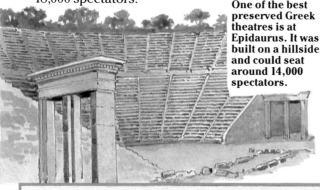
▲ **Scene from a tragedy**

▲ **Scene from a comedy**

▲ **Scene from a *satyr* play**

Tragedies were usually written about the heroes of the past. They concentrated on grand themes such as whether to obey or defy the will of the gods, human passions and conflicts, or the misuse of power. The best known tragic writers are Aeschylus†, Sophocles† and Euripides†.

In comedy, characters were usually ordinary people and the dialogue often included comments on the politics and personalities of the day. However, they also contained much clowning and slapstick humour and many rude jokes. The most famous comic writer is Aristophanes†.

In the comedy competition each author entered one play. However, a writer competing in the tragedy section had to enter three tragedies and a *satyr* play. This was a play which made fun of the tragic theme. The chorus were dressed as *satyrs* – wild followers of Dionysus who were half-man and half-beast.

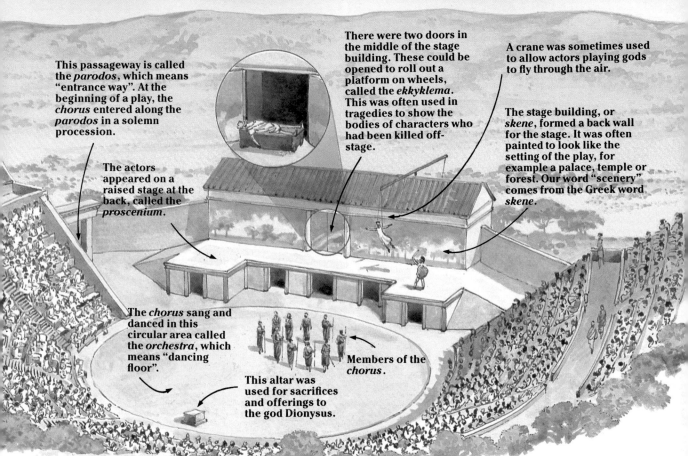

This passageway is called the *parodos*, which means "entrance way". At the beginning of a play, the *chorus* entered along the *parodos* in a solemn procession.

There were two doors in the middle of the stage building. These could be opened to roll out a platform on wheels, called the *ekkyklema*. This was often used in tragedies to show the bodies of characters who had been killed off-stage.

A crane was sometimes used to allow actors playing gods to fly through the air.

The stage building, or *skene*, formed a back wall for the stage. It was often painted to look like the setting of the play, for example a palace, temple or forest. Our word "scenery" comes from the Greek word *skene*.

The actors appeared on a raised stage at the back, called the *proscenium*.

The *chorus* sang and danced in this circular area called the *orchestra*, which means "dancing floor".

Members of the *chorus*.

This altar was used for sacrifices and offerings to the god Dionysus.

The performers

All the performers in Greek plays were men. At first, the play consisted simply of the *chorus* singing and dancing, but later an actor was introduced to exchange dialogue with the leader of the *chorus*. Thespis of Icarus is said to have been the first writer to use an actor in 530BC. Our word "thespian" comes from his name.

A second and third actor were later added, and they often played several roles each. The dialogue between the actors eventually became the most important part of the drama, with the *chorus* only commenting on the action.

Costumes

A *chorus* member dressed as a bird.

Male actor dressed as a woman.

Comic actors

Happy characters wore bright colours, and tragic ones dark colours. Because of the size of theatres, actors had to be visible and clothes were often padded to give them bulk. They wore large wigs and thick-soled shoes to look taller. In comedies, the *chorus* also wore costumes and sometimes even dressed as birds or animals.

Masks

Each actor wore a painted mask made of stiffened fabric or cork. The expression on the mask showed the character's age, sex and feelings. Actors could change parts quickly by simply swapping masks. The masks were easily visible, even from the back of the theatre. They had large, open mouths which amplified the actors' voices.

Athletics and sport

One of the most popular pastimes for Greek men was athletics. The Greek states encouraged their citizens to take part in sport because it kept them fit and meant that they would be in good fighting condition if there were a war.

There were many competitions which athletes could enter. Most were only local affairs, but four events (the Olympic, Pythian, Isthmian and Nemean Games) attracted competitors from all over the Greek world. They were known as the Panhellenic Games. Each one was held as part of a religious festival in honour of a particular deity.

The Olympic Games

The Olympic Games were the oldest and most important of the competitions. They probably developed from funeral games held in memory of the hero Pelops (see page 179). They started in 776BC and were held every four years at Olympia, in honour of Zeus. They lasted five days.

In the year of the Games, messengers travelled through Greece and the colonies, announcing the date of the Games and inviting people to attend.

All wars had to cease until the Games were over to allow people to travel to Olympia in safety.

At Olympia, a group of impressive buildings were built for the Games. These included sports grounds for the various events, facilities for the competitors and spectators, and temples for the religious ceremonies. This is a reconstruction of how Olympia would have looked at its height.

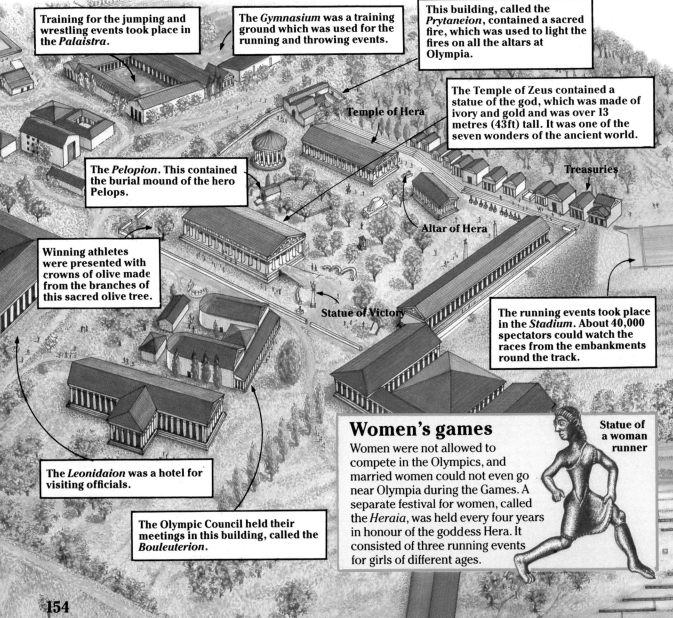

Training for the jumping and wrestling events took place in the *Palaistra*.

The *Gymnasium* was a training ground which was used for the running and throwing events.

This building, called the *Prytaneion*, contained a sacred fire, which was used to light the fires on all the altars at Olympia.

Temple of Hera

The Temple of Zeus contained a statue of the god, which was made of ivory and gold and was over 13 metres (43ft) tall. It was one of the seven wonders of the ancient world.

The *Pelopion*. This contained the burial mound of the hero Pelops.

Treasuries

Altar of Hera

Winning athletes were presented with crowns of olive made from the branches of this sacred olive tree.

Statue of Victory

The running events took place in the *Stadium*. About 40,000 spectators could watch the races from the embankments round the track.

The *Leonidaion* was a hotel for visiting officials.

The Olympic Council held their meetings in this building, called the *Bouleuterion*.

Women's games

Women were not allowed to compete in the Olympics, and married women could not even go near Olympia during the Games. A separate festival for women, called the *Heraia*, was held every four years in honour of the goddess Hera. It consisted of three running events for girls of different ages.

Statue of a woman runner

The events

Running

This vase painting shows a special race in which athletes wore a helmet and greaves† and carried a shield.

Running was the oldest event in the Games. The track in the Stadium was about 192 metres (640ft) long and was made of clay covered with sand. There were three main races: the *stade* (one length of the track), the *diaulos* (two lengths) and the *dolichos* (20 or 24 lengths).

Wrestling

There were three wrestling events. In upright wrestling, an athlete had to throw his opponent three times to win. In ground wrestling the contest went on until one man gave in. The third event, called the *pankration*, was even more dangerous, as any tactic except biting and eye-gouging was permitted.

The pentathlon

This vase painting shows a jumper, a discus thrower and two javelin throwers.

The *pentathlon* was a competition consisting of five athletic events: running, wrestling, jumping, discus and javelin throwing. It was designed to find the best all-round athlete. The *pentathlon* was a very demanding competition, which required great strength and endurance.

Boxing

At first, the contestants' hands were bound with leather thongs. Later, special boxing gloves were developed.

A boxing contest could go on for several hours and was only decided when one athlete lost consciousness or conceded defeat. Athletes therefore aimed most of their punches at their opponents' heads. Virtually any blow with the hand was permitted.

Chariot races

There were chariot races for teams of two or four horses. The course consisted of 12 laps round two posts in the ground. At the start, the chariots were released from a special starting gate. As many as 40 chariots could take part in one race, and collisions were common.

Horse races

The basic horse race was run over a distance of about 1200 metres. In another race the rider dismounted and ran the last stretch beside his horse. Jockeys rode bareback and accidents were common. The jockey was often employed by the horse's owner to race for him.

The winners

Winners were presented with an olive wreath, palm branches and woollen ribbons. They might also have a statue erected in their honour.

Prizes were given on the fifth day of the games. The ideal of the games was that athletes should seek only the honour of competing and the personal glory of winning. However, a winning athlete could also reap many material rewards. By the 5th century BC, some athletes were professionals, making their living by representing the city states at the various games. A city gained prestige by sponsoring a successful athlete, and would pay him well.

The modern Olympics

The ancient Olympics ended by AD395, when Olympia was destroyed by two violent earthquakes. In AD1896 a Frenchman called Baron Pierre de Coubertin was inspired by the ideals of the ancient competition and organized the first modern Olympic Games. Many aspects of the ancient games have been preserved. For example, some ancient games included a relay race in which a torch was passed from one runner to the next. The last runner of the winning team lit a fire on an altar. This event has been adapted for the modern Olympics as the lighting of the Olympic Flame.

Democracy in Athens

At the end of the Archaic Period, some Greek states overthrew their tryants† (see page 117) and adopted a system of government called *democracy*. The name comes from the Greek words *demos* (people) and *kratos* (rule). Under this system all citizens (see page 116) had a say in the government of their city state.

These pages describe how democracy worked in Athens, because this is the state we know most about. Democracy was first introduced in Athens in 508BC by the leader Cleisthenes†. Today, the term democracy is used to describe a system in which everybody has a vote. However, in Ancient Greece only citizens had this right. All other social groups, such as women, foreign residents and slaves, were excluded.

Local organization

Cleisthenes split the people of Attica (Athens and the surrounding area) into different groups for administrative purposes.

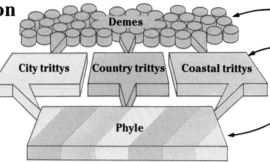

Attica was divided into many small communities called *demes*.

Demes were grouped into 30 larger groups called *trittyes*. Ten *trittyes* represented the city of Athens, ten the countryside and ten the coastal areas.

Trittyes were grouped into ten *phylai*, or tribes. Each *phyle* was made up of three *trittyes*: one *trittys* from the city, one from the country and one from the coast.

The Assembly

Every citizen had the right to speak and to vote at the Assembly, which met about once every ten days on a hill called the Pnyx. At least 6000 citizens had to be present for a meeting to take place. If too few people attended, special police were sent out to round up more citizens. The Assembly debated proposals which were put to it by the Council (see right). It could approve, change or reject the Council's suggestions.

An Assembly meeting on the Pnyx.

The Council

The 50 councillors on duty met in this building, called the Tholos. They kept it manned day and night, in case of emergency.

The Council drew up new laws and policies, which were then debated in the Assembly. The Council was made up of 500 citizens, 50 from each of the ten Athenian tribes. Councillors were chosen annually by lot. Each tribal group took it in turn to lead the Council, taking responsibility for the day-to-day running of the state.

The legal system

One of a citizen's duties was to participate in the running of the legal system. All citizens over 30 were expected to volunteer for jury service. From 461BC jurors were paid, to compensate them for any loss of earnings. There were no professional judges, lawyers or legal officials.

The Athenians tried to make their courts fair and unbiased. Each court had a jury of over 200 men, to ensure that jurors could not be bribed or intimidated.

As there were no lawyers, citizens had to conduct their own cases. Some people employed professional speech writers to prepare their cases for them. Only citizens could speak in court. If a *metic* was accused, he had to persuade a citizen to speak on his behalf.

Any citizen who wanted to serve as a juror simply went to the court. Often more people volunteered than were needed. This machine, called a *kleroteria*, was used to select the names of the jurors for that day.

Coloured balls were dropped in here.

Jurors' names were written on cards and put into these slots.

The colour of ball next to each row decided whether those jurors would serve.

The archons

During the Archaic Period the *archons*† had been the most important officials (see page 117). Under democracy, much of their power passed to the *strategoi* (see below) and the *archons* retained only ceremonial duties. There were nine *archons*, chosen annually by lot from the citizens. Three of them were more important than the others and had special duties.

The *Basileus Archon* presided over the *Areopagus* (see page 117), arranged religious sacrifices, and organized the renting of temple land. He also supervised the theatre festival and other feasts.

The *Eponymous Archon* chose the men who were to finance the choral and drama contests (see page 152). He was also responsible for lawsuits about inheritances and the affairs of heiresses, orphans and widows.

The *Polemarch Archon* was in charge of offerings and special athletic contests held in honour of men killed in war. He also dealt with the legal affairs of *metics*† (foreign residents).

The strategoi

When Athens sent an army or navy into battle, it was led by one or two *strategoi*.

The *strategoi* were military commanders (see page 132) who also had the power to implement the policies decided by the Council and the Assembly. There were ten *strategoi*, one from each of the Athenian tribes. They were elected annually and could be re-elected many times. The *strategoi* had to answer to the Assembly for their actions and for the money they spent.

Ostracism

These *ostraka* show the names of two politicians, called Aristides† and Cimon†.

Ostracism was a system used to remove unpopular politicians. A vote of ostracism could be held once a year in the Assembly. Each citizen present wrote the name of any politician he wished to see banished on a piece of broken pottery, called an *ostrakon*. If more than 6000 votes were cast against a politician, he had to leave Athens for 10 years.

Each juror was issued with two different bronze tokens which were used for voting. At the end of the trial, he handed in one of them to show whether he thought the accused person was innocent or guilty.

The token with a solid centre meant "innocent".

The token with a hollow centre meant "guilty".

Certain jurors, who were chosen by lot, were given special tasks. One took charge as the judge, four counted the votes and one worked a water clock like the one shown here. This was used to limit the time allowed to each speaker.

The upper pot was filled with water.

When all the water had run through into this lower pot, the speaker's time was up.

The Golden Age and the Peloponnesian War

The Persian Wars (see pages 136-137) were followed by an era of great achievement in Athens which is known as its Golden Age (479-431BC). Trade flourished and the city became very rich. Athens became a great centre for the arts, attracting the best sculptors, potters, architects, dramatists, historians and philosophers. This security was shattered by the outbreak of the Peloponnesian War between Athens and Sparta. It lasted for 27 years (431-404BC) and tore the Greek world apart. The city states were left weak and exhausted, and Athens never regained her power.

During the Golden Age, the city was improved and the temples on the Acropolis† were rebuilt.

Pericles

The democratic system (see pages 156-157) was finalized during this period. The most famous politician was Pericles†, who dominated Athenian politics from 443-429BC. He was a very powerful public speaker and could usually persuade the Assembly to vote the way he wanted. He was so popular that he was elected *strategos* year after year. One of his most important achievements was to organize the rebuilding of the Acropolis.

Bust of Pericles

Relations between Sparta and Athens

Soon after the end of the Persian Wars, relations between Sparta and Athens started to deteriorate. As Athens became more powerful and wealthy, the Spartans felt threatened.

In 460BC the *helots* and the Messenians (see page 118) rebelled against the Spartans. The Spartans asked the Athenians for help, but by the time the Athenians arrived, the Spartans had changed their minds. They were so distrustful of democrats that they would not let the Athenians intervene and instead sent them home. The Athenians felt bitterly insulted and abandoned their alliance with Sparta.

The Long Walls

In 460BC the Athenians began building enormous walls linking their city to its port at Piraeus. They are known as the Long Walls. They prevented an enemy cutting Athens off from her navy and made the city into an enormous fortress. The Spartans thought this meant that Athens was preparing for war, and fighting broke out between the two states in 448-447BC. After this, Sparta and Athens signed a treaty known as the Thirty Years' Peace, but relations between them remained hostile.

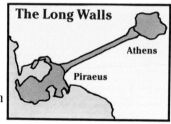

The Long Walls

Athens

Piraeus

The start of the Peloponnesian War

In 431BC hostilities broke out between Corinth and its colony Corcyra (modern Corfu). Sparta supported Corinth, and Athens backed Corcyra. This began the Peloponnesian War, so called because Sparta was supported by a league of states in the Peloponnese (the southern part of mainland Greece). Athens was backed by its allies in the Delian league (see page 137).

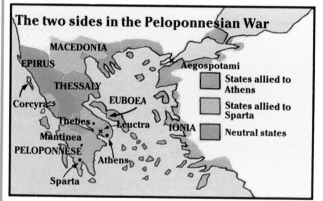

The two sides in the Peloponnesian War

MACEDONIA
EPIRUS
THESSALY
Corcyra
Aegospotami
EUBOEA
Thebes
Leuctra
IONIA
Mantinea
PELOPONNESE
Athens
Sparta

States allied to Athens
States allied to Sparta
Neutral states

The Spartans had a very powerful army and were nearly unbeatable in land battles. They were easily able to invade Attica†. The Athenians had a superior navy and a weaker army than the Spartans. They therefore tried to avoid fighting the Spartans on land. Instead, they stayed inside their city walls and were able to import food by sea. This resulted in a long deadlock.

The Spartan army devastated the countryside around Athens, but could not get through the Long Walls.

The Sicilian expedition

In 430BC a plague broke out in Athens. It lasted four years and about a quarter of the population died, including Pericles. By 421BC both sides were exhausted and signed a peace treaty.

However, war broke out again and events soon turned against Athens. In 415BC a politician called Alcibiades† persuaded the Athenians to send an expedition against the city of Syracuse on Sicily. Before the attack began, Alcibiades was told to return to Athens to face charges brought against him by his enemies. Instead, he fled to Sparta and advised the Spartans how to defeat Athens. The Athenians were defeated at Syracuse and many of their troops were massacred.

About 7000 of the surviving Athenians were forced to work in stone quarries on Sicily, where many of them died.

Political unrest in Athens

After this catastrophe, life in Athens became very unsettled. In 411BC a council of 400 men seized power and abolished democracy†. The news caused the Athenian forces overseas to mutiny. After three months, democracy was restored. The Athenians badly needed a strong leader, so they decided to recall Alcibiades and appoint him *strategos*, despite his earlier treachery. But he failed to fulfil their hopes and was not re-elected. Support for the Athenians declined and several of their allies withdrew from the Delian League.

The Spartans build a fleet

Meanwhile the Persians intervened. They were fighting the Greek colonists in Ionia, who were supported by the Spartans. The Persians persuaded the Spartans to withdraw from Ionia by giving them money to build a fleet. This enabled the Spartans to attack the Athenians at sea as well as on land.

The Battle of Aegospotami

In 405BC the Spartans scored a decisive naval victory. They launched a surprise attack on the Athenian fleet when it was in harbour at a place called Aegospotami in Thrace. The Spartans captured 170 Athenian ships and executed about 4000 prisoners. It was a blow from which Athens never recovered.

The Athenians had gone ashore at Aegospotami to eat when the Spartans attacked.

The Spartans then laid siege to Athens. Without a fleet to support them, the Athenians were unable to import food, and many people starved. In 404BC they had to surrender. The Spartans insisted that the Long Walls were pulled down, ended the Delian League and abolished democracy. They installed an oligarchic† government known as the Thirty Tyrants.

After the Peloponnesian War

The Spartans' victory did not bring peace or unity to Greece. They began to lose control in Athens, where democracy was restored in 403BC despite their disapproval. Wars broke out again between the various states. Most Greeks were too absorbed in these problems to notice a new power rising in Macedonia, to the north-east. The Macedonians began expanding their territory, and took advantage of the lack of unity in Greece. Within 50 years of the end of the Peloponnesian War, the Macedonians had conquered many of the Greek states (see page 168).

Key dates

479-431BC The Golden Age of Athens.

460BC The Spartans reject Athenian help in stopping a rebellion. The Athenians start to build the Long Walls.

431BC Start of the Peloponnesian War.

415-413BC Athens sends an expedition to Sicily which is defeated.

405BC The Spartans defeat the Athenian fleet at the Battle of Aegospotami.

404BC The Athenians surrender. End of the Peloponnesian War.

371BC The Spartans are defeated by the Thebans at the Battle of Leuctra and Thebes becomes a leading power in Greece.

362BC The Thebans are defeated by the Spartans and Athenians at the Battle of Mantinea.

Gods and goddesses

The Greeks believed in the existence of many divine beings, who looked after all aspects of life and death. They thought of the gods as being in many ways like humans – they got married, had children and showed human characteristics such as love, jealousy or deceitfulness. Many legends were told to describe the gods' personalities and teach what pleased or angered them.

The battle between the Titans and the Olympians

How the world began

According to legend, Gaea (Mother Earth) rose out of chaos. She gave birth to a son, Uranos (Sky), who became her husband. They had many children, the most important of whom were the fourteen Titans. One of them, Cronos, led the others in a rebellion against their father and deposed him.

Cronos married his sister, Rhea. Their youngest son, Zeus, led his brothers and sisters against the Titans. He deposed Cronos and became the leader of the new gods. The new rulers lived on Mount Olympus and were known as the Olympians.

The Olympian gods

This family tree shows some of the Greek deities. The most important and powerful of them were the 12 Olympians, whose names are written in capitals. Some of the legends associated with them are told below. Most of the gods had their own special symbols.

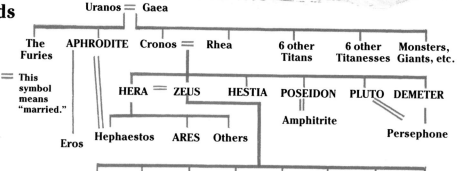

Uranos = Gaea

The Furies | APHRODITE | Cronos = Rhea | 6 other Titans | 6 other Titanesses | Monsters, Giants, etc.

= This symbol means "married."

HERA = ZEUS | HESTIA | POSEIDON | PLUTO | DEMETER

Amphitrite

Persephone

Eros | Hephaestos | ARES | Others

ARTEMIS APOLLO ATHENE HERMES DIONYSUS Herakles Helen Others

Zeus

Zeus was the ruler of the gods and controlled the heavens. He was married to his sister Hera, but was frequently unfaithful to her. He had many affairs with mortal women and appeared to them in various disguises, such as a bull, a shower of gold or a swan. ▶

Zeus' symbols: the thunderbolt, eagle and oak tree.

Hera

Hera was the sister and wife of Zeus. She was the protector of women and of marriage. She was beautiful and proud, and bitterly resented her husband's affairs with other women. She often persecuted his lovers and their children. ▶

Hera's symbols: the pomegranate and the peacock.

Poseidon

◀ Poseidon was the brother of Zeus and the ruler of the seas. His home was an underwater palace, where he kept his gold chariot and white horses. Poseidon was also known as the earth-shaker, because he was thought to cause earthquakes.

Poseidon's symbols: the trident, dolphins and horses.

Hestia

◀ Hestia was the goddess of the hearth. Every Greek city and family had a shrine dedicated to her. She was gentle and pure, and stood aloof from the constant quarrels of the other gods. Eventually she resigned her throne on Olympus, knowing that she would receive a welcome wherever she went.

Pluto

◄ Pluto ruled the Underworld, the Kingdom of the Dead. He guarded the dead jealously, rarely letting any of them return to Earth. He owned all the precious metals and gems of the Earth. Pluto kidnapped and married his niece, Persephone.*

Pluto drove a gold chariot with black horses.

Aphrodite

Aphrodite was the goddess of love and beauty. She was born in the sea and rode to shore on a scallop shell. Aphrodite was married to Hephaestos, but loved Ares. She charmed everyone, as she wore a golden belt which made her irresistibly attractive. ►

Aphrodite's symbols: roses, doves, sparrows, dolphins and rams.

Ares

◄ Ares was the god of war and Aphrodite's lover. He was short tempered and violent. He once had to stand trial for murder in Athens on the hill of the Areopagus (see page 139), which was named after him.

Ares' symbols: a burning torch, spear, dogs and vultures.

Apollo

Apollo was the twin brother of Artemis. He was the god of the sun, light and truth. Music, poetry, science and healing were also under his control. Apollo killed his mother's enemy, the serpent Python, when it was sheltering in the shrine at Delphi. He seized the shrine and made Delphi his Oracle (see page 164). ►

Apollo's symbol: the laurel tree.

Athene

◄ Athene was the daughter of Zeus and Metis the Titaness. Zeus swallowed Metis because of a prophecy that if she had a son he would depose his father. One day Zeus had a headache and ordered Hephaestos to crack his skull open. Athene sprang out, fully armed. She was the goddess of wisdom and war and the patron deity of Athens.

Athene's symbols: the owl and the olive tree.

Demeter

◄ Demeter was the goddess of all plants. When her daughter Persephone was kidnapped, Demeter neglected the plants and went to search for her. This caused winter. When Persephone returned to her mother, she brought the spring and summer.*

Demeter's symbol: a sheaf of wheat or barley.

Hephaestos

Hephaestos was a smith whose forge was beneath Mount Etna in Sicily. He built Zeus' golden throne and his shield, which caused storms and thunder when it was shaken. He was the patron of craftsmen and the long-suffering husband of Aphrodite. ►

Artemis

◄ Artemis was the moon goddess. Her silver arrows brought plague and death, though she could heal as well. She protected young girls and pregnant women. Artemis was the mistress of all wild animals and enjoyed hunting in her chariot pulled by stags.

Artemis' symbols: cypress trees, deer and dogs.

Hermes

Hermes was a precocious and naughty child, full of tricks and cunning, who stole cattle from Apollo and invented the lyre†. He became the messenger of the gods and was also the patron of travellers and thieves. He was said to have invented the alphabet, mathematics, astronomy and boxing. ►

Hermes wore a winged hat and sandals and carried a staff.

Dioynsus

◄ Dionysus was god of the vine, wine and fertility. He wandered the world teaching people how to make wine, accompanied by wild and fanatical followers. When Hestia resigned her place on Olympus, Dionysus became one of the 12 Olympians.

Dionysus carried a special staff, called a thyrsus.

The story of Demeter and Persephone is told in full on page 178.

Temples, worship and festivals

As the Greeks thought of their gods as having the same needs as human beings, they believed that the gods needed somewhere to live on Earth.

Temples were built as the gods' earthly homes. The basic design of temples developed from the royal halls of the Mycenaean Age (see page 109).

Pottery model of an early temple

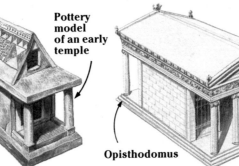

Opisthodomus

Pronaos

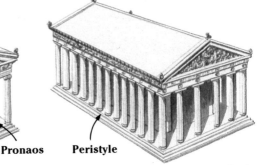

Peristyle

In the Dark Ages, a temple consisted of a room, called a *cella*, with a pillared porch in front. The *cella* contained a special statue of the god, known as the cult statue.

This more elaborate style of temple developed in the early Archaic Period. It had a porch at the front, called the *pronaos*, and another at the back, the *opisthodomus*.

This later Archaic temple was built on a platform and had several steps leading up to the entrance. There was a covered row of columns, called a *peristyle*, round the outside.

The Parthenon

In the Classical Period temples became much larger and more elaborate. This reconstruction shows the Parthenon in Athens, which was built in 447-438BC.

The exterior was decorated with friezes and statues showing mythological scenes, which were painted in bright colours.

A second room behind the *cella* was used as a treasury. Offerings such as jewellery, vases and statues were stored here.

The cult statue of the goddess Athene was made of gold and ivory and was over 12 metres (40ft) high. Athene held a figure of Nike, the goddess of victory, in one hand and a spear and shield in the other.

Cella

The altar

There was a stone altar outside a temple, often situated in front of the main entrance. People brought animals or birds as offerings to the temple deity and they were sacrificed by a priest at the altar.

The building was made of marble.

A *peristyle* surrounded the whole structure.

Festivals

The Greeks held many religious festivals in honour of their gods. The purpose of a festival was to please the gods and persuade them to grant the people's wishes. This could be by making the crops grow or bringing victory in war. Festivals did not consist solely of religious ceremonies – other events, such as athletic competitions or theatrical performances, could also be held. These events included things which would especially please the particular god. For example, at the Pythian Games, which were dedicated to Apollo, victors were presented with crowns of laurel, which was Apollo's sacred plant.

Important citizens

Musicians and dancers

Offering bearers

The dress for the goddess Athene was displayed on the mast of a ship, which was dragged along in the procession.

Priests and priestesses

Soldiers

The period of the festival was a public holiday so that the whole population of Athens could watch the procession.

Sacrificial beasts

The Great Panathenaea

The most important festival in Athens was the *Great Panathenaea*, the feast of the goddess Athene. It was held every four years, and lasted for six days. It included music, poetry recitals and sports events. The climax of the festival was a huge procession from the Dipylon Gate to the Erechtheum temple on the Acropolis†. There a specially made dress was offered to an ancient wooden statue of Athene, which was said to have fallen from heaven in ancient times.

The Anthesteria

A spring festival, called the *Anthesteria*, was held in Athens each February. The wine from the last harvest was put on sale and a statue of Dionysus, the god of wine, was carried in triumph to his temple. On the final day of the festival, each family prepared a meal for the spirits of the dead and left it on the altar in their house.

During the *Anthesteria*, children were given special jugs (see page 148).

Worship

Private worship played an important part in Greek religion. A family would say prayers every day at the altar in the courtyard of their house. During prayers an offering of wine, called a *libation*, was poured over the altar. People would also pray to the appropriate gods as they went about their daily life. For example, someone going on a journey would pray to Hermes, the god of travellers.

If someone wanted to ask the gods for a particular favour, they would go to the temple of the appropriate deity and make a sacrifice. This could be cakes, a libation, a bird or an animal.

There were rules on how to please the various gods. For example, different species of birds and animals were acceptable to different gods. If the rules were not followed, the offering might not be acceptable. Each god had his or her own priests, who ensured that sacrifices were made correctly.

Most gods were addressed with raised arms and hands turned up to heaven.

For Underworld gods the worshipper's palms had to face the ground.

To address a sky god the worshipper had to face the east.

For a marine god the worshipper had to face the sea.

Oracles and mystery cults

The Greeks never began an important project without first trying to learn the will of the gods. Often they would visit an oracle, where a special priest or priestess could speak on behalf of a god.

Other popular ways of learning what the future might hold were reading omens or consulting a soothsayer (someone who could foresee the future).

Oracles

There were several oracles* in Greece where people could ask the gods questions about personal or national problems. The most famous one was at Delphi, where the god Apollo was believed to speak through his priestess, the Pythia. At first the Pythia gave oracles once a year, but Delphi became so popular that they were given every week and two priestesses were needed. Many Greek states regularly sent deputations to Delphi for advice on political affairs.

The temple priests put people's questions to the Pythia. They then interpreted her replies. These were often vague and could be interpreted in more than one way.

The Pythia gave her oracles in an inner sanctuary. First she bathed in a holy fountain, drank water from a sacred spring and inhaled the smoke of burning laurel leaves. This reconstruction shows what a consultation might have looked like.

The Pythia dressed in white and sat on a tripod. She held a branch of laurel in her hand.

The inner sanctuary was closed off from the priests by a curtain.

She gave her oracles in a trance, which was said to be caused by fumes rising from a cleft in the rocks.

Omens

Interpreting omens was a skilled ▶ art, and was only undertaken by specially trained priests. Omens could be read from many different things, such as blemishes on the livers of sacrificed animals, the flight of birds or thunder and lightning.

Soothsayers

◀ The Greeks believed that certain people, called soothsayers or seers, could foresee the future. According to legend, Cassandra, a princess of Troy, had these powers. When she broke a promise to the god Apollo, he decreed that no-one would ever believe her prophecies. Cassandra warned the people of Troy that the wooden horse was a trick, but they ignored her and so the city was destroyed.

Fate and fortune

The Greeks believed that each person's destiny was decided by three goddesses called the Fates. Clotho spun the thread of life. Lachesis wound the thread and allotted a person's destiny. Atropos cut the thread, causing a person to die.

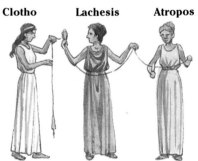

Clotho   Lachesis   Atropos

The goddess of fortune was called Tyche. She could shower people with gifts from her horn of plenty, but she also juggled with a ball, showing how someone could be up one day and down the next.

* The word oracle can mean the priestess who spoke for the god, the sacred place where she could be consulted, or the message she gave.

Mystery cults

Many Greeks who were looking for a deeper religious faith joined one of the mystery cults. These were secret groups of worshippers associated with particular deities. The cults promised their members an answer to the meaning of life and a happy life after death. People who undertook the necessary training and lead virtuous lives were initiated (introduced) by stages into the cult.

The most famous and popular was the cult of the goddesses Demeter and Persephone at Eleusis. The cult's main initiation ceremony, called the Greater Mysteries, was held in September. The mysteries continued to be celebrated at Eleusis until AD394.

The procession

The Greater Mysteries started with several days of sacrifices and purification. On the fifth day, a great procession set out from Athens to travel to Eleusis. They arrived at night, by torchlight.

Priestesses carried the sacred objects of the cult in baskets on their heads.

Statue of the goddess

The initiates wore white robes

The initiation ceremony

No-one knows exactly what happened at an initiation ceremony because it took place in private and the initiates were sworn to secrecy. This reconstruction shows what may have happened during an initiation.

This priestess, holding a pomegranate, played Persephone.

There may have been an enactment of the deeds of the goddesses. This priestess played the part of Demeter.

People waiting to be initiated.

People who had reached the higher stages of initiation were known as "viewers". They were probably shown something special, such as the sacred cult objects.

The origin of the Eleusinian mysteries

The cult of Demeter and Persephone was founded by Prince Triptolemus of Eleusis. According to legend*, when Persephone was kidnapped Demeter wandered the Earth searching for her, disguised as a poor old woman. When she arrived at Eleusis, the royal family took her in and gave her a job, caring for the royal children.

After Persephone was returned to Demeter, the two goddesses went back to Eleusis. They gave the king's son, Prince Triptolemus, a bag of grain and showed him how to plant and reap. Triptolemus travelled all over Greece teaching people how to grow grain and then returned to Eleusis, where he built a temple and established the cult of Demeter and Persephone.

This carving shows Prince Triptolemus with the two goddesses.

*You can read the full story of Demeter and Persephone on page 178.

Death and the Underworld

The Greeks believed that when people died, their souls went to the Underworld. This was an underground kingdom, sometimes known as Hades, which was ruled by the god Pluto. The picture below is an imaginative reconstruction of what the Greeks thought would happen to them when they arrived in the world of the dead.

Many caves and fissures on Earth were thought to be entrances to the Underworld. The soul was guided by the god Hermes through one of these entrances to the banks of the River Styx. The river marked the boundary between the world of the living and the Underworld.

On the other side of the river, the soul passed the three-headed dog Cerberus. His job was to stop living intruders entering the Underworld and to prevent any of Pluto's subjects from escaping.

Next the soul arrived at a cross-roads where Minos, Rhadamanthys and Aeacus judged all the newly-arrived souls. Their judgement was based on how the person had behaved in his or her earthly life.

Souls whose relatives had provided them with a coin (see below) paid Charon the ferryman to take them across the river. Souls without the fare wandered lost and comfortless on the bank.

Funerals

The purpose of Greek funeral rites was to ensure that the dead person's soul arrived safely in the Underworld. Ordinary Greeks were terrified by the thought that they might not receive a funeral. Without proper rituals, they believed that the soul would wander sadly by the River Styx and would not be able to enter the Underworld.

Visitors washed when they left, as death was thought to be unclean.

When someone died, their relatives and friends wore black and women cut their hair short as signs of mourning. The dead body lay in state at home for a day, so that people could come to pay their respects. The body was carefully dressed and arranged. A coin was placed in its mouth to enable the soul to pay the fare to cross the River Styx.

Even after the funeral, the continued well-being of the dead depended to some extent on the care of the living. Families made offerings to their ancestors on the anniversaries of their births and deaths, and at special festivals for the dead.

A wealthy family hired musicians and professional mourners to join the procession.

Early on the morning of the funeral a procession formed at the dead person's house. The body was either placed on a cart or on a bier carried by the relatives and friends. The body was then taken to the cemetery. The procession was a noisy affair, as it was the custom to express grief publicly with tears, sobbing and wailing.

◄ Souls of initiates could ask to be born again. If they got to the Elysian Fields three times by leading virtuous or initiated lives, they could then go to the Isles of the Blessed. This was a place of eternal joy, ruled by Cronos, the leader of the Titans.

▲ People who had led virtuous lives, along with initiates of the mystery cults †, were sent to the Elysian Fields, a happy place filled with golden sunlight.

The Pool of Memory

◄ The souls of people who had led wicked or cruel existences on Earth were sent to Tartarus, where they were condemned to eternal punishment.

Another road led to Erebus, the palace of Pluto and Persephone. By the palace were two pools. ▼

The Palace of Pluto and Persephone.

Initiates of the mystery cults chose the Pool of Memory which was shaded by white poplars. This enabled them to remember the secrets of the cult and pass straight to the Elysian Fields. ▲

Most people had not been very good or very bad in their earthly life and so were sent to the Asphodel Fields. This was a grey, boring place where the souls drifted around aimlessly in the shade, waiting for offerings from the land of the living to cheer them up. ▲

▲ The Pool of Lethe (forgetfulness) was shaded by cypresses and ordinary souls drank there.

Tombs

Cemeteries were usually situated outside the city walls. Each family had its own burial plot, where members of the family were either buried or cremated. It was customary to bury personal belongings, such as jewellery, clothes or armour, with the dead person. Food, drink and bronze or pottery vessels were also buried for the soul to use in the afterlife.

◄ Early tombs were marked by a plain marble slab, topped with a sculptured decoration.

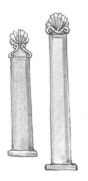

A rich person would be buried in a stone coffin called a *sarcophagus*. This often had elaborately carved reliefs on the sides. ▼

Sarcophagus

◄ By the 5th century BC, people who could afford it built elaborate tombs which looked like small temples. These were often decorated with portraits of the dead person carved on stone slabs, called *stelae*.

Stele

Lekythoi

The women of the family continued ► to bring offerings to the tomb long after the funeral. Perfume was often offered to the dead. It was carried in special white pottery vases called *lekythoi*. They were nearly solid, with only a tiny space for the perfume.

167

The rise of Macedonia

Macedonia lies in the north east of Greece (see map below). The Macedonian people claimed to be descendants of Macedon, son of Zeus. Although they thought of themselves as Greek, many Greeks considered Macedonia to be a cultural and political backwater, whose inhabitants were little better than barbarians†. Although the Macedonians spoke Greek, they had such a strong accent that it was said to be impossible to understand them.

During the 6th and 5th centuries BC, Macedonia was invaded many times. In 399BC the king was murdered and the country entered 40 years of instability and civil war (see date box below).

This ended with the accession of Philip II in 359BC. When he came to the throne, Macedonia had lost a lot of its territory and was split by political rivalries. Many of its soldiers had been killed and the country was impoverished.

Small ivory head of Philip, found in his tomb.

However, within 25 years Philip had united the country, extended the frontiers and turned Macedonia into the greatest military power of the day. He was a brilliant soldier and organizer, a fine speaker and a cunning diplomat with great personal charm. Even so, critics, such as the Athenian politician Demosthenes, saw him as a threat to democracy and independence.

The woman shown on this gold medallion is Philip's wife, Olympias.

The Macedonian royal family

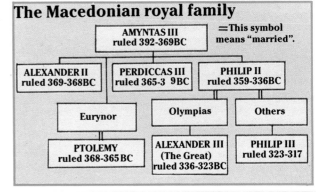

	AMYNTAS III ruled 392-369BC		= This symbol means "married".
ALEXANDER II ruled 369-368BC	PERDICCAS III ruled 365-3 9BC	PHILIP II ruled 359-336BC	
	Eurynor	Olympias	Others
	PTOLEMY ruled 368-365BC	ALEXANDER III (The Great) ruled 336-323BC	PHILIP III ruled 323-317

Philip's conquests

Philip quickly brought Macedonia under control. In 357BC he started to expand his territory, first east and then south. By 342BC Philip controlled the whole of Thrace, Chalkidike and Thessaly (see map).

In 342BC the remaining Greek states, led by Athens and Thebes, formed the Hellenic League against him. Philip defeated them in 338BC at the battle of Chaeronea and gained control of Greece. He joined all the Greek states together in the League of Corinth, of which he was the *hegemon*, or leader. In 337BC he united Greece and Macedonia in a common cause by announcing a war against Persia.

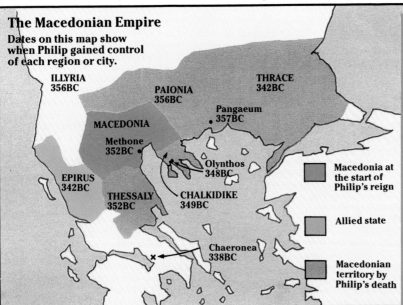

The Macedonian Empire

Dates on this map show when Philip gained control of each region or city.

ILLYRIA 356BC
THRACE 342BC
PAIONIA 356BC
Pangaeum • 357BC
MACEDONIA
Methone 352BC •
Olynthos 348BC
EPIRUS 342BC
THESSALY 352BC
CHALKIDIKE 349BC
Chaeronea 338BC

Macedonia at the start of Philip's reign

Allied state

Macedonian territory by Philip's death

Key dates

399BC King Archelaus of Macedonia is murdered.

368BC The Thebans invade Macedonia. King Alexander II is forced to send his younger brother, Philip, to Thebes as a hostage.

363BC Alexander II is murdered and is succeeded by his brother, Perdiccas III. The Athenians invade Macedonia.

359BC The Illyrians invade and Perdiccas III is killed. Philip takes over as regent, and then king.

338BC Philip defeats the Greek city states at the battle of Chaeronea and unites Greece under his control in the League of Corinth.

337BC Philip unites Greece and Macedonia in war against Persia.

336BC Philip is assassinated.

The army

At the beginning of his reign, Philip reorganized the army and began a programme of intensive training. This produced a tough, well-disciplined army which was the most effective fighting force of the day. Philip led his troops in person, showing great bravery.

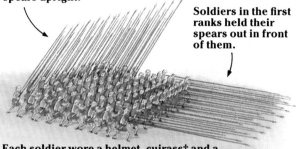

Soldiers at the back held their spears upright.

Soldiers in the first ranks held their spears out in front of them.

Each soldier wore a helmet, cuirass† and a bronze shield. He was armed with a short sword and a long spear called a *sarissa`.*

The Macedonian infantry originally consisted of lightly-armed *peltasts* (see page 133). Philip gave them heavier armour and long spears and taught them to fight in a phalanx, shown above. They attacked by charging into the enemy's lines with their spears extended. This was a very effective tactic and proved to be a decisive factor in Philip's military successes.

There were elite units called the Companion Infantry and the Companion Cavalry. The sons of Macedonian noblemen were often educated at court and served as royal pages before joining the Companion Cavalry. This mosaic shows two royal pages out hunting.

Philip made great use of the Companion Cavalry, which he developed from the king's mounted bodyguard. They wore cuirasses, helmets and boots and were armed with long spears and swords.

Philip's death

Philip had several wives, but only one queen, Olympias. Her son, Alexander, was accepted as Philip's heir. In 337BC Philip took another wife, Cleopatra, and set Olympias aside. He was assassinated soon after. The assassin could have been a political opponent, but it is also possible that Olympias or Alexander had paid him.

In AD1977 archaeologists discovered a new tomb in the royal graveyard at Vergina. In the inner chamber they found a casket, containing the cremated remains of a man aged 40-50. Experts have since been able to piece together the skull.

It had a hole near the right eye. This proves that it was almost certainly Philip, who had been hit in the face by an arrow and lost his right eye.

Philip's tomb was buried under a mound of earth which protected it from grave robbers. This cutaway reconstruction shows the tomb and some of the treasures that were found in it.

This gold casket held Philip's ashes. The star symbol was the emblem of the Macedonian royal family.

Cuirass

Several pieces of Philip's armour were buried with him.

Helmet

This chamber contained the remains of a second body, probably Philip's wife Cleopatra.

Philip's burial chamber

Main entrance

Alexander the Great

Alexander became King of Macedonia in 336BC after the murder of his father, Philip (see page 169). He was only 20. He immediately embarked on a career of military conquests, which gained him the largest empire the Ancient World had known and earned him the title of Alexander the Great. He was a military genius, who inspired great loyalty in his followers and who had extraordinary energy and courage.

In 334BC Alexander led 35,000 troops into Asia Minor to attack the Persians (see page 41). This began an 11-year campaign, during which he captured vast territories in Asia Minor, Egypt, Afghanistan, Iran and India

Picture of Alexander taken from a Roman mosaic.

During his travels, Alexander founded many new cities, most of which he named "Alexandria", after himself. The most famous of these was the port of Alexandria in Egypt, which became the country's new capital.

Alexander did little to change the administration of the lands he seized, although he usually replaced the local governors with his own men. He left Greeks behind in all the areas he conquered, which helped to spread Greek language and culture across an enormous area. This Greek influence lasted long after Alexander's empire had collapsed.

This reconstruction shows the Battle of Issus (333BC), at which Alexander defeated the Persians. It is based on a Roman mosaic in Pompeii.

Alexander realized that his empire was too big to be administered from Greece. In Persia, he tried to include Persians in the government to help unify the empire. He planned to give them equal rights and to let them serve in the army. The whole empire was to have one currency, and use Greek as the official language. Alexander himself adopted Persian dress and married a Persian noblewoman called Roxane.

In 323BC, Alexander died of a fever. He does not seem to have made plans for the government of the empire after his death. Although Roxane was pregnant with Alexander's heir, his generals soon divided the empire up between themselves (see pages 172-173).

Alexander was often shown on coins of the time.

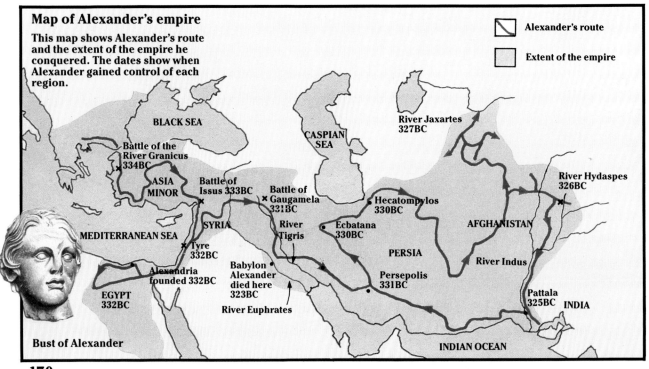

Map of Alexander's empire

This map shows Alexander's route and the extent of the empire he conquered. The dates show when Alexander gained control of each region.

Alexander's route

Extent of the empire

BLACK SEA

CASPIAN SEA

River Jaxartes 327BC

Battle of the River Granicus 334BC

ASIA MINOR

Battle of Issus 333BC

Battle of Gaugamela 331BC

Hecatompylos 330BC

River Hydaspes 326BC

SYRIA

River Tigris

Ecbatana 330BC

AFGHANISTAN

MEDITERRANEAN SEA

Tyre 332BC

PERSIA

River Indus

Alexandria founded 332BC

Babylon Alexander died here 323BC

Persepolis 331BC

EGYPT 332BC

River Euphrates

Pattala 325BC   INDIA

Bust of Alexander

INDIAN OCEAN

Alexander's army

Alexander inherited a large, well-trained army with high morale. He invaded Persia with an army of 30,000 infantry and 5000 cavalry. Macedonian troops, known as the Royal Army, formed the core of the army. It also contained troops supplied by conquered provinces, such as Thessaly and the states of the Corinthian League, along with professional hired soldiers from all over Greece.

The cavalry

The basic cavalry unit consisted of 49 men. It charged in a wedge-shaped formation with the commander at the front. The cavalry was normally used to break up a phalanx† of enemy foot soldiers.

The cavalry often attacked by charging at the right end of the phalanx, which was its weakest point (see page 133). A phalanx of foot soldiers could then move in from behind to finish off the enemy in hand-to-hand fighting.

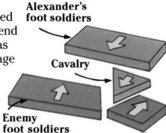

Alexander's foot soldiers

Cavalry

Enemy foot soldiers

The bulk of the cavalry was made up of horsemen from Thessaly, along with troops from the states of the Corinthian League. The elite troops, known as the Companion Cavalry, consisted of eight squadrons, made up of Macedonian noblemen.

Cavalryman from Thessaly

Member of the Companion Cavalry

The infantry

Like the cavalry, the infantry was made up of many different groups – foot soldiers, javelin men, archers and slingers. Alexander continued to use the elite Companion Infantry (see page 169), and he also had a royal bodyguard known as the *hypaspists*.

Foot soldiers continued to fight in a phalanx. Alexander often used the phalanx in an oblique formation, shown here. It enabled him to attack the weaker right wing of an enemy phalanx.

Alexander's oblique phalanx

Enemy phalanx

Under Alexander, many infantry soldiers went back to using the heavy bronze armour of the Greek *hoplites*†, although they still carried the Macedonian *sarissa* (spear). This picture shows a member of the Companion Infantry.

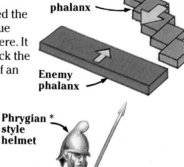

Phrygian * style helmet

Bronze cuirass

Sword

Bronze shield

Sarissa

The army on the move

Each soldier was expected to carry his own weapons and armour, as well as a personal pack containing bedding and cooking equipment. Pack animals and baggage wagons were used to carry bulky equipment such as tents, waterskins and siege equipment, and to move wounded men. The army was accompanied by servants and grooms, and by many women and children.

Key dates

336BC Philip is murdered and Alexander comes to the Macedonian throne.

334BC Alexander invades Persia. He defeats the Persian governors of Asia Minor at the Battle of the River Granicus.

333BC Alexander defeats the Persians, led by King Darius, at the Battle of Issus.

332BC Siege and destruction of the city of Tyre in the Lebanon. Alexander conquers Egypt and founds city of Alexandria.

331BC Alexander defeats the Persians at the Battle of Gaugamela and becomes King of Persia.

327BC Alexander invades India.

326BC Alexander defeats the Indian King, Porus, at the Battle of the River Hydaspes.

323BC Alexander dies in Babylon.

* Phrygia was a part of Asia Minor.

The Hellenistic World

For several hundred years after Alexander's† death, Greek culture and ideas dominated the countries of his empire. The period from 336-30BC is known as the Hellenistic Age, from the Greek word *Hellene*, which means "Greek".

When the news of Alexander's death reached Greece, many cities rebelled against the Macedonians. This began the Lamian War (323-322BC). The Greeks had some initial successes, but were defeated when the Macedonians were reinforced by soldiers returning from Asia.

Alexander was succeeded as ruler by his infant son and his half-brother, Philip Arrideus. Alexander's generals, known as the *Diadochi*, or "successors", governed the empire on behalf of the two kings. But the *Diadochi* began to divide the empire up between themselves and this led to wars over territory, lasting from 323-281BC.

This picture from a later Persian manuscript shows Alexander ascending to heaven.

The division of the empire

By 301BC, Alexander's mother, wife, son and half-brother had all been murdered in the struggle for power, and the empire had collapsed. After the Battle of Ipsus in 301BC, four kingdoms were established, with the rival *Diadochi* as kings. Finally, in 281BC, three kingdoms emerged (see map). They were ruled by the descendants of three of the *Diadochi*: Ptolemy†, Antigonas† and Seleucus†.

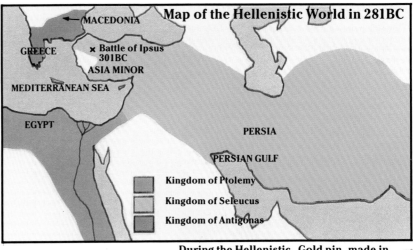

Map of the Hellenistic World in 281BC

MACEDONIA
GREECE
× Battle of Ipsus 301BC
ASIA MINOR
MEDITERRANEAN SEA
EGYPT
PERSIA
PERSIAN GULF

Kingdom of Ptolemy
Kingdom of Seleucus
Kingdom of Antigonas

Macedonia and Greece: 281-146BC

The Antigonids became the new Macedonian royal family. They ruled Greece from Macedonia, and controlled the country by keeping garrisons of soldiers in all the important cities. In 229BC Athens bribed its garrison to leave and became a neutral state. Although it never regained its political importance, Athens continued to be respected as the centre of Greek civilization.

During the third century BC, the Greek colonies in southern Italy became increasingly threatened by the Romans, who were expanding their territory throughout Italy (see opposite page). King Pyrrhus of Epirus went to the aid of the Greek colonists. He defeated the Romans twice, in 280BC and 279BC, but withdrew after a third battle in 275BC.

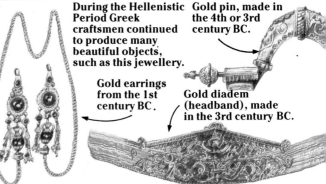

During the Hellenistic Period Greek craftsmen continued to produce many beautiful objects, such as this jewellery.

Gold pin, made in the 4th or 3rd century BC.

Gold earrings from the 1st century BC.

Gold diadem (headband), made in the 3rd century BC.

Conflict with the Romans continued when King Philip V of Macedonia helped the Carthaginian general, Hannibal, in his fight against Rome. This provoked Roman reprisals, which led to three Macedonian Wars between the Antigonids and the Romans (215-205BC, 200-197BC and 179-168BC).

In 168BC the Macedonians were defeated at the Battle of Pydna. The Romans removed the Antigonids from power. After a Macedonian revolt in 147-146BC, the Romans put Macedonia and Greece under direct rule as provinces of the Roman Empire.

When the Romans occupied Greece in 147BC they stole many works of art from temples and houses and took them back to Italy.

The Seleucids: 304-64BC

The Seleucids seized an enormous area of Alexander's empire, but it proved impossible to hold together. Despite inviting in Greek settlers, the Seleucids never had enough Greek manpower to control all their provinces. Gradually large areas began to break away, and by 180BC the Seleucids' territory had been greatly reduced (see map).

Wars with the Parthians, rebellions and disputed successions to the throne caused the gradual decay of the rest of

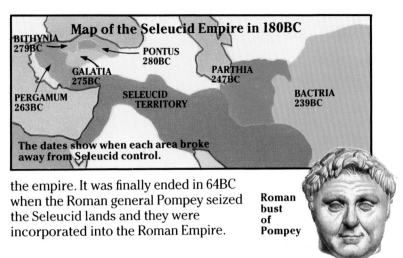

Map of the Seleucid Empire in 180BC

BITHYNIA 279BC

PONTUS 280BC

GALATIA 275BC

PARTHIA 247BC

PERGAMUM 263BC

SELEUCID TERRITORY

BACTRIA 239BC

The dates show when each area broke away from Seleucid control.

the empire. It was finally ended in 64BC when the Roman general Pompey seized the Seleucid lands and they were incorporated into the Roman Empire.

Roman bust of Pompey

The Ptolemaic empire: 323-30BC

Ptolemy was in many ways the most successful of the *Diadochi*. He had contented himself with taking just Egypt, and as a result was able to keep his kingdom intact. At the beginning of his reign, he gained prestige by having Alexander buried in splendour in Alexandria, the capital city of his empire.

Ptolemy and his successors governed Egypt from 323-30BC. They preserved their Greek culture and only the last ruler, Cleopatra VII, even learned the Egyptian language. For more about the Ptolemies, see page 80.

Egyptian carving of Ptolemy.

Confusion over the succession and increasing Roman involvement in Egyptian affairs finally destroyed the Ptolemy dynasty. Queen Cleopatra VII and her Roman husband, Mark Antony, were defeated by the Romans at the Battle of Actium in 31BC. Egypt, the last remaining Hellenistic Kingdom, became a Roman province in 30BC.

The Ptolemies introduced many Greek things to Egypt. This mosaic shows an Egyptian warship, which was based on a Greek trireme†.

The Romans

The Romans developed from a tribe who migrated from central Europe and settled around the River Tiber in Italy in c.1000BC. By c.250BC the Romans controlled most of Italy and began to expand their territory abroad. Thanks to their military efficiency, they soon built up a large empire. For more about the Romans, see pages 193-288.

The arch of Constantine in Rome

The Romans eventually conquered all the Hellenistic kingdoms and were greatly influenced by the Greek ideas they met there. They adopted many aspects of Greek life, such as architecture, literature, religion and social customs. This helped to keep Greek culture alive, even after the end of the Hellenistic Period.

The Roman Empire at its height (2nd century AD)

ITALY
Rome
ASIA MINOR
GREECE
MEDITERRANEAN SEA
EGYPT

Key dates

323-322BC The Greek states rebel against the Macedonians in the Lamian War, but are defeated.

323-281BC Wars of the *Diadochi*, ending in the establishment of three *Diadochi* kingdoms.

275BC Greek colonies in southern Italy pass to the Romans after the defeat of King Pyrrhus of Epirus.

168BC King Perseus of Macedonia is defeated by the Romans at the Battle of Pydna. The Macedonian monarchy is abolished.

147-146BC The Romans suppress a Macedonian revolt. Macedonia and Greece become provinces of the Roman Empire.

64BC The Seleucid empire is conquered by the Roman general, Pompey, and becomes a Roman province.

31-30BC Cleopatra VII of Egypt is defeated by the Romans at the Battle of Actium and Egypt becomes a Roman province.

Learning

Early Greeks used stories about the gods to answer questions about how the world worked or the purpose of life. However, in the 6th century BC some people started to look for new, more practical explanations. To obtain this knowledge, they asked questions and made observations and calculations about the world around them. The Greeks called these scholars *philosophers*, which means "lovers of knowledge".

Today we think of philosophy as the study of the nature of the universe and of human life. However, early Greek philosophers also studied many other subjects, such as biology, mathematics, astronomy and geography.

Scientists and inventors

By observing how things worked, Greek philosophers were able to make many new scientific discoveries, some of which have provided the foundations of modern science.

The astronomer Aristarchus deduced that the Earth revolved on its axis and that it moved around the Sun. This idea was not generally accepted because he could not produce evidence to prove it.

A scholar called Archimedes† discovered an important law of physics. One day he got into a bath and the water overflowed. From this he worked out that an object always displaces its own volume of water.

Thales of Miletus was able to calculate the height of one of the Egyptian pyramids by measuring its shadow. He is also said to have been able to predict an eclipse of the Sun.

Anaximander worked out that much of the land had once been covered in water. He also believed that humans had not appeared on Earth in their present form, but had developed from an earlier creature, perhaps a fish. Another scholar, Xenophanes, examined fossils and discovered that they were the remains of plants and animals preserved in rock.

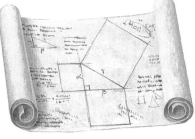

Greek scholars, such as Pythagoras†, Euclid† and Archimedes worked out many basic rules of mathematics. They devised theorems which are still used in geometry. These include Pythagoras' theorem on triangles and the use of pi in working out the circumference or area of a circle.

Another astronomer, Anaxagoras†, realized that the Moon did not produce light itself, but reflected the light of the Sun. He also worked out that eclipses were caused by the Moon passing between the Earth and the Sun and blocking the light.

The Museum

In the Hellenistic Period a temple to the Muses (see page 150) was built at Alexandria in Egypt. It was called the Museion (or Museum). Scholars from all over the Greek world worked there. The Museum also had a library which contained every important Greek book, as well as translations of many foreign books.

We know that engineers at the Museum invented some interesting devices, many of which used water or steam power. However, some of these machines were not very practical and were never widely used. Two of the more useful ones are shown here.

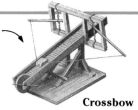

Many inventors at the Museum tried to produce effective new weapons. These were mostly catapults and crossbows. The Greek designs remained in use for many years.

Crossbow

Archimedes built a device which raised water from one level to another. It was in the form of a large screw. Water rose through the screw as it was turned. Pumps like this are still used in parts of Africa today.

Political and moral philosophers

Greek philosophers also examined questions such as how people should behave or what would be the ideal political system. Their ideas were very influential and form the basis of the subject we now call philosophy. Some of the most important thinkers are shown below.

Pythagoras, a mathematician ▶ from Samos, founded a sacred community in Italy. He was interested in what happened to people after they died. He taught that, at death, the soul passed into the body of another creature and so was born again.

Socrates† thought that people would ▶ behave well if they knew what good behaviour was. He challenged people to think about truth, good and evil. He became very unpopular with some Athenians. Finally they charged him with disobeying religious laws and he was forced to kill himself.

Socrates never wrote down his ideas. They were reported by his pupils, one of whom was Plato†. In his own work, Plato tried to find the ideal way of governing a state and set out detailed rules about how this could ◀ be done.

◀ Aristotle† was born in 384BC and was a pupil of Plato. He had a wide knowledge of politics and science. He too was interested in man and society, and finding the ideal way to run a city state. One of his pupils was Alexander the Great†.

In the 4th century BC, Diogenes ▶ founded the school of philosophers known as Cynics. He had no respect for the rules and regulations of society and lived very simply. At one point his home was a large storage jar. He attacked dishonesty and excessive wealth.

The Stoic philosophers ▶ were named after the *stoa* † (porch) where their founder, Xenon, taught. He believed that if people acted naturally they would behave well, because their nature was controlled by the gods. Xenon thought that people should live calmly and reasonably.

Historians

When the earliest Greeks wanted to know about the past, they relied on the stories of gods and heroes that had been handed down to them. They had little interest in the past of other peoples. However, in the 6th century BC when they were threatened by the Persians, the Greeks needed to know more about their opponents. Writers started to gather facts about the Persians and other foreigners. However, these accounts were not always very accurate. It was not until the 5th century BC that more reliable material about the Greeks and other peoples was recorded.

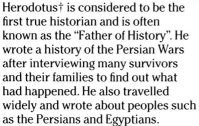

Herodotus† is considered to be the first true historian and is often known as the "Father of History". He wrote a history of the Persian Wars after interviewing many survivors and their families to find out what had happened. He also travelled widely and wrote about peoples such as the Persians and Egyptians.

Another important historian was Thucydides†. He wrote a history of the Peloponnesian War, which is regarded as one of the finest early works of history. Thucydides fought in the war himself and he also interviewed other people who had taken part.

Xenophon† was an army commander, and fought with the Spartans in the Persian Wars. He wrote about many subjects, including the Persian Wars, a history of Greece, military tactics, politics and the care and breeding of horses.

Medicine

Many Greek doctors were priests of Asclepius, the god of healing (see box). By 420BC the cult of Asclepius had been established in Athens, where a festival called the *Epidauria* was held in his honour. Soon there were temples to him all over the Greek world. One of the most important was at Epidaurus, in the Peloponnese.

This reconstruction shows part of the temple complex at Epidaurus.

Asclepius

According to legend, Asclepius was the son of the god Apollo. He was brought up by a *centaur* (a creature that was half man, half horse), who taught him medicine. The goddess Athene gave Asclepius two bottles of magic blood. The blood in one bottle would kill anything, that in the other would bring the dead back to life. Asclepius brought so many people back from the dead that Pluto, the god of the Underworld, complained to Zeus. Zeus was angry with Asclepius and killed him. However, he later relented, brought Asclepius back to life and made him a god.

This statue shows Asclepius with a snake. The snake was the symbol of medicine, and is often still used in this way today.

Religious cures

When they were ill, people visited one of the temples of Asclepius. There priests offered both ordinary medicines and the hope of a miraculous cure. Sick people first had to perform sacrifices and purification ceremonies.

Then they were allowed to sleep for a night in the god's temple. It was thought that Asclepius would heal them while they slept. Sometimes he might appear in a dream to reveal what treatment would cure them.

People who were cured left offerings to Asclepius. This was often a model of the part of the body that had been cured. This relief† shows a man making an offering to Asclepius of a model of a leg.

Developments in medical practice

Later, some doctors adopted a more scientific approach to medicine. They tried to use practical cures rather than religious ones, though they still respected Asclepius. The founder of this movement was a doctor called Hippocrates† of Kos, who is thought to have lived from about 460-377BC. His followers opened schools where the new type of medicine was taught.

Some surgical instruments from the Hellenistic Period.

The new doctors did not believe that illness was a punishment from the gods. Instead they searched for the causes of disease and tried to find out how the body worked. This relief shows a doctor examining a patient to find out what is wrong with him.

Doctors normally prescribed herbal medicines, a special diet, rest or gentle exercise. Sometimes they removed some blood, as it was thought to contain the disease. This vase shows a doctor taking blood from a patient's arm.

As there were no anaesthetics, operations were extremely painful and dangerous. Even if they survived the treatment, patients often died of infected wounds. Doctors therefore tried to avoid operations whenever possible.

Map of Ancient Greece

This map shows Ancient Greece and the surrounding area. All the cities and regions which have been mentioned earlier in this section of the book are marked on this map. The names of regions or countries are written in capital letters. Cities are written in small letters and their positions are marked by dots.

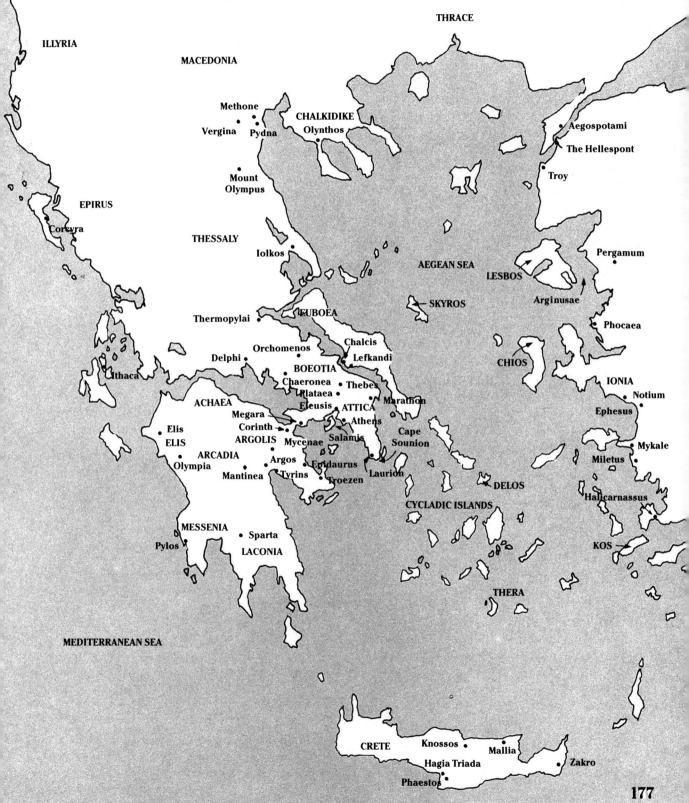

ILLYRIA

THRACE

MACEDONIA

Methone

Vergina · Pydna

CHALKIDIKE

Olynthos

Mount Olympus

EPIRUS

Corcyra

THESSALY

Iolkos

Aegospotami

The Hellespont

Troy

Pergamum

AEGEAN SEA

LESBOS

SKYROS

Arginusae

Thermopylai

EUBOEA

Phocaea

Orchomenos

Chalcis

Delphi

Lefkandi

BOEOTIA

CHIOS

Ithaca

Chaeronea · Thebes

Plataea

Eleusis

ATTICA

Marathon

IONIA

Notium

ACHAEA

Megara

Corinth

Athens

Ephesus

Elis

ARGOLIS

Mycenae

Salamis

Cape Sounion

Mykale

ELIS

ARCADIA

Argos

Epidaurus

Miletus

Olympia

Mantinea

Tyrins

Troezen

Laurion

DELOS

Halicarnassus

CYCLADIC ISLANDS

KOS

MESSENIA

Sparta

Pylos

LACONIA

THERA

MEDITERRANEAN SEA

CRETE

Knossos

Mallia

Hagia Triada

Zakro

Phaestos

177

Greek myths and legends

The earliest Greeks had many myths – stories about gods and goddesses – which they told to explain the world around them. Later, many legends developed which described the lives and deeds of famous heroes in Greek history.

Below are some of the most important Greek myths and legends. Important names appear in bold type to make the main characters easier to identify. You can also read more about the most important gods and goddesses on pages 160-161.

Demeter and Persephone

Demeter, the goddess of crops and harvests, had a beautiful daughter called **Persephone**. **Pluto**, the god of the Underworld, caught sight of Persephone one day and fell in love with her. He had been unable to find a wife, as nobody wanted to live with him in the Underworld where the sun never shone. So he decided to kidnap Persephone and make her his queen. He drove by in his chariot, seized her and carried her off.

Zeus intervenes

Demeter was very upset when she realized her daughter had disappeared. She neglected the plants and trees to look for Persephone. When she found out what had happened, she pleaded with **Zeus** to make Pluto release her daughter. Zeus promised to help her, because no crops would grow and people were starving. So he decreed that Pluto should let Persephone go, on condition that she had not tasted the food of the dead while she had been in the Underworld.

Persephone returns

Persephone had been so miserable that she had not eaten anything, but just before he released her, Pluto persuaded her to taste six pomegranate seeds from his garden. So Zeus decided that she could return to Earth, but would have to spend six months of each year with Pluto in the Underworld, one for each seed she had eaten. Persephone returned to her mother, who was delighted. The crops grew again and it was spring. But after that, for half of every year, Persephone went back to live with Pluto. Demeter became so sad that all the crops died, and it was winter once more.

Theseus

Theseus was the son of **Aegeus**, the king of Athens. As a young man, Aegeus travelled to a place called Troezene and fell in love with a princess called **Aethra**. However he had to return to Athens, and could not take Aethra with him, even though she was pregnant. Before he left, he buried his sword and sandals under a stone. Aegeus told Aethra that if she had a son, when he grew up he should lift the stone and take the sword and sandals to Athens, where he would be introduced to the people as Aegeus' son and heir. Aethra gave birth to a son, and named him **Theseus**.

Theseus travels to Athens

When he was old enough, Theseus found the sandals and sword and set off to Athens to find his father. When he arrived, he went to meet his father, but Aegeus' wife, **Medea**, saw him first. She knew he had come for his inheritance, and wanted to stop him. She handed Aegeus some wine to give to the stranger, but she had secretly poisoned it.

Aegeus recognizes Theseus

When Aegeus saw Theseus' sword and sandals he knew at once who he was, and moved to embrace him. As he did so he dropped the cup of wine. The contents fell on a dog at the king's feet, and killed it instantly. Aegeus then knew that Medea had tried to poison his son. She fled from Athens and never returned.

Theseus and the Minotaur

Some time after Theseus arrived in Athens, the Athenians became anxious and unhappy. When Theseus asked why, he was told that once a year the Athenians were forced to send young men and women to the island of Crete, as food for a monster called the **Minotaur**. It was half man, half bull, and had been born to the wife of **Minos**, the King of Crete (see pages 100 and 105). It lived in a maze called the Labyrinth, which was so confusing that people who entered it never found a way out. The Minotaur ate people who were thrown into the maze.

The voyage to Crete

Theseus volunteered to join the victims in order to kill the monster. Aegeus tried to persuade his son not to go, but Theseus boarded the ship, which had black sails. He promised that if he succeeded, he would change the sails to white ones on the return journey, so that Aegeus would know the outcome as soon as possible.

Into the Labyrinth

When Theseus got to Crete, Minos' daughter **Ariadne** fell in love with him. She gave him a sword to kill the Minotaur, and a ball of thread. Theseus tied one end of the thread to the entrance of the Labyrinth, and went inside. He found and killed the Minotaur, then followed the thread back outside. Ariadne, Theseus and his friends then fled from Crete.

Ariadne is abandoned

On the way back to Athens, they visited the island of Naxos. By this time Theseus was growing tired of Ariadne. While she was asleep, he called his friends back to the ship. They set sail, abandoning her. The gods disapproved, and punished Theseus by making him forget to hoist the white sails. Aegeus, watching from the shore for the ship, saw the black sails and thought that his son was dead. In his grief he threw himself off a cliff. Ever since, the sea where he died has been called the Aegean.

Theseus travels again

When Theseus heard about his father he was griefstricken. To help him forget his sadness, he set out to travel again. He went to the land of a race of warrior women called the **Amazons**, and married the Amazon queen. They returned to Athens, where a son, **Hippolytus**, was born. Shortly after this, the Amazons invaded Athens to take their queen back, but she was killed in a battle.

Phaedra

Theseus married again. His new wife, **Phaedra**, was jealous of Hippolytus and wanted to get rid of him. She told Theseus that Hippolytus had attacked her. The king was very angry, and asked **Poseidon** to punish his son. As Hippolytus was riding on the beach, Poseidon sent a huge wave to scare his horses. The horses bolted and Hippolytus was killed.

The death of Theseus

Phaedra was overcome with remorse. She confessed that she had lied, and then hanged herself. Theseus grew bitter after all these misfortunes, and became a very stern ruler. The Athenians turned against him and banished him to the island of Scyros, where he was murdered. Later Theseus' bones were returned to Athens, where a temple was built in his honour.

Oedipus

Oedipus was the son of **Laius** and **Jocasta**, the King and Queen of Thebes in Boeotia. When he was born, they asked the priests of Apollo to foretell the child's fate. They were horrified to be told that Oedipus was destined to murder his father and marry his mother. To prevent this, Laius made one of his servants take Oedipus away and kill him. The servant did not murder the child, but left him outside to die. A shepherd found the baby and took him to Corinth, where the king and queen adopted him and brought him up as their own son.

Oedipus consults the Oracle

When he grew up, Oedipus went to Delphi to ask the Oracle (see page 164) what the future held. He too was told that he would kill his father and marry his mother. Thinking the king and queen of Corinth were his parents, he left Corinth, vowing never to return.

Oedipus' journey

While travelling he came to a crossroads, where he saw a man being driven in a chariot. The driver called to him to make way, but Oedipus did not move. He was used to being treated as a prince, and would not accept orders. A fight began, and Oedipus killed the driver, the man and his servants. He did not know it, but the man was Laius. The first part of the prophecy had come true.

Oedipus and the Sphinx

Oedipus continued towards Thebes. Near the city he encountered a monster called the **Sphinx** that was terrorizing the area. She sat by the city gates, and would not let people past without asking them a riddle. When they could not answer, she ate them. No-one had yet got past the Sphinx, and no-one dared to attack her.

The Sphinx's riddle

Oedipus was still so sad about having left Corinth that he did not care whether he lived or died. He approached the Sphinx to try and guess the answer to her riddle. This is what she asked him: What has four legs in the morning, two at mid-day, and three in the evening, and is weakest when it has most legs?

Oedipus realized the answer was a human being, who crawls, then walks, then, when old, uses a stick for support. The Sphinx was so angry at being defeated that she killed herself. The happy Thebans made Oedipus their king, and he married the Queen, Jocasta.

The plague

All went well for some years, but then Thebes was hit by a plague. Many people died, and the people turned again to Oedipus to help them. He sent messengers to consult the Oracle at Delphi, who declared that the plague would only cease if Laius' murderers were found and punished.

Oedipus learns the truth

Messengers were sent to find out who had committed the murder. They returned with evidence that it had been Oedipus. The servant who had taken the baby to the hillside confessed that he had not killed the child, but had simply left him to die. Enquiries in Corinth confirmed that the baby had been adopted there. Oedipus realized that the prophecy had come true. Without knowing it he had murdered his father and married his mother. When she discovered what had happened, Jocasta killed herself. Oedipus blinded himself with her brooch, fled from Thebes, and died, ruined, at Colonnus near Athens.

The curse of the family of Atreus

Atreus became king of Mycenae when he married **Aerope**, a Mycenaean princess. But it was said that Atreus was subject to several curses, which caused him and his family great suffering and misery.

Tantalus offends the gods

Atreus' grandfather, **Tantalus**, had been a friend of **Zeus**, and was allowed to eat with the gods. But he offended them by stealing their food and giving it to his friends on Earth. Then he asked the gods to a banquet, and tested them to see if they truly were all-powerful. He killed his son, **Pelops**, and served him up at the feast, though it was forbidden to eat human flesh. The gods knew at once what had happened. Zeus condemned Tantalus to eternal torment in the Underworld, and put a curse on his family.

Pelops returns from the dead

Zeus brought Pelops back to life. When the boy grew up he fell in love with a princess, **Hippodamia**, and asked to marry her. Her father, King **Oenomaus**, had been told by fortune tellers that he would be killed by his son-in-law, and so wished to stop anyone from marrying his daughter. He challenged her suitors to a chariot race, stating that the loser would be executed. The god **Poseidon** lent Pelops some of his horses. In addition, Pelops bribed the king's charioteer, **Myrtilus**, promising him a reward if he would sabotage the king's chariot.

The chariot race

Oenomaus was killed in a crash during the race, and Pelops escaped with Hippodamia and Myrtilus. Instead of rewarding the charioteer, however, Pelops murdered him. As he died, Myrtilus placed a curse on Pelops.

A third curse

Later, Atreus himself was the victim of a curse. He found out that his wife had been seduced by his brother **Thyestes**. He took revenge by killing all but one of Thyestes' sons. Thyestes then put a curse on his brother.

The curses are fulfilled

The curses were fulfilled during the reign of **Agamemnon**, Atreus' son. **Menelaus**, Agamemnon's brother, had married **Helen**, the Queen of Sparta. Helen was so beautiful that all the Greek kings had fallen in love with her, but they had been made to swear that they would help the man she married if anyone tried to steal her away. But the goddess of love, **Aphrodite**, had promised a Trojan Prince called **Paris** that he could marry Helen. He went to Sparta, where Helen fell in love with him, and they ran away to live at Troy.

Agamemnon plots his revenge

Agamemnon was angry about Helen's treatment of Menelaus. He reminded the other kings of their oath and organized an expedition to Troy to bring Helen back. To get good winds for the sea journey he even sacrificed his daughter **Iphigenia**. The war against Troy lasted ten years (see pages 110-111) before the Greeks won and Agamemnon returned home.

Agamemnon is murdered

Meanwhile, Agamemnon's wife, **Clytemnestra**, was angered by the sacrifice of Iphigenia, and by her husband's long absence. She fell in love with **Aegistus**, her husband's cousin and enemy, and married him. She pretended to welcome Agamemnon when he came home, but then murdered him. She and Aegistus then ruled Mycenae.

Revenge, and the end of the curse

Agamemnon's son **Orestes** found out what had happened and took revenge, murdering Clytemnestra and Aegistus. By killing his own mother, Orestes had committed a terrible crime. He was driven mad by the **Furies**, goddesses with dogs' heads and bats' wings who tormented murderers. Finally the gods intervened, seeing that Orestes had suffered enough. They cleansed Orestes of his guilt, and ended the curse. Orestes became king of Mycenae.

Two poems by Homer

The earliest surviving examples of Greek literature are two poems by Homer†, the *Iliad* and the *Odyssey*. Homer only passed his poems on by word of mouth, but when writing was reintroduced in Greece, later scholars and poets wrote them down. For the Greeks, Homer's work was a magnificent source of inspiration about religion and history. For people of later civilizations, the *Iliad* and the *Odyssey* have provided a wealth of information about Homer's world.

The *Iliad*

The *Iliad* takes place during the last few weeks of the Trojan War (see page 110). It concerns an argument between the hero **Achilles** and the leader of the Greek forces, **Agamemnon**. Agamemnon stole a slave-girl from Achilles, who, insulted, withdrew from the fighting. Without him, the Greeks were downhearted and suffered terrible losses. To boost the troops' morale, Achilles' friend **Patroclus** put on Achilles' armour and went into battle. Thinking he was Achilles, a Trojan warrior called **Hector** killed him.

Achilles, full of remorse, returned to the battlefield and killed Hector. He dragged the body round the walls of Troy behind his chariot. Hector's father, **Priam**, paid a ransom to Achilles, who finally returned the body. Hector was given a hero's funeral.

The poem contains many episodes about other heroes and their deeds. The human events are mirrored by episodes about the gods and goddesses, who each take sides in the dispute.

The *Odyssey*

The *Odyssey* tells the story of another hero, **Odysseus**, who suggested the trick of the wooden horse (see page 110). After the Trojan War, Odysseus tried to return home to Ithaca, where his wife **Penelope** was beseiged by suitors. They thought Odysseus was dead, and wanted to marry her. They insisted that she chose one of them as a husband.

Much of the *Odyssey* tells the story of Odysseus' journey home, and of the many dangers he encountered. He had to slay the one-eyed monster **Cyclops**, and survive many shipwrecks. He also escaped from the **Sirens**, creatures whose singing lured ships to crash on to the rocks, and from **Circe**, a witch who turned men into animals.

When he reached Ithaca, the goddess **Athene** disguised him as a beggar, to help him return to his house unnoticed. Penelope had organized an archery competition for her suitors, saying she would marry the winner. Odysseus, still disguised, took part in the competition and won. He then killed the other competitors. Finally Penelope recognized him and the couple were reunited.

Heracles

One of the most famous Greek heroes was **Heracles**. He is also known as **Hercules**, which is the Roman version of his name. Heracles was exceptionally strong and brave, and there are many stories of his adventures.

The birth of Heracles

Heracles was the son of **Zeus** and **Alcmene**. Zeus was already married to **Hera** when he met Alcmene and fell in love with her. However, Alcmene was married to **Amphitryon**. She tried to prevent Zeus from visiting her, so he made himself look like Amphitryon. Alcmene was fooled by Zeus's disguise and let him in. When Amphitryon came home, she realized she had been tricked. She later gave birth to Zeus's son, and named him Heracles ("Glory to Hera") in an attempt to calm Zeus's wife. Unfortunately this plan did not work – Hera hated Heracles. When he was a baby, Hera sent two serpents to kill him in his cradle. Instead, he strangled them with his bare hands. Everyone was amazed by his strength.

Hera's revenge

When he grew up, Heracles married a woman called **Megara** and had a family. He was very happy, and became famous for his courage. Hera was so jealous of him that she drove him mad, causing him to kill his wife and children. When the madness left him, he was horrified and asked the Oracle† how he could make amends. He was told to offer himself as a slave to King **Eurystheus** of Tiryns.

Eurystheus set Heracles twelve tasks or "labours". They seemed impossible, but the king promised that if Heracles could manage them, he would be free of his guilt and become an Immortal.

The Twelve Labours of Heracles

1. To kill the Nemean lion
At Nemea there lived a lion with a skin so tough that no weapon could pierce it. Heracles fought with the beast and managed to strangle it with his bare hands. Afterwards he cut off its skin and wore it as protection.

2. To destroy the Lernaean Hydra
In the swamps of Lerna lived a beast called the **Hydra**, which had the body of a dog and six serpents' heads. No-one had managed to destroy it, because every time a head was cut off it grew again. Heracles found an ingenious way to defeat it. He chopped off the heads in turn, sealing the wounds with a burning torch so that new heads could not grow.

3. To capture the Ceryneian hind
The Ceryneian hind was a beautiful deer with hooves of bronze and horns of gold. Though it would have been easy to kill, Heracles had to capture it alive as it was sacred. It took him a whole year to catch the animal in a net.

4. To trap the Erymanthian boar
Heracles managed to trap the huge wild boar of Mount Erymanthus by tiring it out and chasing it into a snowdrift. He then tied it in chains.

5. To clean the Augean stables
The stables of **Augeus**, king of Elis, had not been cleaned for many years and were piled high with manure. Heracles's task was to clean every single stable in one day. Not even Heracles could have done this had he not come up with a plan. He diverted the course of the River Alpheus so that it swept through the stables and cleared them out.

6. To kill the Stymphalian birds
In woods around Lake Stymphalus lived a flock of man-eating birds with bronze beaks, claws and wings. They seemed impossible to kill because they hid in the trees. Heracles scared the birds from their nests with a brass rattle and shot them with a bow and arrows.

7. To capture the Cretan bull
The bull was the father of the **Minotaur** and lived on the island of Crete. Heracles managed to master the animal and took it back to Eurystheus in Mycenae by boat. After that he released it and it lived near Marathon.

8. To round up the horses of Diomedes
Diomedes was king of the Bistonians in Thrace. His horses ate human flesh and were extremely dangerous. Heracles killed Diomedes and fed him to his own horses. After they had eaten, they were calm enough for Heracles to bring them under control.

9. To fetch Hippolyte's girdle
Eurystheus's daughter wanted a girdle that belonged to **Hippolyte**, who was the queen of the Amazons, a race of warrior women. Hippolyte was happy to give Heracles her girdle, but Hera tricked the other Amazons into thinking that Heracles was hurting their queen. He had to fight her whole army to win the girdle.

10. To fetch the oxen of Geryon
On an island in the far west lived a herd of oxen. They were guarded by the herdsman **Geryon**, who had three bodies above his waist and by **Orthrus**, a two-headed dog. Heracles had to kill both the herdsman and his dog before bringing the oxen to Eurystheus. On the return journey, Heracles set up a pillar on either side of the Straits of Gibraltar to guard the Mediterranean. These were called the Pillars of Heracles.

11. To fetch the golden apples of the Hesperides
The **Hesperides** were a group of minor goddesses who tended a tree of golden apples. To find out where the apples were kept Heracles visited their father, **Atlas**, who supported the weight of the heavens on his shoulders. He agreed to fetch the apples if Heracles would take his place for a while. Heracles accepted, and held up the heavens while Atlas went to get the apples. Atlas enjoyed his freedom so much that, on his return,

he refused to take his burden back. Heracles said that he would keep holding up the heavens, but asked Atlas to take back the weight for a moment while he made himself more comfortable. As soon as Atlas held the heavens once more, Heracles escaped with the apples.

12. To bring Cerberus from the Underworld
This was said to be the hardest of all the tasks. **Cerberus** was a monstrous three-headed dog who guarded the gates to the Underworld and stopped anyone leaving the land of the dead. **Pluto**, the god of the Underworld, agreed to let Heracles take Cerberus as long has he did not harm the animal with any weapons. Heracles managed to drag Cerberus all the way to the court of Eurystheus. He then returned the beast to the Underworld.

The death of Heracles

Hera finally managed to kill Heracles. She tricked his second wife **Deianeira** into giving him a poisoned robe. When Heracles put on the robe it caused him agony, but he was unable to take it off as it had magical powers. The pain was so unbearable that Heracles built a funeral pyre, and climbed onto it to kill himself. However, Heracles's father, Zeus, snatched him from the flames and took him back to Olympus. Heracles finally became an Immortal.

Jason

Jason was heir to the throne of Iolcus, but when he was a baby his uncle, **Pelias**, banished him and stole the crown. When he grew up, he returned to claim the throne. Pelias promised that when he died, Jason could succeed him. He gave one condition. Jason had to fetch a famous golden fleece from Colchis. The fleece was thought to have magical powers. So Jason built a great ship called the Argo, and gathered together a crew of heroes (called the **Argonauts**) to help him on his quest.

King Phineus and the Clashing Rocks

On the way to Colchis, Jason visited King **Phineus** for his advice on the dangers ahead. He agreed to help the Argonauts, on condition that they destroy the **Harpies**, a group of vicious screeching birds with women's heads. When Jason and his companions succeeded, the king told them how to get past their next obstacle. This was a lethal barrier at the entrance to the strait of Bosphorous, known as the Clashing Rocks. Whenever a ship tried to sail between them, they crashed shut and crushed the vessel. Phineus told them to send a bird through first, which the rocks would try to crush, and then to sail through quickly while the rocks were reopening. The Argonauts took this advice and got through safely, though the bird lost a few tail-feathers.

Jason's test

When the Argo reached Colchis, Jason explained his mission to the king, **Aeetes**. Aeetes did not want Jason to have the fleece, so he set him what he thought was an impossible task. He said that Jason could have the fleece if he could harness two fire-breathing bulls, use them to plough a field, and plant some dragon's teeth. Aeetes was sure that Jason would be killed trying to complete this task, but the gods made his daughter, **Medea**, fall in love with him. Medea had magical powers and gave Jason a potion to protect him from the bulls' fiery breath whilst he ploughed. When he planted the dragon's teeth, they turned into armed soldiers and sprang up from the ground. Jason took Medea's advice and threw a stone among them. One soldier thought another had hit him, fighting broke out amongst them and they were all killed.

The Golden Fleece

Jason then had to conquer the monster that guarded the fleece itself. It had a dragon's head and a serpent's body, and never slept. Following Medea's instructions, Jason asked Orpheus to play a lullaby on his lyre. Gradually the monster was lulled into a deep sleep. Jason grabbed the fleece and ran back to the Argo, taking Medea and her brother, **Apsyrtus**, with him. Jason swore to Medea that he would marry her for all the help she had given him.

The journey home

Aeetes chased the Argo as it sailed home, until Medea killed her brother and threw him overboard. Her grief-stricken father stopped to pick up his son, and the Argo was able to escape. The Argonauts met many more dangers on their journey home. These included a group of sea-nymphs called **sirens** whose beautiful songs lured sailors to their deaths on jagged rocks.

Medea's revenge

Back in Iolcus, Medea arranged Pelias's death so that Jason could become king. She told Pelias's daughters that they could restore his youth by boiling him in a cauldron filled with a herbal potion, but when they did this he died. Jason could now be king of Iolcus, but the people were sickened by Medea's cruelty and banished them both. They settled in Corinth, where Jason became ruler and fell in love with Princess **Glaucis**. He broke his oath to Medea by planning to marry the princess. Once again Medea took her revenge. She sent Glaucis a robe and crown as gifts. When Glaucis put them on, they burst into flames and killed her. Medea then fled.

Jason's death

Though Jason ruled Corinth well at first, as time passed he became arrogant and unpopular. Having broken his oath to Medea, he lost the gods' favour and ended his life an outcast. He roamed until he came across the rotting hull of the Argo, the ship in which he had had so many great adventures. Here he sat down and was dreaming of the past when the prow fell and killed him.

Who was who in Ancient Greece

Below is a list of the important people mentioned in this section of the book, with details of their lives and works. If a person's name appears in **bold type** in the text of an entry, that person also has his or her own entry in this list.

Aeschylus (c.525BC-455BC).   Writer of tragic plays. He wrote about 90 plays, but only seven survive. Most of them were stories about the gods and the heroes. His most famous work is the *Orestia*, a group of three plays about King Agamemnon and his family (see page 179). Aeschylus is regarded as the founder of Greek tragedy. He was the first writer to use more than one actor, making dialogue and action on stage possible.

Alcibiades (c.450BC-404BC).   Athenian politician. He was a pupil of **Socrates** and the ward of **Pericles**, who was a close relative. In 420BC he was elected *strategos†*. During the Peloponnesian War, he persuaded the Athenians to send troops to Sicily (see page 159) and was appointed one of the leaders of the expedition. However, he was recalled to face a charge of having mutilated many statues in Athens with a group of aristocratic friends. Instead he fled to Sparta where he advised the Spartans how to fight their war against Athens. In 407BC he was recalled to Athens and re-elected. However, he was held responsible for the Athenian defeat at the Battle of Notium, and retired. He was assassinated in Persia.

Alexander the Great (356BC-323BC).   Macedonian king and military leader. He was a pupil of **Aristotle**, and learned military tactics as a soldier in the army of his father, **Philip of Macedonia**. In 336BC Philip was murdered, and Alexander became king at the age of 20. He was a military genius, and, after taking control of Greece and the areas to the north, in 334BC he began an invasion of Asia. Eventually he conquered the largest empire in the Ancient World (see pages 170-171). Alexander married a Persian princess called Roxane. He died of a fever at Babylon, aged only 32.

Anaxagoras (c.500BC-c.428BC).   Philosopher. He spent most of his life in Athens, and was a friend of **Pericles**. He wrote a book called *On Nature* in which he tried to explain how the universe worked. This book influenced many later philosophers. In the scientific field, Anaxagoras worked out that the Sun was a mass of flaming material and that the Moon reflected its light. He was also the first person to explain a solar eclipse.

Antigonas II.   Macedonian king. He ruled from 279BC to 239BC. As king of Macedonia he also ruled Greece itself, and was one of the most powerful leaders of the Hellenistic World (see pages 172-173). His successors ruled until 146BC, when Macedonia and Greece were conquered by the Romans.

Archimedes (c.287-212BC).   Mathematician, astronomer and inventor. He studied at the Museum in Alexandria (see page 174) and then lived in Syracuse. He invented a type of pulley and a device for raising water. He also discovered an important law of physics – that a body displaces its own volume of water.

Aristides (c.520BC-c.467BC).   Athenian politician and general. He came from an aristocratic family. Aristides was a prominent leader at the time of the Persian Wars and was a *strategos†* at the Battle of Marathon. He was ostracized† in 482BC, but was recalled a year later and took part in the battles of Salamis and Plataea. Aristides also helped to set up the Delian League.

Aristophanes (5th century BC-c.385BC).   Athenian writer of comic plays. He wrote about 40 comedies, of which eleven survive. Some of these make fun of the political events of the time. Many of his works won prizes at the Athens Theatre Festival. His most famous plays are *The Wasps*, *The Birds* and *The Frogs*.

Aristotle (384BC-322BC).   Athenian philosopher. He studied with **Plato** in Athens, then travelled around the eastern Mediterranean. After spending three years as the tutor of **Alexander the Great**, he returned to Athens in 335BC. He set up a school, the Lyceum, but after Alexander's death he was charged with impiety and fled to Euboea. His writings cover many different subjects, such as poetry, political life, and various philosophical theories. Some of his most famous works are *Poetics*, *Politica* and *Metaphysica*.

Aspasia (born c.465BC).   Wife of **Pericles**. She came from Miletus, and was never properly accepted by many Athenians. She was often mocked by Pericles' enemies, and by writers of comedies. However she was very beautiful and well educated, and was highly regarded by **Socrates** and his friends. In 431BC she was prosecuted, but acquitted.

Cimon (late 6th century BC-c.450BC).   Athenian soldier and statesman. He was the son of **Miltiades**, and a sworn enemy of the Persians. After the Greek victory over the Persians at the battles of Salamis and Plataea (see page 137), Cimon led expeditions to free the Greek islands from Persian rule. He was responsible for several later victories against the Persians. In 462BC he persuaded Athens to support Sparta (see page 159). When the Spartans refused Athenian help Cimon's prestige suffered and he was ostracized† in 461BC. Later he was recalled, and negotiated the 5-year peace with Sparta. He led an expedition to Cyprus, where he died.

Cleisthenes (lived 6th century BC).   Athenian politician. He was a member of the Athenian aristocracy, and took power in Athens after the overthrow of the tyrant Hippias. In 580BC he introduced reforms that led to the political system known as democracy† (see pages 156-157). He also introduced ostracism† in the city. **Pericles** was his nephew.

Draco (lived 7th century BC).   Athenian politician. In 621BC he was appointed to improve the Athenian legal system. He favoured public trials so that people could see that justice had been done. He based his reforms on existing laws, but made them much more severe, and introduced the death penalty for many minor crimes. The Athenians became unhappy with such severe laws, and the system was later reformed again by **Solon**.

Euclid (lived c.300BC). Mathematician. He worked in Alexandria, and wrote several books about mathematics and geometry. His most famous book was *Elements*, part of which sums up the teachings of the mathematicians who worked before him. Several of his theories and discoveries remain in use today.

Euripides (c.485BC-406BC). Athenian writer of tragic plays. He wrote over 90 plays, of which we know the titles of 80; 19 of them have survived. Among the most famous are *Medea*, *The Trojan Women* and *Orestes*. He won five first prizes at the Athens Theatre Festival. Later he moved to the court of King Archelaus of Macedonia, where he died.

Herodotus (c.484BC-420BC). Historian. He was born in Helicarnassus in Ionia. He visited Egypt, the Black Sea, Babylon and Cyrene, then lived on Samos. Later he moved to Athens, but he finally settled in Thurii in southern Italy. Herodotus is known as "the Father of History". He wrote a history of the Greek people which centred around the Persian Wars. It also included information on many other, very varied subjects. Herodotus was one of the first writers to compare historical facts and to see them as a sequence of linked events.

Hesiod (lived ?8th century BC). Boeotian poet. He owned a farm at Ascra in Boeotia. He claimed that the Muses (see page 150) visited him one day on Mount Helicon and gave him the gift of poetry. His most famous book is *Works and Days*, which includes practical details of farming, a calendar of lucky and unlucky days, and an explanation of religious ceremonies. He is also said to have written *The Theogony*, an account of the Greek gods and goddesses and their relationships.

Hippocrates (c.460BC-c.377BC). Doctor and writer on medicine. His teachings became the basis of medical practice throughout the ancient world (see page 176). Unlike many earlier Greek doctors, he based his work on close observations of his patients, rather than on religious rituals. His writings discuss many aspects of medical practice, including the way a doctor should behave, and the effect of the environment on disease and illness. Hippocrates lived on the island of Kos, where he founded an important medical school.

Homer (lived ?9th century BC). Poet. Very little is known about him. He was a bard (see page 110) who recited his poems. For many years his work was passed on by word of mouth. Eventually fragments of it were written down by other poets and historians centuries after his death. According to tradition he came from the island of Chios, and may have been blind. His poems *The Iliad* and *The Odyssey* are accounts of events during and after the Trojan War (see pages 110-111).

Miltiades (c.550BC-c.489BC). Athenian soldier and politician, father of **Cimon**. He was sent by the tyrant† Hippias to the Chersonese to make sure that the Athenians kept control of the route through to the Black Sea. Later he fought for the Persians, but joined the Ionian revolt (see page 136) in 500BC. When the revolt was defeated he had to flee to Athens. He led the Athenian forces at the Battle of Marathon, which the Greeks won, largely thanks to Miltiades' superior military skills. Later he led the Athenian fleet in an unsuccessful expedition to Paros, where he was wounded. As a result of this failure he returned to Athens, where he was tried and fined a huge sum of money. He died shortly after the trial.

Myron (lived 5th century BC). Sculptor. He worked in Athens between about 460 and 440BC. His most famous statues included one of the runner Ladas, and one of a man throwing a discus (see page 142).

Peisistratus (c.590BC-527BC). Athenian politician. In 546BC, after two earlier attempts to seize power, he declared himself tyrant† of Athens (see page 117). Under his rule Athens prospered. He reorganized public finances, and spent public money on roads and a good water supply. He also rebuilt and improved much of Athens, and art and literature were encouraged. Athenian trade with the rest of Greece also improved because Peisistratus was an excellent diplomat and wanted good relations with other areas. He died while still in power.

Pericles (early 5th century BC-429BC). Athenian statesman and general. He was a member of the aristocratic Alcmaeonid family, and became the most famous and powerful politician of his day. He was elected *strategos*† every year from 443BC to 429BC, and was such a powerful speaker that he was nearly always able to swing public opinion his way. He was responsible for the rebuilding of the Acropolis, the construction of the Long Walls (see page 158), and for refining the Athenian democratic system. He dictated the Athenian policy during the early stages of the Peloponnesian War. In 430BC he was charged with stealing public funds and fined a huge sum of money. He was still elected strategos the following year, but died in the plague that hit Athens.

Pheidias (c.500BC-c.425BC). Athenian sculptor. He worked as a painter before becoming a sculptor. He mostly used bronze, but was best known for his cult statues in ivory and gold. He made the frieze around the Parthenon and the statue of Athene there, as well as the statue of Zeus at Olympus. He was accused of taking the gold given to him for work on the Parthenon, but escaped and went to work at Olympus. Later he was again charged with embezzlement, and died in prison.

Philip of Macedonia (c.382BC-336BC). Macedonian king and military leader. He began ruling Macedonia in 359BC (see pages 168-169). He reorganized the army, and showed great skill as a military commander and diplomat. Within 25 years Philip had united the country, extended the frontiers, and made Macedonia into the greatest military power of its day. Philip married a princess called Olympias, and they had a son, **Alexander**. He was assassinated in 336BC; it is possible that his wife and son were involved in the murder plot.

Pindar (c.518BC-c.438BC). Athenian poet. He was born in Boeotia, and travelled to Athens at an early age. He was a friend of **Aeschylus**, and quickly became known as a poet. Ancient scholars divided his many poems into 17 books according to themes and styles. Some celebrate victors at games, some are odes to tyrants, and a few other fragments have survived. Many later writers described him as the greatest Greek poet.

Plato (c.429BC-347BC). Athenian philosopher. He was a member of an aristocratic Athenian family, and a pupil of **Socrates**. After Socrates died, Plato fled to Megara, then lived in Syracuse. Later he returned to Athens, where he wrote *The Apology*, an answer to Socrates' enemies. His ideas for the running of an ideal state were set out in his books *The Republic* and *The Laws*. He founded a school on the outskirts of Athens, in a grove called the Academy which gave the school its name. The school was famous throughout the ancient world, and continued for centuries after Plato's death. It was closed in AD529 by the Roman Emperor Justinian, who thought it was politically dangerous. Plato's ideas have remained influential to the present day.

Praxiteles (born c.390BC). Athenian sculptor. Little is known about his life, except that he worked in Athens. His sculpture of the goddess Aphrodite (see page 143) is the first known statue of the female nude. Praxiteles also made sculptures of the gods Hermes, Eros and Apollo.

Ptolemy I. Macedonian general, later King of Egypt. He took over Egypt after the death of **Alexander the Great** in 323BC. He and his successors ruled successfully until Egypt was conquered by the Romans in 30BC.

Pythagoras (c.580BC-late 6th century BC). Philosopher and mathematician. He may have travelled in Egypt and the East. Later he founded a school at Croton in southern Italy. Nothing has survived of his theories, but we know about his teachings from contemporary descriptions. He thought that after people died their souls lived on in other beings. He also developed many geometrical theories (see page 174).

Sappho (born c.612BC). Poetess. She was born on the island of Lesbos, but probably left there to travel to Sicily. For a time she ran a school for girls. It is said that she wrote nine books of poetry, but only fragments survive. Sappho was considered one of the greatest Greek poets. She died in the middle of the 6th century BC.

Seleucus I. Macedonian general, later Middle Eastern king. In 304BC he seized a vast area of the empire of **Alexander the Great**, and became one of the three main rulers of the Hellenistic World (see pages 172-173). But the empire was too big to hold together and it was eventually conquered by the Romans in 64BC.

Socrates (c.469BC-399BC). Athenian philosopher. He wrote no books, but taught his pupils by word of mouth, discussing points of philosophy with them and questioning accepted opinions. Socrates and his pupils pointed out weak points in the government, and in people's beliefs. This made them very unpopular with Athenian politicians. Eventually his enemies charged him with impiety and corrupting the young. He was sentenced to death by drinking poison. We know about Socrates' ideas (see page 175) because they were written down by some of his pupils, including **Plato**.

Solon (c.640BC-558BC). Athenian politician. He became *archon*† in about 594BC, and quickly passed many new laws (see page 117). These included bringing debtors back from exile, and the cancellation of many debts. He set up a new court to which people could appeal if they thought they had been wrongly tried, and also reformed the way the government took decisions. Solon encouraged craftsmen from other parts of Greece to come to Athens, and granted them Athenian citizenship. By making the Athenians use the same money as other Greek states he also encouraged the development of trade and industry.

Sophocles (c.496BC-405BC). Athenian writer of tragic plays. He wrote 123 plays, of which we know the titles of 110, but only seven survive. The most famous are *Antigone*, *Oedipus Tyrannus* and *Electra*. He won many prizes at the Athens Theatre Festival. Sophocles was among the first to write plays with more than two characters, and one of the first to use stage scenery. Before him, plays had concentrated on myths and the affairs of the gods. His plays, though still based on myths, were written from the viewpoint of the human characters.

Themistocles (c.524BC-459BC). Athenian statesman. He was *strategos*† at the Battle of Marathon (see page 136) and persuaded the Athenians to build up their navy. In 480-479BC he organised resistance to the Persians. His strategy helped the Athenians to win the Battle of Salamis (see page 137). Later he organized the rebuilding of the walls of Athens in 479-478BC. Around 471BC he was ostracized† and fled to Argos. He was accused of treason. Then he fled to Asia Minor where the Persians, grateful to him for his part in negotiating peace with Athens, made him governor of three cities.

Thucydides (c.460BC-396BC). Athenian historian. In 424BC he was elected *strategos*†, but he was held responsible for a military defeat and was ostracized†. He did not return to Athens for 20 years. Thucydides wrote an account of the Peloponnesian War which is considered to be one of the first history books. As well as describing the battles and political events, it gives details of life in Athens and elsewhere.

Xenophon (c.430BC-354BC). Athenian historian. He was a pupil of **Socrates**. He fought as a mercenary soldier for both the Persians and the Spartans, and was banished from Athens as a result. While in exile in Sparta he wrote many books, including *The Anabasis*, about his period with the Persians, and *The Hellenica*, a history of the events of his day. He also wrote about farming, horsemanship and finance, and works on Socrates.

Date chart

This chart lists the most important dates in Ancient Greek history. It also includes some of the events that took place elsewhere in the world during same period; these are shown on indented lines.

Early history

from 40,000BC   The first people settle in Greece, hunting and gathering food.

The Neolithic Period: c.6500-2900BC

c.6500-3000BC   First inhabitants settle on Crete and introduce farming. Pottery is made in Greece and Crete.

    c.6250BC   Çatal Hüyük in Anatolia (modern Turkey) becomes the largest town of its time. Pottery and woollen cloth are manufactured there.

    c.5000BC-4000BC   Farming spreads through Europe.

c.4000BC   Evidence of early inhabitants in the Cyclades, including remains of metalware.

    c.3500BC   The wheel is invented in Sumer in the Middle East.

    c.3200BC   Introduction of pottery in Ecuador, South America.

    c.3100BC   Cities develop in Sumer. Writing develops in Sumer and Egypt.

The Bronze Age: c.2900-1000BC

c.2900BC   Metal is now in widespread use. The population of Greece increases, villages grow into towns and some people become specialized craftsmen.

    c.2686-2181BC   Old Kingdom in Egypt.

    c.2590BC   Pyramid of Cheops is built at Giza in Egypt.

c.2500BC   The city of Troy is founded.

    c.2500BC   Beginning of Indus civilization in India.

c.2100BC   Possible arrival of the first Greek-speaking people in Greece.

c.2000BC   The sail is first used on ships in the Aegean.

    c.2000BC   Building of Stonehenge begins in Britain.

    c.2000BC   Middle kingdom begins in Egypt.

    c.1814BC   First Assyrian Empire begins in the Middle East.

c.1900BC   The first Cretan palaces are built. Rise of Minoan† culture on Crete.

    c.1792-1750BC   Reign of Hammurabi, founder of the Babylonian Empire.

c.1700BC   The Cretan palaces are destroyed by earthquakes, then rebuilt.

c.1600BC   Rise of Mycenaean culture in Greece. The first shaft graves† are built.

    c.1600BC   Towns and cities develop in China.

    c.1567BC   New Kingdom begins in Egypt.

c.1600BC   Tholos† tombs are first used in Greece.

    c.1550BC   Aryans settle in northern India and establish the Hindu religion.

    c.1500BC   Writing in use in China.

c.1500-1450BC   Traditional date given for the eruption of Thera.

c.1450BC   The Cretan palaces are destroyed. The palace at Knossos is taken over by Mycenaeans and rebuilt. Expansion of Mycenaean power and wealth.

c.1400BC   Knossos burns down, and is not rebuilt.

c.1250BC   The main defences are built at Mycenae and other mainland sites. Date traditionally given as the start of the Trojan War.

c.1200BC   Mycenaean power declines and many of their cities are abandoned. Migration of Sea Peoples begins.

    c.1200BC   Jewish religion begins.

    c.1166BC   Death of Ramesses III, last great Egyptian Pharaoh.

    c.1150BC   Olmec civilization begins in Mexico.

The Dark Ages: c.1100-800BC

by 1100BC   The Mycenaean way of life has broken down.

    c.1100BC   Phoenicians spread throughout the Mediterranean, and develop alphabetic writing.

    c.1010-926BC   Kingdom of Israel.

    c.1000BC   Etruscans arrive in Italy.

    c.911BC   New Assyrian Empire begins.

c.900BC   The state of Sparta is founded.

    814BC   Phoenicians found city of Carthage on the North African coast.

The Archaic Period: c.800-500BC

Between 850-750BC   Homer† probably lived at this time.

c.800BC   Greek contact with the other peoples of the Mediterranean resumes. The Greeks adopt the Phoenician style of writing, using it for their own language.

    c.800BC   Aryans move southwards in India.

776BC   First Olympic Games held.

    753BC   Date traditionally given as the founding of the city of Rome.

c.750-650BC   Groups of people start to emigrate from mainland Greece. They found colonies around the Mediterranean.

c.740-720BC   The Spartans begin expanding their territory, and conquer the neighbouring state of Messenia.

    c.700BC   Scythians move into eastern Europe from Asia.

c.650BC   The first tyrants† seize power in Greek mainland states. First coins used in Lydia.

    c.650BC   Iron Age begins in China.

c.630-613BC   The Messenians revolt against the Spartans but are eventually crushed.

    627BC   Neo-Babylonian Empire begins.

621BC   Draco† is appointed *archon*† in Athens and introduces a strict set of laws.

c.594BC   Solon† is appointed *archon* in Athens and begins to reform the political system.

c.550BC   Tyrannies are established in the Greek colonies.

c.550BC   Cyrus II of Persia founds the Persian Empire.

c.546BC   Peisistratus† seizes power as tyrant of Athens.

c.530BC   Beginning of Persian Wars.

by 521BC   King Darius I has expanded Persian Empire from the Nile to the Indus

513BC   The Persians invade Europe.

c.510BC   Monarchy in Rome is replaced by a republic.

508BC   Cleisthenes† seizes power in Athens and introduces reforms which lead to democracy†.

500BC-499BC   The Greek colonies in Ionia revolt against Persian rule.

The Classical Age: c.500-336BC

494BC   The Persians suppress the Ionian revolt.

490BC   The Persians invade the Greek mainland, and are defeated at the Battle of Marathon.

486BC   Death of Siddhartha Gautama, founder of Buddhism.

480BC   Battles of Thermopylae and Salamis.

c.480BC   The Persians, the first surviving play by Aeschylus†.

479BC   Battle of Plataea. The Persians are repelled from Greece.

479BC   Death of the Chinese religious teacher Confucius.

478BC   Athens and other Greek states form the Delian League against the Persians.

460-457BC   The Long Walls† are built around Athens and Piraeus. The Acropolis† is rebuilt.

c.450BC   Start of the Celtic culture known as La Tène, named after the site in France where evidence of it was first found.

449BC   The Delian League makes peace with Persia.

445BC   30 Years' Peace declared between Athens and Sparta.

443-429BC   The Age of Pericles†, who is elected *strategos*† every year between these dates.

431-404BC   The Peloponnesian War, fought between Athens and Sparta.

430BC   Athens is hit by plague.

429BC   Death of Pericles.

421BC   50 Years' Peace negotiated by Nicias between Sparta and Athens.

413BC   Athens sends a fleet to Sicily to intervene in a dispute. The fleet is destroyed. War breaks out again between Athens and Sparta.

407BC   Athenian fleet defeated at Notium.

405BC   Athens defeated by Sparta at Battle of Aegospotami.

404BC   Spartan victory over Athens in the Peloponnesian War. The Long Walls are dismantled, the Delian League is dissolved, and Athens is forced to adopt an oligarchic† government, known as the Thirty Tyrants.

403BC   Democracy is reinstated in Athens

399BC   Wars between Sparta and Persia begin. Socrates† is condemned to death.

395-387BC   The Corinthian War. Alliance of Corinth, Athens, Argos and Thebes against Sparta.

394BC   The Persians defeat Sparta at the Battle of Cnidus.

394-391   The Long Walls are rebuilt at Athens.

387BC   Corinthian War ended by the King's Peace, negotiated by the Persians. The Ionian colonies pass to Persian control.

371BC   The Thebans defeat Sparta at the Battle of Leuctra.

362BC   Sparta and Athens defeat Thebes at the Battle of Mantinea.

359BC   Philip II† becomes king of Macedonia.

340BC   Greek states form the Hellenic League against Philip.

338BC   Philip defeats the Hellenic League at the Battle of Chaeronea, and becomes ruler of Greece.

337BC   All Greek states except Sparta form the Corinthian League, led by Philip. The league declares war on Persia.

336BC   Death of Philip. He is succeeded by his son, Alexander†, who becomes leader of the Corinthian League.

335BC   Alexander crushes Thebes.

334BC   Alexander attacks the Persians.

333BC   Alexander defeats the Persians at the Battle of Issus.

332BC   Alexander conquers Phoenicia, Samaria, Judaea, Gaza, and Egypt.

331BC   Sparta joins the Corinthian League. Alexander defeats the Persias at the Battle of Gaugamela.

327BC   Alexander conquers Persia, and advances into India.

323BC   Alexander dies in Babylon.

The Hellenistic Period: c. 323-30BC

323-322BC   The Lamian Wars. The Greek states fight to win independence from the Macedonians, but are defeated.

323-281BC   Wars of the Diadochi† (Alexander's successors).

301BC   Battle of Ipsus. Four rival diadochi kingdoms are set up.

281BC   The Battle of Corupedium ends the Wars of the Diadochi. Three diadochi kingdoms are established: Macedonia (ruled by Antigonas†); Asia Minor (ruled by Seleucus†) and Egypt (ruled by Ptolemy†).

275BC   King Pyrrhus of Epirus is defeated by the Romans in Italy.

266-262BC   The Chremonides War. The Athenians rise against the Antigonids but are suppressed.

221-206BC   Ch'in dynasty in China.

221-179BC   Reign of Philip V of Macedonia.

215BC   Philip V forms an alliance with Hannibal of Carthage, provoking Roman reprisals.

215-205BC   First Macedonian War between Macedonians and Romans.

214BC   Great Wall built in China.

202BC   Philip V forms an alliance with the Seleucid Empire, but Rome intervenes.

202-197BC   Second Macedonian War. Philip V is defeated by the Romans and gives up control of Greece.

179-168BC   Reign of last Macedonian king, Perseus.

171-168BC   Third Macedonian War. The Romans defeat Perseus at the Battle of Pydna. They abolish the Macedonian monarch and set up four Roman republics.

147-146BC   The Achaean War. The Romans destroy Corinth after a Macedonian Revolt, and impose direct Roman rule on Greece and Macedonia.

APPENDIX
Glossary

Many of the Ancient Greek words used in this section are listed and explained in the glossary below. The list also contains some English words that may be unfamiliar. Usually the term given in bold type is the singular. Where the plural is often used, it is given in brackets after the main word.

Acropolis.   A fortified city, built on an area of high ground. The word means "high city" in Greek. In Mycenaean times, much of the city was on the acropolis, but later the acropolis was part of a larger city and was often used as a religious sanctuary.

Agora.   An open space, in the middle of a Greek city, used for markets and as a meeting place. It was often surrounded by shops and public buildings.

Amphora (amphorae).   A large pot with two handles, used to transport and store wine and other liquids.

Andron.   A dining room in a private house, used only by the men of the family.

Archon.   An Athenian official. The *archons* were very powerful during the Archaic Period, but when democracy was introduced they became less important and retained mainly ceremonial duties.

Aristocrat.   A member of a rich, land owning family. The name comes from the Greek word *aristoi*, meaning the best people.

Attica.   Name of the state made up of Athens and the surrounding countryside.

Barbarian.   Any foreigner who did not speak Greek. The name came from the strange "bar-bar-bar" noise which the Greeks thought foreigners made when they spoke. It came to mean any uncivilized people.

Black figure ware.   A style of pottery decorated with black figures on a red background.

Bronze Age.   The period from c.3000-1100BC during which bronze was the most important metal, used for making tools and weapons.

Caryatid.   A column carved in the shape of a young woman.

Cella.   The main room of a temple, in which the statue of a god or goddess stood.

Chiton.   A woman's dress. It was made from a single piece of cloth, fastened at the shoulders.

Chorus.   A group of men who took part in plays at the theatre. They all spoke together, often commenting on the action. Sometimes they also sang and danced.

Citizen.   A free man who had the right to participate in the government of his city state.

Corinthian column.   A style of column whose top is decorated with carved acanthus leaves.

Cuirass.   A piece of armour used by hoplite soldiers. It consisted of a breastplate and a backplate joined together by straps.

Cult statue.   A statue of the god or goddess which stood in the main room of a temple. People addressed their prayers to the statue.

Democracy.   A political system in which all citizens had a say in the government of their state. The word comes from the Greek for "rule by the people".

Diadochi.   The name given to the generals who took over the various parts of Alexander the Great's empire after his death. The word means "successors".

Doric column.   A plain column with an undecorated top. The *Doric Order* was a style of architecture which used this sort of column.

Electrum.   A natural mixture of gold and silver, which was used to make the first coins.

Ephebe.   A young Athenian man engaged in two years' compulsory military training.

Faience.   Coloured, glazed, earthenware used in Minoan Crete to make decorative objects.

Fresco.   A wall painting made by applying paint to wet plaster.

Greave.   A piece of armour used by hoplite soldiers. It protected the leg from knee to ankle.

Gymnasium (gymnasia).   A sports centre where people could practise athletics. In later years a gymnasium was often a centre of intellectual life too, and might be equipped with a lecture hall and a library.

Gynaeceum.   The women's rooms in a private house.

Hellene.   The word which the Greeks used to refer to the whole Greek race. It came from the name of a legendary hero, Hellen, who was said to be the father of the Greek people.

Hellenistic age.   This term is used to describe the period after the death of Alexander the Great, when Greek language and culture dominated the countries of his former empire.

Herm.   A statue of the god Hermes, consisting of a head on a pillar. It usually stood outside the front door of a house and was thought to protect the home.

Hetaira (hetairai).   A woman who was specially educated to make conversation, play musical instruments and sing in order to entertain men. *Hetairai* often had love affairs with their clients.

Himation.   A type of cloak or scarf, worn by both men and women.

Hoplite.   A heavily armed foot soldier who fought in the armies of the Greek city states.

Ionic column.   A tall, slender column, whose top was decorated with a swirl called a volute. The *Ionic Order* was a style of architecture which used this sort of column.

Krater.   A large vase in which wine was mixed with water.

Labrys.   A double headed axe, which was an important sacred symbol in Minoan religion.

Libation.   An offering of liquid (wine, milk or blood). It was usually poured over an altar or onto the earth during a religious ceremony.

Linear A. An early form of writing used by the Minoans.

Linear B. An adapted form of Linear A writing, used by the Mycenaeans.

Long Walls. The walls which linked the city of Athens to its port at Piraeus from 460 to 404BC.

Lyre. A stringed musical instrument, made from a tortoise shell and the horns of an ox. Later lyres were made of carved wood.

Megaron. A large hall in a Mycenaean palace, which usually contained four pillars and a hearth. The king conducted state business in the *megaron*.

Metic. A foreign resident living in Athens.

Minoan. The name that the archaeologist Arthur Evans gave to the civilization he discovered on Crete. The term came from the legendary Cretan king, Minos.

Museum. A temple to the Muses (see page 150). The most famous one was built in Alexandria in Egypt during the Hellenistic age. It was a great centre of learning where many scientists and inventors worked.

Mystery Cult. A religion with rituals that were kept very secret. Only people who had been intitiated into the group of worshippers could attend its ceremonies.

Oligarchy. A political system in which a small group of people govern.

Omen. A sign, said to be from the gods, which warned of good or evil to come. Specially trained priests took omens from marks on the livers of sacrificed animals, or from the flight patterns of birds.

Oracle. The word can mean three things: a sacred place where people went to consult a god or goddess; the priest or priestess who spoke on behalf of the deity; or the message from the deity. The most famous oracle was at the Temple of Apollo in Delphi, where a priestess called the Pythia was thought to be able to communicate with the gods.

Ostracism. A special vote held in the Athenian ¨ssembly to banish unpopular politicians. It is so called because the voters scratched the names of people they wanted to expel onto *ostraka*, pieces of broken pottery.

Paidagogos. A special slave who escorted a boy to and from school and supervised him in class.

Patron deity. A god or goddess who was thought to protect a particular place, person or group of people. For example, Athene was the patron goddess of Athens and Hephaestos was the patron god of metal workers.

Peltast. A lightly armed foot soldier, first used by the Thracians and later by the Greek armies.

Peristyle. A row of columns surrounding the outside of a temple.

Phalanx. The formation in which hoplite soldiers fought. It consisted of a block of soldiers, usually eight ranks deep.

Philosopher. The word comes from the Greek for "lover of knowledge". The first philosophers were scholars who studied all aspects of the world around them. Later, however, philosophy became a more specific subject. Philosophers began trying to understand the purpose of the universe and the nature of human life and behaviour.

Pithos (pithoi). A large, earthenware storage jar used in Minoan Crete.

Polis. An independent Greek state, consisting of a city and the surrounding countryside.

Pythia. The priestess who spoke on behalf of the god Apollo at the oracle of Delphi.

Red figure ware. A style of pottery decorated with red figures on a black background.

Relief. A sculpture carved on a flat slab of stone. The stone was carved away so that the picture stood out against a flat background.

Rhapsode. A man who made his living by reciting poetry at religious festivals or private parties.

Rhyton. A special pot, in the shape of a horn or an animal's head, with a hole pierced in the lower end to act as a spout. It was often used in religious ceremonies to make a libation.

Sarcophagus. A stone coffin.

Shaft grave. An early form of Mycenaean tomb, in which the body was buried at the bottom of a deep shaft.

Soothsayer. Someone who was thought to be able to foresee the future.

Stele (stelae). A stone slab used to mark a grave.

Stoa. A long, roofed passageway with columns on one which provided shelter from the sun, wind and rain. The *stoa* was found in town centres, where it often formed the side of an *agora* and sometimes contained shops or offices. Some religious sanctuaries also had a *stoa*.

Strategos (strategoi). An Athenian army commander. There were ten *strategoi*, who were elected annually. Under the democratic system, the *strategoi* also had the power to implement the policies which were decided by the Council and the Assembly.

Terracotta. A mixture of unfired clay, sand, and particles of clay that has already been baked. It was used to make tiles, and for small statues, which are sometimes called terracottas.

Tholos. A type of Mycenaean grave, consisting of a beehive-shaped room entered through a long corridor. Later the name was also given to circular buildings with conical roofs. These often had pillars round the outside.

Trireme. A warship with three rows of oars.

Tyrant. A Greek word for "ruler". A tyrant was someone who governed with absolute power. In the Archaic Period many Greek states were governed by tyrants. Later the word came to mean any cruel, oppressive ruler.

The Legacy of Greece

The influence of the Ancient Greeks survives throughout the modern world. Many aspects of western civilization are based on ideas that were first developed by them. The Greek legacy comes to us in many forms – language, art, architecture, literature, philosophy and science – which are discussed in more detail in the sections below. The Greeks invented the concepts of democracy, coinage, organized sport, theatre, narrative and personal poetry, scientific theory and the writing of history. They also recorded and passed on to us the knowledge and discoveries of other early civilizations, such as the Egyptians and the Babylonians, in fields like astronomy and metallurgy. The culture of the Greeks and the Romans (who adopted many Greek ideas) is often referred to as classical civilization.

Language

In the early days the people of the Greek city states spoke a number of different dialects, but by about 250BC a common Greek language was in use. This was the language used to write down the New Testament of the Bible. In its written form, Ancient Greek is much the same language as Modern Greek, although the spoken languages have less in common.

Over the years thousands of words derived from Greek have entered other languages. For example, *physics, hippopotamus, hyacinth, diagnosis, theatre, catastrophe, idea, mechanics* and *butter* are all Greek words that have passed into English. It is estimated that one word in eight used in European languages today is derived from Greek.

It is common practice for scientists everywhere to use Greek words, or parts of Greek words, when naming new inventions and discoveries. For example, *telephone, helicopter, astronaut, cinema, symphony, hypnotism* and *electronics* all have their roots in Greek words.

Modern philosophers, psychologists and literary critics use terms which are Greek or have Greek roots (including the words *philosophy, psyche* and *critic*). This reflects the fact that it was the Greeks who first began to explain and construct theories about these aspects of life.

Art and architecture

Greek sculpture and architecture had a profound effect on the Romans, who borrowed and adapted it for themselves. They collected Greek statues and made large numbers of copies. Many 'Greek' works of art are only known to us from these Roman copies. The only surviving examples of Greek painting come from painted pottery, but themes from Greek history and mythology have provided inspiration for artists through the ages.

Classical art and architecture has been imitated and adapted throughout most periods of history, and its influence is still evident today. However, it was particularly important during the period known as the Renaissance. This is the name given to a period of renewed interest in the art and learning of Greece and Rome which began in Italy and reached its height in Europe in the 15th and 16th centuries. It sparked off a series of changes which mark the end of the middle ages and the beginning of modern times. In painting, it stimulated an interest in an accurate portrayal of the human body and the use of perspective, demonstrated by such artists as Masaccio and Leonardo da Vinci. Themes from Greek and Roman mythology were depicted in the work of artists such as Botticelli, and architects such as Alberti, Brunelleschi and Vasari built churches and palaces based on classical designs.

A later revival of classical art and architecture, known as neo-classicism, took place in the 18th and 19th centuries. During this period many civic buildings and monuments in different parts of the world (for example, the White House in Washington and the British Museum in London) were based on Greek designs.

Poetry

The first great epic poems in western literature were the *Iliad* and the *Odyssey* by the Greek poet Homer†. Greek poetry was written according to strict rules of rhyme and metre. Much of western poetry is based on poetic rhythms (such as iambic pentameter) and verse forms (such as the ode) which were originally devised by the Greeks. For example, Shakespeare wrote most of his plays in a metre knowns as blank verse, a non-rhyming iambic pentameter. Many poets have been influenced by the subject matter as well as the form of Greek poetry, like the 19th century poet John Keats whose poems include *Ode to Psyche* and *Ode on a Grecian Urn*.

Theatre

The origins of the theatre in the western world date back to Ancient Greece. The first permanent theatres were built there and the idea of the play itself developed from songs and dances performed at an annual festival in honour of the god Dionysus (see page 152). Greek playwrights included Sophocles†, Euripides† and Aristophanes†. The influence of Greek theatre and Greek subjects can be seen in the works of later European playwrights including Anouilh, Beckett, Goethe, Ibsen, Racine, Shaw and Shakespeare.

The novel

The Greek writer Longus is seen by many as the first true novelist. Rather than simply telling a story, as earlier writers had done, he gave detailed descriptions of the surroundings in which the action took place. He also explained the feelings of his characters, and why they acted as they did.

History

Although the Egyptians and other early civilizations recorded events for the benefit of future generations, their purpose was to enhance the reputation of the reigning monarch, rather than to tell the truth. There was a tendency to gloss over defeats and simply to list the successes. The Greek writer Herodotus† was one of the first to try to record all the known facts as accurately as possible, to analyze them, and to see them as a sequence of linked events. For this reason he is often known as "the father of history". Other Greek historians include Thucydides†, Xenophon† and Polybius.

Biography

One of the earliest biographers was the Greek writer Plutarch. He wrote about the lives of about 50 people and created a series called *Bioi paralleloi*, meaning "parallel lives". Each book in the series related the life history of two eminent people, one Roman and one Greek, and went on to discuss the similarities between the two. This approach was recently reemployed by Alan Bullock who published a book called *Parallel Lives*, comparing the careers of Hitler and Stalin.

Politics

The Greeks invented the system of government known as democracy, which forms the basis for the political systems of many countries today. The name comes from the Greek words *demos*, meaning "people", and *kratos*, meaning "rule". The word democracy is used today to mean a system in which everybody has a vote. In Ancient Greece, however, only male citizens had this right. All other social groups – women, slaves and foreign residents – were excluded.

Philosophy and religion

The stories the Greeks told about their gods (which we call myths) were intended to explain natural phenomena they could not otherwise understand, such as the weather and seasons. However, from about the 6th century BC, some people began to look for more practical explanations and to question the world around them. The Greeks called these people philosophers, which means "lovers of wisdom".

Philosophy has come to mean the study of human life and the nature of the Universe. However to the Greeks it meant the study of all knowledge and so included biology, mathematics, astronomy and geography. Many of the most fundamental ideas in western philosophy are based on the teachings of early Greek philosophers such as Aristotle†, Plato† and Socrates (see page 175).

To the Ancient Greeks the rights of the individual and the spirit of enquiry were very important, and people were not forced to follow any specific system of beliefs. This led many people to challenge the official religion and to look to philosophers, such as Diogenes, Epicurus and Xenon (see page 175), for guidance on how to conduct their lives.

Science

Many of the foundations of modern science were based on the discoveries of Greek philosophers such as Archimedes, Pythagoras and Aristarchus (see page 174). However in many ways the greatest contribution to science was made by Aristotle. He was interested in all fields of learning and worked according to a strict set of rules. He saw the importance of collecting information, analyzing it and classifying the results, disciplines now seen as fundamental to scientific endeavour.

In some areas of science, such as astronomy, it was impossible for Aristotle to test his theories as the necessary equipment had not yet been invented. In biology, however, he was able to use his hands and eyes and succeeded in classifying over 500 animals with considerable attention to detail. One of his observations was that "those creatures have survived which have by chance developed a suitable form; the others have become extinct". This appears to foreshadow the ideas of the 19th century British naturalist Charles Darwin, whose theory of the survival of the fittest (described in *The Origin of the Species*, his book on evolution) came over 2000 years later.

191

Medicine

Modern medicine owes a great deal to the high standards of professional conduct first set by doctors in Ancient Greece. The scientific approach to medicine, traditionally attributed to Hippocrates of Kos†, spread throughout the Mediterranean and provided the foundations of modern medical practice. The Hippocratic Oath, an oath taken by modern doctors to follow a strict code of medical ethics, is named after him.

Greek doctors kept written records concerning patients and their illnesses. Many of these case histories still exist, and it is often possible to recognize the illnesses they describe. The Greeks realized the importance of exercise, diet and cleanliness, although they knew nothing of germs and bacteria, and were not skilled at curing diseases. However, the experience gained by army doctors, and by trainers in gymnasiums, led to the successful treatment of fractures, dislocations and wounds. The Greeks were against the practice of cutting up human corpses and so they knew very little of the workings of the body. However Greek doctors acquired a knowledge of anatomy from the Egyptians, who had been embalming their dead for centuries. Herophilus, a Greek doctor working in the Egyptian city of Alexandria, wrote an account of the brain, liver, eye and sexual organs, and a description of the beating of the pulse (an idea first put forward by the Egyptians).

Eristratus, another Greek doctor in Alexandria, studied the brain, the nerves and various parts of the heart. His writings suggest that he was very close to discovering the circulation of the blood. (It was another 2000 years before circulation was finally discovered by the 17th century English scientist William Harvey.)

Travel and trade

Greek ships carried traders all over the Mediterranean, and colonists established themselves in the Greek islands and on the coast of Asia Minor. The use of coins (probably invented in the 7th century BC in Lydia, a kingdom in Asia Minor) spread rapidly through Greek-speaking areas. When Alexander the Great† and his successors marched through the Middle East and founded hundreds of new cities, they opened up new trade routes and opportunities.

Greek explorers ventured out of the Mediterranean and into the Atlantic Ocean, sailing north and south. The discovery of the monsoon winds by Eudoxus of Cyzicus made it possible, during certain months of the year, to sail in their path from the Red Sea straight across the Indian Ocean to India. This led to the mass importation of gold, ivory, sugar, ebony, cotton and spices into the Mediterranean. At the same time a land route was charted through Afghanistan and Iran. This opened up the silk trade from China and became known as the Silk Road.

The spread of Greek ideas

Greek language and culture spread over a vast area as a result of the conquests of Alexander the Great – from the Crimea in the north to Ethiopia in the south and to India in the east. This influence survived long after the break-up of his empire.

Although Greek independence came to an end with the imposition of direct Roman rule in 146BC, Greek civilization had an enormous impact on the Romans and, in turn, on the countries they conquered. In the 1st century BC the Roman poet Horace wrote: *Graecia capta ferum victorem cepit.* Translated roughly as "Greece was captured and took her fierce conqueror [Rome] captive", it suggests how deeply the Romans felt they were affected by the Greeks and their culture.

After the fall of Rome in the 5th century AD, Greek language and tradition was preserved in the eastern part of the Roman empire, which became known as the Byzantine empire. Ancient Greek and Roman manuscripts were collected and copied there by monks. In the 13th century, as the Byzantine empire began to collapse, there was a steady stream of monks to the West, bringing with them ancient books and manuscripts. This was one of the factors which helped stimulate the revival of classical art and learning which began the Renaissance (see page 190).

In the Middle East the Arabs inherited the Greek libraries in places like Alexandria. Arab scholars were able to develop Greek ideas on subjects such as mathematics and botany. Their discoveries in turn were brought back to Europe by Venetian merchants who traded with the Arab world.

During the 18th century there was an intellectual movement in Europe, known as the Enlightenment. It was characterized by a thirst for knowledge in all areas and it prompted, among other things, an interest in archaeology. Large numbers of Greek and Roman sites were excavated, and treasures were shipped back to museums in European capitals. The Grand Tour, a tour of Europe which included a visit to the classical ruins of Greece and Italy, which was seen as an important part of a young man's education.

THE ROMANS

Anthony Marks

Graham Tingay

Illustrated by **Ian Jackson**
and **Gerald Wood**

Designed by **Radhi Parekh, Robert Walster**
and **Iain Ashman**

History consultant: **Anne Millard**

Edited by **Jane Chisholm**

Map illustrations by **Robert Walster**

Further illustrations by **Peter Dennis, Richard Draper, James Field** and **Nigel Wright**

With thanks to **Lynn Bresler**

Contents

About this section of the book

The city of Rome was founded in about 753BC. By 100BC the Romans had a huge empire centred round the Mediterranean Sea. It lasted for centuries, and its influence has continued to the present day. This section of the book describes both the rise and decline of Rome as a world power and the way people lived from day to day.

Dates

Many dates in this section are from the period before the birth of Christ. They are shown by the letters BC which stand for 'Before Christ'. (Dates in this period are counted backwards from Christ's birth; for example, the period from 100BC to 199BC is called the second century BC.)
Dates in the period after Christ's birth are indicated by the letters AD, which stand for *Anno Domini* ('Year of our Lord'). To avoid confusion AD and BC have been used throughout the book.

Some dates begin with the abbreviation 'c.'. This stands for *circa*, the Latin for 'about', and is used when historians are unsure exactly when an event took place.

Periods of Roman history

Experts divide Roman history into two main periods. The first is known as the republic, which probably began in 510 or 509BC. It is followed by the Empire, which began in 27BC when the first Roman emperor took power. Throughout this section of the book the word Empire has been given a capital letter only when it is used to mean 'the period of rule by emperors' rather than simply 'Roman territory'.

How we know about the Romans

Although Roman civilization began more than two thousand years ago, we have plenty of information about how the Romans lived. Much of it comes from the sources listed below, and has been used as the basis of this section of the book.

Many Roman buildings survive almost intact. They tell us about building technology and styles of architecture. Ruined towns, roads and aqueducts provide information about civil engineering and planning. Buildings and ruins often contain sculptures, wall-paintings and mosaics†, many of which include scenes of daily life.

The Pantheon in Rome remains almost as the Romans built it.

Shoes like this were found near the River Thames in London.

Buildings contain objects that the Romans used, including tools, utensils, ornaments and toys. Some are well preserved, especially at sites where there were volcanic eruptions, because ash and mud have protected them from decay.

Fragments of pottery help us to determine the dates of Roman remains, as different styles of pot are easy to identify and date. If, for example, experts can recognize and date pieces of pottery at the bottom of a well, they can give a rough date to other objects found in the same place.

Archaeologists store and record each item they find.

Many Roman coins are easy to date, as they depict events that are mentioned in Roman books. If found at archaeological sites, they can indicate when buildings were erected or were in use. In addition, coins found in such places as India and Scandinavia suggest that Roman traders travelled far beyond the limits of Roman territory.

This coin commemorates the Roman occupation of Egypt.

Much of our information about the Romans comes from their own writings. Very few Roman books or manuscripts themselves have survived to modern times, but we have copies of them which were made mostly by monks in the middle ages and by later scholars. They include works by many Roman writers about history, politics and philosophy, as well as plays, poems and letters. These give us insight into the lives and characters of Roman people.

Other written evidence survives in the form of stone inscriptions. Details of laws, legal contracts, financial transactions and military records were carved into the walls of public buildings all over the Roman world. In addition, graves and tombs give us details, both written and pictorial, of the lives and deaths of their occupants.

This carving on a stone tomb shows a Roman shipbuilder at work.

Key dates

On some pages of this section there are charts that summarize the events of the particular period. There is also a large chart on pages 280-281 that lists all the events in this section.

Unfamiliar words

Words are written in *italic* type to indicate that they are Latin (the language of the Romans). Words followed by a dagger symbol, such as citizen†, are explained in the glossary that begins on page 273. If a person's name is followed by this symbol, you can read more about them in the 'Who's who' on pages 276-279.

Places

There are small maps on many pages to show where certain events took place. Some of these are based on a projection that may be unfamiliar. This has been used to enable large areas of Europe to be shown in a compact space.

Reference

At the back of this section there is an appendix. It contains a glossary, biographies of important Romans, a detailed date chart and other information. It is followed by an index.

The founding of Rome

The city of Rome was founded in the 8th century BC, in the country now called Italy. The history of the area has been affected by its geography. Most of Italy is rough, hilly country which rises to a central mountain range called the Apennines.

Some of the most fertile agricultural land is near the west coast, on three small plains around the rivers Arno, Volturno and Tiber. Rome was established on the plain of Latium, around the River Tiber.

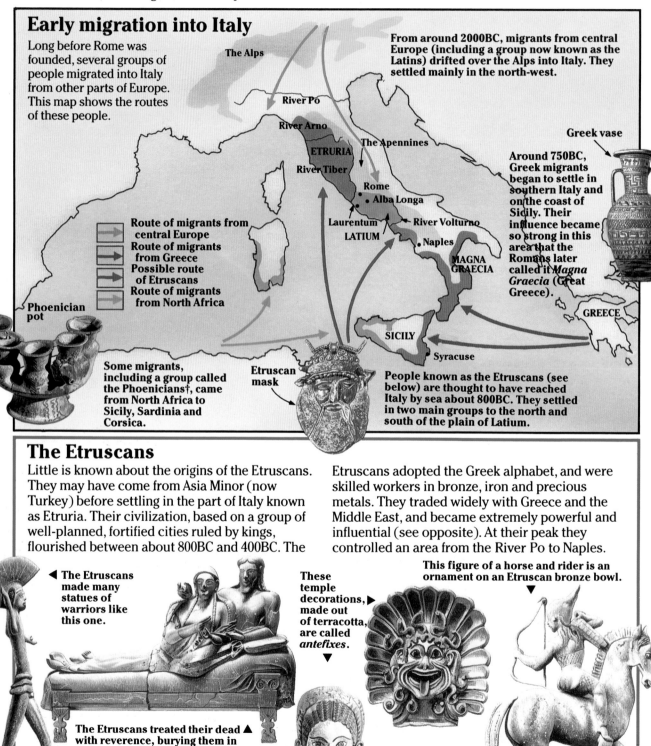

Early migration into Italy

Long before Rome was founded, several groups of people migrated into Italy from other parts of Europe. This map shows the routes of these people.

The Alps

River Po

River Arno

ETRURIA

River Tiber

The Apennines

Rome

Alba Longa

Laurentum

LATIUM

River Volturno

Naples

MAGNA GRAECIA

SICILY

Syracuse

GREECE

Route of migrants from central Europe
Route of migrants from Greece
Possible route of Etruscans
Route of migrants from North Africa

From around 2000BC, migrants from central Europe (including a group now known as the Latins) drifted over the Alps into Italy. They settled mainly in the north-west.

Greek vase

Around 750BC, Greek migrants began to settle in southern Italy and on the coast of Sicily. Their influence became so strong in this area that the Romans later called it *Magna Graecia* (Great Greece).

Phoenician pot

Some migrants, including a group called the Phoenicians† came from North Africa to Sicily, Sardinia and Corsica.

Etruscan mask

People known as the Etruscans (see below) are thought to have reached Italy by sea about 800BC. They settled in two main groups to the north and south of the plain of Latium.

The Etruscans

Little is known about the origins of the Etruscans. They may have come from Asia Minor (now Turkey) before settling in the part of Italy known as Etruria. Their civilization, based on a group of well-planned, fortified cities ruled by kings, flourished between about 800BC and 400BC. The Etruscans adopted the Greek alphabet, and were skilled workers in bronze, iron and precious metals. They traded widely with Greece and the Middle East, and became extremely powerful and influential (see opposite). At their peak they controlled an area from the River Po to Naples.

◄ The Etruscans made many statues of warriors like this one.

These temple decorations, ► made out of terracotta, are called *antefixes*. ▼

This figure of a horse and rider is an ornament on an Etruscan bronze bowl. ▼

The Etruscans treated their dead ▲ with reverence, burying them in elaborate coffins made of terracotta†.

The first settlements

Rome grew from a cluster of villages founded by Latin immigrants about 25km (6 miles) inland on the River Tiber. There was an island there, and a ford where the river could be crossed. This was the furthest point that could be reached by ship before the water became too shallow.

The villages were built on a group of seven hills; one of the first to be occupied was known as the Palatine Hill. They were in a good position for trade, because they were on the most important routes for travelling merchants. As they grew richer, the settlements merged into one town.

An early Roman settlement

Little is known about Rome's early history, so we must rely mainly on legend. The date traditionally given for the founding of the city is 753BC. The actual date is uncertain, but it is likely that the villages merged around this time. According to one legend, the Greeks laid siege to the city of Troy (near the coast of modern Turkey) and killed nearly all the occupants. One Trojan prince, Aeneas, escaped by sea and sailed to Italy.

Aeneas sailing from Troy

Aeneas landed at Laurentum on the west coast of Italy. He formed an alliance with Latinus, the king of the Latins, and married his daughter Lavinia. Aeneas's son Ascanius founded a city called Alba Longa (see map opposite). He was the first of a long line of kings who ruled for about 400 years. When the last king was overthrown, his twin grandsons Romulus and Remus were left to die by the River Tiber. A wolf found them and looked after them.

This statue shows the twins being suckled by the wolf.

A new city

When the twins grew up they decided to set up a new city on the spot where they had been left to drown. They held a sacred ceremony to mark the boundary with a plough, but Remus jumped over the furrow in mockery. Romulus was enraged and killed his brother, gave his own name to the city and became its first ruler. Romulus was followed by six kings: Numa Pompilius, Tullus Hostilius, Ancus Martius, Tarquinius Priscus, Servius Tullius, and Tarquinius Superbus. Parts of a wall around Rome, known as the Servian Wall (see map) and once thought to have been built by Servius Tullius, still remain.

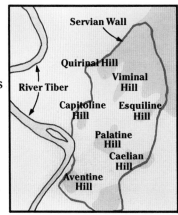

The influence of the Etruscans

For much of this early period Rome was ruled by the Etrucscans, who were more advanced than the Latins. Under their influence Rome became a large city that dominated the Tiber valley. But gradually the Etruscans lost their hold on Latium. Finally the last Etruscan king was expelled from Rome. The date traditionally given for this is 510 or 509BC. After this Rome became an independent republic (for details of how the state was governed, see pages 202-203), but the Romans inherited many things from their Etruscan rulers.

The Etruscans ▲ built Rome's first drainage system.

Romans wore a robe called the *toga* (see page 234). It was based on an Etruscan robe like the one shown on this statue. ▶

Etruscan soldiers had an official symbol called the *fasces* – an axe tied to a bundle of sticks. It was later adopted ▶ by the Romans.

Key dates

From c.2000BC Immigrants enter Italy from the North.

c.800BC Etruscans arrive in Italy by sea.

753BC Date traditionally given for the founding of Rome.

c.750BC Greek migrants settle on the southern coasts of Sicily and Italy.

510BC or 509BC Last king expelled from Rome; republic founded.

c.400BC Decline of Etruscans.

The early republic

Other cities in Latium formed an alliance and challenged the new republic† of Rome. The Romans were defeated at Lake Regillus in 496BC, and forced to join the alliance. Over the next century Rome fought many wars against mountain tribes who attacked Roman territory.

At this time, most Romans were poor farmers who had to fight wars simply to defend their land. However, by 400BC, after years of tough fighting and clever political tactics, Roman territory had doubled in size and Rome had become the dominant partner in the Latin alliance.

Fierce mountain tribes called the Volsci, Aequi and Sabini attacked Roman farms.

The Gauls attack Rome

In 387BC the Gauls, people from northern Europe, defeated the Roman army at the River Allia and invaded Rome. According to the historian Livy†, most of the population had fled in terror. Apart from some troops only the Roman senators† remained, sitting calmly in the courtyards of their houses. The Gauls stared in amazement, but when one of them touched a senator's beard, the senator struck him with his ivory staff.

A massacre followed. The Gauls murdered the senators and then began to destroy Rome. Only the Capitoline Hill survived. According to legend the Gauls attacked it at night, but disturbed some geese that were kept at a temple. The geese warned the Romans of the Gauls' approach. Finally the invaders were bribed with gold to leave the ruined city. The other Latin cities were delighted to see Rome overthrown.

The Gauls attacked Capitoline Hill by night.

Expansion in Italy

Slowly the Romans recovered from this disaster. In about 380BC they rebuilt much of Rome, and constructed a strong wall around all its seven hills. By improving their army (see page 206), they began to regain lost territory. In 338BC, with the help of the Samnites, a tribe from central Italy, the Romans defeated an alliance of Latin cities. This made them the most powerful people in Latium. This map shows the position of the tribes in Italy around 338BC.

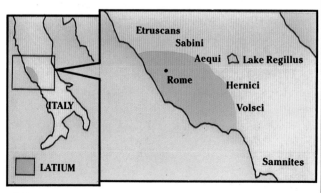

The wars with the Samnites

In 326BC Naples, a city in southern Italy, asked Rome for help against the Samnites. The Samnites objected to Rome's growing influence in the area, and a series of wars broke out. These wars lasted 40 years until the Samnites were defeated, along with their allies the Gauls and Etruscans. During this period, Rome also won important victories against the Aequi and Hernici tribes. By fighting hard and making clever alliances, Rome began to dominate northern and central Italy.

Samnite soldiers

The Pyrrhic wars

In 282BC Thurii, a Greek town in southern Italy, asked Rome to send a force of soldiers to protect them from the Lucanians, allies of the Samnites. Rome did so, and soon other cities had also put themselves under Roman protection. The nearby Greek city of Tarentum resented this and quarrelled with a Roman delegation. Tarentum was a commercial city, unable to match Rome's army, but it had provoked a situation from which it could not retreat. So in 280BC it hired the army of King Pyrrhus of Epirus in northern Greece.

Pyrrhus advanced on the Romans with 25,000 soldiers and 20 elephants.

Statue of Pyrrhus

Pyrrhus defeated the Romans in 280BC and 279BC, but vast numbers of his own soldiers were killed. He said 'If we win one more victory against the Romans we shall be totally ruined.' This is why the phrase 'Pyrrhic victory' is sometimes used when a winner's losses are greater than his gains. Pyrrhus withdrew to Sicily, then returned to Italy in 276BC. He was decisively defeated the following year, and in 272BC Tarentum surrendered. By 264BC Rome dominated the whole of Italy and was recognized as a major power in the Mediterranean.

This plate shows a war elephant from Pyrrhus's army.

Colonization in Italy

The Romans succeeded in dominating Italy by combining military strength and political astuteness. When they conquered an area they offered it an alliance, and drew up a treaty that defined the status of the new ally. Some places, like Tusculum, had full Roman citizenship. Others, such as Spoletium, were given 'Latin rights', which included some of the advantages of citizenship†. Other areas kept domestic independence, but Rome dictated their foreign policies. All allied states had to provide troops for the Roman army.

Rome also formed colonies of Romans or Latins in strategic places throughout Italy. By building roads and improving communications the Romans united the various Italian tribes. Gradually the Latin language and the Roman way of life spread, and linguistic and cultural differences between different areas were reduced.

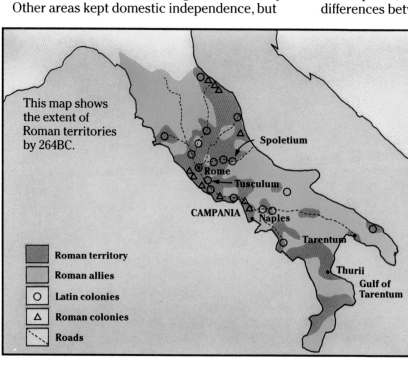

This map shows the extent of Roman territories by 264BC.

Spoletium

Rome

Tusculum

CAMPANIA

Naples

Tarentum

Thurii

Gulf of Tarentum

■ Roman territory
■ Roman allies
○ Latin colonies
△ Roman colonies
‹‹‹ Roads

Key dates

510-509BC Founding of republic.

496BC Romans forced to join Latin alliance after Battle of Lake Regillus.

By 400BC Rome has emerged as the dominant partner in the Latin alliance.

387BC Gauls attack Rome.

338BC Romans and Samnites defeat other Latin cities.

326BC War breaks out between Romans and Samnites.

286BC Rome defeats Samnites, Gauls and Etruscans, and takes control of northern and central Italy.

280BC Beginning of Pyrrhic wars.

275BC Pyrrhus's army defeated at the Battle of Beneventum.

272BC Tarentum surrenders.

By 264BC Rome dominates the whole of Italy.

The expansion of Rome

While Rome was becoming powerful in Italy, the western Mediterranean was under the control of the Carthaginians. Carthage, a city on the North African coast, was founded about 814BC by the Phoenicians, a people originally from the Middle East. Carthage was the centre of a vast commercial empire. While their trading interests did not conflict, Rome and Carthage left each other in peace. But in 264BC, a series of wars began between them. These are known as the Punic wars, after the Latin word for Phoenician. This map shows western Europe at the start of the Punic wars.

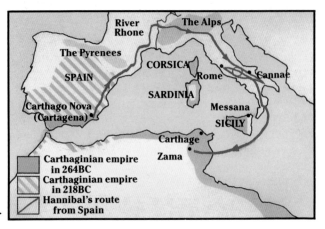

The first Punic war, 264-241BC

In 264BC Carthage occupied Messana in northeast Sicily. The Greek cities in south Italy, under Roman protection, saw this as a threat. The Romans sent an army to Sicily and war broke out. It took the Romans 20

The Romans invented a spiked drawbridge called the *corvus*. It was dropped onto the enemy's ship, enabling Roman soldiers to charge aboard.

years to expel the Carthaginians from Sicily. To do so they first had to find ways of overcoming Carthage's superior naval skills.

The Romans had no experience of sea warfare, but they twice built huge fleets (see page 212) and won victories, then lost all their ships in violent storms. The Carthaginians were eventually defeated by a third fleet in 241BC. Under the terms of the peace, Rome acquired Sicily (its first overseas territory). In addition, over the next ten years, Carthage had to pay the Romans a huge sum of money (known as an indemnity) as compensation for the cost of the war.

The Romans took Sardinia from Carthage in 238BC, and later seized Corsica too. They probably took this aggressive action to deprive Carthage of its island bases in the Mediterranean.

The second Punic war, 218-201BC

In search of a new empire, the Carthaginians invaded and conquered Spain between 237BC and 219BC. Hannibal, the Carthaginian general in Spain and a lifelong enemy of Rome, provoked the second Punic war. He launched a surprise attack on the Romans by marching over the Pyrenees in 218BC with 35,000 men and 37 elephants. He ferried the elephants over the River Rhone on rafts, then forced his way into Italy over the Alps.

The Romans were completely overwhelmed. Hannibal was a great general, and his troops won battle after battle. At Cannae in 216BC they destroyed an entire Roman army. Hannibal fought in Italy for 16 years and suffered no major defeats. However, he never conquered Rome itself, and the Romans remained defiant. After Cannae they waited until the next generation became old enough to form a new army.

Unable to defeat Hannibal in Italy, the Romans invaded and conquered Spain, then attacked

Crossing the Alps in winter, Hannibal lost nearly 10,000 men and all but one of the elephants. But he still had the advantage of being able to surprise the Romans.

Carthage. Hannibal was recalled to Africa and defeated at Zama in 202BC. Rome seized the Carthaginian territories in Spain. In the following decades the Romans conquered much of south-west Europe and became the major power in the western Mediterranean.

The third Punic war (149-146BC)

The third Punic war (149-146BC) ended with the destruction of Carthage itself. The territory became the Roman province† of Africa.

The destruction of Carthage

The Roman conquest of Europe

Gradually the Romans were also drawn into wars to the east of Italy. Some small states asked them for protection, and larger ones pursued aggressive policies that provoked Roman retaliation. Success in a series of wars against Macedonia (215-168BC), and in other conflicts further south, increased the

Romans' military presence in Greece. In 146BC they crushed an uprising in Corinth and destroyed the city, as a warning to others not to undermine their authority. The rest of Greece was put under a Roman governor. Soon the entire Mediterranean came under Roman control.

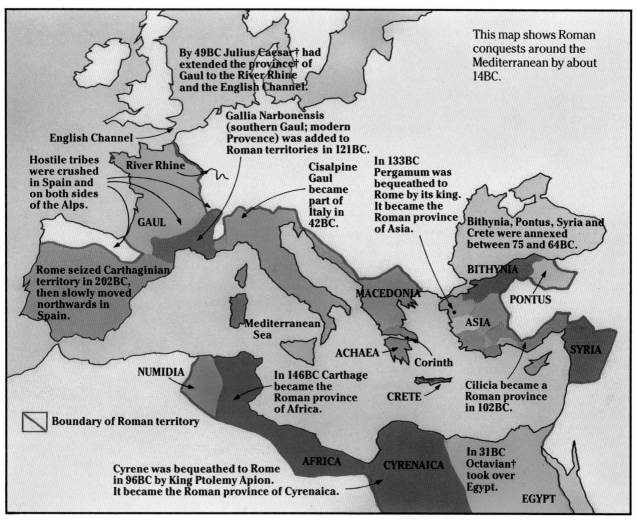

By 49BC Julius Caesar† had extended the province† of Gaul to the River Rhine and the English Channel.

Gallia Narbonensis (southern Gaul; modern Provence) was added to Roman territories in 121BC.

English Channel

Hostile tribes were crushed in Spain and on both sides of the Alps.

River Rhine

Cisalpine Gaul became part of Italy in 42BC.

In 133BC Pergamum was bequeathed to Rome by its king. It became the Roman province of Asia.

Bithynia, Pontus, Syria and Crete were annexed between 75 and 64BC.

This map shows Roman conquests around the Mediterranean by about 14BC.

GAUL

Rome seized Carthaginian territory in 202BC, then slowly moved northwards in Spain.

BITHYNIA

PONTUS

MACEDONIA

ASIA

Mediterranean Sea

SYRIA

ACHAEA

Corinth

NUMIDIA

In 146BC Carthage became the Roman province of Africa.

CRETE

Cilicia became a Roman province in 102BC.

Boundary of Roman territory

AFRICA

CYRENAICA

In 31BC Octavian† took over Egypt.

Cyrene was bequeathed to Rome in 96BC by King Ptolemy Apion. It became the Roman province of Cyrenaica.

EGYPT

Key dates

264-241BC First Punic war.

238BC Romans seize Sardinia. War breaks out again.

218-201BC Second Punic war.

216BC Roman army destroyed at Cannae.

202BC Hannibal recalled to Carthage and defeated at Zama.

149-146BC Third Punic war. Carthage destroyed.

146BC Romans destroy Corinth as a warning to other cities. Start of Roman rule in Greece.

133BC-31BC Major expansion of Roman territories in Mediterranean.

31BC Octavian takes over Egypt.

Rome's social and political structure

The occupants of Roman territory fell into two groups: *cives* (Roman citizens) and *peregrini* (foreigners). Citizens had special privileges. They were allowed to vote in elections and to serve in the army; non-citizens were not. At first only people with Roman parents qualified for citizenship. Later the government began granting citizenship to certain foreigners. These two groups were further divided, as shown below. There were three classes of citizen. These divisions began very early in Rome's history. The non-citizens included provincials (people who lived outside Rome but within Roman territory; see pages 218-219), and slaves (see page 245).

Citizens

The richest citizens, called patricians, were probably descended from early rich landowners and political leaders.

Equites (businessmen) were descendants of the first Roman cavalry officers (see page 206).

Plebeians (commoners) were probably the descendants of poor farmers and traders.

Non-citizens

Slaves were owned by other people. They had no freedom or rights. During the early republic there were very few slaves, but later the number grew.

Provincials did not have the full rights of Romans. They also had to pay taxes to the government in Rome. Citizens did not pay these taxes.

Families

The concept of the family was very important to the Romans. Every family was led by a *paterfamilias* (father), and included his wife and children, his sons' wives and children, and all their property and slaves. When the *paterfamilias* died, each of his sons might become the head of a new family, linked by name to the old one. The resulting chain of related families formed a clan called a *gens*.

The *paterfamilias* commanded awe and respect. He held the power of life and death over the family, and looked after the welfare of its members. He also directed the family's religious activities (see page 254).

The patronage system

The client visited his patron regularly to be given food or money.

People who did not have the legal protection of a family (for example, newcomers to Rome, ex-slaves, or people who had left their own families) could attach themselves to an existing family. They were known as *clientes* (clients), and their protectors as *patroni* (patrons). The *cliens* gave his *patronus* political and social support in return for financial and legal protection.

The government of the Roman republic

Rome was governed by the Senate, originally a group of 100 men who were leaders of important patrician families. Later the number of senators was increased; by 82BC there were 600. Senators normally served for life. Each year citizens voted in an election, known as an Assembly, to select senators to be government officials. The various officials and their duties are shown below.

Two consuls (the most senior officials) were elected each year. They managed the affairs of the Senate and the Roman armies. After their year in office, consuls could become proconsuls (governors in the provinces†).

Eight *praetores* were elected, mainly to be judges in the law courts (see pages 266-267).

Four *aediles* looked after markets, streets and public buildings. They also organized and paid for public games (see pages 250-251), and could become very popular.

Each year 20 financial administrators called *quaestores* were chosen. They did not have to be senators to be elected. After 80BC anyone elected as a *quaestor* also became a senator.

Every five years two *censores* were chosen from the former consuls. *Censores* served for 18 months. They revised the membership of the Senate, removed unworthy members, and enrolled new senators. They were also responsible for making the state's contracts for public works and tax collection.

In emergencies the state could nominate a dictator, who normally ruled for a maximum of six months. He had absolute authority over everyone else. A dictator could nominate his own assistant, called the *magister equitum* (master of the horse).

Social change

At first only patricians could become senators, and they tried to preserve their privileged positions. But many plebeians lived in poverty, and their resentment of the patricians' power caused violent political struggles. The plebeians went on strike five times, threatening to leave Rome whenever they were most needed as soldiers. In 494BC, after the first strike, they set up their own Popular Assembly, which excluded patricians. Each year they chose officials called tribunes to protect their interests.

The plebeians held frequent demonstrations on the streets of Rome.

To pacify the plebeians, the patricians gave them the power to stop any laws passed by the Senate. The plebeians then demanded that the laws be written down and published, to stop judges using unwritten laws against them. A list of laws, known as the Twelve Tables, was published in 450BC.

The plebeians slowly won the right to stand for official positions. The first plebeian consul was elected in 366BC. In 287BC a ruling was passed stating that all resolutions passed by the Popular Assembly should become law. But during the Carthaginian wars (see pages 200-201), plebeian generals misused their power. Many people thought that only the patricians had the ability to run the country during a war. So the patricians still kept political control.

The end of the Roman republic

The expansion of Roman territories abroad led to problems in Rome itself, and placed a strain on the government. There were constant struggles for power between the Senate, the *equites*† and the plebeians†. A period of dictatorships and civil wars finally caused the downfall of the republic†.

During the wars with Carthage, many small farms were ruined by neglect or military devastation. After the wars few farmers could afford to repair the damage. Gradually their land, and much public land as well, was taken over by rich landowners who created new, large farms.

The large farms were worked cheaply and efficiently by slaves, often captives taken in the wars.

Most of the people who had lost their land flocked to the cities, where they remained unemployed. Many others lived in poverty in rural areas. As a result, Rome was left short of soldiers, as only property owners could serve in the army.

Unemployed plebeians

In 133BC a tribune†, Tiberius Gracchus, proposed that public land that had been illegally seized by rich landowners should be given to the landless poor. The Popular Assembly† passed a law, and a committee was set up to redistribute the land. But the Senate disagreed, because many senators were landowners who wanted to keep their farms. Tiberius was killed in a riot that was provoked by the Senate. In 123BC his brother Gaius was elected tribune. Before he too was murdered, he passed radical laws that challenged the Senate's power.

The rise of dictators

For the next 60 or 70 years there was constant political unrest. Some senators, called *optimates*, wanted to maintain the Senate's firm control. Others, called *populares*, were keen to spread the control more widely. They asked the tribunes, *equites* and plebeians for support, but often only because they wanted more personal power.

In 107BC Marius, a military commander, was elected consul†. He was given command of an army fighting in Africa and soon won the war. He was made consul each year from 105BC to 100BC, breaking the rule that consuls had to be replaced annually. The reason given was that he was needed to prevent tribes invading Italy from Gaul.

This coin, showing Marius in a chariot, was issued to celebrate a military victory.

Marius succeeded in his task, but to do so he had to reorganize the army (see page 207). He improved weapons and training, and allowed all citizens† to become soldiers whether or not they owned land. Thousands of unemployed men volunteered. However, the state made no provision for soldiers without property. This meant that when they retired they depended on their generals to obtain money or land for them from the Senate. They were therefore more loyal to the individual generals than to the state.

Marius and his troops

Coin showing head of Sulla

In 88BC Sulla, Marius's former lieutenant, became consul and took command of the army against Mithridates, the king of Asia Minor. When a tribune passed a resolution giving command to Marius, Sulla led his army on Rome. He took control of the city and drove Marius into exile.

As soon as Sulla had been called away from Rome once more, Marius raised an army and took control of the city. After executing hundreds of his political rivals he died in 86BC. Sulla returned in 84BC, destroyed his enemies, and ruled as dictator from 82 to 80BC. He gave supreme power back to the Senate, depriving *equites* and tribunes of most of their influence. He then retired, and died in 78BC.

However, Sulla's arrangements were quickly undermined by a general called Pompey. He won victories in Spain in 71BC, and helped the senator Crassus to crush a slave rebellion led by a slave called Spartacus. In 70BC, Pompey and Crassus demanded to be made consuls, threatening to use military force if they were refused. Once in office they swept away Sulla's legislation, and gave power back to the tribunes.

Bust of Pompey

Pompey and Caesar

In 60BC Pompey, Crassus and a rising politician, Julius Caesar, formed an alliance. Caesar became consul in 59BC. After his year in office he served as a proconsul† in Gaul for ten years. He extended Roman territory throughout Spain and Gaul, and invaded Britain in 55BC. A brilliant general, he became very popular with the army and the people.

Bust of Caesar

In 53BC Crassus died in battle, and a year later the Senate House was burned down in a riot. To restore order, the Senate persuaded Pompey to become consul by himself. Fearing that Caesar would return to Rome and take their power away, the *optimates* turned Caesar and Pompey against each other. They forced Caesar into civil war, relying on Pompey to win. Caesar led his army on Rome in 49BC, and seized power. He defeated the armies of Pompey and the Senate in Spain (49BC and 45BC), Greece (48BC) and Africa (46BC).

Caesar arriving in Rome

Caesar's rule

Once in power, Caesar passed laws to relieve hardship, reduce debts and improve the administration. His rule brought a brief period of political stability, during which he also began many building projects in Rome and elsewhere.

Caesar was a great public speaker and an extremely popular leader.

Caesar was made dictator for life, and became the most powerful ruler Rome had ever known. Although his reforms were popular, he acted as if he were king, taking decisions without consulting the Senate. This worried many people, who believed his power threatened the republic. On 15th March 44BC Caesar was murdered by a group of conspirators led by the senators Brutus and Cassius. They hoped to restore the republic, but they failed. Caesar's heir, Octavian (see page 214), created a military dictatorship which lasted another 500 years.

The murder of Caesar

Key dates

133BC Land reforms of Tiberius Gracchus.
123BC Gaius Gracchus elected tribune.
107BC Marius first elected consul.
88BC Sulla becomes consul, then marches on Rome.
86BC Marius dies.
82-80BC Sulla rules Rome as dictator.
78BC Sulla dies.
70BC Pompey and Crassus elected consuls.
60BC Pompey, Crassus and Caesar form an alliance.
59BC Caesar becomes consul.
53BC Crassus dies.
52BC Pompey becomes consul.
48BC Pompey defeated by Caesar in Greece.
44BC Caesar murdered by Brutus and Cassius.

The army

The expansion of Rome was due mostly to the skill and efficiency of its army. The Roman forces were the best disciplined and among the largest in the ancient world. The army had a very strong influence on political life and many politicians were also important soldiers. The structure of the army changed considerably during Rome's history.

The early republican army

During the early republic†, in a military emergency, all property-owning citizens† were summoned to the *Campus Martius* (Field of Mars, god of war). They gathered in groups called centuries, each of 100 men. At first wars only lasted a few days, so it did not matter if men left their farms for a short time.

— Richer citizens could afford horses, and so served in the cavalry†.

The poorest fought on the edges of the battle, using stones and farm implements.

The rest fought in a block carrying swords, spears, daggers and shields.

By around 340BC wars further away from Rome meant that people were required to leave their farms for longer periods. Wages were introduced to encourage people to join the army. In a crisis the Romans could raise almost 800,000 men, though these emergency armies were often badly trained. Occasionally even slaves† were brought in to increase the numbers, but this was dangerous as armed slaves could turn against their masters.

Soldiers were grouped into units called legions, each of about 4200 men. Within each legion there were groups of different types of soldier. The structure of individual legions varied. This diagram shows the various fighters, and the way in which they were organized in a typical legion.

Legions were divided into groups called maniples. Each maniple contained 120 men. The maniples fought in a special formation called a *quincunx*, shown below, made up of three ranks of soldiers.

In front of the *triarii* fought a second rank, 10 maniples of *principes*, men armed with plenty of weapons and cylindrical shields.

The gaps in each line were covered by the troops in the line behind.

At the rear of the *quincunx* were 5 maniples (600 men) of very experienced fighters called *triarii*.

Maniple of *triarii*

Maniple of *hastati*

Enemy soldiers

Maniple of *principes*

Velites

10 maniples of the youngest, poorest soldiers fought separately from the *quincunx*. They were called *velites*.

10 maniples (1200 men) of young soldiers fought at the front. They were called *hastati* because they carried *hastae* (spears).

The *quincunx* worked well against armies in other formations. First the *hastati* wore out the enemy, then the *principes* moved through to finish the battle. The *triarii* only had to fight if a battle was going badly.

The later republican army

As the empire grew, the army had to be improved to control Rome's distant enemies. By 100BC the army had been reorganized by a commander called Marius. New laws allowed all citizens to join the legion, whether or not they owned property. Wages were improved, and many men became full-time soldiers. Everyone was given the same weapons and training, so the distinction between rich and poor soldiers disappeared. Most troops fought on foot, but there was also a small cavalry. Legions were extremely well organized because they were made up of many small, highly disciplined groups. The main unit was still the century. Below is a plan of how it was made up.

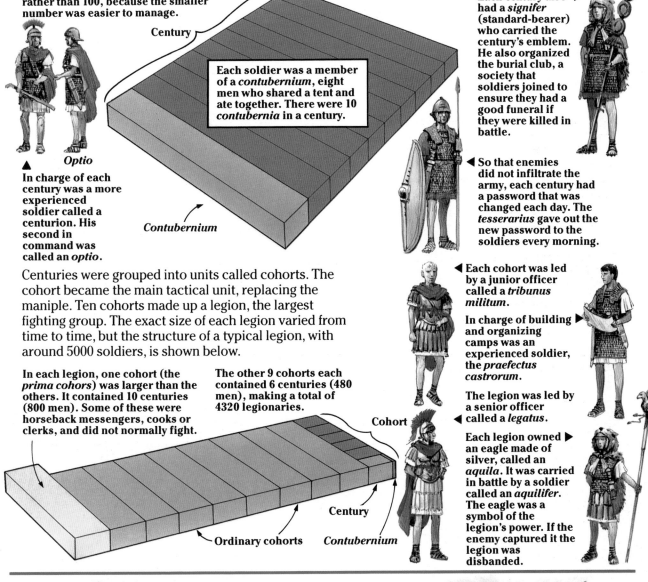

There were now 80 men in a century rather than 100, because the smaller number was easier to manage.

Century

Each soldier was a member of a *contubernium*, eight men who shared a tent and ate together. There were 10 *contubernia* in a century.

Optio

In charge of each century was a more experienced soldier called a centurion. His second in command was called an *optio*.

Contubernium

Each century also ▶ had a *signifer* (standard-bearer) who carried the century's emblem. He also organized the burial club, a society that soldiers joined to ensure they had a good funeral if they were killed in battle.

◀ So that enemies did not infiltrate the army, each century had a password that was changed each day. The *tesserarius* gave out the new password to the soldiers every morning.

Centuries were grouped into units called cohorts. The cohort became the main tactical unit, replacing the maniple. Ten cohorts made up a legion, the largest fighting group. The exact size of each legion varied from time to time, but the structure of a typical legion, with around 5000 soldiers, is shown below.

In each legion, one cohort (the *prima cohors*) was larger than the others. It contained 10 centuries (800 men). Some of these were horseback messengers, cooks or clerks, and did not normally fight.

The other 9 cohorts each contained 6 centuries (480 men), making a total of 4320 legionaries.

Cohort

Century

Ordinary cohorts

Contubernium

◀ Each cohort was led by a junior officer called a *tribunus militum*.

In charge of building ▶ and organizing camps was an experienced soldier, the *praefectus castrorum*.

The legion was led by a senior officer ◀ called a *legatus*.

Each legion owned ▶ an eagle made of silver, called an *aquila*. It was carried in battle by a soldier called an *aquilifer*. The eagle was a symbol of the legion's power. If the enemy captured it the legion was disbanded.

Other soldiers

Each legion was supported by *auxilia*, non-citizens recruited mostly from the provinces. These soldiers were organized into cohorts of 500 or 1000 men. They were paid less than legionaries, served for longer, and were not as well trained. At the end of their service, however, they received Roman citizenship. They provided forces that legionaries were not trained for, such as cavalry.

A soldier's life

In early republican† times any property-owning man aged between 17 and 46 could be called on to serve in the army. It was seen as a citizen's† duty to protect Rome. Soldiers were not required to fight more than 16 or 17 separate campaigns during their careers, but some liked military service and served continuously. By 100BC most soldiers were full-time professionals.

On entering the army a recruit took an oath of loyalty. At first he swore allegiance to his commander, but later this was replaced by an oath to the emperor†.

Training was hard. Each day new recruits did two sessions of military drill, and the entire legion practised swimming, running, jumping, javelin-throwing and fencing.

Three times a month there were route-marches of 30km (18 miles). The pace was forced at 6.5km (4 miles) or even 8km (5 miles) per hour. Legionaries were trained to build and dismantle camps.

Soldiers were flogged if they misbehaved. If a legion disobeyed its rations were reduced; if mutiny was suspected, every tenth man was executed. The word for this was *decimatio*. It is the origin of the English word decimate, which means to reduce by a tenth.

In difficult countryside carts could not be used to transport equipment. Soldiers had to carry all their belongings, food, tools for digging and building, two heavy wooden stakes for the camp fence, and cooking pots. Because of this soldiers were nicknamed 'the mules of Marius'†.

As well as learning to fight, some soldiers were trained as surveyors, engineers or stonemasons, and supervised the construction of roads, canals and buildings.

Under Caesar† legionaries earned 225 *denarii*† per year. Domitian† increased this to 300 *denarii*. Soldiers had to buy their food, which took about a third of their wages. Meals were simple: cheese, beans, and bread or gruel made of wheat or barley. Soldiers drank water or *posca*, a cheap sour wine.

Until AD5 full-time soldiers served for 20 years. Later this was raised to 25 years. The government knew that retired soldiers could be dangerous, and wanted to keep them peaceful. So discharged veterans were given a sum of money, or a small plot of land to farm.

Uniform and weapons

When a recruit entered the army he was given a uniform. All new garments had to be paid for out of his wages. A soldier's basic outfit varied little according to his rank or status. These pictures show what legionaries wore.

Soldiers carried shields made of wood and leather with an iron rim at the top and bottom. They were about 120cm (48in) by 70cm (28in), and curved.

The sword was about 60cm (2ft) long. It hung from the soldier's belt by his right hand.

Soldiers carried two metal-tipped javelins to throw in battle. They had wooden shafts with a section of soft iron. The iron bent when the spear hit the ground, so the enemy could not throw it back. If the spear hit armour it was impossible to remove.

Scarf to stop the armour scratching the soldier's neck.

In cold weather soldiers were given woollen cloaks.

Vests of fine chain-mail were the most common form of armour.

In colder climates *bracae* (woollen trousers) were also issued.

At first helmets were made of leather. Later, metal was used, to give better protection.

Tunic of wool or linen.

Later, some soldiers wore the *lorica segmentata*, a leather tunic with metal strips attached. This allowed more freedom of movement.

A dagger hung from the left of the soldier's belt.

Groin-guard made of leather and metal.

Heavy sandals studded with nails.

Metal leg-protectors, known as greaves.

Making a camp

During the wars to secure the empire, legions spent many days on the march. When they stopped each night they set up camp, then dismantled it the following morning before moving on. The procedure was highly organized.

The camp was always laid out the same way so everyone knew his part in building it. Josephus, a Jewish priest captured by the Romans in AD67, observed Roman tactics and fighting methods. His book, *The Jewish War*, tells how camps were built.

If the ground was uneven it was levelled off. The camp was marked out as a square.

Injured soldiers were treated in a military hospital.

The general's headquarters were at the centre of the camp. This area was also used for meetings, and to house standards and military emblems.

The tents were pitched a long way from the perimeter so that they could not be hit by the enemy's missiles.

The inside of the square was divided into rows, on which the tents were pitched.

A trench was dug around the perimeter. The soil from the ditch was made into a mound, and a fence of stakes was driven into it.

Each centurion† had his own tent, at the end of the row of tents of his century.

Tents were made of goat- or calf-skin. Each tent housed a *contubernium*, a group of eight men.

Branches were woven through the stakes, so from outside the fence looked like a wall. Lookout towers and artillery machines were placed on it.

Streets crossed the camp, dividing it into quarters.

209

Roads

The Romans developed their system of roads out of military necessity. In the early years of Rome's expansion, the army could march from the city to defend the frontiers in a few hours. As the empire grew, however, it became vital to move troops and supplies quickly over very long distances.

The first major road, the *Via Appia*, was begun in 312BC. It stretched south from Rome to Capua and took over 100 years to build. 900 years after its completion, the historian Procopius called it one of the great sights of the world. He noted that despite its age, none of the stones had broken or worn thin.

The *Via Appia* was the first link in a network that eventually stretched over 85,000km (50,000 miles) and reached every corner of the empire (see map below). Much later, the remains of these routes formed the basis of Europe's modern roads and railway lines.

The *Via Appia* as it is today.

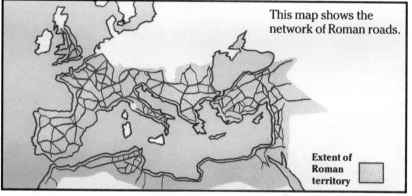

This map shows the network of Roman roads.

Extent of Roman territory

As well as helping the movement of troops, roads brought other changes. Merchants followed armies to sell to the troops, and later to the inhabitants of the new provinces. Trade flourished, and people and goods could quickly reach distant parts of the empire. So roads helped to unite the provinces, as well as to keep them under control.

Travelling

This roadside scene has been reconstructed using information from Roman manuscripts, pictures and remains. We know what Roman vehicles looked like, and also know their names, but it is not easy to match the two. Two-wheeled carriages, used in towns, included the *carpentum* and the more lightweight *cisium*. There were also larger, four-wheeled vehicles like the *raeda*, which could carry a whole family, and the *carruca*, which had enough room to sleep in.

Milestone. The Roman mile was about 1,500m (5,000ft) long. Each mile was was a thousand paces and was marked by a stone. *Mille* is the Latin for a thousand.

Workmen building a new road.

Building a road

When planning a road, Roman surveyors looked for the shortest, straightest, flattest route. To find this they took sights from one high point to another. They probably did this by lighting fires, flares or beacons, observing carrier pigeons, or using a *groma* (see page 264). Once the route had been planned, the turf and trees were cleared in preparation. Then a trench was dug about 1m (3½feet) deep and filled with layers of stone. To prevent puddles (which would crack the road if they froze), the surface was built with a raised curve called a camber, and ditches were dug to drain water away.

Stone slabs (if stone was available locally).

Camber

Gravel or small flints rammed down tight.

Groma

Drainage ditch

Smaller stones, sometimes bound with cement.

Large stones, wedged tightly together.

Minor roads were 3m to 4.5m (10ft) wide, major ones up to 7.7m (25ft).

Roman roads are sometimes steeper than ours. This is because soldiers preferred a short steep climb to a long trudge round a hill.

Taberna

Soldiers

There were post stations on main roads, between 6 and 15 Roman miles apart. They were part of the *cursus publicus*, a postal service set up for government use only. Horse-riders took official messages by relay from one station to the next.

Chariot carrying government mail.

Local workpeople could find food and drink in a *taberna* (tavern). Tradesmen also used these as places to sell their goods, and towns often grew up around them.

Coach taking passengers to the next city.

Farmer taking vegetables to the next town.

Travellers could stay at state-controlled guest-houses called *mansiones*. These were built every 15 Roman miles or so. Some *mansiones* were huge, but they were not always very comfortable.

Mansio

Where the route came to rivers, or valleys that were too steep for men and mules to climb, bridges or viaducts† had to be built. Many of these can still be seen today, and some are still in use, such as this one which spans the river at Alcantara in Spain.

Most Roman vehicles had wheels set about 143cm (60 in) apart. This width (or gauge) became standard once ruts had been worn in the roads. No-one wanted to travel with only one wheel in a rut, so they built their carts at the standard gauge.

Sometimes, instead of a ditch, earth was dug and piled into a mound, with foundation stones on top. This kind of road was called an *agger* and was up to 15m (50ft) wide and 1.5m (5ft) high. *Aggers* were probably built as boundaries or to impress local people.

Ships and shipping

Unlike the Greeks or Phoenicians†, the Romans had no tradition of seafaring. During the early republic they only had primitive shipping forces. However for the first Punic war (see page 200), they had to acquire naval power quickly. They found an abandoned Carthaginian warship, and built 100 copies of it in 60 days; eventually they had over 200 ships. After defeating Carthage the Romans dominated the Mediterranean Sea. They built a merchant fleet, and sea trade flourished. Later they also had a navy that patrolled the seas to prevent piracy.

Warships and naval tactics

There is little information about Roman warships because no wrecks have been found. We know from Roman books that they were called *quinqueremes*. Some historians think that these ships had five banks of oars. Others say this would have made them impossible to row, and think it more likely that each oar was pulled by five men. These diagrams show warships and their weapons.

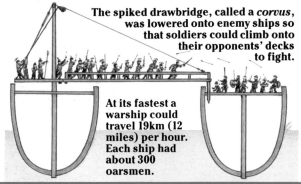

The spiked drawbridge, called a *corvus*, was lowered onto enemy ships so that soldiers could climb onto their opponents' decks to fight.

At its fastest a warship could travel 19km (12 miles) per hour. Each ship had about 300 oarsmen.

120 soldiers were carried on deck to fight.

Other ships were equipped with underwater rams. These were used to break holes in the enemy's ships.

Triremes

After the Punic wars there were no major naval battles, but the Romans kept a fleet of warships called *triremes**. Later during the civil wars between Mark Antony† and Octavian† (see page 214) each side built up huge navies. 900 *triremes* fought at the Battle of Actium. After his victory Octavian set up the first permanent navy to guard the coasts of Italy. A *trireme* is shown in this relief.

A *trireme* had three banks of oars, pulled by slaves below deck.

A *trireme* was lighter and narrower than a *quinquereme*, and therefore easier to manoeuvre.

The crocodile on the front suggests that the ship is from a fleet based on the Nile.

Harbours

When the Romans began using larger merchant ships (see opposite) they needed large, deep harbours. Rome was served by a port called Ostia at the mouth of the Tiber. Claudius† built a vast new port, Portus, nearby. Harbours were also built elsewhere in the empire. Towns grew up around them because they became trading centres. This is what a provincial port might have looked like.

Barges took goods inland along rivers or canals, because many ships were too wide for this journey.

Large merchant ships brought supplies from other parts of the empire.

Naval ships sometimes docked in harbours.

*Triremes were originally invented by the Greeks (see pages 134-135).

Merchant ships

After the rule of Augustus†, the Romans had a vast fleet of merchant ships to carry goods all over the Mediterranean, and as far as Africa and India. Ships had to be sturdy enough for frequent journeys, because Romans relied on imported goods for much of their food. Wrecks of merchant ships have been found which show how they were built.

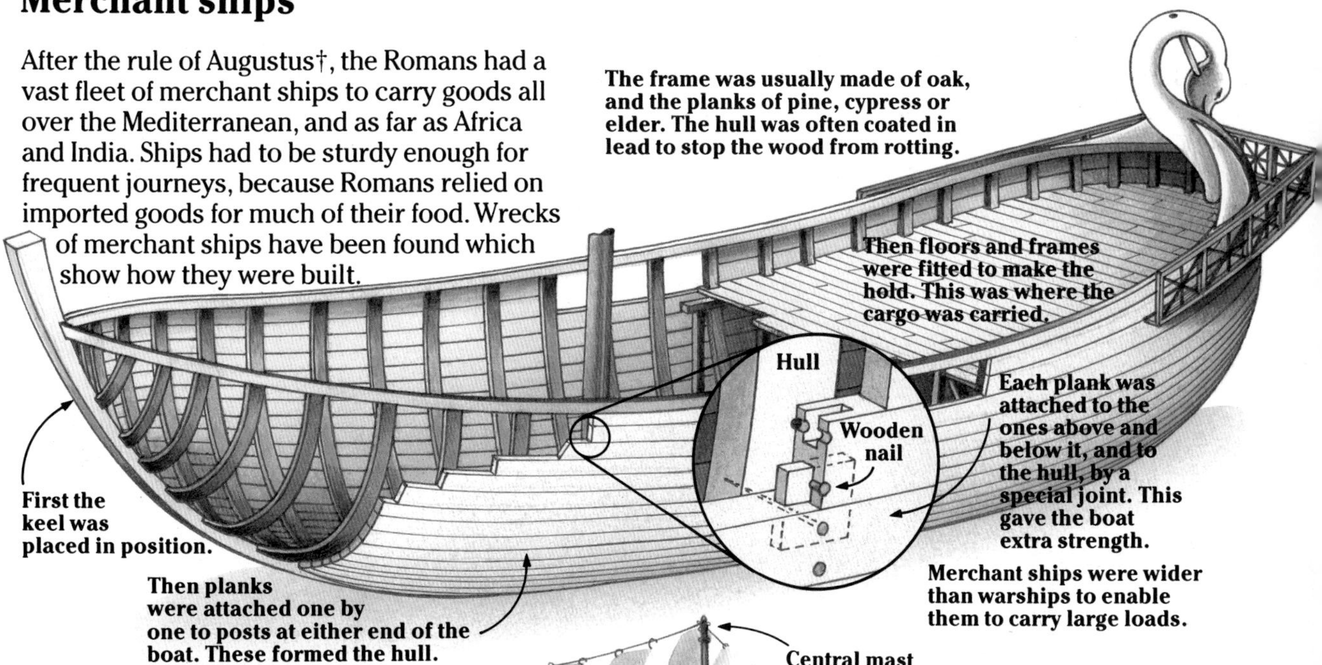

The frame was usually made of oak, and the planks of pine, cypress or elder. The hull was often coated in lead to stop the wood from rotting.

Then floors and frames were fitted to make the hold. This was where the cargo was carried.

Hull

Wooden nail

Each plank was attached to the ones above and below it, and to the hull, by a special joint. This gave the boat extra strength.

First the keel was placed in position.

Then planks were attached one by one to posts at either end of the boat. These formed the hull.

Merchant ships were wider than warships to enable them to carry large loads.

A cargo ship

Roman paintings, carvings and wrecks reveal what cargo ships were like. They varied in size. Remains have been found of small vessels about 18m (60ft) long and 5m (17ft) wide, but the cargo area of some wrecks measures at least 30m (100ft) by 9m (30ft). Ships carried all kinds of goods – such as *amphorae* of oil and wine, or sacks of grain – over large distances.

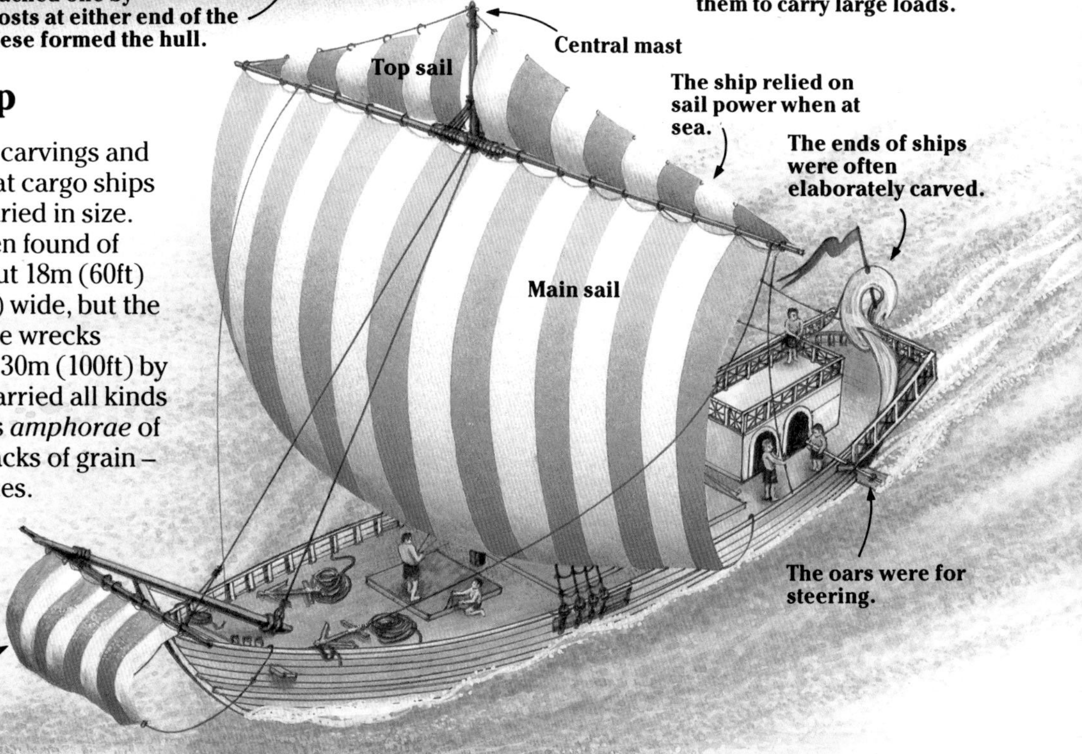

Top sail

Central mast

The ship relied on sail power when at sea.

The ends of ships were often elaborately carved.

Main sail

Ships could achieve speeds of up to 7km per hour (over 4 miles per hour).

The oars were for steering.

Steering sail

Navigation

Roman sailors had no instruments to help them find their way, but they quickly learned many routes across the Mediterranean. There were books that told sailors the best routes and best times to travel. We know from these that navigators did not need to keep the coastline in sight as they travelled.

To calculate his position, a captain looked at the sun, moon and stars. He judged his progress by studying the direction and speed of the wind. There were lighthouses at important harbours. The most famous of these, the Pharos at Alexandria, used huge metal plates to reflect the lights of a fire. It stood over 130m (100ft) high, and was one of the wonders of the ancient world.

From republic to Empire

After Ceasar's death (see page 205) Brutus† and Cassius fled from Rome, realizing they could not restore the republic†. Instead, one of the consuls†, Mark Antony, tried to take Caesar's place.

However many senators disliked him. One of them, Cicero†, made speeches opposing Antony and persuaded the Senate to declare him an outlaw. Antony was dismissed and replaced by another consul.

Coin with head of Antony

In the meantime, Caesar's adopted son, Octavian, formed an army made up of men who had formerly fought for Caesar. He gave control of

Busts of Octavian and his wife Livia†

these troops to the Senate, and they defeated Antony at Mutina in northern Italy. Antony fled to Gaul. The consuls were killed in battle, leaving Octavian as the most likely person to take command.

Octavian wanted revenge for Caesar's death. The Senate refused to support him, so he made a pact with Antony and his ally, Lepidus. The three men led an army on Rome, forcing the Senate to give them official powers for five years. Thousands of people, including Cicero, were killed by Octavian's troops. In 42BC Octavian and Antony defeated Brutus and Cassius at Philippi in Macedonia.

Lepidus soon retired, leaving Octavian and Antony in command. They split Rome's territory into two. Antony took the eastern part and Octavian the west, as shown on this map.

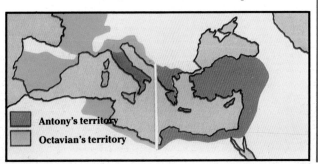

- ■ Antony's territory
- ■ Octavian's territory

Antony lived in Egypt for ten years with his lover Cleopatra*, the Egyptian queen. He seemed to be building a private empire for himself. Meanwhile Octavian defeated his enemies in western Europe, and became accepted by the Senate and the Roman people. But relations between him and Antony deteriorated. War broke out, and in 31BC he defeated Antony in a sea battle at Actium.

This gem depicts Octavian as Neptune, the god of the sea. It was carved to celebrate his victory over Mark Antony at the Battle of Actium.

Octavian takes power

Octavian claimed Egypt for himself, and became the sole leader of the Roman world. In 27BC he offered to return control of the state to the Senate and the people. However he knew that the Senate could not accept his offer because it depended on him to maintain order. The Senate gave Octavian command of three provinces: Syria, Spain and Gaul. These areas contained most of the army, so he retained military power while appearing to want to give it up for the sake of the republic†.

As a result Octavian became the most powerful Roman of all. He was given a new name, Augustus ('revered one'), and has been known by this title ever since. He was the first Roman emperor, though he himself did not use this title. The period of Roman history from his rule onwards is known as the Empire, to distinguish it from the republic before it.

This cameo† shows the head of Augustus.

Key dates

44BC Death of Caesar.

43BC Octavian, Antony and Lepidus form an alliance and seize power in Rome.

c.33BC Growing hostility between Octavian and Antony.

31BC Octavian defeats Antony and Cleopatra at the Battle of Actium.

30BC Antony and Cleopatra commit suicide. Octavian seizes Egypt and becomes sole leader of the Roman world.

27BC Octavian becomes emperor and takes the name Augustus.

For more about Cleopatra, see page 80.

The rule of Augustus, 27BC-AD14

With his new power, Augustus began looking for solutions to his various political problems. He realized that further civil wars would only weaken the empire more and leave it open to threat from outside. So he tried to make his own position safe in order to maintain a firm leadership.

Knowing that too many organized troops could be turned against him, Augustus cut the number of legions† from 60 to 28. He used the vast wealth of Egypt to pay off retired soldiers, who were settled in colonies all over Italy.

Retired soldier

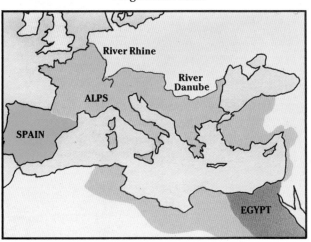
Praetorian guardsmen

To protect himself, Augustus formed a division of soldiers called the Praetorian Guard. These highly paid troops were intended to guard the Emperor, and were stationed in Rome and throughout Italy.

Under Augustus, rebellious parts of Spain and the Alps were brought under control. The empire was expanded along the Rhine and Danube rivers. The map below shows the extent of the empire at the end of Augustus's rule.

River Rhine

River Danube

ALPS

SPAIN

EGYPT

Augustus ruled cleverly and successfully. He formed a system of government in which the Senate and the emperor worked together. This brought peace after years of civil war, and turned a troubled republic into a stable and prosperous empire. When he died in AD14, few people could remember a republican government that had been worth preserving, so the idea of restoring a republic slowly died out.

Tiberius AD14-37

Statue of Tiberius

Augustus had no son of his own, and wanted one of his grandsons or his nephew to take his place, but they all died young. Eventually he had to name his step-son Tiberius as his successor. The two men ruled together for the last ten years of Augustus's reign. Augustus disliked him, but Tiberius was a fine soldier and an experienced administrator.

At first Tiberius ruled well. He took Augustus's advice and did not try to expand the empire. But he was terrified of being assassinated. At first there was no evidence of a plot against him, but Sejanus, the commander of the Praetorian Guard, took advantage of his fears.

In AD26 Sejanus persuaded Tiberius to move to the island of Capri for his own safety. For the rest of his rule, the Senate had to consult him by letter before it could make decisions. In AD31 Tiberius found out that Sejanus was planning to depose him. He revealed this to the Senate and Sejanus and his family were executed. This left Tiberius mentally disturbed. He passed a treason law and prosecuted over 100 leading figures. 65 of these were executed or committed suicide.

Gaius (Caligula) AD37-41

Gaius is often known as Caligula, a nickname he was given as a child because of the soldier's boots (*caligae*) he wore. After a few months in power he had an illness which appears to have left him deranged. He claimed to be a god and tried to have his horse elected consul. He married his sister and later murdered her.

Caligula was extremely extravagant. He financed his spending by forcing rich men to bequeath him their wealth. This, and his cruelty, made him unpopular and he was murdered by a group of officers from the Praetorian Guard.

The early Empire

Claudius AD41-54

Coin with head of Claudius

Claudius was Tiberius's nephew. A childhood disease had left him crippled, frail and nervous. His family and the Senate regarded him as stupid. Because of this everyone thought that he was not suitable to be emperor. After Gaius's murder, however, the Praetorian Guard† found Claudius hiding in the imperial palace. They dragged him off, hailing him as the new emperor, while the Senate was discussing restoring the republic. The senators always resented Claudius because he had been appointed against their will.

Claudius was in fact highly intelligent and wise. He devoted his rule to improving the civil service and extending the empire. He annexed Mauretania and Thrace, and ordered the invasion of Britain. He married four times. His last wife was his niece, Aggripina†. It is thought that she poisoned him so that Nero, her son by a previous marriage, could become emperor.

Nero AD54-68

Nero was only 16 when he became emperor. For the first years of his rule he was guided by tutors (including the writer Seneca†) and ruled sensibly. However, he soon became tyrannical. In AD59 he had his mother, his wife and Claudius's son Britannicus murdered, as well as several advisors. Soon, anyone who opposed him was killed.

Nero liked taking part in theatrical shows, races and games. Many Romans thought his behaviour was very undignified.

In AD64 a fire devastated Rome. It was rumoured that Nero had started it so that he could build a new, more beautiful city in its place. To avert unpopularity, Nero blamed the Christians† for the fire, and had many of them burned or thrown to the beasts. This only made him more unpopular.

According to the Roman historian Suetonius†, Nero sang and played the lyre while Rome burned.

There were many plots against Nero. In AD68 the army rebelled against him and various commanders tried to seize power. Nero was eventually forced to leave Rome, and he committed suicide. He was the last emperor of Augustus's dynasty.

AD69: the year of the four emperors

After Nero's death, an army commander called Galba took power, helped by the Praetorian Guard. But he did not pay the guardsmen enough to win their loyalty. They soon turned against him, had him murdered, and replaced him with Otho, the governor of a province in Spain. Hearing this, the legions on the Rhine declared their own general, Vitellius, emperor. They marched on Rome and defeated Otho at Cremona. Then legions on the Danube decided their own general, Vespasian, should become emperor. He marched on Rome and killed Vitellius and his followers.

Coin with head of Vespasian

Vespasian (AD69-79) and the Flavian Dynasty

Vespasian knew there would be civil war if he did not establish good relations with the Senate. He achieved this, and the Senate granted him imperial power. In addition, he had two adult sons to take over after his death, so he had a strong line of succession. Vespasian ruled well and gave citizenship† to many people in the provinces†. His full name was Titus Flavius Vespasianus, and he and his descendants are known as the Flavian Dynasty.

Vespasian ordered the building of the Colosseum in Rome. This is how it looks today.

Titus AD79-81

Titus was Vespasian's son. He is remembered for his capture of Jerusalem (see page 257) in AD70. This was commemorated by an arch in the *forum* at Rome. Titus became emperor in AD79.

The arch of Titus

Domitian AD81-96

Bust of Domitian

Domitian, Titus's younger brother, was an efficient but arrogant emperor. He despised the Senate and never consulted it. He became unpopular and there were frequent plots against him. His rule became tyrannical, with frequent treason trials and executions. He was assassinated in AD96.

This was probably the last point at which the Romans could have restored a republican government. But the Senate, knowing that Rome needed a strong leader, chose a lawyer called Nerva to replace Domitian. Nerva was the first of a group of rulers known as the Five Good Emperors.

Nerva AD96-98

Nerva ruled successfully and diplomatically. When the Praetorian Guard was indignant at having no say in choosing the emperor, Nerva eased the situation by adopting a famous soldier called Trajan as his son, partner and successor. This started a new method of imperial succession. After Nerva each emperor, who took the title Augustus, carefully chose a younger colleague called the Caesar as his heir. When the Augustus died, the Caesar took his position and title, and then chose his own Caesar.

The imperial succession:

Nerva

The Augustus chose a Caesar to succeed him.

Trajan

The Caesar took over and became the Augustus.

He then chose a new Caesar to succeed him

Hadrian

Nerva treated the Senate with great respect, and this trend was followed by the next four emperors. Gradually senators were chosen from all over the empire, and many non-Italians became senior officials. Nerva also arranged low-interest loans for farmers. The interest from these was used to support orphans and poor children.

Trajan AD98-117

Under Trajan the empire reached its largest extent (see pages 218-219) after his conquest of large areas of the Middle East. His campaigns in Dacia (Romania) are recorded in a series of sculptures on the pillar in Rome known as Trajan's Column.

Trajan's column

Hadrian AD117-138

Hadrian spent more than half his rule touring the provinces. After deciding that the empire was too large he gave up the new territories in the East (except Dacia). Many of his reforms improved the organization of the empire. For example he decreed that senators and *equites*† should receive special training in state administration.

Hadrian ordered the building of fortified barriers to protect the empire. These were put up in Britain (see pages 220-221) and in Germany.

Hadrian's Wall

Antoninus Pius AD138-161

While Antoninus Pius was in power, Rome was seen to be at the height of its wealth and power. But this prosperity aroused the envy of the barbarians†, and of the poor, who were neglected.

Marcus Aurelius AD161-180

Marcus Aurelius spent most of his rule at the frontiers, trying to keep barbarians out. To do this he had to enlarge the army and raise taxes to cover the cost. During his rule a plague killed thousands of people. For the first time people began to doubt that Rome was all-powerful.

This statue of Marcus Aurelius once stood on the Capitoline Hill.

Key dates: the first emperors

27BC-AD14 Augustus	**AD69-79** Vespasian
AD14-37 Tiberius	**AD79-81** Titus
AD37-41 Gaius (Caligula)	**AD81-96** Domitian
AD41-54 Claudius	**AD96-98** Nerva
AD54-68 Nero	**AD98-117** Trajan
AD64 Great fire of Rome	**AD117-138** Hadrian
AD69 Year of the four emperors	**AD138-161** Antoninus Pius
	AD161-180 Marcus Aurelius

The administration of the empire

Roman territory was divided into areas called provinces. These were governed locally by senators representing the republic†, or, later, the emperor. When a province was made part of the empire, a special provincial law was drawn up for it. This differed from the law in Rome, because it took local customs into account and set local levels of taxation. After this, provincials were mostly left to govern themselves. This map* indicates the extent of the empire at its largest, under Trajan (AD98-117), and shows how it was organized.

Barbarians

Outside the empire were many rural tribes. The Romans saw them as inferior, brutal and uncivilized, referring to them as barbarians. Many barbarian tribes threatened the empire's security. Some wanted to regain territory that the Romans had taken from them, others wanted to steal cattle and other goods. To keep invaders out, the Romans built walls along some of their borders. These are shown as blue lines.

Before it was conquered by the Romans, much of western Europe was inhabited by rural tribes and nomads†. The Romans built large towns there, partly to make it easier to govern and partly because they believed urban life was a good thing. Most towns roughly followed the plan shown here.

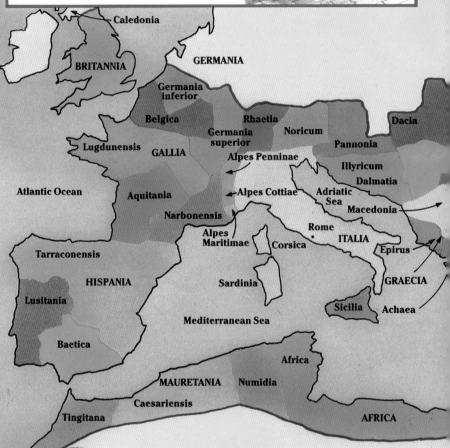

Caledonia

BRITANNIA

GERMANIA

Germania inferior

Belgica

Lugdunensis

GALLIA

Germania superior

Alpes Penninae

Rhaetia

Noricum

Pannonia

Dacia

Illyricum

Dalmatia

Atlantic Ocean

Aquitania

Alpes Cottiae

Adriatic Sea

Macedonia

Narbonensis

Alpes Maritimae

Corsica

Rome

ITALIA

Epirus

Tarraconensis

HISPANIA

Sardinia

GRAECIA

Lusitania

Sicilia

Achaea

Mediterranean Sea

Baetica

Africa

MAURETANIA

Numidia

Caesariensis

Tingitana

AFRICA

The imperial army

When Augustus took power in 31BC the army consisted of 60 legions†. He cut this number to 28, and used them to protect the empire's frontiers. Later emperors varied this number slightly, but there were always around 30. Hadrian† began recruiting soldiers from areas in which they would be stationed. For example German troops were recruited to serve in Germany.

German soldier

Gradually the army became inefficient. Some later emperors thought the legions might turn against them, and to prevent this they gave soldiers special privileges and frequent pay increases. This made generals too powerful, and caused discipline problems. It became harder to recruit soldiers within the empire, because fewer people wanted to join the army. Sometimes the Romans recruited barbarians to defend frontiers, but their loyalty could not be guaranteed.

For a note about the projection of this map, please see page 195.

Most eastern Mediterranean
countries had a civilization
much older than Rome's.
Many had been influenced by
Greek civilization (see page
172). They were urban
societies, accustomed to
central government and
paying taxes.

**Many Roman buildings
were copied from Greek
temples like this one.**

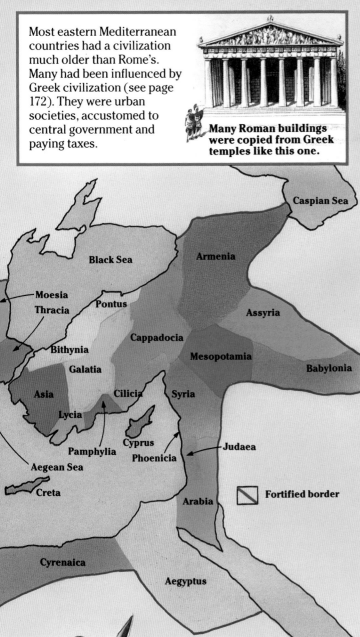

Caspian Sea

Black Sea

Armenia

Moesia
Thracia
Pontus

Assyria

Cappadocia

Bithynia
Mesopotamia
Galatia
Babylonia

Asia
Cilicia
Syria
Lycia

Cyprus
Pamphylia
Judaea
Aegean Sea
Phoenicia

Creta

Arabia

☐ **Fortified border**

Cyrenaica

Aegyptus

Barbarian soldier

Under Constantine† the
frontiers were guarded by
peasant soldiers who had
settled near forts. To support
them Constantine organized
mobile armies, nearly all
cavalry, which were stationed
near the borders. This policy
worked for over a century, but
finally the army disintegrated
and the barbarians moved in
(see pages 270-271).

Government in the provinces

Under the republic, the Senate† appointed
governors for each province. They were
chosen from retiring *praetores*† and
consuls†, and served for one to three years.
Governors had various duties. They
commanded the army in the area, ensuring
that frontiers were safe and maintaining law
and order. They organized the collection of
local taxes, which were used to pay the
army stationed in the area. They also acted
as judges for important trials. Governors
were paid expenses, but no wages. Many,
believing they would not be found out by
the Senate, used their power to extort
money from locals. For this reason they
were often disliked.

The governor was
helped by a *quaestor*,
a junior official who
organized the
finances of the
province and the
collection of taxes.

There were were also
three or four
lieutenants (called
legati) who carried
out the governor's
orders on a day-to-
day basis.

Civil servants called
apparitores worked
as clerks and
messengers. They
came mostly from
Rome, rather than
the province itself.

In imperial times the Senate lost much of
its power in the provinces, because the
emperor took control of the dangerous
areas by the frontiers. Under Augustus only
the legion in Africa remained under
senatorial control. After this, though certain
areas passed from the emperor's control to
the Senate's from time to time,
the emperor always held
supreme power in matters of
provincial government. The
emperor could not manage all
the provinces personally, so he
sent senators to govern for him.

In the emperor's provinces financial
affairs were not managed by
quaestores, but by the emperor's own
agents called *procuratores Augusti*.
They reported directly to the
emperor, so were a useful check on
the governor's behaviour.

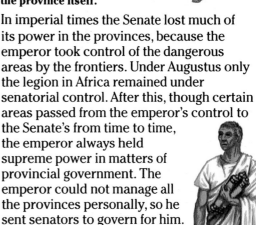

Sieges and fortifications

The Romans were very determined fighters. They even conquered towns that were protected by high walls or built on clifftops. Sometimes the Romans simply surrounded towns. The inhabitants, unable to get in or out, were slowly starved of food and had to surrender. This took a long time, however, so the Romans invented techniques to break down defences more quickly. They also used heavy weapons, or artillery, called *tormenta*. These machines could fire missiles over long distances. Ropes made of horsehair or human hair were twisted and stretched so that when released they shot missiles with great force. This is what a siege might have looked like.

First the Romans surrounded the town.

Some soldiers tried to break holes in the walls.

Others built siege-works, wooden scaffolding and platforms that enabled them to climb the walls.

Most effective of all were siege towers. They were taller than the city walls and could be built away from the fortifications.

When finished, the siege tower was pushed up to the walls and soldiers climbed up inside. A drawbridge was lowered so that the soldiers could enter the city.

If soldiers wanted to approach the wall without being hit by the enemy's arrows, they grouped together and covered themselves completely with their shields. This formation was called a *testudo* (tortoise).

Large stationary crossbows were used to fire spears. Sometimes burning rags were attached to the tips.

The *onager* was a larger, heavy catapult, capable of firing massive rocks over 500 metres (1600ft).

Permanent fortifications

Hadrian† wanted permanent frontiers at the borders of the empire. Walls were built in Germany, Numidia and Britain. The one in Britain, known as Hadrian's Wall, is the best preserved. It runs for nearly 130km (80 miles) from the River Tyne to the River Solway, and was mainly built between AD122 and AD129. It was not only a barrier, like a city wall. It also had a political function, enabling the Romans to control the tribes to the north. This is a reconstruction of part of Hadrian's Wall.

Hadrian's Wall

Built into the wall, roughly equal distances apart, were 16 large forts. Each of these housed an auxiliary cohort of 1000 men, or a cavalry division of 500 men and their horses.

The wall was built by the soldiers in the three British legions. The legions were responsible for the upkeep and administration of the wall but it was actually staffed by *auxilia* (see page 207).

Maintaining frontiers

When legions settled at frontiers they set up permanent camps, laid out much like the temporary ones that soldiers built when they were on the march (see page 209). Legionary camps held about 5000 people. Each followed a similar plan so that soldiers could find their way around wherever they were. At first the soldiers lived in tents, later in wooden huts. In the 2nd century AD they began building forts out of stone, like the one shown here.

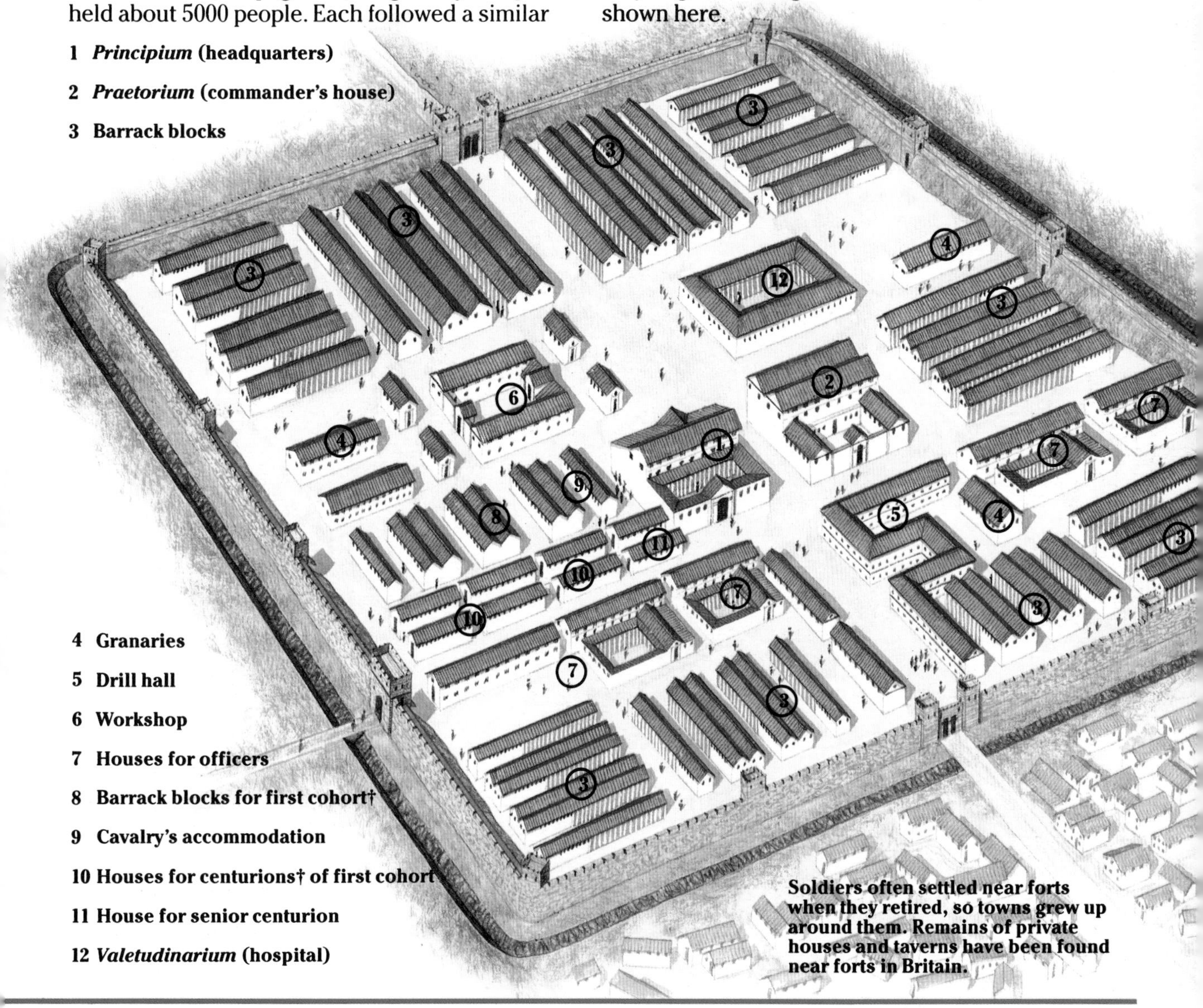

1 *Principium* (headquarters)

2 *Praetorium* (commander's house)

3 Barrack blocks

4 Granaries

5 Drill hall

6 Workshop

7 Houses for officers

8 Barrack blocks for first cohort†

9 Cavalry's accommodation

10 Houses for centurions† of first cohort

11 House for senior centurion

12 *Valetudinarium* (hospital)

Soldiers often settled near forts when they retired, so towns grew up around them. Remains of private houses and taverns have been found near forts in Britain.

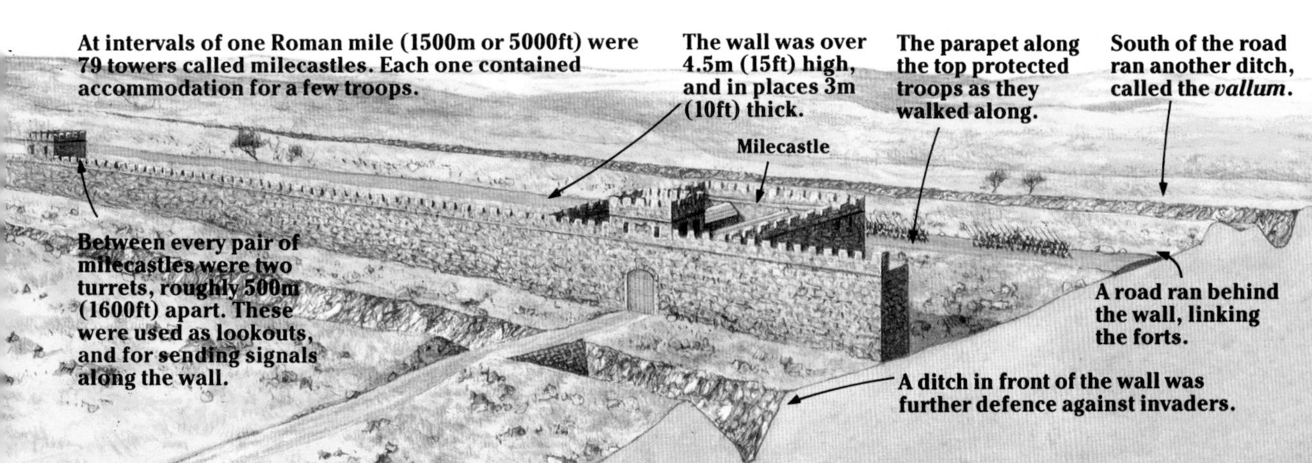

At intervals of one Roman mile (1500m or 5000ft) were 79 towers called milecastles. Each one contained accommodation for a few troops.

Between every pair of milecastles were two turrets, roughly 500m (1600ft) apart. These were used as lookouts, and for sending signals along the wall.

The wall was over 4.5m (15ft) high, and in places 3m (10ft) thick.

Milecastle

The parapet along the top protected troops as they walked along.

South of the road ran another ditch, called the *vallum*.

A road ran behind the wall, linking the forts.

A ditch in front of the wall was further defence against invaders.

Roman towns

Early Roman towns had no particular plan or design, unlike many Greek cities which were built on a grid pattern with streets at right angles to each other. This idea had been introduced about 450BC by the Greek town planner Hippodamus.

When the Romans occupied the Greek cities in southern Italy around 250BC, they quickly adopted the grid pattern for themselves. To it they added the features of the Roman town – the *forum*, basilicas, amphitheatres†, baths, drains and water systems. This is a reconstruction of a typical Roman town. The basic features became standard throughout the empire.

Many towns in the provinces that existed before the Romans occupied them had defensive walls. During the early empire, when these towns were protected by the army, walls were no longer needed. New towns were even forbidden to build them. Later, however, when invaders threatened the empire, earthworks were permitted. Many of these were later made into stone walls.

Library

The *thermae*, or public baths (see pages 252-253).

Gymnasium

Prosperous towns were extremely crowded and busy, with few open spaces. The number of apartment blocks caused a high density of population, particularly as expansion was limited by the town walls.

Most large towns had a theatre (see page 248) and an amphitheatre (see page 251).

Roman towns always had many inns (*tabernae*), snack bars (*thermopolia*) and bakeries (*pistrina*).

A town usually had four or more gates, with roads to neighbouring towns running through them.

Roman towns have been occupied and rebuilt over the centuries, so it is difficult to see the grid pattern in their remains. However it can be seen clearly in the ruins of Timgad in North Africa, because the town was deserted after Roman times.

The roads outside the city were lined with tombs and graves. Burials were not allowed inside the walls.

There were so many traffic jams that some towns barred wheeled traffic, apart from builders' wagons, from their streets during daylight hours.

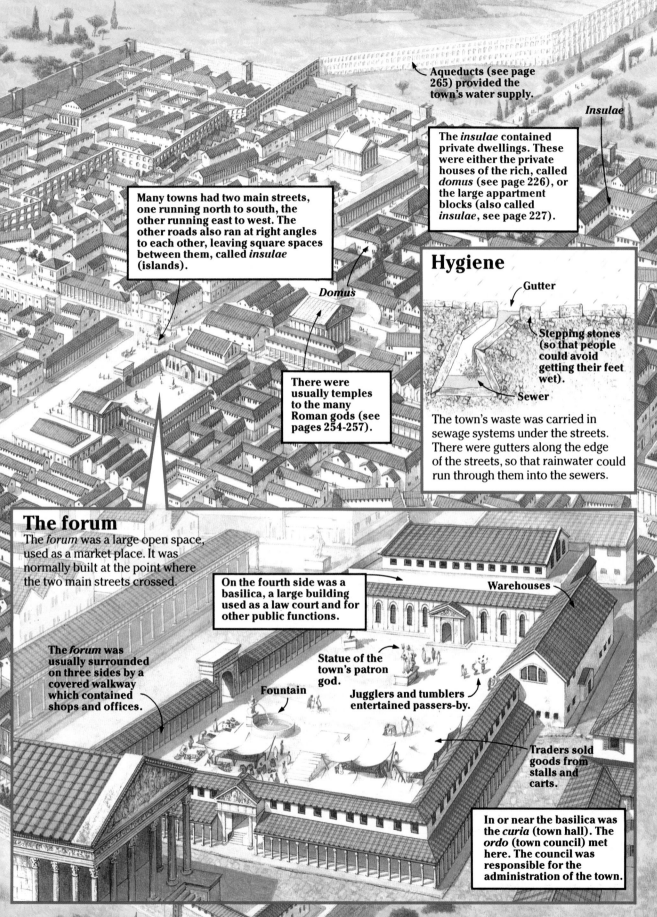

Aqueducts (see page 265) provided the town's water supply.

Insulae

The *insulae* contained private dwellings. These were either the private houses of the rich, called *domus* (see page 226), or the large appartment blocks (also called *insulae*, see page 227).

Many towns had two main streets, one running north to south, the other running east to west. The other roads also ran at right angles to each other, leaving square spaces between them, called *insulae* (islands).

Domus

There were usually temples to the many Roman gods (see pages 254-257).

Hygiene

Gutter

Stepping stones (so that people could avoid getting their feet wet).

Sewer

The town's waste was carried in sewage systems under the streets. There were gutters along the edge of the streets, so that rainwater could run through them into the sewers.

The forum

The *forum* was a large open space, used as a market place. It was normally built at the point where the two main streets crossed.

On the fourth side was a basilica, a large building used as a law court and for other public functions.

Warehouses

The *forum* was usually surrounded on three sides by a covered walkway which contained shops and offices.

Statue of the town's patron god.

Fountain

Jugglers and tumblers entertained passers-by.

Traders sold goods from stalls and carts.

In or near the basilica was the *curia* (town hall). The *ordo* (town council) met here. The council was responsible for the administration of the town.

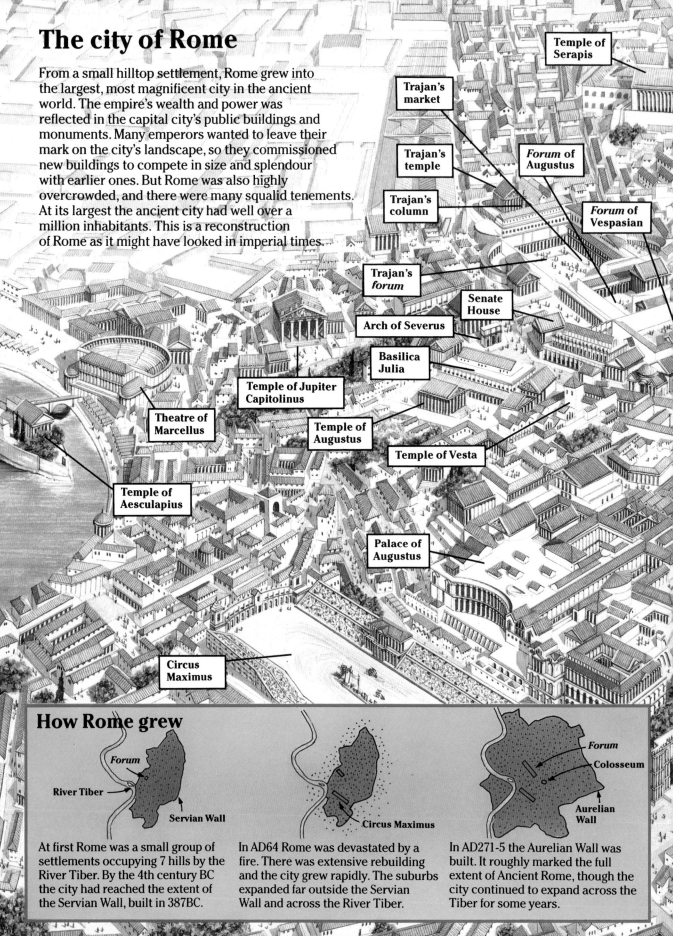

The city of Rome

From a small hilltop settlement, Rome grew into the largest, most magnificent city in the ancient world. The empire's wealth and power was reflected in the capital city's public buildings and monuments. Many emperors wanted to leave their mark on the city's landscape, so they commissioned new buildings to compete in size and splendour with earlier ones. But Rome was also highly overcrowded, and there were many squalid tenements. At its largest the ancient city had well over a million inhabitants. This is a reconstruction of Rome as it might have looked in imperial times.

Temple of Serapis

Trajan's market

Trajan's temple

Forum of Augustus

Trajan's column

Forum of Vespasian

Trajan's *forum*

Senate House

Arch of Severus

Basilica Julia

Temple of Jupiter Capitolinus

Temple of Augustus

Temple of Vesta

Theatre of Marcellus

Temple of Aesculapius

Palace of Augustus

Circus Maximus

How Rome grew

At first Rome was a small group of settlements occupying 7 hills by the River Tiber. By the 4th century BC the city had reached the extent of the Servian Wall, built in 387BC.

Forum

River Tiber

Servian Wall

In AD64 Rome was devastated by a fire. There was extensive rebuilding and the city grew rapidly. The suburbs expanded far outside the Servian Wall and across the River Tiber.

Circus Maximus

In AD271-5 the Aurelian Wall was built. It roughly marked the full extent of Ancient Rome, though the city continued to expand across the Tiber for some years.

Forum

Colosseum

Aurelian Wall

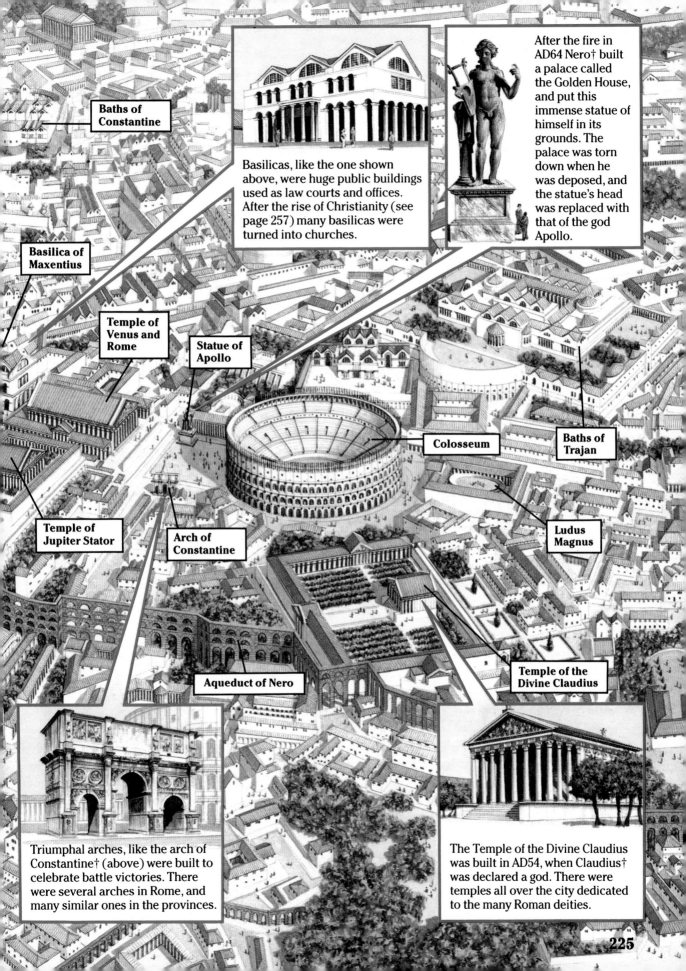

Baths of Constantine

Basilica of Maxentius

Temple of Venus and Rome

Statue of Apollo

Basilicas, like the one shown above, were huge public buildings used as law courts and offices. After the rise of Christianity (see page 257) many basilicas were turned into churches.

After the fire in AD64 Nero† built a palace called the Golden House, and put this immense statue of himself in its grounds. The palace was torn down when he was deposed, and the statue's head was replaced with that of the god Apollo.

Temple of Jupiter Stator

Arch of Constantine

Colosseum

Baths of Trajan

Ludus Magnus

Aqueduct of Nero

Temple of the Divine Claudius

Triumphal arches, like the arch of Constantine† (above) were built to celebrate battle victories. There were several arches in Rome, and many similar ones in the provinces.

The Temple of the Divine Claudius was built in AD54, when Claudius† was declared a god. There were temples all over the city dedicated to the many Roman deities.

225

Town houses

By the time of the later republic, most townspeople lived in large apartment blocks called *insulae*. Each individual apartment was called a *cenaculum*. Only very rich people could afford to live in a private house, or *domus*. A survey of Rome in AD350 listed 1790 *domus* and 46,602 *insulae*, though elsewhere the proportion of private houses may have been higher.

A domus

Most town houses were variations of the same basic plan. Some, like this one, had rooms on a second storey, but this was not very common.

The tiled roof of the *atrium* † sloped down to an opening called a *compluvium*. In cold weather it could be covered by canvas.

Rain collected in a shallow pool called the *impluvium*. When the water rose to a certain level, it was piped to a tank underneath the house.

The family lived in the rooms at the back of the house between the *atrium* and the garden.

Guests were received in the *atrium*. The word comes from the word *ater*, meaning black. In early times the *atrium* was the only room, and it was blackened by smoke from the fire.

The rooms at the front opened on to the street. They were often rented out as shops.

Tablinum (study)

In warm climates windows were left open, or covered with wooden shutters, animal skin or layers of semi-transparent stone. Glass windows were rare.

A walled garden like this was called a *peristylium*.

The *lararium*, a shrine to the household gods, was kept in the garden or the *atrium*.

Kitchen (see page 232)

The dining room was called a *triclinium* (see pages 230-231).

Most houses had no bathrooms, because in every town there were many public bath-houses (see pages 252-253).

Central heating

The Romans developed their central heating system, called the hypocaust, in the first century AD. In warm climates, like Italy, it was used mainly in bath-houses, but in colder parts of the empire it could be found in town houses and country villas. This diagram shows how the hypocaust system worked.

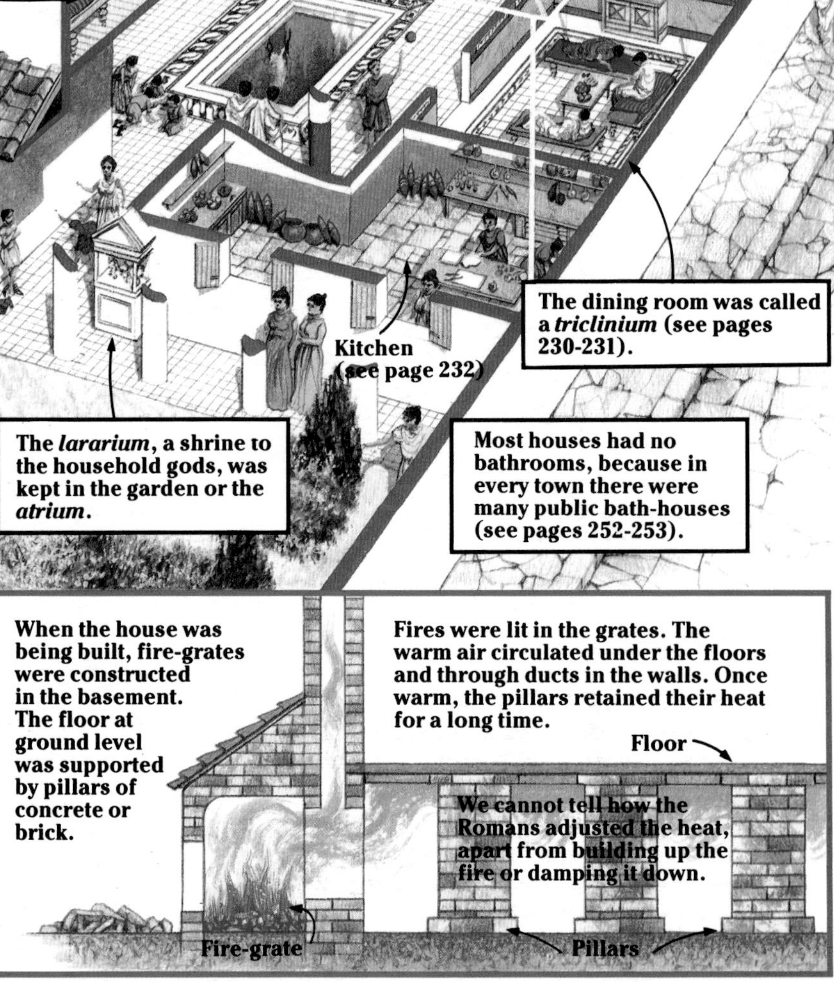

When the house was being built, fire-grates were constructed in the basement. The floor at ground level was supported by pillars of concrete or brick.

Fires were lit in the grates. The warm air circulated under the floors and through ducts in the walls. Once warm, the pillars retained their heat for a long time.

Floor

We cannot tell how the Romans adjusted the heat, apart from building up the fire or damping it down.

Fire-grate

Pillars

226

Insulae

Some apartments were luxurious and spacious, while others were cramped and squalid. They could have many rooms, or only one. Limits were imposed on the height to which *insulae* could be built – normally only four or five storeys were allowed.

Poorer tenants lived in the upper storeys, which were built of wood. The rooms were smaller and often in very bad condition.

Landlords often built extra rooms so that they could make more money, but these were often badly constructed of cheap materials. This made buildings very unsafe, and many collapsed.

Woodburning braziers were the only form of heating used, but these were a great fire risk and there were no chimneys.

The *insulae* had no internal drains, so people threw their waste into gutters in the streets.

Rich occupants often had several well-furnished, comfortable rooms to live in.

Few *insulae* had their own toilets. People had to use public lavatories like this.

Cooking was impossible in the flats, so people ate cold snacks, or went to inns and bars for their meals.

The lower storeys, usually built of stone, were for richer tenants.

There was no running water, but people fetched water from the many public fountains nearby.

The rooms at street level were sometimes let as shops or taverns. People rarely lived in the ground-floor rooms of *insulae*.

The storeys were connected by a staircase.

Firefighting

Fire was a constant risk in Rome, because of the hot, dry climate, the overcrowded conditions, and the use of open fires in wooden buildings. Augustus† set up a fire service for Rome. There were seven brigades, called *vigiles*, each with 1000 men. The city was divided into 14 regions and each brigade was responsible for two of them. These fire brigades were copied in other towns, though on a smaller scale.

Simple hand-held pumps were used to fight small fires, but they could only deliver a small amount of water.

Sponges and leather buckets were used to dampen undamaged walls to stop the fire spreading.

Furniture

Roman houses were quite sparsely furnished. Apart from the *atrium* and the *tablinum* (see page 226), many rooms were too small to hold much furniture. Most surviving Roman furniture is made of marble or metal, but this may be misleading. Wooden furniture may have been more usual, but most of it would have since decayed.

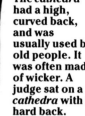

A back, head, or foot-board might be added, depending on the purpose of the bed.

Cushions and mattresses were filled with wool or feathers.

Webbing of leather or cloth.

A blanket was the only covering.

Beds

Beds and couches were important items of furniture. They were used in studies and dining rooms as well as bedrooms, in place of sofas.

Luxurious bed-frames were often inlaid with precious metals.

Some other kinds of Roman bed

Chairs

Scamnum

A Roman stool was called a *scamnum*. Stools usually had three legs and a round wooden top, or four legs and a square or rectangular top, often made of bronze.

Folding chair   *Sella*   *Bisellium*

A *sella* was a chair with four legs, arms, and no back. A larger version, the *bisellium*, was used by important people. The Romans also had folding chairs.

The *cathedra* had a high, curved back, and was usually used by old people. It was often made of wicker. A judge sat on a *cathedra* with a hard back.

Tables

Tables varied a lot in price, and Romans were prepared to spend large sums of money on them. As the Romans frequently ate outside, marble or stone tables were common.

Marble table

Table made of metal and wood

The one-legged table, called a *monopodium*, was particularly expensive. The central support could be carved in ivory, or be made of elaborately cast metal. Precious, rare woods were sometimes used for the tops.

Storage

For storage, the Romans used heavy chests and cupboards.

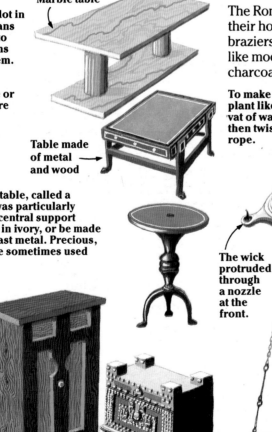

Heating and lighting

The Romans used oil lamps and tapers to light their houses. For heating they used small bronze braziers, or enclosed heaters which looked more like modern stoves. For fuel they used wood, charcoal, or coke, a refined form of coal.

To make a taper, the stalk of a marsh plant like papyrus was dipped in a vat of wax or tallow. The tapers were then twisted together into a sort of rope.

A brazier

Thousands of oil lamps have survived. They were made of terracotta† or metal, and burned vegetable oil (from olives, nuts or sesame) or fish oil. This produced a light similar to a candle.

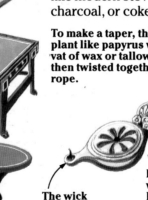

The wick protruded through a nozzle at the front.

Lamps were long and flat, with a handle at the back.

There were also hanging lamps with chains and hooks.

Lanterns were widely used. The flame was protected by pieces of horn, or animal bladder. Later lanterns were made of glass.

Decorations

The Romans were more interested in how houses looked inside than how they appeared from the outside. While many town houses looked drab from the street, their interiors were lavishly decorated with wall paintings and mosaics. At first the styles and techniques were adopted from the Greeks. Many Romans employed Greeks to decorate their rooms, because they were thought to be the best artists. This reconstruction shows decorators at work in a Roman house.

Artists began painting pictures on the walls while the plaster was still damp. Paintings done in this way are called frescoes.

Paintings of the countryside were popular. They included pictures of wildlife and decorative panels of fruit.

Architectural scenes were also common. Some used tricks of perspective to make the room seem larger.

When the background was dry the details of the painting were added. For this stage the paints were mixed with egg-white to thicken them.

Paints were made from ground rocks, plant extracts or animal dyes.

Mosaics (pictures made of small pieces of tile or stone) were popular in Rome by the 1st century BC.

Figures from Greek mythology were often depicted.

Walls were also painted with portraits, possibly of the owner of the house. These are often very realistic.

Wet plaster was spread over a small area, then stones were pressed into it.

At first, regular patterns in black and white were most common. These remained fashionable around Rome.

Coloured stones were used to make detailed portraits, or patterns like the one shown here.

There were companies of mosaicists who designed the mosaic away from the house. Then someone came to the house with a plan, and the stones already cut.

Statues

Rooms were decorated with statues. They were brightly painted in Roman times, but the paint has now worn off.

Statues of sea creatures were sometimes built into fountains.

Gods and goddesses were common subjects.

Animals were also popular.

Food and dining

For breakfast most Romans ate bread or wheat biscuits with honey, dates or olives. They drank water or wine. The *prandium* (lunch) was a similar meal of bread, or leftovers from the previous day's main meal. However, instead of eating at lunchtime, many Romans waited until the main meal of the day, the *cena*. This was in the afternoon, after the daily visit to the baths.

During the early republic, the *cena* was very simple. The commonest food was wheat, often eaten as a kind of porridge, with sauces and vegetables. Meat was eaten only after animals had been sacrificed at religious festivals, or on special occasions. Later, however, meat became more common, and, for the wealthy, meals became more elaborate.

A dinner party

In rich imperial households, the *cena* was often very lavish. It was a way to entertain friends or important people, and hosts displayed their wealth by giving luxurious meals. This is how a banquet might have looked.

During the republic, only men could attend formal dinners. By imperial times, women often dined with the men. In early Rome people sat on chairs at tables. Later it was fashionable to dine lying on couches.

Romans did not use knives and forks. They mostly ate with their fingers, or sometimes with spoons. Slaves wiped the guests' hands between courses.

Some dining rooms were decorated with mosaics† showing scraps of food.

Poet waiting to read to the guests.

The fourth side of the table was left clear for slaves to bring food to the table and remove empty dishes.

The slaves also served wine with the meal. Sometimes it was heated in a warmer.

The menu

The dinner came in three courses. The first consisted of such appetizers as salad, radishes, mushrooms, oysters and other shellfish, sardines and eggs. This course was followed by a drink of *mulsum* (wine sweetened with honey).

The main course contained as many as seven dishes, including fish, meat and poultry. These were served with vegetables and sauces.

Rather than clearing the dishes after the main meal, the slaves removed the table and replaced it with another one, on which fruit, nuts and honey cakes were served. This part of the meal was called the *secundae mensae* (second tables).

The food was served with plenty of wine. The Romans had more than two hundred varieties from various parts of the empire. The best was said to come from Campania, near Naples.

Roman recipes

A recipe book from the fourth century AD, written by an expert on food called Apicius, gives us details of some Roman dishes and tells us how they were cooked.

Sauces were made with great care. The commonest, called *liquamen* or *garum*, was made from fish, salt and herbs. Some people made it themselves, but it was so popular that it could be bought ready-made.

Defrutum, another sauce, was obtained by boiling fruit juice until it reduced by a third. This was then added to other dishes.

Dining utensils

The food was brought into the dining room on serving dishes. Most of these were made of glass or pottery, but if the host was very rich there would also be ornately decorated platters made of gold and silver. Some examples are shown below.

Glass was made throughout the empire. It was often extremely ornate.

Silver drinking cup

Spoons

Silver strainer

Red, decorated pottery like this was popular all over the empire. It is known as Samian ware.

The Romans were highly skilled metalworkers. Intricately decorated serving dishes like this were often found in rich households.

The seating plan

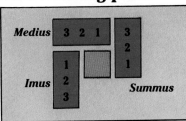

Medius 3 2 1		3 2 1
Imus 1 2 3		*Summus*

At formal banquets each couch seated three people. The couches were named *summus*, *medius* and *imus* (top, middle and bottom), and diners were seated according to their social status. The most honoured guest sat at *medius* 3, and the host often sat next to him at *imus* 1. A very rich host might have two tables of nine people each. Less formal dinners often had fewer than nine people.

The host also provided entertainment. Musicians, dancers, acrobats, conjurers and jugglers performed during the feast. At more elegant banquets the works of poets were read or sung.

Music and musicians

Though some rich citizens learned to play musical instruments they always remained amateurs, because they thought it was undignified to play, sing or dance in public. Professional musicians and dancers were usually slaves or freed men. As well as performing at dinner parties they also played in processions and parades, in the theatre and at the games. Here are some of the instruments they played.

Pipes   Lyre   Flute   Cymbals

Tambourine

Stuffed dates

For dessert Romans often ate stuffed dates. You can make these yourself.

Mash together some chopped apple and nuts, bread or cake crumbs, a pinch of cinnamon or nutmeg, and a little wine or fruit juice.

Cut the tops off the dates and remove the stones.

Push the filling in with a spoon.

In the kitchen

Most simple houses or apartments had no kitchens. The occupants could not cook in their living rooms because of the fire risk, so they had to visit a tavern whenever they wanted a hot meal. But rich people often had large, well-equipped kitchens in their houses. These were staffed by many slaves, each a specialist at preparing a particular type of food. They spent most of the day preparing the main meal. A typical Roman kitchen is shown below.

Pots like this, with pointed bottoms, were called *amphorae*. They were used for storing wine or oil.

Small *amphorae* were laid on shelves.

Large *amphorae* were propped up in the corner.

Food was cooked in earthenware or bronze pots on a stove full of hot charcoal.

Meat and poultry were roasted on spits over fires.

The cooks had sharp knives to chop vegetables.

To make sauces, ingredients had to be ground with a heavy pounder called a pestle, in a stone bowl called a mortar.

Kitchen utensils

Unlike the elaborate glass and metal utensils used for serving meals (see page 231), cooking pots were simply and strongly constructed to withstand a lot of use. Many utensils have been found at archaeological sites. Here are some examples.

Jugs were often made with very thick sides and only a small opening at the top, perhaps to keep water cool during hot weather.

This pottery strainer may have been used to drain liquid from curd cheese.

There were also pans that could be used for cooking or serving. This one also had a close-fitting lid.

Knives were beaten or cast out of metal, then sharpened. Some were given handles of wood, bone or ivory.

Metal sieves were used for straining wine or sauces. The holes in the bottom formed a decorative pattern.

Cooking pots were often placed on pottery or iron stands so that they did not rest directly on the fire.

This Roman relief shows slaves at work in a kitchen.

Two slaves are stoking the furnace.

A third is scooping flour from a sack.

Another is making dough or pastry.

Jewellery

At the beginning of the republic ornate jewels were rare. The law allowed only the upper classes to wear gold rings. However jewellery became more common after the Romans gained territories in the east, where precious metals were readily available. The materials most often used were gold, silver, bronze and iron, set with precious and semi-precious stones such as opals, emeralds and sapphires, and also with pearls. The Romans also polished glass and used it in place of precious stones. Both men and women wore rings. Women also wore a variety of earrings, necklaces, anklets, hairpins and brooches. In later imperial times these were very ornate. Pieces of jewellery have been found all over the Roman world. Here are some examples.

Gems often had designs cut into the surface, like this one found at Herculaneum.

A gold bracelet shaped like a snake was said to bring the wearer long life. These were found at Pompeii.

Others were set into rings made from several pieces of gold.

Fine gold chains were common. They were often made of many strands of metal, and worn as necklaces.

This bracelet is made from many strands of fine gold wire.

Each leaf in this necklace from Pompeii was stamped out of a sheet of gold.

Earrings were mostly made of gold, sometimes with semi-precious stones attached. This pair, set with emeralds, was probably made around Naples.

Pearls were very popular. Earrings like this were common around Pompeii and Herculaneum.

Pins such as these were made of ivory or gold and carved with various decorations. They were worn in the hair or pinned to clothing.

Provincial jewellers used local materials. This bangle, found in England, was carved out of a stone called jet.

Cameos

Miniature carvings in semi-precious stone, known as cameos, were also popular. They were made from sardonyx, a rock with layers of different colours. Cameos were often worn as brooches or medallions.

The carver first chose his stone carefully to make sure that the colours would be clear and sharp after it was carved.

Then he cut the design so that the raised portion was a different colour from the base.

The most popular designs were pictures of the imperial eagle, or portraits of famous people.

This skeleton, found at Herculaneum, shows that Romans might have worn rings between the first and second joints of the finger, as well as below the second joint. Some people wore more than one ring on each finger.

Clothes and fashion

Roman paintings, statues and writings all provide information about clothes. Fashions in Rome changed very little for nearly a thousand years. Most people wore clothes made from wool or linen. In imperial times fine cotton cloth was imported from India, but was very expensive. Silk, from China, cost three times its weight in gold. Fur and felt were also used, especially in cold climates.

Most garments were made from large uncut pieces of cloth which were folded and pinned with pins called *fibulae*, or tied with belts. Garments needing a lot of sewing were rare, as most needles were made of bone and therefore very clumsy. Clothes were mainly the natural colours of their fibres, but some were bleached white or dyed various shades.

Men's clothes

A man's only underwear was a loincloth. He probably slept in one of these as well. Over this he wore a tunic, made from two rectangles stitched at the sides and shoulders, and tied with a belt. Augustus† is said to have worn four tunics at once when the weather was cold.

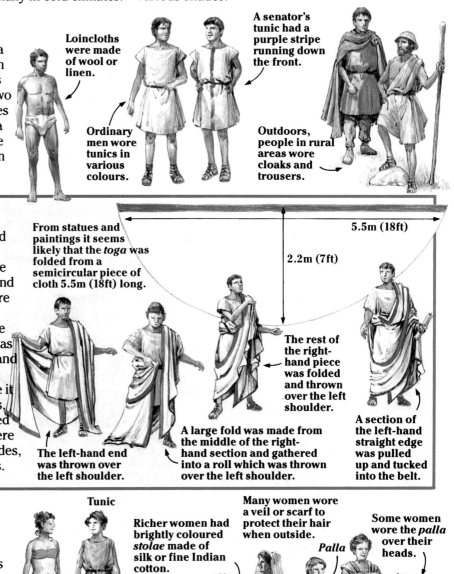

Loincloths were made of wool or linen.

Ordinary men wore tunics in various colours.

A senator's tunic had a purple stripe running down the front.

Outdoors, people in rural areas wore cloaks and trousers.

The toga

Originally only citizens† could wear the *toga*. Worn over the tunic, at first it was just a large woollen blanket wrapped round the body. Later it became more elaborate with complicated folds and drapes. Many people disliked the *toga* because it was heavy and awkward to wear, and hard to clean. But emperors tried to keep it in use because it was so distinctive. Like tunics, senators' *togas* were decorated with a purple stripe. *Togas* were sometimes worn in other shades, particularly black for funerals.

From statues and paintings it seems likely that the *toga* was folded from a semicircular piece of cloth 5.5m (18ft) long.

5.5m (18ft)

2.2m (7ft)

The rest of the right-hand piece was folded and thrown over the left shoulder.

The left-hand end was thrown over the left shoulder.

A large fold was made from the middle of the right-hand section and gathered into a roll which was thrown over the left shoulder.

A section of the left-hand straight edge was pulled up and tucked into the belt.

Women's clothes

As underwear women wore a loincloth and, sometimes, a brassière or corsets. Over this went a tunic, probably of fine wool or linen. On top of this was worn the *stola*, a robe which reached the ankles.

In early times women wore the *toga*, but later a garment called the *palla* became fashionable. It was a large rectangular piece of cloth which could be draped over the *stola* in many ways.

Tunic

Richer women had brightly coloured *stolae* made of silk or fine Indian cotton.

Stola

Many women wore a veil or scarf to protect their hair when outside.

Palla

Some women wore the *palla* over their heads.

Tunics were often made of plain, undyed cloth.

Children's clothes

Most boys and girls wore tunics like those of their parents. Some young boys wore the *toga praetexta*, a garment with a purple stripe. At about the age of 14 a special ceremony took place and they began wearing adult clothes (see page 240).

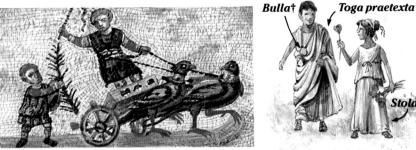

This mosaic shows children in tunics.

Bulla† — *Toga praetexta*

Stola

Some young girls wore the *stola*.

Men's hairstyles

During the early republic, many men wore beards, but from the 2nd century BC until the rule of Hadrian† it was the fashion in Rome to be cleanshaven. Most Roman men wore their hair short, but during imperial times some fashion-conscious men had longer hair which was oiled and curled. Some popular hairstyles are shown here.

Republican hairstyle

Later hairstyle

Early imperial hairstyles

The barber's shop was a place to meet friends and gossip. Being shaved was painful. Although the razor was sharp the barber used no oil or soap, so cuts and scars were frequent.

Women's hairstyles

Rich women spent a lot of time and money on their hairstyles, and had slaves to do their hair for them. Some of the most popular styles are shown here.

During the republic most women wore a simple bun.

Women sometimes cut the hair of blonde or red-headed slaves, and made it into wigs to wear themselves.

In imperial times hairstyles were very ornately plaited and curled.

Makeup

Women used various substances as makeup. They stored these in small pots and bottles.

Eyelids were darkened with ash or a substance called antimony.

It was fashionable to look as pale as possible. Women whitened their faces and arms with powdered chalk.

To colour their lips and cheeks red, they used the sediment from red wine, or a plant dye called *fucus*.

Pins

Heated tongs were used to curl hair, and pins made of bone or ivory were used to keep the hair in place.

Makeup pot

Hair-comb

Shoes

During the early republic, many Romans went barefoot most of the time, especially indoors. Outside they wore leather sandals. Later, footwear became more elaborate, and shoemakers became skilled at creating ornate sandals, shoes and boots out of canvas and leather.

Sandals were made out of leather.

Soldiers often wore boots that had soles studded with nails.

Women wore elegant sandals like these.

Outside men wore *calcei*, heavy boots.

Slippers were made out of soft leather or cloth.

The Roman villa

The Romans used the word *villa* for a country house, as opposed to *domus* (town house; see page 226). Wealthy Romans saw the countryside as a source of income and as a place to rest. Many villas were owned by rich city-dwellers who only spent part of the year in the country. At other times the estate was run by a manager and a team of slaves. Most villas were centres of farming (see overleaf). A few were supported by such other industries as pottery or mining. A very small number were lavish palaces that existed simply for their owners' pleasure.

An Italian villa

Most of the villas that have been excavated date from late imperial times. Few earlier villas remain, as their sites were often rebuilt or improved at a later period.

This reconstruction is based on remains found at various Italian sites. It shows a villa on an estate that made its money from farming and the production of olive oil and wine.

Decorations

The interiors of villas were often lavishly decorated. Mosaics (see page 229) were used to cover floors and walls. This one was found at a villa near Pompeii.

Triclinium (dining room)

The part where the owners from the city lived was very luxurious. It was called the *villa urbana*.

Kitchen

Paintings

The walls were also painted with colourful murals. Countryside scenes like this one were very popular.

A villa in the provinces

When the Romans conquered northern Europe, the population there consisted mostly of peasant farmers who lived in simple huts. The conquest opened up new opportunities for many of them. Gradually a new class of natives emerged – wealthy landowners who adopted Roman customs. They built large, important farmhouses based on Roman ones.

The pictures below show how this new style of farmhouse developed. They are based on details taken from excavations at a villa known as Lockleys, near St Albans, England.

One of the wings had two storeys

▲ Before the conquest (c.AD50) the farmhouse was round with a thatched roof.

▲ Around AD60, after the conquest, it was rebuilt as a rectangular hut.

▲ About ten years later it was rebuilt and enlarged, with five rooms and a verandah.

Towards the end of the 2nd century the villa was redesigned. The new style is known as a winged-corridor villa, because the verandah was replaced by a corridor with an area known as a wing at each end. Later, in some villas, the wings were extended and linked with a wall, forming a courtyard inside.

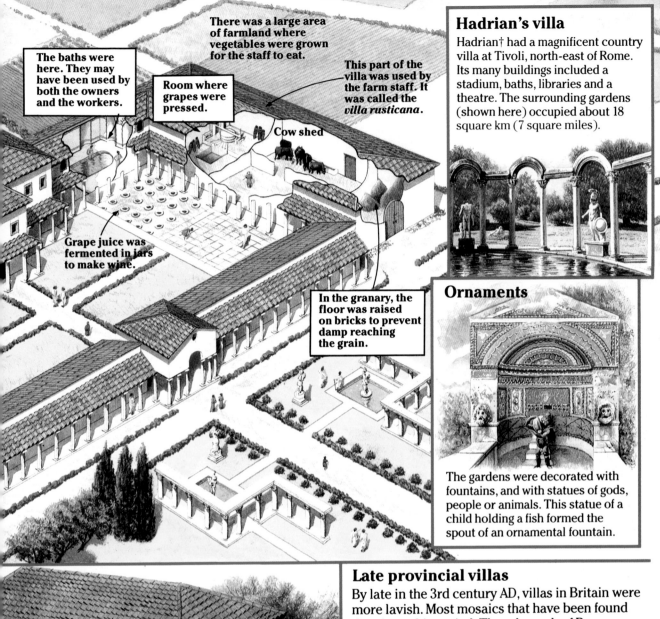

The baths were here. They may have been used by both the owners and the workers.

Room where grapes were pressed.

There was a large area of farmland where vegetables were grown for the staff to eat.

This part of the villa was used by the farm staff. It was called the *villa rusticana*.

Cow shed

Grape juice was fermented in jars to make wine.

In the granary, the floor was raised on bricks to prevent damp reaching the grain.

Hadrian's villa

Hadrian† had a magnificent country villa at Tivoli, north-east of Rome. Its many buildings included a stadium, baths, libraries and a theatre. The surrounding gardens (shown here) occupied about 18 square km (7 square miles).

Ornaments

The gardens were decorated with fountains, and with statues of gods, people or animals. This statue of a child holding a fish formed the spout of an ornamental fountain.

Late provincial villas

By late in the 3rd century AD, villas in Britain were more lavish. Most mosaics that have been found date from this period. Though much of Roman Europe was under attack from barbarians†, Britain was quite a safe place to live. Some rich citizens† from more dangerous provinces may have sought refuge there. This is a reconstruction of a 3rd-century villa at Chedworth, Gloucestershire.

The Roman courtyard alone was bigger than the modern manor house that was later built on its grounds.

The foundations were built of chalk and flint.

The lower parts of the walls were made of flint and mortar.

237

Farming

Farming was one of the Romans' most important industries. Although basic farming methods changed little over the centuries, the Romans developed ways of making farms more efficient and productive. They introduced these ideas all over the empire and took better equipment to primitive countries like Britain. They also spread new crops, fruit and vegetables through the empire.

During the early republic most farms were very small, often worked by just one family and maybe one or two slaves†. These farmers grew enough to live on, and sold any surplus.

During the Punic† wars many farmers had to leave their farms to join the army. Their lands were neglected; some were devastated by battles and marching soldiers.

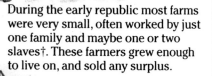

After the wars, many owners of small farms could not afford to repair the damage. Their land was bought by rich landowners and turned into large farms which were staffed by slaves.

An imperial farm

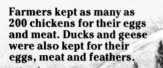

Many imperial farms produced a variety of goods, including crops, cattle, oil and wine, but some concentrated on just one or two of these products. The farm shown here has been reconstructed using details from Roman paintings, reliefs and mosaics, some of which are shown in the inset boxes.

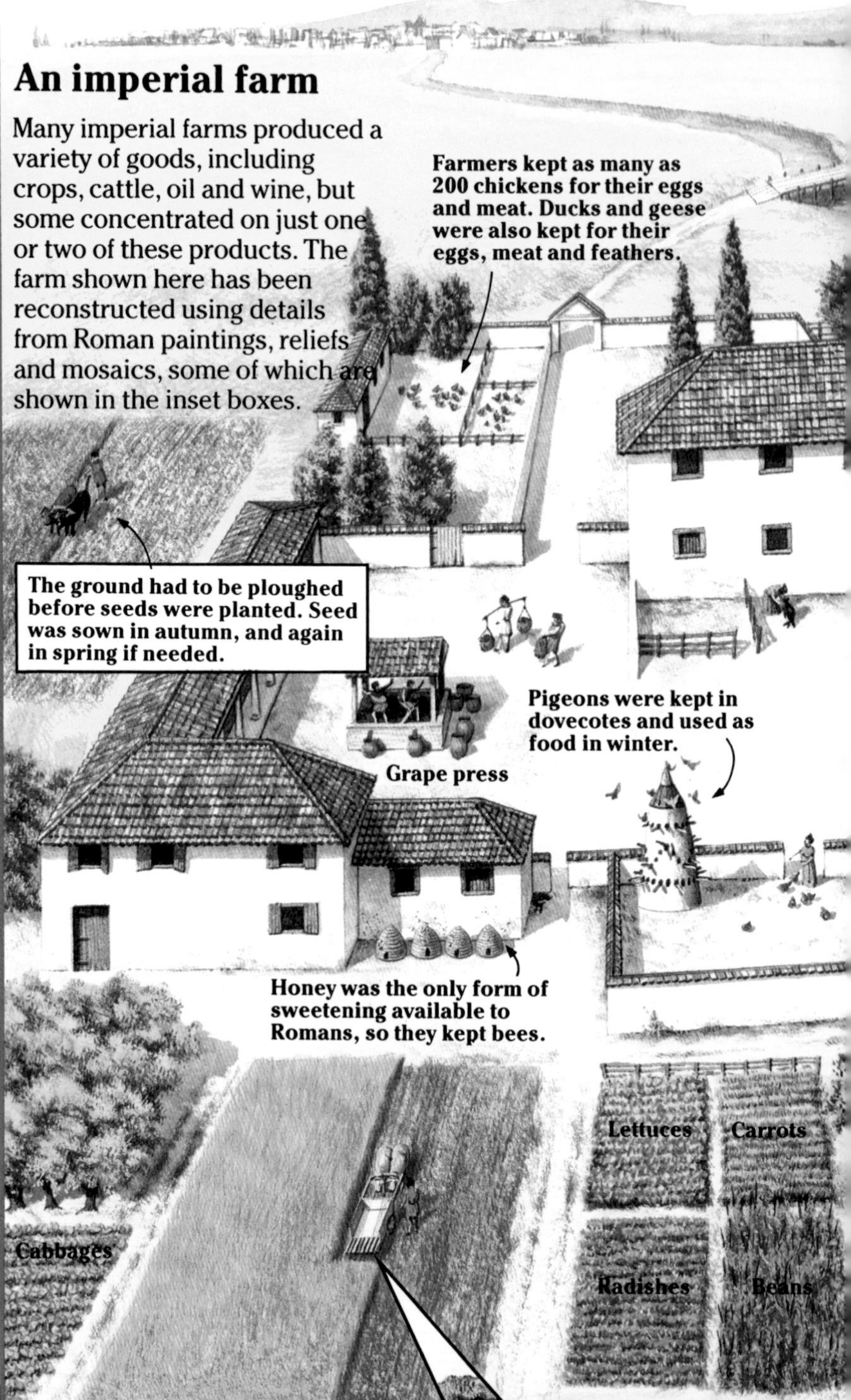

Farmers kept as many as 200 chickens for their eggs and meat. Ducks and geese were also kept for their eggs, meat and feathers.

The ground had to be ploughed before seeds were planted. Seed was sown in autumn, and again in spring if needed.

Grape press

Pigeons were kept in dovecotes and used as food in winter.

Honey was the only form of sweetening available to Romans, so they kept bees.

Lettuces   Carrots

Cabbages

Radishes   Beans

Many farms were dedicated to growing food for the inhabitants of nearby towns. Market gardens were very prosperous, and we know from the remains of rubbish tips that the Romans had many different types of fruits and vegetables.

The most important working animal was the ox, which pulled ploughs and carts. The ones in this relief are pushing a threshing machine.

Horses were rarely used as farm animals, though they were bred for the army.

Donkeys and mules had many uses. They were used to pull carts, turn flour-mills and carry heavy loads.

When ripe, grapes were picked, put into a stone trough, and trodden to extract the juice. The juice was stored in jars to ferment into wine.

Grapes were a very common crop. Vines were grown to provide fruit for eating and for wine-making.

Olive trees grew all over Italy. Olive oil was used in cooking, as a form of soap, and as fuel for lamps. It was extracted from the olives in a special crusher like this.

On the threshing floor, horses were driven over grain to prepare it for grinding into flour.

Figs

Pears

Apples

Sheep were kept for their wool and milk. Sheep's milk was a very popular drink.

The Romans had large herds of pigs, because pork was the most popular meat.

The rural ideal

Belief in the merits of rural life continued even among sophisticated imperial city-dwellers. This is partly why villas† were so popular with the urban rich. The countryside inspired Roman artists to create scenes like this, showing a rural goddess looking after a flock of sheep.

There were also many books about farming. Some, like Cato's *De Agri Cultura* (c.160BC), were manuals about how to run an estate. Others, however, like the *Georgics* by Virgil†, are lengthy poems in praise of rural life. But while city-dwellers idealized the country, the reality for farmers was often poverty, famine and disease.

Goats gave milk, and their hair was used to make rope and sacks. This relief shows a farmer milking a goat.

Cattle were also used for ploughing, and kept less often for milk or meat.

Marriage and childbirth

Young Romans had little choice about whom they married. Parents chose husbands and wives for their children, and often arranged marriages for political, business or social reasons. Girls could marry at the age of 12, but most waited until they were at least 14. There were different types of marriage contract. In republican times a woman's money and possessions could become the property of her husband's father. Later, women controlled their own belongings and had more freedom.

The wedding day had to be carefully chosen because many days in the Roman calendar were thought to be unlucky. Weddings often took place in the second half of June, which was considered a particularly lucky period.

To celebrate an engagement, a party was held and the marriage contract was written out. The bride was given a ring for the third finger of her left hand. The night before the wedding, she offered her childhood toys to the gods at the household shrine.

On the wedding day, the bride's house was hung with flowers and ribbons. She wore a white tunic, a head-dress of flowers, and a red veil and shoes. Her hair was braided.

When the guests and bridegroom arrived the priest asked the gods if the day was a lucky one. If the answer was favourable the ceremony continued.

The contract was signed and the chief bridesmaid led the bride forward and joined her hand with the groom's. The couple prayed to the gods, and the bride promised to follow her husband wherever he went.

After the ceremony, there was a party at the house of the bride's father. Then the bride and groom led a procession of guests, flute players and torch-bearers to the groom's house. When they arrived, the groom carried the bride over the threshold.

Childbirth

Childbirth was very dangerous in Roman times. Medical science was primitive, and we know from tombstones that women often died giving birth. Children often died when they were still very small. Women married early partly because they believed that childbirth was safer when they were young. Some richer women, after giving birth to an heir, avoided having more children by using sponges as contraceptives.

A new baby was bathed and placed at its father's feet. The father picked up the child to show formally that he had accepted it into the family.

On the ninth day after the birth a ceremony took place at which the child was named. It was given a *bulla*, a charm to ward off evil spirits.

Becoming an adult

When a boy was about 14 years old, normally after he had finished his basic education, a ceremony was held at which he formally became an adult. With family and friends he went to the *forum*†, where he discarded his childhood clothes and *bulla*. He was given an adult's *toga*† and his first shave, and was registered as a citizen†. A party was held to celebrate.

Funerals and burial

When someone died, the Romans performed rituals based on their beliefs about what happened after death. Most people thought a dead person's spirit was rowed across a mythical river (the Styx), to the underworld (Hades†). The spirit was judged, then went to heaven (Elysium) or hell (Tartarus). Funerals prepared the dead person for the journey. A coin was placed under his or her tongue to pay the ferry fare to Hades. This is what happened after the death of a very important person.

The body lay in state in the *atrium*†, surrounded by lamps and candles.

When a nobleman died his body was washed and covered in oil.

If the man had held political office he was dressed in his official robes. Otherwise he wore a *toga*.

Important citizens lay in state for several days, an emperor for a week. During this period people came to pay their respects.

The body was covered in flowers and wreaths.

On the day of the funeral the body was placed on a portable bed known as a litter. Eight men carried the litter to the *forum* as part of a procession.

Praeficae (professional mourners) and torch-carriers followed the corpse.

Musicians

The procession stopped in the *forum*, where a speech was made in praise of the dead person.

In republican times relatives of the dead person rode in front of the procession. They wore death masks and mourning robes. This practice stopped in imperial times.

The body was taken to the grave; by law this had to be outside the city. Main roads were lined with magnificent tombs. The body was placed in a coffin made of stone or marble called a *sarcophagus*.

Sarcophagi were often intricately carved with scenes of daily life, hunts and battles.

The site of the grave was marked with a tomb, monument or mound of earth. Sometimes pillars or even high towers were built, such as this one at Igel in Germany, which is 23m (75ft) high.

Sometimes, instead of burying the body, the Romans cremated it. In simple ceremonies they dug a pit, filled it with wood, and burned the body. When the fire died down they covered the ashes with earth.

In more elaborate rituals the body was burned on a ceremonial fire known as a pyre. Relatives threw clothes and food into the flames, in case the dead person needed them later.

After the fire had died down it was doused with wine. The ashes were collected and placed in a jar called an urn. The urns were sometimes placed in a special underground chamber called a *columbarium*.

Education

Roman children were educated according to the wealth of their families. Many poorer children never learned to read or write because their parents needed them to work. Richer children started school when they were about six years old, attending a *ludus* (primary school). Most children left the *ludus* at the age of 11, and had any further education at home. But girls often began preparing for marriage, which could take place when they were 12 years old.

The school day

Most schools only had one room, on the ground floor of a house or behind a shop. There was usually only one class, of about 12 children. Remains of pupils' exercises, and descriptions by Roman writers of their education, tell us about the school day.

Teachers were often slaves brought back from Greece by the Roman army. The Romans respected the knowledge and learning of the Greeks.

Young children recited the alphabet and practised reading and writing.

Rich families employed a slave called a *paedagogus*, who took the children to school and supervised them while they were in class.

Older children had to learn and recite the works of famous authors.

Some pupils wrote on wooden tablets coated with wax.

Some pupils scratched their writing on bits of pottery.

The grammaticus

Around the age of 11 some boys went to a *grammaticus* (secondary school), where they learned such subjects as history, philosophy, geography, geometry, music and astronomy. One of the most important subjects was Greek, because Greek culture was such a big influence on Roman life. Works of Greek and Roman literature were studied in great detail. Pupils were expected to be able to imitate the styles of famous authors. Greek was also necessary for Romans because most of the best books on other subjects were written by Greeks.

Further education

One purpose of secondary education was to prepare the student for study with a teacher of public speaking called a *rhetor*. Anyone who wanted to be a politician or lawyer had to learn to speak in public. This training began when a youth was 13 or 14, and could take many years; Cicero† continued his studies until he was nearly 30. If parents were very rich they might send their sons to Athens or Rhodes to learn these skills from the best Greek teachers. Only the wealthiest people could afford to give their children this education, so few poor people became politicians or lawyers.

The *rhetor* taught his pupils how to write speeches properly and how to present them well.

Rhetor

Writing

In school, pupils practised writing by scratching on panels of wood coated with wax, using a pointed metal pen called a *stylus*. When the space on the tablet was used up, the wax was scraped off and more was applied. Some children scratched writing exercises on pieces of broken pottery. Older pupils were allowed to use pens made from reeds or metal. They wrote on sheets of papyrus (see below) with ink made of gum and soot.

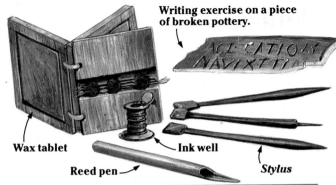

Writing exercise on a piece of broken pottery.

Wax tablet

Ink well

Reed pen

Stylus

Papyrus

In Roman times paper made from wood-pulp had not been invented. Instead the Romans used a material made from an Egyptian reed called papyrus. When papyrus was not available, parchment made from washed animal skin was used, but it was regarded as inferior to papyrus, probably because it was much heavier. The method of manufacturing papyrus is shown below.

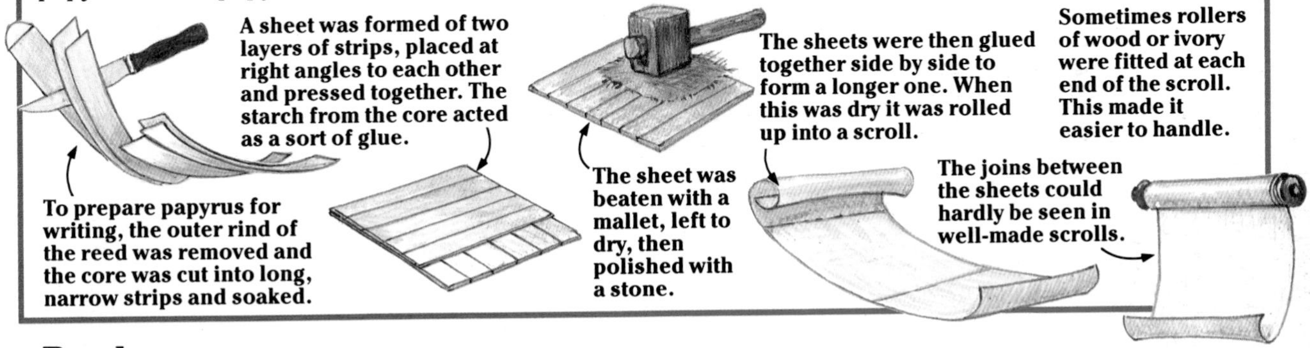

A sheet was formed of two layers of strips, placed at right angles to each other and pressed together. The starch from the core acted as a sort of glue.

To prepare papyrus for writing, the outer rind of the reed was removed and the core was cut into long, narrow strips and soaked.

The sheet was beaten with a mallet, left to dry, then polished with a stone.

The sheets were then glued together side by side to form a longer one. When this was dry it was rolled up into a scroll.

Sometimes rollers of wood or ivory were fitted at each end of the scroll. This made it easier to handle.

The joins between the sheets could hardly be seen in well-made scrolls.

Books

The Romans were very fond of books. In large cities like Rome and Alexandria there were numerous bookshops and publishers. Many people treasured books, and built up large collections of them. The state, and also some rich individuals, set up libraries for the public to use.

By the late Empire there were 29 libraries in Rome. Books took a long time to make, because each one had to be written out by hand. They were copied by scribes who were often Greek slaves. This picture shows how a manuscript was copied.

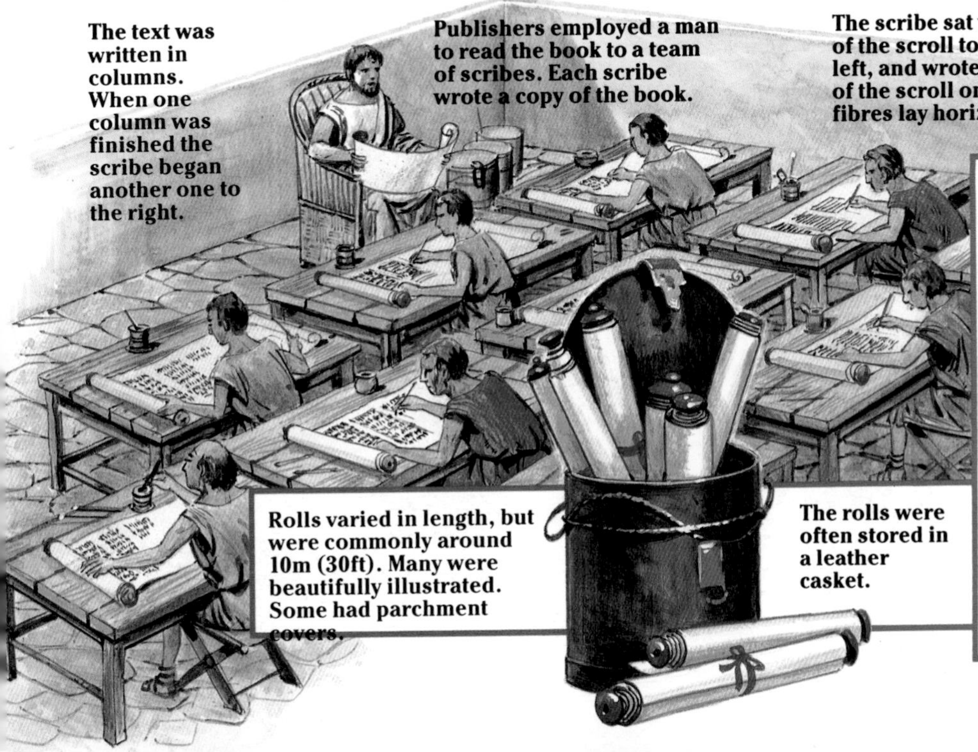

The text was written in columns. When one column was finished the scribe began another one to the right.

Publishers employed a man to read the book to a team of scribes. Each scribe wrote a copy of the book.

The scribe sat with the ends of the scroll to his right and left, and wrote on the side of the scroll on which the fibres lay horizontally.

Rolls varied in length, but were commonly around 10m (30ft). Many were beautifully illustrated. Some had parchment covers.

The rolls were often stored in a leather casket.

The codex

In the 4th century AD the scroll began to be replaced by the *codex*, in which the pages were secured at one side. The *codex* was adopted by the Christian † Church because it held more information than a scroll, and was easier to store, carry and read.

Jobs and occupations

Upper-class Romans did not respect physical labour, and would consider only a few careers, such as the army, politics, or some forms of financial work. Skilled jobs like architecture (see pages 70-73) or medicine (see pages 68-69) were done by educated members of the middle class, foreigners, or freed men (see opposite). Most poorer citizens† worked as craftsmen or shopkeepers; those in rural areas owned or worked on farms (see pages 46-47). Manual labour like building or mining was done almost entirely by slaves (see opposite).

Most craftsmen worked in small workshops, with a few apprentices and perhaps one or two slaves. They worked at the back of the shop, and sold their goods in the front. Other shopkeepers bought their goods from wholesale markets and then sold them to the public from their shops. A typical Roman street might have contained some of the shops shown here.

> Meat, produced from specially bred cattle, was sold wholesale to butchers at a market called the *forum boarium*. The butcher then sold to the public. Some butchers sold poultry as well.

> Carpenters made furniture or worked in the building trade. The workshop was equipped with many types of tool still in use today.

> Potters designed and made crockery of all kinds. They cast the pots on wheels and baked them in kilns over wooden fires.

> Bakers ground flour and baked bread at the back of their shops, then sold it over a counter at the front. The loaves were given distinctive patterns.

> Metalworkers made tools, weapons, and household goods, most commonly out of bronze, iron and copper. Jewellers made brooches, rings and ornmaments out of gold, silver and precious stones (see page 41).

Working women

The lives of Roman women depended on how rich they were. Rich families thought it inappropriate for women to go out to work. Instead wealthy women directed the work of slaves and organized the running of the home. They were also expected to have babies, and slaves helped them to bring up their children. We know that a few women became doctors or teachers, but these were rare.

In ordinary families women had to spin and weave woollen cloth to make clothes. All women were taught these skills, but most rich families bought ready-made cloth.

Poorer women worked in markets, as needlewomen, or as attendants at the baths. Some served in shops, like the one shown in this relief.

In the country, women worked on farms and as shepherdesses. A farmer's wife worked on the estate with her husband.

Slaves and slavery

Slaves were workers with no rights or status who were owned by Roman citizens, or by the state. They were bought and sold like any other property, and their lives were controlled by their owners. Like other ancient peoples, the Romans thought this situation was quite natural. There were very few slaves during the early republic, but after the 3rd century BC the number grew as Rome conquered other countries. After each new victory prisoners of war were brought back to Rome. They were exhibited at markets with signs round their necks advertising their qualities.

Slaves were sold by auction to the highest bidder.

A slave's life

In imperial times there was a vast workforce of slaves. Their lives varied depending on the jobs they did and whom they worked for. The law allowed slave-owners to treat their slaves however they wished. Many slaves suffered terribly at the hands of cruel masters, but others lived well. Here are some of the jobs that slaves did.

Greek slaves were thought to be the cleverest, so they were the most expensive. They worked in richer Roman houses as doctors, tutors, musicians, goldsmiths, artists and librarians. Other slaves worked as hairdressers, butlers, maids and cooks. Some helped their owners in shops or factories.

Slaves owned by good masters in the country often lived better than poor citizens in towns. They worked in pleasant surroundings, and could marry and have children. Many also ran small farms of their own.

The government itself owned many slaves, who maintained buildings, bridges and aqueducts. Others worked as civil servants, helping the administration of the empire. Some became very powerful and important.

Slaves who worked in mines suffered particularly bad conditions. They were harshly treated and forced to work constantly in mines that were often unsafe. Many died as a result of injuries or beating.

There were several rebellions by discontented slaves. The most famous was led by Spartacus, who formed an army of slaves in 73BC. It had up to 90,000 members until it was defeated by the Roman army two years later.

Some slaves were paid wages. If they saved enough, they could pay their masters to set them free. Others did not have to pay, as some owners freed their favourite slaves as a reward. By imperial times freed

At the freedom ceremony the slave wore a special cap and was given a *toga praetexta* †.

men were a large, rich sector of the population. Many became businessmen, and were a vital part of the economy. Others became important administrators or civil servants (see page 219).

Money and trade

The Roman economic system changed as the empire grew. During the early republic money was not used; people simply exchanged one kind of goods for another (this is known as bartering). Later, economic transactions were conducted using blocks of bronze weighing one Roman pound (327g/11.44oz). But as the Romans gained territory, they became richer and the economy became more complex. Coins were introduced, and trade and taxation reorganized. By imperial times an intricate economic system co-ordinated money and trade all over the Roman world.

Republican coins

Coins were first widely used by the Greeks. After seeing Greek coins in central Italy, the Romans opened their first mint around 290BC. Soon there were several Roman mints, all producing their own coins. The names and styles changed often, and, as prices kept rising, so did the values.

The first Roman coin, the *as*, was ▶ bronze. Asses had the heads of gods or goddesses on one side and pictures of ships on the other.

Around 269BC the first silver ▶ coin, the *didrachm*, was introduced. This one shows Mars, the god of war.

◀ Later a silver coin called the *denarius* was issued. This one shows a man voting in the elections. There were at first 10, and later 16 asses to a *denarius*.

Another silver coin, the ▶ *sestertius*, was first worth 2.5 asses, later 4.

The *aureus*, Rome's first gold coin, was introduced during the second Punic† war.

◀ Coins were used to mark important events. This one from about 42BC shows Brutus† on one side. The other shows a cap and a pair of daggers. 'EID MAR' means 'The Ides of March', the date of Caesar's assassination.

Early imperial coins

When Augustus became emperor he took control of the mints, and all gold and silver coins were made under his supervision. But mints in the provinces were allowed to produce their own bronze and copper coins, because they were less valuable. Augustus standardized the monetary system and gave all coins a fixed value. They were used all over the empire, and this encouraged trade (see opposite).

Every coin had the emperor's head on it ▶ to prove it was genuine. The largest gold coin, still called the *aureus*, was roughly 8 grams (¼oz) of gold.

The silver *denarius* ▶ now weighed about 4 grams (⅛oz). An *aureus* was worth 25 *denarii*.

During the Empire the *sestertius* was minted in bronze, not silver; ◀ there were 4 *sestertii* in a *denarius*.

A *dupondius* was ◀ worth half a *sestertius*.

The *as* was made ▶ of copper. There were 4 to a *sestertius*.

There were 2 ◀ bronze *semis* to an *as*.

There were 4 copper *quadrans* ▶ in an *as*.

Later imperial coins

Prices rose constantly, so people could buy less and less with their coins. New ones of higher values had to be minted. But the cost of precious metals increased too, so mints were forced to reduce the weight of coins, or to make them in copper with only a thin coating of precious metal.

This type of coin, known as the *solidus*, was first issued by Constantine†. He intended it to become the standard coin, as it was difficult to forge and everyone knew what it was worth. The *solidus* was made from about 5g (⅙oz) of gold.

Towards the end of the Empire people became suspicious of money because prices rose so quickly, coins contained less precious metal and forgeries were common. Many Romans abandoned coins and returned to bartering.

Banking

After the Punic† wars, the Romans controlled a huge trading network. Merchants and businessmen needed money to finance trading projects, so money-lending and banking became important parts of the economy. These services were provided mainly by *equites*† and freed men†, as patricians† thought financial work was undignified. Many members of the middle classes became very rich.

This relief shows a banker at his desk. There were moneychangers and bankers all over the empire. Some were controlled by the government, but others operated individually.

Many people found themselves unable to repay their debts. When this happened they had their property confiscated. Some were even sold into slavery.

Taxes

The government imposed taxes to raise money to run the state. Taxation changed from time to time, and differed in each area. Some of the main types of tax are described below.

Provincials†, and later Roman citizens† themselves, paid tax on their property, houses, farms, slaves and animals. Travelling inspectors assessed how much tax people had to pay.

Some financial transactions were subject to tax, including buying and selling property or slaves. People also paid tax on money they inherited. This stone relief shows people paying a tax collector.

There was no centrally organized system of distributing food to soldiers. Instead farmers had to reserve a portion of their grain and other goods for any troops based on their land.

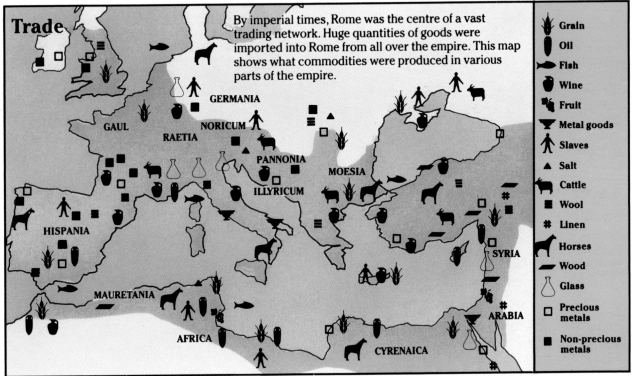

Trade

By imperial times, Rome was the centre of a vast trading network. Huge quantities of goods were imported into Rome from all over the empire. This map shows what commodities were produced in various parts of the empire.

GERMANIA

GAUL

NORICUM

RAETIA

PANNONIA

ILLYRICUM

MOESIA

HISPANIA

SYRIA

MAURETANIA

ARABIA

AFRICA

CYRENAICA

Key	
🌾	Grain
	Oil
🐟	Fish
	Wine
	Fruit
	Metal goods
👤	Slaves
▲	Salt
🐂	Cattle
	Wool
#	Linen
	Horses
	Wood
	Glass
◻	Precious metals
◼	Non-precious metals

247

Entertainments

Many Roman citizens had a lot of free time, as slaves† did most of their work. Evidence of Roman leisure activities comes from archaeological finds, mosaics and paintings, and the writings of Roman authors. Some popular amusements are described here and on the next five pages.

Pastimes

Public gardens and parks were popular places to relax and chat. Romans also enjoyed many forms of exercise, including running, javelin throwing and wrestling. For these activities there were exercise grounds like the Campus Martius in Rome. There was also space for less energetic activities like the ones described below.

People scratched criss-cross patterns on the ground to play games like draughts with counters like these.

Gambling games with coins included *capita et navia*, the Roman equivalent of heads and tails.

Tali (knucklebones) was played with pieces of bone or pottery. The pieces had numbers on the sides and were thrown like dice.

Rich men were fond of hunting and fishing. They wore the special costumes shown in this mosaic.

We know from the writings of Horace† that children built toy houses, used whips and tops, kites and hoops, and played on see-saws and swings. Reliefs, paintings and mosaics show pictures of the games that children played. Many of their pastimes imitated the activities of adults.

Dolls like this were moulded from clay, then carved and painted.

Rag dolls and jointed dolls made of wood were also common.

Sometimes children rode in carts pulled by geese, as shown in this mosaic.

For more about Greek theatre, see pages 152-153.

The theatre

The theatre became popular in Rome during the 3rd century BC after the Romans came into contact with the Greeks*. At first plays were staged in primitive wooden theatres but in 55BC the first stone theatre was built in Rome by Pompey†. It held up to 27,000 people. Stone theatres were later built all over the empire. The remains of these show us what the inside of a theatre might have looked like.

Each part of the auditorium was reserved for a different class of people. The poorer they were, the higher up they sat.

In early days the public stood to watch the play. Later theatres were built with stone seats.

People brought cushions to make the seats more comfortable.

People could leave the theatre very quickly because there was an intricate network of corridors and stairs.

To keep the sun off the spectators, canvas covers were spread over the auditorium, stretched from poles at the back of the top row of seats.

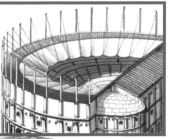

Roman actors wore masks on stage. This was because most Roman plays included the same types of characters, and the masks made them easier to identify from a distance.

Scenery and backcloths were sometimes hung behind the actors.

The scenery was manipulated by complicated machinery, and was often very elaborate and realistic.

Scene changes were hidden by a curtain which was lifted from a slot at the front of the stage.

The actors appeared on the *pulpitum* (stage).

At first only men were allowed on stage. Later, women performed too.

Some benches were also arranged in front of the stage with the best seats reserved for senators.

The audience was rowdy, clapping, booing, hissing and often fighting. Some actors were so popular that they were mobbed by their fans.

Plays and writers

The first play was shown in Rome in 240BC. It was a Greek drama, translated into Latin by a Greek former slave called Livius Andronicus. Though serious plays were popular at first, audiences began to want comedies. The most famous Roman comic writers were Plautus† and Terence†. This wall-painting at Pompeii shows a scene from a play by Plautus.

Gradually theatrical shows became more spectacular, to compete with races and public games (see pages 252-253). Eventually people went to the theatre more for the special effects than the plays themselves.

Races and games

Public entertainments in Rome were called *ludi* (games). Many were paid for by the government as they were part of the religious calendar (see pages 258-259). There were three kinds of entertainment: theatrical performances (*ludi scaenici*; see page 248), chariot races (*ludi circenses*), and gladiator fights and beast hunts (*munera*). At first these events were staged together to form a whole day's entertainment. By imperial times, however, each event could be seen separately, often in its own specially designed building.

Chariot races

Chariot racing was the most popular spectator sport in Rome. Races were held at a racecourse called the circus or hippodrome. As many as 24 races took place in a day, with up to 12 chariots from four different teams. This is what a chariot race would have looked like.

The races were directed by an important person (sometimes the emperor himself) who started each race by throwing a white cloth from his raised platform.

A central rib, the *spina*, ran down the centre of the course, with three pillars at each end.

Each race usually lasted for seven laps. These were counted by removing objects shaped like dolphins or large eggs from racks on the *spina*.

The four different teams were identified by the colours red, green, blue and white.

The drivers jostled for a position close to the *spina*. This was to secure the shortest route round the bend, the most dangerous part of the race.

The driver wound the reins around his body, and carried a knife to cut through them if he was thrown from the chariot.

The *Circus Maximus* in Rome, shown here, was the largest and oldest racetrack in the empire. It was 550m (over 1800ft) long and 180m (almost 600ft) wide, and held up to 250,000 spectators.

Usually either two or four horses pulled each chariot, but sometimes special races were held with six or even eight horses to a team. The more horses, the harder it was to control the chariot.

Each team had its own stables and trainers. Supporters of the teams were fanatical, and unpopular results could lead to riots. Champion drivers, like the one in this mosaic†, became very rich and famous.

Gladiator fights

Gladiators were prisoners, criminals, slaves, or paid volunteers, who fought for the public's entertainment. Gladiator fights and shows involving wild animals were very popular in Rome. At first, like chariot races, they were held in the circus, but later they were staged in stone buildings called amphitheatres†. Games were often put on by individuals to mark an important event like a battle victory. The earliest games were small, but they gradually became more extravagant. Trajan† presided over a show that lasted 117 days in which 10,000 gladiators took part.

There were amphitheatres all over the empire. The largest held up to 50,000 spectators. Rich citizens sat in the best seats, near ground level. Poorer people sat higher up.

Games began in the morning with a procession past the seat of the emperor or presiding official. The gladiators were accompanied by dancers, jugglers, priests and musicians.

Next came the beast shows. Some rare animals were simply displayed. More common animals, like bears, panthers and bulls were forced to fight each other, hunted in the arena by archers, or let loose on defenceless prisoners. Many fights involved the bloody and violent killing of thousands of animals and humans. After the beasts came comic acts, mimes and mock fights.

Vats of incense were used to disguise the smell of the blood.

Retiarius

Murmillo

Samnite

Thracian

The sand was often coloured so that the blood did not show up so much.

The gladiators fought in the afternoon. There were four types, distinguished by their weapons and costumes. To make the show more interesting, gladiators in different categories fought each other; for example a *retiarius* might fight a *murmillo*. They normally continued to the death, but defeated or wounded fighters could appeal for mercy. After listening to the crowd, the official in charge signalled with his thumb whether the man should live or die. We think that the 'thumbs up' signal meant that the gladiator should live, but we have nothing to prove this.

A successful gladiator received money, a crown, and great adulation. After many victories he might be awarded a wooden sword, which signified his freedom. Many freed fighters became trainers at special schools for gladiators.

The baths

The first bath-houses, built in the 2nd century BC, were simple washing facilities for men only. But by the time of Augustus† there were 170 privately owned bath-houses, and in AD20 the first large state-owned public baths were opened. Baths grew in size and splendour in imperial times; they became huge centres where thousands of people spent their leisure hours. We know from the ruins of baths that they were sophisticated buildings with complicated heating and plumbing systems. This is what a Roman bath-house might have looked like.

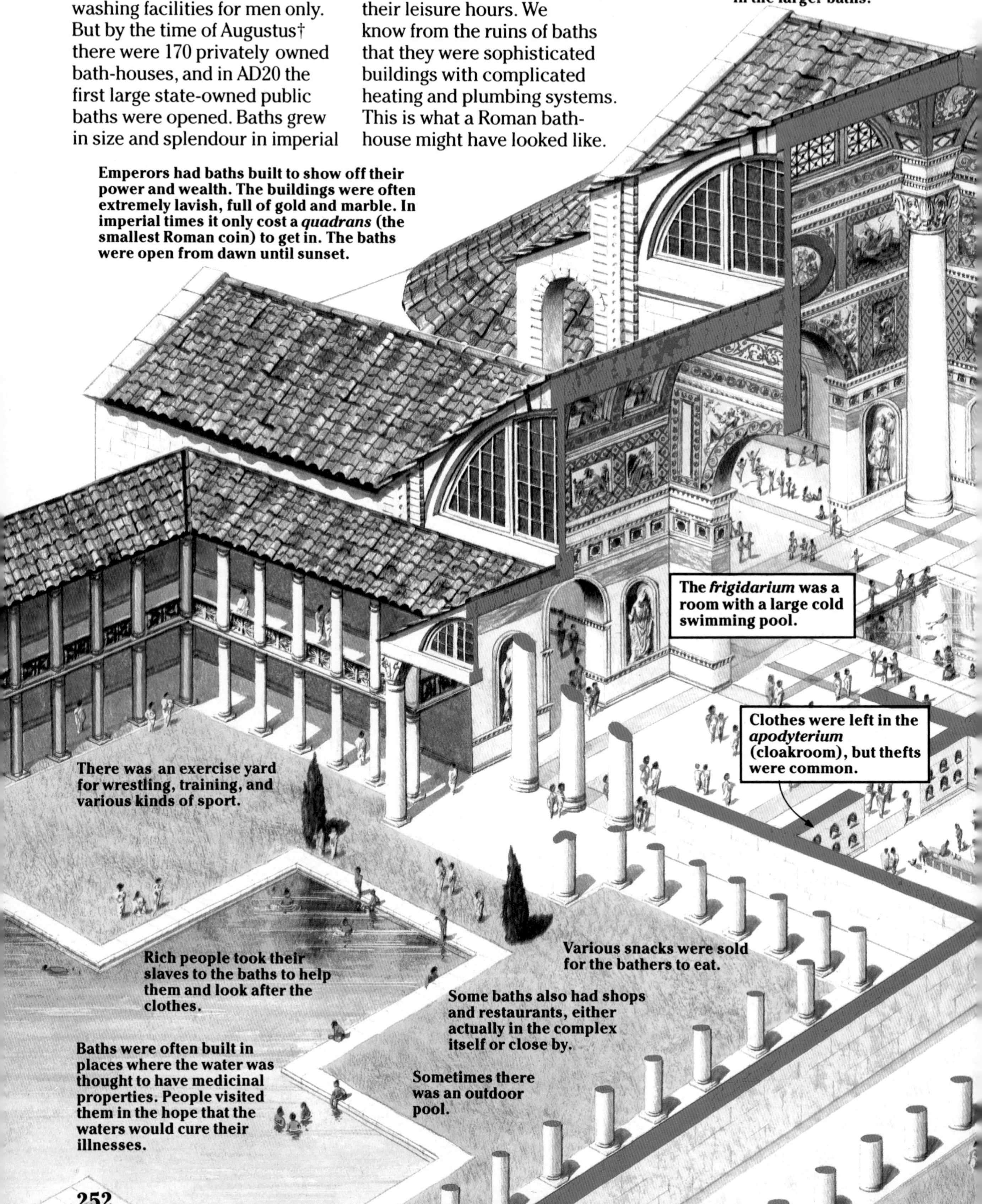

Emperors had baths built to show off their power and wealth. The buildings were often extremely lavish, full of gold and marble. In imperial times it only cost a *quadrans* (the smallest Roman coin) to get in. The baths were open from dawn until sunset.

Libraries and reading rooms were also common in the larger baths.

The *frigidarium* was a room with a large cold swimming pool.

Clothes were left in the *apodyterium* (cloakroom), but thefts were common.

There was an exercise yard for wrestling, training, and various kinds of sport.

Rich people took their slaves to the baths to help them and look after the clothes.

Baths were often built in places where the water was thought to have medicinal properties. People visited them in the hope that the waters would cure their illnesses.

Various snacks were sold for the bathers to eat.

Some baths also had shops and restaurants, either actually in the complex itself or close by.

Sometimes there was an outdoor pool.

There were several types of bath at different temperatures.

A huge wood-fired hypocaust system (see page 226) conducted heat under the floors and into the room.

The hottest room of all, the *laconicum*, was used mainly by invalids. A tub of boiling water in the centre kept it steamy.

The hot room, the *caldarium*, had a pool for bathing. In this damp atmosphere people sweated a lot.

After bathing, customers could hire attendants for a massage. Barbers and hairdressers were also available, as were beauty treatments.

The *tepidarium* was a warm room with a small pool.

Keeping clean

The Romans did not have soap. To remove dirt and sweat they covered their bodies with oil which they then scraped off with strigils (scrapers made of wood, bone or metal).

People played games of knucklebones (see page 248), dice or chequers.

Famous baths

By AD284 there were around 1000 private bath-houses and 11 public ones. Among the most impressive in Rome were those opened by the emperors Caracalla and Diocletian. This is a reconstruction of the Baths of Caracalla.

There were gardens where people could stroll before or after their baths. They were a good place to socialize and catch up with all the latest gossip.

253

Religious beliefs

The Romans had many different gods and goddesses. They fell into two main groups: spirits that were thought to protect houses and were worshipped domestically, and the gods and goddesses of the formal state religion who were worshipped at public ceremonies. Worship of household spirits was the earliest form of Roman religion; the rituals of the organized state religion (see below) became more elaborate during the expansion of the empire.

Worship at home

Romans believed that their homes were controlled by groups of *numina* (household spirits). One group, the *penates*, protected the stores; another, the *lares*, looked after the whole household. Each family also had its own guardian spirit, the *genius*, and ancestral spirits, the *manes*. These beliefs began among early farmers, but were retained in the sophisticated urban houses of imperial Rome. Some *numina* took on individual personalities and names. These included Vesta, goddess of the hearth, and Janus, god of the doorway.

Each house had a shrine to the *lares* called a *lararium*, where the family prayed each day, and offered small gifts such as wine, bread or fruit.

The growth of religion

As the Romans conquered areas outside Rome itself they met people who worshipped other gods and goddesses. Rather than suppressing these other religions, they often adopted them. As the empire expanded the number of deities grew.

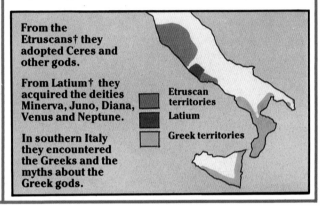

From the Etruscans† they adopted Ceres and other gods.

From Latium† they acquired the deities Minerva, Juno, Diana, Venus and Neptune.

In southern Italy they encountered the Greeks and the myths about the Greek gods.

Etruscan territories

Latium

Greek territories

The state religion

The Romans were attracted to Greek mythology. They matched their Roman gods (see overleaf) with the Greek ones, making them the basis of their state religion. This required worshippers to observe strict rituals at elaborate ceremonies. Romans could worship any number of gods, and did this by praying and making sacrifices. Most people believed that they were protected by a particular god or goddess. They also believed that each deity looked after a particular aspect of life. For example, people prayed to Venus for success in love, or to Mars for success in war.

Temples and ceremonies

Large and impressive temples were built for the state deities. Their layout was adopted from those of the Etruscans and Greeks (see page 162). Temples contained treasures won in battle or donated by individuals as a way of thanking the gods. People were also allowed to store their own gold in the temple, which was looked after by priests and priestesses.

On public holidays and festivals (see pages 258-259) a long procession of priests, government officials and musicians approached the temple, leading animals which were to be sacrificed.

The temple housed the statue of the god.

Ceremonies were held outside the temple, but individuals could go inside to say private prayers.

Making sacrifices

Animals were sacrificed at an altar in front of the temple. Only priests could conduct the ceremony because it was very complex. If any detail of the ritual went wrong, the Romans believed the gods would not accept the sacrifice. Priests were therefore very important. The chief priest was called the *Pontifex Maximus*. From the time of Augustus† this position was held by the emperor himself.

Citizens† wishing to make offerings brought beasts to the temple. The animals most frequently used were oxen, sheep, pigs, goats and doves.

The priest washed his hands, called for silence, and sprinkled salt, flour or wine on the animal's head. When he signalled that all was ready, attendants carried out the sacrifice.

Parts of the animal's carcass were thrown onto the altar fire for the god to consume.

Foretelling the future

The Romans believed strongly in supernatural forces. They had many ways of predicting the future and learning the will of the gods. People performed all kinds of rites to ensure their safety and wellbeing, and consulted various fortune tellers. Some of these are shown below.

Haruspices were special priests who examined the innards of sacrificed animals. It was thought that the shape of an animal's liver, and the presence or absence of blemishes on it, would reveal the attitude of the gods towards public projects and government policies.

In Rome there was a group of 16 prophets called augurs. They examined the sky for flocks of birds, cloud shapes, lightning, and other natural events. They believed that these things were omens that could tell them the opinions of the gods.

In times of national crisis, the Romans consulted books of prophecies written by the Sibyl†, a prophetess who lived in caves at Cumae in early republican times. The books were closely guarded in Rome, and contained advice about how to interpret the will of the gods.

Astrologers told fortunes by examining the position of the stars at the time of a person's birth. By imperial times the practice was very widespread. Even emperors consulted astrologers, to try to protect themselves from assassination.

Poorer people had ways of foretelling the future, including palm reading and throwing special dice.

People also thought that illness could be cured by miracles or by treatments suggested in dreams. To have such dreams the patient slept in the temple of Aesculapius, the god of medicine (see page 261).

Gods and goddesses

This family tree shows the most important gods of the state religion (see page 254) and their spheres of influence. Each Roman name is followed by its Greek equivalent in brackets*.

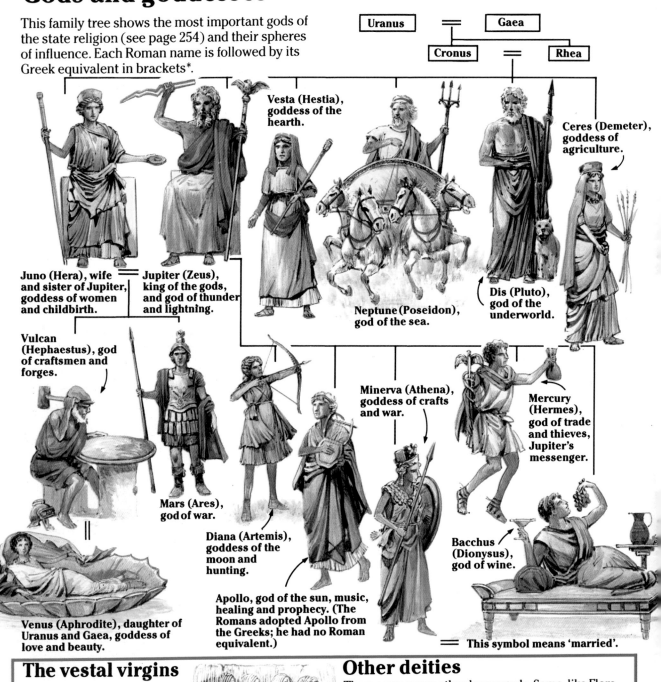

Uranus = Gaea

Cronus = Rhea

Juno (Hera), wife and sister of Jupiter, goddess of women and childbirth. = **Jupiter (Zeus)**, king of the gods, and god of thunder and lightning.

Vesta (Hestia), goddess of the hearth.

Neptune (Poseidon), god of the sea.

Ceres (Demeter), goddess of agriculture.

Dis (Pluto), god of the underworld.

Vulcan (Hephaestus), god of craftsmen and forges.

Mars (Ares), god of war.

Diana (Artemis), goddess of the moon and hunting.

Apollo, god of the sun, music, healing and prophecy. (The Romans adopted Apollo from the Greeks; he had no Roman equivalent.)

Minerva (Athena), goddess of crafts and war.

Mercury (Hermes), god of trade and thieves, Jupiter's messenger.

Bacchus (Dionysus), god of wine.

Venus (Aphrodite), daughter of Uranus and Gaea, goddess of love and beauty.

= This symbol means 'married'.

The vestal virgins

Vesta was a household deity before becoming a state goddess. She had a shrine in the *forum*, where a fire burned constantly. It was tended by six women called Vestal Virgins, who are shown in this relief. They were chosen from Rome's leading families. It was an honour to be selected, but they had to do the job for 30 years and were not allowed to marry.

Other deities

There were many other lesser gods. Some, like Flora, Faunus, Pomona and Silvanus, were responsible for growth and fertility. There were also several gods and goddesses of war, including Quirinus and Bellona. The god of love was Cupid. Roma was the goddess of Rome itself.

Flora   Cupid   Quirinus   Roma

Alternatives to the state religion

Many Romans lost faith in the state religion, as it offered little more than rituals and did not satisfy their personal needs. Also, when affairs of state went badly people found it increasingly hard to believe that sacrifices and prayers had any effect. By the start of the Empire many Romans had abandoned the state religion. Augustus† tried with some success to restore it, but people wanted other religious experiences and turned to the various cults that reached Rome from other countries as the empire grew. These required people to take part in ceremonies rather than just watch them. Some promised life after death and offered more personal involvement than the state religion could. Here are some of the gods, goddesses and religions that the Romans adopted.

◀ Epona, the Celtic goddess of horses, was first worshipped in Gaul. But her cult was spread, probably by Gaulish soldiers, to Spain, Germany, the Danube, Scotland, and into Italy itself.

Mithras

◀ Worship of the god Mithras began in India and Persia. Mithraism became popular all over the Roman world, especially among soldiers. It offered life after death, and asked people to treat others with kindness and respect. The religion stated that all men were equally worthy, whether senators or slaves, but women were not allowed to join the cult. Mithraic temples have been found throughout the empire.

Cybele, an important foreign goddess, ▶ was also known as the Great Mother. She ruled fertility, healing and nature, and was very popular with women. Her cult was brought to Rome from Asia Minor in 204BC, when a prophet warned that the Romans would lose the Carthaginian wars without Cybele's help. The ceremonies included wild music and dancing, processions and sacrifices. This made some Romans suspicious of the cult, but Claudius† gave it public status.

Cybele

Judaism was an ancient religion that the ▶ Romans encountered when they conquered Palestine in 63BC and made it the province† of Judaea. Many Romans turned to Judaism instead of the state religion, and at first it was officially tolerated. But later Jews were badly persecuted because they believed in only one god and refused to worship the emperor as the state demanded. There were many revolts against Roman rule, and in AD70 the Romans destroyed the Jewish temple at Jerusalem. This event is depicted on the arch of Titus.

◀ The cult of Isis began in Egypt (see page 20) and later spread all over the empire. Isis was the ruler of heaven and earth, and goddess of wheat and barley. The cult became fashionable when the Egyptian queen Cleopatra spent the year 45BC in Rome. The Romans were attracted to the cult because it was so ancient. Ceremonies were very elaborate and mysterious.

This early Christian wall-painting shows Jesus as a shepherd.

◀ Christianity was founded in Palestine by the followers of Jesus of Nazareth (c.5BC-AD29), and spread rapidly through the empire. It was particularly popular with the poor, who found comfort in its promise of everlasting life. Like Jews, Christians believed there was only one god, and refused to worship the state gods. This angered the Roman government. Christians had to meet in secret, and were often harshly persecuted. But the religion continued to grow and in AD313 official toleration of Christianity was declared by Constantine (see page 269). It became the official religion in AD394.

Phoenician gods

Baal

Baal and Tanit were ancient Phoenician gods that the Romans encountered in Carthage. At first the rituals of their cult included human sacrifices, but these were forbidden after the Romans conquered Carthage in 146BC. The cult survived in parts of Spain and North Africa into the 1st century AD.

A shrine to another Carthaginian god, Melkart, was founded in 1100BC at Cadiz in Spain. By 400BC the Romans had linked Melkart to the god Hercules (himself derived from the Greek god Herakles). The cult continued into the 5th century AD.

When the Romans conquered ▶ new areas they took their gods with them. Locals were not forced to adopt Roman gods, but they were often curious about them. Native deities were merged with Roman ones, so local versions of the state gods emerged all over the empire. This temple at Trier in Germany was built for Mars Lenus, a god of healing.

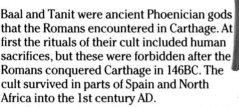

Festivals

The Romans had many festivals, each with its own social or religious significance. They were often public holidays, although business was forbidden on only the most solemn occasions. During the rule of Augustus† there were at least 115 holidays each year. Under some later emperors there were more than 200 festival days a year. Many festivals were celebrated with games, races and theatrical performances (see pages 248-251). Below is a calendar of some of the most important events. The reason for the celebration is given, and, where known, the festival's Latin name.

1 January

New consuls† were sworn in. Bulls were sacrificed to Jupiter as thanks for his protection in the past year. The consuls promised that their successors would do the same the following year.

Early January — Compitalia

In the country, each farmer built a small shrine with an altar at the boundary of his farm. He placed a plough there and a wooden doll for each person in his household. The next day was a holiday. A sacrifice was made to purify the farm for the coming year.

In the city, the president of each *insula*† sacrificed a hen on an altar built at each crossroads. Three days of celebrations followed.

13-21 February — Parentalia

Parentalia was a ceremony to honour dead parents. Romans visited the cemeteries outside the city where they placed flowers, milk and wine on the graves of their parents. This was to stop the dead feeling hungry and returning to plague the living.

15 February — Lupercalia

Two teams of youths met at the Lupercal, a cave on the Palatine, and raced round the hill. Crowds gathered to watch. The runners dressed in the skins of sacrificed goats and were smeared with blood. As they ran they whipped the spectators with strips of goatskin. This was said to promote fertility, so women wanting children stood close to the race.

22 February — Caristia

This was a ceremony to conclude the *Parentalia*. It was an occasion on which families gathered together for a joyful dinner.

1 March

A ritual took place in the temple of Vesta at which the perpetual fire was re-kindled. This day was also the beginning of the dances of the *Salii* (college of priests). Twelve young patricians† danced around Rome holding sacred shields. This continued for 19 days. The dancers feasted at a different house each night.

14 March

Horse races were held in the *Campus Martius*† to mark the feast of Mars, the god of War.

15 March

This was a festival for Anna Perenna, goddess of the year. People took picnics to the River Tiber. Some Romans believed that they would live as many years as they could drink cups of wine.

23 March — Tubilustrium

On this day sacred trumpets of war were purified at a ceremony to the god Mars. This was to bring success in the coming battle season.

4-10 April — Ludi Megalenses

Games were held to honour Cybele, the Great Mother (see page 257).

12-19 April — Ludi Ceriales

Games were held to honour Ceres, goddess of corn.

21 April — Parilia

Parilia began as a country festival to purify sheep and keep disease from the flock. But later it was celebrated in Rome itself because the date was said to have been the birth of the city. Each area of Rome organised its own festivities. These included bonfires onto which offerings were thrown. People danced in the flames. *Parilia* ended with a large outdoor feast.

28 April-May 3 — Ludi Florales

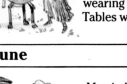

This was a carnival in honour of Flora, the goddess of flowers, and a celebration of fertility. It was also known as *Floralia*. People danced wearing brightly coloured garlands. Tables were piled high with flowers.

9 June — Vestalia

Married women went to the temple of Vesta with gifts of food for the goddess. *Vestalia* was a holiday for bakers, because the Vestal Virgins produced loaves made from *mola salsa*, a salted flour.

24 June — Fors Fortuna

This was the festival for the goddess Fortuna. There was a great public holiday. People rowed down the River Tiber to watch sacrifices at the two shrines to Fortuna, just outside Rome. The rest of the day was spent picnicking and drinking.

6-13 July — Ludi Apollinares

During the republic this festival was connected with religious ceremonies to the god Apollo. But by imperial times it was simply an excuse for theatrical shows, games and races.

12 August

The god Mercury was known for his sly practices and cunning. He was particularly popular among businessmen and traders, who paid 10% of their profits to his shrine. The money was used to pay for a public feast which took place on this day.

13 August

This day was a feast to Diana. Slaves had a holiday. It was also traditional for women to wash their hair.

5-19 September — Ludi Romani

At first this 15-day festival of games, races and theatre was to honour Jupiter, but later much of the religious significance disappeared. On 13 September a cow was sacrificed at Jupiter's temple, and the Senate and all the magistrates ate a banquet there. Statues of Jupiter, Juno and Minerva were dressed up and placed on couches so that they could share the feast with the humans.

4-17 November — Ludi Plebeii

Theatre, games and races marked this feast to Jupiter. On 13 November there was a banquet for senators and magistrates.

Early December — Rites of the Bona Dea

This festival was in honour of the Bona Dea ('Good Goddess'), whom the Romans believed protected women. The rituals were secret, and men were strictly forbidden to attend. The rites may have involved dancing, drinking and the worship of sacred objects.

17 December — Saturnalia

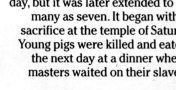

At first *Saturnalia* lasted only one day, but it was later extended to as many as seven. It began with a sacrifice at the temple of Saturn. Young pigs were killed and eaten the next day at a dinner where masters waited on their slaves.

Medicine

The Romans gained most of their knowledge of medicine from the Greeks. Hippocrates (see page 182), a Greek doctor who lived in the 5th century BC, described all the illnesses he encountered and recorded how he treated them. His writings formed the basis of Greek and then Roman medical teaching. During the republic, medical schools opened in Rome, and the organized teaching of medicine began. Doctors had to learn many skills, for Roman medical methods often combined scientific treatments and religious rituals. Some doctors trained in army hospitals. They learned about anatomy and surgery from the wounds of soldiers. This is what a hospital tent might have looked like.

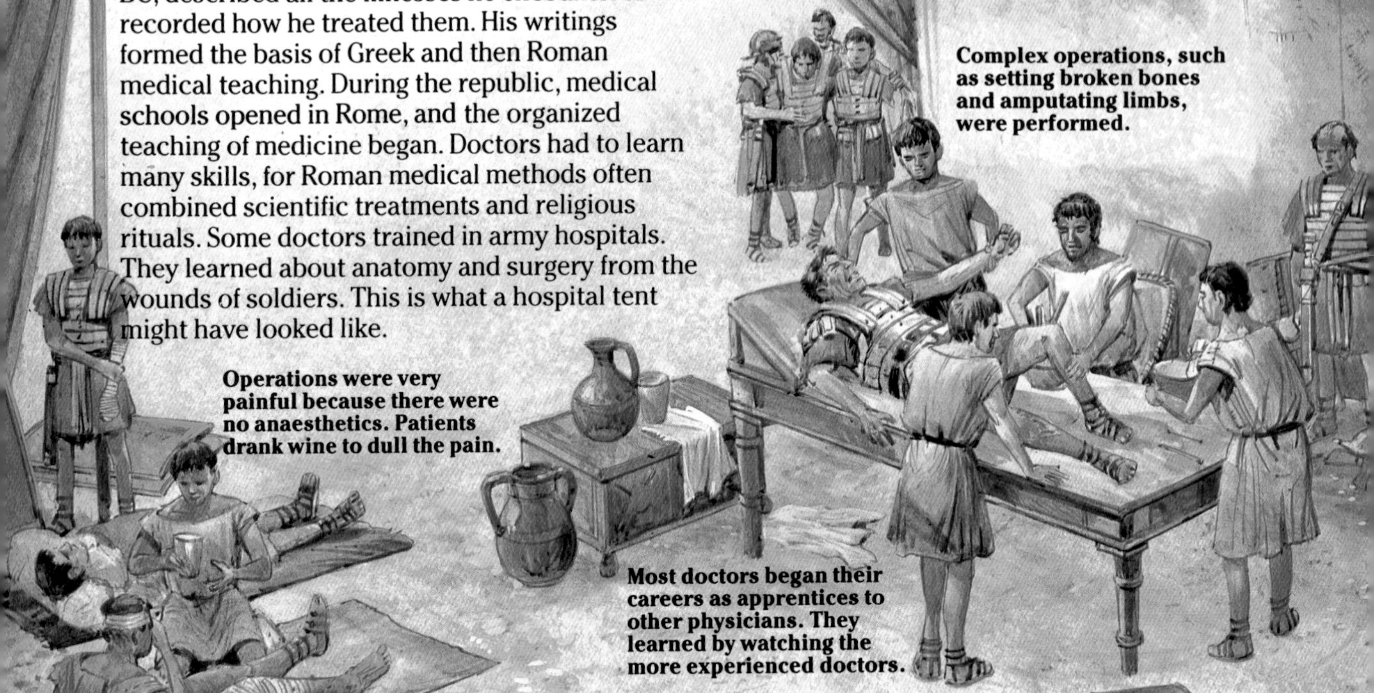

Operations were very painful because there were no anaesthetics. Patients drank wine to dull the pain.

Complex operations, such as setting broken bones and amputating limbs, were performed.

Most doctors began their careers as apprentices to other physicians. They learned by watching the more experienced doctors.

Surgical instruments

Archaeologists have found evidence of bronze and iron instruments that doctors used. Some of them are shown here.

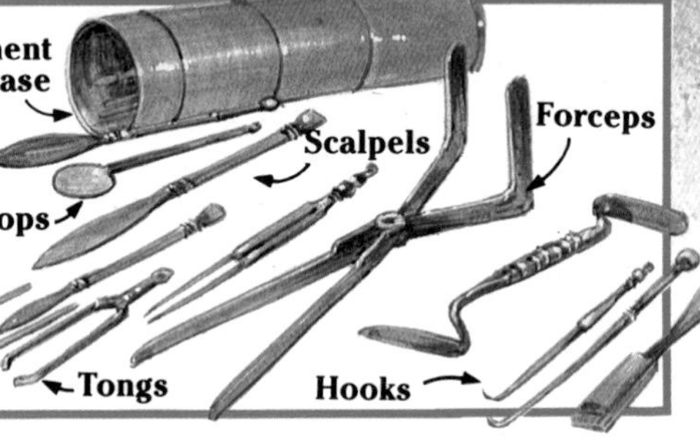

Instrument case

Scalpels

Forceps

Scoops

Needles

Tongs

Hooks

Treatments and remedies

Roman doctors used many kinds of remedies. They knew that people's health was affected by what they ate, and often advised patients to alter their diets. They knew the benefits of exercise, fresh air and regular visits to the baths.

Doctors also used medicines made from plants, minerals and animal substances. The remains of medicines have been found. It is hard to tell what they were made of and what they were used for, but we know about some of them because many documents about medicine have survived. Discorides, an army doctor, wrote a catalogue of 600 plants and 1000 drugs which he had tested on patients.

Eye infections were treated with ointments made with lead, zinc or iron. The sticks were often stamped with the maker's name.

The sap of certain plants was used to cure skin problems and snake bites.

Medicinal herbs were added to wine. The mixture was drunk to cure coughs and chest complaints.

Pill-box

Ingredients were sometimes ground in a pestle and mortar then made into pills.

A visit to the doctor

The richest Romans had personal physicians to look after them. Other wealthy patients could afford to pay doctors to visit them at home, but ordinary people had to go to a hospital or surgery. In the 1st century AD a sort of state health service began. Under this scheme, each town had a number of doctors who were exempt from tax. They could accept fees, but were expected to treat the poor free of charge. Some doctors saw patients in ordinary shops open to the street. Others had quieter rooms, like the one shown here.

Garden for growing herbs used to make medicine

Cabinet with scrolls containing medical writings

Examination couch

Writers on medicine advised the doctor how to behave so as to make the patient feel at ease. Here the doctor is examining a young child.

Boxes containing medicines and ointments

Surgical instruments

Other doctors

Archaeological evidence like this tombstone suggests that there were some female doctors. They probably worked as midwives, assisting women in childbirth.

Some doctors travelled from town to town, treating people at each place they came to. They probably carried medicines with them to sell to their patients.

Dental treatment was also available. Technicians riveted extracted teeth to gold bridges to form false teeth. This technique was probably invented by the Etruscans†.

Religion and medicine

The Romans linked religion and medicine because they believed that their deities had powers to heal people. To obtain cures, many Romans performed complex religious rituals, while others relied on superstition and spells. Some doctors used these treatments because they too held these beliefs.

Throughout the Roman world there were temples to Aesculapius, the god of medicine. They contained statues of the god, like the one above. People slept in shrines, believing that their dreams would tell them how to cure their illnesses.

If they were cured, people gave offerings to the gods. Some were stone models of the part of the body that had been healed. Others showed the deities themselves. This one shows Aesculapius and his daughter Hygieia, the goddess of healing.

There was a temple to Aesculapius on an island in the River Tiber. Slaves who were too old or ill to work were often left there. Claudius† granted them freedom. Later the temple became one of the first public hospitals.

Architecture

In architecture, as in other areas, the Romans were influenced by the Greeks*. They borrowed Greek styles, architects and craftsmen. However, the Romans were quick to adapt and develop Greek ideas. Their interest in architecture was mainly practical, and their great skills lay in the construction of huge buildings – amphitheatres†, baths, basilicas†, bridges and aqueducts†. The introduction of concrete enabled them to build stronger and bigger structures than before.

Temples

The Romans copied Greek temple architecture very closely. Greek temples were mostly built in open spaces and could be seen from all sides. Roman temples, however, were often constructed in town centres, surrounded by tall buildings, and only visible from the front. This picture shows the Maison Carrée, a Roman temple, built in the first century AD at Nîmes, France.

While the Greek pillars were detached from the rest of the temple, the Roman peristyle was joined to the inner room (*cella*). This made the *cella* more spacious.

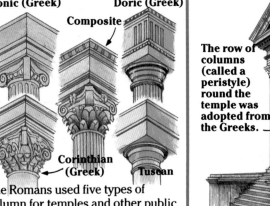

Ionic (Greek)

Doric (Greek)

Composite

Corinthian (Greek)

Tuscan

The Romans used five types of column for temples and other public buildings. They were adapted from those used in Greek architecture.

Cella

The row of columns (called a peristyle) round the temple was adopted from the Greeks.

The temple was raised from the ground to make it look more impressive. A long flight of steps led to the porch.

Arches

Before the Romans, most buildings were constructed with walls and columns topped by beams of wood or stone (known as trabeated architecture). The largest known roof span built this way is 7.3m (25ft). The Romans used these methods for buildings like the Maison Carrée, but they also developed the arch and the vault, which had been used earlier by the Etruscans†. The arch enabled builders to span greater distances. The method of building an arch is shown here.

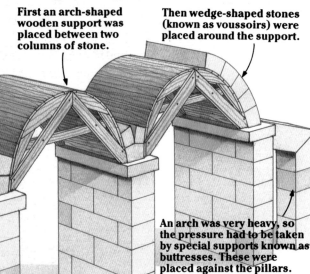

First an arch-shaped wooden support was placed between two columns of stone.

Then wedge-shaped stones (known as voussoirs) were placed around the support.

An arch was very heavy, so the pressure had to be taken by special supports known as buttresses. These were placed against the pillars.

The development of the arch enabled the Romans to build fine bridges and aqueducts, such as the Pont du Gard in France. In this case the hillside acted as a buttress.

For the Colosseum in Rome, shown here as it looks today, architects used arches to support the structure. The columns outside were only for decoration.

262

*For more about Greek architecture, see pages 140-141.

Vaults and domes

The Romans realized that a line of arches side by side could produce a tunnel vault to enclose large areas. But this allowed very little light to enter a building.

Later architects developed crossed vaulting by overlapping two tunnel vaults at right angles to each other. This was lighter in weight and easier to illuminate.

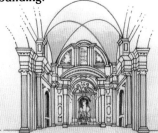

The groin vault was first used at the baths in Rome. Shown here is the *tepidarium* (warm room) at the Baths of Diocletian. This was transformed around AD1550 into the church of Santa Maria degli Angeli.

A further development of the arch was the dome, made by crossing a number of arches over each other to enclose a circular area.

The Pantheon

The best example of a Roman dome is the Pantheon in Rome. It was built in 25BC as a new form of temple, by Augustus's lieutenant Agrippa.

In this picture part of the dome has been cut away so that the details can be seen.

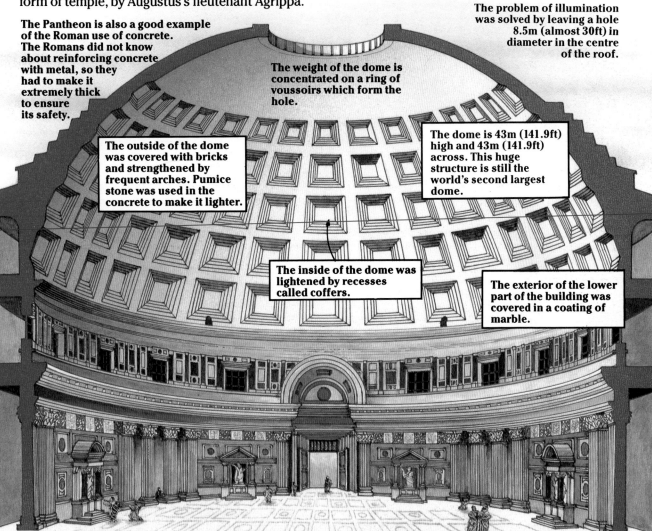

The Pantheon is also a good example of the Roman use of concrete. The Romans did not know about reinforcing concrete with metal, so they had to make it extremely thick to ensure its safety.

The weight of the dome is concentrated on a ring of voussoirs which form the hole.

The problem of illumination was solved by leaving a hole 8.5m (almost 30ft) in diameter in the centre of the roof.

The outside of the dome was covered with bricks and strengthened by frequent arches. Pumice stone was used in the concrete to make it lighter.

The dome is 43m (141.9ft) high and 43m (141.9ft) across. This huge structure is still the world's second largest dome.

The inside of the dome was lightened by recesses called coffers.

The exterior of the lower part of the building was covered in a coating of marble.

Building technology

We know that the Romans were highly skilled builders because so many of their constructions have survived into modern times. Their spectacular innovations in the fields of civil and mechanical engineering enabled them to construct vast, strong buildings and public works. Archaeological evidence tells us that the Romans chose the finest materials and devised many sophisticated construction methods to ensure that their buildings were safe and lasted many years. This is how a Roman building site might have looked; the scene shows some of the methods, materials and equipment they used.

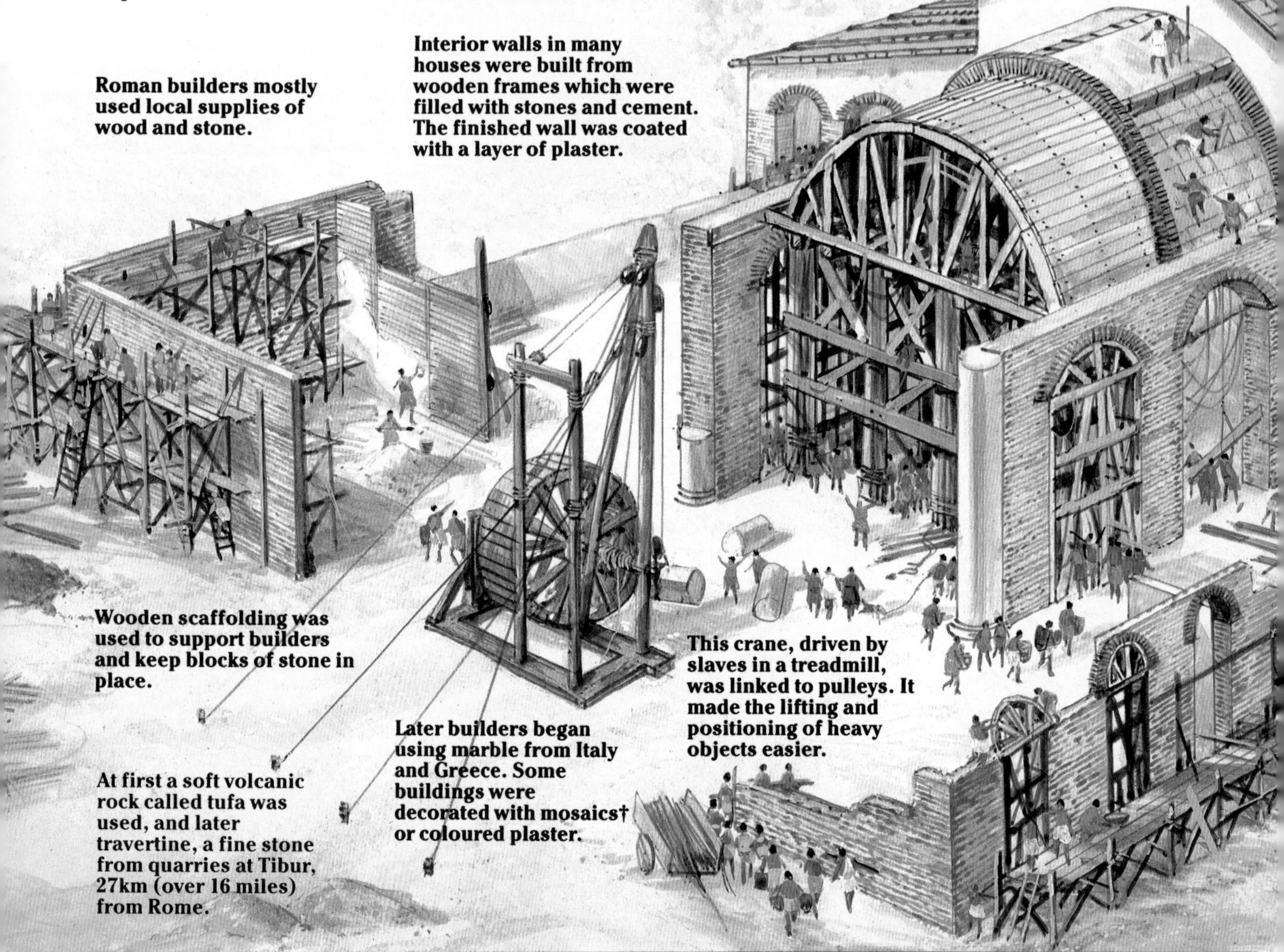

Roman builders mostly used local supplies of wood and stone.

Interior walls in many houses were built from wooden frames which were filled with stones and cement. The finished wall was coated with a layer of plaster.

Wooden scaffolding was used to support builders and keep blocks of stone in place.

Later builders began using marble from Italy and Greece. Some buildings were decorated with mosaics† or coloured plaster.

At first a soft volcanic rock called tufa was used, and later travertine, a fine stone from quarries at Tibur, 27km (over 16 miles) from Rome.

This crane, driven by slaves in a treadmill, was linked to pulleys. It made the lifting and positioning of heavy objects easier.

Concrete

The use of concrete was developed in the 2nd century BC. The Romans discovered how to make an excellent mortar out of volcanic ash, and so were able to build very strong structures. The stages of building a wall are shown here.

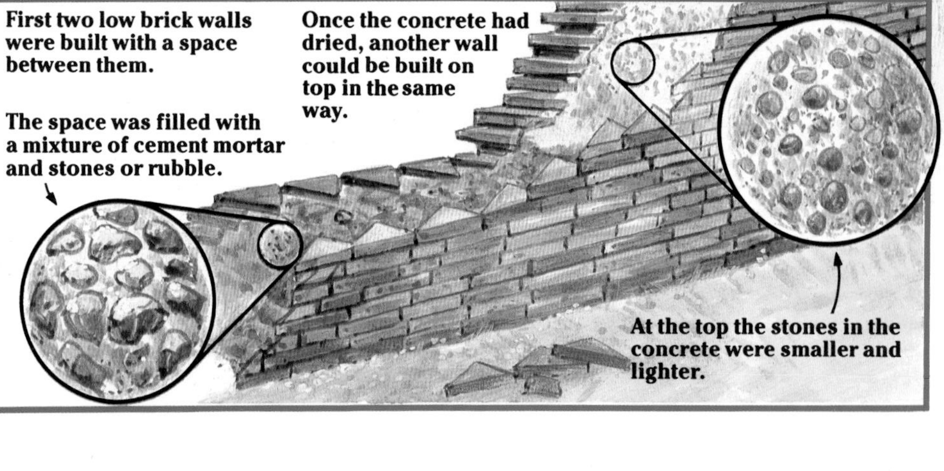

First two low brick walls were built with a space between them.

The space was filled with a mixture of cement mortar and stones or rubble.

Once the concrete had dried, another wall could be built on top in the same way.

At the top the stones in the concrete were smaller and lighter.

Tiles and gutters were moulded from clay then baked to harden them. Every brick and tile had the name of the factory stamped on it.

Bricks were often laid in elaborate decorative patterns.

The Romans produced excellent bricks, often rather flat and small. Bricklayers were highly skilled.

Civil engineering

Roman roads, bridges, buildings and water systems were all carefully planned. The success of so many of these projects shows how well the Romans dealt with complex mathematical and technical problems. Below you can see some Roman advances in civil engineering.

The Romans needed a good water supply for public baths and lavatories. Water flowed into huge cisterns along aqueducts (pipes set into bridges or laid underground). It was then distributed through a complex system of lead or earthenware pipes.

Water power was used to turn chains of waterwheels. This is a reconstruction of a set of wheels near Arles in France which was used to drive flour mills.

Treadmills turned by slaves or oxen were used to raise water from underground shafts such as mines. The water collected in troughs at the top of each wheel. Each trough was emptied by the wheel above.

Bridge building

First a temporary bridge was built over a row of boats. Wooden stakes, chained together in circles, were driven into the river bed. The water was then pumped out of this space.

Blocks of stone were placed inside the stakes, forming the pillars to support the bridge. When the pillars were tall enough, wooden frames were fixed between them. Arches were then built on top of the frames.

Tools and equipment

Roman metalworkers and carpenters made excellent tools for builders. Here are some examples.

The *groma* was used to estimate straight lines to make sure that buildings and roads were straight.

Stonemason's square

Cutting tool

Tongs

Trowel

Axe

The legal system

The first document to describe the Roman legal system in detail, known as the Twelve Tables, was published in 450BC. It was a list of rules and statutes, and covered many aspects of the law. Although only a part of it has survived, we know it contained laws about money, property rights, family and inheritance, and public behaviour. There were also sections about court procedure, crimes and punishments. The legal system changed considerably over the years, but it continued to be based on the Twelve Tables throughout imperial times.

Courts and trials

Trials had to be set in motion by individuals, as the government itself did not prosecute people. Courts were managed in Rome by *praetores*†, and in the provinces† by governors. These men decided whether or not cases were worthy of trial, then chose the judge or tried the case themselves.

Anyone claiming that a crime had been committed had to summon the suspect to appear at court. People who did this gained great honour and prestige. In Rome, trials were held in basilicas† near the *forum*†. This is what a Roman court might have looked like.

If the suspect refused to attend the court the accuser could use force to take him. This often led to fights before trials.

Interesting or scandalous cases drew large audiences who often participated by shouting and jeering.

Trials themselves took place in the rooms off the main hall.

In serious cases the accused paid a lawyer (called an *advocatus*) to speak on his behalf. Good lawyers were highly respected.

In important cases a jury of up to 75 people was called. Jury members had to be citizens†.

Sometimes the accused put ashes in his hair and wore rags, or brought his weeping wife and children to court. This was to make the judge and jury feel sorry for him.

After everybody had spoken the jury decided by voting whether or not the accused had committed the crime. The judge announced the verdict and decided the punishment.

Crimes and punishments

Roman writings about law contain details of crimes and punishments. In imperial times the punishment depended on the status of the accused. Judges placed each defendant into one of two categories: *honestiores* and *humiliores*. The *humiliores* were usually poorer, and got worse punishments.

Many people were tried for crimes like not paying debts, not fulfilling contracts, or fraud. As punishment they had to pay fines or compensation.

Criminals were not imprisoned. Instead they were exiled to distant parts of the empire for a period. Others lost their citizenship and had their property confiscated.

Laws and lawyers

Roman law changed constantly throughout Rome's history. The legal system outlined in the Twelve Tables grew into a vast code of laws and their interpretations, from which a ruling could be found to suit most circumstances. This diagram shows how the law was put into practice.

Republican law

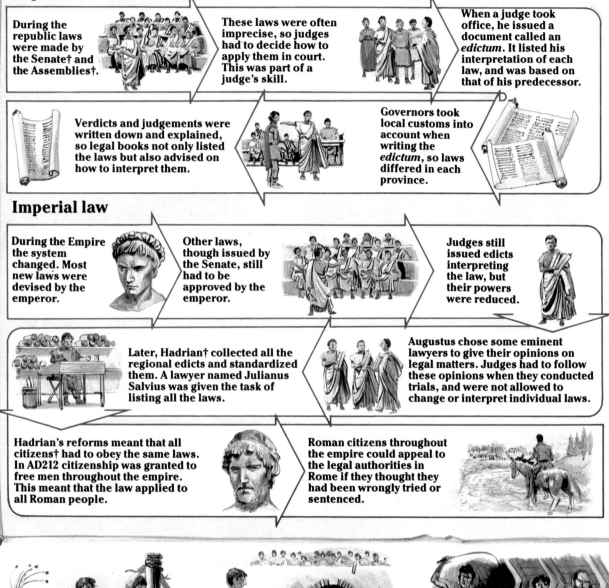

During the republic laws were made by the Senate† and the Assemblies†.

These laws were often imprecise, so judges had to decide how to apply them in court. This was part of a judge's skill.

When a judge took office, he issued a document called an *edictum*. It listed his interpretation of each law, and was based on that of his predecessor.

Verdicts and judgements were written down and explained, so legal books not only listed the laws but also advised on how to interpret them.

Governors took local customs into account when writing the *edictum*, so laws differed in each province.

Imperial law

During the Empire the system changed. Most new laws were devised by the emperor.

Other laws, though issued by the Senate, still had to be approved by the emperor.

Judges still issued edicts interpreting the law, but their powers were reduced.

Later, Hadrian† collected all the regional edicts and standardized them. A lawyer named Julianus Salvius was given the task of listing all the laws.

Augustus chose some eminent lawyers to give their opinions on legal matters. Judges had to follow these opinions when they conducted trials, and were not allowed to change or interpret individual laws.

Hadrian's reforms meant that all citizens† had to obey the same laws. In AD212 citizenship was granted to free men throughout the empire. This meant that the law applied to all Roman people.

Roman citizens throughout the empire could appeal to the legal authorities in Rome if they thought they had been wrongly tried or sentenced.

In republican times the death penalty was rare, but during the Empire crucifixion (death on a cross), flogging, beheading or drowning were more common.

Many *humiliores* who were sentenced to death had to appear in public games. They either fought as gladiators or were savaged by wild animals (see page 253).

Others were sent to be oarsmen on warships or to work in mines. The conditions were harsh and many prisoners died as a result of maltreatment and overwork.

The later Empire

After the rule of Marcus Aurelius (see page 217), political problems increased, caused by dishonest, brutal or incompetent emperors and rebellious soldiers. The Praetorian Guard† became very powerful, often choosing or deposing emperors without consulting the Senate†. This led to frequent changes of ruler, so the empire lacked the continuity and strong leadership it needed.

Commodus AD180-192; Pertinax AD192

Aurelius abandoned Nerva's method of choosing a successor (see page 217). Instead he appointed his son Commodus, who made peace with the barbarians†, but then ruled irresponsibly, ignoring the needs of the empire. He was mudered in

AD192. His successor, Pertinax, was killed after only three months by the Praetorian Guard, who auctioned the throne. The winner was Didius Julianus.

Didius Julianus AD192; Septimius Severus AD193-211

Three army groups on the frontiers became jealous of the Praetorian Guard's power. They chose their own emperor, Septimius Severus, who returned to Rome and deposed Julianus. Severus kept the barbarians out of the empire for 14 years, but he had to raise taxes to pay the army. For the first time even Romans in Italy were taxed.

Caracalla AD211-217

Caracalla, Severus's son, raised the army's wages again, and paid barbarians to stay away from the borders. He is remembered for the baths that he built in Rome. To increase the number of people he could tax, in AD212 he granted citizenship† to all free males in the empire. He was murdered by his Praetorian† Prefect, who seized power until he too was assassinated.

Bust of Caracalla

Elagabalus AD218-222

Elagabalus became emperor when he was 15. He was fanatically dedicated to worship of a Syrian sun-god. The Praetorian Guard killed him and chose his cousin Alexander as the new emperor.

Severus Alexander AD222-235

Alexander was only 13, so his mother Julia Mamaea ruled for him. She brought the army under control and gave management of the empire to a small group of senators. She also improved social conditions. Teachers and scholars were subsidised, as were landlords who repaired their property. Julia achieved relative peace, but after 12 years the eastern frontiers of the empire were invaded. The army rebelled against the government and murdered Alexander and Julia.

The Anarchy AD235-284

Chaos followed. The throne went to an army leader, Maximinus Thrax, a barbarian who could hardly speak Latin and had never been to Rome. After this the empire was torn apart by civil wars. Various army factions nominated more than 50 different rulers. Huge areas of the empire were ruined by famine, plague or invasion. Taxation was heavy and prices rose; many people left their homes to join bands of outlaws. Finally the wars ground to a halt, but the country was devastated.

Diocletian AD284-305

In AD284 Diocletian, a general in the Danube, was declared emperor by his troops. To establish order, he enlarged the army and made it responsible for the administration of the empire. Aware of the threat posed by ambitious soldiers, he increased the number of generals but gave each one fewer troops. He split the provinces† into smaller areas – 70 at first, later 116 – to make them easier to manage. More civil servants were appointed to handle the new administrative work.

Diocletian's most radical change was to divide the empire into two. Each half was governed by its own Augustus† and Caesar†. Diocletian was Augustus of the East, and set up his court at Nicomedia (see map). In AD286 another soldier, Maximian, was appointed Augustus of the West.

This statue represents the new system of leadership.

This map shows how the empire was divided.

☐ **Western half of empire**
☐ **Eastern half of empire**

To stop prices and wages rising, Diocletian issued lists of the maximum sums that people could charge for goods and labour. But this did not work. In addition, the cost of defending the empire made it necessary to increase taxes. To make taxation more efficient, a census† was taken every five years. At first people had to stay on their land while the census was counted; later they were forced to remain permanently where the census takers had first found them.

The empire ran much more efficiently, but people had less freedom. The law was enforced by the army, which as a result became very influential.

Soldiers were now less able to depose the emperor, but they had more power over ordinary people. The Senate lost most of its authority, and in effect simply became the city council of Rome.

Diocletian convinced the people it was the will of the gods that he was emperor, and declared himself a god. It was impossible for others to challenge him. In AD305 he resigned, persuading Maximian to do so at the same time. He retired to a huge palace which was built for him at Spalatum in Dalmatia (now Split in Yugoslavia).

Diocletian's palace

Diocletian expected the two Caesars to take over, but this arrangement did not last long before the army interfered. Once more soldiers tried to choose emperors to suit themselves. By AD311 there were four contenders for the throne.

Constantine AD312-337

One contender, Constantine, was leading the army in Britain. In AD312 he returned to Rome with his troops and defeated Maxentius, his main rival, at the Milvian Bridge. It is said that before the battle Constantine saw a cross in the sky and the words *'In hoc signo vinces'* ('You will conquer with this sign'). After his victory he granted tolerance to all religious groups, including Christians† (who under Diocletian had been badly persecuted).

Constantine adopted the Christian symbol shown on this tomb. It is made up of the first two letters of Christ's name in Greek: *chi* (χ) and *ro* (ρ).

Constantine began reuniting the empire. He defeated various rivals, and became sole emperor in AD323. He granted freedom of worship to Christians and gave people special privileges if they adopted the religion; in AD337 he formally became a Christian on his deathbed. Constantine demanded to be treated as the earthly representative of the Christian God, and began taking part in religious disputes and discussions. In this way he cleverly transferred the ideas of the state religion – that the emperor had divine status and religious authority – to Christianity.

Constantine wanted a capital city to rival the splendour of Rome. In AD330 he moved his court to Byzantium, a former Greek colony at the entrance to the Black Sea, where he founded a city called Constantinople (now Istanbul; see page 272). It remained an imperial capital for 1000 years.

This head of Constantine, once part of a statue 10m (30ft) high, was probably an object of worship.

Constantine was tolerant in religious matters, but he ruled in an authoritarian manner. The security of the empire depended on huge armies, and taxes had to be collected by thousands of civil servants. Workers were increasingly tied to their land and professions. But these measures still failed to halt the decline of the economy, and could not prevent the threat of the barbarians (see overleaf).

Key dates

AD180-192 Commodus

AD192 Pertinax, Didius Julianus

AD193-211 Septimius Severus

AD211-217 Caracalla

AD218-222 Elagabalus

AD222-235 Severus Alexander

AD235-238 Maximinus Thrax

AD238-284 Civil wars

AD284 Diocletian takes power.

AD286-305 Maximian rules western empire; Diocletian rules eastern empire.

AD293 Galerius and Constantius appointed Caesars; new system of government is formalised.

AD305-312 Struggles for power

AD312-337 Constantine (East and West united again from 324).

The Empire after Constantine

After Constantine's death the empire was divided among his three sons, but struggles for power soon arose. After the death of two of them the third son, Constantius II, reunited the empire, but himself died in AD361.

His successor, Julian (AD361-363), was known as the Apostate (someone who abandons one religion for another). Julian restored the old Roman gods and rebuilt their temples. Though Christianity† was not banned, people who worshipped the old state deities were favoured.

Julian

Julian was very hardworking and conscientious. He cut the number of palace workers and gave back independence to city councils throughout the empire. Julian's successor, Jovian (AD363-364), restored Christianity to its former supremacy.

Soon events outside the empire threatened its frontiers. The Huns, a tribe from eastern Asia, began moving west. They invaded the territory of other tribes, who in turn had to move further west to escape them. In AD367 the Visigoths†, Vandals† and Suebi began to set up their own kingdoms on Roman territory. This coincided with a series of short-lived emperors who were too weak to prevent the invasions.

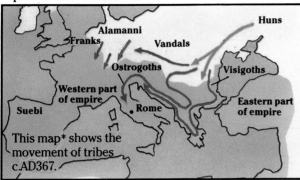

Huns

Alamanni
Franks

Vandals

Ostrogoths

Visigoths

Western part of empire

Suebi • Rome

Eastern part of empire

This map* shows the movement of tribes c.AD367.

Theodosius AD379-395

During the frontier unrest, Theodosius took power (AD379). Unable to expel the barbarians from Germany, he made a treaty with them. This granted them safety if they provided soldiers and farm-workers for the Romans. Barbarian Germans, and later Huns themselves, became a regular part of the Roman army. Many Romans disliked this, but it was necessary as not enough Roman citizens were willing to become soldiers.

This silver relief shows Theodosius in his official robes.

Barbarian soldiers

Theodosius fought against the break-up of the empire, and was the last emperor to rule both East and West. In theory Theodosius's sons were joint rulers of the whole empire, but they split it down the middle again and each ruled half. This scheme continued for another century; usually each emperor was succeeded by his eldest son. But these rulers were often interested only in personal power and wealth. Meanwhile the barbarians continued to advance, further contributing to the downfall of the western half of the empire.

Honorius AD395-423

During Honorius's rule the barbarians shattered the security of the empire. In AD402 Italy was invaded by a tribe of Goths led by a commander called Alaric. Scared by this, Honorius moved the imperial court to Ravenna on the east coast of Italy. Gradually Ravenna grew from a poor town into a properous city, and it remained an imperial centre for centuries.

Ivory plaque showing Honorius.

This is one of the oldest surviving buildings in Ravenna. It is known as the Baptistry of the Orthodox, and was built during the 5th century AD.

While Honorius lived in splendour and safety until his death in AD423, the empire was being overrun by the barbarians. In AD409 the Vandals invaded Spain. In AD410 Rome was sacked by Alaric, who rapidly invaded the rest of Italy. That same year the Romans abandoned Britain and recalled the British legions† to defend the shrinking empire. Disease and famine weakened the population. It is also likely that people stopped wanting to fight the barbarians, because they no longer had any faith in a Roman government that kept taxing them and restricting their freedom.

The barbarians take over

The barbarians swept across Europe. Part of Gaul was occupied by the Burgundians†, and northern Europe by the Franks. In AD429 the Vandals moved from Spain to North Africa. In AD451 the Romans drove the army of Attila the Hun out of central France. But this was the last Roman victory.

The empire was continually under attack. In AD455 the Vandals sailed to Italy, invaded Rome and destroyed it. The city's administrative services collapsed. Chaos and famine followed. Rome's population fell from over 1 million to about 20,000. Romulus Augustulus, the last emperor of the West, was deposed in AD476 by Odoacer, a German captain who declared himself king of Italy and ruled from Ravenna. The western empire had ended.

This map * shows the position of the barbarian tribes by AD476.

BRITAIN
Franks
Burgundians
GAUL
Ravenna
Ostrogoths
Eastern Roman Empire
Visigoths
Rome
SPAIN
ITALY
Vandals
NORTH AFRICA

Many barbarians, such as the Vandals in Africa, were violent fighters who wanted to remove all trace of the Romans. Others, like the Burgundians, did not destroy the areas they conquered, and tried to preserve Roman buildings. But often they failed to do so because they did not have the skills to keep the buildings in good repair.

Each barbarian tribe ruled the area it conquered in its own way. Romans were badly persecuted in some areas. In others the invaders were tolerant. They could not keep strict control over large areas, so local Roman governments were able to preserve the Roman way of life for years. But in the West the idea of the empire, once so important to the Roman people, gradually faded away.

The rise of the Christian Church

In the 4th century AD the Christian Church became richer and more powerful. Educated men began to choose careers as religious officials rather than entering the army or politics. The Church began to influence the way the empire was governed. Bishops, not generals, organized resistance to the barbarians. They also converted many barbarians to Christianity. The developing Church produced many writers and philosophers. Even after the barbarian invasion the Church remained very influential.

This mosaic shows Ambrosius, a Roman bishop. He was highly respected for his teaching and writings.

As Christianity grew, Christians founded communities called monasteries all over the empire. In monasteries men called monks lived away from the rest of society and observed strict rules of behaviour. Some monasteries became famous places of learning, and monks saved and copied ancient books. In this way they preserved many works of Latin and Greek literature and history which otherwise might have been destroyed.

Key dates

AD337-361 Rules of Constantine II, Constans, and Constantius II.

AD361-395 Many emperors of East and West, including Julian ('the Apostate') and Jovian.

AD379-392 Theodosius rules as emperor of East.

AD392-395 Empire re-united under Theodosius.

AD395-423 Rule of Honorius.

AD402 Italy invaded by Alaric the Goth. Honorius moves the imperial court to Ravenna.

AD409 Vandals invade Spain.

AD410 Sack of Rome by Alaric.

AD455 Vandals invade Italy from Africa and destroy Rome.

AD476 Romulus Augustulus, last emperor of the West, is deposed by Odoacer.

The Byzantine empire

While the western half of the empire declined, the eastern half flourished. It preserved many of the traditions of the western Romans, including their administrative skills and military system, and the Christian† religion. The eastern empire after the fall of the West became known as the Byzantine empire, after the original Greek name for the area.

Constantinople's position (see map) made it an ideal link between Europe and Asia, and it became a great and powerful city at the centre of a huge empire. The eastern Church became almost as influential as the

Roman Church, and eastern rulers dreamed constantly of reconquering the old Roman empire. Art and culture flourished in Byzantine times. Mosaics became very lavish, inlaid with polished glass and precious stones and metals.

This mosaic†, in the Church of San Vitale, Ravenna, shows Theodora, the wife of Justinian (see below). Ravenna became the base of the eastern Church in Italy.

Justinian AD527-565

Justinian was one of the greatest emperors of the eastern empire. His armies reconquered most of Rome's former territory in the West. But the cost of this was enormous, and many areas they recovered were delapidated after years of barbarian rule. The inhabitants did not care who ruled them. Except for the southern part of Italy, all the areas that Justinian regained were lost once more within a century.

Justinian's most important achievement was his codification of the Roman legal system (see pages 266-267). This became the basis of the law throughout western Europe. He also launched a programme of building to enlarge and enhance Constantinople. This included the building of the Church of Santa Sophia (AD534-537). For centuries it was the largest church in the Christian world.

This reconstruction shows Santa Sophia as it might have looked in Byzantine times.

The later Byzantine empire

The eastern empire remained powerful for several centuries, but gradually links with Rome were broken. Latin was replaced by Greek as the official language, and the eastern Church and the Roman Catholic Church grew apart. The eastern Church was the forerunner of the modern Greek and Russian Orthodox churches.

The empire was soon challenged by Islam, the religion founded in Mecca, Arabia, by the prophet Mohammed (c.AD570-632). Within a century of Mohammed's death much of the old Roman empire had been conquered by the religion's followers, known as Muslims.

The Byzantine empire slowly shrank, until only Thrace and the Peloponnese were left (see map bottom left). Constantinople itself was attacked by many different invaders and grew weaker, until it had very little political power. In AD1453 it fell to the Muslim armies of the Turkish Sultan Mehmet II. This event is seen by many historians as the point at which all remaining political links with imperial Rome were finally broken.

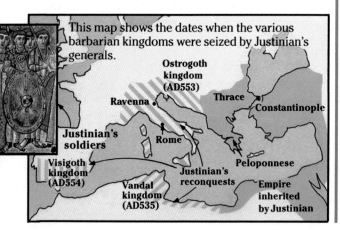

This map shows the dates when the various barbarian kingdoms were seized by Justinian's generals.

Ostrogoth kingdom (AD553)

Thrace

Ravenna

Constantinople

Justinian's soldiers

Rome

Visigoth kingdom (AD554)

Peloponnese

Justinian's reconquests

Vandal kingdom (AD535)

Empire inherited by Justinian

Key dates

AD491-518 Rule of Anastasius I, traditionally thought of as the first Byzantine emperor.

AD527-565 Rule of Justinian

AD528-534 Codification of the Roman law (known as the Justinian Code)

AD535 Justinian retakes the Vandal Kingdom in North Africa.

AD553 Justinian retakes the Ostrogoth Kingdom in Italy.

AD555 Justinian retakes the Visigoth Kingdom in Spain.

AD1453 Constantinople conquered by Sultan Mehmet II.

Glossary

Many Latin words in this section of the book are listed and explained in the glossary below, which also contains some English words that may be unfamiliar. Other words related to the term appear in **bold** within the text of the entry. When a word in the text of an entry is followed by a dagger, that word has its own entry in this list. When the sign follows a name, see the 'Who's who' that begins on page 276.

Aedile. A government official. Four senators† were elected every year to become *aediles*. They were responsible for markets, streets and public buildings, and also organized public games.

Amphora. A large pot with two handles. *Amphorae* were used to transport and store oil and wine.

Amphitheatre. A circular or oval building in which gladiator fights and shows of wild beasts took place. The first amphitheatres were wooden; stone ones were later built all over the empire.

Aqueduct. A channel or pipe for carrying water. Rome and other cities of the empire had excellent supplies of water which was piped into urban centres from rivers and springs in the countryside. The pipes were either built underground or set into large bridges – also known as aqueducts – like the Pont du Gard in France.

Assembly. A meeting of Roman citizens† in Rome. **Assemblies** were held for various purposes, including the election of government officials, the passing or confirmation of laws, and the declaration of war or peace. The plebeians† also held their own **Popular Assembly**, which excluded patricians†, to elect their own representatives called tribunes†.

Atrium. The central area of a Roman house (*domus*†) on to which most of the other rooms opened.

Augustus. Imperial title. It was first taken by Octavian† when he became emperor† in 27BC. Later, under the system of succession devised by Nerva†, it was given to each new emperor when he took power. As the Augustus, the emperor chose a successor known as the Caesar†. The two men ruled together until the Augustus died. Then the Caesar took over, became the Augustus, and chose his own Caesar.

Barbarians. The name generally given to people who lived outside Roman territory. The Romans saw them as brutal and uncivilized because they did not conform to the Roman way of life. Invasions by various barbarian tribes was one cause of the collapse of the empire.

Basilica. A large public building, often near the *forum*† of a Roman town. It was used as law courts or offices, and sometimes also contained shops and markets.

Bulla. A good-luck charm. Each Roman child was given a *bulla* to keep evil spirits away.

Burgundians. People, originally from northern Europe, who around AD406 invaded the Roman empire and set up their own kingdom in the province† of Germania.

Caesar. Imperial title. Under the scheme of succession devised by Nerva†, each emperor decided who would take his place. The successor, until he himself became emperor, was given the title Caesar.

Cameo. A miniature carving in semi-precious stone.

Campus Martius. The Field of Mars, god of war. An open space near Rome where, in early republican† times, Roman armies assembled to go to war.

Carthage. A city on the coast of North Africa founded by the Phoenicians† about 814BC. The growth of **Carthaginian** power in Sicily caused the Punic† wars.

Cavalry. The part of an army that fights on horseback.

Censor. A government official. Two *censores* were chosen every five years. They served for 18 months; during this period they revised the membership of the Senate† and negotiated contracts for public works.

Census. A survey of the population. The Roman government gathered statistics and details about the inhabitants of the empire, mostly for taxation purposes.

Century. A unit of the Roman army. At first each century contained 100 men; later this was reduced to 80. Each century was led by an officer called a **centurion**.

Christianity. A religion founded in Palestine by the followers of the prophet Jesus of Nazareth (c.5BC-AD29), later known as Jesus Christ. His teachings spread rapidly through the Roman empire, though **Christians** were often badly persecuted until Christianity became the official state religion towards the end of the 4th century AD.

Citizen. A Roman man who had the rights to vote and to serve in the army. At first, to qualify for **citizenship** people had to be born in Rome to Roman parents. As the empire grew, however, the conditions were changed to include other people. Finally, in AD212, citizenship was granted to all men in the empire except slaves†.

Cohort. A unit of the Roman army. After the reforms of Marius†, a cohort became the main tactical unit. In each legion there were 10 cohorts; one contained 10 centuries, the others contained 6 centuries. It was led by an officer called a *tribunus militum*.

Consul. The most senior government official. Two consuls were elected each year; they managed the affairs of the Senate† and commanded the armies.

Contubernium. A unit of the Roman army. Each *contubernium* contained eight soldiers who ate together and shared a tent.

Denarius. A Roman coin. In early imperial times *denarii* were made from about 4 grams of silver.

Dictator. A government official. In times of crisis, such as during a war, the Senate† could appoint a dictator to rule for a maximum of six months. He was given complete control of all other officials and of the army, and took all important military and political decisions.

Domus. A private house, normally occupied by one family.

Emperor. The supreme ruler of all Roman territories. The first emperor was Augustus†, who took power in 27BC when the Roman republic† collapsed. The period after this date is known as the **Empire** (the capital letter is used in this book to denote 'the **imperial** period' rather than simply 'Roman territory').

Equites. A class of Roman citizen†. The *equites* were descendents of the first Roman cavalry† officers. In later republican† times the term denoted a powerful middle class of businessmen, traders and bankers.

Etruscans. People, perhaps originally from Asia Minor, who arrived in Italy about 800BC. The area they inhabited, in north-west and central Italy, is called Etruria. For parts of its very early history, Rome was ruled by Etruscan kings.

Forum. An open space at the centre of a Roman town. It was used for markets and trade, and was also the centre of social and political life.

Freed man. A slave† who had been released from slavery by his master.

Gauls. People who lived mainly to the north and west of Italy. There were many tribes of Gauls, who from around 500BC occupied much of what is now France, and areas as far north as the River Rhine and as far south as the Italian Alps. During the early republic† the Gauls attacked Rome frequently; by Caesar's time, however, most of them had been conquered. Their lands were seized by the Romans to form the various Gallic provinces†.

Goths. People who lived originally in Scandinavia. Around the beginning of the 1st century AD they began moving south, and by AD200 they lived north of the Black Sea. From here they attacked Roman territory in Asia Minor, but were defeated. Shortly after this they divided into two factions, known as the Visigoths† and the Ostrogoths†.

Hades. Originally, in Greek, the god of the dead. Later, for the Romans, the place where a person's spirit went after death. To reach Hades the spirit was rowed across a mythical river called the Styx by a boatman called Charon.

Huns. A tribe from eastern Asia who began moving west in the 4th century AD. They invaded the lands of the Ostrogoths†, Visigoths† and Vandals†, who had to move west into the Roman empire to escape them.

Hypocaust. A form of central heating. Buildings were constructed with spaces between the inner and outer walls and below floors. Fires were lit in special furnaces, and the heat flowed into these cavities.

Insula. A block of flats or apartments. Most occupants rented their living-quarters from a landlord. Each individual apartment was called a *cenaculum*.

Lararium. A shrine, kept either in the *atrium*† or garden of a *domus*†, which contained statues of the Roman household gods. The family said prayers at the *lararium* every day.

Latins. People, originally from central Europe, who entered Italy around 2000BC. They settled on the plain of **Latium** (an area of flat land on the north-west coast of the Italian peninsula which surrounds Rome).

Legatus. A government official. In republican† times *legati* worked in the provinces†, serving on the staff of the proconsul†. In imperial times *legati* commanded the legions or acted as military and political advisors or administrative assistants.

Legion. A unit of the Roman army. The size of the legion varied throughout Rome's history. It is thought that in the earliest times it was made up of about 3000 soldiers; by the 4th century BC this number had risen to about 4200. After the reforms of Marius† there were about 5000 soldiers in a legion.

The number of legions also varied. In late republican† times there were 60, but Augustus† cut this number to 28. After his rule there were always around 30 legions.

Ludi. The general name given to sporting events, public games and theatrical performances. Most *ludi* were held to mark religious festivals, funerals or battle victories.

Mosaic. A picture or abstract pattern made up of small pieces of stone, glass or glazed earthenware.

Nomads. People who do not live permanently in any one area but move from place to place.

Ostrogoths. A subdivision of the Goths† who built up a huge empire north of the Black Sea in the 3rd and 4th centuries AD. Around AD370 they were overrun by the Huns†, and so had to move west. From around AD455 they lived in the Balkans. They overran Italy in AD489, led by Theoderic, who deposed the barbarian ruler Odoacer and then declared himself king of Italy.

Paedagogus. A slave†, often Greek, employed by Roman parents to look after their children at school.

Papyrus. A reed used to make a form of writing material (itself often also called papyrus). It was cut into strips which were pressed, dried and polished to create a smooth writing surface.

Patricians. A class of Roman citizen†. Patricians were descended from the oldest families of noblemen. In early republican† times, only patrician men could become senators†. They also held all the most important political, religious and legal appointments.

Peristylium. A row of columns round a building or open space. The word is also used to mean an outdoor walkway or garden surrounded by a row of columns.

Phoenicians. People who lived in the eastern Mediterranean (now Lebanon) from around 1200BC. They were avid traders and seafarers and rapidly occupied many Mediterranean islands and parts of North Africa. Their most important colony was Carthage. The growth of the Carthaginian power in Sicily caused the Punic† wars.

Plebeians. A class of Roman people. The plebeians were the poorest citizens† who were probably descended from Rome's first farmers and traders.

Praetor. A government official. At first the word was used for the two most important officials who replaced the kings at the beginning of the republic†. Later these men became known as consuls†; the word *praetor* instead came to mean the senior judges, administrative officers elected each year by the Assembly†, and governors in some of the provinces†.

Praetorian Guard. An army of around 9000 soldiers formed by Augustus†. It protected Italy and the emperor, as there were no legions† to do this. Because it was the only part of the army stationed in Rome, the Praetorian Guard became very powerful.

Proconsul. A government official. A proconsul was a consul† who, after his term of office, was sent by the Senate† to another job, usually as governor in one of the provinces†.

Province. From later republican† times (after the expansion of Roman territory), any area outside Rome (later outside Italy) that was controlled by the Romans. The inhabitants of these areas are known as **provincials**.

Punic wars. Three wars, fought at intervals from 264BC to 146BC, between the Romans and the Carthaginians. The word Punic is derived from the Latin word *Punicus*, meaning Phoenician†.

Quaestor. A government official. Twenty *quaestores* were chosen each year to be financial administrators.

Republic. A state or country without a king, queen or emperor which is governed by elected representatives of the people. Rome became a republic at the beginning of the 6th century BC when the last Etruscan† king was expelled. Though after this it was occasionally ruled by dictators†, it remained a republic until 27BC when Octavian† became emperor†.

Senate. The group of officials that governed Rome. In early republican† times the Senate consisted of around 100 patricians†; by 82BC there were 600 **senators**, selected from all classes of citizen†. The Senate took most political, military and legal decisions that related to Rome and Roman territory, but gradually the **senatorial** system broke down. After a period of dicatorships† and civil wars, Octavian† took power. During imperial times, the Senate's powers were gradually reduced as emperors took more and more power for themselves.

Slave. A person owned by another and used as a worker. In Rome most slaves were non-Romans, such as prisoners of war and their descendants. They were owned by citizens† or by the state, and were bought and sold like any other property. They had no rights or privileges, and were forced to work at any jobs their masters gave them.

Terracotta. A mixture of clay and sand, used to make tiles and small statues.

Toga. The official garment of a Roman citizen†. It was a roughly semi-circular piece of woollen cloth which the wearer draped around his body in an elaborate series of folds. The most popular colour was white; senators wore a *toga* with a purple border. Young boys also wore a *toga* with a purple hem, called the *toga praetexta*.

Tribune. An official elected by the plebeians† to represent them in the Senate† and protect their interests. In the first Popular Assembly† of 494BC two tribunes were elected; later this number was increased to ten. Tribunes could prevent any actions of the Senate or laws passed by magistrates if they believed that these threatened the rights of the plebeians.

Vandals. People who lived originally in Scandinavia. At the end of the 1st century BC they began moving south; by about AD200 they occupied an area south-west of the River Danube. In AD406, moving west to avoid the Huns†, they crossed the River Rhine into Gaul and devastated large areas of the country. In AD409 they entered Spain, where some of them settled; others moved on to North Africa. From here they sailed to Italy and in AD455 attacked and destroyed Rome.

Viaduct. A bridge built to carry a road across a river or a valley.

Villa. A large house in the country. Most villas were owned by rich city-dwellers who only visited the country from time to time. When the owner was absent the estate was run by a manager. Many villas were centres of farming or other industries.

Visigoths. A subdivision of the Goths† who settled in Dacia in the 3rd century AD. In AD376, escaping from the Huns†, they moved south across the River Danube and into Moesia. Led by Alaric, they advanced through Greece, continued to Italy and in AD419 attacked Rome. After this they moved to Gaul, and finally settled in Spain, where their kingdom survived until the 8th century AD.

Who was who in Ancient Rome

Below is a list of important Romans, with details of their lives and works. If a person's name appears in **bold** in the text of an entry, that person also has his or her own entry in this list.

Agrippina (AD15-59). Mother of **Nero**. She became involved in various political intrigues and was banished from Rome in AD39. Her uncle **Claudius**, however, allowed her to return and married her in AD49. She encouraged him to adopt Nero, her son by a previous marriage. It is said that she later poisoned Claudius so that Nero could become emperor. Later, when she opposed Nero's intention to marry Poppaea Sabina, Nero had her murdered.

Augustus. The title taken in 27BC by Octavian when he became the first Roman emperor†.

Octavian was the great-nephew and adopted son of Julius **Caesar**. After Caesar's death he formed an alliance with **Mark Antony** and Lepidus; the three men seized power and in 42BC defeated **Brutus** and his troops. When Lepidus retired, Octavian and Antony split Roman territory between them, but later disagreed. Octavian defeated Antony in the Battle of Actium in 31BC.

After so many years of civil war the Senate knew that Rome needed a strong ruler, so they gave Octavian command of the armies, sole control of foreign policy, and power to reform the Roman administration. He was given the title Augustus ('revered one') in recognition of his status as the head of the Roman government.

By working closely with the Senate and involving it in his decisions Augustus brought peace and prosperity to the Roman world after decades of unrest and civil war. In addition he reformed the army and made the provinces more secure. Building schemes were begun in Rome, and welfare was improved for the poor. According to **Suetonius**, Augustus was fair and honest; his rule was so successful that the idea of restoring a republican† government gradually died out.

Brutus (85-42BC). Politician, leader of the plot to murder **Caesar**. A famous soldier, and a firm believer in the ideals of the Roman republic†, he thought that Caesar was too powerful. Hoping to restore republican traditions, he and several others murdered Caesar in 44BC. After this he fled to Macedonia and later committed suicide.

Caesar, Julius Gaius (c.100-44BC). Politician, general and writer. He was born in Rome and was educated there and in Rhodes. He already had a reputation as a fine soldier when his political career began in 68BC. From 58BC to 49BC he led troops in Gaul and Illyricum, and extended Roman territory as far as the Atlantic coast and the English Channel. He recorded this period of his life, and details of his military campaigns, in seven books called *De Bello Gallico* (The Gallic Wars).

Disputes with Pompey and the Senate caused Caesar to return to Italy in 49BC, supported by his army. After defeating his enemies he became the most powerful man in Rome. He described these victories in three books called *De Bello Civili* (The Civil Wars). He was declared dictator† for life, but despite his popularity with the Roman people many senators believed he was too powerful. A group of these, led by **Brutus**, murdered him on 15 March 44BC.

Caligula. See **Gaius**.

Cato (234-149BC). Politician and writer. He fought in the second Punic† war, then held political positions in Sicily, Africa and Sardinia. In 184BC he was a censor†. Cato believed in the republican† values established when Rome was a small semi-rural settlement: restraint, dignity, and simple living. These are described in his book *De Agri Cultura*, which is the oldest existing work of Latin prose. He also wrote *Origines*, a history of the Roman people from the earliest times. His great grandson, also a politician, was one of Caesar's bitterest enemies.

Catullus (c.84-c.54BC). Poet. He settled in Rome as a young man. Details of his life, including travels to Asia and his final illness, are recorded in his poems. These include laments, witty parodies and elegant descriptions of incidents from Roman life. Catullus was one of the first Roman poets to adopt the forms and styles of Greek poetry.

Cicero (106-43BC). Politician, lawyer and writer. He was educated in Rome and Athens, and in 81BC his first speeches in the law courts earned him recognition as the greatest public speaker of his day. He became a famous lawyer, and was a consul† in 63BC. However he made political enemies by speaking out against people in the Senate and courts. After **Caesar**'s murder Cicero made many speeches in the Senate opposing **Mark Antony**. As a result, when Antony and **Octavian** took power, Cicero was murdered by their troops.

Many of Cicero's speeches were written down; they tell us a lot about life in late republican† times. His letters and philosophical writings also survive, and show that Cicero was responsible for introducing many Greek ideas to the Romans. His style of writing and speaking were imitated by scholars for centuries after his death.

Claudius (10BC-AD54). Emperor AD41-54. He was declared emperor by the army after the death of **Gaius**. Childhood illnesses had left him weak and crippled, and most of his relatives thought him stupid. But he was in fact very intelligent; contemporary accounts tell us he was a good public speaker, an excellent historian (he wrote several books of history, though none survives) and a wise and sympathetic ruler.

Constantine (c.AD274-337). Emperor AD312-337. He was leading the army in England when his father, the emperor Constantius, died. Constantine returned to Rome and defeated his rival for the throne, Maxentius, at the Milvian Bridge. Once in power he moved the imperial court from Rome to a new city on the Black Sea which he called Constantinople (now Istanbul). Constantine was the first Christian emperor; in AD313 he issued the Edict of Milan, granting freedom of worship to Christians.

Crassus (c.112-53BC). Soldier and politician. He defeated the uprising led by the slave Spartacus in 71BC, and was consul with **Pompey** the following year. In 60BC he joined an alliance with Pompey and **Caesar**; his extreme wealth enabled him to support Caesar's political ambitions.

Diocletian (AD245-313). Emperor AD284-305. He was declared emperor in AD284 by his troops. He made many radical reforms to coinage, taxation, the army and, most importantly, the way in which the empire was organized. After splitting Roman territory into two he ruled the East and appointed another emperor, Maximian, to rule the West. The administrative systems he devised, implemented by an expanded civil service, lasted for centuries.

Domitian (AD51-96). Emperor AD81-96. He took power after the death of his brother **Titus**, and quickly began to strengthen the frontiers of the empire to protect them from the barbarians. A patron of the arts, he also restored and improved many of Rome's buildings. But he was an arrogant ruler who did not respect the Senate. The end of his rule was marked by constant political quarrels. He solved these by ordering the murder of anyone who disagreed with him. He was eventually assassinated.

Gaius (AD12-41). Emperor AD37-41. He grew up in various military camps by the River Rhine, where his father was an officer. He was nicknamed Caligula because of the small soldier's boots (*caligae*) he wore as a child. **Suetonius** and others describe him as arrogant, cruel and extravagant. After ruling for four years in a wilful, inconsistent manner he was murdered by the Praetorian† Guard.

Hadrian (AD76-138). Emperor AD117-138. He succeeded his relative and adoptive father **Trajan**. A great soldier, he spent much of his rule with the armies in the provinces, and set up permanent barriers against the barbarians, including Hadrian's Wall in Britain. He was also a scholar and patron of the arts. He built a library in Athens and a villa for himself at Tibur near Rome. Around AD135 he set up an organization called the Athenaeum to sponsor writers and philosophers.

Horace (65-8BC). Poet. He was educated in Rome and Athens, then worked in Rome as a government clerk and began writing poetry. He became friendly with **Virgil**, and with Maecaenas, a patron of poets, who gave him a farm where he settled to write. **Augustus** asked Horace to be his secretary, but he refused. From their letters, however, it appears that the two men were friends. Horace's most famous works are the *Odes*, short poems on various subjects including the joys of the country, food and wine. His poetry became famous almost immediately and has remained widely read and studied.

Julian (AD332-363). Emperor AD360-363. On becoming emperor he began to restore worship of the ancient Roman deities, going against the official religion of the state which was by that time Christanity. He is known as 'the Apostate' – someone who abandons one religion for another. He greatly reduced his palace staff and improved the civil service, but was unpopular because of his religious views. He was killed fighting in Persia. Some of his letters and other writings survive, which give us details of political and religious life at that time.

Justinian (c.AD482-565). Emperor of the East, AD527-565. His most important political achievement was to recapture many of the territories in the West that had been overrun by barbarians. He also commissioned a huge codification of the Roman legal system, which formed the basis of his reforms of the political administration.

Juvenal (c.AD60-c.AD130). Poet. Almost nothing is known about his life. The first of his poems still in existence were probably published around AD110. His works are called *Satires*; they criticise what Juvenal saw as the evils and defects of life in Rome – poverty, immorality and injustice. The attacks, though bitter, are delivered with biting humour and wit. It is thought that his poems led to him being banished from Rome for a time.

Livia (58BC-AD29). Wife of **Augustus**, and, by an earlier marriage, mother of **Tiberius**. She was an aristocrat from one of the oldest Roman families, and had considerable influence on Augustus's rule. Roman historians tell us she was shrewd and wise; it is possible that she persuaded Augustus against his will to appoint Tiberius as his successor.

Livy (59BC-AD17). Historian. He spent much of his life in Rome writing *Ab Urbe Condita*, a huge history of the city and its people. It was published in instalments and brought him wealth and fame. It charts the development of Rome from the earliest times, and provides us with much detail of both historical incidents and everyday life.

Marcus Aurelius (AD121-180). Emperor AD161-180. Much of his rule was spent at the empire's frontiers, trying to keep the barbarians out. Aurelius's journals, known as *Meditations* and written mostly in army camps, show him to have been a peace-loving, philosophical man.

Marius (157-86BC). Soldier and politician. He fought successful campaigns in Spain, Africa and Gaul. During this period he was consul† six times (107BC, 104-100BC) and used his power to reform the army and make it more efficient. After this he was hardly involved in political life until 88BC, when tensions arose between him and **Sulla**. The struggle for power between the two men was one of the causes of the civil war that brought about the collapse of the republic†. Marius seized control in 87BC and the following year was appointed consul for the seventh time just before his death.

Mark Antony (82-30BC). Soldier and politician. He was a consul† with **Caesar** in 44BC. After Caesar's death he formed an alliance with **Octavian**; they split Roman territory and Antony ruled Egypt with his lover Cleopatra, the Egyptian queen (see page 84). Later the two men disagreed and war broke out between them. Antony and Cleopatra committed suicide after their defeat by Octavian at the Battle of Actium.

Martial (c.AD40-AD104). Poet. He was born in Spain, and lived in Rome for many years. His poems, known as *Epigrams*, provide details of everyday life and describe some of Rome's more colourful characters. While much of his work is bitterly satirical, attacking various individuals for their faults, his writings also include poems to his friends and touching laments.

Nero (AD37-68). Emperor AD54-68. At first Nero's rule was effective and stable, but he freed himself from the influence of his advisors (including **Seneca**) and became arrogant and obsessed with power. Anyone who opposed him was murdered (including his mother **Agrippina**). According to **Suetonius** he sponsored public shows and games in which he himself appeared, and had to increase taxes to pay for them. It is thought that he caused the fire that destroyed much of Rome in AD64, and then began organized persecution of Christians, blaming them for the blaze. Eventually he left Rome and was forced to commit suicide.

Nerva (c.AD30-98). Emperor, AD96-98. He was appointed emperor by the Senate after **Domitian** was assassinated. A respected lawyer, he restored faith in imperial rule by treating the Senate and others with consideration. The army, at first uneasy about his appointment, was won over when he chose a famous soldier, **Trajan**, to succeed him. Nerva is best remembered for devising this system of succession (after him each emperor chose and trained his own replacement), and for increasing aid to the poor.

Octavian. See **Augustus**.

Ovid (43BC-AD18). Poet. He was educated in Rome and studied to become a lawyer, but gave this up to write poetry. His work became very popular in Rome, and he was friendly with **Horace** and others. In AD8, however, he was banished to the shore of the Black Sea by Augustus; the reason for this is not entirely clear, but he never returned to Rome. His most famous work is *Metamorphoses*, fifteen books of poems on a variety of subjects, chiefly legends or myths, all involving changes of shape and character. Ovid's poetry is notable for its pictorial detail; his writing later influenced many artists, including Rubens and Picasso.

Petronius Arbiter (lived 1st century AD). Author. Little is known about his life, but several of his works survive. The most famous of these is the *Satyricon*, a rambling narrative about the experience of three characters as they travel through southern Italy. The work is most important as a report on the social customs of the day, and as a description of the lives of people of various classes; it also contains historical poems and snatches of political commentary.

Plautus (c.254-184BC). Playwright. He is said to have written more than 130 plays, though only 21 survive. These are all based on Greek comedies, but introduce features of Roman life, often affectionately parodied, probably to make them more interesting to Roman audiences. The works of Plautus have inspired many later playwrights, particularly Shakespeare and Molière.

Pliny (c.AD61-c.113). Writer and lawyer. During **Trajan**'s rule he served as a consul†. He published nine volumes of his correspondence with the emperor, his friend **Tacitus** and others. Written in a clear, elegant style, they are an excellent source of information about the Roman world at that time.

Plutarch (AD46-126). Writer. He was born in Greece, but later lived in Rome. Many of his writings survive. They cover several different subjects, including science, literature and philosophy. His most famous work, known in English as *Plutarch's Lives*, is a series of biographies of Greek and Roman soldiers and statesmen. They are grouped in pairs, one Greek, one Roman, and their lives and careers are carefully compared.

Pompey (106-48BC). Soldier and politician. He fought with **Sulla** against **Marius**, and later suppressed the slave rebellion led by Spartacus. Asia Minor was added to Roman territory as a result of his campaigns there. He joined an alliance with **Caesar** and **Crassus** in 60BC, and remained in Rome while Caesar was fighting in Gaul. Owing to political tensions the alliance broke down, and in 49BC Caesar returned to Rome and seized power. Pompey was defeated and died in Egypt.

Seneca (c.5BC-AD65). Writer, philosopher and lawyer. He was born in Spain, but spent most of his life in Rome. In AD41 he was banished by **Claudius**, but was recalled by Agrippina eight years later to be **Nero**'s tutor. For a time Nero governed well, probably because of Seneca's influence, but the administration deteriorated and in AD62 Seneca asked to retire. Three years later he was accused of being involved in a conspiracy against Nero, and was forced to commit suicide. Seneca's most famous works are the *Apocolocyntosis*, a satire on the deification of Claudius, and his *Moral Letters*, which outline his philosophical beliefs.

Sibyl. A name used by the Greeks and Romans for several prophetesses active all over the Ancient World. One of them offered nine books of her prophecies to Rome's early king Tarquinius Priscus. When he refused to buy them, she burned three books and offered him the remaining six. Priscus refused again; the Sibyl burned another three books and offered the last three at the original price for nine. Priscus bought the books, which were kept in Rome by special priests; they were thought to be so sacred that they could only be consulted in extreme emergencies.

Suetonius (c.AD69-AD140). Historian. After a period as a lawyer he became a government assistant to **Trajan**, Hadrian and others. His most famous work is *Lives of the Twelve Caesars*, which has survived in complete form. It discusses the careers of each Roman ruler from **Caesar** to **Domitian**. As well as studying the political careers of the emperors, it also passes on a wealth of detail about their personalities, appearances, families and habits. In addition Suetonius also recorded the gossip, scandal and rumours surrounding the lives of his subjects.

Sulla (138-78BC). General and politician. His first military successes were as a lieutenant to **Marius**, who later became his fiercest rival. Between 88 and 86BC the two men were involved in constant struggles for power; after Marius's death in 86BC Sulla and his troops seized control of Rome and he declared himself dictator†. A man of highly conservative views, he tried to return power to the Senate and the patricians†.

Tacitus (c.AD55-c.AD116). Historian. He served as a military officer and held several government posts, including consul†. According to contemporary sources he was an excellent public speaker. His most famous works are the *Annals* (about the period from **Tiberius**'s rule to the death of **Nero**) and the *Histories* (about the lives of the emperors from Galba to **Domitian**).

Terence (c.195-159BC). Playwright. He was a slave†, freed by his master. His six plays – including *Phormio* and *Adelphoe* – were adapted from Greek comedy. Contemporary sources tell us that many audiences found Terence's plays dull, possibly because they are less exuberant than those of **Plautus**. But his work was performed in imperial times, and was known in the middle ages. Many later writers, including Sheridan and Molière, were inspired by his plays.

Tiberius (42BC-AD37). Emperor AD14-37. He had already retired from army life to Rhodes when he was called to Rome to become emperor. He appears to have been an excellent administrator, but many of his reforms were very unpopular. Terrified of being assassinated, he withdrew to the island of Capri and ruled through his deputy, Sejanus. Eventually Sejanus tried to seize power for himself, and Tiberius had him executed. After this he became suspicious and tyrannical. Anyone who he thought opposed him was forced to commit suicide.

Titus (AD39-81). Emperor AD79-81. He was the elder son of Vespasian, and had a distinguished military career. His capture of Jerusalem in AD70 is depicted on a triumphal arch in Rome. According to **Suetonius** he was extremely popular, generous and merciful. He gave financial aid to people who had suffered in the volcanic eruptions at Herculaneum and Pompeii (AD79) and in a huge fire in Rome (AD80). The Colosseum in Rome and other public buildings were completed during his term of office.

Trajan (?AD53-AD117). Emperor AD98-117. He was born in Spain and was an outstanding soldier and general; his military successes are commemorated on a huge sculpted pillar in Rome known as Trajan's Column. During his rule the empire grew to its largest with the conquest of Dacia and Parthia. Among his public works at Rome were baths, markets, a basilica and a new forum.

Vespasian (AD9-AD79). Emperor AD70-79. He came to power after the murder of **Nero** and the short rules of Galba, Otho and Vitellius. Rome was in civil and financial turmoil, but he quickly restored order. His improvements of the administration and the army achieved political stability, and he began an extensive programme of public building. This included the Colosseum, temples and restorations to the forum and elsewhere.

Virgil (70-19BC). Poet. He was educated at Cremona, Milan, and Rome. His first published work, the *Eclogues*, is a series of poems about life in the country. In 42BC his land was confiscated to provide farms for retired soldiers, and he lived for a time near Rome, and later near Naples and elsewhere. He completed his next great poems, the *Georgics*, in 30BC. During the last 10 years of his live he worked on the *Aeneid*, a poem in twelve books about the origin and growth of the Roman empire.

Vitruvius (c.70BC-early 1st century AD). Architect and engineer. He is most famous as the author of *De Architectura*, a series of ten books about architecture and building. They include information about civil engineering, construction, town-planning and materials, as well as sections about the techniques and styles of decoration. *De Architectura* brought together much information about Ancient Greek architecture, and is the only work of its kind to have survived ancient times.

Date chart

This chart lists the most important dates in
Roman history. It also includes some events that
took place elsewhere in the world during the
same period; these are shown on indented lines.

Dates BC

from c.2000BC Immigrants enter Italy from the North.

c.900BC First settlements on Palatine and Esquiline hills.

>**c.900BC** State of Sparta founded in Greece.

c.800BC Etruscans arrive in Italy by sea.

>**776BC** First Olympic Games held in Greece.

753BC Date traditionally given for the founding of Rome.
The city is ruled by a series of kings, some of whom are
Etruscan.

c.750BC Greek migrants settle on the southern coasts of
Sicily and Italy.

>**c.650BC** First coinage appears in Lydia
(Asia Minor).

>**c.550BC** Cyrus the Great founds Persian Empire.

510 or 509BC Last king expelled from Rome; republic
formed.

>**c.505BC** Democracy established in Athens by
Cleisthenes.

496BC Romans defeated by an alliance of Latin cities at
the Battle of Lake Regillus.

494BC Plebeians go on strike for the first time.

>**494BC** Ionian revolt crushed by Persians.

493BC First two tribunes appointed.

>**490BC** Battle of Marathon: Persians defeated by
Greeks.

>**486BC** Death of Siddhartha Gautama, founder of
Buddhism.

450BC Publication of the list of Roman laws known as
the Twelve Tables.

>**450BC** Celtic La Tène culture appears in Europe.

449BC Number of tribunes increased to ten.

>**431-404BC** Peloponnesian War, fought between
Athens and Sparta.

by 400BC Rome has become the dominant partner in
the Latin alliance.

367BC Law is passed declaring that one consul must be
a plebeian.

366BC First plebeian consul is elected.

338BC Romans defeat the other members of the Latin
alliance; the alliance is terminated.

>**334BC** Alexander the Great invades Asia Minor. He
conquers Egypt in 332, Persia in 330 and by 329 has
reached India.

326BC War breaks out between the Romans and the
Samnites.

>**323BC** Death of Alexander the Great in Babylon.

312BC The Appian Way is begun.

287BC Lex Hortensia passed, stating that all resolutions
of the Popular Assembly should become law.

286BC Final defeat of the Samnites.

280-272BC Pyrrhic wars.

by 264BC Rome dominates the whole of Italy

264-241BC First Punic war.

241BC Sicily becomes the first Roman province.

238BC Romans seize Sardinia.

220BC Via Flamina built.

218-202BC Second Punic war.

>**214BC** Great Wall built in China.

204BC Rome invades Africa.

202BC Rome seizes Carthaginian territory in Spain.

179BC First stone bridge built over the River Tiber.

>**171-138BC** Reign of Mithriades I of Parthia, who
extends Parthian empire to Persia and Mesopotamia.

>**from c.170BC** Greeks establish small settlements
in parts of the Punjab, India.

149-146BC Third Punic war ends with the destruction of
Carthage.

133BC Rome acquires the province of Asia. Tiberius
Gracchus becomes tribune.

123BC Gaius Gracchus becomes tribune.

121BC Province of Gallia Narbonensis acquired.

107BC Marius becomes consul, and begins reforms of
the army.

88BC Sulla marches on Rome and drives Marius into
exile.

87BC Marius recaptures Rome, but dies the following
year.

82-80BC Sulla is dictator.

73-71BC Rebellion of discontented slaves, led by
Spartacus.

70BC Crassus and Pompey are consuls.

63BC Pompey acquires provinces of Bythnia, Pontus,
Cyrene, Syria and Crete.

59BC Caesar is consul.

58-49BC Caesar's campaigns in Gaul.

55-54BC Caesar's invasions of Britain.

53BC Death of Crassus.

49BC Caesar returns to Rome and seizes power. Civil
war breaks out between him and the Senate's forces (led
by Pompey).

48BC Pompey is killed in battle.

45BC Caesar finally defeats the Senate's forces and
becomes sole leader of the Roman world.

44BC Caesar is assassinated by Brutus and Cassius.

42BC Deaths of Brutus and Cassius.

c.33BC Growing tension between Octavian and Mark
Antony leads to civil war.

31BC Octavian defeats Antony and Cleopatra at the
Battle of Actium.

27BC Octavian becomes first Roman emperor, and is
given the title Augustus.

>**c.5BC** Birth of Jesus Christ in Bethlehem, Judaea.

Dates AD

AD14   Death of Augustus. Tiberius becomes Emperor.

AD14-37   Rule of Tiberius.

AD17   Death of the historian Livy.

AD37-41   Rule of Caligula.

AD41-54   Rule of Claudius.

AD43   Conquest of Britain.

AD54-68   Rule of Nero.

AD64   Rome burns down; Nero begins persecution of Christians, blaming them for the fire.

AD68-9   After Nero's death, struggles for power lead to civil wars.

AD69   Reigns of Galba, Otho, Vitellius, before Vespasian takes power.

AD69-79   Rule of Vespasian.

AD79   The Colosseum in Rome, one of the empire's largest amphitheatres, is opened.

AD79-81   Rule of Titus.

AD79   The volcano Vesuvius erupts, destroying the towns of Herculaneum and Pompeii on the west coast of Italy.

AD81-96   Rule of Domitian.

AD96-98   Rule of Nerva.

AD98-117   Rule of Trajan.

AD112   Trajan's forum in Rome is completed.

AD117   The empire reaches its largest extent after the conquests of Dacia and Parthia.

AD117-138   Rule of Hadrian.

AD122   Building of Hadrian's Wall and other frontiers begins.

AD138-161   Rule of Antoninus Pius.

AD161-180   Rule of Marcus Aurelius.

AD180-192   Rule of Commodus.

AD193-211   Rule of Septimius Severus.

AD211-217   Rule of Caracalla.

AD212   Roman citizenship granted to all free people throughout the empire.

AD217-218   Rule of Macrinus.

AD218-222   Rule of Elagabalus.

AD222-235   Rule of Severus Alexander.

AD235-284   Short reigns of many emperors. Barbarians threaten the empire's borders. Plague and famine sweep through Europe.

AD260-275   Gaul declares independence from Rome.

AD270   Romans begin to abandon parts of the empire, withdrawing from Dacia.

AD271-5   The Aurelian Wall is built around Rome.

AD284   Diocletian takes power and splits empire into two parts, East and West.

AD284-305   Rule of Diocletian (East).

AD286-305   Rule of Maximinian (West).

AD286   Britain declares itself independent from Rome (until AD296).

AD301   Edict of maximum prices issued to regulate inflation.

AD305-312   Rule of Constantius I, followed by struggles for power which end when Constantine defeats Maxentius at the Battle of the Milvian Bridge.

AD312-337   Rule of Constantine. Empire is reunited from AD324.

AD313   Constantine issues Edict of Milan, tolerating Christian worship.

AD330   Constantine moves his court to Byzantium, where he founds the city of Constantinople.

AD337   Constantine baptised into Christian faith.

AD337-361   Rule of Constantine's sons.

AD361-363   Rule of Julian the Apostate; old state religion restored.

AD363-364   Rule of Jovian. Christianity restored.

AD364-379   Rules of Valentinian I, Valens, Gratian, Valentian II.

AD367   Barbarian tribes, moving west to escape the Huns, begin to set up their own kingdoms on Roman territory.

AD379-392   Theodosius rules as emperor of the East.

AD392-395   Empire re-united under Theodosius.

AD394   Christianity becomes official state religion.

AD395-423   Rule of Honorius.

AD402   The Goths invade Italy. Honorius moves the imperial court from Rome to Ravenna.

AD404   First Latin version of the Bible (known as the Vulgate) is completed.

AD406   The River Rhine freezes, allowing the Goths to cross it and enter Roman territory.

AD409   Vandals invade Spain.

AD410   Sack of Rome by Alaric the Goth. Rome abandons territories in Britain and Gaul.

AD449   Angles, Saxons and Jutes invade Britain.

AD455   Vandals invade Italy from Africa and destroy Rome.

AD475   Visigoths declare an independent kingdom in Spain.

AD476   Romulus Augustulus, last emperor of the West, is deposed by Odoacer, a barbarian captain who delcares himself king of Italy.

AD486   Clovis founds Frankish kingdom.

AD491-518   Rule of Anastasius I, traditionally thought of as the first Byzantine emperor.

AD527-565   Rule of Justinian.

AD535-555   Justinian's troops recapture much of the former Roman empire from the barbarians, but these territories are later lost again.

AD1453   Constantinople is conquered by Sultan Mehmet II.

The legacy of Rome

The Roman empire in western Europe came to a close in AD476 when the last emperor in Italy, Romulus Augustulus, was deposed. But the Roman way of life was so widespread and firmly established that it did not simply disappear when the barbarians took over. Some elements of Roman civilization remained as strong as ever after the fall of the empire, and had a huge impact on the cultures that followed them. Other aspects of Roman life – chiefly ideas and literature – all but disappeared in the middle ages. But they were maintained for centuries in monasteries and other centres of learning until they were rediscovered by writers, artists and scholars.

The Romans also transmitted to us skills and ideas learned or borrowed from other ancient cultures. Without the Romans, much information about more remote civilizations would be lost. Greek sculptures and many Greek writings exist almost solely in the form of Roman copies. Technical innovations of other ancient peoples only survive because they were adopted by the Romans. Below are examples of the ways in which the influence of the Roman world continues to be felt today.

Towns and cities

Much of western Europe had no urban civilization before the Romans, and they profoundly influenced its geography. They nearly always chose excellent positions for the towns they created, assessing physical and political factors before beginning to build. Many modern cities occupy the sites they do only because the Romans built there first, or developed tiny hamlets into large, prosperous towns. These include London, Paris, Lyons, Bordeaux, Cologne, Toledo, Milan and, of course, Rome itself.

Some European town centres are still laid out as the Romans planned them, with a large open space at the centre corresponding to the *forum* and roads that intersect at right angles. Bridges, markets and other public landmarks often occupy the sites where the Romans first placed them. In addition, other cities built or rebuilt long after Roman times were created by town planners in imitation of the grid pattern of the Greeks and Romans; these include New York and Lisbon.

Travel and communications

The Romans established trade and military routes all over Europe and into North Africa and Asia. Many can still be seen in ruins; far more, though no longer in existence, form the basis of modern main roads and railways, their directions being followed by modern planners. In addition, the wheel-gauge of Roman wagons became fixed at about 143 cm once ruts were worn in their roads. This is now the gauge of many railways, as early steam trains were tested on tracks in mines developed by the Romans.

Architecture

Very few barbarian tribes were able to maintain Roman buildings, and some actually destroyed them. Cities fell into disrepair and were plundered for stone and marble. But many Roman buildings lasted because they were so well made. The Romans' innovations and developments in architecture and building technology – the arch, the dome and the use of concrete – enabled them to create huge structures that still survive. Some are still in use, like the Pantheon in Rome and theatres and amphitheatres all over southern Europe.

In centres where building continued after Roman times, such as parts of the Eastern empire and certain cities in Italy, architects at first imitated the great buildings of Rome. Later in the Byzantine world architectural styles gradually changed, but many buildings were still based on the large domes and basilicas of late Roman times. In addition, many Roman basilicas were turned into churches during this period.

During the Renaissance (see opposite) Italian architects like Palladio (1518-80) discovered the books of the Roman architect Vitruvius. These codified the rules and styles of the classical architecture of the Greeks and Romans. Renaissance architects followed these guidelines; some copied Roman buildings in their entirety, others incorporated the rules into new designs. In addition, at this time many original Roman buildings were restored. The Baths of Diocletian in Rome, for example, were turned into the church of Santa Maria Degli Angeli by the Renaissance artist Michaelangelo.

Though new styles of architecture later developed, many architects continued to use Greek and Roman principles of proportion and design. In the 19th century many civic monuments were built with columns, domes and arched halls in an attempt to capture the imposing grandeur of ancient Rome. The National Gallery in London and the Louvre in Paris are good examples, but the European imperial powers also constructed buildings like this in many parts of the world, including India, Africa and Asia. Some large state buildings in the USA, including the Capitol in Washington, DC, also follow this style.

Painting and sculpture

In Renaissance times artists became fascinated with the classical statues (mostly Greek but preserved in Roman copies) that were being rediscovered. Michaelangelo and others adopted their realistic style and their proportions and moods, often altering them subtly to suit their own purposes. Myths and legends from the classical world were often used as the basis for paintings by such artists as Botticelli. At that stage, however, very few Roman wall-paintings had been found; when, in the 18th century, excavations began at Pompeii, classically inspired painting and sculpture received a fresh impetus. The classical legacy remains a source of inspiration for many modern artists.

Language

When the Romans conquered a new area, its inhabitants had to learn the language of their conquerors, because the new administration was conducted in Latin. This was not the language of literature or public speaking, but the everyday speech of peasants and soldiers. It survived after the fall of the empire, spoken all over the Roman world in various provincial forms. These dialects, when later fused with the languages of the barbarian invaders, grew into the modern European languages. Many of them – particularly Portuguese, Italian, French, Spanish and Romanian – are very closely linked to Latin. Others, like English, are more distantly related, but still contain thousands of Latin words.

A more formal, official Latin was preserved by the Christian Church. All church ceremonies were conducted in Latin, and it was the language spoken in monasteries. As these places were the main centres of learning during the middle ages, Latin became the language of scholars. By the 16th century Latin was used all over Europe by scholars, diplomats and scientists. This tradition has survived into modern times; a qualification in Latin is still an entrance requirement for some universities and colleges, whatever subject the student intends to study.

Law

The Roman legal system survived the collapse of the empire for many reasons. It was widely established, well integrated into Roman society on a local level, and meticulously codified and documented. The Romans' ideas of justice and rights, as outlined in the Justinian Code, (AD528-534), remain relevant today. Some modern legal systems, such as that in France, are based in a large part on the Justinian Code; others, though now very different from it, still display their origins in the Roman system. In the USA, the state law of Louisiana still follows Roman law very closely.

Government

The concept of an empire – a territory unified by one set of laws and governed by a central body – was not a Roman invention. The Macedonian ruler Alexander the Great conquered large parts of the eastern Mediterranean and Asia, hoping to unite them under a single political administration, but died before he could carry this out. The Romans not only acquired a vast empire but also succeeded in governing it smoothly and effectively. The Romans brought many benefits to the areas they conquered: improved buildings; trade; a legal system; and the vast economic resources of the empire.

The imperialist system was later copied by many rulers, with varying degrees of success. In AD800 the Frankish king Charlemagne was crowned 'Emperor of the Romans', in imitation of earlier Roman rulers. Later Frankish and German leaders continued this tradition, and named their territories the Holy Roman Empire. This institution remained in existence in Germany until 1806. Though Roman in name only, it demonstrates the potency of the Roman empire as a historical model.

In the 18th century the revolutionary movements in France and America were inspired by the ideals of the Roman republic to overthrow monarchic rule. The USA is still governed by a body called the Senate. By the 19th century some western European countries had empires all over the world, to which they, like the Romans, tried to export their culture and governmental systems. In modern times the European Community can be seen as an extension of the Roman ideal; it aims to bring the various member states together with a common monetary and taxation system, a central government, and an international court of justice.

Elements of Roman local government survive today in the Roman Catholic Church. Its managerial units, known as dioceses, were invented by Diocletian for civic purposes and only later adopted by the church. The idea of a religious empire with its own leader – the Pope – and its own laws is itself derived from the Roman imperial administration.

Literature and ideas

The great works of Latin literature, and histories of the Romans written by Romans themselves, were preserved in the middle ages by monks, who collected ancient books and copied the original manuscripts. From the 13th century there was a steady drift to the West of monks from the fast crumbling Byzantine world. The books they brought with them provoked new interest in Greece and Rome; this in turn brought about gradual cultural changes (first in Italy, later throughout Europe) known collectively as the Renaissance.

The Renaissance influenced all aspects of European life. Greek and Roman writings taught Renaissance thinkers to stress human possibilities rather than dwell, as most medieval theorists did, on human failings. Learning began to develop independently of the Church; schools and universities were founded by bankers, statesmen and others in non-religious walks of life. Scientific and medical experiments flourished. The political, religious and technological changes of this period mark the end of the medieval age.

Renaissance poets like Petrarch and Boccaccio imitated Latin verse forms (particularly those of Virgil); the Dutch scholar Erasmus perfected his Latin prose style by detailed study of Cicero. In this way writers incorporated Latin styles and ideas into contemporary culture, and in turn passed them on to later ages. Aspects of classical literature and thought appear throughout later literature and philosophy: for example, episodes from Roman history provide the material for plays by Shakespeare, operas by Verdi and novels by Robert Graves. Latin verse and prose styles have been imitated by countless authors, including Pope and Keats in English and Racine and Molière in French.

283

Index

Page numbers in italic denote map references.

Acknowledgment

The publishers wish to thank the Museo della Civiltà Romana, Rome, for permission to base the reconstruction of Rome on pages 224-225 of this book on their model of the ancient city.